Severn River Publishing
www.SevernRiverBooks.com

ISBN: 978-1-951249-77-9 (Paperback)
ISBN: 978-1-951249-86-1 (Hardback)
ISBN: 979-8-719942-71-1 (Hardback)

ALSO BY JOHN J. GOBBELL

The Todd Ingram Series

The Last Lieutenant

A Code For Tomorrow

When Duty Whispers Low

The Neptune Strategy

Edge of Valor

Dead Man Launch

Somewhere in the South Pacific

Other Books

A Call to Colors

The Brutus Lie

Never miss a new release! Sign up to receive exclusive updates from author John J. Gobbell.

severnriverbooks.com/authors/john-gobbell

TO THE FALLEN

Sleep my sons, your duty done
For Freedom's light has come.
Sleep in the silent depths of the sea
Or in your bed of hallowed sod
Until you hear at dawn the low,
Clear reveille of God.

Monument on Corregidor Island
Manila Bay, Philippine Islands

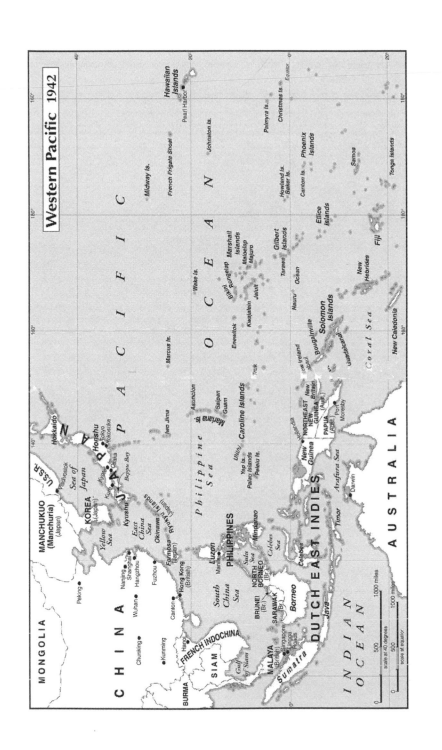

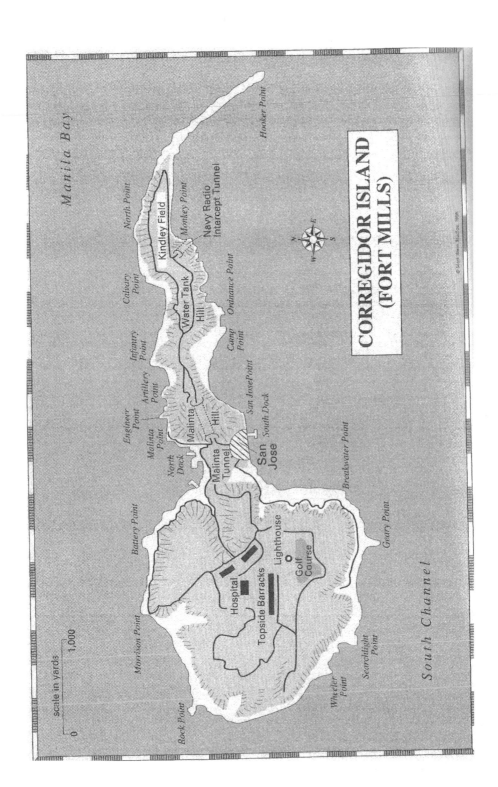

Manila Bay

North Point

Kindley Field

Monkey Point

Navy Radio
Intercept Tunnel

Calvary
Point

Water Tank
Hill

Ordnance Point

Infantry
Point

Camp
Point

Artillery
Point

Malinta
Hill

Engineer
Point

San JosePoint

Malinta
Point

South Dock

Battery Point

North
Dock

Malinta
Tunnel

San
Jose

Breakwater Point

Morison Point

Geary Point

Rock Point

Hospital

Lighthouse

Topside Barracks

Golf
Course

Searchlight
Point

Wheeler
Point

South Channel

scale in yards

0   1,000

CORREGIDOR ISLAND
(FORT MILLS)

Hooker Point

N

E

W

S

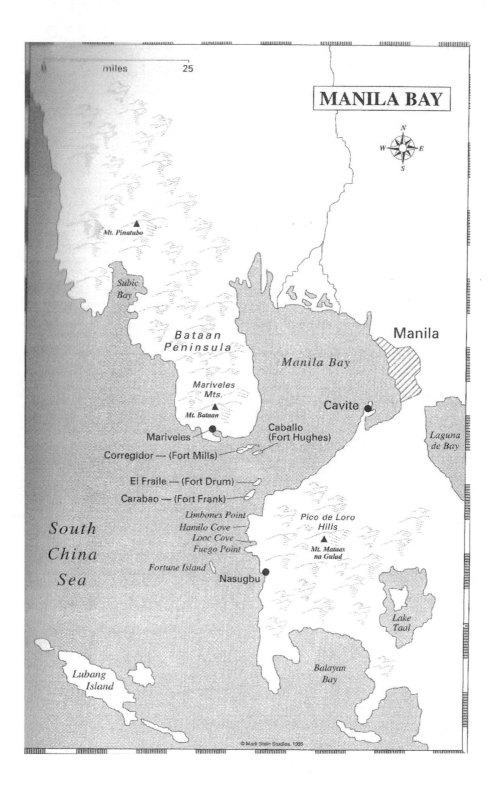

CAST OF CHARACTERS

AMERICANS -- U.S. NAVY, ABOARD MINESWEEPER USS *PELICAN* (AM 49), MANILA BAY

Alton C. Ingram, Lieutenant. "Todd," Commanding Officer
Frederick J. Holloway, Lt. (jg), Operations Officer.
Oliver P. Toliver, III, Lt. (jg) "Ollie," Gunnery Officer.
Bartholomew, Leonard (n), Chief Machinists Mate, "Rocky," Chief Engineer.
Farwell, Luther A., Quartermaster Second Class, Top helmsman.
Hampton, Joshua P., Electronics Technician 1st Class, Crew
Whittaker, Peter L., Engineman 3rd Class, Crew
Forester, Kevin T. Quartermaster 3rd Class, Crew
Forester, Brian I., Quartermaster Striker, Crew
Yardly, Ronald R., Pharmacist's Mate Second Class "Bones," Crew.
Sunderland, Kermit G. Gunner's Mate 1st Class, Crew.

AMERICANS -- CORREGIDOR ISLAND GARRISON (FORT MILLS), MANILA BAY, PHILIPPINES

Helen Z. Durand, First Lieutenant, U.S. Army, Nurse
Otis (n) DeWitt, Major, USA, Garrison Adjutant
Dwight G. Epperson, LT. USN, Commander, Naval Radio Intercept Tunnel at Monkey Point; Station CAST

Radtke, Walter, Cryptographer Technician, 2nd Class, USN, Monkey Point B Abwehr Military Intelligence see GERMANS.

Leon V. Beardsley, 1st Lieutenant, USAAF, B-17 pilot.

Carl R. Mordkin, Captain, USA Stockade Commander.

George F. Moore, Major General, USA, Garrison Commander, Corregidor Island (Fort Mills)

Jonathan M. Wainwright, Major General, USA"Skinny," Commander US Forces, Philippines.

Gordon F. Plummer, Captain, USA, Commander, Battery Craighill, Fort Hughes, (Caballo Island).

La Follette, Bruno (n), Sergeant, USA. Mortar Fire Control man, Fort Hughes (Caballo Island)

AMERICANS - U. S. NAVY, HAWAII

Chester W. Nimitz, Admiral, USN. Commander in Chief Pacific Fleet and Pacific Ocean Areas (CinCPOA).

Robert H. English, Rear Admiral, USN. Commander Submarine Forces, Pacific.

Elphege Alfred M. Gendreau, Captain, USN, Pacific Fleet Surgeon; Nimitz' housemate.

Milo F. Draemel. Rear Admiral, USN, Nimitz' Chief of Staff and housemate.

Edwin T. Layton, Lieutenant Commander, USN, Nimitz' Fleet Intelligence Officer.

Joseph J. Rochefort, Commander, USN, Commander station HYPO; OP-20-G, Naval Intelligence Unit.

AMERICANS -- U.S. NAVY, ABOARD SUBMARINE USS *WOLFFISH* (SS 204)

Roland M. Galloway, Lieutenant Commander, USN, Commanding Officer.

Gordon E. Chance, Lieutenant, USN, Executive Officer.

Morton A. Sampson, Lieutenant, USN, Operations Officer.

Raleigh T. Sutcliff, Lieutenant, USN, Engineering Officer.

Wallace Gruber, Ensign, USN, Torpedo Officer.

Hall, Ernest, Radioman Chief, Chief Radioman.

Lorca, Dominic Federico Radioman 2nd Class, Top radioman.

FILIPINOS

Don Pablo Amador, Philippine Deputy Finance, Minister, sawmill owner and lumber baron, Nasipit, Mindanao.

Manuel Carillo, Runs Amador's lumber mill.

Rosarita Carillo, Carrillo's wife.

Don Fito Diaz, Fishing Fleet Owner - Northern Marinduque Island.

Doña Valentina Diaz, Wife of Don Fito Diaz.

Don Emilio Aguilar, Marinduque Island plantation owner.

Doña Carmella Aguilar, Aguilar's wife.

Augustine Vega, Aguilar's foreman.

Luis Guzman & Carlos Ramirez, Ex-Filipino scouts working for Amador.

GERMANS

Helmut Döttmer, Kapitänleutnant *Kreigsmarine, Abwehr*--military intelligence, Posing as Cryptographer, Technician Second Class Walter Radtke, Corregidor Island; code named HECKLE.

Kurt Döttmer. Helmut's Father.

Elsa Döttmer, Helmut's Mother.

Wilhelm Canaris, Admiral, *Kreigsmarine,* Head of the *Abwehr* military intelligence, code named BESSON.

Hans Oster, Colonel, Canaris' Chief Assistant.

Karl Dönitz, Admiral, *Kreigsmarine,* Germany's Chief Flag Officer of U-boats with the title of *Befehlshaber der U-boote* (BdU).

JAPANESE

Kiyoshi Tuga, Lieutenant, Commander *Kempetai* (Thought Police) garrison, Northern Marinduque, later Nasipit, Mindanao.

Akihiko Watanabe, Lieutenant Tuga's *Kempetai* second-in-command on Marinduque.

Isoroku Yamamoto, Admiral, *"Rengo Kantai"* Commander in Chief Imperial Japanese Navy Combined Fleet.

Kawai Chiyoko, Umeryu (Plum-Dragon), Yamamoto's mistress.

PREFACE

Imperial Japan expanded her conquests at a dizzying rate beginning with the Pacific war's outbreak in December 1941. By mid-1942, she controlled an area equal to one-seventh of planet Earth. To support a voracious war-machine, she desperately needed raw materials to the south, namely the Dutch East Indies and New Guinea (now Indonesia), French –Indo China (Viet Nam, Thailand, Cambodia, Myanmar), and the Philippines.

But one of these objectives lay beyond her grasp: Manila Bay on Luzon's west coast in the Philippines. Manila Bay is an enormous natural harbor; so large, that it could easily have anchored all ships in the world at that time.

Four US Army fortified islands stood at the entrance to Manila Bay: Corregidor Island – Fort Mills; El Fraile Island – Fort Drum; Caballo Island – Fort Hughes; and Carabao Island – Fort Frank. The Bataan Peninsula forms the northern part of the entrance to Manila Bay. Tragically, it became known for the Bataan Death March after the Fil-American forces surrendered it to the Japanese in April, 1942.

The final hold-out in Luzon became the three mile-long, tad-pole shaped Corregidor Island. This was the largest and most heavily fortified island that guarded the entrance to Manila harbor; a harbor desperately needed by Japan so she could fulfill the strategic objectives of her so-called Greater East Asia Co-Prosperity Sphere.

But Corregidor held out, the 5,000-man garrison swelling to 11,000 after the fall of Bataan. After a sustained round-the-clock artillery barrage, Corregidor fell on May 6, 1942 to a Japanese night time amphibious assault. To stop the hideous slaughter of wounded and civilians, Major General Jonathan M. Wainwright surrendered to General Masaharu Homma, commander of the Imperial Japanese 14th Army. But Homma refused to cease fire on Corregidor. He continued his attacks on the surrendered troops demanding that Wainwright give up all forces in the Philippines. With great reluctance, Wainwright did so, resulting in the capitulation of well over 120,000 Fil American forces in the Central and Southern Philippines. Overall, 135,000 allied troops fell to the Japanese in that campaign; the worst defeat in American history.

But some got out including the late John H. Morrill, II rear admiral, USN, -- then a lieutenant commander. With sixteen men off his sunken minesweeper *Quail*, Lieutenant Commander Morrill escaped Corregidor the night it was surrendered to the Japanese. He navigated to Darwin Australia and freedom through 1,900 miles of enemy-controlled waters, much of it under the cover of night -- a heroic voyage by any measure. Morrill wrote about this in his book, *South From Corregidor*, Simon & Schuster, 1943. Thus, Todd Ingram's voyage through the Philippine Archipelago loosely approximates that of Lieutenant Commander Morrill.

The *Dugüello*: We learn about this historic piece in this novel's prologue and then throughout. At first, a simple tune, the *Dugüello* was played by a Mexican bugler at the Battle of the Alamo in 1836. This was when Mexican General Santa Ana and his army of 2,000 men attacked the Alamo in Texas defended by only 300 Texans. *Dugüello* comes from a Spanish noun meaning to cut one's throat. More figuratively, it means "...give no quarter,' or "...no prisoners." Few Texans survived the Alamo, but the battle became a rallying cry for Texans and their fight for independence from Mexico. In modern times, The *Dugüello* was given prominence by the well-known composer and conductor, Dimitri Tiomkin (winner of four academy awards) in the 1960 film, *The Alamo*, a United Artists release. On my website, we hear a beautiful and mournful rendition of Tiompkin's *Dugüello* played by Nelson Riddle and his orchestra – courtesy of the Nelson Riddle Foundation. You can enjoy this selection at: http://www.johnjgobbell.com/the-last-lieutenant.htm#. And yes, speakers up.

FOREWORD

9 August 1941
Placentina Bay, Newfoundland
Canada

Two warships, the cruiser USS *Augusta* (CA 31) and the battleship, HMS *Prince of Wales*, stood into the misty, cold waters of Placentia Bay, Newfoundland. Embarked were two heads of state. U.S. President Franklin D. Roosevelt, who had sailed from Maine aboard the *Augusta*, and from the United Kingdom, Prime Minister Winston Churchill. The ships anchored in a nest near Argentia, a fishing village on Placentia Bay's eastern shore. Meeting for the first time, the leaders were accompanied by their military and senior civilian staffs. Right away, the two found a common ground and talked amicably, one of the Brits soon commenting "...the cigarette-in-holder and the long cigar were at last being lit from the same match."

There was much to discuss. The Germans had overrun the European mainland. By June 1940, the Brits and French had been pushed into a pocket and savaged on the Beaches of Dunkirk. Eventually rescued to fight again were nearly 400,000 British and French soldiers. And later, in September, the brave fighter pilots of the RAF stood against the *Luftwaffe* and won the Battle of Britain. And for the time being, the *Wehrmacht*, the German Army, was no longer a direct threat to Britain. The previous June, via *Operation Barbarossa*, the Germans had invaded Russia along an unheard of eighteen-hundred-mile front and were now half-way to Moscow. At the same time, the Japanese were driving deep into China and were separately capturing parts of Southeast Asia, threatening British and American assets.

FDR knew his United States, whose citizens were recovering from a terrible depression, were seventy-eight percent isolationist. But eventually, they were to be pulled into a war whether they liked it or not. Churchill knew it too. One way or the other, it would be the Germans or the Japanese, against the Americans. Maybe both. What to do?

After four days, the two great leaders shook hands, hoisted anchor, and sailed home, where they announced to their respective nations that they had formed the *Atlantic Charter,* a precursor to the United Nations: Hands across the water. A series of agreements to support Britain in her fight against Nazi tyranny.

The *Atlantic Charter* was received well by the respective nations. But what Churchill and Roosevelt didn't tell the media was that they had also agreed on something else: *Europe First*. That for the time being, until the United States could catch up with its mighty industrial base and manpower pool, Asiatic bases would be left alone if Japan attacked. There would be no effort to rescue anyone. In other words, they would be sacrificed. Buying time. Both nations could ill afford to go after the thousands of men scattered in a vast array of possessions over the Pacific. And this included Singapore and the Philippines.

Europe First.

Among other evils which being unarmed brings you, it causes you to be despised.

The Prince
Niccolo Machiavelli

PROLOGUE

16 June 1941
Union Station
El Paso, Texas

The killer's code name was HECKLE. He looped his garrote around the sailor's neck and yanked. The sailor straightened to his tiptoes, then jounced while grabbing futilely at the cord crushing his windpipe. His hat tumbled into the restroom sink.

In the mirror, the killer watched his victim's eyes bulge in disbelief. He renewed his purchase and pulled the garrote tighter. With what air was left, the sailor gurgled pathetically and sunk to his knees.

Thirty seconds will do it.

But, there it was again. From the cantina, a block to the west of the station drifted a haunting trumpet solo. The sailor's writhing grew weaker. The melody was locked in the killer's mind, making it hard to concentrate on the task at hand.

The sailor wrenched to his side, pulling the killer off balance. The garrote loosened and the sailor sucked a prolonged sobbing breath. Avoiding his victim's grappling hands; the killer held on, took one step back and pushed open a toilet-stall door with his right elbow. While jabbing his right knee in the sailor's back, he pulled the garrote tighter.

The sailor fell face-first onto the cold, tile floor while the killer dragged him into the stall. The killer stumbled against the commode then slipped in a urine puddle, once again losing his hold. The sailor's feet jinked and pounded on the tile as he pushed his left hand on the floor, loosening the garrote further. As he drew another gurgling lungful of air, he slumped back onto his stomach.

This is going badly.

The killer moved precisely dropping his right knee into the sailor's back, and putting all his weight on the sailor's spine. With clenched teeth, the killer pulled the garrote again and, this time, counted to 120. Slowly.

The tinny music once again drifted into the rest room from the cantina. HECKLE cocked his head as the trumpeter finished his solo. The musician was talented and put his soul into what he played. HECKLE could tell by the trumpeter's breathing. When the other instruments joined in, HECKLE could still pick out the solo trumpeter. He closed his eyes and tried to visualize what the man looked like.

The body twitched. The killer leaned over, finding the sailor's eyes shut and his face blue. He thumbed an eyelid: The pupil was completely dilated. Checking the carotid artery, he found no pulse. This sailor would give no more trouble; he was dead. Surprised he was winded, the killer sat on the toilet and forced himself to take a brief rest.

A long way to go...take your time.

He looked out the high, half open transom window seeing brilliant stars in the moonless Texas night.

It must be the heat.

It had been 106 degrees yesterday when he had crossed the border and, even at this hour, it was stifling. He ran the back of his hand over his brow and listened while catching his breath. The little band played another song, but that same melody floated in HECKLE's mind.

What the hell was that song? The melody was victorious yet...at the same time, oppressed. How could that be?

He listened for another moment, then checked his watch: 0317. Two minutes behind schedule.

Only nine minutes before the train pulls out.

The killer gave a quick whistle and his lookout stepped inside the restroom, wearing an Army MP uniform. He was thin and mousey and had a long-pointed nose. Giving the corpse a sour look, his large beak wiggled as he sniffed. "Gott!"

The killer took in the odor and realized the sailor had soiled himself during his last throes. With a scowl, the lookout quickly changed his clothes. He put on a pair of overalls and stuffed the MP uniform in a paper bag. While wiping sweat from his bald head, he jammed on a straw hat and moved toward the door.

The killer looked up with his brow raised.

The lookout responded, "Car four three six one, seat fourteen A. The duffle is there. Hurry." The door closed and the lookout resumed his vigil outside the men's room, this time as a civilian.

The killer expelled a huge sigh. Without that duffle, the operation would have been almost impossible. The sailor's uniforms, orders, and personal gear were all there.

Nice going. How did that little turd find the duffle so quickly? No, forget him. With that nose, the man can find anything.

Hurry.

He pulled off his mufti, revealing a dress white uniform identical to his victim's and, taking everything from the sailor's pocket, stuffed it into his own. The wallet seemed unusually thick and he flipped it open, finding singles, fives, tens, and twenties; close to five hundred dollars.

Strange.

A quick look at the United States Navy identification card verified he'd killed the right man. A mournful wail drifted through the transom window. HECKLE cocked his head and analyzed the beautifully pitched chord. E-minor? Or was it A-minor? He couldn't tell as the whistle blew again, nearer this time. At first the floor tingled, then shook mightily as, moments later, an eastbound freight thundered past.

The lookout peeked in; they nodded, and together pulled the sailor to his feet with an arm draped around each of their shoulders. Walking past the washbasin, the killer stopped, tightened the faucet, and retrieved the sailor's white hat. He jammed it on the man's head with the edge resting on the bridge of his nose.

An Army sergeant blasted in, unzipping his fly. He looked at them with a bleary-eyed grin and yelled something. But the chuffing of two steam engines pushing the same eastbound train obliterated conversation.

The sergeant stood weaving and studied them, making the killer feel so self-conscious that he casually tucked his left hand in his back pocket. The sergeant nodded to the dead sailor and mouthed against the roar, "he okay?" He squinted and braced a hand against the wall, blocking their path.

They waited while the mighty engines snarled their way eastward dragging the last of the train's rumbling cars.

The sergeant had Fort Bliss Calvary written all over him.

Do Something, the killer thought. "He'll be fine. Puked like a waterfall. Must be that damned Mexican beer." He said in a loud voice. The killer broke out in laughter and his lookout had the good sense to join in.

Finally, the sergeant chuckled with them as the train faded in the distance. The sergeant said, "Better use the side door. MPs are out on the platform."

"Thanks," said the killer.

"Wheooow." The sergeant held his nose as he eased past the threesome and stepped to the urinal.

Hauling their victim outside, it took five precious minutes to drag the dead man to a Ford pickup truck parked on Overland between Durango and Leon streets. Looking both ways, they stuffed the body under empty tomato crates. Their excess gear followed. The lookout climbed in and slammed the door. He turned the key, shoved in the clutch, and jammed his foot on the starter pedal, giving the killer an odd look while the engine cranked. The four-banger caught, the lookout jammed it into gear, and the Ford waddled off to Stanton Street, turning right to cross over the Rio Grande into Juárez, Mexico, where the body would be disposed of.

The killer looked at his watch.

Three and a half minutes before the train pulls out.

He ran, making it to the station in two minutes and twenty seconds. A conductor stood outside car four three six one checking his timepiece. The killer stepped aboard, finding the car almost empty: three civilians and two army enlisted. All were asleep. No Navy. He walked past 14A, eased the duffle from 14B, noting the stenciling on the thick, olive-drab canvas:

RADTKE, W. A., BU3, USN, 1187526

Hoisting Bugler Third Class Walter A. Radtke's duffle over his shoulder, he quietly walked forward two cars, found an empty seat, 12A, dumped the duffle in 12B, and sat.

The killer looked out at Union Station thinking about how the sailor had obliged them by jumping off the train just as it pulled in for a twenty-minute layover. Their plan was to have the lookout, in his MP uniform, pull him off the train and lure him to a dark corner. But their target made a beeline for the men's room, the killer followed, and that was that. On reflection, the killer remembered he'd waited forty-five seconds for the sailor to empty his bladder meaning the toilet in car four three six one was stopped up. He was glad he'd moved forward two cars.

HECKLE had entered the United States yesterday via the El Paso bridge and had registered in a cheap hotel near the rail yards, wanting a good night's rest. But next door was a Cantina with a glowing red-neon blinking sign: *Preston's*. Sleep was impossible with those insane mariachis, or whatever they called themselves. They played endless music with brass, violin, and guitar haphazardly coordinated. But the more HECKLE listened he realized the music had wonderful character, even though the violin player sometimes did a terrible job. He mused; was it the rhythm or was it what the musicians were trying to say that made some of their material so haunting?

Especially that one trumpet solo. The man played it two or three times during the night. He couldn't get to sleep even after Preston's closed at four. Now HECKLE thought about it as he slumped in his seat and nestled his head next to the open window. It reminded him of another trumpet solo: "Parsifal", slow, deliberate and pure; Wagner's bold arrogance was absent in "Parsifal." And yet, if one listened carefully, the passage offered something new each time one heard it. Messages, imbued with filigreed secrets, drifted from each beautifully crafted phrase.

Something rustled across the aisle and he looked up, seeing a corporal unload a duffle in the seat opposite. Pretending to ignore the soldier, he dropped his hat over his eyes and looked at his watch: 0325.

The soldier studied the man in the white uniform for a minute, then tipped two fingers to his brow and said, "Where ya'll from, swabbie?" The corporal, another Fort Bliss Cavalryman, had one of those interesting Texas dialects.

"Minneapolis," the killer mumbled, and casually spun his duffle turning the stenciled name and serial number away from the corporal. Then he rested his head against it, keeping his face in shadows and making sure his left hand, with its gnarled ring finger, didn't show.

"What ship ya on?"

He scrunched further. "*North Carolina*." Even as he said it, he knew he'd made a mistake.

"Hot damn! Another guy on the train's off the *North Carolina*. You must know him. "

"She's a big ship." the killer feigned a snooze.

The engine gave two short toots and the conductor's voice wafted to them, "...board."

"Ya like poker, swabbie?" the corporal asked gently.

The train jerked backwards then, with couplings clanking, started ahead with the Mountain, MT-4 locomotive's great eighty-inch driving wheels spinning on the rails as the engineer fed in too much steam. At last the drivers found traction and the "4-8-2" type engine rolled smoothly out of Union Station, resuming its journey to Los Angeles. From there HECKLE would transfer to a train for San Diego where, for the next six weeks, he would take his victim's place in the U.S. Navy's cryptography class 41-B-276 at the U.S. Naval Station.

"I said, 'do you like poker?' Your buddy back there cleaned me out. So how 'bout a chance to get even?"

That's where all the money in the sailor's wallet came from, thought the killer. He wondered how well the corporal had become acquainted with the sailor. They passed within fifty feet of the cantina which had denied him so much sleep last night. There it was again. That mournful strain from a solo trumpet.

"Sorry. I didn't mean to wake you," the corporal said.

HECKLE snapped from his reverie. "Poker? Sure. Look, soldier, do you know what they call that music?"

"What?"

"Listen." HECKLE nodded to Preston's. The glow of the cantina's red neon sign flicked across his face as the train labored by. And they heard the lone trumpeter: His notes were full and pure and triumphant. This trumpeter, his instrument and his music were as good as anything he'd heard his father play.

The corporal slumped back. "Shit, man."

"Yes?"

"Damned Mexicans love pissin' off gringos now and then."

"I don't understand."

"That's the '*Deguello*.' Ain't you ever heard the '*Deguello*'?"

"Guess not."

"Shit. Santa Ana played it at the Alamo. Where you from, anyway?"

HECKLE felt a rush of blood to his head. He had no idea about Santa Ana and the Alamo. "Uh, Minnesota."

The corporal folded his arms over his chest and yawned. "Ah'm tired. I'll take a raincheck on the poker. Wake me when we get to Deming."

Deming, New Mexico, was their next stop. Afraid he would lose his chance, HECKLE said, "you getting off there?"

"No," the soldier mumbled. He jabbed a thumb over his shoulder. "Damned toilet's stopped up."

The killer thought that one over then said, "You going all the way to Los Angeles?"

"Yup."

Realizing he had plenty of time, HECKLE relaxed. The wheels clicked on the rails and the coach car wobbled a somnolent rhythm, easing him off to a welcomed sleep; yet, even as he drifted, the "*Deguello*" played again and again in his mind.

PART I

And lay siege against it, and build a fort against it, and cast a mount against it, set the camp also against it, and set battering rams ...

Ezekiel 4:2

I cannot stand this constant reference to England, to Europe... how typically American to writhe in anguish at the fate of a distant cousin while a daughter is being raped in the back room...

Manuel L. Quezon, President of The Philippine Republic
January 26, 1942

1

19 April 1942
Naval Radio Intercept Tunnel, Lateral Four
Corregidor Island, Manila Bay, Philippines

The radioman's foghorn voice rattled through the door, "Hey, rat-man! Front and center. Hawaii calls. Hubba, hubba."

The cryptographer second class wiped the last of the shaving cream from his face, slapped on some Bay Rum after shave, and stepped into the radio room, just as Portman finished tapping his key acknowledging the message's receipt. "Almost done, rat-turd."

"It's Radtke," the cryptographer said, tucking his left hand in his back pocket.

Portman, clad in shorts and filthy tank T-shirt, was a first-class radioman, who somehow managed to look fat in spite of his half-starved condition. He ripped the flimsy out of his typewriter and handed it over his shoulder without looking.

"Gotcha rat-brain. Now, hurry up and decode it. Maybe it says when the fleet's coming."

"You'll be the last to know."

"Guess what?" Looking both ways, Portman leaned toward Skinner, a parrot-beaked third-class radioman. Motioning them closer, Portman cleared tunnel dust from his throat and, turning down his resonant bombast said, "One of the guy's in Army intelligence told me they raised the *Oklahoma*."

Skinner whistled, "No shit?"

"But she won't be fixed in time to relieve us." Portman said.

"So, who's gonna relieve us?" asked Skinner.

"All the rest of them battleships, dope! They raised 'em all. Like the *Nevada* and the *Pennsylvania*. He even said my old lady, the *Arizona* is all set to go."

"Army BS," spouted Skinner.

"Skinner, you stupid jerk!" Portman roared. "This is straight from Watkins. Don't you know that..."

Radtke walked in the crypto room and shut the door. He took another step when everything shook. Thunder raged overhead and he instinctively eyed the reinforced concrete ceiling and reached to a cabinet for support, hearing Skinner yelp next door.

With the fall of Bataan two weeks ago, Corregidor staggered under a twenty-four-hour artillery and aerial barrage. This felt like a stick of Jap 250-kilogram bombs. Chips fell, dust swept through the room, and the single forty-watt lamp swayed, casting a pool of itinerant, stygian light. Dust caught in his throat and, while he coughed, he picked up a towel and covered Lulu, his sensitive crypto machine. He would have to wait a minute or two before he decrypted the message.

Dust. Always the dust. Still, this wasn't as bad as two days ago when a Jap artillery shell exploded smack at the entrance to the tunnel. Dust, trash, even tin cans blew over wounded and dying all the way through the tunnel's length and out the other side, belching a large cloud of black, pungent detritus.

Sweat ran in his eyes and he blinked. The dust had settled. Pushing aside the towel, he flipped on Lulu's power switch and placed the message in a holder. It read:

TOP SECRET

041920152Z

FM COM OP-20-G HYPO
TO COM OP-20-G CAST
BT
28876 89761 53086 67443 89130 86531 76124 22317 77312 67321
78226 23078 66731 93220 71532 97013 29641 55066 71322 15266
67132 87331 85162 39253 56618 27828 87661 87395 34116 75041
76552 98776 13023 86297 97746 98736 85512 71324 25553 87351
85673 73619 73669 84612 17429 28619 33672 33265 61543 83266
33527 18854 94529
BT

Radtke was thirty-one and had matted blond hair that once proudly stood in a crew cut. Wearing only T-shirt, shorts, and boots, he licked his lips and pecked at the keyboard. He had just decrypted the message's protective buffer when an enormous explosion shook the room. That one landed directly overhead. Gripping the desk, he figured it for one of the huge 240 millimeter howitzers the Japanese were sighting in from Bataan. A strange noise, like a steam locomotive chuffing around a bend from two miles away, reached him. It was the wounded and dying in the main tunnel, and offshoots called *laterals*. They didn't have the strength to scream or moan or even wail like Skinner was doing out there.

Dust swirled in the crypto room. The man covered Lulu and sat back, hearing Mr. Epperson walk in the radio room behind him.

"...hey Portman. This says sixteen B-25s bombed Tokyo yesterday. I thought you said twelve." Epperson's voice carried the scratched record sound from dust-shrouded vocal chords. They called it the tunnel voice.

Portman rasped back, "That's what the Fox broadcast said, Sir."

"Well, which is it?" Epperson asked.

"This one amends this morning's message, Sir. I'd say sixteen is the--"

"Damnit, you better be sure..." Epperson's fist slammed in the next room.

While Epperson chewed on Portman, Radtke pulled the towel off Lulu and methodically crunched the keys. He stripped the code's protective padding and started on the text. Hair stood on the back of his neck as the five-digit groups arranged themselves into:

TOP SECRET

04192015Z
FM COM OP-20-G HYPO
TO COM OP-20-G CAST
BT

1. EPPERSON, D. J., LT. USN, 476225; RADTKE, W. A., CT2 USN, 1187526
DETACHED CAST.
2. REPORT SOONEST TO HYPO AVAILABLE XPORT VIA DARWIN.
3. SEA CONDOR ETA 04202100H, SW CRNR YY2. EPPERSON/RADTKE
MANIFESTED HIGHEST PRIORITY.
4. CAST ENSURE COMPLETE DESTRUCTION REMAINING EQUIP-
MENT AND MATERIALS.
5. ACKNOWLEDGE.
BT

"Jeepers!" Radtke jumped up. "Mr. Epperson!"

The small shuttered door opened just as three enemy shells landed on Water Tank Hill, barely six hundred yards away. *Krumpf, krumpf* and *WHOOM!* It was the third one; it sounded like it got something, maybe an ammo dump. He knew people had died when that third shell hit. And soon, more maimed Americans and Filipinos would be stacked among those already gasping in the tunnels.

Epperson's skeletous five-foot-five-inch frame walked in the crypto room. Like Radtke, the lieutenant was clad in only boots and shorts. He had deep sunk eyes and his ribs and clavicles protruded, making his head look much too big for his body. All of his black hair had been shaved off, and abscessed heat sores on his head were painted with methylate. Oddly, a hopeless case of pimples he'd sported until last December were gone.

Radtke knew that, except for his own six feet four inches, he looked as emaciated. In fact, he was afraid to look in a mirror. They had started with one-half rations last January; now they were down to three-eighths. Invari-ably, it consisted of hotcakes made without eggs for breakfast; no lunch; rice, tinned salmon, and murky water for dinner.

Epperson's peripatetic eyes darted about the room and Radtke, knowing it was better not to interrupt, waited patiently. The radio squealed next door;

Portman fine-tuned the receiver and Glen Miller's rich, syncopated tones saturated Lateral Four.

After Tuxedo Junction, the voice of Tokyo Rose echoed before Portman could turn down the volume. "...nations of Nippon. Honored members of the Greater East Asia Co-Prosperity Sphere bordering the Western Pacific and Indian oceans. You have well benefitted from the noble sacrifices of divine Japanese liberators--"

"Portman! Turn that shit off," someone yelled outside.

"Hold on, Chief. Benny Goodman's up next," Portman yelled back.

"...as proof," Rose went on, "I offer our stunning victories in Pearl Harbor, Wake Island, Hong Kong, Singapore, the Dutch East Indies, New Guinea and, two weeks ago, Bataan. And now tonight I'm proud to announce the *Kido Butai* has swept the--"

"What's the *Kido Butai*?" moaned Skinner.

"Jap attack carriers. Now, shuddup," hissed Portman

"...and other sections of the Indian Ocean as far west as Ceylon where, outside Trincomalee Harbor, our glorious naval-dive bombers sank the British aircraft carrier *Hermes*."

Rose paused. Explosions rumbled from Corregidor's western end and someone wailed "...shiiiit."

"You on Corregidor!" Rose's tone was sharper than usual. For once, she forgot to lilt her inflection in a beckoning timbre. "Hasn't General Wainwright told you that eleven thousand are there with you. Soon, you will have no food nor water. Time runs out. General Masaharu Homma, Commander of the Imperial Fourteenth Japanese Army, has set up a land, sea, and air blockade from which no one can escape.

"You're trapped. Why resist?" Adding a coquettish curl to her syllables, Rose said, "The Rising Sun flies proudly over Manila. And with our glorious victory on the Bataan Peninsula, the entire Philippine Archipelago will soon be free from American oppression. Further resistance is useless. Surrender now and you'll receive preferential treatment--"

"Where the hell's Benny Goodman?" someone yelled.

The radio squealed again as Portman tuned it, "In a minute, damnit." The rig still screeched.

"Turn it up!" another voice screamed.

Portman said, "Okay, okay, Chief."

Rose's moon-pearl voice drifted back, "...for your wives and sweethearts. When was the last time you saw them? And when was the last time you had fried ten ounce steaks topped with onions and mushrooms? Baked potatoes dripping with butter? Corn on the cob and mounds of chilled salad all chased with frosted pitchers of cold beer..."

"...Rrradtke, damnit!"

The cryptographer blinked. He'd fallen asleep standing up. It happened to everyone. With Corregidor's siege, nobody had had uninterrupted sleep for over three months.

Dumbly, he handed over the message making sure his left hand was tucked in his belt. Epperson's gold U.S. Naval Academy class ring flashed as he snatched it and held it under the swaying lamp.

Epperson whistled. "That's it then. CinCPac wants us out. You can play your trumpet again. How about that?"

"Yessir."

"Send an acknowledgement; then let's get things ready for the incinerator. Any ideas on how to destroy Lulu and the rest of this stuff?" Epperson's hand swept toward an IBM tabulating machine.

"Yessir. I know a shipfitter. Big sledgehammers."

"Okay, but just you in here, Radtke. Nobody else. And it has to be dumped in the bay. Deep water. Understand?"

"Yessir."

Epperson's eyes flicked around a room that once held over fifty code and intelligence analysts, their crypto machines, and the IBM tabulator. Now the room was bare except for the tabulator, twelve gaping floor safes, two filing cabinets, a destitute water cooler, Epperson's double-bolted locker, and Lulu. Corregidor had been part of a network of four major radio intercept and cryptographic analysis posts. The others were in Honolulu, Washington, D.C., and Melbourne (previously Singapore before the Japanese overran it two months ago).

Corregidor was station Cast: phonetic for the letter C. Hawaii was Hypo. Melbourne was Mike. The network pooled information about decoded enemy messages. Hypo and Cast, in particular, cooperated extensively to crack messages in the Japanese naval code, designated JN-25, by the Allies.

Corregidor was going to be tough to lose, he knew. Cast's proximity to the Japanese homeland provided an effective base for reception of radio traffic.

And it was because Corregidor was a rock, a natural fortress festooned with tunnels, provisions, long-range coastal guns, and gigantic mortars that it remained in American hands. For the Rock sat squarely in the entrance to Manila Bay, a staggering body of water twenty miles wide, capable of providing safe anchorage for fifty percent of the world's navies at one time.

Until three months ago, Cavite, on Manila Bay's southern shore, was homeport for the U.S. Navy's Asiatic Fleet. The Cavite and Batangas provinces shared the mouth's southern edge, while the mouth's northern shore was formed by the Bataan Peninsula. There, a small harbor accommodated the Mariveles Naval Station now occupied by the Japanese.

But use of Manila, Cavite, and Mariveles was denied to enemy shipping because Corregidor and three smaller island fortresses guarded the entrance to Manila Bay. Corregidor--Fort Mills--was a tadpole-shaped island a little over three miles long and lay closest to the southern edge of the Bataan Peninsula. Only four miles away: Caballo Island, two miles south of Corregidor, was headquarters for Fort Hughes; Fort Frank was perched atop Carabao Island, only two miles from Luzon's Batangas Province. Also, an extensive minefield had been laid across the entrance, controlled by an Army electronic detonation station on Corregidor.

An oddity was tiny El Fraile Island lying nearest the Batangas shore. From 1919 to 1929, Army engineers had poured an enormous reinforced concrete casement, thirty feet thick, around the islet in the shape of a battleship with its "bow" pointed into the South China Sea. Indeed, when the tide swept in, Fort Drum, as it was called, cut a bow wave with the uninitiated estimating the "battleship's" speed at three to four knots. Two massive fourteen-inch twin gun turrets rotating on barbettes were mounted on Fort Drum's "foredeck." Aft, four six-inch "stern" mounted guns looked into Manila Bay.

Only remnants of the U.S. Navy's once-proud Asiatic Fleet were left: Minesweepers to tend the minefields, a couple of old China river gunboats, and utility craft.

Even the PT boats were gone. Last month, the four remaining boats of MTB 3 whisked MacArthur and his staff to Mindanao. There the general and his entourage rendezvoused with a B-17 which took them to Australia.

Like the minesweepers, Epperson and his assistant were the skeleton crew left to man station Cast's crypto room. But it was a surety they would be tortured if captured. Secrets would spill; their invaluable information would make the war's course graver for the Allies. And if Epperson and his assistant didn't get out, OP-20-G Hypo would issue orders through CinCPac to someone on Corregidor to shoot them before the enemy stormed ashore.

But this message changed all that. And their priority was so high that Lieutenant Dwight Epperson and Cryptographer Second Class Walter Radtke would be the first to step aboard that submarine tomorrow night. Ahead of brownnosing colonels and generals, ahead of nurses, even civilian kids.

Epperson checked his watch. "Twenty-six hours before that sub shows up. I'll--"

Epperson's voice was wiped out by a thunderous explosion. The room shook. Papers slid off the filing cabinet and a drawer shot open. A large shell had landed nearby: Kindley Air Base, he judged. The two watched each other's faces jiggle for three whole seconds. With dust shooting through ceiling cracks, Radtke automatically pitched the towel over Lulu.

It wasn't until the shaking was over that Epperson eased away from the file cabinet. He blinked and wheezed "...I have to find someone to take us through the minefield."

"How, Sir?" He knew the Japanese had just about bombed everything that floated in Manila Bay.

Epperson was distant. "...Todd Ingram. He could do it."

"Who's that?"

"...a classmate." Epperson's eyes snapped up to his assistant's. "I'll take care of it. Draft an acknowledgement, then get those damned sledge-hammers."

"Yessir."

Epperson turned and opened the door; Benny Goodman drifted through. The door hadn't quite slammed when a series of shells, one hundred millimeter howitzers by the feel of it, blasted along the North Shore Road. Radtke held on, as yet another salvo walked across Ordnance Point, obliterating Epperson's prolonged swearing.

With the door closed, he whipped open the drawer under Lulu. A .45 lay atop four blue mimeograph master sheets which were labeled:

TOP SECRET

COMPACFLT EYES ONLY
PREDICTIONS
IMPERIAL JAPANESE COMBINED FLEET ACTIVITY
MAY - JUNE 1942

He pulled out the .45 and quickly dumped the clip. In a flash he worked the action, making sure the chamber was clear, thumbed off the safety, then pointed it at the door. After steady pressure on the trigger, the pistol's hammer clicked loudly.

"Good-bye, Mr. Epperson," the cryptographer said.

2

19 April 1942
U.S.S. *Pelican* (AM 49)
Manila Bay, Philippines

Smoke rising from Corregidor's round-the-clock bombardment masked a full moon which otherwise would have well illuminated the *Pelican*. At 2 a.m., the temperature and humidity were unified at eighty-eight, while the 187-foot minesweeper sat deep in the water off Corregidor's South Harbor. Manila Bay was oily and flat, allowing the ship to keep her anchor at short stay for a quick escape. Except getting underway was impossible. The *Pelican* was hopelessly without power.

They had thrown everything at her today. Mitsubishi A6M5 Zeros strafed from deck level, while simultaneously, Aichi D3A2 "Val" dive-bombers tried their best to kill her with screaming plunges from ten thousand feet. But the 1,250-ton *Pelican* twisted and turned in Manila Bay, avoiding eight of those dive-bombers and all they could toss.

The skies cleared and the *Pelican*'s gunners cheered and looked for paint to scribe two Val silhouettes on their bulwarks. Suddenly a ninth Val dove out of the sun. The *Pelican* was just able to spin from under two 250 kilogram bombs, but the effects of the near misses were as deadly as direct hits.

One bomb landed close off the starboard bow, its concussion decimating the forward three-inch gun while throwing Hampton, a first-class electrician, through the air where he slammed against a bulwark, breaking the bone in his thigh. The other bomb landed amidships, causing serious damage in the *Pelican*'s engineering spaces. Two minutes later MacRoberts, a third-class gunner at the forward three inch, was killed when a twenty-millimeter shell from a strafing Zero ripped through his chest.

Now the *Pelican*'s gunners toiled frantically on her forward three inch to replace the recoil spring shattered by the same bullet that killed MacRoberts. Two other gunners and a bosun worked feverishly on the gun's broken breech block.

In the engine room, the battle lantern's ghostly beams illuminated men fighting to offset the disastrous effects of the second bomb. Humidity, intolerable in the daytime, was ninety-two in the cramped space with the thermometer stuck at 104 degrees.

The bomb's concussive effect had buckled the metal plates, allowing sea water to rise dangerously close to the minesweeper's silent diesel engine. Topside, a portable P-250 pump barely kept up with the flooding as one hose, dangling through the engine room hatch, sucked up the dark water and spewed it back into Manila Bay.

Aft of the main engine, the refrigerator sized reduction gear box had jumped its bed, shearing the mounting bolts. Also, the bomb's shocking jolt had caused the diesel's camshaft to hopelessly wobble out of alignment and burn up its bearings.

Four men stood on the main engine catwalk installing a new camshaft, while to starboard, shipfitters swung mallets, pounding thick wooden strong backs to shore the metal plates back into place. Welders, wearing bug like goggles, worked their torches to re-seam the plates into some measure of their original watertight integrity.

A shirtless Todd Ingram, the *Pelican*'s skipper, stood in the shaft alley where water, fouled with hydraulic fluid, fuel oil, and trash, sloshed around his hips. Standing beside the gear box, five sweating enginemen stooped to put their weight on two long crowbars.

Ingram yelled, "One...two..."

"Hold on." Bartholomew, the ship's balding chief engineman squeezed among the men taking a grip on the forward crowbar. He looked back with a grin. "Okay. This time does it."

Ingram growled, "One...two...three...Go!"

The men grunted and cursed and slipped, raising their backs to the crowbars.

Ingram counted to five and shouted, "Stop!"

As one, they exhaled and braced their hands against the bulkhead to catch their breath. While the men rested, Ingram bent to examine the reduction gear mounts. Like everyone else, he was twenty-five to thirty pounds below his normal weight of 175. What seemed stupid was not the ribs or even his hip bones sticking out; it was the skinny arms. His hands, too; he'd lost so much weight he had to wear his Naval Academy class ring on his thumb. Ingram looked like a frail orphanage reject, just like everybody else. Fractional rations of tinned salmon and rice took its toll, and the lifting and the sweating wasn't going to put weight back on.

"Anything move?" wheezed Jennings.

Ingram shook his head.

Jennings's face mirrored the frustration of the other men.

Bartholomew sloshed aft and pulled out a flashlight. Even in the humidity, the chief wore the traditional engineer's dark green coveralls. And these, of course, were soaked with sweat, grease and innumerable other indelible blotches, which he displayed more proudly than the four rows of campaign ribbons on his dress uniform.

The light clicked and they bent close.

"Still a half-inch, Rocky," Ingram said.

Bartholomew looked at him strangely for a moment, then rose and walked back to the crowbar. Spitting on both hands, he roared, "This is it, girls. Put your backs to it now." He nodded at Ingram.

Ingram backed into the shaft alley where he could sight the reduction gear box.

"Wait." He went forward, stooped, and slipped the tip of one crowbar aft six inches. Then he splashed back in the shaft alley. Taking a deep breath he bellowed, "Alright, now. One, two, three! Mule haul!"

The red-faced sailors growled in unison, and the stout gear box thumped. "Okay, okay!" Ingram yelled, sloshing to the aft mounts.

Bartholomew joined him and they nodded to one another.

"Forward?" croaked Bartholomew.

"All set, Chief," Jennings yelled, from in front of the housing.

Bartholomew stood saying, "Whittaker. Start here with the studs." He turned to Ingram. "Okay, Skipper. Once the cam is in, we can start up and begin pumping."

"How long do you think--"

"Todd," someone yelled.

Ingram looked up. "Yeah?"

Lieutenant Junior Grade Fred Holloway was the midwatch officer of the deck (OOD). A chemistry major at Stanford, he was halfway through his master's program two years ago, when he became restless and decided to join the Navy. His twenty-three-year-old hairless babyface peered down from the main deck hatch. "A guy's here to see you."

"Who?"

A shadowy face appeared behind Holloway. Ingram shined a battle lantern into it. Gaunt eyes, prominent cheekbones and a shaved head with methylate-painted suppurating sores made him think of an Eric von Stroheim horror movie.

"Ace, it's me," the shape said.

That dry voice. It had the scratchiness of the tunnel people, yet there was a familiar resonance.... And no one had called him "Ace" since his days at the U.S. Naval Academy. His full name was Alton C. Ingram--ACI--and they called him Ace.

It hit him. They had been plebes together. And roommates. This man had patiently tutored him in trigonometry and calculus at the Naval Academy. After graduating in 1937, Ingram had lost track of him. "Dwight? Dwight Epperson?"

"You bet."

"I'll be damned." Ingram scrambled up the ladder to the main deck where they shook hands and clapped shoulders.

Ingram lead him aft a few paces. "What are you doing here? Are you on the Rock?"

"Yes."

A large round flashed atop Malinta Hill, illuminating Epperson. Even at this distance they felt the concussion. "You look like hell."

His friend choked out a raspy laugh. "Looked in a mirror lately?"

Ingram sighed.

Epperson looked around the ship, spread his arms and croaked, "What happened?"

Ingram told him.

"What's wrong with the other engine?"

"This ship's about as old as Dewey. One decrepit diesel, one screw, that's it."

Epperson said, "Oh."

"The nips laugh at anything we have floating out here. Today was target practice for them. Except we got lucky and turned the tables."

"It's about time."

"That's right. But reality sinks in. You want a minesweeper with twin screws? How--"

"Todd--"

"--about a brand new one? Well, all you have to do is go stateside. Plenty of everything just sitting around."

Epperson waited.

"Sorry, one of my guys was killed today. And it's hot as hell down there." Ingram paused. "Last I heard, you were on the *Portland*."

"Radio officer. After that, intelligence school." Epperson's nod toward Corregidor was barely noticeable. "I've been here for eighteen months."

It struck Ingram. His classmate had lived in Tokyo for ten years where his father had worked for Western Union. The whole family spoke fluent Japanese. "You're in the radio intercept gang?"

Epperson said nothing.

"And you read their traffic?"

A shrug.

Ingram waited. Finally, he said, "I was gun boss on the *Hayes*, a tin can. She was blown out from under me in the first raid on Cavite last December. They sent me here." He grinned. "My first command."

"I know."

"Why didn't you look me up?"

Epperson's face was illuminated by stroboscopic flashes from Calumpan on the south shore: more incoming.

They waited. Five rounds landed on Fort Hughes, four miles away. Gasoline ignited and consumed itself inside a mushroom shaped cloud. A vehicle, perhaps a small boat had been hit. Just then Fort Hughes's Battery Woodruff roared back with dual fourteen-inch disappearing cannons. Soon Woodruff's seven-hundred-pound projectiles erupted in the Pico de Loro Hills just above Calumpan.

Ingram said, "I think Corregidor is completely sighted in."

"Sighted in?" Epperson, the cryptographic whiz-kid, had forgotten his gunnery courses.

"One particular artillery piece is sighted and checked at one particular spot. Then they leave it alone and don't shoot it until--"

"--Tojo blows his whistle?"

"Something like that. Everything goes off at once. One cannon is aimed at the tunnel mouth, another at the fuel docks, another at the mortar batteries and so on." He paused. "It won't be pretty when Tojo blows his whistle."

They turned as a round exploded on Fort Drum's concrete casement. Ingram said, "What brings you over?"

Epperson's eyes glistened.

Ingram prodded, "I haven't got all night."

"Alright. If someone asks, you didn't see this." Epperson reached in his shirt, pulled out a stained flimsy, and handed it over.

In darkness, Ingram tried to look at Epperson. But even if it were full sunlight, he somehow knew his classmate would be poker faced. "Fred!" he called.

"Yo." from darkness forward.

"Flashlight."

Holloway walked up, handed one over, and walked back to the quarter-deck. Ingram covered the flashlight lens with his fingers; a dim reddish glow washed the paper. He got as far as item one before his spine stiffened ramrod straight. "My God."

Epperson walked to the rail and leaned on his forearms.

Ingram finished, then reread the message, imagining his own name substituted in the section that read..."EPPERSON, D. J., LT., USN, 476225...DE-TACHED CAST." And then, "REPORT SOONEST TO HYPO..."

After running his hand through his hair, Ingram took two deep breaths. He didn't realize his heart had been racing. And his hand shook; he couldn't make it stop. "Shit."

"What?" Epperson moved back.

Strangely, Ingram had an urge to touch his ex-roommate. Just for the briefest of moments he could lay a hand on someone who suddenly had an excellent chance of completing his natural lifetime. Epperson would escape this hideous siege to enjoy the decades to come. He could marry, have kids, go to football games. They could cook in the backyard and--

"Todd?"

--and go trick or treating on Halloween. "Are you married?"

"What? No."

"Sorry. Hypo is what--Honolulu?"

Epperson gave an imperceptible nod. "We had fifty guys with a full commander in charge over there. The *Tambor* took them out two months ago."

At length Ingram asked, "what's OP-20-G?"

Epperson's head shook.

"Who's Radtke?"

"Uh-uh."

"Dwight. Damnit! I've got a sinking ship on my hands."

"I'm sorry. Look. Can you tell me where area Yoke Yoke two is?"

"You want me to take you out there." It was a statement.

"Yes."

"What's wrong with the Rock's boat pool?"

"All but wiped out. Besides, piloting through a minefield without navigational aids in the middle of the night is not their strong suit. Nor is it mine."

Ingram looked at the message again. "I see." Then he barked, "Fred!"

"Here." Holloway's bass voice echoed from the quarterdeck.

"Minefield chart."

Holloway ran to the bridge. In two minutes, he returned with the chart. They unrolled it and lay it on the deck next to the engine room hatch.

Just then, the *Pelican*'s diesel coughed into life.

Bartholomew's head popped out the hatch, his chief's hat at a rakish angle. "Sweet sound, huh, Skipper?"

"I'll say."

Bartholomew whipped off his hat and scratched his bald head. "Keep your fingers crossed. That's our last spare cam shaft. We'll have the bilge pump on the line in a few minutes."

"Good work, Rocky."

Bartholomew looked skyward, "What's the word on Hambone?" Hampton was the electrician injured at the forward three-inch gun mount.

"Yardly thinks it's a broken femur. He's on an IV and we may have to send him over to the beach."

"That's the last thing we want."

"I know."

Taking a last look at the stars, Bartholomew filled his lungs with fresh air. "Have to make sure the injectors are okay." He disappeared down the hatch.

Ingram looked at Epperson. "A lot of good it'll do. We only have a few gallons of fuel oil left. Maybe a day's worth of steaming."

"Why not scuttle and go ashore?"

"That's what General Moore wants. But I convinced him to let us stay out here."

"Why?"

"We can still fight. We can still kill Japs. Hitting the beach would split up my crew. And those damned tunnels do something to me. An hour or so in there and I'm jumpy as hell. I can't sleep. I don't see how you put up with it."

Even without the bombardment, Epperson had the tunnel heebie-jeebies, too, but he wasn't going to say anything. "What are you going to do? Sooner or later..." Epperson's crackling voice trailed.

"Wish I knew. Stay together as long as we can. Maybe make a break for it."

"Where?"

"I don't know. China."

"You're kidding."

"I heard some sections of the coast aren't patrolled. Make our way inland, maybe."

"Yeah?"

Ingram went back to the chart and ran a finger over a crosshatched strip blocking the mouth of Manila Bay. "Minefield."

"Here?" Epperson pointed to a grid-work off Luzon's coast labeled with double letters and a number.

"Ummm. Yes." Ingram jabbed a finger. "Southwest corner of Yoke Yoke two. That's two and a half miles straight out. But I won't waste fuel taking you in this thing. Any other ideas?"

"How 'bout a thirty-six-foot shore boat?"

"That would be nice."

"Right there."

Ingram peered outboard. Through the darkness, a shore boat's silhouette bobbed alongside.

Epperson said, "I think there's three left. The rest are matchwood."

Ingram had seen the wreckage at South Dock; his recollection was there had been twenty-five to thirty boats in the pool. Clicking off the flashlight, he said, "I'll make you a deal."

"Todd--"

"You heard my chief engineer. We have a seriously wounded electrician. Broken femur my quack says. He can die without proper care. Take him with you. Submarines usually carry a pharmacist's mate. They...Dwight?"

"What's wrong with the hospital?"

"That's what I'm afraid of. It's like a damned death sentence. All they can do is lay him out in the tunnel with all the others...to wait for the Japs."

Epperson's head shook slowly. "I can't. This is top secret. You weren't supposed to see that message."

"Hell, I know the *Sea Condor*. Remember Bob Fox? He's her exec. I know he'd take Hampton if I asked."

"Todd, no. Radtke and I are manifested with thirty people." He ticked off on his fingers. "Eighteen nurses, a couple of generals, leftovers from MacArthur's staff and three civilians. As it is, that sub is taking a big chance breaking through the Jap pickets. With all of us on board she'll be stuffed to the gills."

Ingram yanked Epperson's lapels bringing the code analyst to his tiptoes; he felt feather light. "The hell with all those people and the hell with MacArthur. Hampton will die without proper care!"

"No."

"Screw you. Get your own pilot." Ingram let go.

"I can order you."

"Bullshit!"

"I have the authority. I can have the commandant order you. If you don't obey, they'll arrest you and put you in the brig."

Ingram said, "Fred!"

Holloway replied, "Sir?"

"See that Lieutenant Epperson is safely escorted to his boat," Ingram said in a thick tone.

Holloway walked up and cocked his head just as a thunderous shell exploded between San José Point and Malinta Tunnel.

Epperson flinched.

Holloway's pointed teeth gleamed. "If you'll follow me, Lieutenant?"

Epperson turned to Ingram as cannon flashes flicked from Cavite. "You'll be under arrest within the hour." Epperson waited. After a prolonged silence, he walked to the rail as the Cavite-launched rounds erupted near the Topside Barracks. With the *Pelican* low in the water it was an easy jump into the shore boat. Three sailors moved lethargically to get her going. The engine started after a lot of cranking.

Ingram had to yell, "Dwight?"

"Yes?"

"Would you really do that to me?"

"What's that?"

"Let them toss me in the brig?"

"Yes."

"To Hampton?"

"Who?"

"My electrician, damnit."

"Yes."

Holloway threw the bow line into the night; it dropped into the shore boat with a "plop." Farwell, a second-class quartermaster, another of the *Pelican*'s starving wraiths, did the same with the stern line.

Ingram paused as the boat drifted. Two bullet holes decorated the starboard bow almost at gunnel level. One hole pierced a stained white "51."

Corregidor's Battery Geary belched a twelve-inch mortar round toward Bataan, making everyone stand out in backlighted cameo.

"Okay," Ingram shouted.

Epperson's boat had drifted ten feet. "What?"

Ingram cupped his hands to his mouth. "I said "okay". Can you give me five cases of tomato juice?"

Epperson said at length, "I know where I can lay my hands on at least three."

"That's something, anyway. When do you want me?"

"Ten hundred. Bring your charts."

"Can't. We're underway at dawn."

"Very well. Make it 0430. You'll be back here by first light."

"Where are you?"

"Conference room in Lateral Four. I'll leave your name with the guard. See you later, Ace." Epperson nodded to his cox'n who clanked a bell. The engineer shoved her into gear, eased in throttle, and the boat roared toward what was left of the South Harbor Docks.

The *Pelican* wallowed in darkness. Residual heat from the day's sun penetrated Ingram's soles. He looked fore and aft, finding exhausted off-watch men laying on blankets tossing and turning in a demented synthesis of sleep. Others, with gaunt eyes, stared at the heavens, watching the masthead scribe slow arcs across constellations.

He followed their gaze and tracked the *Pelican*'s yardarm as it swept over Venus. "Holloway!"

The jaygee stepped up. "Sir?"

"What's the word on the forward three inch?"

"Recoil spring is fixed, but they're still working on the breech block."

"And?"

"It doesn't look good."

Ingram rubbed his eyes and started forward. "We're gonna need that-- damn!" Ingram stopped. "Is the stokes litter fixed yet?" It had been mutilated by a Zero's twenty-millimeter cannon.

"Nossir."

"I want it ready to go before tomorrow night."

"Is it for Hampton?" A round exploded halfway up Ramsey Ravine, illuminating the OOD's grin.

"Just get it fixed. Okay?"

"Yessir."

3

20 April 1942
Naval Radio Intercept Tunnel, Lateral Four
Corregidor Island, Manila Bay, Philippines

Radtke stood behind Portman watching the radioman pound his key. As he waited, he glanced again at the clock: 0305. So what? he thought. In here, it could be three in the afternoon as far as anyone knew.

Portman finished and yanked the five-digit group message from his typewriter. Without looking, he handed it over his shoulder.

Radtke reached; Portman pulled back. "Com' on rat's-ass. Tell us when our battlewagons are gonna blow the nips to smithereens, huh?"

"The message please, Portman."

The once rotund radioman made a show of passing the message over his other shoulder, making Radtke reach with his left hand, the one with the deformed ring finger. He jerked it away. "I wanna know when to start packing, claw-fist. You should--"

With both hands, Radtke grabbed a corner of Portman's chair and jerked it out from under.

Portman spilled to the floor. Sputtering, he turned to pick himself up. "You sonofa--"

Radtke was on top of the sweating radioman within a half-second. His knee pinned Portman's throat, two fingers spread to gouge his eyes. With tunnel dust in their lungs and limited diets, both wheezed horribly. Without breaking eye contact, Radtke reached over and grabbed the message from Portman's fist.

"Hey, you two! Break it up." Hadley, a lieutenant junior grade rushed over, slapping a palm on Radtke's shoulder.

Radtke shook off Hadley's hand and kneed a little more pressure into Portman's throat, making the radioman choke and gurgle.

"Hey! Hey! Radtke, stop. You're on report" Hadley squealed.

Getting up, Radtke stood over Portman and hissed. "Make fun of me again and I'll rip out your fat guts before the Japs get their chance."

Radtke walked to the crypto room just as the door burst open. Epperson stuck out his head. "What the hell's going on?"

"Your man's fighting with one of mine," said Hadley, standing between Radtke and the crypto room door.

Radtke said, "Shove it, Hadley." He eased past the two officers and padded into the code room.

With a roar, Portman sprang to his feet, jumped around Hadley and charged after Radtke. Epperson barred his way. "Classified area, Portman. Forget it."

"That sumbitch been askin' for it."

"Get back," barked Epperson.

Hadley peered over Portman's shoulder. "Your man profaned a United States Naval officer, Dwight. I'll have him on charges."

Epperson bellowed, "Sergeant!"

Just then a shell hit the mountain. The room shuddered; dust and papers swirled.

Through the fog, two Marines clumped from their position at the front door. One was a sergeant, the other a corporal. Both wore jungle-rotted fatigues and carried .45 caliber Thompson submachine guns, .45 caliber pistols, grenades, and bayonets. Both had fought the Japanese on Bataan; both of their faces were shrouded with the "thousand-yard stare."

Epperson stepped before the Marines. "Sergeant. These are my orders to you. For the rest of this watch, your post is on either side of this door. If any unauthorized personnel attempt to enter this room without my permission, you will shoot them. Is that clear?"

The sergeant's eyes were hooded as he said, "sssir." To Epperson, it sounded like a cobra's hiss.

Portman moved closer and glared. The sergeant swiftly raised his hand to his neck and scratched. Portman jumped back, his mouth open. Slowly, the sergeant shouldered his Thompson and leaned against the wall. His left hand produced a Lucky Strike from his top pocket and he stuck it between thin lips. With a flourish, the corporal produced a Zippo and lit the cigarette. After a long drag, the sergeant blew smoke directly in Portman's face.

Portman stepped forward with a low growl, but stopped, finding the sergeant had silently drawn his bayonet. With a mirthless smile the marine raised his eyes to Portman's and thumbed the blade's tip, the Lucky dangling from his lips.

"Sheyyaatt." Portman turned and walked back to his radio, righted his chair, and sat making a show of putting on earphones and twisting knobs.

Epperson watched Portman, making sure he remained seated. Satisfied, he drew Hadley in the doorway saying, "We've been down here too long, Jim."

Hadley's face turned ashen when a round exploded directly above, making the whole lateral shake.

Skinner screeched, "Yipppi-i-yay. Ride 'em cowboy." He slapped his thigh and mimed riding a horse. "That wuz one of them one-hundred-fifty millimeters."

"Nah, dope." Portman roared. "It was a two hundred forty-millimeter mortar."

"I tell yah, Portman. It wuz a one-fifty." Skinner yelled.

"Two forty, lame-brain..."

Hadley's voice quivered as he watched the bickering radiomen. "We're not getting out, are we?"

Epperson shrugged.

The young jaygee looked around and spoke softly. "What do you think the Japs'll do to us?"

"Prison camp."

"They didn't sign the Geneva Convention. Those guys captured on Bataan...they..."

"Easy!" Epperson said. "They won't have any reason to--"

Hadley's voice cranked up a notch. "Remember what that Filipino Scout said? They marched them on the Cabcaben Road, bayonetted the guys who couldn't keep up and threw 'em into binjo ditches."

The Marine sergeant turned to them with a curious look. Epperson grabbed Hadley's forearm. "Come on, Jim. Easy."

Epperson waited until Hadley's breathing slowed then nodded to the front door. "Better call the guard shack and get another detail up there."

Hadley nodded slowly.

Trying to smile, Epperson backed in the crypto room, closed the door, and walked to his desk.

The cryptographer sat before Lulu, lining the message on the board. Without turning he said, "you want to do this one, Sir?"

"Go ahead. I'll keep working the burn bags." Cramming documents in the canvas sack, Epperson was amazed how much material Op-20-G Cast had left behind: Stuff he wasn't cleared for. They'd been in such a hurry to rendezvous with their submarine.

He watched Radtke peck for a minute, then said, "And lay off Portman. I know you lead him on."

Radtke's ramrod-straight index fingers punched Lulu's keyboard. "The guy is a jerk."

Epperson opened his mouth to speak just as another shell landed nearby. The room shook, dust rose reducing visibility to ten feet. Radtke's key crunching stopped. Lulu was covered, Epperson knew.

The dust cleared and both went back to work. Epperson decided to let the Portman matter go and kept pitching classified papers and manuals in canvas sacks called "burn bags".

It was another five minutes before Epperson heard, "Lieutenant?"

He looked up finding his assistant standing patiently before his desk, his arm outstretched with the message in hand. He took it and read:

TOP SECRET
042OI754Z
FM COM OP-G-20 HYPO
TO COM OP-G-20 CAST
BT

1. SEA CONDOR DEPTH CHARGED BASHI CHANNEL HEAVY DAMAGE. ENROUTE HYPO.
2. WOLFFISH ASSIGNED.
3. ETA 04252130H SW CRNR YY2.
4. PRIORITY SAME.
5. PREPARE DESTRUCTION MATERIALS/EQUIPMENT MOMENT'S NOTICE.
6. ACKNOWLEDGE.
BT

Epperson felt like he'd been kicked in the stomach. Another five days! With this barrage, they'd be dead and the Rock reduced to cinders in five days.

Sledgehammers loaned by the shipfitters stood in the corner. The IBM tabulating machine had been smashed and dumped in Manila Bay, but somehow they had put off wrecking Lulu. Epperson rubbed his chin. The irony was, had they put Lulu to the sledges earlier, they wouldn't have been able to decrypt this message. And tomorrow night, they'd be bobbing with Todd Ingram in the southwest corner of area Yoke-Yoke two waiting for a submarine that would never come. Now, Lulu gave them something to do for five days.

Another thought touched Epperson. Those Marines outside. They'd been conveniently posted just last week, having relieved two wobbly-kneed Army privates. The bayonet wielding sergeant and the cigarette lighting corporal would be the ones who could easily carry out orders to kill both him and his assistant. Epperson would have to keep watch if he wanted to live. Possibly bring Radtke in on it; maybe devise a plan of escape.

Todd Ingram.

China.

That's an idea. He wondered if--

Radtke interrupted Epperson's train of thought. "Somehow, I knew it wasn't true. This dump will be crawling with Japs before that sub gets here."

Not looking up, Epperson filed the message on his clipboard, "We'll still be here. The Japs will still be over there. Don't worry. Now, send an acknowledgement."

"Yessir."

Trying to look nonchalant, Epperson grabbed a sheaf of papers he'd worked on with Commander Joe Rochefort at HYPO. They were labeled:

IJN COMBINED FLEET
PROJECTED CENTRAL PACIFIC CAMPAIGN

"What are you looking at?"

Tucking his left hand behind his back, Radtke's eyes quickly darted from the papers in Epperson's hands. "Nothing, Sir."

"Forget you ever saw these."

"How can I Mr. Epperson? I ran the mimeograph."

"We're not supposed to talk about it."

"Yessir."

"Give the encrypted message to the marine sergeant. Let *him* hand it to Portman."

"With pleasure."

Epperson watched his assistant set up the acknowledgement to HYPO. Sitting back, he was afraid to admit he agreed with Radtke, the man who was so self-conscious about his left hand he kept it tucked behind his back, making him appear as though he were on a drilling compound ready to snap to parade rest.

But all one had to do was cock an ear to the bombardment outside; any fool could tell the tempo had increased. He didn't give much for their chances of lasting another five days.

Epperson lifted the phone, telling the Army signal crew to send a flashing light message canceling Todd Ingram's visit. He sent another message to Major Otis DeWitt over in Malinta Tunnel. DeWitt, General Moore's adjutant, would pass the new schedule to the rest of the evacuation party.

That done, Epperson yawned, grabbed the IJN COMBINED FLEET report, stood, and shuffled to a cot in the far corner. He lay down and, in spite of the dust, lit a Chesterfield. Artillery rumbled as he absently flipped dog-eared pages marked TOP SECRET.

Another shell landed overhead; Epperson didn't notice the shaking and spewing dust. He picked at a scab on his head and scanned familiar text, having worked on it three weeks nonstop. Ernest J. King, Chief of Naval Operations, had ordered it through Admiral Nimitz who in turn, assigned Joe Rochefort in Hawaii and Dwight Epperson in Corregidor to do the analysis exclusively. The objective was to give King their best estimate of what the Japanese Navy would be up to for the next two or three months.

Ignoring thick dust motes, Epperson took another drag off his cigarette thinking about how interesting his collaboration had been with Rochefort. They'd communicated by guard mail, radio, and the direct telephone connection to Hawaii. To be safe, they'd decided to draft separate reports. Epperson wrote his and sent it on to Hawaii two weeks ago in a PBY.

Once compared, their predictions were remarkably similar. Both Rochefort and Epperson concluded Fleet Admiral Isoroku Yamamoto would unleash his *Kido Butai*, the same carrier group that mauled Pearl Harbor, against Midway Island the first week in June.

Epperson was amazed when the cable came back, tersely stating Rochefort' s analysis was basically the same: that Yamamoto was going to hit Midway with an invasion force of over one hundred ships and submarines in early June. Four carriers of the *Kido Butai* were to be in the vanguard to deliver the knockout punch: *Kaga*, *Akagi*, *Hiryu*, *Soryu*. With two other carriers, these ships were the ones that had terrorized the Pacific Ocean the last five months, starting with the attack on Pearl Harbor.

It was almost worth the starvation, the hideous suppurating sores, the diarrhea, the "tunnelitis," the specter of being trapped with eleven thousand other desperate men. He only hoped his luck would hold out and he'd be out of here in another five days.

Now, the future of what remained of the U.S. Pacific Fleet was in the hands of Nimitz, King, and Roosevelt. The ship's deployment around Midway would ultimately be up to Nimitz. But for the sake of the proud cities of San Francisco, Los Angeles, and San Diego, Epperson hoped he and Rochefort had been right.

4

For the next three days, the Japanese seemed to have forgotten the *Pelican*, giving full concentration to their aerial and artillery bombardment of Corregidor and the other three islands, which denied access to the much-needed docks at Manila and Cavite. General Homma and his Imperial Japanese 14th Army was losing face. Not only had he augmented his original contingent of 100,000 with another 100,000 troops, but Homma was far behind his time schedule. The Americans had held out way too long and he was under pressure from Tokyo to do something.

And now, Thursday afternoon, Ingram had anchored the *Pelican* close to the precipitous cliffs of Caballo Island's Fort Hughes. Standing at general quarters, the minesweeper blended into the background, while the men from Nippon intensified Corregidor's bombardment, two miles away.

Ingram leaned against the port bridge bulwark wearing, like everyone else, his World War I style "tin hat." With binoculars, he watched a formation of Japanese "Betty," twin-engine G4M2 Mitsubishi bombers drone overhead, their sinister outlines standing out against a high, cirrus overcast. Operating from Clark Field, they flew formations in groups of nine. Three plane vees formed one large vee, with their station keeping so precise it reminded Ingram of the tight formations that flew over Annapolis during his graduation ceremonies.

The *Pelican*'s gunnery officer, a lanky, tow-headed jaygee, stood aft, near the signal bridge, pointing his binoculars skyward. He, too, wore a tin hat, shorts, boots, and nothing else. His skin, long tanned under the near-equatorial sun, glistened with sweat.

The man's name was Oliver P. Toliver, III. At times, Ingram wondered what else Toliver's Long Island parents had done to him. A graduate of Yale, it was well-known that his father, a partner in the Manhattan Law firm of McNeil, Lawton & Toliver, expected his son to follow in his footsteps and become a tax attorney after the war.

Ingram shouted, "How many, Ollie?"

"Twenty-seven, Skipper. I'd say they're at fifteen-thousand feet today."

Ingram braced his binoculars. With a slight adjustment to the focus knob, the entire formation snapped into view. After a moment, little black missiles simultaneously spewed from the bomber's bellies. "They've salvoed."

The cluster of deadly specks gracefully carved a long, ballistic path ending with explosions that sprinted along Corregidor's Kindley Field.

"East end, again," said Holloway, referring to the tail section of the tadpole-shaped Corregidor.

Ingram said. "Yeah. Not Topside or Water Tank Hill or a gun battery. Just the east end. What does that tell you?"

Holloway looked up to him. "Beach assault soon."

"Umm."

Just then, Chicago Battery, the navy 1.1-inch pom-pom gun opened up. Other ack-ack followed suit. Cheering ranged from the foredeck as Ingram and Holloway swung their binoculars skyward to see a Betty burst into flames and plunge almost straight down. Another Betty trailed smoke from its starboard engine and, losing speed, dropped out of formation and made a shaky turn north toward Clark Field.

"On the way," said Ingram hearing Japanese field pieces erupt on Bataan. Fired in defilade, the counter-battery was zeroed in to silence Corregidor's anti-aircraft guns. But the Army gun crews on Corregidor knew thirty seconds was time enough to put up a few rounds and safely take their shelters before the Bataan-launched shells roared in.

"Hey, bucket mouth," said Forester. "What the hell's that?"

Farwell, a once robust quartermaster second class, had an oversized, jutting lower jaw; only his lower teeth showed when he spoke. Still, his were the best eyes on the bridge. He said, "I'll be damned."

Ingram and Holloway swung their binoculars.

"Sonofabitch," laughed Holloway.

Ingram twirled his focus knob, finding a jungle-green camouflaged hot-air balloon rising above a low ridge line on Bataan. Three helmeted figures were barely distinguishable in the basket, which was tethered by a thick line.

"Close to Cabcaben, I'd say," yelled Toliver.

"What can they do, skipper? Throw rocks?" laughed Farwell.

A battery of cannons erupted from Bataan.

"They can spot," said Ingram.

Toliver spread his elbows on the bulwark to steady his binoculars. "One hundred millimeters, I think."

"Yes," said Ingram.

For the next ten minutes, they watched expert gunfire "walk" back and forth across the 1.1 inch Chicago pom-pom battery.

"Jesus," said Farwell, his oversized jaw clanking shut. He ran a hand through thinning hair. "One P-40. That's all we need." He spoke for them all, knowing American air-power in the Philippines had long been obliterated.

Stockade Battery, with its French, 155-millimeter GPFs (*Grande Puissance Filloux*), roared in defiance, lofting ten rounds toward the Cabcaben-tethered balloon. Soon, explosions stopped raining around the Chicago Battery.

"Give it to 'em," yelled a shadowboxing Farwell. The forward three-inch crew caught Farwell's chant and echoed, "Give it to 'em. Give it to 'em."

Just then, a series of coughs ranged along the Bataan Peninsula announcing Japanese counter-counter-battery. In seconds, explosions fell beyond Stockade Battery. Then five or so rounds fell short. Silence reigned for a moment or two as the smoke cleared. Then the enemy gunners methodically pumped their rounds into Stockade Battery for the next fifteen minutes. For insurance, an airburst followed every tenth round.

Suddenly the barrage stopped, the silence overwhelming. Ingram looked over his shoulder into the South China Sea, seeing the sun touch the western horizon. And, as if on cue in a bizarre rendition of a Gilbert and Sullivan play, the olive-green balloon descended behind the Cabcaben ridge.

It became serenely quiet. Nobody spoke, afraid the tiniest noise would bring back Japanese artillery. At length Ingram took off his tin hat and lay his binoculars in a bracket with a clatter. He felt their eyes fix on him; heard their breath exhale, as the wind dispersed smoke over what was left of Stockade Battery's 155s. "They're standing down for chow," he said.

Their eyes wandered back to the smoke.

Ingram clapped his hands. "Come on!" Their heads jerked. He stuck his head in a pilothouse porthole and shouted at the lee helmsman, "Forester! Anchor detail to the fo'c'sle!"

Forester, operating the engine room telegraph, blinked for a moment. "Aye, aye, Sir. Secure from GQ?" he asked, reaching in his top pocket.

"Negative. Just station the anchor detail."

Forester pressed his lips, shoved the cigarette back, and gave orders on his sound-powered phones.

As the *Pelican's* foredeck sprang to life, Ingram called Toliver and Holloway into a corner. "I got a message from General Moore last night."

"Yeah?" said Holloway.

"He wants me to scuttle."

"Come on," said Holloway.

"I'm afraid so. We're sucking dregs out of the fuel tanks. He knows we're only good for another day or two."

"When?" asked Toliver.

"He's left it up to me."

Holloway asked, "Why don't we just bottom her off, say, Fort Drum and act as an AA platform."

"No dice. They're worried about her falling into Jap hands. He said to send her into deep water when we do it."

"That's that." Toliver looked down.

"I don't like it either. But we've no choice," Ingram said.

"We'll be tunnel termites," said Toliver as the sun's upper rim disappeared.

Holloway said, "The Rock's goin' anyway. One way or the other, they got us."

"We'll anchor off South Harbor tonight. I have to go ashore to talk to Epperson," Ingram said.

"What's he want?"

"I'm becoming boat pool officer."

"Huh?"

"Tell you later. Another reason is Yardly says Hampton should go ashore."

"Why?"

"Broken thighbones are dangerous. Hampton could die. Yardly can't handle it as well as the Rock's doctors, so I'm taking him over."

"We're gonna miss him," said Toliver.

"I know." Ingram dug his shoe at the deck.

Toliver stared at the horizon leaving Holloway to figure it out. "Todd?"

"What?" said Ingram.

"What's on your mind?"

After a pause, Ingram said, "I want to get out of here."

"Me, too," echoed Holloway.

They looked at Toliver who finally said, "Get to what?"

Ingram said, "Soon, we'll be on the Rock sitting in the tunnels or filling sandbags or manning batteries. We can get killed just waiting it out."

Holloway stood in the early twilight with his hands on his hips. "Go on."

Ingram took a breath. "And then the Rock falls and the Japs come along waving flags and sticking swords in the air. We'll be prisoners with thousands of others."

"Yes."

"It's a crock. We remain under orders after surrender. Which means we're obligated to lay down arms and turn ourselves over to the Japs.

"While I'm away tonight, take a straw vote and see what the crew wants to do. Start with Bartholomew."

"You mean escape?" asked Toliver.

"Yes."

"Where?"

"China. I'll bet they love us after Doolittle's B-25 raid. I've heard some sections of the coast are not patrolled. And they'd take good care of us if we could get far enough inland."

Holloway's eyes gleamed. "You know, I heard--"

Twenty-millimeter cannon shell spouts raced through the water and across the *Pelican*'s fo'c'sle. A shadow zipped over them, gunned its engine then whipped around the northwest corner of Caballo Island.

Ingram found himself piled on deck with the others. He cursed, picking himself up. "Damn Zero cut its engine and snuck right up to us."

Toliver squirmed free, ran aft, strapped on his head phones and helmet, and roared orders to his gun mounts.

Ingram yelled aft to Toliver, "Tell mount one heads up. I'll bet he has a buddy."

Toliver had no sooner spoken when more cannon spouts raced toward them. The forward three-inch mount opened fire just as the second Zero's shadow flicked astern. Instinctively, Ingram and the bridge crew dropped to their haunches, then spun to watch. "Damn!"

The aft three inch opened up as the sleek fighter gunned its engine to reach for altitude. But then its left wing dipped, and a light-blue haze trailed from its cowling.

Corregidor's 1.1-inch Chicago Battery joined in. Two seconds later, the Zero exploded in an orange ball at five hundred feet.

Ingram shouted to Forester, "Tell the fo'c'sle to hoist anchor. Stand by for turns on the main engine."

Apparently, the first Zero hadn't learned of his wingman's fate; the forward three-inch mount was ready for his next run. The Mitsubishi's outline whipped around Cabala's headland, seven hundred feet away. Five rounds snapped from the forward three inch before the Zero's pilot could shove in throttle. At first, the single-wing monoplane shuddered, then straightened out weaving toward Corregidor. Then, the propeller stopped and the plane mushroomed. Desperately, the pilot pulled up. But the dark-green Zero stalled and smacked the water, disintegrating in a giant plume.

Forester shouted over the cheering, "Engine room ready to answer all bells, Captain."

Ingram checked forward and said, "Very well. What's taking the anchor detail so long?"

The lee helmsman cupped his hand to his earphone and turned white. He bit his lip with, "Oh, shit."

"What?"

"Nothing, Sir."

"Forester, damnit! Talk to me."

In the pilothouse, Farwell yanked his sailor hat from his rear pocket and walloped Forester's arm.

Forester looked up. "Anchor's aweigh, Sir." Forester said.

"About time," said Ingram.

Ingram walked to the starboard bridge wing to watch the anchor detail on the fo'c'sle. A deck ape, Forester's younger brother, stood on tiptoes jabbing a long pole over the side.

"Forester, is the anchor clear of the water, yet?"

The lee helmsman's voice was distant. "Yes."

A second wallop from Farwell and Ingram's "WHAT?" were simultaneous.

"Sorry, Sir," Forester said mechanically. "Anchor's clear of the water, Sir."

"Very well. Rudder amidships, Farwell. Main engine ahead two-thirds."

Forester said into his mouthpiece, "Bridge, aye." He turned to Ingram and said in a quiet voice. "Fo'c'sle requests you back from the anchorage, Sir."

"What?"

"That's what they said, Sir."

"Whose ship is this?" demanded Ingram.

Forester shrugged; but there was something in his voice.

Forward, the anchor detail still leaned over the starboard rail. A glance aft told Ingram it wouldn't be difficult to back away. The precipitous cliffs of Caballo Island towered above his starboard quarter and he'd tucked the *Pelican* in fairly tight for protection this morning. But there was perhaps fifty yards maneuvering room between the minesweeper and the shoreline.

Ingram rubbed his chin, knowing he would find out soon enough. He ordered, "Main engine back two-thirds. Right full rudder."

With Farwell spinning the helm to starboard, Forester rang up the engine order, and froth kicked under the *Pelican*'s transom. She pirouetted counterclockwise and edged toward the beach. Soon, Ingram said quietly, "Main engine ahead full, rudder amidships. Steady on course three-two-zero."

The *Pelican*'s sternway slowed; she stopped, shuddered momentarily, then moved ahead.

With a look forward, Ingram saw what it was and made a course correction. "Come further left to three-one-zero. Main engine ahead two thirds."

Farwell saw it, too. Easing in more left rudder, he growled through clenched teeth, "Three-one-zero, aye, aye, Sir."

Holloway, Toliver and Forester, the latter two trailing sound powered phone cords, joined Ingram at the starboard bridge-wing. "Bastards," Toliver hissed.

Four bloated corpses drifted facedown along the starboard side. Recognizable were US Army fatigues with name and serial number stenciled on the back. Their legs and hands were tied and on one, long, wispy red hair undulated with the current. The corpse next to it had no head. They'd seen this many times since the fall of Bataan, but were never accustomed to it.

Toliver ran aft and gagged over the signal bridge rail. Holloway, looking green, stumbled to the pilothouse bulkhead, leaning against it with one hand.

Ingram waited for his own stomach to stop jumping before saying, "Mr. Holloway!"

"Sir?" croaked the pale jaygee.

A look at a pallid Forester sent him back to the pilothouse. Taking Holloway by the elbow, Ingram moved aft out of earshot. Beckoning to Toliver he said, "I'll be damned if I'm going to let that happen to us."

With unfocused eyes, Holloway watched the cluster of dead men bob as the *Pelican*'s quarter wake washed over them.

"Tonight, Fred. While I'm on the Rock. Start with Bartholomew, like I said."

Looking at the deck, Holloway straightened his hat.

"Ollie, you talk to the deck force. Got it?"

Toliver nodded.

Ingram squeezed harder on Holloway's elbow. "Listen to me," he hissed. "We're going to take inventory of what's in this harbor and grab what we need."

"Yeah?" asked Holloway.

"Ask Rocky what we need for a long trip."

"How long?" said Toliver.

"I'm not sure. But see if he knows where we can get things. Diesel fuel, lube oil. Stuff like that."

"Todd," asked Holloway. "How do we take eighty-two people to China?"

"I don't know. We have to plan. Start with Rocky."

After twilight, the *Pelican* pulled into her anchorage. An accelerated night bombardment provided all the light needed to find a place near the South Dock. But she laid off the Rock further than usual so as not to be hit by a wild shot.

On the bridge, Ingram ordered "finished with engines,' left Holloway in charge of the ship, and went to his cabin and grabbed his charts. He walked aft toward the quarterdeck where the motor whale boat rocked alongside, but a bursting shell on Breakwater Point illuminated a group of men gathered in a semicircle around Hampton laying in a stoke's litter on the main deck. Yardly bustled among them making sure his patient's IV and Thomas Splint were well secured. Ingram drew up in darkness to await their good-byes, marveling that the crew had pooled their rations so Hampton had three squares a day. The result was that, in spite of his broken leg, he looked better than his shipmates.

Kowalski, a second-class machinist's mate, stooped and patted Hampton's shoulder saying, "about time they kicked you off the old bird. Now we can get a replacement who knows what the hell they're doin'. I been tired of you tripping out the electrical load all the time." He took Hampton's outstretched hand.

Hampton said, "I'll be back, Ski. You owe me."

"Owe you what?"

"I still say you didn't draw into that full house."

"Meaning?"

"Meaning you cheated me out of two hundred thirty bucks."

"Horseshit!" Kowalski withdrew his right hand, but Ingram saw the machinist's left hand tuck a dark, pint sized flask in Hampton's armpit.

Hampton said, "And next time I catch you dealin' from the bottom, you're going over the side."

"You and who else?"

"Just wait."

Kowalski rose and stepped back.

Bartholomew took out a clarinet case and tucked it between Hampton's arm and blanket. "Here's Benny."

"Forget it! I'm only gonna be there for a couple days." He handed it back. "Stick it back in my locker, Rocky."

Bartholomew said, "I know. I know. But, I figured you could entertain those guys while you're there. You know, a little Moonglow never hurt no one."

Kowalski said, "Yeah, how 'bout a few bars, now, Hambone?"

Hampton fumbled at the case's latch.

"Skipper's waiting," said Yardly. "We have to get going."

Hampton swallowed and the men looked away.

Bartholomew helped tuck the clarinet under a blanket. "Let us know if you need anything. Come back, soon."

"Yeah, Rocky."

Bartholomew stood. He and Hampton knew there was no coming back from the Rock's hospital. The doctors would do what they could, then lay him out in the tunnels with everyone else...to rot...and await the Japanese.

Kevin Forester, the third-class quartermaster, edged his brother aside and started to lift the stokes litter.

"What you pullin'?" said Junior Forester.

"You're on the back end, dope."

"I had the front."

Kevin Forester pushed his younger brother, "Shove off. Do what I say."

Junior Forester wailed, "Listen. I'm not takin' anymore--"

"Sssst," from Bartholomew.

Ingram walked up. "Ready Cox'n?"

"Yessir," said Forester. "As soon as we load Hampton."

Ignoring the tradition that the ship's captain board the whale boat last, Ingram hopped in the whale boat and held the IV as Hampton's litter was passed over.

Whittaker jumped in and began cranking the engine. Junior Forester followed to act as bowhook. His brother stood at the tiller as Cox'n.

"...hey Sonny," Hampton called.

"Finally rid of you," replied Sunderland, a barrel chested first class gunner's mate who chomped the stub of an unlit cigar. Except for intermittent cannon shells, one could barely see their faces as they leaned over the rail looking into the motor whale boat.

"Just to set the record straight, Sonny."

"Yeah?"

"My mount got that Val, not yours." Hampton was the ship's best gun pointer. His battle station had been on the forward three-inch mount.

Sunderland shot back, "That's a crock! You couldn't hit the broad side of a hog's ass from three feet in Central Park."

The whale boat bumped softly against the *Pelican*'s fenders while a cursing Whittaker cranked the engine.

Hampton feigned disbelief. "Hear that skipper? I got witnesses that'll prove this nincompoop is cheat'n me."

Whittaker kept cranking the diesel. One or two cylinders announced life, then wheezed to an oiled silence. The engineman muttered, "Same old shit."

A saboteur had poured a wax like substance in the diesel fuel they had taken just before the frantic evacuation from Cavite. They had cleaned the fuel system constantly, but residue still clogged the lines and, on occasion, worked its way to the injectors.

Ingram cringed thinking about the contaminated fuel. It reminded him of Cavite and that first horrible air raid on December 8, only a few hours after Pearl Harbor. The dive-bombers had left the fuel tanks alone, but hit everything else. They were so unprepared: Many had been killed, especially civilians in the workshops. Some of the dead were horribly maimed and the burial detail refused to collect body parts strewn about. The only way to get the job done was to break out the booze. It became grisly. In Ingram's dreams, he still saw the pimply faced buck private weaving down the cratered thoroughfare kicking along a human head like a soccer ball. The kid laughed demonically; a fifth of bourbon clutched in his hand as he sang a ditty--

"You're nothin' but a sponge-brained electrical jock," Sunderland roared. "Just come aft to my mount and I'll teach you how to shoot straight."

Hampton said, "Captain? You believe that crap? The Val was smokin' by the time it drew aft."

Ingram took a deep breath and said, "It was the second Val that--"

"What the hell you mean, 'drew aft?'" Sunderland roared at Hampton.

"Exactly what I said," Hampton yelled up into darkness. "Your mount was in the stops. You couldn't have opened fire, damnit!"

A flashing shell caught Sunderland spitting thick tobacco juice over the side. "Stops, my ass--"

The diesel roared. Ingram shouted, "I'll order a complete inquiry. Let's go Forester."

The whale boat pulled away from the *Pelican*. Sunderland's voice drifted across the widening chasm, "...Hambone! Gimme a call when you need help with the nurses..."

Hampton raised on his elbows; his clarinet spilled out. He shouted and grappled for it at the same time, "Don't you wish, goldbrick? For once, the Navy's sending someone qualified to do a man's job!"

"Shut up, Hampton. Quit wiggling!" Yardly caught the clarinet and put a hand on the man's shoulder easing him back to the stokes litter. Whittaker helped him tuck the clarinet away.

Ten minutes later, they nosed along the outskirts of South Dock. It was a wharf with a rail line built to receive cargo from ships. But now, most of it had been blasted into useless splinters. Twisted rails hung down and dead, creosoted pilings jabbed from the water like rotten teeth.

As they closed the beach, an air burst flashed over San José Village, a small barrio where civilian laborers had lived before war broke out. Another shell hit at the tide line, raising a fifty-foot water column that settled into a hissing, misty curtain.

Forester slowed the boat to idle, leaned forward, and rubbed his chin. "Skipper?" His voice was tense.

Ingram waved an arm. "Try for the boat pool area. Closer to the beach the better. Watch for broken pilings.

"And listen to me, all of you." Ingram raised his voice. "Take a look. Shells are landing all over the Rock. It's dangerous anywhere outside. People who come outside for a breath of fresh air get killed. So, stay inside in spite of the tunnels!"

He continued with, "Forester!"

"Yes Sir?"

"After you drop us, lay five hundred yards off the wharf."

"Yessir," Forester said.

"Try and anchor. If you can't. Cut the engine--"

A mortar shell landed near Breakwater Point with a bone-piercing crack that echoed for five seconds.

Ingram had to catch his breath. "...cut the engine and drift. Or tie up to a piling out there. I don't want you near the beach and don't waste fuel. I'll signal with a flashlight when we're ready. Okay?"

Five shells thundered up Malinta Hill obliterating Forester's response. Then it was silent. The whale boat's gurgle sounded oppressive in the absence of cannon fire. Forester nosed around half-submerged work boats looking like dead, bloated whales.

Hampton said, "Skipper?"

"Yeah?"

"Don't do this on my account. I'll get better. I promise"

"It's okay, Hambone," said Yardly. "You'll have good care."

"Skipper, please!"

"You have a broken femur, Hampton," said Ingram. "They can do a better job on you than we can. We'll pick you up in two or three weeks. Okay?"

"...okay." Hampton sighed and lay back.

Forester eased in, further working them to the small boat docks. His younger brother jumped off to moor the bow, Whittaker took the stern line.

Ingram stepped off with Hampton's duffle bag and watched as the others passed the stokes litter to the dock. Ingram stepped out of their way and stumbled on something. Turning, he saw a chunk of twisted metal. He stooped and picked it up.

"Owww." It was a red-hot piece of shrapnel; it hissed when he threw it in the water.

"Come on!" someone yelled.

"What?" Ingram said.

"You stupid bastards. Hurry up!"

Ingram looked toward the beach as another round landed in what was left of San José barrio. In the shell's flash, he spotted the outline of a soldier running up to them. Wearing the pancake tin hat, he turned out to be a Marine Corps second lieutenant.

Ingram said, "I'm Lieutenant Ingram, skipper of the *Pelican*. We're bringing one of our wounded to the hospital."

The Marine said, "Well, if you hang around any longer Sir, there won't be any wounded. Just dead. Me included. So let's haul ass."

"Okay. Here, take this." Ingram handed Hampton's duffle to the Marine and yelled, "Come on."

Yardly and Forester jogged past with the stokes litter. Ingram ran back to the boat where a shell bursting over Topside illuminated the cox'n' s face.

Forester stuttered, "Need us anymore, Skipper?"

"Head on out. Watch for my signal in about an hour or so," said Ingram."

He tossed in the bow and stern lines. Forester, not needing further encouragement, backed into darkness.

Two twelve-inch M-1890 mortar shells roared from Battery Geary. Ingram turned to run, but slipped on another piece of shrapnel falling headlong on the dock.

Yardly yelled from darkness, "Skipper, hurry!"

Ingram rose, but sharp pain throbbed in his right knee. "Go on. Check him in and stand fast," he yelled. "I'm headed for the Navy tunnel. See you in a while."

"It's your ass, Captain," said the Marine, just as another round dropped on Water Tank Hill.

"Move, damnit," yelled Ingram.

"Yessir!" Two shells silhouetted Yardly and Forester running with the stokes litter. In front, the marine second john, held Hampton's IV bottle and ran interference like a pulling guard.

Ingram sat back to massage his knee. The Japanese counter-battery rained on the Geary mortar emplacement with deafening, ripping explosions that lighted up wrecked boats and torn pilings. In the flashes, he saw Forester had gained a position about five hundred yards offshore.

The counter-battery ceased and he rose, finding his knee felt better. It must have been his funny bone. He took two shaky steps knowing it would be okay.

A Japanese air burst lighted up San José. What was that? He waited for another shell.

His eyes had almost readjusted to the dark when a shell hit near the Navy tunnel. It was enough to light up a nest of three thirty-six-foot shore boats. One looked familiar. He walked over, seeing twin bullet holes neatly stitched in the starboard bow; one hole had nearly obliterated a white stained numeral '51'.

5

23 April 1942
Naval Radio Intercept File Room, Lateral Four
Corregidor Island, Manila Bay, Philippines

HECKLE opened the door a crack and was relieved to see Epperson talking with that insipid Portman at his radio console. Easing the door closed, he walked to the back of the file room and stepped up to a large oak table like the ones in public libraries. He was tempted to use the darkroom's enlarging equipment but was afraid Mr. Epperson would come in when the bulb was on. It was so damn bright! It would be a sure tip-off.

Quickly, he picked up the folder and laid it flat on the library table directly under the 150-watt bulb. It was the brightest he could find, and he paused to consider how to set the shutter speed. It was only a five-page report, so he decided there was enough film for three exposures for each page shot at 60, 250, and 500th of a second.

The room shook with artillery overhead. Afraid he might not have heard the door squeak open during the artillery's rumble, he ran to the door and once again opened it a crack to double-check. Peering back from the other side was a human eyeball.

"Need something?" the Marine sergeant said.

"Trying to find Mr. Epperson," said HECKLE looking at the eyeball in fascination. It was bloodshot.

"Off to the commissary."

"It'll wait." Perfect, he thought. HECKLE shut the door and ran back to the library table. Quickly, he pulled out what looked like a common matchbox from his pocket. But then he extended it lengthwise revealing a subminiature Minox camera. He set it up for the first exposure marveling at its construction. About three inches long, it fit well in the palm of his hand, and the film was only 9.5 millimeters in width giving decent exposures with reasonable light. What fascinated him was that the Minox wasn't made in Germany like the Leica. The Minox had been invented by a Latvian named Walter Zapp in 1937 and was made in Riga by Valsts Electrotechniska Fabrika.

HECKLE leaned over the paper, extended the camera body and, with a little trouble from his deformed ring finger, was able to hold the camera correctly and sight through the little viewfinder. The image he saw was:

TOP SECRET
COMPACFLT EYES ONLY
PREDICTIONS
IMPERIAL JAPANESE COMBINED FLEET ACTIVITY
MAY - JUNE 1942

He clicked off the first three shot at different exposures then flipped the page and shot that. He was halfway through the third page when he heard the door squeak open. An artillery shell rumbling overhead seemed louder with the door open.

"Radtke?"

Epperson! "Sir!" Quickly he snapped off the light, pocketed the camera, and shoved the folder in the back of his trousers.

Epperson walked up. "Anybody call?"

"Nossir. You expecting one?" asked HECKLE, hoping he wouldn't have to turn around lest Mr. Epperson see the folder. But just in case, his eyes darted about looking for a weapon. He soon spotted a holstered .45 hanging from a hat rack. Too loud. What else? he thought.

"Todd Ingram. If he does call, I'll be just outside with Commander Jacobson. Got it?"

"Yessir. You're not going to the commissary?"

"Who the hell told you that?"

"I thought--"

"Never mind. I'm expecting Ingram. Let me know if he calls at once. Understand?"

"Yessir!"

Epperson walked out.

HECKLE held his breath for another ten seconds then let out a long exhale. Then he took the folder from the back of his trousers and quickly put it back in the file cabinet marked TOP SECRET. Sometime soon, he resolved. Sometime soon.

Ingram stood rubbing his jaw, momentarily unaware of an explosion near the Topside Barracks. The 51 Boat bobbed at its mooring and except for the bullet holes in her bow, seemed oblivious to the destruction that rained on the Rock. It seemed as if on signal, the barrage's tempo had stepped up a notch with a shell landing somewhere on Corregidor every fifteen seconds.

It wasn't until a monstrous explosion knocked him over that he came to his senses. He scrambled to his feet and ran, dodging barbed-wire weaved in hideous patterns, toward Hooker Point. But another explosion raised a misty curtain, making it difficult to keep his bearings. Cursing, he stumbled through smoke until the cordite laden cloud dissolved.

He sensed, rather than saw, a smoking crater before him and, congratulating himself, deftly skirted its edge--only to trip on a sandbag and topple headlong into another. He blocked his fall with his hands just as another shell landed, its blast deafening.

Dirt and rocks tumbled about as he wiggled snakelike, finding himself atop an ammunition belt. In panic, he discovered he was sprawled among the cordite-infested debris of an armed outpost.

He raised his head, seeing a machine gun barrel's ugly snout within inches; his hands found something soft and yielding...

Just then, an airburst lighted up the wide-open, surprised eyes of a dead Army corporal. Pulling his hands from dark stickiness, Ingram took endless seconds to untangle himself from the corpse, ammo boxes, and radio equipment. Gasping and cursing that he'd not taken the longer, but safer route through Malinta Tunnel, he rose and ran east stumbling among rocks, bomb craters, and wreckage.

He trudged along the coastal path trying to shake the horror of what lay behind. Reassuring was the familiar outline of Water Tank Hill as it rose above his left shoulder. At Ordnance Point, he was challenged by Marines and gained the Naval Radio Intercept Tunnel. With some fumbling, he showed his ID to the sentry and passed into relative quiet of the reinforced concrete throughway.

Red night lights, surrounded by a curious fog, illuminated the tunnel's single lane. Visibility was only ten feet and two wheezing breaths made him realize it wasn't fog but dust that shrouded his path.

The first offshoot was labeled: Lateral One-Commanding Officer-Marine Garrison. Trying to squint at the "Lateral Two" sign ahead, he tripped on something soft. He barely caught his balance, and stumbled over another bundle which went "uhhh." He looked down seeing he'd stepped on two men sleeping on blankets. One man sat up and rubbed his finger at his lip.

Knowing his boot had connected with the man's head, Ingram crouched and said softly, "Sorry, buddy. You okay?" Someone else moaned; Ingram looked up, seeing similar heaps stretched as far as he could see.

The man raised slowly to an elbow and studied blood that ran over his finger. He was perhaps nineteen years old with thickly matted, dark curly hair that grew to his neck and covered his ears and forehead. He wore a dungaree shirt without insignia and oddly, cutoff corduroy shorts and unmatching tennis shoes. Scarecrow-thin arms and legs, far worse than Ingram's own, protruded from the young man's sleeves and shorts.

"Can I get you anything?" Ingram said louder.

The man hadn't shaved for a long time. His mouth twisted open to a foamy drool and one could see three upper front teeth were missing. Raising his eyes toward Ingram's, he focused somewhere on the tunnel's ceiling.

Ingram said, "Maybe some water. Here, let me--"

"Shut up!"

Ingram spun to the mound behind. "What?"

"Move on!" This hirsute creature wearing sergeant's stripes, had no distinguishable facial features except for an oval shaped mouth.

"All I was trying to do was--"

Ingram looked into the barrel of a .45 which the man quickly cocked. The muzzle leveled between his eyes. "Me and Hughie took orders from pimps like you on Bataan. He ain't said nothin' since and I don't talk to you bastards, either. Get on." The muzzle waved.

Where were his eyes? Ingram couldn't see the sergeant's eyes. Slowly, he raised his hands, then stood and edged further into the tunnel until the hideous apparition disappeared into the mist. It wasn't until then that he exhaled and took deep, choking breaths.

His focus was better, perhaps the dust was less or he'd become used to the light. He picked his way among the prostrate bundles and reached Lateral Four.

He presented his ID to a Marine sergeant and Epperson soon appeared and showed him into a room labeled: *Radio Intercept File Room, Authorized Personnel Only.*

They sat at a conference table while Epperson--the sores on his head looking worse--prepared a mysterious concoction that was to become coffee. Ingram was surprised he had sugar.

Grumbling to his classmate about the deranged sergeant Ingram said, "I didn't have time to be incredulous or indignant or even to put the guy on report. I just walked away. I had to. I think he would have pulled the trigger."

"Ace, you did the smart thing."

"What?"

"He would have pulled the trigger."

"Come on."

"Happens all the time. We lost a full commander two days ago."

"And now, if I went back with a squad of Marines, I don't think I could find the sonofabitch," said Ingram.

Epperson sat and stirred his own cup of thick gluttonous liquid. "Most of them out there are off Bataan. They just don't care. They've had it. They're tired of seeing their buddies blown to bits. Can you blame them?"

Ingram thought for a long time. "I suppose not."

"Surviving Bataan for this is not any better, especially with all this Jap artillery pining us down."

"Send them someplace else?"

"No room. And we can't just order them outside to...to...die." He raised gaunt eyes to Ingram and sipped his ersatz coffee. "We sort of co-exist. Don't bother them and they don't bother you."

"And they want me to scuttle and bring my crew ashore to live..." He waved a hand toward the main tunnel.

Epperson's voice was soft. "Todd, I overheard a guy on Moore's staff say they *are* ordering you to scuttle in the next two or three days, fuel oil or not."

"No!"

"The Army wants your crew--experienced gunners--to man the mortar pits."

"Screw 'em. What's wrong with their people?"

"Wounded. Dead. They're losing a lot of guys with the shelling and need replacements. Except for a direct hit, the guns survive. People don't."

A shell thundered overhead, making dust and pebble-sized concrete chips rain down.

Ingram stood and swept a forearm across the table sending his mug shattering against the reinforced concrete wall. "How do you stand it in this garbage pit?" he shouted.

"Didn't take long for the sugar to hit your system," muttered Epperson as Ingram quickstepped around the table.

Waiting until the end of the second circuit, Epperson nodded to a pouch slung around Ingram's neck. "Are the charts in there?"

With nostrils flared, Ingram walked two more circuits then sat and waited for his breathing to calm down. "Tomorrow night?"

"No. The next one. I want to get this set, now. Then I can tell DeWitt to--"

"Who's DeWitt?"

"A major. He's General Moore's adjutant who is organizing the evacuation. He wants to make sure transport is set. That's the riskiest part."

"You're telling me." Ingram spread a chart and they talked for five minutes. At length he said, "How about the tomato juice?"

Epperson jabbed a thumb over his shoulder, then walked to a desk and picked up a phone saying, "Major DeWitt, please." He sat, put his feet on the desk, and spread the minefield chart across his lap.

As Epperson talked, Ingram walked to a canvas-covered heap against the wall. He raised a corner, finding four cases of tomato juice. Epperson palmed the mouthpiece and whispered, "I had two more, but I figured it would have gone to waste since you're going to scuttle."

Ingram turned and faced Epperson. "I want 'em."

"What for?" Epperson wheezed.

"Never, mind. Can you get them?"

"I suppose so. But why--hello? Otis? Look. Everything's set on our end. Ingram will use the 51 Boat. I had it double-checked this afternoon. They-- what? Just a moment." Epperson covered the mouthpiece, "You have a crew?"

"I'm not sure."

"What? How can you not be sure? You must have--just a moment, Otis--I don't understand."

Ingram raised the canvas and offered a palm to the pile of tomato juice crates.

"Shit. Alright. Six cases."

"I have a very good crew." Ingram allowed a smile.

"All set with crew, boat and skipper, Otis. Yes, good-bye. Epperson hung up. "You sonofabitch. Why pull--"

"And there better be six cases, Dwight, or I swear I'm throwing you over the side on the way out. The Rock's gonna fall. One less guy to show up at the submarine won't make any difference."

"Todd. Be--"

"Now get someone to help me with all this."

Epperson's mouth curled to a confused grin. "You're serious?"

Ingram stared at his classmate.

"Okay. Okay." He walked to the door and called a sentry. "Sergeant, tell Radtke to report in here, please."

Ingram and Epperson, too tired to fume at one another, sat and twiddled until a lanky man entered to the accompaniment of three shells landing near Calvary Point. He had matted blond hair and wore boots and shorts. But he was freshly shaven and Ingram caught a slight wisp of Bay Rum.

"You wanted me, Lieutenant?" the man asked standing stiffly.

Epperson said, "At ease, Radtke. This is Mr. Ingram."

"Our transport?" Epperson's assistant relaxed and broke into a smile.

Ingram raised his eyebrows.

"Radtke. Besides being my friend, Mr. Ingram is a lieutenant in the United States Navy--his collar devices should tell you that. Also, he is skipper of the U.S.S. *Pelican* and, indeed, is not your personal," Epperson hissed, "transport. Is that clear?"

"Yes, Sir." Radtke arranged himself to a listless form of attention.

"I need six cases of tomato juice carried to the..." he looked at Ingram.

"South Dock, berth one-oh-one or what's left of it, " said Ingram.

"Here are four cases." Epperson gestured to the stack. "Take the other two in the crypto room--"

"But Lieutenant. Those two are for..." said Radtke. His eyes darted for a moment.

Epperson waited, "Yes? Do you plan on staying here long enough to drink two whole cases of tomato juice, Radtke?"

"No, Sir."

"Fine. You'll need help. Call the guard shack for two men. You'll each carry two cases."

"Dwight. I'd like them to drop one off in the Hospital Tunnel." Ingram said.

"Radtke?" said Epperson.

The man said, "Can do, Sir. Who gets it?"

"One of my men," said Ingram. "We brought him in tonight. Broken femur." He glared at Epperson who conveniently found a sheaf of papers to study. "He's a first-class electrician. Admittance will tell you where he is. Name is Hampton. Joshua Hampton."

Epperson said, "not *the* Joshua Hampton?"

"You know him?" said Ingram.

"East Coast sailor? Plays clarinet. A really hot stick."

"That's him. How'd you know?"

"They had a concert a couple of years ago when I was on leave in D.C. How did you get him?"

"Came to us from the *North Carolina* we...what's wrong with you?"

Radtke's eyes opened and closed for a moment and he jammed a hand behind his back. "Nothing, Sir. Tunnelitis, that's all."

When he said no more, Ingram prompted, "Yes?"

Radtke licked dust off his lips. "Going crazy inside. Afraid to go outside. Don't know what the hell to do. Japs everywhere."

Ingram said, "Where you're going you won't have to worry about Japs."

Radtke turned to Epperson, "He knows about us, Sir?"

Epperson ran a hand over his bald head, "He has a need to know. Now, that's all."

Radtke walked out. "Smart kid," Ingram said.

"Whiz-bang cryptographer. He played bugle and trumpet on the *North Carolina*."

"Maybe he knows Hampton."

"Could be. Anyway, they sent him to me after three weeks of crypto school. Showed up just a day before Pearl harbor. It's too bad. Apparently had a swell career going in big bands. Word is he was a backup to Ziggy Ellman. But then money ran out and he joined the Navy. And now he ends up with me."

Interesting. Ingram had heard that musicians from battleships sunk at Pearl Harbor had been sent to crypto school. The Navy had discovered their natural ability at understanding complex relationships within structured musical formats gave them a significant head start learning cryptography. And at war's outbreak, the Navy needed legions of cryptographers instead of piano players or trumpeters or drummers. "Heard him play?"

"Haven't had a chance. This place has been topsy-turvy since the Japs bombed Cavite."

Epperson leaned back in his chair seeing Ingram's mind clicking. "Todd. I say this to you as a friend. It's best not to ask much about what goes on with stuff I'm involved in."

"Okay."

"I was trying to tell you that the other night. The people I work for play for keeps."

"I said, 'okay.'"

Epperson nodded. "Why tomato juice to the hospital?"

"It's miserable in there. And it's gonna get worse. Hampton will need something for himself plus something to barter with--I don't know--food, clothing, medicine."

"Tell him he better stay awake, Ace."

"Yes?"

Epperson turned to study charts. "Otherwise someone will steal it. They may even kill him just for the fun of it."

6

---

23 April 1942
Navy Radio Intercept Tunnel
Monkey Point, Corregidor Island, Philippines

Ingram finished twenty minutes later and, dodging an occasional shell, made it to the Hospital Lateral of Malinta Tunnel. The barrage had slackened. Maybe the Japs were tired, he figured. A corpsman gave him directions and, picking his way through red fog, he found Yardly and Junior Forester curled against the concrete wall.

Forester snored loudly but Yardly' s eyes snapped open the instant Ingram tapped his shoulder.

"Tomato juice show up?" whispered Ingram.

Yardly nodded. "You made Hambone the richest man on the Rock."

Ingram's eyebrows went up.

"Me and him bargained a cot and two bottles of quinine from a corpsman. And we got a bottle of aspirin from a blind guy. Just two lousy cans of tomato juice. That's all it cost. Here." Yardly reached over and patted a bulging pouch. "Hambone wanted the quinine and aspirin for us."

Yardly looked up and down the tunnel. "Good thing about the cot. They were going to stick him out in the main tunnel with all the other ghouls." He shuddered, his eyes rolling up to Ingram. "Can we go back to the ship now, Skipper?"

"In a minute. I have to see Hampton. Where is he?"

"Skipper. You don't wanna go back there."

"I have to give him something." Ingram slapped the .45 on his hip.

Yardly watched Ingram's hand and slowly nodded. "I'll show you."

"No. Stay with Forester and guard the quinine."

"Okay." Yardly gave directions.

"Be right back," said Ingram.

The lateral seemed endless as Ingram worked his way through anguished groans of the sick and wounded. Odors of rotting flesh, ether, vomit, alcohol, urine, and sweat pulled at his nostrils.

There was another smell common to everyone on Corregidor: fear. Naked fear, which, it seemed to Ingram, was more pronounced here than on the *Pelican*.

And while on cold, concrete walls, stark shadows of medical teams silently danced their bizarre renditions of mercy, Ingram tread further, dodging heaps that moaned and writhed. Some, he grimly noticed, were forever silent, covered from head to foot.

Catching a patient's eye was to be avoided, Ingram learned. Some had the distant stare of hopelessness and acquiescence. Others looked with envy at healthy passersby. One sensed the driving, wrenching, denial in these sick and wounded, that this was not really happening to them; that in who ever walked by, there was the desperate hope of cure, or escape, or hidden relief.

Ingram found his way blocked by three people hovering over a man on a stretcher. The supine figure groaned louder, longer; it was an army major whose torso glistened darkly. For the moment, they ignored his right leg which was crooked in an obscene direction. A freckled army captain with a full mustache stood opposite with arms folded and feet spread. Flanking him were two sergeants whose cigarette smoke beckoned oddly in wisps and coils inscribing symmetric halos against the red lights.

One of those kneeling called, "How much is left?"

"I'll check, Doctor." It was a woman's voice. She turned from the stretcher and opened a large bag next to Ingram's foot.

She wore coveralls, boots, and a baseball cap. Bottles and instruments clanked when she reached in.

Ingram stooped beside her and whispered, "Mam?"

Dark ebony hair was pulled back under the cap fixed with an Army first lieutenant's devise. A name tag on the breast pocket said HELEN Z. DURAND. But it was her eyes: dark brown, quick, intelligent, calculating. This one, he could tell, was as used to triage as the doctors who decided which ones lived while ignoring the terminal ones, letting them die.

She gave him an efficient glance. "Navy."

"That's right. We brought one of my men in here tonight. A first-class electrician named Hampton. Broken thigh."

One corner of her mouth raised slightly as she knelt closer to her bag. "The guy with the tomato juice. And you're the skipper?" Durand didn't waste words.

"Well, yes."

"Idiots. Your corpsman and all his razz-ma-taz. Those three couldn't have done better if they'd flashed the Hope Diamond." She looked up and nodded further into the lateral. "I think your man is in the cots area starting about twenty feet over there. Third row back."

"Thanks."

The major moaned again, softer than before.

The army captain's voice had a deep rumble, "Doc? What's going on?"

Ingram didn't rise as Nurse Durand reached in the bag. He barely saw her hoist a large bottle labeled *Ether*. A half-inch or so swirled on the bottom.

"Helen, goddamnit. Where is it?" The doctor demanded.

"All gone, Sir," was Helen Durand's answer.

"Very well. Kelly and lap sponge, please."

Ingram had seen it, she knew. Helen's eyes implored for a moment, then she reached in the bag, drew the instrument, crawled to the stretcher and slapped it in the doctor's palm. The major gurgled and his arms spasmed for a moment.

"What is this shit? What do you mean, no ether?" growled the captain. He stepped around the stretcher and walked toward Helen.

Ingram stood as if to pass but stumbled against him. "Oh, sorry buddy."

The captain didn't notice. Instead, he reached at the doctor's back, grabbing a handful of shirt and roared, "You dirty bastard! He's hurting. Give him ether!"

The doctor, trying to ignore the man, wiggled to free his shirttail and work on his patient at the same time.

"You can't let him die, you sonofabitch!" yelled the captain.

"Come on, Captain." said one of the sergeants.

The captain yanked harder on the doctor's shirt. "If he dies, you die!" The captain pulled his .45 and started to cock it.

With his fist, Ingram hit the captain in the left temple. The blow felt weak to Ingram and he was surprised when the man collapsed at his feet with the pistol clattering alongside. The two sergeants quickly moved around, pulled the captain against the wall and propped him to a sitting position.

"Water's over there." Helen Durand pointed to a steel jug on a small table. She looked up to Ingram. Her eyes said *thanks*.

"Yes Mam," said one of the sergeants. He stepped over, poured a tin cup and returned to feed it to his captain.

Ingram felt the other sergeant's eyes fixed on him. A shell boomed overhead, shaking the tunnel. He stooped, picked up the captain's .45 and dumped the clip. Handing them over he said, "Wait 'til tomorrow before you give it back."

"Yessir." The sergeant stuffed the pistol and clip in his belt.

They all turned to hear the major give a long expulsion of breath releasing him from the world. The doctor rubbed his cheeks and closed his eyes for a moment. At length he gasped, "You said there was someone else?"

Helen said, "Over there. It's his left arm."

Moving farther back in the tunnel Ingram found it quieter; the shells weren't as loud and he heard occasional snoring. He counted along the cots until he found the third row. He looked down seeing an open case of tomato juice. An I.V. drip was set up at the head of a cot and with a smile, Ingram bent to see Hampton asleep on his back. He was without shirt and trousers and his blanket had fallen to the floor. Ingram picked it up to cover Hampton but noticed the man's mouth was wide-open. On a whim, Ingram felt at Hampton's neck. No pulse.

"Jesus!" he roared, and put an ear to Hampton's chest. No heartbeat; his skin was clammy. Joshua Hampton was dead.

"Hampton!" Ingram yelled, and shook the electrician's shoulders.

A heavily bandaged man in the next cot said, "Knock it off, damnit. People are trying to sleep."

Ingram stood and doubled his fists. "Shut up!" he yelled.

Snoring stopped. Men stirred and their eyes flicked open; he saw the dim reflections; their blinking. One cursed while voiding his bladder in a metal urinal.

Ingram put his head in his hands and swayed slightly until the urinal clanked on the concrete floor. Blankets rustled. A man snored nearby. Others soon took up the cadence.

Something nudged his leg. He turned seeing the shirtless patient sit up and hand over a dark, slim object. "Huh?"

It was the one who said, "knock it off." His head was covered with bandages. "Here." He raised the object toward Ingram. "You want this back?"

Something roared in Ingram's ears. He swayed for a moment and put out an arm to keep his balance. Finally, he sat on a corner of Hampton's cot.

The clarinet case waved at Ingram's chest. He grabbed it and looked back to Hampton's vacuous face and--Good God! Hampton's thigh was the size of a tree stump. "What the hell?" he muttered.

"That's what I'd like to know, Mac. You said you were going for water," the bandaged face man said.

"Who?" asked Ingram.

"You, dim wit. I held on to your case. Now where's my damned water?"

Ingram turned the clarinet case in his hands. "Someone was here?"

"I thought it was you."

"No. How long ago?"

"About eighty shells ago."

"What?"

"Only way I tell time is to count shells."

Fifteen to twenty minutes, figured Ingram. "What's at the other end of the tunnel?"

"Don't know, Mac. The last thing I saw was the inside of our bunker before we took a direct hit.

"Which one?"

"Searchlight command bunker on Topside. I'm the only one that survived. I don't know why. My face is so sliced up I'm one gigantic scab. I don't even know if I'll see again. But, twenty-two other guys were luckier than me. They got to go home."

Maybe it was the medical team. "A woman? A nurse?"

"Nah. Helen and Doc Taft are still at the front of the lateral. This was a guy. He gave your buddy morphine after Filby left."

"Yardly?"

"Yeah, the smooth-talking corpsman. I traded aspirin for tomato juice."

Ingram stood and looked at Hampton. "I didn't realize he was that ill," he muttered.

"What?"

Ingram spoke up. "You said morphine? He wasn't in pain."

"*Wasn't* in pain? What's wrong with him?" the sightless man demanded.

Ingram didn't know what to say. "Shhh. You'll wake everybody."

The man lay back. "Look who's talking."

Ingram stood then looked at the man's chart. He was a first lieutenant; an Army Air Corps pilot from De Moines, Iowa, named Leon Beardsley. They had brought him in yesterday suffering flash burns, multiple facial lacerations, and severe cornea abrasions. He looked around and saw a metal pitcher in the corner. He walked over, found a tall dented cup, and filled it and brought it back. "Leon." He nudged Beardsley's arm.

The pilot arranged the cup's lip at the hole over his mouth and drank; some dribbled to mix with sweat on his chest. He lay back and said. "You read my chart."

Ingram couldn't deny that. "Um."

"Did the chart say when I'll be able to see again?"

"It says you're allergic to sulpha."

"Crap makes my face swell like a basketball. Lookit my eyes."

Ingram forced himself to look in the eye openings. All he could see was gooey flesh. "Glued shut?"

"Tighter than Fort Knox."

"Something you don't need right now."

"They won't tell me when I'll see again."

"What does it matter?"

Beardsley thought about that. "Okay."

"What do you fly, Leon?"

"B-17s. When there are some to fly. We lost all ours at Clark Field."

"And they stuck you with the ground pounders."

"At least I wasn't on Bataan." He handed back the cup and wiggled it.

With a nod, Ingram refilled the cup and walked back. "Here, Leon." He put it in the man's hand and leaned close, whispering, "Hampton didn't make it."

"I wondered. He just breathed less and less but I thought you knew what you were doing."

"Not me." Ingram rose.

"Who the hell are you?"

"His skipper. We're off a minesweep. The *Pelican.*" Ingram stooped and shoved the tomato juice case under Beardsley's cot. "The juice is yours. You have a weapon?"

Beardsley reached under his back and whipped out a .32 nickel-plated automatic. "My Uncle ran booze in Chicago."

"Very good." Ingram found an opener and popped a can. "Here, Leon. Drink up. Better have another can before someone steals..." He almost completed the sentence with "you blind." "Maybe another can before someone takes it all. Here's the opener."

"Thanks, Mac."

He waited until Beardsley finished sucking at the can. "Anything you can tell me about the guy with the morphine?"

"No." Beardsley held the can all the way up and sucked. Blood-red juice dribbled around the mouth opening. "Ahhhh."

"Okay, Leon. Good luck." Ingram patted the pilot's shoulder and took a last look at Hampton. As an afterthought, he reached in the dead man's duffle and retrieved Kowalski's flask of booze.

"Hey!"

"Yeah?"

Leon sat up. In a flash, he pulled his shiny .32, dropped the clip, cocked it and pulled the trigger. The hammer clicked loudly.

"That's good, Leon. Thanks for taking out the clip."

"I remember something. The guy with the morphine smelled like he was groomed for the evening. You know? My girl got some for me for my birthday last year."

"What?"

"Bay Rum."

"Sure."

———

Helen Durand nodded when Ingram walked up. She held the ether bottle and gauze over a Filipino corporal as Doctor Taft finished amputating his left hand.

"Can I talk to you?"

She looked at the doctor who kept working. With a slight nod, she finally said, "What's it like out there?"

"Not as bad as in here."

"People get killed for just going outside for a breath of fresh air." Sweat beaded on her forehead and both hands were busy.

Ingram picked up a towel. "Okay?"

"Please."

He dabbed at her forehead and cheeks. "I found my man back there."

"Good."

"He's dead."

"Sorry." Her eyes blinked and she bit at her upper lip. "Funny..."

"What's funny."

"He didn't seem that bad."

Ingram pushed a wisp of hair from her forehead and dabbed again. "That's what I thought." He turned his head for a moment. The ether made him woozy. "What made his leg swell up?"

"What?" She looked at him.

"Yeah. His injured thigh. Like a balloon."

"Doctor?" she said.

"Mosquito, please," said Taft.

She handed him one. "That man with the broken femur? We saw him about an hour ago."

Doctor Taft bent close to the Filipino's hand to clamp bleeders. "Haven't the foggiest."

"He and his friend had the tomato juice."

Doctor Taft smiled. "The cumshaw artists?"

"The lieutenant here says he's dead," said Helen.

Ether fumes made Ingram see double. He turned his head again and took a deep breath. How do they stand it? he thought.

"Must have tried to move around. Got up to take a leak, maybe. Was he in a Thomas Splint?" asked Doctor Taft.

"Yes," said Helen.

"Was he strapped in?"

Helen Durand looked at Ingram. "Was he strapped?"

Something was wrong. "I don't understand. He wasn't strapped. At least I don't remember. What does that--"

Doctor Taft said, "We keep 'em strapped so they can't move. Your man was scheduled for work tomorrow morning because I agreed with your corpsman. He had a broken femur. But if he moved around much then the jagged edges of the break probably lacerated the femoral artery."

They stared at him.

Ingram said, "Yes?"

"Bleeds to death. The entire blood supply is pumped into the thigh; makes it blow up like a balloon," said Doctor Taft.

"Gone," said Helen. They looked down. The ether bottle was empty.

Doctor Taft bent to his work. "Call over to Lateral Eight."

"They're out," she said.

"Shit." Taft sewed. The Filipino moaned slightly.

He dabbed at her brow. "Why give him morphine?"

She looked at him then took the towel and wiped her face. "I asked if he had pain. He said 'no.' We didn't order morphine."

Ingram's voice rose. "Well, then. Who did?"

Doctor Taft said, "Gonna have to leave now, son."

Ingram yelled, "Damnit. Somebody pumped morphine into Hampton."

The Filipino's moaning became louder. Helen stroked the man's forehead and said, "I remember a helpful man a few minutes ago that kept a certain army captain from shooting Dr. Taft."

"I..." Ingram sat back. "What should I do with Hampton?"

Helen said, "We'll take care of it. Go back to your post. Where are you?"

"*Pelican*. A minesweeper."

"Okay."

He put his hand on her shoulder. "I gave the tomato juice to the pilot."

"That was nice," she said.

"What's next?" asked Doctor Taft.

Helen nodded toward a Marine private leaning against the wall. "Broken elbow, I think."

The doctor said as Ingram rose to shuffle out, "Thank God. Sounds like something I can handle for a change."

7

24 April 1942
Hospital Tunnel
Corregidor Island, Manila Bay, Philippines

They waited until midnight for a let-up in the bombardment. There was none, so Ingram, Yardly, and Junior Forester put their heads down and ran to South Dock sprinting as if they were in a 440-yard race. Someone screamed. Ingram realized it was his own voice as his legs pumped furiously. Forester was the fastest and raced ahead, leaving Yardly, also screaming, alongside Ingram their cacophony like two wailing imbeciles.

Offshore, Forester's older brother saw Ingram's frantic flashing. He bore in just as two enormous shells erupted alongside the wharf raising twin hissing water columns. Everyone was drenched as the shore party scrambled aboard, hauling in their tomato juice. Whittaker anxiously revved the engine as the sandy mist dissipated. Forester clutched his tiller, pointed at the crates, and screeched, "What the hell's that?"

"Skipper got lucky in a crap game. Shove off!" yelled Yardly, jumping in with the last case.

Three minutes later they sliced easily into Manila Bay with Forester setting a course for the *Pelican*'s anchorage. Words weren't necessary. They all looked at one another, breathing collective sighs of relief over the hell they'd just escaped. Yardly found a rag in the bilge, wiped mist off his face, and nonchalantly handed it to his skipper. Ingram wiped and passed it on to Junior Forester as the little Buda four-banger diesel purred; the bow wave sizzled alongside while they collected themselves and looked back at the Rock, watching the bombardment.

"Funny," said Yardly.

The pharmacist's mate's voice was almost normal and it made Ingram realize the last time he'd heard Yardly the man had screamed in terror. For that matter, he had, too.

"Yeah Bones?" His throat was raw.

"Lookit that. They're shootin' at just the Rock. Nothing else."

They all looked around, seeing the barrage crash into Corregidor. Strangely, the other three fortified islands were not under bombardment for the moment.

"Why is that?" asked Forester.

It dawned on Ingram that he'd have to say something. Aside from MacRoberts and an executive officer who had been with them for a short while, Hampton was their only casualty since war broke. He and his crew had done well together. The man with the scythe and dark, musty robe had finally boarded the *Pelican* in earnest. A debate raged in his head on how to break the news. "Yes," Ingram said, "they're leaving the other forts alone tonight."

"Must mean something." Whittaker said.

Ingram tapped Yardley's knee. "Listen, Bones, I--"

"I'll bet the Japs are going to land, soon. Maybe tomorrow morning." Yardly said.

"Let 'em try it," said the gnarly faced Whittaker. "The gunners on the Rock'll chop 'em to pieces."

Yardly cocked both thumbs and with arrow-straight forefingers, aimed at Bataan and shouted, "Make the little saps pay. Rat-a-tat-tat-tat. That's for MacRoberts."

"Yeah, pay for Hambone, too." Whittaker said. "How's he gettin' along, anyway?"

Yardly grinned. "You shoulda seen us. We had this tomato juice--"

"He's dead," said Ingram.

"Nah. Skipper. We traded for--"

"Listen to me! He's dead." *Damnit! Why did I lose my temper?*

While catching his breath he watched their eyes and the silent, inaudible, *"how"* that crossed their lips. "'Dead', I said." He threw Kowalski's flask in Yardley's lap. The corpsman stared at it then back at Ingram as the diesel rumbled on. Finally, he told them.

"Bastards!" roared Forester from his tiller. "I say let's go and ice that doctor."

Whittaker pulled a bayonet and plunged it into a kapok life jacket. "Yeah. What was his name, Bones?"

Yardley's eyes were wide; the rage in his voice barely checked. "Skipper, Hambone didn't need morphine. He wasn't in pain. Why do that? Who the hell did it, anyway?"

Ingram shook his head and spread his palms.

"Maybe some asshole pay clerk doing double duty?" said Whittaker.

Ingram said, "I don't know what they had in mind. Nobody seemed to know--"

Something whooshed right above their heads. Instinctively, they ducked and threw their hands over their heads. Whatever it was felt big, metallic, and warm. But it didn't smash the water like the howitzer shell Ingram expected. Instead, engines revved up and roared.

"PBY!" yelled Forester from his tiller.

"Bullshit," said his younger brother. "That was a Zero. The sonofabitch is probably out lookin' for--"

"Quiet!" barked Ingram. He stood watching where the airplane had gone...when...another flew right over. He looked up in time to see the dark shape whip by, no more than twenty feet overhead. Hull-shaped fuselage, single tail, high wing, twin engines; blue flaming plumes shot from the exhaust stacks as the pilot revved engines like the other amphib.

It dawned on him. They were in the seaplane lane used in peacetime just a few months ago. And now it seemed strange it was to be used again; that seaplanes, American seaplanes, were returning. These past few months seemed like forever and Ingram now wondered if there had ever been a time without war.

He shouted. "It's two PBYs, Forester. We have to clear the lane. Head toward the Rock so these guys can land."

Forester leaned into his tiller, making the boat slug around and aim once again toward Corregidor. He'd just put their nose on Geary Point when a PBY whooshed over again. Something popped, lighting the area in a hoary brightness making them shade their eyes. In the flare's brightness, they saw they were almost directly upwind of the other PBY's final approach. In fact, they were right in the way, Ingram realized. "Step on it, Whittaker. I don't think he sees us." Ingram yelled.

Whittaker leaned into the engine compartment and fiddled with the throttle linkage, making the engine run a little faster. "He probably sees us, Skipper. Just doesn't give a shit."

Ingram sliced a hand through the air. "Head more to the left, Forester. Take a fix on--good, that's it."

The PBY flared, squatted, and splashed hard. Water spewed as she bounced high in the air.

"Ouch," said Yardly, as the amphibian settled once again to Manila Bay. "Pensacola guys call that kind of landing a pile driver."

Ten or so fifty-five-gallon drums bobbed in the flare's light loom. "Noooo," they yelled.

The PBY settled among them, with her hull hitting two drums, making her wobble a bit. Three seconds later, her right pontoon ripped off when it snagged another drum. Even then, the Consolidated PBY-5 Catalina flying boat probably would have survived, except she still yawed and skipped from the first blow. Without the pontoon, her right wingtip dipped and caught the water, making the amphibian cartwheel over the water, spewing mist and wreckage.

"Get over there!" yelled Ingram.

Forester needed no urging and jammed his tiller hard right to head directly for the stricken craft.

"Life jackets on," Ingram ordered.

His crew struggled into bulky kapok vests as they closed the crash site. Forester yanked one bell and Whittaker throttled to an idle where they drifted through unrecognizable pieces of wreckage.

Yardly sniffed, "What's that?"

"Avgas: one hundred octane. Don't light a cigarette." said Ingram.

"Hold it," called Junior Forester, from the bow. Whittaker reversed and they drifted next to a face down body. Junior Forester reached and lifted the head.

"Brian?" said Forester's brother from the helm.

"He's dead all right," said Junior Forester. "A lieutenant. Must have been the pilot."

They dragged the body in as the other PBY whooshed overhead to land with a large splash about two hundred yards upwind.

Ingram found a battle lantern and shined it around, seeing another body. They recovered that one, finding it was an enlisted man. "It's too dark for anyone else. We better check in with the other PBY in case--"

Something gurgled off to their right. "Hold it," Ingram said. He shined the light on a man whose head barely rose above water. The man waved a hand weakly then let it plop.

Forester maneuvered the boat alongside a lieutenant commander with a deep gash in the side of his head. Ingram reached over to secure a hold under his armpits. "Anything broken?"

"Don't think so," was a weak reply.

"Okay. Here we go."

They eased him in the boat and lay him in the bilge beside the two corpses. All three-looked like bloated fish.

"Head for the other PBY." said Ingram.

"Yessir," Forester rang bells for full speed.

Yardly opened the lieutenant commander's shirt while Ingram asked, "How do you feel?"

"Not sure." The man grimaced. "What happened?"

"You hit some oil drums." said Forester.

"Who stuck 'em out there?" The commander said "theah." His accent was New England, maybe Boston.

"Junk's floating all around the bay. They should have--hey buddy. You all right?" Ingram made room for Yardly, who checked the man's pupils.

"What do you think, Bones?" asked Ingram.

Yardly gently probed the head, neck, and shoulder area. He said softly, "Concussion at least. In shock. Might be ripped up inside, too. I don't know what else."

The corpsman probed the lieutenant commander's lower extremities.

"Skipper?" Reaching behind the man's back, he produced two items: a .25 caliber automatic and a cylindrical device.

Ingram palmed them. "A silencer?"

The man groaned.

Yardly dug at the man's left calf finding a stiletto strapped on the inside and handed that to Ingram.

They looked at one another. At length Ingram said, "Cox'n. Slow down for a moment."

Forester rang the bell and the whaleboat idled over an oily smoothness. "Where's the other PBY?" asked Ingram.

"Last time I saw it was at our ten o'clock," said Forester.

They drifted, not seeing anything except explosions flashing from Corregidor.

Ingram said, "That's it then. Back to the Hospital."

Forester cursed then asked, "Why not take him to the ship?"

Ingram said, "not with this--"

To their left, two Pratt & Whitney R-1830 Twin Wasp engines wound up to full throttle.

"What the hell?" said Whittaker. "Taking off? That was quick. Adios, Pal."

They listened, savoring every stroke of each of the Twin Wasp's fourteen pistons. And for an extra delicacy, the Pratt & Whitney's superchargers delivered a certain authoritative whine, unlike the tinny Japanese engines they'd heard for the past few months.

In the night, each man visualized her on the step now, with her pilot sighting a star to momentarily steer by so he could hold her steady and build speed. The PBY's copilot would be synchronizing the R-1830s until they gave a unified, triumphant, bellow.

The Cat's engines faded, but they still hung on to it. Even when a shell rattled the foundations of Monkey Point, they cocked their ears. And when the shell's reverberations were consumed by Corregidor, they again picked up the receding heartbeat of the Catalina, knowing she was safely airborne and heading into the South China Sea and on her way to Australia.

More damned generals or colonels, probably, just a pittance out of Corregidor's eleven thousand. But those men were safe now. They couldn't help but feel relieved as they settled back knowing they would soon be among friends; maybe even home in a few days.

At this very moment, Ingram realized, while he and his sailors bobbed aboard a stinking motor whaleboat in the carnage of Manila Bay, the ten or so colonels and generals would be drinking coffee handed over by a grinning crewman. After a few sips, they would lay back exhausted, prop a parachute or two for pillows, and grab some shuteye before they refueled in Mindanao. The long, boring leg to Darwin would be a Godsend as they continued with uninterrupted rest. After landing, they would stand beneath long, hot showers, and nestle between clean sheets. Soon they would be in Melbourne. And if the evenings were still balmy, they would drink a smooth, single-malt scotch with ice cubes, or perhaps one of the Aussie's strange, dark ales while a juicy top sirloin sizzled in--

"I have immediate business on Corregidor," the lieutenant commander gurgled.

Ingram jumped.

"Okay, Commander, we'll take care of it," said Ingram."Come on, Forester! South Dock."

"Yessir." The cox'n rang up full speed and pushed the tiller to head for Corregidor.

Ingram stuck out his hand, "Todd Ingram. Skipper of the U.S.S. *Pelican*."

"...Richardson. Fred Richardson..."

Ingram bent close, finding the lieutenant commander had lost consciousness again.

Yardly pulled out the man's soggy wallet and handed it over. Keeping his fingers over the lens, Ingram switched on his flashlight, giving the wallet's contents a glistening, hemoglobin cast.

Yardly looked over his shoulder as Ingram compared the picture to the face before him. "Too dark to be certain," he muttered, and squinted at the ID: 'Fowler, Robert T., CWO, USN.' The ID bore the seal of the United States Navy Department with an added inscription: 'Office of Naval Intelligence.'

"Says the guy's a chief warrant. What gives?" Asked Yardly.

With a look at the corpsman, Ingram grabbed the lieutenant commander's dog tags: Richardson, F. T., 149047, USN, PROT, O.

"I don't know what to believe." said Ingram nodding at the pistol and stiletto. "ONI people live in their own world and fight their own wars. The sooner we get him on the Rock the better I'll feel."

"Skipper!" Forester called.

Ingram looked aft, seeing a bow wave overtaking them.

"Shit! Japs," yelled Whittaker.

A shell flashed on Corregidor. The boat was not a landing craft, Ingram had seen it before. "Take it easy," he said watching the bullet riddled nose of the 51 Boat climb over their wake.

Soon they were abeam, and a hail pealed over engine noise.

"Heave to, Forester," Ingram said.

The boats slowed to an idle. Silhouettes of men in tin hats and four or five civilians formed against a murky horizon: two looked female.

One man stood high. Shell flashes illuminated a barrel-chested man who had a pug nose, cauliflower ears, short crew-cut, and carried a .45 low where a leather thong secured the holster's bottom to his leg. From the grim set of his mouth he looked like he knew how to use his pistol. "Carl Mordkin, captain, United States Army, military police. Have you seen another aircraft?"

"What are cops doin' out here?" Whittaker chortled softly.

"Shhht," whispered Forester. "I know that guy."

"You should," laughed Whittaker. "Brig rat like you probably had 'is butt kicked by Mordkin. You big buddies by now? First names, maybe? You call him Carl, and he sez," Whittaker twirled a finger in the fetid air and squeezed his vocal chords in a gangster falsetto, "'Oh Kevin, sweetie. Time for us to beat the shit out of you, again. Remove your shirt, please, and Sergeant Brutus Crushus here will warm up with--'"

"Shuddup, Pete. You don't screw with this guy," hissed Forester. Due to a preference for liberal quantities of cheap alcohol and barroom brawls, Forester had been reduced in rate several times and had spent time in military prisons. "He runs the stockade on Caballo. I know guys who have gone in there and never returned. One time I--"

"Pipe down," said Ingram. He turned to the 51 Boat and called, "Ingram, skipper of the *Pelican*. Affirmative. We saw a PBY crash and recovered a survivor and two bodies. I'd like to return to my ship, now. Can you take them?"

The 51 Boat cruised in silence for a moment. "Yes, Captain. We'll take them in."

The boats slowed and bobbed close together, their crews propped fenders between the hulls.

Yardly said, "Skipper, I hate to say this, but this guy has a concussion. Maybe internal problems, too. I don't think we should move him."

Whittaker whispered, "Buzz off Bones. Send him over so we can head back to the ship."

Ingram bit a thumbnail while the two bodies were passed. "Major?"

"Yes?" The stockade commander stood high on a thwart with hands on his hips.

"I don't think we should move this one. He has a concussion at least, possible internal injuries, and we're not sure what else. He lost consciousness a few minutes ago."

"Can I help, Captain?" It was a woman's voice; she sounded familiar.

Her outline popped up and a round exploded on Corregidor, lighting up the face of Helen Durand. "Yeah, come on over," said Ingram.

Ingram reached for her and, along with Junior Forester, helped her over the gunwale. She wobbled a moment and Ingram held her hands until she adjusted to the whaleboat's bobbing.

"Is Doctor Taft with you?" he asked.

"Still there." She nodded at Corregidor.

"You were supposed to go out on that PBY?"

She drew a deep breath. "Nobody knew what happened. They couldn't find the other plane so we drew straws." She tilted her head toward the '51 Boat. "They were yelling. The lottery was a joke."

"Who yelled?"

"The men in the boat. A general panicked and screamed at Mordkin. Mordkin screamed at us and ordered take-off in sixty seconds. It all happened so fast. Two out of nine nurses made it out."

"Who else?"

"Couldn't tell, it was so dark. That fat general. Some other brass. Two or three civilians."

"Lucky." He rubbed his chin. "How'd you get out here so fast?"

"Soon after you left, they rounded us up with five minutes to pack a duffle...with all those shells falling, I had to run for the dock."

She released his hand and bent with Yardly to examine the lieutenant commander.

Captain Mordkin called. "Captain?"

Ingram answered, "Yes."

"Uh, you ID your survivor?"

"Told me his name is Richardson. lieutenant commander."

"Anything else?"

"No. He passed out."

The Army captain exhaled. "Very well, Captain. We'll wait for you at South Dock."

"As fast as we can make it."

Lines were untied, they eased away from the 51 Boat which, being the faster of the two, roared ahead to Corregidor. Ingram sat back, watching Helen Durand and Yardly work on Richardson, or whoever he was.

Yardly said, "Skipper, you better hear this."

With the two corpses gone, Ingram found room to kneel beside Richardson. "What is it, Bones?"

Yardly said in a half whisper. "Looks like he's slipping."

Helen, still probing, said, "I think he has a lung puncture."

"Anything we can do?" Ingram asked.

"Keep him warm; hope we get him to the hospital in time," said Yardly. "But the guy said--"

"...Epperson." Richardson's eyes fluttered open. He blinked rapidly and searched their faces. "Any of you know Epperson?"

"Skipper. That the guy who came out the other night?" asked Yardly.

Ingram nodded and said softly, "You're going to be okay, now, Commander. We're taking you to the hospital."

"Mark Hopkins...Market Street..." Richardson's focus wandered and his eyes closed.

"Commander," said Helen. She bent close to his face. "Stay with us."

"Come on, Commander, don't go away." Yardly said loudly.

Richardson's eyes blinked open. He searched the stars then found Ingram. "You know Epperson?" His voice was weak.

Ingram nodded and held up his Naval Academy ring. "Both of us were class of 1937."

A shell landed perhaps two hundred yards away. Without looking, Ingram knew they were getting close to South Dock.

Richardson tried to wave a hand. Helen wrapped her hands around it and held on. "...my pouch," he said, looking to his right.

Ingram spotted it. "This one?"

Richardson wheezed deeply. Blood trickled from his mouth. He gurgled, "...deliver to Epperson."

As frail as Richardson was, Ingram detected an urgent tone. He picked up the letter-sized pouch and looked inside. "Empty, Commander."

"...nooo..."

Forester rang one bell and Whittaker eased the throttle to idle. With an upward glance, Ingram saw the dead, saw-toothed creosote pilings of South Dock glide by. "Hold on, Commander, almost there."

Richardson went rigid.

"Jeez," moaned Yardly.

With clenched eyes, Helen Durand grabbed both of Richardson's hands and held them to her neck.

Blood foamed at his mouth. It was a tremendous effort for Richardson to capture another breath. "Tell him...me." His eyes searched Ingram's.

"I will," Ingram said.

"...tell him, Pontiac."

"What?" asked Ingram.

Forester rang three bells. The whale boat's engine roared in reverse and stopped at a dock where Whittaker cut the engine.

Richardson's mouth and eyes were wide open as if propped with sticks.

"What?" Ingram put his ear close to Richardson.

"...Pontiac." Richardson's pupils grew large and his last breath escaped in a prolonged hiss.

Yardly shook his head. "Liked cars, I guess."

Helen eased Richardson's hands down and crossed them over his chest.

"I don't think he was talking about cars," Ingram said.

8

---

24 April,1942
South Dock, Corregidor Island
Manila Bay, Philippines

"Captain?" Carl Mordkin's stance on the wharf was silhouetted by an exploding seventy-five-millimeter shell, arms folded, feet wide apart.

Ingram looked up.

"We can take him now." The fireplug-shaped captain waved two men into the *Pelican*'s whale boat.

"He's dead."

"I see. Did he leave anything?" Mordkin looked at the ground and kicked cement shards.

"Not a thing," said Ingram.

"You sure? We're lookin' for a pouch."

"Sorry," said Ingram.

Mordkin swore just as a shell whacked Stockade Battery, reverberating thunderously down Government Ravine. Almost simultaneously, Battery

Geary's M-1908 mortar roared in defiance, the blast so loud they slapped their palms on their ears.

The nurses wailed, Helen among them, as they looked about for cover. The mortar roared two more times, while Richardson's body was lifted out. Suddenly, staccato flashes of Japanese counter-battery rained on the mortar pits with a machine gun swiftness. The battery was about a mile away, but even at that distance, the rapid concussions were so penetrating no one could move, except to crawl to a low wall and crouch with their hands over their heads. Shells crashed and the souls around Ingram, men and women alike, moaned and wailed. He, too, was shaking and with all the cataclysmic blasts one of the people moaning could well have been him.

Five minutes later it stopped. Blessed silence reigned for a moment then a distant shell fell on Monkey Point, sounding like a firecracker. Mordkin was the first to stir. "Pack up and get inside," he yelled.

Whittaker rose, dusting himself off. "That's it for them mortar pits."

"Those poor bastards," said Junior Forester.

Mordkin walked up and nodded to the three nurses who struggled to their feet. "Too bad about the ladies. They should be halfway to Mindanao by now."

"Too bad about all of us," muttered Forester.

"I know you?" asked Mordkin, squinting his eyes.

"No, Sir!" Forester walked to the dock and fiddled with mooring lines.

Mordkin turned to Ingram. "We have to go back out, Captain. Appreciate your help." He called his men; they jumped in the shore boat, cast off, and disappeared into South Harbor's gloom.

Helen Durand stood and watched them go.

Ingram stood beside her and said, "I'm sorry."

"I don't know why...guilty..." she said looking at the ground.

"Nonsense. You're not guilty of anything."

"Why I don't--" Her eyes glistened and she pulled her ball cap low to her eyes.

"Go on."

Her chin jutted out. "Alright, damnit. I don't know why I don't feel guilty. I don't. Maybe it's because I had a chance to live. And I wish with all my soul I was aboard that airplane right now."

"You mean guilty about leaving everyone here? Walking out on us? Leaving us to face the Japs? Forget it. You deserve the chance."

"So do you. So does everybody."

"Maybe."

She grabbed his shoulders. Ingram was surprised at the strength of her grip. "Why us?"

"What?"

"Why is Roosevelt throwing us in the toilet?"

His temperature rose and he realized it wasn't the tropical heat. "I don't know what he has in mind. Why don't you--

"Where is your damned Navy?"

Navy. Where is the Navy? My Navy! He'd heard that so many times. Ingram jerked. Her hands flew away as he shouted, "Honey. I'll tell you where the Navy is. The Pacific Fleet is on the bottom of Pearl Harbor. The Asiatic Fleet is on the bottom of Cavite or the Sunda Straits. And the Japs are kicking leftovers to Timbuktu."

Helen Durand took a step back.

He stepped with her. "Our warships have been sunk needlessly while the brass dithers in Washington trying to come up with another foolhardy scheme. All the while, thousands of good men are being killed.

"There is no Navy. You and I are next, honey. Maybe we can wave to each other when the Japs stand us against the wall and..."

She folded her arms.

With an effort, he controlled his breathing. "...sorry."

"The apology is mine. Those men in the PBY gave everything tonight."

"Their number came up."

"And Richardson's."

"And Richardson's."

"Good-bye."

Helen Durand picked up her duffle.

Ingram caught the stenciling on the side: HELEN Z. DURAND. "What's the 'Z' stand for?" he asked.

"Not now."

"What?"

"I'll tell you, sometime." Helen caught up with the other nurses; the three disappeared in the direction of the hospital tunnel.

Ingram watched for a moment then called, "Forester!"

The cox'n' said, "Yessir."

"Take the boat and lay offshore for an hour. I have to go to the Navy Tunnel."

"Yessir."

Two mortars belched from Battery Geary flinging their projectiles toward Sisiman Cove on Bataan.

"Let's move," yelled Forester.

"I'll be damned," said Whittaker, marveling that the mortars had survived the Japanese counter-battery.

Ingram didn't hear. He was already running for the Naval Intercept Tunnel.

Ingram walked up to Epperson's door as Tokyo Rose moaned, "...so I plead with you men of Corregidor. Give up. While General MacArthur basks in Australia you are dying. While he and his staff grow fat on fried shrimp and play eighteen holes of golf each day, you are dying. While your own admirals and generals hide like rats in the tunnels, you are dying. What is the use?"

The Marine sentry knocked. Epperson stuck out his head and waved. "Todd! Be right there," he said, and closed the door.

The loudspeaker hissed and Portman, wearing a splotchy-gray T-shirt, skivvies, and shower sandals, adjusted the squelch. Ingram sat on a table and, looking at his own skinny arms, wondered, how can that radioman be so fat?

With a screech, NHK's signal was clean again. Ingram kicked his feet back and forth, having no choice but to listen. "...four more days, boys. Four more days. April twenty-ninth is his Imperial Majesty's birthday, and it will be on that day you will experience artillery like none has ever seen or felt on this earth before.

"I beg you, listen to reason. Give up now, before it is too late. Once the bombardment starts, General Homma cannot stop until you are all dead.

"Lay down your arms. Save yourselves for your wives and sweethearts who at this very moment are entertaining 4-F cowards back home. Back-biting weasels with phony disabilities and falsified records. You know the weak ones who are getting rich off the black market and spending time with your ladies.

"Men of Corregidor! You've proven yourselves. You've put your lives on the line. But unlike you, the 4-Fs are too afraid to die for your country. Too afraid to stand for principle." Rose's voice softened, her timing perfect. "Too afraid to fight for the ones they love.

"And now..." she whispered. A record, *Harbor Lights* sung by Rudy Vallee began.

Ingram closed his eyes. It was "their" song. He was dancing with Miriam again in the Coronado Hotel's Crown Room. A whirlwind marriage. Crossed swords at the wedding chapel. They'd only known each other for six months. They met in San Diego, his first duty station where he was assigned to the U.S.S. *Hayes*, a swift, four stack destroyer that sported four, five-inch guns.

For four of those six months, he was at sea on the *Hayes* fighting the Battle of San Clemente Island returning to San Diego harbor for weekend liberty and steamy lovemaking to the tune of "Harbor Lights."

He lowered his head thinking of her and why it didn't work out. Why, on December 6, 1941, her letter dated two months earlier caught up to him in Cavite, announcing she had moved to Reno to commence divorce proceedings. That she wanted a "Nevada quickie" was evidence enough for Ingram to believe Tokyo Rose was right in his case.

But the image of some poor, unsuspecting 4-F ending up with Miriam made him laugh. She'd inherited her father's hair-trigger temper and would eat the little bastard alive the first time he got in her way. A little 4-F slob wouldn't have time to backbite. And if he did, Miriam would bite back with a ferocity that could rip up a mountain lion.

Miriam. After the wedding, he discovered she liked art. He liked sailing. She liked Chopin. He liked Louie Armstrong. He wanted children; she didn't. She liked cruising in her father's Packard. He admitted he liked that on occasion, especially when her father wasn't there.

Finally, he screwed up his courage and told her he liked walking on the beach more than riding in daddy's Packard. Her eyes turned to slits and, as expected, Miriam reached for something to throw, but Ingram stymied her by standing before the large bay window of their Point Loma rental overlooking San Diego Harbor.

After fumbling a grip on a Wedgewood pitcher, Miriam oddly stopped.

She gave a long exhale and simply walked from the room. Miriam moved back to Beverly Hills; Ingram to the BOQ. For a while neither started paperwork. It grew to a marriage of convenience with both becoming complacent. He wondered if--

"Todd. What goes on?" Epperson stuck out his hand.

"Where can we talk?" asked Ingram.

Epperson nodded to a conference area and they walked in and sat.

Ingram explained about the PBY crash, noting Epperson sat a little straighter with the subject of Richardson.

"What did he look like?" asked Epperson.

Ingram pulled out Richardson's water-soaked wallet and looked at the picture, still unsure if it were Richardson or not. "Here." He flipped the wallet over. "Don't tell the Army I kept this. Mordkin will toss me into his stockade."

"Who?" asked Epperson.

Ingram told him.

"Guy is a dope." Squinting at the wallet for a moment, Epperson pulled out Richardson's photo ID, rubbed it on his shirt, and held it to the light. "Beantown accent?"

"Yes."

"He talk about anything? A city?"

"San Francisco."

"Photo is all screwed up. He had a mustache, but it's Fowler, all right."

"How do you know him?"

"Taught a security class when I was at Treasure Island. We tipped a few in town. Picked up girls at the Top of the Mark."

Ingram smirked.

"Made fools of ourselves. Fifteen minutes later, they went for flyboys because they had gleaming brass wings and flashy campaign ribbons on their blouses."

Ingram blurted, "And now you're bald. They'll never let you in the Mark, again."

Epperson gave him a "not funny" look and said, "Anything else?"

"I think he had something for you. Like guard mail or something. He had a pouch around his neck and asked me to look in it. But it was empty."

"Empty? Did it have a lock?"

"No. Just a flap. Whatever it was, he wanted it delivered to you. But it was gone."

"You didn't find the inner?"

"Inner what?"

"Pouch. There is an inner section. That must be what they went looking for."

"Oh."

Epperson rested his chin on his forearms and stared for a moment. At length, he said, "Is that it?"

"Cars."

"What?"

"He likes cars. Just before he died he said 'Pontiac.' That mean anything?"

Epperson said, "You sure?"

Ingram nodded.

Epperson stood and walked past Portman's floor-high radio unit and stooped at a large, open safe. He rose and returned with a thick, three-ring binder and flopped it on the table.

Ingram caught the typed front label as Epperson flipped pages:

SECRET
STANDING ORDERS
COMMANDING OFFICER, U.S. ARMY, FORT MILLS,
CORREGIDOR ISLAND, PHILIPPINES.

"Here it is. It's how Wainwright plans to end the party." Epperson sat back and picked at a scab on his head.

"Stop it, damnit!"

"Sorry." Epperson sighed, and said, "We have enough food for another two months. I think that's when Wainwright plans to surrender."

It roared over Ingram. Within weeks for sure, maybe even days he would be in a Japanese prison camp. "Surrender," he mumbled. A shell hit, making the room shake violently like a shark worries living flesh off its victim. "This place won't last two months," he said softly.

With a nod, Epperson said, "That's why Nimitz wants me out. Now." He folded his arms on the table and rested his chin. "If I'm captured and they find out where I worked, then all they have to do is shove hot pokers in my eyes."

"Dwight. I don't think you would--"

Epperson held up his hand. "And I'll tell 'em all."

"No."

"The Japs have exquisite methods. Another favorite is one they learned from the Russians. They pound nails into your skull. Then they--"

"Okay. Okay."

"I'm no hero. Neither are you." Epperson gave a long exhale, his eyes unfocused. "I radioed my own analysis last night. Tokyo Rose is right. The Japs can't screw around anymore. They can't afford to wait two months or however long they think it will take to starve us out. They need Manila Bay, now. An all-out bombardment on Hirohito's birthday makes sense. They'll throw everything they have at us, then they'll try a landing. Amphibious probably."

"They haven't enough landing craft."

"Yes, they do." Epperson looked up. "More than enough. Tanks, too. They'll roll the damn things through the tunnels squashing sick and wounded while firing into laterals."

Deep in his spine, Ingram felt cold. "My God."

"Yeah."

"What's Pontiac?"

Epperson picked up the Army manual, ran his finger down a column and looked back to Ingram. "It means 'destroy everything above .45 caliber.' *PONTIAC* would precede a surrender order. It means prepare to give your-selves up but destroy large weapons and ammo so they can't fall into Jap hands." Ingram's mind drifted back to the terrible night Bataan surrendered. The Army had touched off several ammo bunkers on the peninsula. Even on Corregidor, the earth shook violently and flames roiled thousands of feet skyward. It was all the more macabre when an earthquake shook Bataan at the same time. With ammo belching into the sky and the earth shaking, it was as if Vulcan stood tall above them, laughing, toying with them.

They stared at the walls, as shells exploded outside. "But why did Richardson--"

"Fowler," corrected Epperson.

"Fowler said *PONTIAC*? Wouldn't he want that relayed to Wainwright instead of you?"

Epperson said, "I don't think Fowler meant that at all. Without whatever was in the pouch, I think he was trying to tell me something. *PONTIAC* means he wants me to destroy something."

"What?"

Running a hand over his scalp, Epperson eyed fresh Marines relieving the detail at the crypto room door. "I'm not sure."

9

25 April 1942
U.S.S. *Pelican* (AM 49)
Caballo Island, Manila Bay, Philippines

Ingram's eyes flipped open and he focused on the overhead tracing cable arcing its way around a ventilation duct. He moved an arm. It was stuck to the sheet with last night's sweats. This morning promised another day of miserable, perspiring humidity.

He rolled his eyes to check the bulkhead mounted clock: 0627.

After turning in at two-thirty, he'd slept four hours in his skivvies and his bunk was, as usual, drenched in sweat. He rose, ran his hands through his hair, and bent over--what the hell? It was quiet. Where was the artillery?

A salvo, 150s perhaps, landed on Corregidor answering his question. While flipping the fan switch to high, another string of Japanese shells established the plan of the day on Caballo Island as well.

He looked out the porthole seeing Caballo' s barren cliffs rise sharply. At the top of the cliff, green jungle jutted out making the facade look like a man with a high forehead; two boulders almost level with one another formed beady eyes while a feral pig trail (the pigs were extinct, having been run to ground by hungry defenders) scribed a mouth with a cruel smile. With air attacks in mind, Ingram felt safe from artillery tucked in here. There wasn't much of a swell. Another reason he lay close to the mile-long island was he hoped General Moore, stuck in Corregidor's Malinta Tunnel, would forget his plans to have the *Pelican* scuttle: Out of sight--out of mind, he thought.

With MacArthur's departure on March 11, two other minesweepers and three ancient river gunboats were all that remained of the once mighty Cavite-based Asiatic Fleet. Now all they could do was defiantly ply the waters of Manila Bay. With critically low fuel and obsolete weapons, they still put up effective antiaircraft barrages. Ironically, the Japanese let them alone and even ignored the plight of their own bombers which occasionally spilled from the sky in fiery plumes from American ack-ack.

It wasn't until they became hungry for targets that the Japanese finally swooped down to take the little ships under fire. Usually, it was just one ship at a time, with twenty or thirty airplanes doing their best to pound her to junk. The *Pelican* had been lucky last week. She'd been underway and was able to avoid the strafing and all but two crippling near misses.

In one way, the atmosphere was circus like. Survivors of the minesweeper *Finch*, paddling about while their ship wallowed in death throes, watched three Zeros fly upside-down at deck level in a perfect vee. The plane's canopies were cranked open and the damned pilots flipped them the finger as they zipped overhead. The waterlogged sailors asked in amazement, *how the hell did they know what that meant*?

Otherwise, it was bloody, macabre; war as usual. Like a shark frenzy, Zeros and Vals and Kates bored in from all directions, making it impossible for a ship to effectively direct its antiaircraft barrage. Soon the ship would be smothered with explosions and begin her trip to the bottom. Some straggling attackers simply buzzed the stricken ship as the crew abandoned her. Other aircraft strafed men in the water or aboard lifeboats. Now, all were gone except the *Pelican* and her sister ships, *Quail* and *Tanager*.

Ingram shuffled to the stainless washbasin and bent over to sponge himself off.

Someone rapped on the door.

"Come."

Fred Holloway walked in, pulled up a chair, and sat.

Ingram sloshed brackish water in his eyes and groped at a rack. "Yeah?"

Holloway threw a towel. "Rocky likes your idea."

"What?"

"He thinks we should head for China. He's an old Yangtze sailor. He was on the *Panay* and knows some of the lingo."

"Yeah?"

Holloway grinned. "Knowing Rocky, it's probably just dirty words. Anyway, he talked to the engineering gang. He says they're for it."

"Okay."

"Our motor whaleboat isn't good, he says. The engine is a wreck."

"Ran swell last night."

"Claims he stuffed Fuller's earth in the crankcase. He's going to look for something else."

Drying his face completed Ingram's morning ablutions. He buttoned up a stained sleeveless khaki shirt and was ready for the day. "What about Ollie?"

"Don't know."

"Come on, Fred."

"Shit. Alright. He hasn't talked to the deck force yet."

"I better fire a blast at him. We need to get this thing moving." Ingram rubbed the stubble on his chin. "Look. I think we might have something. There are three shore boats at the South Dock. It would be tight, but I think we can get everyone in."

"Wow."

"Food and water is a big problem."

Holloway made a wry face. "If the price for escaping the Japs is eating canned salmon and rice for another couple of weeks, I'll go for it." He looked out the port for a moment. "But, what if we get there to discover rice and canned salmon is all the Chinese have?"

"That may not be a problem."

"Oh, yeah?"

"I've been thinking of another route. One that takes us--"

Someone rapped on the door. "Come," said Ingram.

Toliver poked his head in the door. "Shore boat headed our way, Captain. Army guys."

Ingram reached for his garrison cap. "Be right there."

Toliver left and Ingram asked, "What's with him?"

Holloway tipped his hand from side to side. "I think he's tired. A lot of the guys are. They're ready to throw in the towel and let the Japs run things."

Ingram said. "They're not worried about what happens to them?"

"They don't care anymore."

He squared his cap and stood in the doorway. "It's their choice. I'll try to fix it so everyone on this ship has a chance to go with me. Put the word out."

Holloway stood. "Yes, Sir."

Ingram turned and walked to the quarterdeck to find the 51 Boat pulling in with Mordkin and another nervous looking Army captain. With them was an Army major with a lightly pockmarked face, wearing Jodhpurs. A thin mustache underlined a large hawk billed nose. Deep-set eyes hid in shadows under a campaign hat.

After salutes, Mordkin introduced Major Otis DeWitt, and the other officer, Captain Henry Fletcher of the Quartermaster Corps, who wore large round glasses that obscured constantly darting eyes. Ingram lead them to the wardroom and poured coffee. Mordkin acted as if he hadn't had any for years, finishing his cup in three gulps. DeWitt took his time, savoring his portion while Fletcher sipped slowly with a cocked pinkie. Finally, DeWitt spoke with a resonant Texas twang, "I understand you're taking the party out to meet the submarine."

Come on. Epperson's deal is supposed to be top secret, thought Ingram. "Who says so?"

DeWitt sat back and sniffed. "Are you not the one assigned, Lieutenant?" For whatever reason, DeWitt had tossed a poorly conceived gauntlet; he'd addressed Ingram by his actual rank, one junior to DeWitt which was technically correct. But Ingram figured this staffer and his two weenies who sat slopping up *his* coffee on *his* eleven-hundred-ton United States Navy fighting ship for which *he* had been commissioned to command should favor *him* with the traditional honorific of captain.

He rose, snatched a phone from the overhead bracket and punched a call button. "Mr. Toliver? This is the captain. We're two minutes late for General Quarters. And set the anchor detail." He looked at DeWitt. "I may want to get underway at a moment's notice."

The 1MC screeched, "General Quarters. General Quarters. All hands man your battle stations." A bell gonged, hatches crashed shut and were dogged.

First Fletcher, then Mordkin stood and looked about nervously as the exhaust and vent blowers--the ship's breathing system--wound down making it immediately fetid. Without the blowers, the bulkheads began to sweat with the humidity. Little rivulets of condensation worked their way to the deck. More hatches slammed shut as men clumped in adjacent compartments, energizing their equipment and hooking up their telephone headsets to report in.

The wardroom hatch banged open. DeWitt jumped up as Yardly and two perspiring hospital corpsmen pounced into the wardroom.

"Excuse me, gentlemen," said Yardly, handing DeWitt, Mordkin, and Fletcher their cups and saucers. With a practiced flourish, he yanked the green-felt cloth off the wardroom table while another hospital corpsman flipped out a white pad. Quickly, the three men spread surgical instruments and a portable medicine chest on a side table. Yardly plugged in sound powered telephones and said, "Bridge? Wardroom. Manned and ready."

Yardly looked at the other two and said, "Who's gottum?"

"Me," said one of the hospital corpsmen. He reached in the portable medicine chest producing poker chips and a deck of cards. Judiciously, the three glanced at Ingram then took seats in a far corner and began playing.

Ingram checked his watch: Forty-three seconds to set GQ; not bad. The average was forty-six; the best time ever was thirty-four. He enjoyed watching DeWitt's wild eyes wishing it could be prolonged. But then war was the *Pelican*'s business and his men were paid to be quick and professional.

Mordkin recovered first and with a glance at Ingram, nonchalantly walked over and poured more coffee. DeWitt opened his mouth to speak but Ingram beat him to it.

"Major. You need authorization to discuss something like that. Now, if you'll excuse me, I must take my place on the bridge." He started to walk out.

"My apologies, Captain. Please read this." DeWitt's voice was full of ice as he pulled a sheet of paper and handed it over. It was a note from Epperson:

Todd--

The bearer is Major Otis DeWitt--adjutant to General Moore. He's in overall charge of the evacuation party, so he's important to Radtke and me. He told me he needs help with something else, so give it your best.

Bad news for us. The sub's been delayed again until, guess what?--the 29th—Hirohito's birthday.
   Thanks,
   Dwight

Ingram read it twice and looked at DeWitt. "What can I do for you?"

   DeWitt nodded toward Yardly. "Was all this necessary?"

   "Actually, Major, we should have been at GQ a half-hour before sunrise. But it was relatively quiet and I allowed the ship to stand at a condition three watch so others could catch up on sleep."

   "I don't understand what that means."

   Ingram exhaled, "What can I do for you Major?"

   "It's top secret. Where can we talk?"

   "What's wrong with right here?"

   "Captain, I mean it." DeWitt's eyes narrowed.

   "Very well. Yardly!"

   "Sir?" said Yardly.

   Ingram said, "The three of you lay to the quarterdeck. Stand by the phone and report here immediately if there is any indication of enemy action. You may leave the hatches open."

   "Yessir." The three hospital corpsmen undogged the hatch and filed out.

   Ingram sat. DeWitt took a place opposite and said conspiratorially, "Are you aware of a submarine that called here last January?"

   "There have been quite a few submarines."

   "Fletcher?" DeWitt said.

   Captain Fletcher sat, licked his lips, and said dramatically, "This submarine brought in ammo, food, and medicine."

   Ingram thought, this guy is going to shift his gaze from side to side like the nervous Neanderthal sucking on pterodactyl eggs. "You mean the gold on the *Trout*?"

   DeWitt looked perturbed. "How the hell did you know?"

   Ingram said, "January twelfth. We were the ones who guided her through the minefield. She was five thousand pounds' light when she tied up. Offloading ammo and stores meant she needed more ballast. Since they couldn't give her sand she had to take bullion."

Fletcher took a deep breath, looked from side to side, and lowered his voice. "She took on two and a half tons of gold and silver bullion plus U.S. securities and currency. Now," he rubbed his hands together, "there's another half-ton that has to be removed. MacArthur kept it here in case the Japs lifted the siege and he needed something to restart the Philippine economy."

"I see. And you want to send it out on the next sub," said Ingram.

"Yes," said Fletcher.

Interesting, thought Ingram. Epperson and his crypto whiz-kid were to be mixed with nurses, MacArthur's imperial residue, a few civilians, and a thousand pounds of gold. He rubbed his chin. "What's a brick weigh?"

Fletcher said, "About seventy pounds."

Ingram started doing the math but DeWitt already had it in his head. "We have fifteen bars, Captain. That's worth close to a half million dollars."

Fletcher looked at DeWitt. "$535,815, Sir."

DeWitt gave Fletcher a sour look then flicked an imaginary ash from his shirt.

"That'll buy quite a few war bonds," Ingram said.

"Actually, it belongs to the Philippine government," Fletcher drawled.

"If that's the case, what was MacArthur's plan for it?"

Fletcher's mouth opened.

"I find that insolent, Lieu..." DeWitt said.

Ingram smiled. "Relax, Major. I'm on your side."

DeWitt returned the smile, albeit a thin one.

Ingram sat forward and said, "Okay gentlemen. If you're worried about the load, I think one boat can do it all. Perhaps the people in your party wouldn't mind forming a work detail to help transfer the bricks?" Ingram's eyebrows raised, visualizing sweating, cursing, stumbling, top brass manhandling seventy-pound bricks of solid gold as ten-foot ocean swells slammed the shore boat against the submarine.

"Very funny, Lieutenant," said Mordkin. He stood close with his arms crossed.

Ingram glanced at Epperson's message and said, "This says the pickup is delayed until next Wednesday. I'll bring my crew over about 2000 and we--"

The 1MC's loudspeaker squawked. "Captain to the bridge."

10

Ingram grabbed his hat and said, "Excuse me gentlemen." He dashed through the passageway to the main deck hearing the drone of multiple aircraft engines at high altitude.

He stopped halfway up the ladder and looked back, seeing DeWitt and his men had followed him to the main deck. "Our day is about to begin, so you better shove off. I'll see you Wednesday evening."

Ignoring further formalities, Ingram bolted to the bridge and strapped on his helmet. Holloway and Toliver were looking almost straight up through their binoculars. "See 'em?" he asked, grabbing his own pair.

Holloway strained, looking toward Caballo' s cliffs. "Nossir. They're masked behind--there!" He pointed. Vee after vee of Mitsubishi G4M2 "Betty" bombers flew into view.

Soon explosions rumbled on the island with the bomber formation receding in a lazy arc toward the northeast.

"They're plastering Caballo on command salvo." said Holloway.

Ingram shouted at Forester, "Fo'c'sle. Up anchor, on the double!" Then, he leaned into the pilot house saying, "Engine room, stand by for maximum turns."

The explosions finally died and it became quiet.

He said to Forester, "How's the anchor?"

The man blinked and said, "I just told them, Captain."

Toliver yelled, "Thirty-nine in that formation." He cocked an ear, listening to the engine's reverberation. "Altitude about ten thousand. More on the way."

"Tell 'em to slip the anchor now," Ingram barked at Forester.

"You want them to slip the anchor, Sir?"

"Do it!" Ingram yelled.

Explosions rumbled again. Ingram stood on a platform and shouted to the fo'c'sle, "Chief, slip the anchor."

"What?" Chief Bender, standing seventy-five feet away, cupped an ear.

"Slip the dammed anchor. Now!" yelled Ingram, as explosions sprinted Caballo' s length.

As Bender dashed to the anchor-chain's brake release, Ingram ordered, "Forester! All ahead full!"

The bomb-salvo raced over the cliffs sooner than anyone expected. The cliff's face was disintegrated in a bizarre, anthracite blast pig trail and all, with tons of dirt and rock shooting directly above them. Boulders rained, tree limbs and enormous clumps of soil fell on the ship. Just then the anchor chain's bitter end whipped out of the hawse pipe and ran into the bay, while Bender and his men raced aft for cover.

Ingram leaned into the pilot house as a bomb hit the *Pelican's* windlass, flinging Bender, with legs still pumping, high in the air. Four more bombs raced past them into Manila Bay, their detonations deafening.

Picking himself up from the deck, Ingram looked up, seeing formations droning overhead. Then, more bombs hammered Caballo and spilled into the ocean exploding about the ship. Smoke cleared on the fo'c'sle; he looked to see if he could find Bender, but there was no bow. Twenty feet of the *Pelican's* forward section had disappeared--all that was left were mangled, smoking beams bent out like the end of an exploded gag cigar. Even as he watched, the *Pelican* started a drunken list to starboard.

Ingram stumbled into the pilot house and helped Forester struggle to his feet. "Report damage."

Forester gaped at his mouthpiece and tapped his earphones. "Line's dead, Captain."

"Keep trying. Messenger!" Staggering, he looked down seeing Quinn, their GQ messenger, sprawled on the deck, his neck bent to an obscene angle. Farwell stooped next to him, then glanced up shaking his head.

He checked forward again, seeing the *Pelican*'s nose lower. Aft, the screw was almost out of the water. Men poured out of the engine room hatch as he watched and, oddly, an enormous blast of air rushed up the companionway, flipping off Farwell's hat.

Holloway was at his side. "Just got word from Junior Forester. Near miss blew a hole in the mess decks' s hull plating. Almost totally flooded down there. They can't control it. And Rocky says that weak seam opened up again in the engine room. They're taking on water, too."

The *Pelican* screeched, rumbled and listed farther to starboard. Ingram put out his hand to grab--he fell.

The next thing he knew Holloway had his hands under his armpits, helping him to his feet. He blinked, finding he'd tripped over a large tree branch, banging his head on a helmet-stowage rack.

"What's that doing here?" he muttered, putting his hand to his cheek and wiping off blood. Slipping on dirt clods, his right foot flew out and his hand almost landed on a green, bug-eyed lizard that twirled in panic on the blistering deck. "Damnit!" Ingram yelled and yanked off his helmet.

"Come on, Todd." said Holloway.

"Where's Ollie?"

Holloway shook his head.

Ingram had to squint momentarily to capture a focus. Finally, he struggled to his feet and shouted, "Anything on the forward magazines?"

"Flooded," grunted Holloway heaving the branch overboard.

They looked aft, hearing a long ululating scream.

"Okay," shouted Ingram. "We'll abandon. Take the port side and start yelling."

"Right." Holloway trotted through the pilot house.

Ingram ran aft to the signal bridge, cupped his hands around his mouth, and shouted, "Abandon ship."

Within seconds, men started jumping. The *Pelican* tipped further to starboard. It hit Ingram, *we only have seconds. She's going fast.*

He yelled at the radioman to destroy their confidential material. Then, his eye caught fifteen or so men in the starboard motor whaleboat. The bow floated free in the water, but the stern was still suspended; the aft davit falls hadn't fully paid out. A shirtless sailor in the stern sheets frantically hacked at the thick lines with a knife, even as men piled in quickly overloading it.

Ingram saw the trouble: Someone had carelessly released the aft davit line near a cleat, where it had caught and snagged. He leaned over to yell at the men in the boat, when Toliver walked by the davit.

"Ollie!" yelled Ingram.

Toliver's gait was like one strolling down Fifth Avenue on a Sunday afternoon. Men ran past, a few bumping into him, as he sauntered with his hands in his pockets.

"Mr. Toliver!" Ingram tried again.

Toliver slowed and looked around as the *Pelican* lurched farther to starboard. Finally, he blinked and looked up.

Ingram pointed to the aft davit. "Ease the boat falls. It's snagged on that cleat."

Toliver stared.

"Do it! Quick."

"Huh?" Toliver's mouth fell open.

"Uncleat the boat falls, Ollie!" Ingram shouted as Pelican's roll increased.

"Captain. Time to go." It was Farwell. "I got the log books."

"Wait." Ingram yelled.

The *Pelican* was listed almost to forty degrees. Storage lockers burst open. Their contents spewed into screaming men as they clung to the starboard rail. A fifty-five-gallon drum of hydraulic oil fluid broke from its lashings and tumbled over a screaming man fifteen feet from where Toliver stood.

Ingram tried again. "Ollie!"

Water swirled around Toliver's ankles. Suddenly, he bent to the deck, took off his shoes, and methodically tied the laces of one to the other making sure he used square knots. After hanging the pair around his neck, Toliver dove over the side and stroked for safety, while the *Pelican* rolled suddenly to a perilous angle.

"Let's get down there," Ingram yelled to Farwell.

As the *Pelican* started her capsize, the wooden whaleboat floated momentarily, while men frantically tried to knock away the davit hook. Too late, the ship kept rolling with the after davit smashing through the whale boat's aft section. Three shrieking sailors were crushed as the rest leaped out of the way.

Ingram poised on the signal flag locker with Farwell ready to jump. But the *Pelican* lurched and thumped. With another metallic screech, it became quiet.

A sea gull squawked. Groans punctuated the morning air. Ingram looked at Farwell and said, "Bottom." He reached to brace his hand on the bulwark, seeing the *Pelican* had settled at a near fifty-degree list. A quick glance fore and aft told him bow and stern were below the surface. Only the minesweeper's superstructure remained above water.

Ingram and Farwell stepped off the flag locker and wobbled to find a foothold, half on the bulwark, half on the deck. "Get them back aboard," Ingram shouted.

Farwell nodded at the three bodies floating among the men who flailed in the water near the smashed whaleboat. "With respect, Sir. I'm going to kill that yellow sonofabitch."

"Who?" Ingram said.

"Toliver," Farwell spat. "All the stupid bastard had to do was uncleat the falls and let the boat go. Because of him, those guys died!"

"That's enough," barked Ingram, waving his sailors back to what remained of the *Pelican*. He looked Farwell in the eye. "I'll deal with Mr. Toliver. Do you understand?"

Farwell's nostrils flared. He glared for a moment, then looked down. "Yessir."

A thoroughly soaked Holloway scrambled up to the bridge. "Did you see what Ollie did?"

"Forget it. Help me get everyone aboard."

To their surprise, the 51 Boat returned and cruised among the survivors with the ashen-faced DeWitt, Mordkin, and Fletcher pulling in dead and wounded. Eventually, they lay alongside. DeWitt stood beside his cox'n and cupped his hands over his mouth. His twang rippled across the water, "You all want us to take your casualties ashore, Captain?"

Ingram cupped his hands to his mouth. "How many?"

Fletcher stumbled among them, counted, and said something to DeWitt. "Four dead. Nine need medical attention," Dewitt shouted.

"Hold on for a moment." Ingram looked aft finding Yardly bent over a man on the 01 level.

The hospital corpsman caught his eye saying, "Fifteen dead at least, Captain. I have seven wounded I'd like to send over."

"Very well, do it," said Ingram, hearing a distant drone. He looked up seeing another formation of Betty's wheel toward Caballo and straighten out for their bomb run.

Holloway said, "Shit, here we go again."

Ingram leaned over the rail and shouted to the 51 Boat. "Major, can you take seven more to the hospital?"

DeWitt stared at the formation. "Alright, but hurry it up."

"Sheeyat," spat Holloway.

"Shut up, Fred," said Ingram through clenched teeth. He cupped his hands and called, "Chop, chop, Major. And please send the boat back."

DeWitt scratched his head. "What the hell for?"

Ingram did his best to stifle his anger. "As you can see, Major, our whale-boat has been reduced to kindling. We need a means to take our men ashore."

"Oh."

"I'll send a boat crew with you."

"Okay."

The 51 Boat bobbed alongside as explosions rumbled on Caballo. The Bettys had salvoed, but this time their load fell at Caballo' s eastern end. DeWitt, Mordkin and Fletcher, their uniforms splotched with blood, worked among the *Pelican*'s hospital corpsmen to help the wounded and arrange the dead. Soon, the transfer was complete, and Forester and Whittaker jumped aboard.

With a whine of its gear box, the 51 Boat backed away. DeWitt yelled, "Can we still do business, Lieutenant?"

"Do what?" Ingram yelled back.

"Wednesday night."

Their wardroom discussion seemed like years ago. Ingram had no idea where he'd be by next Wednesday. "Hell...I don't know...I guess so."

"We're depending on you, Captain," DeWitt shouted.

"Alright. Don't forget to send the boat back."

"We will. And make sure you destroy this hulk before sunset. Leave nothing for the Japs."

"Will do."

The 51 Boat twirled and roared on its way to Corregidor.

"Fred," Ingram said. "Find Sunderland and get him up here. Toliver, too. And get someone to take a muster."

"Aye aye, Sir." Holloway eased down the canted companionway while Ingram hobbled forward to look in the pilot house.

Soon, a soaked and breathless gunner's mate first, class Kermit Sunderland stumbled up. "Captain?" he said, wiping water off his face.

Ingram said, "Sunderland, the Japanese will be able to salvage this ship if we don't blow it up. Are the demo charges in place?"

"As far as I know, Sir."

"Are the ones in the magazines still there?"

"Yes, Sir. I checked those day before yesterday."

"How do we get to them?"

"Forester's a qualified diver. He could set the timers."

"Very well. Tell him--"

They stepped aside to let Yardly and his corpsmen carry Quinn's body aft. Toliver and Holloway, having reached the bridge, stepped aside to let them pass.

"--to get ready. We'll set the charges as soon as everyone is off."

"How much time, Sir?"

"Four hours. Have you seen Bartholomew?"

"Down there." He nodded toward the main deck.

"Send him up." After a beckoning nod to Toliver, Ingram turned to the pilot house hatch. With the ship at a fifty-degree list, he had to hoist himself up, finding the once well-arranged orderliness of the ship's navigation center strewn with junk on the starboard bulkhead.

Farwell crashed about, throwing tools, flashlights, and cushions into a heavy duffle bag.

"Navigation gear, too, Farwell."

"Sir?"

"Sextants, all three of them. Nautical Almanac, chronometers, sight reduction tables, charts, dividers, pencils, pads, binoculars. Anything else you can think of."

Farwell gave a blank stare. "You're..."

"Do it. Get someone to help you. Take as much as you possibly can."

"Yes, Sir." Farwell scrambled out, making sure he brushed roughly against Toliver.

"Come on in," said Ingram.

Grunting and wheezing, Toliver wiggled in, pushed aside Farwell's duffle, and flopped against the bulkhead.

"What happened, Ollie?"

Toliver's head shook slowly. He folded his arms on his knees and rested his head.

Ingram, close to the boiling point, waited a full minute. "You better start talking. What the hell happened?"

Farwell reappeared and grappled at the hatch with Junior Forester standing just behind.

Ingram raised a palm and shook his head. Farwell turned to Forester and drew a forefinger across his throat, then eased out of sight.

"Ollie. I don't know if I can handle this. Those guys want to kill you."

Toliver's head rolled back and forth.

Ingram shouted, "I haven't time for sniveling, damnit. I've got a ship to blow up and a crew to take care of. Now say something or I'm throwing your ass to the sharks!"

"I don't know what happened," Toliver blurted. He raised his head, tears ran down his cheeks. "I saw their eyes. Someone kicked me, I think it was Whittaker. Something terrible happened, didn't it?"

"Ollie, you were there. Three men were crushed to death under the whaleboat davit."

"Wheat?"

"You were right there. You could have saved them. All you had to was unwind the line off the boat falls cleat."

"No. I was in the water."

Ingram pointed. "Look, damnit."

"What?"

"Your damned shoes. Still hanging around your neck. Don't you remember stooping on the deck and taking them off?"

"No."

"I yelled at you then, remember?"

"All I know is that I was in the water!" With hands to his face, Toliver cried openly.

Yardly poked his head in the hatch. "Captain?"

"Yes?"

"Muster complete, Sir. Nineteen dead. Twenty-six wounded."

Ingram shook his head. Forty-five casualties out of eighty-two reasonably healthy men. Forty-five men who just minutes before lived in unmutilated bodies.

"Sir?" asked Yardly.

"Got their dog tags?"

"Yessir."

Ingram couldn't help himself. "Did you recover the bodies of the men crushed beneath the davits?"

Toliver's head dropped on his forearms.

Yardley's voice was surprisingly soft. "On their way ashore with the Army major."

Ingram said, "Any wounded still aboard?"

"Ten, Sir."

"Serious?"

"Not too bad. Worst one is a broken clavicle."

"Very well. Get some men. Have them help you pack as much of the medical supplies as you can carry. Now, send in Mr. Holloway."

"Yes, Sir."

Holloway's head popped in the hatch. Bartholomew stood just behind.

"Come on up, you two."

They crawled in and looked curiously at Toliver.

Ingram caught it, too. Toliver's eyes seemed ablaze. In fact--

"Eeeeaagh." Toliver leaped for a bayonet lodged against the binnacle. Ingram was closest and reached for it. But Toliver's fist smacked into his cheek, opening the cut further. He fell toward the bulkhead. Pain shot through his back as he crashed over an upended stool.

Holloway and Bartholomew jumped on Toliver, and all three groped at the bayonet.

Holloway managed to yank Toliver's hand away while Bartholomew bear-hugged the struggling officer's waist, holding him down. Somehow

Toliver managed to grab the bayonet and, with a bellow, drove the point at his throat. At the last moment Holloway grabbed his arm, stopping the thrust. He screamed, "Shit! I can't hold him."

Ingram shook off his pain and rose to his feet, falling atop the writhing trio. With a superhuman effort, Toliver wrenched his arm free and swiped the bayonet within inches of Ingram's eyes.

Ingram, looking down into the most tortured face he'd ever seen, drew back and punched his gunnery officer, Lieutenant Junior Grade Oliver P. Toliver, III, full in the jaw.

Toliver sagged and went limp. The bayonet clattered to the starboard bulkhead. For a moment, the only sound was their wheezing. They looked at one another, seeing the horror they'd endured that morning reflected in each other's faces.

"Sonofabitch is stronger than I thought," puffed Bartholomew.

A strange thumping assailed Ingram's eardrums. He shook his head, realizing a convoluted semblance of normality had returned, signaled by Japanese artillery falling sporadically on the fortified islands guarding the entrance to Manila Bay.

Several openmouthed sailors pressed in the hatchway, but Ingram was too tired to compose himself. At length, he took deep breaths and found himself close to Bartholomew's red, craggy face. "Very strong," Ingram agreed.

11

25 April 1942
Hospital Tunnel
Corregidor Island, Manila Bay, Philippines

Carefully, Helen rested her thumb on Ingram's jaw and examined the wound. "Pretty deep. It needs sutures."

"How many?"

"Ummm, nine or ten."

"Look. I have to check on my men." said Ingram,

"Later."

"Nonsense." He tried to rise from the gurney.

"Take it easy." She dabbed a damp cloth with one hand and pushed back with the other.

Ingram asked, "Will Doctor Taft do it?"

"Doctor Taft is dead. Doctor Drake has this lateral now."

"What happened?" With more pressure from Helen's thumb, he eased back on the gurney.

"Patching up a colonel in a command bunker above the mortar pits. A shell went directly down the air shaft...twenty-six people..."

"My God." Ingram blinked at the concrete overhead. Condensation beaded the walls. The dust was thick. Like sporadic little earthquakes, the Rock shook with the continuous apocalyptic bombardment. She dabbed a saline solution into the wound. "Ouch! Damnit!" He sat up holding his cheek.

"That shouldn't sting."

"It does."

"You'll have to do better. And we're out of Novocain. So, stand by, sailor."

"I don't need this." Ingram made to rise.

She stood in his way. "We're out of anesthetics. We have to do everything without them. Even amputations."

"I know. I was there. Remember?"

"...no." She reached for instruments. "Now, be good and I'll have Doctor Drake sign your purple heart recommendation."

"Thanks. Before you do that, slap on a bandage and I'll be on my way."

"Lay down. That cheek's going to be sewn up."

"No dice, sister."

The saline bottle gurgled menacingly as she stopped it and banged it on a metal table. "Okay. You're free to go outside and grovel. I give you three, maybe four months."

"Four months for what?"

"Then you're dead." She looked at him.

Ingram's shoulders sagged. Even minor wounds in the tropics were subject to virile infections if left untreated. With Corregidor's filthy conditions, the gash could easily become infected and spread; yes, he could die.

He lay back and she dressed his cheek with damp grayish towels. He forced a chuckle as she casually flopped the saturated material over his eyes. "Do I die from an infected wound or grimy towels?"

"They're boiled." Instruments clanked on the table.

Another nurse came up and whispered, then moved away.

Helen said, "Doctor Drake won't be available for another half-hour. You can wait for him or you can let me do it."

"...you do it?"

"Yes. Me."

"Where'd you go to medical school?" He made to rise.

She pushed him back. "University of Corregidor. Which is it?"

Ingram's Adam's apple bounced several times as he tried to swallow. "Okay."

"My rates are cheaper, anyway. So shut up."

Ingram said hoarsely, "Can I have a bullet to bite?"

"Use the rails, cowboy."

He grabbed the gurney's smooth, shiny rails. Even in the tunnel's gruesome heat and humidity, they felt cold, clinical, devoid of life. He let go, wondering how many men had died on this gurney. How many bodies this four-wheel squeaky contraption had shipped outside where burial details, making sure dog tags were removed, threw them into shell craters. They did their best to cover up the common graves, but on occasion another shell would impact, strewing body parts about the area. The morgue had long been cleared out because it was too small for what would become stacks of bodies. And they couldn't afford to keep it refrigerated. Thus, the irony was the morgue had been converted to an aid station for the sick and wounded.

Something cool, clear, and mildly burning ran into the wound. "How did this happen?" she asked.

"I got run over by a truck."

"Please?" She sounded clinical.

"Fell into the hat rack when the ship capsized."

"Hat rack?"

"Well, yes. On the bridge wing. It's where we stow the helmets. We stack 'em in there."

"Is your hat rack painted?"

"Of course."

"I see." Her rubber gloved fingers probed at the gash.

"Owww...shiiit!" An instrument ranged inside the wound and plucked. Lightning coursed in his cheek; he spasmed briefly with the sharp pain and grit his teeth. "Wh--the hell are you doing? Felt like you ripped out a tendon or something."

"Chunk of paint."

A pair of feet shuffled. Holloway's voice rumbled overhead, "Sure 'nuff, Skipper. It's a paint fleck the size of a dime. Haze gray and underway."

"Okay." Helen's voice was near. Her breath drifted about his neck and chest, taunting him and feeling cool on his skin. She swabbed around the wound. For some reason, he thought of Miriam. "You're lucky," she said.

"Why?"

"I have some sulfa left."

"That's peachy."

"And I'll leave it open a little so it'll drain." Her forearm rested on his shoulder. She was poised.

"Wonderful," he said.

"--okay, Skipper?" Holloway patted Ingram's shoulder.

Ingram asked, "Fred. What's the latest on Hopkins?"

"He'll pull through, but two more died."

"Who?"

"Fairfield and that new signalman."

"Redding?"

"Yes."

"Damnit!" Sweat beaded on Ingram's forehead. Someone blotted it with a towel. He raised his wrist. "I can't see my watch."

Two hands cupped his shoulders ready to press. It was Holloway who said, "It's okay, Skipper, about thirty minutes to go."

"For the Saturday matinee?" asked Helen.

Holloway said, "That's when the old bird blows sky high. That is if Forester--"

"--arghhh--!" A hand clamped over Ingram's mouth breaking off his scream as Helen debrided the wound. Then, without hesitation, she ran the first of the interrupted sutures. For sure, he was three feet off the table; yet he found the rails and held on fiercely. He managed to hold his scream to a muted gurgle. His ankles beat a tattoo on the gurney, making it squeak and rattle.

Holloway's hands pressed. "Come on, skipper."

Something hot ran down his cheek. He felt pressure and soon his face throbbed. "You finished?"

"Pumper," she said. She pushed with a sponge. Then the pressure eased and--

"eeeeoooyhou!"

"Captain, damnit! Shut up," said Holloway.

"You can do better than that, Lieutenant." The voice was familiar. Ingram tried to place it as Helen clanked her instruments. Finally, it came to him. The blind B-17 pilot. "Leon?"

"Yeah."

"What are you doing out here?"

"I can see a little bit."

"Yeah? That's neat."

"So, I practice by walking to the crapper. Then I hear you yowlin'"

"Glad your eyes are back, Leon. Maybe you'll fly again."

"Maybe...just maybe."

"You still got your .32 nickel plate?"

"Yes. Why?"

"Hand it over so I can shoot this sonofabitchin' nurse."

Laughter rippled among them until someone jammed a section of warm, damp towel in Ingram's mouth. Helen continued suturing and he screamed into the towel while his heels pounded the gurney.

"Damnit, Sir." It was Bartholomew who grabbed his knees.

The needle pierced his flesh once more making Ingram certain Helen had dragged a fifty-foot-length of barbed wire through his cheek. His chest heaved as he fought to control his breathing.

"Water?" asked Helen.

"No. Keep going," gasped Ingram.

"Right. Nine more to go."

"You said nine or ten, total."

"What would you have done if I had said twenty?"

"I would have--eaagh! Damnit! Run like hell."

"Hey, Skipper she's a lady just doin' her job," said Bartholomew.

...another suture: Ingram clutched the rails and yelled through clenched teeth, "does it...?"

Her voice was soft "Does it what?"

"Does it really need twenty?"

"Hold still. Just one more." He did his best to crush the gurney's rails with his hands while she worked. Something clanked in the metal tray and she pulled off the toweling, dabbed a sponge, and bandaged the wound. "Up, Captain."

Ingram sat up feeling woozy. His cheek throbbed and he blinked for a moment, seeing shadows in the background. Five or so men stood in a group. He recognized Whittaker, Kevin Forester, and Sunderland. Bartholomew, still in engineer's overalls and filthy chief's hat, had stepped away and now leaned against the wall, hands in his pockets.

He turned to Helen. "Only seven stitches?

"Out of suckers. Sorry." A corner of Helen's mouth turned up.

He held her gaze for a moment and nodded his thanks. He hadn't been this close to a woman since...when was the last time? Strange, he thought. It's hard to think of a woman as a woman in this garbage pit, even this good-looking nurse. Japs on all four sides: Japs overhead, explosions everywhere, day and night, bodies outside, bodies in the gullies, bloated corpses in Manila Bay. The *Pelican* was now one of them, laying in Caballo' s shallows with her back broken. And like Doctor Taft and those guys in the mortar pit command bunker, no one knew when their number would be called.

Reading his mind, she patted his shoulder. Her hand lay there for a moment then she turned, fussing with her instruments. It flooded over him. What a wonderful recollection was the universal comfort of a woman. How much he had taken such a thing for granted. How much he had taken *any* simple thing for granted like a cool glass of orange juice or an afternoon nap or stepping outside in the snow for the Sunday paper.

But nothing was simple while one lived under the specter of being horribly maimed by artillery fire, or tortured when captured, or prolonged dying while sandwiched shoulder to shoulder with those other hideous creatures in the main tunnels. One needed to survive; one needed to hope, but with all prospect of escape gone, one lived from moment to moment. That was all. Simple pleasures on Corregidor consisted of drawing the next breath; of sleeping for fifteen minutes, when perhaps one wouldn't hear an ear-splitting explosion. But more often one heard the groans of the dying, knowing full well the next anguished groans could be your own. Normality was denied on the Rock. Nobody ate or slept properly. Nobody bathed; they couldn't even defecate properly. In desperation, men crept outside seeking fresh air and a moment of solace. Many times, they were ripped apart in the artillery fire.

Nobody gave a thought to sex. Quite simply, they were too scared to think of it. Only food, sleep, and survival counted. One rarely eclipsed the other.

Ingram thought about the last woman he'd dated. It was last Thanksgiving at Manila's Polo Club. He danced with Nancy Goodkin, a delightful, overly made-up nineteen-year-old supply clerk in Cavite. Nancy Goodkin was Lieutenant Colonel Lucien George Goodkin's daughter. With an overwhelming smile, she was an Army brat who loved to tango. He thought he could smell her perfume: a sharp, penetrating imitation of Chanel No. 5. They'd swayed until two in the morning. He took her home finding Colonel Goodkin on his porch exuding San Miguel fumes. With a crimson face, Goodkin pointed a bony finger and gurgled "what have you been doing to my daughter?"

Ingram had done nothing with Goodkin's daughter, but he yelled back, "the hell with you Colonel". He marched out and was surprised Nancy followed. They went back to the restaurant and--

"I said, 'how do you feel?'" It was Helen. She looked directly into Ingram's eyes.

He eased off the gurney. "Still throbs. But thanks. Send me your bill."

"Fine. Please leave your address, phone number, and five-dollar deposit with my receptionist."

12

25 April 1942
Malinta Tunnel, Lateral Three
Corregidor Island, Manila Bay, Philippines

Voices rumbled incoherently as Ingram and Holloway waited for General Moore, Corregidor's garrison commander. The general's deep resonant voice echoed from behind heavy black drapes drawn across the lateral. Sergeants, corporals, and privates stepped about the antechamber with exaggerated purpose. Colonels and majors, with jaundiced faces somberly fixed, swooped in only to swoop out minutes later, their faces drawn even tighter.

"Do you suppose Wainwright is back there?" Holloway asked.

Ingram whispered, "Sergeant said he's over at Fort Hughes."

"Why?"

"I just thought I--"

A brigadier bumped into Holloway, shouldered past a corporal, whisked the curtain aside, and walked through. "Look at that guy," muttered Holloway with hands on his hips. "You'd think he had to give up his afternoon round of golf."

"Quiet, Fred," said Ingram.

"Pasty-faced tunnel rats." Holloway grumbled. "These guys haven't seen daylight since Roosevelt beat Willkie."

Ingram said. "Fred. Be quiet. I don't want to--"

"This where 'Dug-out-Doug' was holed up?" Holloway referred to General MacArthur.

"I think so."

Holloway raised his hands taking in rows of file cabinets, desks, chairs, and map tables. A bank of radios stood against one side of the tunnel, their operators hunched close, tweaking dials and making the speakers squeal. "Look at those goldbricks," Holloway whispered loudly. "Two, three to a desk. Nothing to do. Why not stick *these* guys in the mortar pits instead of sharpening pencils?"

"The Army takes care of its own." Ingram couldn't help adding his own bitter tone. When one of their sister ships, the *Finch* had been sunk, her crew was taken ashore and dispersed among the gun batteries and mortar pits of Corregidor and Caballo Islands. Many had since been killed in the lopsided artillery duels.

"That's probably where we'll end up. Eating Jap shrapnel made from our own scrap iron. They'll--"

"Fred, shut up," Ingram hissed through clenched teeth. Without looking up, the men fixed their eyes on the desks, as they bent paper clips to impossible contortions or bounced pencils or flipped erasers with little wooden rulers. "They can hear you, dope."

"I don't care."

Otis DeWitt stepped out. "Ingram?"

"Yes, Sir?"

The major walked up wearing a sleeveless khaki shirt; thin bony arms stuck out. An incongruous balance was jodhpurs and shiny boots. Sweat ran down his deeply tanned face and Ingram wondered what had become of his campaign hat. DeWitt looked Ingram up and down. "Your ship. Have you blown her up yet?"

"Not yet, Sir. We--"

"Damnit, Lieutenant. You had specific orders to take care of all that. Now, tell me why--"

Holloway interrupted, "Major. We lost twenty-one men today. There were other things to take care of."

"What the hell is this?" DeWitt's gaze wandered over Holloway.

"Sorry Major. This is my operations officer, Lieutenant Junior Grade Holloway."

"Tell him, Mr. Ingram, the next time he interrupts me his next *operations* assignment will be operating a machine gun post outside."

Holloway turned red and doubled his fists. Ingram raised his eyebrows.

DeWitt continued, "You can also tell Mr. Holloway that I lose close to fifty men a day. Now," he fixed his gaze on Ingram, "I suppose we'll have to send engineers out to blow up your ship."

"They won't find much, Major. Magazine charges will go off in about fifteen more minutes. She'll be ripped to shreds."

"Why didn't you say so?"

"Todd," said Holloway. "Tell this goldbrick--"

"Major DeWitt," said Ingram, "We need to see General Moore about our assignments."

"Yes. Follow me. Leave your mascot here." DeWitt turned and walked toward the curtains.

"Shiii--"

"Mr. Holloway! Outside. Now." Ingram barked.

The quiet was oppressive. The men. Everyone. With eyes to the wall, they kept bending paper clips or spinning erasers or flipping pencils. Holloway stared at DeWitt, then turned and walked toward the entrance to Lateral Three.

Ingram nodded and preceded DeWitt through the curtain, finding a large room. In the center was a large table with maps spread about. Paper coffee cups were scattered, and ten or so senior officers dressed like DeWitt--all were in shorts, some wore long sleeved-shirts--were gathered around the table. Two walls were taken with tote boards ranging from floor to ceiling. Ratings with sound-powered phones stood at the boards with pieces of chalk updating the data. Another wall was crammed with filing cabinets. From the fourth wall hung three enormous maps; one of Corregidor and Manila Bay, another of the Philippine Archipelago; the last was of the Western Pacific. Crumpled papers lay on the floor; folders stamped TOP SECRET spilled from filing cabinets;

papers littered desktops and chairs. Of the six desks wedged between filing cabinets, four were occupied by men clacking on typewriters. Men were slumped asleep at the other two desks. Both were full colonels. Another colonel lay asleep on a plush eight-foot leather couch snoring, loudly.

There were two small, glassed-in anterooms off the main command center. Labels over the doorways indicated one was for target designation and command of Corregidor's artillery; another housed electronic controls to detonate the mines guarding the entrance to Manila Bay.

The ripe smell of human feces hit him like a blast of hot, desert air. To Ingram's right was an open doorway. It was dimly lit with three unpartitioned wall-mounted toilets: Tissue paper hung over the commodes onto a wet, unpainted concrete floor. Inside, Ingram saw a tech sergeant tucking his shirt in his trousers.

DeWitt walked over and said, "Flannigan, damnit. Keep this door shut."

Flannigan buckled his belt. "Sorry, Mr. DeWitt. It's hard to--"

DeWitt slammed the door then nodded toward another small room situated in the corner of the control room. "Come on."

They walked up to General Moore, a man with a full head of white hair and wire-rim glasses. DeWitt said, "Lieutenant Ingram, Sir."

General Moore waved irritably while peering into the anteroom. Ingram was surprised to see Dwight Epperson standing next to Moore. They nodded to one another, and Ingram moved alongside and stood on tiptoes to look over Moore's shoulder. Two men were inside wearing head phones; one stood and the other sat before a large electronic console where gauges and dials surrounded a large tube giving off a phosphorescent glow. "Oscilloscope?" whispered Ingram to Epperson.

"Long distance radar, dummy," Epperson whispered from the side of his mouth."

"I'll be damned!"

"PPI display. One of the newest."

Ingram nodded slowly, having no idea what a PPI display was. "What is a--"

DeWitt put a finger to his lips as the radar operator droned, "...Skunk Tare-Victor. Bearing two-six-one; range thirty-one thousand, five hundred yards. No bearing drift."

"Headed right toward us again. What's he doing?" mumbled General Moore.

"Testing?" offered Epperson. "Probing the effective range of our guns. He may try to--"

"Tell Batteries Smith and Hearn to stand by," ordered Moore. He referred to the pride of Corregidor's artillery: The twelve-inch "disappearing Naval rifles," so named because the gun barrel mechanism lowered itself below ground level to its carriage when not firing. Hearn and Smith were pointed into the South China Sea and could hurl a seven hundred-pound projectile almost thirty thousand yards: fifteen miles. The disappearing feature had provided effective cover from ground spotters in the great European land war, fought twenty-five years ago against fixed positions. But the twelve-inch rifles were defenseless against Homma's artillery, now sighted from behind their backs and worse, they were totally vulnerable to air attack.

The talker muttered in his phone then asked, "Hearn wants to know if they should load and elevate, General."

Moore rubbed his jaw. "Does plot have a solution?"

The talker spoke into his headset, then held his hand to the earpiece. "Yessir. Plot says they're ready to engage the target at maximum range."

"Right. Tell Hearn and Smith they have permission to load. Don't elevate, yet. And man the batteries with only essential personnel."

The talker relayed the instructions.

"Skunk Tare-Victor evaluated as three ships," the radarman droned into his headset. "Looks like a possible cruiser and two smaller ships, maybe destroyers. Still at two-six-one. Range thirty-one thousand yards."

Moore looked out into the room and yelled, "Where the hell is Ingram?"

DeWitt's mouth opened but Ingram said, "Right here, Sir."

Moore looked startled for a moment. "Oh, there you are, Lieutenant. Sorry about your ship. How are your men?"

"Lost twenty-one, General."

"I'm sorry." Moore shook his head. "Great job I'm doing protecting my navy. *Quail* and *Tanager* are all I have left... three river gunboats...damnit!" He paused, then said, "In here, Ingram."

Epperson and DeWitt made way, letting Ingram stand beside General Moore. The room was dark except for the green glow from the radar's cathode ray tube. A cursor, extending from the center of the tube to the edge, swept slowly around like a side view of a single plank on a Mississippi River stern-wheeler. Corregidor was in the center and, on the tube's northern hemi-sphere, Ingram recognized the landmass shapes of Bataan, Manila Bay, Caballo, El Frail, and Carabao islands. Except for the Cavite Province's distinct shore line to the south, ground clutter confused the return from the Pico de Loro Hills above Calumpan. On the scope's left side, he spotted the three blips the radarman tracked. "What do you make of that?" General Moore asked.

Ingram raised his hands and let them fall to his sides. He'd barely heard of radar, let alone PPI, or whatever the hell Epperson swooned over. He knew a few ships had the super-secret detection device, but nobody talked about it. A cruiser had dropped anchor last fall with a bed-spring-like contraption twirling atop her mast. He supposed that was the antenna. And he'd heard rumors of radar directing anti-aircraft guns and searchlights here on Corregidor. But this was the first time he'd seen it. Amazing.

"...Skunk Tare-Victor twenty-nine thousand yards, bearing two-six-one. Still looks like one large and two smaller ships."

"Vanguard for an amphibious attack?" offered Ingram.

Moore snorted. "Maybe, but not tonight. They're barely within gun range of my twelve inchers. But they'll pull back soon. The question is, if they're out there four days from now, will they be able to detect the submarine rendezvous from that position?"

Ingram nodded and bent to the scope. "Any way to check the plot?"

"Impossible, Lieutenant," DeWitt chirped. "The plot room is in another lateral. This is a command center."

"Major?" asked the General. "Don't we have a plot running in there?"

DeWitt paused, "Well, Sir. I--"

"Looks like they have it up, General." Epperson nodded to a wall chart where a talker plotted Xs with a grease pencil.

"That's it," said Moore, tossing DeWitt an icy glance.

Ingram squinted at the chart. "Could be, General. Your targets are about ten miles northwest of area Yoke-Yoke two. If they have one of these they might pick us up."

"Pretty sure Japs don't have radar," Moore said. "How 'bout visually?"

The talker's voice wafted around the room in a monotone, "...Skunk Tare-

Victor drawing right bearing two-six-six, range opening; now thirty-thousand, five hundred yards..."

"Turned north." Moore's chest heaved. "Tell Batteries Hearn and Smith to stand down." While the talker relayed the message, Moore walked from the room with everyone in trail. "Always the same. The little bastards run straight in, then turn left at the last minute and head up the coast." He drew up to the table. "Well, Mr. Ingram? You're the leading Navy man around here, now. Would the enemy be able to detect the rendezvous if they were in that position? Should we reschedule the submarine rendezvous?"

Ingram scratched his head. "I..."

The prone colonel on the couch belched loudly and smacked his lips. "Is dinner ready, yet? I'll take the rack of lamb, please. A tall, cool San Miguel and mint sauce. You know, the green shit. Make sure there's plenty of green shit."

"Roll over and shut up, Tom," said Moore.

Epperson caught Ingram's incredulous glance and whispered, "He's Moore's G-2."

"George." The colonel opened his eyes and stared at the ceiling. "You can't reschedule the pickup. That sub's en route."

"I can radio Darwin and have them put out a recall or change of rendezvous," said Moore.

"Unlikely the sub will pick it up in time," said the colonel, interlocking his hands over his stomach, and closing his eyes.

"They come up at night to charge batteries, don't they?" Moore looked at Ingram who nodded. "That must be when they clear all their radio traffic. They'll get the message."

The colonel snored slightly then muttered, "...wouldn't do it George. We need that sub to take those people out along with the damned gold. Besides we're finished, here. Not enough time for another--"

Moore spun quickly and yelled, "Get up!"

The colonel's eyes blinked open. "George. I only meant--"

"Get up!" Moore roared again.

With groans, the colonel worked his way to his feet.

"We're not giving up. Is that understood?" Moore yelled spewing saliva, his face red.

Typewriters stopped clattering; the room fell quiet as little earthquakes jiggled the command room. Even the radarman, whose ears were covered by headphones, looked up, forgetting his radar contacts designated Skunk Tare-Victor.

Moore walked in a circle waving his arms in the air. "We're not dying for nothing out here. Don't forget we owe the ones who went before us. And just as much, we owe the ones who will follow. The longer we hold," Moore's fist crashed on the map table making coffee cups jump--one toppled to spill cold, dark liquid on Luzon. "the better off for the ones who will follow. And they, likewise, will owe us. We will prevail!"

He stopped in mid-space. "We will. We will."

The colonel walked up and put a hand on General Moore's shoulder. "I know George. It was only a figure of speech."

General Moore shrugged then looked at Ingram. "Well?"

Ingram peered at the wall chart of Manila Bay and said, "area Yoke-Yoke two is about ten miles from their closet point of approach tonight--that's twenty thousand yards. The shore boat' s silhouette is negligible; so is a sub's conning tower at that range."

Epperson said, "The moon will be full." At a glare from Ingram he spread his palms saying, "So says the nautical almanac."

Ingram said, "Dwight, I'm proud of you. Your next billet is navigator on a battleship."

"Don't push your luck."

"Okay. We'll be up-moon from them," said Ingram. "Even with that we'll be masked by the ground swell. The sub would have plenty of time to dive if we are detected. At the same time, we can run for the beach."

"Okay. It's on." General Moore said, "And it's come down to this I'm afraid. You're the only one who knows the minefield well enough to get them through at night. Do you mind doing that, Ingram?"

"General, after today, I'm in the market for another seagoing command."

"Good." General Moore clamped a hand on Ingram's shoulder then walked toward the lavatory saying, "Otis. Are those damned toilets fixed?"

DeWitt trailed after him, "Soon, General. Engineers are jury rigging a new sewer line. Should be ready in a couple of hours."

"...tell 'em to shake a leg. Place smells like..." Moore closed the door in DeWitt's face.

Epperson said, "Todd. You gonna be able to bring this off?"

"Getting you out there?" Ingram replied.

Epperson nodded, scratching a sore. Some were healing and covered with thick scabs. His hair grew in patches.

"Stop that, damnit."

"Sorry. How you going to do it?"

"With a full moon, we'll have plenty of landmarks. What's the matter? You getting anxious?"

Epperson grabbed Ingram's forearm and drew him next to a file cabinet. "Todd, I can't afford to miss that sub."

"A lot of guys would like to go with you."

"I know. I don't mean it that way. It's just that..."

"What?" prodded Ingram.

Epperson looked from side to side and lowered his voice. "Look. I'm not yellow. You ought to know that."

"If I didn't believe you, I wouldn't be talking now."

"I'd gladly trade places with someone here to have a go with the Japs. You. Anybody."

"Dwight, I said I believe you."

"Alright. There are some things I know..."

"You told me."

"Right."

"The Japs will pound nails into your skull to make you talk."

"Wrong. They make me watch while they pound nails in *your* skull. Then I talk."

"Oh."

"Todd. This stuff is so hot, nobody here knows about it. Not DeWitt. Not Moore. Not even Wainwright." He raised his hand and ran a finger at a scab.

"Stop it!"

"Sorry, itches like hell. Look. Those PBYs the other night--Fowler? I'm sure Rochefort wants me out of here. If he can't get me out he'll have to order me dead."

Dead. Strange. Ingram had seen plenty of dead people in the last few hours. He rubbed a hand over his face and leaned against the cabinet washed with fatigue. Just hours ago, he'd lost his ship and he hadn't eaten today. And they hadn't posted him yet. He had no idea where he was to sleep; no clothes, nothing. DeWitt would tell him when he was ready, he supposed.

Ingram looked longingly at the couch where Moore's G-2 colonel had fallen back to sleep; the man's mouth was wide open but he didn't snore. With the bright lights shining on his pallid, sweaty skin, the colonel looked...dead. "Who is Rochefort?"

"In Pearl. He's my real boss."

"What's he do. Command an aircraft carrier?"

"Uh, uh."

"Who do you report to here?"

"No one really. Moore, I suppose from an administrative standpoint. But he doesn't know what I do."

"What do you do?"

"Todd, damnit."

"Why does Rochefort want you dead?" Ingram asked.

"He knows that I know something big. Hell, I helped him work on it."

"In Hawaii?"

"No. From here."

"Ah. Radio intercept stuff. That means you guys collaborate or something."

Epperson looked irritated. "Todd, like I said before, don't draw too many conclusions."

"Okay."

"The Rock is going to fall soon and Rochefort can't let the Japs take me."

"Look. I'm tired. My men. They're tired. Could we come over to your tunnel?"

"I think so. How many?"

"About thirty-seven if my operations officer doesn't end up in the stockade.

"We can handle that. What's the deal with your ops officer--is that the smart-mouthed jaygee?"

"You remember?"

"Yep."

"Well, he took on DeWitt out there."

"Keep them apart. DeWitt is dangerous. And with the Rock falling, he'll be like a wounded rattlesnake. Thinks he's at the Alamo or something. Look. There's something else."

"I don't need anything else today."

"Do you still plan to make a break for it?"

Ingram said. "I've been thinking about it."

"Because if you are, I'd like to go if this submarine deal falls through."

Ingram said, "Of course. We can--"

DeWitt walked up. "I have your orders Lieutenant."

Ingram supposed he should be at attention, but he was so tired he felt as though his elbows were glued to the top of the file cabinet. He tilted his head and looked through the crook of his elbow. "Yessir?"

DeWitt gave an exasperated snort then said, "You are to augment the garrison on Caballo Island. You will take half your men and report to Captain Plummer. Your mascot is to take the other half and report to Major Lattimer over there. By the way, don't you have an executive officer?"

"Killed last month. Never got a replacement."

"I see. Well, that's all."

"Major?" asked Ingram.

DeWitt darted an owlish glance.

"I'd like a chit for diesel fuel."

"For what?"

"To top off the shore boat' s tanks for our trip Saturday night. Also, we're thinking of making a break for it when the Rock falls. I'd like to use one of those boats."

"You what?" yelled DeWitt.

"What's wrong, Major," Ingram asked.

"You said you were going to try and escape?" squealed DeWitt.

Ingram stood. "That's right."

"Negative. You'll do no such thing. When--if we surrender, we surrender as a cohesive unit. We're American servicemen, damnit. I can't afford mavericks running around the countryside making the Japs angry."

"Major DeWitt, I--"

"Shut up, damn you." DeWitt slammed a fist.

Ingram couldn't help notice the surrounding activity continued. This was no General Moore interlude.

DeWitt said, "The Japs will take hostages while tracking you down. Innocent civilians--maybe even our own people will be tortured. Shot as reprisals."

"General Moore is my commanding officer," Ingram said. "I'd like to take this up with him." He looked around the command center. Moore was not in sight.

"Let me remind you I'm the general's adjutant. You'll do as I say."

"But--"

"No chits. Every drop of fuel is precious. We need it more for our diesel generators than for your yachting foray into the South China Sea. Where the hell were you thinking of going, anyway?"

"Not sure, yet. China. Mindanao. Maybe Australia."

DeWitt's lips twisted into a demented grin. "That's preposterous. Permission denied. You'll have enough fuel for the submarine rendezvous and that's it. Now. You are to report to Captain Plummer at Battery Craighill tomorrow morning on Caballo Island. Is that clear?"

"Major, I--"

"I'll hear no more of this. I don't have time. You may bunk and feed your men here tonight. Then tomorrow, Plummer will take care of you. And make sure you're here on time Saturday to take the evacuation party. Is that clear?"

Ingram looked around the room. The men quickly averted their eyes. "Yessir," he said.

DeWitt spun and walked away.

Epperson muttered in a low voice, "See what I told you?"

Ingram's hands were on his hips as he watched the major. "I'll say."

Epperson said, "What the hell is Battery Craighill, anyway?"

Ingram turned to Epperson and gave a long exhale. "Mortar pits, Dwight. Four big, stupid, obsolete mortars."

13

29 April 1942
Fort Hughes, Craighill Battery Command Center
Caballo Island, Manila Bay, Philippines

It had rained and the late afternoon heat was oppressive. Steam rose off Caballo Island with the thermometer shooting to ninety-five degrees.

Inside the command center, Ingram wiped sweat from his brow while looking through a jagged hole in the three-foot-thick concrete bulkhead. It was the result of a direct hit last week, killing all inside the command center and destroying much of the equipment. This is what happened to Doctor Taft, he mused darkly.

As promised by Tokyo Rose, the bombardment's tempo had increased to a vengeful, unending, hideously rhythmic, concussive level. An unofficial noon tally radioed from Corregidor reported 7,500 rounds had fallen on the Rock since midnight.

Midnight, Ingram remembered: Wednesday April 29, 1942. Thus, began the birthday of the Divine Ruler of Japan, Emperor Hirohito.

Seven thousand, five hundred rounds since midnight. That's fifteen thousand a day, and they were taking the same medicine here on Caballo. Except, with all the thunderous rumbling and bouncing and tearing and dust and anguished screams, it felt like 150,000 rounds.

Yes. Happy birthday Your Highness.

Battery Craighill was one of the last intact batteries where defenders of the fortified islands could serve up a defiant round or two against Homma's artillery. With heart-stopping explosions, the twelve-inch smooth-bore, M-1912 mortars belched enormous projectiles ten miles into the Bataan Peninsula. But over the months, Japanese spotting improved keenly taking in the tell-tale smoke or muzzle-flash to summon immediate retribution in the form of merciless, counter-battery. Thus, the pit crews died quickly if they weren't in their shelters as soon as a round was launched.

Two days ago, five loaders had been killed as they ran for the shelter. Dead among them was Saunders, a third-class gunner's mate from the *Pelican*.

Every ship had a kid that looked like Saunders: He was the one with long, sandy hair, glasses, and a stupid, lopsided grin from Olathe, Kansas, or Sharon Valley, Connecticut, or Walla Walla, Washington. The *Pelican*'s Saunders was just a little different. A new arrival, he'd been a semipro baseball pitcher. Last spring, the crew challenged the wardroom to a baseball game and put Saunders on the mound. The crew trounced the officers eleven to three. But it didn't matter. It rained that day, and everyone returned to the ship, covered with mud and full of beer. A grinning Saunders, his once white T-shirt now soaked with muck, sat weaving and cheering atop their shoulders, his fists in the air. One of the men carrying Saunders, so covered with muddy slime as to be unrecognizable from the others, was a shouting Ensign Oliver P. Toliver, III.

Saunders. They had dragged his broken body into the shelter and had to wait two hours for a lull so the burial detail could take him away.

Ingram winced with the thought. *Pelican gone. Saunders gone. What's next? When does my number come up?*

Now, he peered through the hole, deeply hurt to see the kids out there loading that damn mortar. Except they weren't kids. They were twenty years old, terribly thin, half-starved skeletons, whose eyes were gaunt with terror and lack of sleep. They trudged like mechanical erector toys, ignoring a sergeant who bellowed at them in a hoarse, tunnel voice. Trapped in emaciated bodies with no hope for the future, they cursed the steaming heat, swatted flies, and wrestled their projectile onto the loading tray, knowing full well a shell could erupt among them at any moment.

This crew finished loading without incident, then did a quick shuffle to the far side of the mortar pits. One loader moved among them, his gait a little slower, and his head hung further than the rest. He was third in line as they ran to their bunker entrance, but at the last moment stood aside, letting the others dash inside to safety. He paused, looking at the sky for a full twenty seconds before someone pulled him inside and shut the hatch. This was the third time in as many days Ingram had seen him linger like that, defying the artillery. Or perhaps, did he beg for an enemy shell to euthanize him, excusing him from the misery and privation and hunger of the others?

Could be. The man was Ingram's former gunnery officer, Oliver P. Toliver, III.

Pug-nosed Sergeant Bruno La Follette stood on a platform above Ingram peering out of one of the command bunker's slits. He turned and yelled, "Okay. Mount Three is loaded and they're clear. We ready to shoot, yet?"

A sweating Gordon L. Plummer, captain, U.S. Army, sat shirtless at the firing console. Badly in need of a haircut, he constantly brushed long blond hair from his eyes. "Still no power to the panel. We'll have to shoot locally," he said.

"Getting close, Captain," shouted Sunderland, his voice distant.

La Follette swore in exasperation. Nothing had worked right since the Japanese shell had blown the place apart. But, he had to admit to himself, it was good having these Navy guys, Ingram and Sunderland helping in the bunker, patching things up as best as they could. At the moment, they were trying to set up Mount Number Three so they could again aim and shoot it from the control panel.

"Okay to test the firing circuit?" Sunderland's voice echoed. The *Pelican's* first class gunner's mate was jammed almost upside-down in a combination air-conditioning and cable duct.

"Permission granted," shouted Plummer. "Shake a leg. The major wants to get this one off. Says there's a Jap convoy on the--"

KARRUMPFF! Dust blew through the hole. Ingram found himself sitting on the floor wiping dirt from his eyes. The mortar had fired, making his ears ring from the impossibly loud muzzle blast. La Follette tumbled to the floor beside him. Plummer rocked back in his chair as dust and papers swirled about.

With a wisp of a smile, La Follette climbed to hands and knees and yelled at the air duct, "Sunderland! You-stupid-son-of-a-bitch. You fired the fuckin' thing."

"I hope you had it aimed right for once." Sunderland's voice seemed more distant.

"Fat chance. You just sank a hospital ship steaming into Manila Bay. It went down with six thousand GIs, doctors, and nurses. Part of a thirty-ship relief column. Now, they've all turned back. How do you feel about that?"

"Not my fault. Wires were crossed. Either that or some jerk out there closed the firing key."

"I wasn't even close to it," protested Plummer, brushing concrete chips off the console with a dirty rag.

"Just the three of us up here, Sunderland. Where'd you Navy guys learn your gunnery? In ice-cream school?" yelled La Follette. He and Ingram rose, dusted themselves off, and walked over to the duct, finding Sunderland had slid down and become wedged again. This was the fifth time. Unlike the first, Sunderland no longer panicked. Now he waited patiently to be pulled free.

They grabbed his legs and feet, and hoisted.

"Hold on a minute," Sunderland's hoarse echo was muted. "There's a junction box here. It's under a ledge. Yeah, hold on. Damned thing is ripped open. Everything is all screwed up. Looks like a typical Army wiring job."

Ingram and La Follette widened their stance to hold Sunderland in place. Soon sweat rolled down their faces and chests.

Tools clanked in the duct as Sunderland muttered, "...put together with the cheapest shit. Third-rate insulation. Lookit this! Can't tell one wire from another. Things are all brown. Just like your damned clothes. Is that why your uniforms are brown, La Follette? To disguise the fact you guys are so scared you shit your pants twice a day? Even your toilet paper is brown. You guys save money reusing it?"

La Follette rolled his eyes and yelled, "I'm surprised you know about something like that."

"Meaning what?" asked Sunderland, clicking a ratchet wrench.

"Word around here is you don't use toilet paper," croaked La Follette.

Ingram glanced at Plummer who spread his hands with an I-can't-control-La-Follette look.

Ingram nodded back with a look saying I-can't-control-Sunderland-either.

Sunderland's voice echoed up, not missing a beat, "True enough. But you must admit I'm discrete."

Silence. La Follette looked at Ingram who shrugged and sweated, holding half of Sunderland's weight in the duct. La Follette exhaled knowing he'd lost. "Okay, bright boy. Discrete about what?"

Sunderland squeezed his voice to an aristocratic falsetto, "I refrain from using toilet paper, Bruno," he rolled the "r" delicately, "when I know I'm going to be shaking hands with Army sergeants."

La Follette jiggled the man's feet.

Sunderland bellowed, "Hey, hey! Almost done. Shit! You want your mortars to fire?"

Plummer, at the fire control panel, jumped in his chair as red, yellow, and green lights blinked on and off. "Yay! We have power."

La Follette shouted into the duct, "Panel's working, Sonny."

"Shrapnel ripped up the junction box," said Sunderland, as more tools clanked.

"Right," said La Follette. "Everything looks normal. You almost done? You're getting heavy, fatso."

"I wish I was," the gunner's voice echoed.

They held on. Sunderland's weight seemed to increase by tens. "Sunderland, damnit!" yelled Ingram.

"In a second, Skipper...there! Okay."

"We ought to leave his ass in there," La Follette said loudly, pulling on the gunner's feet.

A profusely sweating Sunderland, naked from the waist up, slid out easily. He pulled with him a dirty canvas bag of tools and wrapping tape. Raising an eyebrow to La Follette he said, "Okay, I've fixed your precious mortar. You ready now for me to teach you how to shoot straight?"

La Follette turned and walked to the water barrel, snatching a paper cup from the rack.

"Where's my cigar," said Sunderland.

La Follett shrugged his shoulders.

There was an edge in Sunderland's voice, "You promised, Bruno."

With a grunt, La Follett reached over and raised the lid of a wooden box trimmed in intricate patterns of inlaid ivory. Realizing the others were watching, he reached in his humidor with a flourish and produced a cigar wrapped in cellophane secured by a gleaming silver band. "Just for you, Sonny," he said, with a mirthless smile.

Ingram counted five remaining cigars just before La Follette quickly slammed the lid.

Sunderland closed his eyes and slowly drew the cigar under his nose. "Ummm. It really is a Don Ortega."

"Damn rights," growled La Follette.

Sunderland carefully put the cigar in his shirt pocket and buttoned it. "Tonight, after chow," he said, with a smile. Then he wiped his face with a greasy towel and called after La Follette, "We can start winning the war, now that the place is wired properly."

"Shiiit."

Sunderland asked Captain Plummer with innocent eyes, "You want me on the panel, Sir?"

Plummer rose from his chair saying, "Take a seat." He looked at Ingram and they walked to an observation slit. "What time do you take off?"

"What?" Ingram weaved for balance as the floor bounced. A series of explosions sprinted the length of Caballo Island. Another bombing attack, Ingram supposed, like the one that got the *Pelican*. His teeth jiggled. The constant artillery shelling felt like an enormous creature out there at work with a gigantic jackhammer.

Plummer stepped closer. "When do you go?"

Ingram supposed Plummer meant the submarine rendezvous. He checked his watch. "In an hour. You have anything else for me?" A stick of bombs roared overhead, spilling dirt through cracks in the concrete, making them reach out to steady themselves.

"More sandbagging tomorrow. We have to get that wall plugged."

Ingram looked at the hole in the concrete bulkhead and groaned.

"You better grab some sleep." Plummer had to shout. "DeWitt said to make sure you're fresh."

Suddenly the bombardment let up. It was strangely quiet. Ingram rotated his index fingers in his ears and said, "I'd love some shut-eye but this isn't exactly the Mayo Clinic."

"Try anyway." Plummer trudged to a cabinet and fished for a clipboard. He kept his voice low, "You want us to get rid of that guy?"

Ingram froze, knowing Plummer referred to Toliver. "What are you talking about?"

Plummer nodded toward the mortar pits. "Mr. Long Island yellow streak."

"Where'd you hear that?"

"Everybody's talking about it."

"What do you want me to do? Shove a .45 in his ear and pull the trigger?"

Plummer looked down saying nothing.

"He has a right to live just like everybody else, doesn't he?"

"Don't like cowards around my mounts. Those are brave men out there."

"We were strafed and bombed many times, and Ollie stood his post in the open just as bravely. He has lots of Jap planes to his credit. That's more than I can say for you. So, who the hell says he's a coward?"

Plummer looked from side to side. Sunderland and La Follette were hunched over a wiring schematic at the firing panel. They were quiet and it was hard to tell if they were listening.

"Your guys say so, Todd. And keep your voice down, damnit. Didn't five people die when your ship rolled? Didn't they--"

"It was three."

"Yeah. Three guys. Froze, didn't he? All he had to do was untie a rope or something. He's yellow. My people don't like it and yours don't either. Let's face it. The guy's miserable. Doesn't eat. He wants to die."

"He's an officer, and he helps load your dammed mortars," Ingram hissed.

"That's all one of your officers can do?"

"Better than those slouches you have hiding in tunnels counting paperclips."

"At least they want to live. This guy's askin' for it." Plummer slowly shook his head. "Okay, Todd. Let it go. Sorry I mentioned it. Go get some sleep."

Suddenly, it didn't seem to matter: Toliver, Epperson, Corregidor. Nothing.

Suddenly, it didn't seem to matter. Toliver, Epperson, Corregidor. Explosions rumbled. He headed for a lower bunk in a cramped alcove. "Okay."

14

29 April 1942
Navy Radio Intercept Tunnel, Monkey Point
Corregidor Island, Manila Bay, Philippines

The bombardment's tempo was the worst Radioman First Class Cyrus L. Portman had endured. Distractions were harder to find, as round after round thumped overhead, shaking the tunnel, and rattling equipment and light fixtures. Malinta Hill, to the west, seemed to be taking most of it. But the Naval Radio Intercept Tunnel, burrowed under Monkey Point, also received its measure.

Without knowing why, Portman had shaved and bathed as best he could before going on watch this evening. Everyone was surprised as he relieved Henderson, dressed in his last set of clean dungarees, shirt, and polished shoes. He even wore a white hat. Just like the old days on the *Arizona*, he told them as he took his seat next to Skinner, his third-class assistant. Why didn't anybody laugh or snicker? And Lieutenant Hadley looked as if he were nodding appreciatively. They seemed to know something Portman didn't and it was connected to his dressing in clean dungarees.

A series of thuds rattled the tunnel, and Portman did his best to look nonchalant, tweaking radio dials. He checked the black-faced twenty-four-hour clock, which miraculously held to its wall mount. Damn! 1909. The Japs had been at this for over nineteen hours.

The floor heaved with another shell burst. Popping noises rippled up and down the tunnel, as Portman and Skinner fiercely gripped the table.

"Wha-wha the hell's that?" Skinner looked from side to side, as the lights dimmed, and then went bright again.

"Expansion joints," Portman growled. He looked over, seeing the two usually unperturbed Marines at the crypto room door put on their helmets and secure chin straps. Their eyes were hidden but their lips were pressed almost white. Even after what those two had been through on Bataan; they looked scared--it was something one couldn't hide.

KRUUMPF! Their world shook, the concrete seeming to jump from all sides.

"Big sumbitch!" yelled Portman, looking from right to left. He held the table in a death grip with his left hand bracing the radio console against the wall with his right, as a smaller unattended receiver crashed to the floor, taking with it a case of light bulbs. "You all right?"

Skinner screeched an unintelligible reply that was soon lost among other shouts and groans up and down the tunnel. Lieutenant Hadley kneeled in an alcove with tin hat on. The lights dimmed momentarily; the overhead fixtures swayed, masking a shape running full speed down the tunnel. Portman watched the figure for a moment, then said, "Another two hundred forty-millimeter, I'll bet. Japs throwin' that shit around like they was bowling balls."

"I can't take this," Skinner squealed, shooting to his feet.

Portman reached, barely in time to grab a handful of Skinner's shirttail. "Easy, kid," said Portman, pulling the squirming, panting Skinner back into his chair. "You go outside and them shells'll rip you to pieces. Remember Bogoslawski last week? Relax. They don't have enough ammo to keep this--

Three shells hit almost simultaneously plunging the tunnel into darkness. One landed near the entrance and they felt the concussion. Dirt and papers blew through. Portman knew he was screaming and, at the same time, a macabre, detached sense told him Skinner screamed louder and more hysterically. Cabinets crashed to the floor; pictures and crockery shattered on the concrete.

As if a diabolical ghoul controlled a master rheostat, the lights, swinging pendulously from the ceiling, cycled from full bright to dark to full bright again. Groans and hoarse shouts ranged up and down the tunnel. A glance over his shoulder told Portman that Skinner had bolted. His chair was empty. And the two Marines sat hunched on the ground with their backs pressed against one another, their submachine guns ready.

The dust congealed into a thick, foglike mist. Portman couldn't see more than six or seven feet, as he tied a handkerchief around his face, and tucked it into what was recently his last clean shirt.

He'd just finished when he heard horrible gurgling, worse than the general cacophony now dying in the tunnel. Someone was wheezing, maybe choking to death nearby.

Damnit! It was getting closer.

The fog eased a bit yielding the shape of a muted apparition.

Ten feet visibility. The Marine sergeant and his corporal were crouched side by side now; they clacked the actuators on their Thompson submachine guns and flipped off safeties. The corporal tucked the stock of his Thompson in his shoulder and sighted down the barrel into the roiling muck.

Needing no further urging, Portman jumped to his feet and reached behind the radio for his own weapon--a .45. Fumbling, the butt slipped away as the shapes came nearer. He secured a purchase, frantically worked the action, and aimed in a two-handed stance, as two dark profiles emerged weaving beneath the swaying lamps.

"Take it easy. Damn! What's wrong with you guys?"

"Who goes?" the Marine sergeant bellowed.

"Lieutenant Ingram calling for Lieutenant Epperson. And I think I have someone who belongs to you."

Their faces materialized. Ingram pulled a choking, wheezing Skinner by his belt. The man's tongue protruded and his eyes were bugged wide open. Glancing at his chair, he wailed uncontrollably.

Portman tucked his .45 in his belt and took Skinner's arm. "Come on, Ernie. Sit down."

The radioman shook his head and tried to wiggle away just as another shell hit.

"It's okay," said Portman, holding a squirming, shaking Skinner. Ingram's grip slipped and he grabbed with both hands.

The Marine sergeant walked up and threw a pitcher of water in Skinner's face and slapped him twice. Skinner blinked with surprise, then indignation. Still panting, he looked at the sergeant. Finally, the young radioman caught his breath, dropped his head, and braced his hands on his knees. "Okay."

Ingram eased his grip.

Skinner looked at him sideways. "I'm okay, Lieutenant. Thanks." He grappled at the back of his chair and sat shakily.

Ingram eyed Portman. "Mr. Epperson here?"

A shell landed, but it didn't seem as near. Portman nodded over his shoulder. "In there, Sir."

Through a hoary haze laden with concrete dust, Ingram squinted to make out a sign that read: *Radio Intercept File Room*
Authorized Personnel Only.

Portman leaned close and whispered, "That's where the Lieutenant stores his tomato juice. Other goodies, too. Malone is supposed to be standing sentry duty inside, but I think the guy pissed his pants and bolted with the last barrage. Go on in, Sir."

"Thanks." Ingram nodded and walked across the tunnel, opened the door and stepped in, just as a large shell smacked into Monkey Point. He stumbled backwards to pitch against the door, making it slam shut.

He waited a few moments, regaining his balance and savoring the temporary calm. The room was much larger than the door indicated. The area was perhaps twenty by thirty, arranged with row upon row of light-beige file cabinets. Most of the drawers were open and empty of contents. Except, in one corner, he spotted a bank of cabinets of more sturdy construction with combination locks. Tucked in their drawer handles were large, striped red tags marked SECRET or, in a few cases, TOP SECRET. He wondered if the tomato juice and the rest of Epperson's hoard really was stacked in the rear, perhaps by the conference table.

The dust was still thick; lamps swayed from the ceiling washing the cabinets to a mummified complexion. A desk stood near the front door. Papers were scattered on top. A mug half-filled with coffee stood near the corner. He spotted the conference table and stacked behind it were a dozen cases marked "Tomato Juice." He was surprised to see behind that, another pile of cases marked "Pineapple Juice." Stretching along the wall to the corner were boxes marked "Coke syrup," "Toilet Paper," and "Hershey Candies."

"Dwight?" Ingram called.

Four rounds thudded into the Rock in quick succession. But they seemed far away; perhaps at Corregidor's western end.

"Hello?"

The dust motes twirled more lazily. Now he could see across the file room; he took a few steps. Absent the impact of distant shells, the room was quiet and, even without air-conditioning, unnaturally cool. Solace washed through him. He'd been elbow to elbow with a horde of sweaty, terrified human beings for the past five months. What a wonderful place to retreat and read or just be quiet for a while. Or, even sleep.

"Dwight. Where the hell are you?"

Nothing. Ingram checked the aisles. Zero. That radioman, like everyone else on the Rock, was out of his--

"...uhhhh."

Something thumped on the floor. Ingram spun and looked down an aisle on the far side of the room. At the end was a doorway. A sign over the top read: "Darkroom."

There! Something thumped again. Ingram walked down the aisle. At the end, cabinets labeled TOP SECRET stood guard around a library-sized study table. A pair of supine, booted feet stuck out of the darkroom's doorway.

"Son of a bitch!" Shoving aside armchairs, he rushed past the table. Looking inside, he saw an Army private stuffed under the sink. His face was blue and he stared at Ingram with surprised, wide eyes. But there was no blood. Ingram jabbed the wall switch. Nothing. But enough light crept in to illuminate another man on his back. He had a shiny bald head.

"Dwight! What the hell?" Ingram kneeled down. Epperson's face was pale and his eyes were open. His mouth was a large oval expanding and contracting as a fish does when out of water.

"Damn!" Ingram drew his hand away from a warm stickiness. He knew what it was. He'd seen too much, smelled too much of it over the past five months. He looked closer, finding a large stomach wound.

Epperson's eyes followed him.

"Dwight. What happened?"

"Ace?"

"Yeah."

"Cold. Can't move my feet."

"Hold on, buddy. Let me get a doctor. We'll fix you--"

"No time," Epperson wheezed. A bony hand gripped Ingram's lapel.

"Come on, Dwight. I'll get you jiving again."

"Listen, damn you." Epperson's eyes focused. He tried to take a deep breath. Instead, he coughed foamy pink spittle.

"Jesus. Dwight. Hold on. Lemme get help."

"...Todd. Radtke shot me with Malone's .45. Blew me across the room...uhhh...tried to garrote me first. I got the bastard by the nuts."

Ingram looked to his left, seeing the .45 laying within arm's reach. "Who?"

"Radtke. My assistant."

Ingram nodded to the sentry. "What happened to him?"

"Strangled, garrote, I think."

Ingram choked, "Why did...Radtke do this?"

"Bastard had a Minox."

"A what?"

"Tiny camera. Disguised as a matchbox. Microfilm. He was shooting those files...up..." Epperson's hand raised toward papers and files scattered across the table just outside the darkroom. His hand fell. "He knows. Damn. The bastard figured it out."

"What, Dwight?"

"You have to stop him. You have to." Epperson's eyes glowed for a moment, then went watery as his chest heaved. As if in cosmic unity, the lights dimmed and Epperson's breathing stopped.

Ingram moved an ear toward Epperson's clammy chest. He jumped when Epperson's lungs heaved; he wheezed and said loudly, "The Japs are going to invade Midway!" He blinked and his eyes darted.

"I wouldn't be surprised," Ingram said. "They've bombed everything else. Why not Midway?"

"AF," Epperson's voice turned to a gurgling rasp.

"Huh?"

"...shut up. Rochefort and I figured it out. AF." Epperson's eyes blinked rapidly as he focused on the ceiling. "We cracked their damn code. AF was the key."

It dawned on Ingram. Epperson really was lucid and knew what he was talking about. His classmate had dealt with important material. While Ingram and his ship had squirmed in its own milieu of survival, Epperson's outlook was global. "What's AF?"

"Midway. Damnit." Epperson's tone was almost conversational. "That's their code. AH is Hawaii. AG is French Frigate Shoals. And damnit! AF is Midway! Nimitz believes us."

"He does?" Reference to the Commander of the Pacific Fleet gave Ingram a heady feeling.

"Yeah. The Nips will hit AF on June fourth. Gigantic force. Shit. Over a hundred Jap ships spread from Alaska to Midway."

Both of Epperson's hands pulled on Ingram's collar. His voice was weak. "They outnumber us three to one. But we can win, Todd. We can win. Surprise the little bastards. Knock the wind out of all this *Kido Butai* bullshit. Sink their Imperial asses...buy time...why is it so damned cold?"

A shell impacted overhead making the floor surge. Epperson's eyes squeezed shut with pain. He swallowed and his eyelids fluttered. "Todd?"

"Yeah?"

"Find Radtke. Kill him."

"Dwight," Ingram almost wailed. "I don't understand any of this."

"I don't either...except Radtke...he shot meeee...he knows too much...uhhh...shit it hurts..."

"Dwight! Stay with me. Hold on 'til I get the Doc."

"...cold..."

"Dwight? Dwight! Damnit. Come on--"

"On your feet, mister!"

Ingram looked up into the barrel of a .45 caliber Thompson submachine gun. A helmeted figure stood above him with legs splayed, ready to fire. It was the Marine sergeant. The corporal hovered alongside; his eyes darting about the room.

"Get up, I said. Now," said the sergeant.

"This man's dying. He needs a doctor," said Ingram.

"Sir," the sergeant said. "If you don't stand now, I'm blowing your damned head off."

Ingram stood.

"Kick that over here. Easy with it."

Ingram caught Malone's .45 with his instep, sliding it across the linoleum to bounce off the corporal's foot. He pointed at Epperson. "Ask him if you don't believe me."

The corporal stepped around Ingram, knelt, and put his hand on Epperson's neck. "Lieutenant's dead." He nodded toward the prone sentry. "Looks like Malone don't feel too good, either."

"No!" roared Ingram. "He was just talking to me."

The corporal stepped back and, to prove his point, gestured with a palm to Epperson's corpse.

Ingram's jaw fell open.

"What is it, Sergeant?" Lieutenant (jg) Hadley stepped through the main door and walked down the aisle. Looking around he said, "Jeeze this place is bigger than I thought."

Seeing Ingram, he said, "You were right, Sergeant. Who let you in here, Lieutenant?"

Ingram stuttered. "The radioman. He--"

"Sonofabitch!" Hadley's mouth fell open as he drew up, seeing the two bodies in the darkroom.

"I can explain," said Ingram.

"Better keep your hands where we can see 'em, Lieutenant," said the sergeant.

"Who did this?" asked Hadley.

"A man named Radtke, I think." said Ingram.

"Where is he?"

"How the hell should I know?" Ingram spread his hands.

Hadley looked around the room. "Looks like he's off duty." His eyes squared on Ingram. "Who are you?" demanded Hadley. "And what are you doing in a classified area?"

Two shells thumped overhead and they waited, staring at one another, until the ground stopped jiggling. Finally, Ingram identified himself and said, "Your radioman told me to come in. Said it was okay."

"Who?" asked Hadley.

"The guy in the dungarees. A first class."

Hadley rubbed his chin for a moment. He looked at the sergeant. "Have Portman come in here."

"Ssssir." The sergeant jogged out.

A moment later, Portman's once thick frame stood before them. Seeing feet sticking from the darkroom door, his adam's apple bobbed up and down. With wavering voice, he said, "You wanted me Mr. Hadley?"

Without taking his eyes off Ingram, Hadley said, "Portman. Do you know this officer?"

Silence.

"Portman?" shouted Hadley.

The Marine sergeant stood at Portman's back and hissed in his ear.

Portman gulped. "Seen him a couple of times, Lieutenant."

"Did you authorize him to come in here?"

Ingram swung and looked at Portman.

Beads of sweat stood on Portman's forehead as shells rumbled in the distance.

Hadley croaked in a tunnel voice, "Portman. I haven't got all day, damnit."

The Marine sergeant prodded Portman's back.

"...nnn...no-nossir."

"What?" said Ingram.

"Are you sure, Portman?" asked Hadley.

"Y-yessir," said Portman.

"Back to your post," ordered Hadley.

Portman scurried back to his radio, while the sergeant closed the door and walked back to the group.

Ingram was incredulous. "That man is lying. I came in here because I'm detailed to lead an evacuation party," he checked his watch, "that is supposed to shove off in twenty-five minutes. Lieutenant Epperson and Radtke were supposed to go. I came here to pick them up."

"Lieutenant Epperson said nothing to me about evacuation," said Hadley. He spotted the .45 and nodded to the sergeant who bent and picked it up.

"Call Major DeWitt over in Malinta Tunnel if you don't believe me."

"We will," said Hadley. He looked at the sergeant. "Well?"

With a flourish, the sergeant snapped the action and released the clip which dropped in his palm. He sniffed the breech and checked the clip saying, "One round fired recently."

For a moment, all four looked at Epperson's unblinking eyes and wide-open mouth frozen in a last, futile gasp. His stomach was an enormous red blotch and blood pooled beneath his corpse.

Hadley and the two Marines looked to Ingram.

Ingram felt like an ice-cold spike had been driven through him. Unaccountably, his cheek wound throbbed beneath the blackened bandage. "You're crazy."

"Turn around, please, Sir, " said the sergeant, grabbing a length of twine from atop a file cabinet. "Put your hands behind your back."

Ingram was astounded. "What the hell are you talking about?"

Hadley stepped back two paces. "Better do as the sergeant says, Lieutenant."

15

29 April 1942
South Dock
Corregidor Island, Manila Bay, Philippines

Within seconds of one another, a pair of shells smacked the water a hundred yards offshore. Strangely, they seemed not to explode, but lifted twin fifty-foot columns of hissing, debris-laden water, which hung in midair for a moment before cascading down.

A residual mist enveloped the 51 Boat as her passengers lined up to await boarding. In twilight, Todd Ingram stepped away from the two Marines detailed to accompany him to the dock. He squinted at his watch's radium dial: 8:14. A glance told him it was calm out in the South China Sea: No wind chop and only low ground swells rolled toward land. They would have a smooth passage which was lucky, for the boat would be overloaded with passengers and their gear. Plus, fifteen gold bars were stored in the bilges: That was over a thousand pounds right there. The 51 Boat would ride low in the water tonight, but with the weather as it was, he reckoned they would have a smooth trip.

Major Otis DeWitt, wearing campaign hat, jodhpurs, and shiny boots, raised a clipboard and screeched the names of those with the highest priority. A half dozen AAF pilots, none older than twenty-five, raised their hands.

"Step forward, damnit, and get in the boat. Sit in the front." DeWitt took their names and checked them off as they filed past.

One of the pilot's eyes was bandaged. His hair was gone, allowing his combination cap to rest on his ears; his face was a mass of oozing sores and scabs. He had great trouble finding his footing. Two other pilots helped him along. "Leon," Ingram yelled, and walked over, the Marines in tow.

Beardsley raised his head as if sniffing the wind. "That you Skipper?"

"Any tomato juice left?"

Beardsley's voice dropped to a conspiratorial tone. "Four cans. I stashed them under the--"

"Haven't all night, gentlemen," said DeWitt. "Stand back, Ingram."

Mordkin materialized between them and called to the Marines. "I have him now." He pat a .45 on his hip. "Return to your post."

"Ssssir," said the sergeant. The two Marines turned and jogged toward Monkey Point.

"No crap from you, Ingram," Mordkin said.

"No crap intended, Captain," said Ingram. He walked to the dock's edge to watch Beardsley being helped into the boat. "Hey, tough guy. See you in Chicago," he yelled.

"Rat-a-tat-tat-tat," said Beardsley, taking a seat.

Next, DeWitt passed aboard fifteen or so nervous Army brass, including two brigadier generals. Three Navy commanders were after that, followed by a handful of blue jackets and Army enlisted. The rest of the contingent was civilian, mostly Filipinos.

While they boarded, Ingram stood on an empty fifty-five-gallon drum and carefully scanned out to sea for mast tops. There were none. Apparently, the Japanese had pulled their picket ships farther out. Satisfied, he jumped down and walked up to DeWitt. A series of artillery rounds sprinted along Kindley Field lighting up the major's thin moustache.

"Worried about something, Lieutenant?" said DeWitt.

Ingram said. "There's a forty-minute boat ride ahead of us. We better shove off soon, if you want to make that nine o'clock rendezvous. Submarine skippers get nervous hanging around on the surface."

"Three to go."

"It's your show." Ingram nodded and walked over to the Forester brothers, who stood with Whittaker smoking cigarettes. All three looked nervously at explosions pummeling Corregidor's east end. Kevin Forester, who Ingram had appointed as cox'n asked, "Any word, Sir?"

"Waiting for stragglers."

Whittaker asked, "How're we going to find that damned submarine, Skipper?"

"Full moon will pop up in fifteen minutes. If we steer a descent course, the *Wolfish* will find us, if worse comes to worse." He dropped his voice to a whisper. "All we do is just steer straight out there."

"What about mines?" the Forester brothers asked in unison. Kevin Forester looked at his younger brother and scowled.

"Pass right over them." With a nod to his cox'n, Ingram said, "After we clear the dock, full throttle and steer two-six-two. Should take about forty minutes." Ingram rubbed his chin thinking of the irony that he was out here at all. Technically, he was a prisoner; a murder suspect. Yet, here he was, still doing his job because he was about the only one left who knew the way over the minefield. But the mines were laid deep for big ships. DeWitt didn't know a child could have driven the 51 Boat straight out.

He bit on a thumbnail thinking what could he say to his former crew members? What could he tell men who had looked up to him as their commanding officer? Men he had lived with in close quarters and had fought with. As the *Pelican*'s captain, Ingram once had the power of life and death over these men. And now...he was under arrest for murder. After fifteen minutes of sputtering histrionics, DeWitt ordered Ingram to continue his duties with the evacuation party, assigning himself and Mordkin as watch dogs. Justice would have to wait until after the 51 Boat returned from the submarine rendezvous.

A number of shells smacked into Malinta Hill. Roiling dust clouds shot up, obscuring the last of the twilight. A light breeze carried the muck over South Dock, and soon they were gagging and choking.

DeWitt caught Ingram's eye and looked at his watch. With a nod, he yelled in his high-pitched drawl, "Move 'em out!" The major might as well have been ordering a cattle drive.

"Let's go," said Ingram to his crew.

Forester jumped in the boat and stood on the aft conning platform. Whittaker followed and cranked the diesel into life. Junior Forester kneeled by the bowline while Ingram, breaking protocol that officers don't do enlisted men's jobs, grabbed the stern line taking all but two turns off the cleat.

There was a commotion on the dock as the smoke cleared. Three figures ran out of the haze and staggered to a stop before DeWitt. The major nodded solemnly, his pencil twirling on his clip board. Finally, he jabbed a thumb at the boat and yelled, "All present and accounted for. Let's go!" He jumped in and held a hand up to the three on the dock.

The figures, bundled in overcoats and ball caps, leaned against one another, out of breath. They were female: Nurses. One looked familiar. Ingram stepped over, finding Helen Durand last in line. "Hello."

She managed a nod as she passed her satchel and hesitated.

With the dock lines loose, the boat drifted out a bit. "Come on," said Ingram.

"Thanks." She took his hand and stepped aboard.

Ingram whipped the stern line off the cleat and said, "Shove off, Forester." Whittaker fed in throttle and the 51 Boat plowed out of South dock, its engine growling.

Ingram jumped aboard and stood beside Helen at the port gunnel. "Glad you made it, this time."

She gasped, "ten minutes. That's all I had. A tunnel creep came in and said we had a place on the boat. Then the ghoul looked at his watch and said, 'too bad, the boat most likely has left' and walked out."

"What did you do?"

"Ran after the little jerk. Got him to tell us how to find you. I'll be dammed if I was going to miss another chance."

"Was he a medical type?"

Still wheezing, she said, "Just a tunnel rat. No insignia. Could have been in the Eskimo Army for all I know. But the doctors were great. They made us drop everything. We grabbed what we could and ran."

Her voice. There was something he couldn't identify, a lilt of some sort that captivated him. Even out of breath, it was intriguing. "This time you'll get out."

"I hope so. How's your cheek?"

"Still throbs. I may have to sue for malpractice."

"Nonsense," she said. "You'll have to prove it. Besides, my attorney specializes in frivolous--look at that!" She palmed his chin and turned his head for a closer examination. "What have you been rolling in? A slag heap? When was the last time you changed the dressing?"

Aside from occasional throbbing, he hadn't paid attention to the wound let alone change the dressing. Actually, hunger pangs were worse than the throbbing.

Helen Durand sighed. "Okay mister. You're my last patient."

"In a minute. Be right back." He stood.

"I'm serious. You'll probably have a scar as it is. I won't hurt you. Don't chicken out on me."

"I said I would 'be right back.'" Ingram moved aft, where Forester stood casually on the helmsman's platform with the tiller resting between his legs. The cox'n yelled over the diesel's roar, "course two-six-two?"

"Right." Ingram motioned to Junior Forester and Whittaker and said, "Get up there with him. Keep a sharp eye for Japs."

"Yessir." The two jumped up standing behind Forester.

Ingram climbed up with them and squinted into the gloom, finding nothing discernable on a dark horizon. Everything looked alright. Checking the compass--two-six-two--he eased down and stepped forward again.

Helen had taken a seat beside a Filipino with hands tucked in the pockets of a Navy windbreaker. His hair was gray-streaked, round wire rimglasses accented quick, clear eyes.

"Excuse me," said Ingram, wedging in. They nodded to one another, then he turned to Helen, "Okay, amputate my head."

"By the looks of your bandage I'd say that would be an improvement. Inez?" she called. "The kit, please."

A small bag was passed over the passenger's heads from two rows forward. The boat rolled, and the bag pitched into the Filipino's hands. He caught it and handed it over.

Helen thanked him then turned and squatted before Ingram. While unzipping the bag, the boat slewed down the back of a wave and she fell against the man. "Sorry," she said.

"It's alright," he said. His voice had a deep, cultured timbre. "Can I help?"

"Yes. Thank you." Helen clanked inside the case and pulled out a bottle.

She handed the case to the Filipino as the boat yawed steeply. "Hold this open, please," she said.

The 51 Boat's diesel purred smoothly. They were through the minefield and almost in open ocean. The trip was going well, Ingram figured. In fact, it seemed strangely peaceful. They drew farther from the barrage, and were almost out of earshot of the explosions for the first time in months. In a way, it seemed odd that deadly, ear-splitting concussions, which had for so long been macabre companions, should fade in the distance. His ears rang and he wondered how long it would take for these people to get over that? Worse, how long for them to forget the sickening revulsion of the dead and dying?

He glanced at their lolling heads. They kept to themselves, not quite ready to believe, he was sure, that they could be really escaping Corregidor's horrors. Now, it depended on a safe passage to the rendezvous, and on a submarine surfacing at the right time in the right place.

He looked back at the Rock seeing explosions pop about its length. How can I return to that hell-hole, he thought? His mind turned black for a moment. End it now. Jump over the side and drift down into nothing. He peered into the South China Sea as it swept past the 51 Boat with a somnolent gurgle; the quarter wave a deadly, green phosphorescence. I could never do that. Stand and fight, he decided grimly.

And in that moment, he thought of Dwight and the man who murdered him: Radtke. What about Midway? How to find Radtke? Start with... "What?"

"'Hold still,' I said." It was Helen dabbing something cool on his face. She picked at the bandage, got a purchase with thumb and forefinger, and tore off the old dressing.

"Ouch. Damnit!"

"Hurt?"

"No." It did hurt. The throbbing seemed worse.

She leaned close to inspect the wound. Even with ten knots of relative wind, he felt her warm breath on the nape of his neck. She said, "Yes, infected. You should be ashamed."

"Glad you're getting out of here, Helen."

"Why didn't you change this?"

"You'll be home, soon."

"You should have done it a long time ago."

"Will you be going to the States?"

She paused and looked into his eyes. She said, "Is there anyone I can...you know...talk to? Maybe deliver a letter?"

"No."

"Okay now. Put your head down and turn your cheek up to me." He leaned forward; she took a small penlight from the bag, and covering the lens, worked on him for a moment. "You can sit up now. I dumped in some sulfa. But the stitches should stay in for a few more days. Have you ever been to Heidelberg?"

"Where?"

"Germany."

"Of course not."

"Well, if anyone asks, you have now. Because that's where you got it."

"What the hell are you talking about?" demanded Ingram.

The Filipino chuckled. "Your dueling scar. It's almost perfect."

"Will it show?" asked Ingram, touching his hand to his face.

The Filipino said, "in Germany, they go to extreme lengths to have such a scar."

Helen dabbed alcohol. "A dueling scar, Captain, is very distinguished."

"Am I gonna look like a damned Nazi?"

"The Student Prince couldn't be more proud," said the Filipino.

Ingram gave the man a how-the-hell-do-you-know-about-the-Student-Prince? look.

"Excuse me," The Filipino offered his hand. "Pablo Amador. I went to Harvard, then did my post-graduate work at Oxford."

Ingram shook Amador's hand saying, "Todd Ingram. Are you in the government?"

Amador said, "Undersecretary of the Treasury. Or, what's left of it." He nodded toward the gratings over the bilge where the gold bars had been laid. "They assigned me to accompany that."

For some reason, Ingram felt it was more than gold bars that brought Amador out here, but he decided not to pursue it.

Helen Durand finished taping on the new dressing and repacked her bag. "All is finished, Herr Kapitain. Sieg Heil!" She tossed something into his lap.

"What's this?" asked Ingram.

"A clean dressing. Put it on day after tomorrow. Get someone to pull the stitches in about three more days."

"Otherwise, I will look like a German."

"More like Quasimodo."

"Thanks."

"Sorry. Maybe, you'd rather look like a German?"

"No," said Ingram.

"You're going to tell me your ancestors are German and I've been insulting you."

Ingram shrugged. "Don't know. I was born in New England. We moved to Oregon when I was ten."

Amador offered, "Are you a Cabot? That's all I heard about at Harvard."

Ingram didn't feel like playing. "I'm not a Cabot. I'm just a mutt."

Helen sat back. "Well, you're a clean mutt now. I got that filthy island out of your cheek."

Amador coughed lightly. Instinctively, they sensed he was used to commanding attention this way, and turned to him. He leaned forward putting a hand on each of their shoulders. His voice shook as he said, "God bless you for who you are, and what you are doing for the Philippine Commonwealth."

Ingram was a bit embarrassed, but then he looked at Helen; her expression confirmed the Filipino wasn't daft. He didn't know what to say and an awkward silence followed, with all three watching flashes and listening to crumping thuds of exploding shells on Corregidor. Out here it seemed like fireworks, but on the islands, each knew the terror that reigned.

Something seemed different about Amador when Ingram stole another look. A ghostly radiance brightened over the Filipino's shoulder that seemed to deepen the crevices in his face. It was the rising full moon over the Pico de Loro Hills, making Amador look far older, in a way, sage-like, as he braced his palms against the 51 Boat's slow roll.

Ingram checked his watch: 8:43. He stood and looked toward Luzon, then peered at Forester in the moon's rising light. Forester waved, and then returned to concentrating on his compass. A glance at Whittaker and young Forester confirmed they were keeping a vigilant watch.

"How are we doing?" asked Helen. Her face was lost in darkness.

"Okay. Pretty soon, now," said Ingram taking a seat. "We're making good--"

"There is something you should know about Corregidor," Amador said, waving a hand at Luzon.

"I've had enough of Corregidor," said Helen.

"After this is over, he will have gotten what he deserves," Amador said.

"Who?" Ingram and Helen said in unison.

"Corregidor."

"He? Who's Corregidor?" they asked.

Amador looked at them. "An evil magistrate." When neither spoke, he continued. "Look," he said, sweeping his hand toward the mountain on the Bataan Peninsula. "Do you know what that peak is called, Lieutenant?"

"Mariveles," said Ingram.

"That's right. And Mariveles was a lovely young nun who lived in a convent at the bottom of that mountain." He paused, finding Helen's eyes wide, her mouth slightly open.

Ingram muttered to himself and checked aft to catch a reassuring nod from Forester. When he again looked at Amador he couldn't tell if the scorn in the Filipino's face was real or imagined.

Amador continued, "Nearby was a monastery. A young friar lived there. It was inevitable. They met. They fell in love, but they could only have stolen moments together. Finally, they decided to marry..."

The boat rolled, pitching Ingram into Amador. The man was well braced and didn't budge. Ingram sensed he was strong, without an ounce of fat. The moon had climbed higher, washing the coast line in a gray-green phosphorescence. Corregidor and the other fortified island stood out vividly.

"...in those days, you must understand this was long before the Renaissance, the area at the entrance to Manila Bay was a salt marsh; there was no sea, as we know it, between Bataan and the Cavite headlands."

A series of explosions flashed through Corregidor's Middleside. Barely audible, they lighted Amador's face like a child's sparkler on the Fourth of July. More bombs hit, and Ingram stood looking out to sea to search for the *Wolfish*. Nothing. He checked his watch. They were five minutes past rendezvous time. Maybe it was aft. He looked over their starboard quarter searching...

"...the lovers decided to run for it. They stole a horse from a nearby village and started across the marsh. Almost immediately, the villages learned of their disappearance and followed after them. Deep into the marsh the horse bogged down and they transferred to a Carabao. Then they--"

"A what?" asked Helen.

"Like a domesticated water buffalo. A sturdy, draft animal." Pablo Amador paused, then went on. "The villagers came closer, and the young friar and Mariveles grew desperate. Finally, they jumped off the carabao and ran on foot."

Amador paused and looked up at Ingram.

Feeling the man's eyes Ingram said, "Please don't stop."

Amador sighed and was silent. The 51 Boat's engine purred, and her wake sizzled in a calm, flat sea. Finally, he spoke again in what seemed a super-modulated voice, "The Villagers caught them. They were very angry and demanded justice for the sins of the nun, Mariveles, and her young Friar."

Ingram's eyes darted about the sea, knowing any number of subtle shadows could mask the *Wolfish*. Worse, the night could cover an enemy patrol boat until it was too late. They could be murdered with deadly machine gun fire from close range as they sat listening to Amador's insipid fairy tale. But despite that, and despite hunger and exhaustion, Ingram found himself compelled to listen.

With a nod, Amador said, "They took them to their magistrate. His name was--"

"Corregidor," said Helen.

"How did you know?" asked Amador.

"You said so. He was evil." Helen said.

"Yes," Amador continued. "Corregidor was evil. He was arrogant and contemptuous of everyone. He ordered that Mariveles and the friar be forever separated, to live on opposite sides of the marsh, never to see one another ever again."

"How awful," said Helen.

"Yes," said Amador. "But a merciful deity who watches over lovers pitied them. And he was displeased by the prideful magistrate. He said, 'I will show this proud Corregidor. He is not to decree eternal punishment for anyone, much less a pair of faithful lovers.'"

"Ah," said Helen. "He gave them mercy and they lived happily ever after."

Amador shook his head. "Sadly, my dear, no. He could not ignore that Mariveles and the friar had broken solemn vows of their orders taken before God. The deity had no choice but to make them a lasting example. But he needed something to exemplify justice for the lovers on the one hand, and fidelity to their oaths on the other."

The diesel droned on, driving the bow sideways into a wavelet. Water slapped ten feet in the air forming spray that found its way aft to the threesome, covering them in a fine mist.

"His decree was that the young nun should rest in an eternal state atop that mountain." Amador pointed to the peak dominating the Bataan Peninsula.

"Mariveles," said Ingram.

"That's her," said Amador. "A silhouette of her figure can be seen from the marsh, which is now the entrance to Manila Bay.

"The friar--now El Fraile Island--is on the opposite side of the channel where, mercifully, he gazes up to his beloved Mariveles."

"That doesn't seem just," said Helen.

"Possibly not," said Amador. "But then evil Corregidor himself was frozen in stone and turned into an island, keeping the two separated forever."

Ingram's hand went to Helen's shoulder as the boat slewed through a trough. She looked up at him as he steadied himself saying, "Carabao and Caballo islands," said Ingram.

"Yes," said Amador. "The water buffalo and the horse separate Corregidor from El Fraile." He bent down and took Helen's hands in his. "It may not seem just. But at least they can see each other. Perhaps, some day..."

"I think..." Ingram began. Something distracted him. He stood and searched the ocean off their starboard quarter.

Helen looked back to the islands, where artillery flashes threw sparkles across her pupils. She said, "perhaps with Carabao and Caballo close by, El Fraile can someday mount one of them and dash across the marsh to rescue Mariveles."

Amador sat back and lightly slapped his knees. "Perhaps."

Helen stood and waved a hand across Ingram's face. "Hello? Captain Midnight? If El Fraile drinks Ovaltine, can he bring Caballo back to life and rescue--

"Shhh!" said Ingram, seeing that Junior Forester and Whittaker peered aft, too.

Amador stood and looked over the starboard quarter with them.

"It's her. The *Wolfish*. Can't you hear?" said Ingram.

16

29 April 1942
U.S. Naval Operating Area YOKE YOKE 2
South China Sea

Framed in their vision, Corregidor lay three miles astern, the hulking island like a staggering boxer. Shells pummeled its ridges and ravines as they peered aft looking for the *Wolfish*. "Where is it?" Helen searched the darkness.

Ingram pointed, "Out there. That 'whoosh.' That was her ballast tanks."

DeWitt and Mordkin stood with them to look aft. In ones and twos, almost all the passengers rose to their feet, making the shore boat top-heavy and slew drunkenly.

"Seats, please," barked Ingram. "Wait till she's alongside and your name is called." He drew a finger across his throat, and Whittaker throttled back to an idle.

DeWitt said to Ingram, "Lieutenant? Where's your submarine?"

Ingram pointed in the darkness.

A Fairbanks-Morse, nine-cylinder, opposed piston, model 248 engine bellowed into life. Three other mighty diesels started, each one generating 1,535-brake horsepower. Even though the exhaust's deep rumble was close off the starboard quarter, they still couldn't see her. But that didn't stop the passengers from cheering and thumping each other on the back.

DeWitt stood on a thwart and yelled something but the cacophony was too great. He tried again, but they cheered louder and hugged each other and clapped shoulders as the sound of the *Wolfish*'s diesels drew near.

With very little headway, her snout popped into view not fifty yards distant; then, her conning tower and periscopes quickly materialized. Barely above the surface, she was a new *Gatos* class fleet submarine, 311 feet long displacing 1,526 tons. Her topsides were camouflaged a dull black, blending well into the nighttime seascape. "She's awash," Ingram said. Her skipper had partially surfaced so as to reduce her silhouette and keep her main deck near the water, making the personnel transfer easier. It would be easier handing the seventy-pound gold bars over, too, he figured.

Junior Forester and Whittaker needed no urging to make bow and stern lines ready as the submarine's bullnose wallowed near their starboard side. Dark figures stood on her deck as Forester worked the 51 Boat under the *Wolfish*'s port bow with a bump. The lines were made fast and Whittaker dropped a fender over the side.

DeWitt blew a whistle. "Line up in order of priority, goddamnit!" He may as well have tried to stop a Texas-style stampede as the evacuees swarmed to the starboard side and started boarding en-masse. "Bastards!" He turned and yelled at the Navy enlisted evacuees. "You, there! Line up for bullion detail."

Six sailors shrank back into the 51 Boat and waited for instructions like rebellious sixth-grade pubescents.

DeWitt said, "Fall into ranks, I said. Right here. Otherwise, you're not going home."

The men were sullen but did as they were told. One was taller than the rest and went to extra lengths to keep his face averted. He had been close enough to hear Amador tell his Corregidor legend. Now he shifted positions and took a place a bit farther away.

Pablo Amador, with a broad smile, shook Ingram's hand. "I enjoyed talking to you, my friend."

"And you, Mr. Amador. Perhaps we'll meet again." He lowered his voice making sure DeWitt couldn't hear. "We may run for it."

The boat rocked, then slammed against the *Wolfish*. Amador had to shout over the noise and confusion. "Escape?" he said. "Where?"

"Not sure. Australia, maybe."

"Well, if you do, make sure you stop in Nasipit. North coast of Mindanao. It's my hometown and I have many friends there. They have a big radio and the resistance grows daily. It would be a good resting place, before you transit the Surigao Strait into the Pacific." Shadowy figures gestured from the submarine's deck. "I'm up next." Then he took Ingram's hand again. "Use my name. Pablo Amador. They'll take good care of you."

"Pablo Amador. Thanks. I won't forget."

"Everywhere our resistance gains momentum. They may try to enlist you. Good luck. Excuse me." Amador stepped between the rank of sailors, braced a foot on the starboard rail, and accepted a hand from a burly torpedoman who pulled him onto the submarine's deck. He climbed down the hatch to the *Wolfish*'s forward torpedo room.

Helen stood at the starboard gunnel. "Thanks, Lieutenant. I--what is your name, anyway?"

"Ingram. Todd Ingram." He shook her hand.

"Okay, Todd. Best of luck, and take care of that cheek." She reached for a hand on the submarine, but withdrew and kissed Ingram just above the bandage.

"Why did you do that?"

"Take care of yourself."

Ingram put his hand to his face as she gained another foothold on the gunnel. He choked out, "Where do you live?"

She turned. "What?"

"Yes. Damnit. How do I find you?"

Her eyes darted for a moment. "Ramona. I live in Ramona, California."

"Like the movie with Don Ameche?"

"He was the star."

"Here." He twisted his Naval Academy ring off his thumb and stuffed it in her pocket. "Keep it safe for me."

He was glad she didn't make a show of mock resistance. "You'll get it back," she said.

"I hope so." He had no idea why he'd given her the ring. Perhaps it was because a part of him--even though it was an inanimate object--was on its way to safety. But he wasn't sure.

"Where do *you* live" she asked.

"Why?"

"Where do I send the ring in case it doesn't fit?" Helen's eyes glistened.

"Echo. Echo, Oregon."

"Where's that?"

"Eastern Oregon. Farming town just outside--"

A *Wolfish* sailor took her hand and pulled her on deck with a rough yank.

Ingram tossed her satchel up to the sailor. "California's a big state," he shouted.

She looked back yelling something and patting her pocket.

"What?" Ingram stepped on a thwart.

She could only manage a wave as she was hustled down the forward hatch.

"Todd? Is that you?" An officer towered above Ingram on the *Wolfish*'s deck.

Ingram squinted up into darkness. "Foggy?" There was no mistaking that voice and for a moment, he felt warm inside just hearing it. The tall, thin, Lieutenant junior grade Raleigh T. Sutcliff was so named because of his deep, baritone voice and bobbing Adam's apple. Although Sutcliff had been two years behind Ingram at the Academy, they were good friends. "What the hell are you doing up there?" said Ingram.

"Engineering officer. What the hell are you doing down there? Last I heard your ship was blown out from under."

Ingram told him about the *Hayes* and the *Pelican* as DeWitt and Mordkin organized their work party. Soon the sailors passed up the bullion.

"Sounds rough."

"It is."

"Look, Todd, we have some food, medicine, cigarettes, candy. They--" Sutcliff looked away, "didn't give us any ammo for you." All the other submarine relief missions had brought in ammunition.

Ingram said, "It's okay, Foggy. Give it to my boat crew."

Sutcliff spoke to a group of men and soon a line formed with boxes being handed down to the Foresters and Whittaker.

"What's the news from home?"

Sutcliff squatted so he could see Ingram better. "Don't know about home. We're stationed in Fremantle."

"Nice duty." Ingram looked to the bow of the shore boat. Mordkin's work party was hard at it. He was surprised to see Beardsley still in the boat. Helped by a nervous looking pilot, he stumbled aft toward him. Ingram looked back up to Sutcliff. "New pig-boat, huh? How do you like her?"

Sutcliff said, "Beautiful. Commissioned eight months ago. Everything a man can want. Newest sonar. Even an air-search radar. Hell, they threw in an ice-cream making machine for good measure. But there's one snafu I wanna tell you."

"What's that?"

"Torpedoes aren't worth a shit."

"You're pulling my leg."

"Had a perfect setup on an anchored Jap cruiser two nights ago off Cebu. Fired four. Three hit and didn't go off. Duds. The other missed and detonated at the end of its run, waking up the Japs. Damn destroyers almost depth charged us to hell. Held us down for eleven hours. Everyone is pissed."

"I don't believe this."

"Same in the other boats," said Sutcliff.

"What are you going to--what?" It was Beardsley yanking on his sleeve. "Time to go, Leon. They'll be diving, soon,"

"Yeah, better get 'em aboard. See you later, Todd. Good luck." Sutcliff stood and walked to the torpedo room hatch.

Beardsley's voice was low and conspiratorial, Chicago style, making Ingram suppress a smile. "Uh, Skipper," Beardsley said. "You remember the night that sailor of yours died? The guy with the morphine?"

Ingram stopped smiling.

"Lieutenant?" said Beardsley.

"Yes."

"He's here." Beardsley nodded forward where four sailors worked with the last gold bricks.

"Who?" demanded Ingram.

The other pilot, a young redhead said, "Leon. Knock off the crap. We gotta get aboard." He grabbed Beardsley's sleeve and tugged.

Beardsley pulled away. "Damnit, I know the guy's here."

The pilot helping Beardsley said loudly, "How do you know? You're half blind you dumb shit. Come on!"

Beardsley reached out, finding Ingram's shirt and grabbed a lapel. "Didn't I tell you? Bay Rum. Remember? My girl gave me a bottle. The guy is wearing it," he yelled.

"Get moving," shouted DeWitt.

The red-headed pilot spat, "You're on your own, Leon." Taking the submariner's outstretched hands, he jumped up to the *Wolfish's* deck and headed for the torpedo room hatch.

It swarmed over Ingram: Hampton and his swollen leg. "You sure?" He looked forward. Two sailors knelt to replace the bilge gratings while another pair, under Mordkin's supervision, passed up the last seventy-pound gold bar.

"Come on Leon." Ingram helped turn Beardsley around, and they walked forward.

"Hey. Hey. You. Ingram, stay away from there," screeched DeWitt.

"Leon. There are four guys up here. Have any idea which one?" growled Ingram.

"I think he was low; maybe on his knees." Beardsley said.

One of the sailors working at the bilge casually turned away from Ingram and crouched at the grating with a screwdriver.

DeWitt yelled from behind. "Is the gold loaded?"

"Last bar just went up," said Mordkin, watching Ingram and Beardsley.

"Then send those swabbies to the submarine and let's get out of here," said DeWitt.

"You!" shouted Ingram. "Turn around!"

"What's your problem?" rumbled Mordkin.

"I said turn around." Ingram grabbed the tail of the man's shirt and spun him.

The sailor fell on his side and, grappling for a handhold, looked at Ingram with wild eyes.

Ingram gaped into the face of Cryptographer Second Class Walter Radtke. "You!"

With surprising alacrity, Radtke sprang for the gunnel. He was quick, grabbing the bowline to pull himself on *Wolfish's* deck.

"No!" Ingram roared. He jumped after Radtke and chopped at his wrists.

The man squirmed and kicked and bit and squealed. But slowly, Ingram tugged him back into the 51 Boat. Just as he let go, Radtke reached in his pocket and spasmodically tossed something looking like a box of matches over the side.

He yelped in pain as Ingram dragged him back in the boat and jumped on him, driving a fist in his face. Radtke turned his head just in time to deflect the blow. And somehow, during all this, the smell of Bay Rum played at Ingram's nostrils.

"What the hell you doin'?" Mordkin shouted, pulling at Ingram's arms and shoulders.

Radtke's hand grabbed at Ingram's crotch. His other hand sent two splayed fingers to gouge his eyes. Ingram ducked and hit Radtke again, this time in the neck.

Radtke gurgled. But to Ingram's amazement, he powerfully raised himself off the deck.

Mordkin and DeWitt stood over them yanking and pulling at the flailing pair with DeWitt shouting, "Turn this man loose. He has to get aboard the--"

A tall column of water erupted two hundred yards to port. The four stared, unbelieving at the tumbling, cascading water.

"What's going on with the--"

Another shell landed off to starboard somewhere making ocean hiss.

"Shit! We're bracketed," yelled Sutcliff running for the conning tower. "Get below before..."

His voice was drowned out by the diving klaxon and ballast tanks venting. The forward torpedo room hatch clunked shut and the *Wolfish* gathered way.

Looking up in horror, Ingram saw the dock lines were still attached to the submarine's cleats. The *Wolfish* pulled them through the water and soon, would tow them under.

"Forester!" He shouted aft. "Cast off the stern line. Cut it, you have to."

Whittaker and Forester needed no encouragement. Both hacked at the line with knives. Junior Forester sprang to the bowline, as the submarine picked up speed. Looking aft, Ingram saw the port bow plane unfolding from the superstructure. For a terrifying moment it looked as if the diving plane would crash down on the boat's transom. But it cleared by two feet and sliced into the water in the full dive position.

The next shell was to port and much closer, the explosion cracking their eardrums. Water and hot shrapnel chunks rained on the deck. Forester madly sawed at the line. Ingram scrambled over Radtke to assist him. He reached the young quartermaster, wrapped his hands around his wrists, and helped him bear down.

Through gritted teeth, Junior Forester sobbed, "Dull blade."

Another shell landed close to starboard, raining more water and shrapnel. But by now, the *Wolfish*'s entire forward section was submerged with water peeling off her conning tower.

Whittaker got the engine started just as the bowline snapped with a twang. Ingram looked aft, seeing the stern line had been cut. Forester leaned into his tiller and veered away from the diving *Wolfish*.

The submarine was under. Her periscope, pulling a large wake, swept by as Whittaker opened the throttle.

Ten seconds later another shell landed where they would have been. Then another.

Breathless, they watched for a minute or two. It became quiet. Finally, DeWitt took off his campaign hat and slapped it against his thigh, making the water shake out. With the other hand, he wiped drops off his face and said, "Damned accurate. The bastards had us. Think that's the one we picked up the other night?"

Ingram recalled the Japanese cruiser's feint toward Corregidor on General Moore's radar. On a moonlit night like this, they wouldn't have needed radar. They were in gun range. Their optics were excellent, their night fighting gunnery and torpedo tactics the best.

He stood on a thwart and looked to the west. Sure enough. The moon glinted off something metallic just above the horizon, perhaps a yardarm. He pointed toward the cruiser, "We're safe now, Major. They won't fire at small potatoes."

"Shit!" yelled Beardsley, slamming a fist on a thwart.

"Sorry, Leon," said Ingram.

"Double shit!" roared Beardsley. "I can't believe those bastards dived without me."

Ingram jumped down and tried to help Beardsley sit, but the pilot wouldn't have any of it.

"You son-of-a-bitch!" Beardsley yelled toward the bow, waving his fists in space.

Epperson's assistant moved to the forward thwart, sat with hands in his pockets, and looked out to sea.

Beardsley lurched forward and found a handhold on a thwart. "I'll kill that bastard myself. Where is--"

An enormous explosion erupted on Corregidor, sending roiling flames and pieces of rock and machinery hundreds of feet in the air. Flames cascaded in an enormous mushroom cloud, which illuminated the island from end to end. Even at this distance, they felt the heat.

"My God!" said DeWitt bracing himself on the gunnel.

A cloud of fire spilled down Government Ravine, where shipwrecked sailors from the submarine tender, *Canopus*, had made camp. Ingram looked away knowing men were being consumed in that inferno. Squeezing his eyes shut, he still couldn't stop imagining their screams and burning, writhing bodies.

Flames and concussions and reverberations racked Manila Bay for another ninety seconds. Afterwards, a few fires broke out, but without combustible material on the island's surface, they quickly flicked out.

"Come on." Ingram helped lift Beardsley off the deck onto a thwart.

"What happened?" the pilot asked.

"Ammo bunker, most likely. Hard to tell which one. Could be Way." Ingram referred to Battery Way with four, twelve-inch M-1890 mortars.

"People died," said Mordkin, matter-of-factly.

"A lot, I think," said Dewitt.

They sat for a moment, consumed in their own horror, still feeling the heat from the magazine's explosion.

After a while Beardsley said, "How 'bout the guy I fingered?"

Ingram said, "We got the bastard. He's sitting up forward. And he killed another guy, it turns out. This time--"

"That's yet another charge against you, Lieutenant," said DeWitt walking up.

"What?" said Ingram

"Assaulting an enlisted man."

17

---

3 May 1942
Baker Cellblock, Fort Hughes Stockade
Caballo Island, Manila Bay, Philippines

Major Otis DeWitt walked in waking Ingram from a troubled sleep. Trudging behind DeWitt was Captain Carl Mordkin. He was followed by a nervous looking Navy jaygee, the one who turned Ingram over to the Marines the other night.

Ingram's skin prickled when next he saw Cryptographer Second Class Walter Radtke trudge in, immediately followed by the two Marines.

The thin, mustachioed major stepped to his cell and signaled to Mordkin, "Okay, Mr. Ingram let's hear what you have to say."

Ingram rose off the wooden bunk, his cheek throbbing with pain. He patted it and was satisfied that at least it wasn't bleeding. A Marine corpsman had pulled the stitches two days ago, but the thing still hurt.

Trying to ignore the thumping and swelling he did his best to concentrate on the lieutenant jaygee. He hadn't seen the man since last Wednesday, the night of Dwight's murder. Undernourished like everyone else, the man's hollow eyes darted nervously around the cellblock. And when a shell landed he seemed to shrink into himself as the ceiling shed plaster chips and dust. Like everyone else he was scared.

Except Radtke. With an aloof air, the cryptographer leaned against the wall with folded arms, one foot crossed over the other. He carried a small duffle and casually swung it. Last time Ingram had seen the man his hair was matted and deranged; he had worn ragged trousers, boots and a grease-spotted jacket. Now, his hair stood in a crew cut and he wore clean dungarees and black shoes, as if standing for inspection. *How the hell did he manage all this?*

Nearby, the two Marines looked cool enough, with their Thompson submachine guns slung over their shoulders. And they carried their usual array of pistols, grenades, and bayonets. These Marine's boots had seen their share of Bataan's muddy foxholes, Ingram was sure. Worn, sweat-soaked fatigues gave a ripe odor Ingram somehow associated with formaldehyde. The corporal's eyes shifted endlessly around the room, while the sergeant watched Radtke's every move.

Mordkin stepped over to the Navy jaygee to offer his hand. "Carl Mordkin. Welcome."

The jaygee shook. "Jim Hadley," he muttered.

DeWitt stepped up to the cell and said, "Alright Ingram. Let's go over your accusation that Lieutenant Epperson was shot by this man."

Radtke, Ingram noticed, had pulled himself to a semblance of parade rest. Even the bastard's hat brim is squared to the regulation two inches above the nose, he thought as he rolled his eyes.

DeWitt said, "Lieutenant. I'm talking to you. The Japs are poised to invade any minute. I have no time. What do you have to say?"

"That's the man who killed Dwight and the guard," said Ingram.

"Um, huh." DeWitt turned to Hadley, who somehow had wedged himself in a far corner. "You there, Lieutenant. What's your name, again?"

"Hadley, Sir."

"Aren't you the one who preferred charges against Ingram?"

Hadley stood straighter. "Yes, Sir."

"Why?" DeWitt said.

"Well, Sir..."

"Haven't you been listening? I don't have all day, Lieutenant. Nor do the

Japanese," snapped DeWitt. "Come out here where I can see you."

Hadley stepped to the room's center and swallowed several times. His eyes were fixed on the ceiling with the look of a submariner who knows the next depth charge will be the one that crushes the hull.

DeWitt said, "What was the first thing that made you think something was wrong?"

Artillery rumbled overhead. Hadley's eyes swept the ceiling. "The sentry was not at his post."

"Who was that?" said DeWitt.

"Private Malone, Sir. He was supposed to be on guard outside the file room door."

"And," prompted DeWitt.

"Portman, my radioman," said Hadley, "saw him go inside for reasons unknown. Mr. Ingram showed up a few moments later and also went inside. To me it looked like Mr. Ingram entered a secure area without permission."

"Wasn't Portman supposed to be here?" said DeWitt, looking at the stockade doorway.

"Well...there was a..."

"Please hurry."

"Broken jaw. He's in a lot of pain and barely conscious."

"How'd that happen?" asked DeWitt with some irritation.

"Skinner, a third class went sort of berserk last night. Three two-forties hit almost on top of each other and he bolted. Portman tried to stop him and got clobbered."

"Alright, go on."

A shell rumbled overhead making the ceiling jiggle. Hadley's Adam's apple bounced. "Well, Sir, I..."

"Lieutenant Hadley," said DeWitt, "if you don't hurry along, you'll be testifying before a Jap tribunal."

"Yes, Sir.

"Did anyone come out of the file room?" asked DeWitt.

"No, Sir. But then I remember we took a hit that really rattled our teeth. Maybe a two-forty. Damn thing must have landed at the tunnel entrance. A bunch of dirt and trash blew through."

"So, someone could have come out of the room," said DeWitt.

Hadley scratched his head. "Maybe, but not likely, Sir."

"You don't think this man, Radtke, was in the room?" said DeWitt.

"Hard to tell, Sir. But he wasn't there when I went in. So, where was he?" answered Hadley.

"I see," said DeWitt. He turned to the cell. "Tell me Mr. Ingram. Was Radtke in the file room when you went in?"

Ingram felt like the walls were closing in. "No."

"And you say he is a spy?"

"Must be. Why would he want to kill Dwight?"

"Lieutenant Ingram." DeWitt clasped his hands behind his back. "You're charged with the murders of Lieutenant Epperson and Private Malone. And the way it looks, I wouldn't give your defense counsel a plugged nickel for his chance of winning his case. Even so, we owe it to this command to hear your allegation that Radtke is the murderer. And," DeWitt's eyes narrowed, "a spy?"

Ingram nodded slowly.

DeWitt said loudly, "You'll have to do better than that, Lieutenant. We must know if there is anything to this. Radtke's scheduled for evacuation tonight."

"How?" Hot anger welled up in Ingram's throat.

"The *Wolfish* has been ordered back in."

"She's already stuffed full of people." Ingram snorted.

"I know." With his boot, DeWitt toed the pavement for a moment. "Apparently your Navy boys...think there's not enough time for another pig-boat to get here. The *Wolfish* is the closest. So, they were ordered to drop the first batch on Marinduque and skedaddle back." Marinduque was an island about one hundred miles southeast of Manila.

Ingram was glad when Mordkin said, "What happens to them?"

"Resistance cell is there. Amador will--"

"Who?" said Mordkin.

"Amador, Captain." DeWitt was more than a bit bothered. He swung on Mordkin and almost shouted, "That Filipino we took out that night the Jap ship almost sunk us. He's supposed to hook up with the resistance there and make their way to Mindanao via interisland steamer. Nasipit, if I read his orders right."

Ingram thought of Helen Durand. He'd given her his ring. "And then?"

"Another sub picks 'em up off Nasipit."

A prolonged silence set in. Each let his own thoughts range over the two lucky groups rescued by the *Wolfish* and how precious that freedom was. And Ingram had thought a lot about Helen Durand during his time in jail. Soon, she would, be headed for Australia. Then home, maybe on leave, to a little town in California: Ramona, where she would have clean sheets, steak, and potatoes, long hot showers, cool beer beside--"huh?"

"I said, Mr. Ingram," DeWitt stood close to the bars, "unless you provide tangible evidence, we have no choice but to send him out."

"Who?"

"Radtke, damnit."

"No!" roared Ingram. He pointed to Radtke. "That bastard killed Epperson." Ingram's hair was wild; sweat ran down his face. "You can't let him go. He's a spy, "he gasped his voice raspy. He cleared his throat, knowing he didn't sound convincing.

"Prove it!" said DeWitt.

Feeling weak, Ingram held his head. "That PFC... the one under the sink..."

"Malone," said DeWitt.

"Yeah, Malone. Radtke must have strangled Malone, then shot Dwight with Malone's .45."

"Why?"

"Dwight says he photographed secret documents."

"Photographed? With what?" demanded DeWitt.

"Little camera, Dwight said it was a Minotaur. Disguised as a matchbox."

DeWitt rubbed his chin for a moment, then looked at Radtke. "Minox?"

Ingram shrugged.

DeWitt said to Radtke, "Turn out your pockets."

"Yes, Sir." Radtke stepped to a table and emptied his belongings. DeWitt's eyes roamed over a small pen knife, a key chain, and a can opener.

"No matchbox," said DeWitt. "Radtke. Do you smoke?"

"No Sir."

"Hold out your hands," ordered DeWitt.

Radtke held up splayed fingers. DeWitt stepped close looking for nicotine stains. Satisfied there were none, he moved away saying, "Sergeant, search this man. His duffle, too," DeWitt ordered.

The Marine sergeant said, "Ssssir." With a nod to Radtke he said, "Hands on the wall, swabbie. Feet spread."

Radtke rolled his eyes, turned, slapped his palms on the concrete wall and leaned against them. The sergeant patted, while the corporal emptied the duffle. It didn't take long for the Marines to finish. They looked at DeWitt shaking their heads.

DeWitt walked up to Ingram's cell and said, "No secret cameras, Mr. Ingram. Anything else?"

Ingram could only stare. Why *had* Dwight been shot? Why didn't they believe him? What sort of magician was this man Radtke, anyway? Artillery thumped somewhere on Caballo and he spread his hands in desperation saying, "Sir, you can't let this happen. That man knows we've cracked the Jap code and have learned their plans for a major invasion early next month. Dwight said he photographed documents that prove it."

"What the hell are you talking about, Lieutenant?" said DeWitt, his eyebrows raised.

"The Navy radio intercept tunnel. It's connected by long-line to Pearl. Dwight talked to them all the time."

"Nonsense," said DeWitt. "We would have known."

"It's true," said Ingram, his words rushing faster. "And Dwight said we could beat the hell out of the Japs with sort of a trap; a surprise counterattack. But let Radtke go free and he'll warn them."

DeWitt studied the floor. "Warn who? The Japs?"

"I don't know."

DeWitt paced up and down for a few minutes. His gaze swung back and forth between Ingram and Radtke. At length, he stopped before the cell, looked straight at Ingram, hooked his hands in his belt loops and rocked on his heels. "You really think this man murdered Lieutenant Epperson?"

Ingram looked around the room, finding everyone's eyes fixed on him.

"Well, come on, Lieutenant-Captain of the minesweeper. Did he do it?" growled DeWitt.

Ingram straightened to his full height. "I believe he did."

"And the reason he shot Lieutenant Epperson is that he's a spy," DeWitt shook his head slightly.

Ingram said, "That must be what happened."

DeWitt's voice dropped to an almost gentle tone, "Lieutenant. Are you aware of the precautions our security people go through before they send a cryptographer to us?"

The green metal lampshades swayed in concentric orbits as shells rumbled overhead, making their faces turn from gray to white and gray again.

"We're wasting our time," DeWitt said softly. He turned to Mordkin. "See that Ingram is released when the enemy takes the island. He'll receive the same treatment as the others. I'll get to the bottom of this somehow in prison camp. That is, if we survive." He headed for the door.

The realization sank in with Ingram feeling as if he'd been skewered with an ice-cold, heavily barbed sword. DeWitt had said matter-of-factly "*when the enemy takes the island,*" not "*if they take the island.*" Looking around, he noticed the others stared at the ground. But suddenly a thought struck him. "Wait!" he shouted.

DeWitt took two steps then hesitated. "What?"

Ingram pinched the bridge of his nose and snapped his fingers several times. "A musician. Dwight said...he plays...the trumpet!" His voice rose a notch. "This guy's supposed to play the trumpet. A virtuoso or something. He was in the ship's band aboard the *North Carolina.* And...and he's supposed to be as good as Ziggy Ellman in civilian life. I--"

DeWitt turned, seeing Ingram's red face. "What's wrong, Lieutenant?"

"The Sonofabitch!" roared Ingram. He yanked at the bars making his door rattle. "My electrician, Hampton, was on the *North Carolina* before he came to us. He must of known the real Radtke." He pointed, "You bastard! You killed Hampton, in case he discovered you weren't Radtke. What's your real name? You work for Tojo, maybe? Or is it Uncle Adolph?"

All eyes settled on Radtke.

Radtke stuffed his belongings in his pocket, jammed his left hand behind his back, and said to DeWitt. "Sir, I'm sorry about all this. Mr. Epperson was like a friend to me. We were close. He taught me a lot. Encouraged me to go to college. Become an officer. I intend to do that if I... well, if I live through this."

He looked at the ceiling and took a deep breath. "I don't know why the Lieutenant here persecutes me. But I do know that I'm going to be late for that sub. He already made me miss her once."

DeWitt stepped close to Radtke looking him up and down. "How, Lieutenant Ingram, do you think your spy got in our Navy in the first place? Maybe he crawled up the *North Carolina*'s anchor-chain?"

Ingram barely heard what DeWitt said. He thrust an index finger through the bars and yelled louder. "My God. The poor bastard. You doped Hampton then twisted his leg to make him bleed to death."

Radtke's voice was close to a bored exhaustion. "Sir. Can I go now?"

DeWitt said, "Lieutenant, these are serious charges. And if you can't prove them, I have no choice but to release this man. I'm under orders. We have a message from Nimitz, himself."

Ingram's chest heaved and sweat ran freely down his face. In his mind, a voice kept saying, get a handle on it, you're making a fool of yourself. But he didn't listen and raged again, "See? That proves it. The long-line to Pearl Harbor. Radtke, or whatever his name is, has access to the highest levels. You must believe me. He must know our plans for counterattack!"

DeWitt sighed. "Counter-attack, Lieutenant? Just where is this great battle to take place?"

Ingram was ready to say "Midway," but, for some reason, chose to remain silent.

"You have proven nothing, Lieutenant." DeWitt walked to the door.

"A trumpet," shouted Ingram. "If he's so hot, let's hear it."

DeWitt said, "Sorry, no time."

Mordkin said, "Actually, Major, we could easily check this out. Do you remember the night that PBY crashed?"

DeWitt snorted. "Which one?" They had lost many aircraft during the siege.

"I was there that night," said Ingram.

"That's right," said Mordkin. "We had word to pick up an ONI guy who was coming in on a serious security matter. The message was very cryptic, and we were told to throw out the red carpet for the guy. But the PBY crashed on landing. It..." He swung to Ingram.

Ingram picked it up. "We were on our way back to the *Pelican*." His eyes rolled. "The PBY's pontoon snagged an oil drum, just as it landed. Damn thing ground-looped. We got there a few minutes later and fished Richardson out of the water. He died just as we got back to South Dock."

"Why wasn't I informed?" demanded DeWitt.

"Actually, you were, Major. I told you about that," said Mordkin. "And then I--"

"His real name was Fowler," Ingram blurted.

"What?" They all turned and looked at him.

Now Ingram was sorry he hadn't turned the ONI man's wallet over to Mordkin that night. He said, "Later, I described the incident to Dwight. He knew Richardson. Said his real name was Fowler. Taught a security class at Treasure Island. You're right, Captain. Dwight thought Richardson was here to investigate a security problem."

"What else?" asked DeWitt.

Ingram rested his hands on the bars and shook his head.

DeWitt said, "Unless there is something significant to add, I find nothing more conclusive about this, one way or the other."

"The point is," said Ingram, "that guy flew out here and gave his life for us."

"Maybe he has something," muttered Mordkin.

DeWitt absently pulled at his lower lip. "What are you suggesting?"

Mordkin said, "The band equipment room is just down the hall. Shouldn't be too hard to find a trumpet. If he can play one, fine. Send him on his way. Otherwise, we talk a little more with Cryptographer Technician Second Class Walter Radtke."

Artillery rumbled overhead making the ground vibrate. The lamps swung on their cords again, this time in an oval pattern. Furniture rattled and concrete dust and chips cascaded, adding to the coat of thick, hoary pumice coating the cellblock's horizontal surfaces. Finally, DeWitt sighed, "Alright. Hurry."

Radtke said with an edge to his voice, "Sir, I'm overdue at the boat landing."

"You'll wait, Sailor," DeWitt said.

DeWitt nodded to Mordkin, who dashed out. He paced up and down, hearing a prolonged squeak echo from down the passageway. That was followed by a ripping and tearing of wood. Something clattered to the concrete and soon, Carl Mordkin jogged inside with a shiny black case. He handed it to Major DeWitt with a smirk.

DeWitt nodded to Radtke.

Mordkin stepped to Radtke handing the case to him.

Radtke said, "Sir, this isn't fair. I'm being harassed."

Mordkin said in a low gravelly voice, "Play it, or you're up shit's creek."

Radtke stood straight. "I'm sorry, Sir, but this is extremely unfair. And as you pointed out, I'm under orders from Admiral Nimitz. I respectfully request that I be released and allowed to proceed in accordance with my orders."

Ingram mimicked a falsetto. "'...proceed in accordance with my orders.' Play the trumpet, you bastard," he yelled. Even as he said it, it struck Ingram that Radtke was very cool. And, for some reason he felt wary, almost scared. How could this man, the one who murdered Dwight Epperson, stand there and lie? Radtke was very controlled and didn't act like the sailors who stood before Ingram at Captain's Mast, accused of drunkenness or petty theft. Unlike those, who sniveled and begged to stay out of the brig, this one was very composed. Very much in control. An actor.

"Sir. I protest," said Radtke.

All eyes fixed on Radtke.

Ingram grinned. "He protests, gentlemen."

The Marine sergeant stepped silently before Radtke. Looking the sailor up and down, he eased the case from Mordkin's hands and flipped the latches open. A gleaming brass-lacquered Conn trumpet lay nestled in purple velvet lining. A filigreed brass placard inside announced the owner's initials: LTS. The sergeant removed the trumpet and lay the case on a table. With a dirty thumb, the sergeant flipped open a small compartment in the case, found the mouthpiece, and tapped it in the trumpet.

"Well?" said DeWitt.

Radtke took in their faces, then peered at the ground with pressed lips.

The Marine slapped the trumpet against the man's stomach, none too gently.

Radtke sighed and braced his back against the wall. Staring at Ingram, he accepted the trumpet from the sergeant. His fingers worked the piston valves and he licked his lips two or three times.

Mordkin said, "Go on, swabbie. Blow the damn thing."

Radtke blew. The horn shrieked erratically like a child playing for the first time.

DeWitt said, "I'll be damned."

"No one touches him. The bastard is mine," yelled Ingram triumphantly.

In a semicircle, they started toward Cryptography Technician Second Class Walter A. Radtke.

Radtke raised the gleaming Conn to his lips and blew again. The first two bars of The Star-Spangled Banner floated beautifully from the instrument's bell.

"Son of a bitch," said Mordkin. The men stopped in mid step.

Radtke took a deep breath and played again. The rest of the national anthem pealed elegantly from the trumpet, with the men mesmerized as if hearing it for the first time. They almost stood to attention. Radtke's notes were long, confident, and exquisitely executed as he played with closed eyes.

He finished. The room was silent. It took long moments for them to realize shells pounded overhead.

"Wow," said Mordkin. "That was beautiful, Sailor."

"May I go now, Sir?" Radtke asked.

DeWitt's mouth worked. At length he said, "Yes, of course."

"Thank you, Sir." Radtke grabbed his duffle and walked out.

DeWitt said to Hadley, "Lieutenant, take your men and return to Corregidor. I'm staying the night in Captain Plummer's quarters, if you need me. I caution all of you not to repeat anything you heard in here. Is that clear?"

"Yes, Sir," said Lieutenant Hadley. He and the two Marines walked out.

DeWitt said to Mordkin, "That's all we can do for now. I don't want this man assigned to punitive duties. No filling sandbags or nonsense like that. He might talk casually of something we don't want the Japs to hear. And I mean what I say about everyone here keeping their mouths shut. Is that clear?" DeWitt walked toward the door saying, "Make sure he doesn't--" He paused in mid-sentence.

Mordkin said, "Uh, what's wrong, Sir?"

DeWitt said, "Shhh."

They listened, hearing shells pound. Then, long mournful notes of a horn echoed to them. They almost stood on tiptoe while straining to hear.

Ingram's eyes snapped to the open trumpet case. The lacquered brass Conn was not there.

Mordkin cocked his head. "Far away. Must be up on A-level by now near the entrance."

DeWitt's eyes darted through the bars to Ingram.

Ingram sat back on the cot. Looking straight at DeWitt he said, "Son of a bitch is laughing at you."

"Bastard," growled DeWitt.

"You think that's him?" asked Mordkin.

"Has to be," said DeWitt. His face was flushed.

Mordkin said, "What the hell's wrong, Major?"

DeWitt's fists bunched. "I grew up in San Antonio."

Mordkin smirked, "You never let us forget that."

DeWitt said absently, "Ingram may be right. That guy's laughing at us."

"What?" said Mordkin.

"He's playing the 'Deguello.'"

Mordkin took a chance. "Texas bullshit."

Whether serious or in jest, DeWitt normally would have taken profound issue with his subordinate's wisecrack. But he ignored Mordkin. Veins bulged on his face and he turned red saying, "1836. Santa Ana took the Alamo. It was a thirteen-day siege and he lost over fifteen hundred men for only one hundred eighty-three Texans. That's about the odds the Japs have on us now, isn't it? And that Sonofabitch killed all the defenders; Colonel Travis, Jim Bowie, Davy Crockett, everybody."

Mordkin said. "That's right. Jack Armstrong and Captain Midnight got Congressional Medals of Honor posthumously," he snickered.

DeWitt grabbed Mordkin's lapels and pulled him close. He yelled making spittle flew in Mordkin's face. "I'm serious, you stupid bastard! That man's playing the *'Deguello.'* It was played during the Alamo's siege--like the Japs are doing to us right now. *Deguello* means 'no prisoners.' Think about that!" He thrust Mordkin against the wall and walked to the door, looking up the stairwell.

Mordkin shook his head and straightened his soiled khaki shirt, in a beleaguered attempt to recover dignity.

Ingram stood and turned his head slightly. The trumpet's notes came again to him true, whole, and mournful. And although the soloist was farther away now, the bars still drifted from A-level down the stairwell with authority and determination. As if what had happened in 1836 was happening again. A curse.

Gripping the bars tightly, Ingram looked down feeling as if he stood before a firing squad. The hood yanked over his head had been used before; the black cloth had the smell of death. The squad had just worked their bolts home with a clatter and were poised to pull triggers. At that time, all that remained of his life on this planet would be the last guttural shout.

He sat and muttered, "No prisoners.

PART II

The Imperial Japanese forces have entered on the wings of victory.

Hideki Tojo, Prime Minister Of Japan

Corregidor needs no comment from me. It has sounded its own epitaph on enemy tablets. But through the bloody haze of its last reverberating shot, I shall always seem to see a vision of grim, gaunt, men, still unafraid.

General Douglas Macarthur
On Learning Of Corregidor's Surrender

JAPANESE IMPERIAL HEADQUARTERS ORDER, 5 MAY, 1942:

BY COMMAND OF HIS IMPERIAL MAJESTY TO COMMANDER IN CHIEF YAMAMOTO OF THE COMBINED FLEET:

1. THE COMMANDER IN CHIEF OF THE COMBINED FLEET IS TO COOPERATE WITH THE ARMY IN THE OCCUPATION OF MIDWAY AND STRATEGIC POINTS IN THE WEST OF THE ALEUTIANS.
2. DETAILED DIRECTIONS WILL BE GIVEN BY THE CHIEF OF THE NAVAL GENERAL STAFF.

18

3 May 1942
Marinduque Island
Philippines

Helen Durand hid behind the staircase of Fito Diaz's house. Bullets stitched the walls, the noise like knives punching into a rice-filled gunny sack. Kneeling beside her was Doña Valentina Diaz, Fito's petite wife. She held her ears, swallowing rapidly with soundless cries. Everyone was pulled within themselves fighting their fears, real and imagined. In the living room, Helen saw two Army colonels and a Navy commander huddled under the piano, whimpering each time a bullet zipped through or glass tinkled.

The reason the Japanese hadn't yet stormed the house was those crazy Army pilots upstairs wouldn't give in. Seven enemy bodies littered the veranda as the pilots fought back with ancient regular army, and were untrained in coordinated assault, merely bullies, thugs, detritus. And fighting beside the pilots upstairs was Pablo Amador, the Filipino resistance leader and statesman who told the legend of Corregidor the night Helen had been evacuated to the *Wolfish*.

Someone shouted on the second floor. "Grenade!"

There was an explosion, screams, tinkling glass. Someone ran down the staircase, tore open the front door and stood in the doorway shouting unintelligibly. A breathless Amador charged after him. "Catch him. Gone berserk," he wheezed.

Helen stood, but it was too late. The man, a lieutenant colonel, seemed frozen in time, jerking and jinking as slugs tore through him. She jammed a fist in her mouth as the lieutenant colonel pitched into the black and white tiled foyer and fell on his back, his arms splayed.

Still having great momentum, Amador dove over the corpse and tumbled into the living room as Fito Diaz ran behind the door kicked it shut, and fell flat. A submachine gun opened up, drilling four holes diagonally across the door's ornate paneling.

Doña Valentina screamed. "Fito!"

Quickly, Diaz rolled across the hardwood floor into the relative safety of the dining room just as another fusillade of bullets hit the door, chewing it to pieces, blowing it off its hinges. But somehow, it didn't fall over, and stood jammed in the doorway.

There was a lull. Helen sank against the wall incredulous at how fast this had happened. The *Wolfish* had landed them on Marinduque the night before last when two bancas appeared and Fito Diaz, a local fishing baron, took them ashore around midnight. The Diazes had treated them well, scattering the thirty exhausted evacuees around the beautiful, twelve-room, antebellum home. There was plenty to eat, clean sheets, even hot water for bathing, something Helen had not luxuriated in since last January. Up until a few minutes ago, they were preparing to catch the interisland steamer and head to Mindanao with Pablo Amador.

Instead, Japanese had surrounded the house and opened fire without warning.

Amador, lying in the broad living room doorway shouted across the foyer, "Fito. That's Lieutenant Tuga out there."

"Tuga? Here?"

"Can't miss that stupid white suit. Too bad we're such poor shots. How did he find out?"

"Roberto, I think." spat Diaz. "He didn't show up for work yesterday morning. Nor today."

Amador rolled over, looked up at the ornate ceiling and sighed, "The Hapons pay well."

"Roberto won't live out the week. You can be sure his head will end up in a Hapon stewpot. Even if I am dead." He looked over to Valentina and gave a wan smile. Valentina, now twenty-four, was Diaz's second wife. The fifty-five-year-old Diaz had lost his first wife to tuberculosis eight years ago. He'd married Valentina as a child bride five years ago and they were very happy, with two daughters, ages two and four, fortunately visiting an uncle on Cebu. Diaz also had a son by his first marriage, now serving in the Filipino Scouts on Mindanao.

"Fito." she said softly.

The house shook as another grenade exploded in back. This time there were screams outside and cheers from upstairs.

Doña Valentina hugged herself with her arms and fell against the wall. Helen moved close and put an arm around her shoulder, "Valentina, I'm sorry."

The woman shrugged. "Fito, always talking. Always so flamboyant. His bluster helped him to become Marinduque's fishing king. But look at this..." She waved a hand.

"Who is Tuga?" Helen asked.

Doña Valentina sobbed something.

"Who?"

"*Kempetai.*"

"What's that?"

"Thought police. They torture you." Patterned after the Nazi SS, the civilian-clad *Kempetai* was a stepchild of Prime Minister General Hideki Tojo. Years ago, he had used it with great effect to crush the rebellious officer corps of Japan's Kwangtung Army based in China. Now, the *Kempetai* were responsible for ferreting out those suspected of improper loyalties at home and in the new provinces of Japan's Greater East Asia Co-Prosperity Sphere. Citizens everywhere were encouraged to spy on one another, then inform the *Kempetai*.

Helen shuddered. "What can I do?"

"I don't know. I think we're finished. The best thing we can do is to get Senior Amador out of here."

"How?"

"The cellar. There is a secret closet. A cache actually, where Fito keeps all his stupid guns." Tears ran. She turned. Helen and Doña Valentina threw their arms around each other. "There is only room for one. Not even," her body racked with sobs as the Japanese started firing again, "room for my babies."

Helen looked in the living room. One of the Army colonels had taken heart and now popped away with an old Springfield bolt-action rifle. "Why Amador?"

Valentina turned and looked at Helen. "You don't know?"

"No."

"The Amador and Diaz families have been close for decades. Fito and Pablo are among Manuel Quezon's favorites; both are important to the resistance. Fito here, Pablo in Mindanao." Helen nodded having heard about the situation in Mindanao, the southernmost of the major Philippine Islands. The politics there were hideous; fractionated cells jabbed at each other from village to village, some with warlords who went on killing sprees. And then there were the Moros of Western Mindanao.

The colonel cranked his bolt trying to get off a shot, but instead screamed as enemy rifle fire chewed the window frame. The Springfield clattered to the floor and the colonel fell next to it holding his head.

"Pablo, go!" said Diaz. He rose and crawled into the living room, picked up the rifle, and fired out the window. Three other Americans joined him and began shooting. The four were doing a decent job snapping off their rounds, Helen noticed, and there was plenty of ammunition.

"Fito," said Amador.

"Damnit, Amador, get going," shouted Whitney, a blond, curly haired pilot.

"Si!" The silver- haired Amador ran around the staircase and hugged Doña Valentina fiercely. "I won't let them take you to Santo Tomas."

She howled, burying her face into Amador's chest, "It'll be Santiago for Fito." Soon after the Japanese occupation of Manila in January of 1941, Santo Tomas, a university founded in the 1700s, was converted to house civilian prisoners. Santiago, on the other hand, was an old Spanish prison on Manila's Pasaig River. Used for military prisoners, it had original Spanish implements of torture such as quartering racks and giant cauldrons for boiling humans alive. There was one feature the *Kempetai* appreciated with relish.

Locking prisoners in one particular subbasement ensured they drowned when the tide gushed in through barred windows.

Amador pressed his lips together. "I won't let that happen, either."

She took a deep breath, then took his hands and looked up. "No matter. Pablo, you're our future. Go."

Amador kissed her on the forehead. Then he looked at Helen Durand. His eyes flicked down to the Naval Academy ring hanging by a lanyard around her neck. He palmed it for a moment, and then said, "He's a fine man."

"I hardly know him," Helen said. *Why did I say that?*

"Better not let the Hapons see it." With a thin smile, he kissed Helen's forehead as well. "*Via con Dios.*" Amador ran across the foyer, opened a small door, and was gone.

Within minutes, the shooting became louder, more intense. Multiple explosions shook the house, and guttural screams from outside mixed with the screams of death and pain from inside. Smoke grenades crashed through the window. Helen couldn't breathe, smoke filled her lungs; claustrophobic and desperate for air, she jumped up and ran for the kitchen. Tearing open the door, she charged into a grunting Japanese soldier, a stocky, grotesque man wearing a bug-eyed gas mask with a hose connected to a canister mounted on his back. He thrust her aside and ran into the foyer firing his rifle. Several more soldiers followed, their shouts muffled by gas masks.

Helen fell against the door jamb and back into the foyer as more soldiers careened through. Several Americans tumbled down the stairs. One was thrown through the rail upstairs and fell screaming horribly, crashing on the tile floor right before Helen as another soldier stepped up and shot him through the head.

A rough hand grabbed Helen's elbow. With a howl of pain, she rose and stumbled across the foyer. At a shout, the front door heaved open and fell across the lieutenant colonel's body with a crash. Immediately, there was a breeze and the smoke cleared. The Japanese soldier holding Helen took off his gas mask and breathed deeply, turned to her and smiled, speaking Japanese in a low voice. Another soldier found Doña Valentina and dragged her beside Helen.

Behind them more prisoners were pitched down the stairs. Soldiers shouted and the Americans who couldn't rise immediately were shot where they lay. After a while, ten or so of the original thirty stood on the veranda, their hands in the air.

A soldier at the door snapped to attention and saluted. The soldiers guarding Helen and Doña Valentina did the same.

First, Helen saw a shadow, then a civilian stepped over a body and walked into the foyer. He was tall for a Japanese, at least six three, weighed close to 195, had a pockmarked face and a long, curved nose with a thick, almost Hitleresque moustache; his eyebrows were bushy, and a thick lower lip hung halfway down his chin. He wore an immaculate, starched white suit and white buckskin shoes.

He walked up to Doña Valentina and examined her for a moment, then shouted something in Japanese. Two other soldiers dragged Fito Diaz through the doorway and dumped him on the door.

"So, your lordship. Been having fun with your little spy games?" Helen was amazed at how good the man's English was.

Diaz's face was bloody and his left arm hung at a grotesque angle. Sobbing quietly, Diaz rose to his knees and looked at the white-suited man. "I am a fisherman, Lieutenant Tuga," he gurgled.

"A fisherman, we'll see." Lieutenant Tuga pointed to the beautifully crafted paneling under the staircase and spoke quietly to the soldier at the door.

"*Kashikomarishita!*" The soldier stepped in the foyer and with his rifle butt bashed at the paneling. Splinters flew as he grunted, thumped and smacked. Soon, he found a spot that made a hollow sound and gave four hard whacks. The paneling gave way, revealing a radio transmitter receiver and several manuals. The soldier bowed and stepped back.

Tuga stepped up, waved at the radio, and said, "Ummm, Halicrafters, I see. A nice one, too. And you're a fisherman you say?" He spoke as he pulled a pistol, a Nambu, from his waistband, sighted it at the ceiling and ran the action. "How often do you radio the fish?"

"The devil with you, Tuga," Diaz shouted, red spittle spewing before him.

"You first!" Tuga whirled and shot Diaz twice, both quick rounds going through his head.

Doña Valentina screamed and rushed for her husband. Tuga waved a hand and four grinning soldiers dragged her off to the dining room.

Through Valentina's screams Helen heard Tuga say, "And you are the nurse, Helen Durand?"

Clothing ripped, men laughed, Valentina's screams ripped at the morning's cool air.

"Nurse Durand?" Tuga said louder.

"What?" Helen looked at Tuga. "Who are you? What kind of animal are you?" Helen pointed to the dining room door. "Make them stop."

"You're lucky I don't give you to them. You're mine. We'll have our own private sessions." Tuga nodded to another soldier. Helen was led out and with the others, loaded into a stake truck. Over the next twenty minutes, everyone except Tuga took their turn. Valentina's screams became raspy, then pitiful, scratching moans.

Finally, a single shot rang out: It was quiet. The American's bodies were stripped where they lay. Next, the soldiers dumped gasoline in the house. The broken American corpses were pitched through the front door, and then the house set afire, the captives looking on in horror.

The five-truck convoy drove off into a morning that grew hot and dusty. Helen's truck bounced heavily on the dirt road and the Japanese sergeant sitting next to her let himself fall across her lap from time to time. With a broad smile, he pushed himself off by placing his hands on her thighs and letting them linger. Giving him the foulest of looks, Helen Durand scooted forward and looked back just once, seeing a tall column of smoke rise above Marinduque's thick forest.

19

6 May 1942
Malinta Tunnel, Lateral 3
Corregidor Island, Manila Bay, Philippines

Otis DeWitt cradled the field telephone and stood to one side, as generals Moore and Wainwright argued. Both looked drained. In fact, all in the command center were haggard; most hadn't slept in two days. And last night the bombardment reached a terrible peak, where it seemed a shell rattled their teeth every two seconds.

About ten-thirty it abruptly stopped. A half-hour later, the first landing craft wallowed ashore at East Point and Japanese troops poured out. The fighting was bloody, with Americans and Filipinos almost throwing them back into Manila Bay. But by morning, the counterattack fizzled and the Japanese fought their way over Water Tank Hill. Now, at nine-thirty, they stood two hundred yards from Malinta Tunnel's east end.

Inside the command bunker the air was dense and humid, condensation beaded on the walls, and all three toilets were stopped up. Even with doors closed, the place smelled like a sewer. Everything remotely classified was being burned, and smoke crowded the ceiling. To go outside and burn the stuff gave one a good chance of being killed by artillery, so they wore soaked handkerchiefs over their faces and breathed as lightly as possible.

Moore slammed his fist. Pencils and paperclips jumped on DeWitt's desk. "Damnit, Jon," he shouted. "I'm not going to have my boys chopped up like on Bataan. I say we hold."

In spite of the living hell overhead, General Wainwright looked tall and cool, and in command. Incongruous was that his nickname was "Skinny"; a tag that followed him all the way from West Point. Especially now, he was a tall sack of bones and sinew with red blotches around his temples. His eyelids drooped and his voice seemed hoarser than usual. Yet, he was steady and self-assured. "Here's the crux, George," said Wainwright. "Hong Kong and Singapore surrendered at night. The Japs raped and shot everything in sight until--"

"That's what I'm saying, Jon," said Moore. "We can hold out. Two, three days. Maybe a week. Make 'em negotiate."

"Listen to me, damnit," yelled Wainwright. "Those surrenders were at night. The little bastards were full of saki. Jap officers couldn't control their troops. That's why I'm thinking of doing it now."

With his buttocks, DeWitt edged aside a pile of SECRET documents and sat on his desk waiting for the machine gun outpost to come back on the line. He picked up a message Wainwright had handed him and read it again:

TO: MAJOR GENERAL JONATHAN M. WAINWRIGHT
FROM: THE COMMANDER IN CHIEF
DATE: 5 MAY, 1942
YOUR DEFENDERS OF CORREGIDOR ARE LIVING SYMBOLS OF OUR WAR AIMS AND THE GUARANTEE OF VICTORY.
FDR

An anemic looking corporal, wearing a stained, olive-drab T-shirt, boots, and shorts walked up reaching for a pile of classified documents. The corporal raised his canvas burn bag and stuffed papers into it.

DeWitt moved aside noticing the corporal's face was ulcerated with running sores. Handing the man FDR's flimsy, he said, "Here, you might as well take this one, too."

Bony fingers clawed at the message. The corporal's eyes darted over the words and he looked up with a twisted grin. "Shit, Roosevelt. If he wants to be a living symbol of our war aims, I'll gladly trade places with him." Without a glance at DeWitt, the corporal moved to the next desk to stuff more papers in his burn bag.

The corporal vanished behind a bank of filing cabinets before DeWitt could think of something with which to chastise the man. He gave a disgusted grunt and opened a drawer to prop a foot. While Wainwright talked, DeWitt listened for Hager to come back on the line. Hager was a first lieutenant they had sent to the machine gun nest for an assessment. The line was open. Occasionally he heard snapping like fire crackers. Two minutes ago he'd heard a voice shout, "They're over that rise. Try again." Then there was a hollow thump and, strangely, no machine gun fire.

DeWitt bent to knock mud off his once shiny boots. The drawer was empty but for a rogue pencil stub and paper clips. Except, deep in the back of this drawer, he spotted something in the shadows. Reaching in, he discovered a water-stained leather pouch, drew it out, and flipped it in his hand absently as he listened.

"Any news, Otis?" said Moore.

DeWitt said, "Not yet, Sir."

"Is Hager still alive?"

"Yessir. I can hear him once in a while. Gunfire sounds closer, though."

"Keep at it."

"Yessir."

Wainwright and Moore kept bickering while DeWitt flipped the pouch in the air. Suddenly, he stopped. This pouch, he remembered, was the one Mordkin had fished out of Manila Bay the night the PBY crashed. It was off the dead man. Mordkin had made a special trip to go back out there that night. After three hours of poking among wreckage, he found a sodden lump and brought it to DeWitt, who promptly threw it in his drawer to dry out. With that, he forgot about it.

Curious.

DeWitt turned it in his hand for a moment, then unzipped it and looked inside. It reeked of mildew but his eyes fixed at the top of the first page. He drew a sharp breath. The stamp of the office of Naval intelligence--ONI--was blemished by green mildew blotches. The letterhead was ONI. It was a memo addressed to COMPHILIPPINES--stamped TOP SECRET. It was to Wainwright.

DeWitt's eyes jerked along the text. Suddenly, he felt cold. "Epperson! Good God," said DeWitt.

"What?" said General Moore.

"Nothing, Sir," said DeWitt. He sat up, rubbing his chin, and scanned the memo again. Flipping inside, he found a photograph of a grinning blondish man with long hair parted in the middle. "No!" said DeWitt.

"Otis, what the hell's wrong with you?" growled Moore.

"General. There's been a mistake," said DeWitt. "I should have--" DeWitt put a hand to his ear, hearing machine gun fire.

A whispering voice crackled on the line. "...Major, can you hear me?"

DeWitt said, "Go ahead Hager."

"The Japs landed a tank. It's fifty yards away, now," Hager's voice was choked. The thirty-caliber machine gun pounded.

"How many tanks?" yelled DeWitt.

"Tank?" Wainwright and Moore looked at DeWitt with open mouths.

The thirty-caliber stopped chattering. In the background, DeWitt heard the loader arguing with the gunner about a fouled breach. "...don't know, Sir." Hager's voice shook. "All I can see is one for now. He's--Jeez--" Something roared and the line went dead.

"Hager! Hager!" shouted DeWitt. He looked at Wainwright and Moore. Both general's faces were ashen.

"Tank, Sir," DeWitt offered. He looked around the command room. All the clerks and messengers and officers stared, their faces incredulous. It became very quiet.

Wainwright's head drooped. An artillery shell rumbled overhead, making concrete chips tinkle down. The general rubbed his face and looked at Moore. Quietly, he said, "Tanks get in the tunnels and a lot of our boys will be squashed. Is that worth holding for?"

Moore dumbly shook his head.

"Sound *PONTIAC*, George."

Moore knew better than to argue. "Yes, Sir."

"Got a pad, Otis?" said Wainwright, sitting heavily.

"Yes, Sir." DeWitt reached in a drawer.

Taking a deep breath, Wainwright looked at the ceiling and said, "This goes to Roosevelt. Make that to the Commander in Chief, Otis."

Everyone's eyes were fixed on Wainwright. Sitting straight up, DeWitt nodded and started writing.

Wainwright was silent for a moment, then said, "With broken heart and head bowed in sadness, but not in shame, I report to your Excellency that today I must arrange terms for the surrender of the fortified islands of Manila Bay. There is a limit of human endurance, and that limit has long since been passed. Without prospect of relief, I feel it is my duty to my country and to my gallant troops to end this useless effusion of blood and human sacrifice."

Wainwright stared at his fingernails. Across the plotting table, a burly sergeant DeWitt had known for ten years, broke down and sobbed.

Another man, the thin corporal with the ulcerated face yelled, "Shit! They ain't takin' me alive. I'm going to the--"

"Silence!" barked Wainwright, slapping a hand on DeWitt's desk. Rising to his feet, his eyes swept the room and he stared each man down. Finally, he said, "Major Drake?"

A man stood. "Yes, General?"

Wainwright's eyes continued sweeping the room. "Make arrangements to detonate the minefield."

"Yes, Sir." Drake said.

"Andrews!" he barked.

"Sir." A youngish colonel shot to his feet.

"Same goes for all ammo bunkers. Make sure they're blown. The artillery, too. You will ensure everything is well spiked. Now, go!"

"Yes, Sir!" Andrews and Drake walked out.

Shells rumbled overhead. Everyone was speechless as Wainwright sat back on a couch and put his head in his hands.

General Moore stared dumbly at the floor.

DeWitt flipped his pad shut and started for the radio room.

"I'm not finished, Otis," said Wainwright.

"Sir?" said DeWitt, turning around.

"I'd like to add this," Wainwright said. He looked to the ceiling and dictated, almost in a gasp, "If you agree, Mr. President, please say to the nation that my troops and I have accomplished all that is humanly possible, and that we have upheld the best traditions of the United States and its Army.

"May God bless and preserve you and guide you and the nation in the effort to ultimate victory. With profound regret and with continued pride in my gallant troops, I go to meet the Japanese commander. Good-bye, Mr. President."

Wainwright looked up to DeWitt with wet, red eyes. "Got that, Major?"

"Yes, Sir," said DeWitt.

Wainwright drew a long breath and said, "George?"

"Huh?" said Moore.

"Come on, George. We have a lot to do."

"Okay, Jon."

"When was the last time we had contact with Caballo?"

"Hour ago," said Moore. "We still can't get through."

"Alright, Otis," Wainwright said. "Take the message to the radio room. Then, I want you to shag over to Caballo and tell them we surrender, effective noon today. I guess white flags will do it for now. Detail two others to Carabao and El Fraile with the same message. I'll send teams later with the formal surrender arrangements."

"Yes, Sir."

Wainwright turned to Moore and sighed, "Let's figure out how we get in touch with the Japs without getting our heads blown off."

DeWitt sat for a moment formatting Wainwright's message for transmission. He started to walk for the radio room, but stopped and retreated to his desk. He stooped and snatched the pouch from his drawer, ensuring no one watched him. All had returned to burning papers and gathering personal articles. Stuffing the pouch in his pocket, Major Otis DeWitt took a long look around Malinta Tunnel's command bunker. Wainwright and Moore were over in a corner bent over a chart. Unaccountably, he swallowed a couple of times and his eyes welled with tears. He loved "Skinny" Wainwright. And he loved George Moore, too. Both had been avuncular, close to being like fathers. He had played poker with them on hot summer evenings and had swilled too many beers with them on the golf course.

Unaccountably, Otis DeWitt knew he wouldn't be seeing generals Wainwright and Moore for a long while. Maybe never. He was leaving Malinta Tunnel for the last time.

20

6 May 1942
Baker Cellblock, Fort Hughes Stockade
Caballo Island, Manila Bay, Philippines

Hands folded under his head, Ingram lay on his back in dank, semidarkness listening to the shelling. A damp handkerchief was stretched over his mouth, but even with that, putrid dust seeped so that he breathed in shallow gasps. Rivulets of sweat soaked his shirt and trousers and occasionally, his body spasmed as a shell landed overhead, shaking the cellblock and making powdered concrete and loose dirt sprinkle down.

A corporal had brought water and canned salmon twice a day, the mixture tasting like slurried cardboard. But once, Ingram had been given hot tea: It felt wonderful on his throat. Bunk rest had helped, the bombardment notwithstanding. His facial bruises didn't hurt as much and the throbbing in his cheek had subsided. Trouble was, his Bulova watch had wound down during one of his catnaps and he'd lost track of the time and even what day it was.

Now, the bombardment seemed different. Its rhythm was deliberate, spaced. Each shell seemed thoughtfully positioned and more powerful than the last. Like rolling thunder, the intensity cycled up and down Caballo Island like a sine wave peaking every ten minutes.

Winding his watch, he reckoned they were in the cycle's seventh minute and due for another pasting overhead, when an iron door grated loudly outside. Men shouted, then another iron door clanked and rattled. The yelling became louder. Lights snapped on and a bony Fred Holloway stumbled into the cellblock.

His eyes were savage as he scanned the cells. "Skipper!" he yelled.

Ingram jumped up and grabbed the bars. "Over here."

Holloway ran up, his face flush.

Mordkin followed closely behind saying, "You can't do this. I don't have authorization to release him yet."

"Forget it. We're surrendering," Holloway yelled over his shoulder. "Where's the key?"

Mordkin waved a .45 and cocked it. "Step back you sonofabitch."

"Look out!" yelled Ingram.

As Holloway spun, Junior Forester piled through the door and, with feet churning, jumped on Mordkin's back, knocking the pistol aside. Sunderland charged in, hitting the stockade captain in the side of his head with a beefy fist. Mordkin groaned and sank to the floor unconscious.

Holloway rattled the bars. "Where the hell are the keys?"

Ingram pointed to Mordkin. "In his pocket."

While Sunderland and Forester bent to search Mordkin, Ingram asked, "What time is it?"

"Almost 1530," Holloway answered.

Ingram shook his head, thoroughly confused. "What day?"

Holloway covered his ears, the bombardment near the ten-minute intensity peak. "Jesus. Sounds like a damned freight train in here. It's Thursday, May sixth. Todd, are you alright?"

"I think so. What's going on?"

"No keys," shouted Sunderland, looking up from Mordkin's body.

Ingram pointed toward the door, "Try the cabinets. Isn't there a desk of some kind out there?"

Sunderland and Forester dashed out the door. Holloway turned and said, "Japs made an amphibious assault on Corregidor's east end about midnight last night. By this morning, they'd taken over half the Rock. Then, a couple of hours ago, white flags popped out over Topside and Monkey point."

Holloway took a deep breath. "Big snafu in HQ here. We lost radio contact with the Rock. Nobody knows what's going on. Just before noon, the brass decided to surrender and ran white flags up, too. It was quiet for a while but the damned Japs started shelling and bombing again! During the lull a bunch of guys ran for the tunnel entrance for fresh air." With wide eyes, Holloway spread his arms. "Wham! Direct hit. Everybody dead. Forty dumb, happy guys just standing around breathing fresh air and thinking their war was over. You should see--"

"Fred," said Ingram. "Take it easy."

Looking at the floor, Holloway grit his teeth, then pounded withered hands on the bars. "They didn't have a chance. I wish I knew what all this means."

"Fred, damnit!" Ingram said sharply. "What it means is that it's time to get out of here."

Forester lunged into the room jangling a key ring in the air. He tried several. After a half-minute of cursing and scraping, he found one that twirled in the lock. The door opened and they ran past a groaning Mordkin up the stairs to the main level.

Their running was more of a wheezing fast walk, as they carved a path through men of all ranks and uniforms. Some stood or sat by themselves, while others gathered in little groups. With slumped shoulders and hung heads, their sweaty, unshaven faces were gaunt; their bodies scarecrow thin. Some spoke in low, stilted tones, while others smoked in spite of the humidity and dust. Most just stared at the wall.

MPs walked up and down shouting with hoarse voices, "...weapons. Weapons, please. Turn in your weapons. Here, Sailor. That goes for you. Toss that knife..."

Every fifty feet or so, they ran past a pile of rifles, pistols, swords, bolo knifes, hand grenades, loose ammunition, and web belts. On second glance, one could pick out the odd weapon such as stilettos, ice picks, even zip guns.

Hazy sunlight beckoned from the tunnel's mouth and they broke into a breathless jog. Suddenly, a young Army captain with a bandaged face and wild eyes moved before them on crutches and held out stick-thin arms. "Stop! Where are you going?"

They dashed past the man with Ingram sputtering, "Where is everybody?"

"Not sure," puffed Holloway. "Rocky was supposed to have rounded 'em all up. We were to meet up front."

They drew up twenty feet from the entrance. Ingram looked around saying, "Well, where are they?"

"Don't know. Should we wait?" said Holloway.

Even with shells erupting and thick smoke curling, Ingram felt drawn to the living hell outside. Especially after his seven days in the cellblock and the constant thunder overhead. He looked at the tunnel faces. Most stared at the concrete. Some watched with doomed, forlorn eyes. Yes, freedom was outside no matter what happened.

"Have you lined up anything?" Ingram said.

Holloway said, "We have that shore boat. The 51 Boat."

"Good. Anybody guarding it?"

"No."

"Wonderful. How about fuel?"

"Half a tank," said Holloway.

"Anything else?"

Holloway shrugged. "We just broke from our assignments. I grabbed Forester from the mortar pit and bumped into Sunderland in the main tunnel, near the command post. We really haven't had a chance to do a damn thing."

Ingram turned to Sunderland. "All that stuff we pulled off the bird. Do you know where it is?"

Sunderland coughed and cleared his throat. "We stashed it in a shed near the small boat landing."

"Good," said Ingram. "Let's load up, find our boys, and get out of here."

"Uh, Sir?" said Sunderland.

"What?"

"That shed took a direct hit two days ago, Sir."

The three stared at Sunderland for a moment.

"This isn't looking too good," said Holloway. He thought of the *Pelican*, wishing they hadn't been so careful planting demolition charges. Nothing was salvageable and only a portion of her mast stuck above the water on the other side of Caballo. He muttered, "No gas, no chow. No navigation gear. No nothing."

"You want to join up with the rest of these guys and get captured?" said Ingram, nodding back in the tunnel.

"I didn't say that, Skipper," Holloway said quickly.

The men studied the pavement and kicked concrete chips for a minute.

Ingram said, "Okay. I've got an idea."

"What?" said Holloway.

"The *Pima*," said Ingram.

They stared at him.

Ingram said, "There's a lot of work to do. Come on! Let's get down there!" He started toward the entrance.

"Hold on there." A man stepped up and grabbed Ingram by the shoulders. Ingram shook loose and stumbled into a metal cabinet, hitting his face. He staggered away holding a throbbing cheek and it took long moments to shake the cobwebs. Finally, Ingram focused into the pallid face of Otis DeWitt.

Holloway slipped in between them saying, "Outta the way, Major."

DeWitt blinked and stepped back. "Wait," he said. "I want to go."

Ingram was about shake his head when they heard a commotion deep inside the tunnel. He stepped on an ammo crate and peered into the gloom. After a moment he said, "Mordkin."

DeWitt said, "Look. I'll take care of him. What's important is that you were right about Radtke. I have to go with you. He must be stopped."

Stripped of pomposity, DeWitt seemed comical standing before them with a plaintive expression. Ingram opened his mouth to speak, but just then an aerial bomb smacked just below the entrance, sending smoke twirling around them. At length, he croaked out, "Where is Radtke?"

"Made it aboard the submarine as far as I know." DeWitt patted the pouch now jammed in his belt. "That's why I'm here."

Shouts echoed from Mordkin's direction. The commotion grew, and Ingram peered seeing the Stockade Captain was closer. And he had two MPs in tow. All three brandished .45s. Mordkin's face lighted up when he picked out Ingram. "Stop! Those men are deserters." he yelled.

Ingram jumped off the ammo case shaking his head. "Where the hell does he think we're going to desert to? Mexico City? Can't you reason with him?"

DeWitt said, "Certainly." He stood on the crate and thrust both hands in the air. "Captain Mordkin," he shouted. "I order you to--"

From twenty feet away, Mordkin fired his .45. The shot zipped over DeWitt's shoulder and spent itself in the ceiling; the booming echo rang in their ears.

Mordkin shrieked, "Everybody! On the floor, now!"

All within fifty feet hit the deck. Still standing, Ingram and the others were easy targets.

"Raise your hands," shouted Mordkin.

"That Sonofabitch gone loony," growled DeWitt. "Captain," he yelled, "You are subject to my orders. I'm--"

A series of rounds landed near the entrance, knocking them to the ground. Quickly, an enormous dust cloud swirled over them.

"Now!" barked Ingram. As one, they rose and charged into the murk, not seeing two feet before them until well outside the tunnel. They burst from smoke and falling dirt and stones. Ingram took the lead, running toward a concrete stairway with a rusted iron railing and long treads that wound toward the beach.

They ran as fast as their emaciated bodies could stumble. They had scrambled a quarter of the way down when a twin-engine Betty bomber roared over at treetop level. A salvo of eight 250-kilogram bombs whistled toward them. Ingram sprang off the stairway into a shell crater.

He tumbled in just as the stick of bombs raced over the hill. The concussion knocked Ingram across the crater where he balled up clutching his hands over his head. Dirt, concrete chunks, pieces of metal, and sticks of jagged tree limbs cascaded around him.

Ingram rose, choking. And he realized he couldn't hear. DeWitt and Holloway moved close, with DeWitt opening and closing his mouth while rapidly slapping a palm against his ear; Ingram realized the man was shouting and most likely couldn't hear either.

They looked at one another dully then weaved to their feet. Ingram shook his head to regain his vision, then checked the tunnel but it was still engulfed in smoke. Mordkin and his MPs hadn't followed.

He nodded toward the landing, and they bumped and stumbled their way down the steps, gaining the beach five minutes later. Staggering around barbed wire and shell craters, they fell into an abandoned machine gun pit. After staring at Holloway's back for five minutes, Ingram realized the shelling had stopped and the droning of airplane engines receded. He also realized he could hear again and looked up to see a formation of twelve Bettys heading north over Bataan.

What struck him was that there were no explosions. Wisps of smoke drifted among them and he blinked, trying to remember the last time his world wasn't filled with thumping, shrieking explosions. There were no massive air-compressing concussions; no ground-lifting, ear-splitting eruptions; no incredulous screams of the dying. Instead, there was silence, sweet silence.

"What the hell?" said Holloway. Sunderland stood and spun slowly with his arms straight out. Soon they all rose with grins, realizing the bombardment had really stopped. At first, it seemed stifling as if imaginary bindings had been cast loose. But they were unsure of which direction to tread. To the best of Ingram's recollection, it was the first time in weeks a single minute had elapsed without a shell detonating nearby.

He looked toward Corregidor seeing what looked like a bedsheet waving on Topside. Another flew over Monkey Point. Even so, explosions rained along the three-mile-long Rock with thick smoke engulfing much of the west end. "Why do the Japs keep shooting? Our white flags are out." Ingram said.

DeWitt put his hands on his hips. "The surrender's not well coordinated. See that?" He pointed to the west end. "Some guys are still holding out. Looks like hand-to-hand fighting."

Ingram checked the sun's angle, judging the time to be about four o'clock. "Let's go!"

They rose and walked a few paces for the dock. Suddenly, Sunderland raised his hand. "Back," he urged in a raspy whisper.

They jumped into an empty machine gun nest, watching a long, narrow launch, flying a Japanese naval ensign, round the pier and tie up. Four Japanese officers, wearing swords, got out and walked toward them, stopping at the bottom of the stairway, not thirty feet from their refuge.

"There," whispered Holloway.

A tight-lipped sergeant, carrying a white flag tied to a bamboo stick, walked down the steps and drew up to the officers. Soon, the GI was joined by a U.S. Army colonel, two majors, and a captain.

Ingram pointed to the army captain and whispered, "Isn't that Plummer?"

Sunderland nodded, recognizing men he'd served with in Caballo's mortar pits. "And La Follette's carrying the flag."

Junior Forester, on his haunches, stumbled and put his hand out to brace himself. His knuckles grazed a half-empty ammunition case which fell over, spilling thirty-caliber shells. The bright brass rounds clanked and tinkled, and another ammo box toppled on Forester's hand, cutting it. "Ouch," he yelped.

Japanese and American officers swiveled their heads in their direction.

"Sorry." Forester sheepishly bit his hand.

"You stupid dodo. If we die, I'm gonna kill you," Sunderland whispered savagely. Then, realizing what he'd said, his face turned crimson.

Ingram counted to two hundred, then peeked over the berm. La Follette, Plummer, and his party walked up the steps. At the launch, the Japanese climbed in, took in their lines, and shoved off.

"Let's not push our luck," Ingram said.

They dashed for the docks and jumped in the 51 Boat. Sunderland hit the starting switch and the engine cranked and cranked. "Com' on, com' on."

But La Follette didn't' get in the boat.

"I don't believe it," said Bartholomew.

"It's time." Ingram grabbed the tiller and nodded to Forester who untied the lines and threw them in. "Let's go," barked Ingram.

Instead, Forester backed away, standing on the dock.

The 51 Boat drifted farther from the dock. "Get in," yelled Ingram.

"Have to find my brother, Sir," said Forester, jabbing his thumb at the hill. He whipped off his white hat and nervously fumbled with it.

Ingram rubbed his chin. "Right. Dig up as many of the rest as you can, too. We'll be back after sunset. Right here."

"Yes, Sir."

"Down!" yelled Holloway.

They dropped, as a sleek, low-wing Japanese Zero curved around, leveled at about fifty feet, and headed toward them. Its two fuselage-mounted 7.7-inch machine guns and twin wing mounted twenty millimeter cannons sputtered, raising ten-foot water spouts. The bullets smashed into the pier, tearing great sections of wood chunks and shredded metal.

The plane roared over at deck level, but miraculously, the 51 Boat was unscathed. Ingram rose, finding Sunderland's thumb still on the starter switch, with an ominous, black greasy cloud slithering from the exhaust pipe. Forester scrambled to his feet, slapping his white hat against his thigh. He jammed it over his head yelling, "Bastard."

"Forester!" Ingram shouted.

"Sir."

"Make sure you find Whittaker. Yardly, too. Now, get going."

"Yessir." Junior Forester ran up the hill to Fort Hughes.

Suddenly, the engine sputtered and burst into life. Ingram grabbed the tiller as Sunderland slammed the boat into gear. With water boiling under her transom, the 51 Boat charged out of Caballo Island harbor.

21

6 May 1942
Abwehr (German Military Intelligence) Headquarters
Berlin, Germany

Rain roared down in sheets as the staff car pulled in front of 74-76
Tirpitzhufer, a four-story stucco building. The driver jumped out and immediately yanked the rear door open. Admiral Karl Dönitz, wearing his white
cap and navy blue great coat, shrugged off his orderly's umbrella and dashed
up the steps into the building. Quickly he gained the top floor and burst into
Admiral Wilhelm Canaris' office unannounced. "Leave us," he yelled at
Colonel Hans Oster, a cavalry officer and Canaris' chief assistant.

Oster, with tunic unbuttoned, walked halfway to the double doors. His
palms spread, the young colonel turned on his heel and looked at his boss,
the head of all German armed forces intelligence.

Canaris smiled, saying, "It's alright, Hans." He turned to Dönitz. "Do you
care for anything, Karl? Schnapps, perhaps?"

Dönitz, wearing dress blue uniform, strode to the window, took off his
hat and greatcoat, pitched them on a small leather couch, and stood

watching sheets of rain cascade down the glass. Through pounding rain, mist, and glistening green leaves of chestnut trees, Dönitz barely made out the oily sheen of the nearby Landwehr Canal.

He was Germany's Chief Flag Officer of U-boats, with the title of Befehlshaber der U-boote or, for short--BdU. Now, BdU stood with his back to them, his hands in his pockets. The humid and stuffy office was made more so by books, reports, magazines, and papers stacked everywhere.

Canaris shrugged. Oster gave a slight bow and backed out, pulling the doors closed silently.

Canaris rubbed deep-set eyes, threw a pencil on his desk, and leaned back. He cursed his luck, for the years had taught him Dönitz was given to moods: The lean and balding admiral would decide where he wanted to sit when he was ready to talk. So Dönitz fumed; Canaris' wooden armchair squeaked as he rocked and waited. At length, he gave up and tried to get things going. "Nice weather you bring from Kiel, Karl. Next time you drop by be sure to bring a case of--"

Dönitz whirled and pointed at the closed door. He hissed, "You'd better muzzle that little clown of yours, Wilhelm."

Canaris' eyebrows went up.

"I just came from Himmler."

"Yes?"

"Colonel Oster does a wonderful goosestep imitation of the führer, Wilhelm. But it's not funny. There is serious innuendo all over the place about him."

"Yes?"

"Damnit, Wilhelm. Don't patronize me. You could get sucked into it, too. The little bastard will drag you down." Dönitz's voice was barely audible.

Canaris had heard every syllable. The World War I U-boat veterans glared at one another. Finally, Canaris looked away and said, "Himmler should go back to what he does best. Pig farming."

Dönitz patrolled the Abwehr office, kicking aside boots, packages, and magazines that lay in his path. "Himmler wants to set you up. His goal is to have all military intelligence units under him. And Oster, if he keeps shooting off his mouth, will be the perfect excuse to pop your balloon."

Canaris' spine stiffened. He was a rival to Himmler, and this had been brewing for a long time. He could no longer depend on his old submarine friend for help. Dönitz, a consummate politician, enjoyed an impeccable reputation for strong loyalty to Hitler.

Without looking, Dönitz knew Canaries' reaction. They'd discussed this before. "That's right, Wilhelm. Himmler. He put a proposal through Bormann, who endorsed it."

Canaris steepled his fingers and rocked in this chair. In spite of the heavy, knit white sweater, dark wool slacks, slippers, and the fire Oster had laid, he suddenly felt cold. "Directly to Hitler?"

"Yes." With thumb and forefinger, Dönitz lifted the front page of the *Völkischer Beobachter* which neatly camouflaged a half-full crystal decanter of schnapps. Searching for a glass, he stooped to look under the couch. "He's thinking of putting your precious little Abwehr under Heydrich."

Canaris couldn't help himself. "Another pig." He pulled open a drawer and handed Dönitz a glass. "Thanks for the tip. Now, what brings you to Berlin?"

Dönitz took the glass and said, "I want you to promise--"

"Karl, I--"

"Promise, damnit, to be careful. And to shut your little Colonel Oster up. Otherwise, Himmler will do it for you. You should consider transferring the little bastard to Russia maybe."

They listened to rain gush down window panes.

"Alright," said Canaris.

BdU nodded and poured. He plunked the decanter precariously near the edge of Canaris' monte verde desk, then, with a forearm, swept a stack of books off the leather couch and sat. "They sent me to Rostok for an on-site report."

"And?"

Dönitz swirled his schnapps, then sipped. "It's as bad as they said. Worse. Thousands dead. Bodies everywhere. The place stinks. You can't see. Smoke. Soot. Rubble. Seventy percent of the city burned to a crisp. The Tommys must have flown two, three hundred planes. They dropped incendiaries into the fire, time and time again."

Canaris looked out the window. "The docks?"

"They'll be alright. Two destroyers damaged. Not as bad as Kiel."

"And was Goering at your meeting?" Reichsmarschall Hermann Goering was Reichsminister of the Luftwaffe, thus responsible for

Germany's air defense. The horror of Rostok was ultimately his responsibility.

Dönitz shook his head. "At Karinhall playing with his shotguns and toy trains."

And you talk about Oster having a big mouth, thought Canaris. "What can I do for you, Karl?"

BdU was silent while Canaris dug out a glass and poured schnapps for himself. The U-boat admiral took the bottle, refilled his glass, sipped; and looked out the window.

Canaris lost patience. "Karl, damnit. I'm busy."

"Yes, yes. I think your report has merit."

"Which one?" The Abwehr generated kilos of paper.

"American torpedoes. How did you do it?"

"Ah, yes. We got two of our people in through basic training in the Great Lakes Naval Station. Then, they were assigned duty in the Navy ordnance laboratory."

"When was the last time you heard from them?"

"Nine weeks ago."

"Then..."

"Yes. They're way overdue."

Recently, Canaris' spies had confirmed American magnetic exploders and depth engines were defective, with their torpedo failure rates soaring to fifty percent. Dönitz's torpedoes suffered similar problems, and he needed to know more. The irony was that the Americans copied early German torpedoes. Then during the 1930s, Germans copied the American designs. But now, BdU shook his head, it seemed Canaris' spies were caught. Dead probably. Hoover didn't waste time.

Dönitz sighed. "Both of them?"

"It looks that way. Have you been able to do anything with what we've given you?"

"At least I stopped the investigation."

"I didn't realize there was one."

Dönitz drank up. "Oh, yes. Himmler sent in Kaltenbrunner to investigate our torpedo experimental laboratory. He court-martialed three of my best technicians. Two were hanged. The other, he sent to the Eastern Front as a private." The admiral slapped his knees. "And, now it turns out the American design is faulty. Too bad Kaltenbrunner can't go to America and hang a few people there. Ehh?" He looked up to Canaris with mirthless eyes.

"And you want us to do what?"

"Penetrate that laboratory again. We need more data on the magnetic exploder designs so we can retrofit."

"I'm not sure. Hoover's G-Men scoop up our people like acorns."

"That's your problem. Fix it." Looking up, BdU's tiny pupils were like embers. "Wilhelm. We've had to revert to the old contact exploders. It could take well over a year to develop a new magnetic design. I must find out what the Americans are doing to retrofit their exploders and depth engines. It will save us an enormous amount of time."

Dönitz had somehow changed, and Canaris felt uncomfortable. BdU had no compassion for anyone, he decided. With no remorse, the man would cut him down as easily as one of his U-Boats putting a helpless tanker under. Canaris shrugged, "We will do our best, Karl."

"Good. And don't let Oster in on this. My torpedo laboratory has been tainted enough."

"Alright." Canaris nodded solemnly hoping his old U-boat friend would never learn he and Oster shared everything. Both were up to their necks in the resistance movement against Hitler. He decided to take a chance and sat forward. "It's well you're here. I need help, too."

Dönitz's face turned blank.

Canaris said, "I need to get word to Oshima right away."

"Then talk to--"

Canaris waved a hand. "Ribbentrop is such an ass. There's just no cooperation. I'd like you to do it." Foreign Minister Joachim von Ribbentrop was the primary contact to General Hiroshi Oshima, Japan's ambassador to the Reich. But what Canaris didn't tell Dönitz was that he had met the Japanese ambassador two years ago during a Führer reception. Then he'd learned from an operative in Britain that the Americans had cracked one of the Japanese political codes. He'd gone to Oshima's office and told him directly. Oshima as much as said Canaris was crazy and that honorable Japanese codes were impenetrable. Canaris lost patience and made the mistake of arguing with the little twit. With loss of face, Oshima sat frozen in his chair. The interview was over. After three minutes of silence, Canaris stood, bowed stiffly, and walked out. None of this was explained to Dönitz.

BdU asked, "What is it?"

"We picked up an NHK broadcast fifteen minutes ago. Corregidor surrendered."

BdU looked in the distance. "The Japanese have all the damned luck." Like an attack periscope, he swung his gaze on to Canaris. "What does Oshima have to do with that?"

Canaris said, "We have a man in there. He could be in a very sensitive position."

"Doing what?"

"Cryptography. He works in the U.S. Navy Radio Intercept Tunnel."

"Wilhelm!" Dönitz almost smiled.

"I inserted him almost a year ago hoping he would be assigned to Hawaii. Instead, he received orders to the Philippines. Before he left, Döttmer told us--"

"Döttmer?"

"Kapitänleutnant Helmut Döttmer. One of my best. But we haven't heard from him since early December. I'm sure he's onto something."

"I see," said Dönitz, rubbing his chin.

Canaris slowly twirled in his chair and looked out seeing the rain had dwindled to a foggy mist. He took a slow sip of schnapps, let it burn on his tongue for a moment, then knocked it back. He spun to face Dönitz. "I need Oshima to tell the Japanese general in the Philippines to order his people to make sure Döttmer is not killed when they occupy Corregidor and sort out prisoners."

"I don't think you have to--"

"Karl," said Canaris, spreading his hands. "Hong Kong. Singapore."

Dönitz slowly nodded

"Tell Oshima at once. I want Döttmer back, please."

"You have specifics?"

"I'll send a description with photo. He's impersonating a sailor by the name of Walter Radtke, cryptographer technician second class."

Dönitz scratched his cheek, "Döttmer. Döttmer. Hmmm. Isn't there a Döttmer that plays for Furtwängler?" Wilhelm Furtwängler was the music director of the Berlin Philharmonic Orchestra.

"His father. Kurt Döttmer. Leads the brass section."

"That's the one."

"One of the best on trumpet. Played for the New York Philharmonic when he lived in America. Was good at jazz, too. Made recordings and formed a quintet when he returned. Himmler had him investigated for playing decadent music and tried to concoct a story passing him off as Jewish. Furtwängler put up such a stink to Goebbels that even Himmler had to back off."

"And the son?"

"Plays as well as his father. Strange though." Canaris stroked his chin. "I had a long talk with the lad one night before his first taste of action."

"Where was that?"

"Greece."

"A cakewalk."

"We didn't know that at the time. He was nervous and handled it well. Turns out he's a virtuoso on the trumpet but hates it. Wanted the violin, but then some roughneck urchins did something to his left hand when he lived in New York making it impossible to play with his left. Outwardly it doesn't look bad. His fourth finger is flexed--cocked and he has no feeling in his little finger. They're both very stiff."

"Is this significant?"

"We were worried about them catching him with the medical records. The real Radtke doesn't have a deformed ring finger. And Döttmer keeps his left hand out of sight anyway from embarrassment. We thought it was worth the chance."

"Elaborate operations have been tripped up for tinier reasons than that."

"I know."

"Tell me. What happened after they wrecked his hand?"

"He was forced into the trumpet. Interesting don't you think? Döttmer hates Americans--they ruined his chance to play the violin and crawl out from under his father's shadow. After the injury, Papa Kurt--his father--tutored him, forced him. Even at that he was a natural and became very accomplished. In fact, his code name for this operation is 'HECKLE.' Because of his--

Dönitz snapped his fingers, "Heckle, Heckle. Don't we do business with them? Electronics, isn't it? Something like that. What do they build?" BdU leaned forward.

"Heckle builds trumpets. The finest available. My code name in this operation is 'BESSON.'"

"So many makers of musical instruments. Why don't we convert them to war production?"

"Besson is French. They make piston-valve trumpets. The best. Heckle is rotary-valve."

"What?" Dönitz's tone was incredulous. "Have you been getting enough sleep, Wilhelm?"

Canaris shrugged.

"Döttmer could be already dead."

"Maybe. But Corregidor is laced with tunnels. He's had a safe place to stay."

Dönitz looked at the crystal schnapps decanter for a moment.

Canaris picked it up and waved it.

Dönitz gave a long sigh, "*Nein*." He stood and picked up his coat. Working his arms into the sleeves, he said, "Very good. Helmut Döttmer known as Walter Radtke. Code name HECKLE. Yes. I can handle Ribbentrop. He sees Oshima almost daily. I'll make sure he takes care of it." Dönitz finished with his buttons and looked down to Canaris. "And you'll put some people on the torpedo project right away?"

"Absolutely."

With thumb and forefinger, BdU placed his cap on his head and squared it over his nose. "Keep Oster away from it."

"Absolutely."

22

6 May 1942
U.S.S. *Pima* (ATF 63)
Aground Caballo Island, Manila Bay, Philippines

Ingram tied the thirty-six-foot shore boat to the *Pima*, a battered tugboat of World War I vintage. The old workhorse had taken a mortal bomb hit in her engine room a few weeks before, and her crew had beached her a few hundred yards north of Caballo's docks. With a thirty-degree list to port, her tall funnel had fallen over, her main deck was awash, and junk littered her topsides. Bobbing next to such a miserable derelict, he figured the 51 Boat would look abandoned, too. And so, the hungry Zeros left Ingram, DeWitt, Holloway, and Sunderland alone to roam inside the wreck.

Almost immediately, Ingram found what he wanted lashed beside the *Pima*'s towing reel on the main deck. For the next forty-five minutes, the four of them, sweating and cursing in the thick, humid heat, wrestled four barrels of diesel fuel aboard the 51 Boat. Each fifty-gallon drum weighed 350 pounds. When it was done, Ingram's tongue hung comically as he sank to the deck splayed on hands and knees.

After resting he went scavenging for whatever else the *Pima* offered, finding charts, sextant, binoculars, flashlights, dividers, and a *Nautical Almanac*; even a *Bible, Book of Common Prayer*, and a hymnal. But there was no Bowditch or Hydrographic publication, both essential for star shots. In the crew compartment, Holloway and DeWitt rescued blankets, clothing, and foul-weather gear. A resourceful Sunderland broke the lock on the gun locker producing four BARs, two Springfield rifles, ammunition, and some dynamite with caps and fuses.

At about five-thirty, Ingram instinctively ducked, hearing the wheeee of artillery shells. Incredulously, he cursed, as the Japanese barrage resumed on Caballo Island, while white flags continued to pathetically flutter from the flagpoles. In short order, the twin engine Bettys once again droned overhead to bomb. Soon, a magazine erupted on the other side of the island, sending trees, boulders, roiling flames and smoke hundreds of feet in the air. Ingram held his ears and thanked God, knowing they would have been killed had the explosion been on this side of the island.

His relief was short-lived when a moment later a stick of bombs raced down the beach, no further than fifty yards past the tilted *Pima*. In a hideously detached way, he listened to his own screaming as he was thrown off the pilothouse deck against tables and bulkheads, while red, garish flames lighted up the space.

It was over. Ingram looked out the porthole finding the bombs had been powerful enough to shift the *Pima* slightly in her grave. Turning back, he sat and stared at DeWitt staring at him. For fifteen minutes, he lay in a world of hideous, horribly vibrating explosions, watching a drop of blood creep from a cut on DeWitt's forehead down the side of his face. But with the return of his hearing came ringing ears and a terrible headache.

The bombardment raged on with artillery, machine gun and rifle fire rattling on Corregidor's west end. On occasion, a flamethrower plume would arch across a hill or into one of the Rock's gullies, eating at pillboxes and artillery bunkers. It was hard to tell who was on which end and, finally, Ingram asked DeWitt, "Our guys have flamethrowers?"

DeWitt choked back a sob, "Not us. Never seen one until now."

The sun's lower limb touched the South China Sea as the barrage raged on. With the others still scavenging the ship, Ingram and DeWitt sat on the pilot-house deck, watching the *Pima*'s bulkhead mounted chronometer: 1806. The clock seemed to go slower and slower. Every minute passed in agony, as the secondhand jerked its spasmodic circular path.

During a lull, a ripping sound echoed up to the bridge.

"What the hell's that?" demanded DeWitt.

"Don't know." Ingram shouted, "Holloway!"

It took a few moments for Holloway, his face bathed in the sunset's crimson glow, to labor up the deckhouse ladder. He was out of breath and finally managed, "Skipper?"

"What's going on?"

Holloway puffed, "Found a void near the after steering lazarette. Damn hatch was double-locked and labeled 'flammable.' Seems the snipes had chow squirreled away. Found several cases of corned beef, canned salmon and a case of tomato juice, large cans."

"Really?" DeWitt licked his lips.

Holloway clambered up the rest of the way and panted, "It's all loaded. Everything. Damn. I'm done in." He flopped to the deck, breathing deeply.

Unspoken was Ingram's worry that the enemy could storm the island before sunset, blocking their departure. He looked at the bulkhead chronometer for the tenth time in the last five minutes: 1817. Then he shot a glance at Holloway and, despite his anxiety, almost laughed. Holloway's eyes had been fixed on the clock. DeWitt watched too. All of them willed each tug of the second hand to bump faster; to end this damning sunlight.

At length, DeWitt's Adam's apple bounced a couple of times. He said, "Lieutenant. About Radtke."

A shell landed close by making everything rattle.

DeWitt continued, "Do you remember the night the PBY crashed?"

"What about it?"

"Mordkin went back out that night and fished out--"

Holloway interrupted, "Do we have enough gas, Skipper?"

"No," said Ingram.

"Damnit. I'm speaking, Mister," said DeWitt.

Holloway turned redder than the sunset. He moved to say something but Ingram interrupted, "Knock that stuff off, both of you."

The jaygee and the sputtering Major glared at each other.

Ingram cleared his throat and said, "I figure at least eight and a half barrels of fuel oil are needed for the nineteen hundred miles to Australia. That means we need five barrels more."

Holloway's eyes slid from DeWitt to Ingram. "Maybe we won't need to go all the way. What about Mindanao?"

Ingram quickly did the math. It was about 450 miles due south to Mindanao. The four barrels they now had gave them a range of almost double. "We have plenty for that, but I want to grab more fuel if there's a chance."

They fell silent and fixed their eyes on the clock again, with DeWitt deciding to table his discussion about Radtke.

Twilight deepened, and Sunderland crawled up the ladder to join them on the pilothouse deck chomping the stub of La Follette's cigar. He groaned, "No cigars, no cigarettes, no nuthin'. We looked everywhere."

With the *Pima*'s thirty-degree list, it was easy to plop against the port bulkhead. "What's wrong with everybody?" he asked, looking at the clock.

"Diesel fuel," said Ingram. "We need five more barrels."

"Bunch of it in that generator shed at the head of the pier," said Sunderland.

Holloway sighed. "Is it still intact?"

"Last time I looked," said Sunderland.

"That's what we'll do, then," said Ingram.

The bombardment intensified with the deepening twilight and hearing the shells crumff augmented their tension. Ingram felt the others staring at him. Imploring. Begging. "Go!" their faces said.

He closed his eyes intending to count to five hundred. But after a while, his mind drifted and he lost his place. Then, he looked at the clock. A detonation close by shook the *Pima* and the flash was enough to tell him it was 1848.

He rose and peered out the porthole.

Instantly, the others stood. It was still hot and humid but reasonably dark. Good enough, he thought. Another shell flashed, making the sweat on their foreheads glisten.

He drummed his fingers for a moment, then said, "Think you can start that thing, Sunderland?"

"You bet!" said the gunner's mate.

They scrambled into the 51 Boat and Sunderland got her going without too much trouble. They cast off, and five minutes later eased into a mooring at the Caballo Dock. The island was grimly silhouetted by shells lighting up the area like gigantic flashbulbs.

"Why are the Japs still shooting?" yelled Holloway.

Ingram shrugged and pointed to a miraculously undamaged generator shed twenty yards away. "Go," he said.

Holloway and Sunderland ran.

Ingram said to DeWitt. "You, too."

A bomb exploded, highlighting DeWitt's but-I'm-an-officer look.

"Get over there," bellowed Ingram.

DeWitt ran for the shed. Soon the three men rolled a gurgling barrel toward the 51 Boat. But the dock was eight feet above the boat's gunnel, making it almost impossible to hand the barrel down. Ingram was thinking of tying a line around it when thirty or so figures materialized above him. Illuminated among them by shell flashes were Whittaker, the Forester brothers, and Yardly with a bulging medical kit. They scrambled aboard. Bartholomew was among them and extended his hand. "Good to see you, Skipper."

"Welcome back, Rocky," said Ingram. "Can you figure out a way to get this fuel on board?"

"Right away." Bartholomew grabbed some heavy line, organized a work party and, soon, all nine barrels of diesel fuel were lashed amidships.

The bombardment raged on Caballo, but it didn't seem to faze the crowd on the wharf which grew to fifty or so. Their faces were gaunt, their eyes wide open as if propped with sticks: lifeless, unseeing. Ingram counted ten men in the boat. He looked up and shouted, "There's still room."

"Easy Skipper. Only eight inches or so of freeboard," said Bartholomew in a low voice.

"I know, Rocky." Ingram looked up into the crowd and yelled, "Anybody else? We're going to Australia. I can't promise we'll get there but I figure anything's better than what the Japs have to offer. Who's for it? We still have room."

Heads jiggled in the back row, the group parted, and a figure stepped forward. "How about one of Big Al's boys?" Leon Beardsley, wearing leather bomber jacket and combination cap with the "fifty mission crush," pushed his way through and stumbled against a cleat. His face was not as scabbed since Ingram had last seen him. His hat fit better, but his eyes were still covered with a bandage wrapped around his head. Someone grabbed his elbow to keep him from pitching headlong into the boat. The B-17 pilot steadied himself and wavered in place. "Alright, Skipper?"

"How'd you get over here, Leon?"

Beardsley smirked, "Sent me with the surrender team to coordinate radio procedures." He waved a hand at explosions, "How about that?"

Ingram studied the bilge, knowing this voyage would demand the utmost of everyone's mental and physical faculties. It did not look promising for Beardsley who might be permanently blind.

Holloway said in a low voice, "Xnay Ipperskay."

Ingram almost had to shout, "The other day you said you could see well enough to walk to the crapper, Leon."

"Medic gave me sulfa day before yesterday. Dumb shit didn't read my chart. I'm allergic, all swollen up again. Third time, damnit. I'll be alright in a few hours. A day or two tops."

Yardly gave Ingram an *it's possible shrug.*

"Got your nickel plate, Leon?" said Ingram.

Beardsley reached behind, whipped out his gleaming .32 automatic, and waved it in the general direction of Corregidor.

"Jeez." Men on both sides quickly ducked.

Yardly moved alongside and whispered, "I'll take care of him, Skipper."

Ingram nodded then said, "Rocky, help Bones bring him aboard."

A shell exploded nearby, raising a hissing plume of water, as Bartholomew and Yardly reached up, helping Beardsley in the boat. Mist rolled toward them and Ingram held a hand over his forehead as he shouted, "There's still room. Who else?"

Nothing. The wraiths above him said nothing. With hands in their pockets, they just stared into the boat. In flashing explosions, he saw wide, unblinking eyes and sagging faces devoid of purpose, hope, and motivation. Hearing an escape was underway, the curious had shuffled to the pier, hungry for something benign; seeking sanity in this surrender, where white flags finally flew after a protracted, miserable siege, only to see death still spitting from Luzon's shores. They were deprived and wounded and abandoned. Without any purpose, whatsoever, they were beaten. Without any connection to home, they were forgotten. Without knowing why, they were being sacrificed by the country they served and loved.

Ingram spotted one of his crew. "Hastings. What are you waiting for?"

Shaking his head, Hastings stumbled back, forcing the man behind him to step aside. Before the face disappeared in shadows, Ingram recognized Lieutenant Junior Grade Oliver P. Toliver, III.

Ingram stepped on a thwart and cupped a hand to his mouth. "We may not be going all the way to Australia. First, we're going to try for Mindanao. Maybe get a ship or a sub out. Maybe make a stand with the resistance. There's a lot you can do besides stay here and let the Japs have you. Come on!"

"Mindanao is gonna fall, Todd." It was Plummer, the commander of Caballo's Battery Craighill.

"How do you know?" Ingram shouted louder as explosions rumbled up a gully.

"That's what all this is about." Plummer waved an arm. "Wainwright surrendered Corregidor and the fortified islands. But the Japs won't stop shooting until all the other Philippine bases give in, including Mindanao."

Ingram felt their eyes fixed on him. He shook his head and said grimly, "It's Australia, then."

He spotted another of his crew hunched over a single crutch. "Kowalski, get in."

Bartholomew yelled, "Yeah, Ski. What the hell you doin'? Get down here."

Kowalski pressed his lips and shook his head slowly.

"What's the matter?" said Bartholomew.

Kowalski said, "Dunno. Weak as hell. Dysentery is driving me crazy. I can hardly walk. And besides, you don't know for sure. Do you? Maybe the Japs will treat us fairly. All I know is, I can't take any more of this."

Farwell moved close and said, "Skipper. It's getting late."

Explosions shook Caballo as Ingram nodded and checked his watch. "Start her up, Whittaker," he said.

Whittaker fumbled with levers, hit the switch, and the engine rumbled into life.

Sunderland, taking in the bowline, spotted Sergeant La Follette and said, "Bruno. Come on. We got plenty of room."

La Follette said in a hoarse voice, "I'm all in, Sonny."

Sunderland said, "Damnit, Bruno. You once told me--"

"Malaria," said La Follette. "Sometimes my head feels like it's going to explode."

Sunderland turned in the boat and said, "Bones. We got any quinine?"

Yardly bent over and fumbled in a bag, muttering and jiggling bottles and wrappers.

"I think we got some stuff to take care of you, Bruno," Sunderland wailed.

La Follette said, "I'd only hold you back, Sonny. Take this. Sorry I'm out of cigars." He tossed a .45; Sunderland caught it and stuffed it in his belt.

Sunderland looked up, finding La Follette had disappeared. "Bruno!" he shouted.

The lines were all aboard. Kevin Forester palmed his tiller. "Skipper?"

In desperation, Ingram scanned the men standing above him. They looked like cardboard cutouts. Something caught in his throat and it tightened. His chest heaved and his eyes welled up. He found it hard to speak. "Anybody else?"

"Yeah," yelled Plummer. "Take this piece of shit with you. It's yours, anyway."

A horribly moaning figure catapulted into space and smacked the water. Bartholomew and Yardly reached over and pulled the man aboard. The saturated body slipped over the gunnel and flopped in the bilge like a dying fish. Bartholomew rasped caustically, "Mr. Toliver is back aboard, Sir."

A round landed on a fuel dump at the base of the pier sending flames two hundred feet in the air. The blast should have knocked everyone down but somehow, they swayed like drunken men keeping their footing as the 51 Boat drifted away.

Unable to speak, Ingram nodded to Forester. The engine roared, and Forester put the tiller over to head into the South China Sea. They stood watching the figures recede on Caballo. Even Leon Beardsley, the near-blind B-17 pilot, faced in that direction. Had somebody even halfheartedly waved from that wharf, Ingram would have turned instantly and grabbed him, even if he had to force the man into the boat.

But nobody waved. Backlighted by flames roaring on the pier, they stood rooted to their fate as Japanese troops swarmed victoriously over Corregidor and, by the next day, the rest of Manila Bay's fortified islands. The Philippines and all of Japan's coveted maritime routes leading to the riches of Indochina were at last in their hands. Just as the *Kido Butai* had wiped out the Pacific Fleet at Pearl Harbor, General Massaharu Homma's Imperial 14th Japanese Army had conquered all of Luzon. Secure were the goals of Japan's vaunted Greater East Asia Co-Prosperity Sphere.

23

6 May 1942
Limbones Point bearing 125E/2.2 nm
Luzon, Philippines

The 51 Boat wallowed in light ground swells, as thousands of stars glistened overhead. Aft, Kevin Forester stood at the tiller steering a near southerly course with Ingram, Holloway, and DeWitt watching the fortified islands recede over their port quarter. The men, thoroughly debilitated and exhausted, were scattered across thwarts. One or two had fallen asleep, but the others cast nervous glances, as artillery rained on Corregidor and Caballo islands.

Suddenly, a series of concussive whacks sounded five hundred yards astern, pulling Ingram from his malaise. Somehow, Army holdouts on Corregidor had thrown the minefield's remote master switches, turning the entrance to Manila Bay into a tormented cacophony of gray-white upward thrusting plumes. Each mine, containing five hundred pounds of high-explosive, thumped three hundred feet in the air one after another, row after row, until all four fortified islands were obscured by mist.

Ingram blinked with each concussion and, as the boat dipped in a wave, stumbled and grabbed the binnacle and stood again looking into DeWitt's eyes. They mirrored his own: sheer unabated terror. Both knew they would have been high in the air, shredded to glistening pulp, had they left the dock two minutes later.

DeWitt yelled in his ear. "Lucky."

Ingram shouted back, "I'll say. Why didn't they trigger them sooner?"

"Don't know. Wainwright gave the order early this morning," DeWitt said, squinting at the reverse waterfalls.

"Was that part of the *PONTIAC* routine?" yelled Ingram, referring to Wainwright's code word to destroy all weapons above .45 caliber.

DeWitt cocked his head and shouted back, "How did you know about that?"

"Epperson."

"He should have kept his mouth shut."

The major was being petty. Ingram ignored it. Besides, he hadn't the strength to argue over the explosions. Instead, he tried, "It's like abandoning ship. You do the drills, but nothing goes as planned."

"Very few people knew of *PONTIAC*, Lieutenant," DeWitt persisted. "I'm interested in why--"

The minefield stopped detonating, leaving mist to hang over Manila Bay's entrance as if someone had drawn a gigantic, opaque curtain. DeWitt lowered his voice. "I'm interested in why Epperson felt compelled to tell you."

Ingram ground his teeth. DeWitt's triviality distracted him from the impossible task at hand: Escape. Being drawn into such a stupid debate was pointless. This just wasn't the time to argue about Epperson's murder. Nor was there energy to even begin considering the monumental task of preventing Radtke from alerting the Japanese that the U.S. Navy knew their plans to attack Midway. "Who the hell cares?" he said. "It's not as if we've had a lot of practice blowing up our own cannons and mortars."

"Yes, but you must admit--"

"Major, damnit. All I'm trying to do is save our skins. One thing at a time. Okay?"

DeWitt's eyes narrowed for a moment, then he let it go with a sigh. He nodded toward Caballo. "Funny. I was in the mortar pits when *PONTIAC* came through. Nobody did a damn thing about it."

"How come?"

"Who knows? Too scared? Too confused? All I know is their crews gave up and headed for the tunnels. They were so far gone, they could hardly stand. So, I figured I would give it a shot." DeWitt snorted. "Imagine me. A ground-pounder trying to spike those damn mortars."

"How the hell do you spike mortars?"

DeWitt shrugged. "There wasn't much time, and those things are so solid and so enormous I couldn't find anything to break. So, I started tossing grenades down the tubes. But then some colonel came running out, screaming at me to report to the command tunnel."

Ingram waited.

An uncharacteristic smile formed over DeWitt's face. "We argued. Can you believe that? I said it was my duty to destroy the mortars. And that stupid sonofabitch told me it was our duty to turn ourselves and our equipment over to the Japanese in a military manner."

"Had he heard of *PONTIAC*?"

"I'm sure he had, but he was scared. Didn't want to piss off the enemy." DeWitt fiddled with his moustache, "So it looks like the Japs took Caballo with the mortars intact."

Ingram looked aft. "So what? A lot of good they did us."

"Hmmmf." DeWitt folded his arms.

Something tugged at Ingram's memory. Caballo. For some reason, Helen Durand's image swam into focus. Caballo. The Horse. That crazy fairy tale they heard on the way to the *Wolfish* rendezvous. Both of them looking up to the silver-haired Filipino like a couple of open-mouthed preadolescents. What was his name? "...Amador."

"What?" said DeWitt.

"Nothing," said Ingram. He wouldn't forget Pablo Amador, nor would he forget Helen Durand. He touched his cheek. The wound hadn't knitted properly and a little pus leaked. He made a note to have Yardly look at it.

Where would she be now? Australia? Maybe on a plane for San Francisco? Where did she live...Ramona? Where the hell is Ramona? Somewhere in California's backwoods, he remembered.

Why had he asked where she lived? He'd acted like a pubescent teenager. Everybody, Ingram included, was so thin and so debilitated, not only from lack of rations but from terrible sicknesses such as malaria, dysentery, and beriberi, that thoughts of sex were a rude intrusion on the business of survival. Like the others, he looked like a cadaver. His weight was down to 130 pounds and his beard grew in scraggly patches. Yet somehow, he had felt compelled to give her his Naval Academy ring that night. Just as well, he thought. The damned thing would have been lost; already it had fallen off his thumb twice.

But now, he couldn't stop closing his eyes and imagining the scent of Helen's hair. She had bent close that night in the hospital hellhole, sewing up his cheek while the maimed and dying groaned and thrashed. Her face was very near and for a moment or two her breath tickled his neck, and he saw her smile and listened to the subtle humor in her voice.

There was something else. On the way out to the *Wolfish*, she'd laughed once. A quick chuckle. That was all; about a second and a half--it was the nicest sound he'd ever heard. And now, as the 51 Boat wallowed and rolled, he clung to that rich sound, as if it were a recording playing over and over.

The boat hit the face of a wave, water popped in the air dissipating spray all over them. Dripping, he wiped a hand over his face, realizing that he'd almost fallen asleep thinking of Helen. But then a shell went crumff on Corregidor's Topside and another image swam into his mind, one he would never forget: The Caballo docks.

Even now he closed his eyes seeing those hulking shapes through the mist, those skeletous, pathetic creatures weaving on the wharf. They looked down at him with hands jammed in their pockets, shells exploding all around. Terrified of what captivity would bring, they were exhausted beyond comprehension and totally without will to escape. The image of those hollow-eyed men he'd left behind was something he knew he'd dream of for the rest of his life.

The four-cylinder Buda purred with conversation trailing off to nothing. Like the others, Ingram's eyelids grew heavy and he fought sleep, yawning and holding his face to the breeze, wordlessly watching the eastern horizon as it grew brighter with moonrise.

Stay awake, damnit! He'd heard of a Filipino scout who had been court martialed and sentenced to death for falling asleep on watch. The Japanese did the poor fellow a favor when they hit his truck convoy in a bombing raid, killing him with fourteen others.

Ten minutes later a three-quarter moon rose above Luzon. Ingram's eyes fixed on the shimmering, platinum disc, and he almost dropped off again.

Stay Awake!

He swung his arms and looked down moon into the South China Sea. As if blasted with a fire hose, three silhouettes on the western horizon brought him to full consciousness. They were Japanese destroyers patrolling with running lights, which defiantly glowed as if there never had been a war. It was something Ingram hadn't seen since the fighting began six months ago. The red and green side lights and white masthead lights made the South China Sea seem tranquil, even festive in a way. His mind drifted again and he actually asked himself if the gruesome atrocities of Cavite, Manila, Bataan, and Corregidor were only hideous nightmares.

Holloway groaned, sat up, and stretched for a moment. Then it was evident he too saw the ships. He stood and stepped alongside. "What do you think, skipper?"

"Tin cans."

"Wonderful. What do we do?"

"Damned if I know. And look at that," Ingram pointed south. Two more destroyers steamed across their track, running lights also blazing. "Looks like they've set up a picket line between Fortune Island and Nasugbu."

"How about going outboard?"

Ingram rubbed his chin. "Don't think so. We better duck in and hide. Too much heat out here."

DeWitt rose and joined them. With the boat rolling in swells, he braced himself, putting a hand on Ingram's shoulder. "Lieutenant. How far can we travel in one night?"

"Assuming this thing has a clean bottom, which I doubt, seventy miles or so."

DeWitt said, "Hell, It's only thirty miles to Cape Santiago. What's wrong with holing up somewhere in Balayan Bay?"

Realizing DeWitt hadn't seen the pickets, Holloway jabbed a thumb over his shoulder, "Major. There's at least--"

"Mister Holloway," DeWitt said evenly. "I'm speaking to Lieutenant Ingram."

"But--"

DeWitt, campaign hat and all, put his nose in Holloway's face. Like a drill sergeant, he said, "Is that clear--"

"Otis," said Ingram sharply.

Major Otis DeWitt bristled at being so addressed by one of lesser rank.

Ingram said, "Are you familiar with Navy regs?"

"Years ago, I--"

"They state in this situation, the senior Navy line officer is in command. So, that's me, Otis, I'm the captain."

"Yes, well--"

"But in case a Jap bullet takes me out, Mr. Holloway is the Captain. And when Holloway is killed, it's Mr. Toliver."

DeWitt and Holloway said, "Toliver!" Both looked forward for a moment studying Toliver's inert form.

Holloway said, "Over my dead body."

"That's right," said Ingram, jabbing a finger at Holloway's chest. "Toliver becomes skipper when your body is dead. When Toliver gets it, Otis, you'd be smart to let Chief Machinist Mate Bartholomew take over. And then, depending on how much you know about lifeboat navigation and survival at sea, you should strongly consider allowing First Class Gunner's Mate Sunderland to become captain after Chief Bartholomew falls through the deck."

DeWitt fell silent and gazed in the distance.

Ingram said, "Look at it this way, Major. If I had a tank battle on my hands, I'd be well advised to turn it over to you, the Army officer. Wouldn't I?"

Holloway suddenly took great interest in water sloshing in the bilge. DeWitt stared at Luzon.

Ingram growled, "Look, damnit. Both of you. It's nineteen-hundred miles to Darwin. We're going to be cozy for a while. So, get used to it. I want you guys to keep away from each other's throats. There's too much at stake. If you have something to say, say it to me. Then that's it. I'll take it from there. That goes for everyone here, because if anything is going to get us through, it's brains, not rank. Got it?"

DeWitt nodded. Holloway said, "Yessir."

Thirty minutes later the 51 Boat closed to within three miles of the destroyers. With running lights flamboyantly blazing, the ships steamed in opposite directions, stiffly passing one another like strutting wooden soldiers.

Ingram shook his head, "No sense getting too near. Let's take a look." He handed Holloway a flashlight, then opened a duffle, stooped, and pulled out a chart. Holloway kneeled alongside, wrapped his fingers over the lens, and flicked on the light letting a hemoglobin redness ooze across the chart.

Ingram ran his finger along the coastline and muttered, "...about here." Then he barked over his shoulder, "Forester!"

"Sir?" replied the helmsman.

"Head for the beach," Ingram said.

"What?" said Forester.

"Right there," said Ingram, slicing a forearm at the coast. Steer for that hill. Looc Cove should be just to the right."

"Aye, aye, Sir." Forester's tone carried a touch of doubt. But he swung the tiller, and the 51 Boat headed toward Luzon. Her motion changed as she settled on her new course. With the waves off her stern, she wallowed deeply, making Forester curse and swing his tiller in wild arcs to maintain rudder control.

Ingram rolled up the chart and said to Holloway. "Wake everyone. Put 'em in life jackets and post two bow lookouts."

"Right." Holloway lurched forward, shaking the men.

DeWitt asked, "How far do you think we've come?"

"Seven, eight miles," said Ingram, looking back to the entrance to Manila Bay. A fine mist still obscured Corregidor and Caballo.

"Not far."

"No, not far. But we were almost on those damn destroyers. It's too risky trying to sneak through the picket line tonight," said Ingram, stepping aside to let Whittaker stumble aft to his engine controls.

With eyes drooping they fought sleep for twenty minutes as the 51 Boat dipped and wallowed. But then, her pitching motion became more pronounced with the swells growing sharper. Then the waves started to tumble and break.

Ingram said, "Slow ahead."

Whittaker ran the throttle down to idle and over the exhaust's muted gurgle; they heard waves crash in the distance. Again, the 51 Boat climbed the back of a wave, crested it, and surged majestically down the front with Ingram enveloped by the perfumed heaviness of vegetation and sodden earth. Suddenly, as if someone had switched off the lights, he looked up seeing they had surged under tall bluffs masking them from moonlight.

"Shit," muttered Forester.

Something loomed ahead, and Ingram opened his mouth to shout--

Sunderland, the bow lookout, beat him to it, "That way, damnit!" He waved frantically to the right.

Forester shoved the tiller over, turning the boat to starboard. Abruptly, a rocky islet, at least eighty feet high, emerged from darkness.

"Watch out!" several shouted.

"Jeez!" Forester again leaned into his tiller, leaving the jagged islet only twenty-five yards to port, where waves crashed at its jagged base, shooting misted water thirty feet in the air. After a moment, Forester straightened to parallel the coast, heading for a bright patch of water where the bluff line dipped. They rolled and pitched back into moonlight where Ingram, spotting a gap in the headlands, gasped, "There."

Forester nodded and steered for it.

"This place inhabited?" said Dewitt.

Ingram unrolled the chart. His fingers were so stiff they seemed like they were made from brass cartridges. DeWitt flipped on the light and they stooped again to examine it. "Hmmm, seven fathoms of water in Looc Cove but it doesn't indicate any villages or people."

"We better be ready," said DeWitt.

Ingram nodded and said, "Sunderland. Pass out the weapons."

The muttering gunner's mate upended boxes and duffels, digging out the Springfield 30-06s, BARs, and ammunition.

Holloway said, "Lot of good those pop-guns are going to do."

"You'd rather be without them?" said DeWitt.

"I didn't say that," said Holloway.

Rolling up the chart, Ingram said, "Knock it off, you two!"

Holloway muttered, "Sorry."

The Buda's exhaust gurgled as moonlit ripples danced in their wake. Soon they were abeam of Looc Cove's yawning mouth where inside, trees and vegetation grew in a dark, hodgepodge fashion all the way to the water's edge.

Forester grunted, "Well, Skipper?"

Ingram pointed to a clump of low palms near a rocky outcrop. "Under those trees."

With the 51 Boat weaving drunkenly in confused ground swell, Forester eased his tiller and they headed through the entrance. The next moment found them suddenly inside, where the waters were smooth and shimmered in moonlight.

To them, it was too quiet and too peaceful. They cocked weapons and flipped off safeties. Ingram found himself swallowing rapidly and, suddenly, his stomach felt as he'd eaten a pound of cement. His eyes flicked from object to shadowy object, convinced each shape was a deadly menace. Over there, he was sure a dark, low mound was really a platoon of Japanese riflemen. And that clump of coconut trees directly ahead masked a machine gun nest. Barely visible in the palm grove to starboard was a 105-millimeter howitzer pointed right at him, with grinning gun crew hunched behind the splinter shield ready to yank the firing lanyard.

Thirty yards from shore, Ingram croaked, "Cut."

Whittaker shifted to neutral, and soon Sunderland and Yardly jumped in shallow water and caught the bow just as the boat squeaked into sand. Grunting and sweating, they worked the boat another twenty feet, where it finally was wedged among thick tree stumps, fallen logs, and dense foliage.

Ingram said softly, "Okay."

Whittaker switched off the engine.

The absence of sound was devastating. Ingram could have sworn the thumping of his heart and the crunching of his blood circulating was audible to others. And the low buzz of insects and the occasional bird squawk was eerie, something he hadn't heard for at least three months. No pillboxes, no riflemen, no howitzers shot at them. Looc Cove was empty, and nature thrived as if the hideous atrocities eight miles to the north had never occurred.

A mosquito buzzed in his ear. He slapped it, finding it almost felt good.

Others slapped and swore. Holloway popped one on his neck saying, "Haven't done this for a while."

"Time for the goop," said Yardly, digging into his medical kit for repellent.

In filtered moonlight Ingram caught their vacuous stares as they slowly smeared on Yardley's potion. Quietly he said, "We sleep aboard. Major DeWitt and I will take the first watch. Good night."

For the first time in over three months, the men settled into sleep uninterrupted by thundering explosions, putrid smoke, and screams of the dying. While their snoring organized itself into a rhythmic pattern, DeWitt sat heavily on a thwart, folded his arms, and said, "Think we should go ashore and look around?"

"Let's stay aboard and get our rest."

DeWitt nodded in and soon his eyelids began to droop.

"Otis."

"Huh?"

"Come on."

"Yeah."

They stared at one another for a moment. Then DeWitt looked dully over the side at shimmering wavelets that occasionally slapped the hull's boot-topping.

Like DeWitt, Ingram watched the little waves. And like DeWitt, he started to slip. Luckily, a mosquito landed on his cheek and he slapped it. It helped a little, and he peered into the South China Sea where those damned destroyers relentlessly paced back and forth. Their lights still glistened as if it were Christmas.

Christmas...red and green...when would...he shook his head. What day is it? Not December 25. This is May 6. So what? Damnit! He shook his head and rubbed his eyes, seeing the destroyer's lights swim into focus.

Between Fortune Island and the coastal city of Nasugbu, another two destroyers marched on east-west courses. "Got us trapped in here," Ingram muttered. "Any ideas Otis?

"Otis?" Ingram turned finding Major Otis DeWitt's chin rested solidly on his chest. But he didn't snore.

24

The 1500-ton *Gatos* Class submarine raced from the South China Sea into the Balabac Strait at flank speed. She was surfaced on a near easterly course and at 0415, cleared Cape Melville by three miles to port. Heading toward the Nasubata Channel, she hoped to poke her snout into the Sulu Sea by sunrise. With number two engine on battery charge, the other three bellowing Fairbanks Morse diesels drove the *Wolfish* at eighteen knots, pulling an enormous phosphorescent wake over a sea unencumbered by wind. But the Balabac Strait swirled with ominous turbulence from a two-knot tidal current gushing from the South China Sea into the Sulu, a body of water in the southwestern Philippine Archipelago the size of New Mexico.

After picking up the second load of evacuees from Corregidor, the *Wolfish* had assumed her patrol station in the southeast corner of the South China Sea. Her passengers were surprised they weren't going to Australia, immediately. They were told the U.S. Navy wasn't there just to run a bus service. The

Wolfish was in the Philippines on the submarine's stated mission: Sink enemy ships and shipping through offensive patrols at focal points.

The night was overcast, and Helmut Döttmer found himself on the sub's bridge, with binoculars in hand, wedged against another sailor. After four days, the Abwehr agent finally felt better. With half the evacuees, he'd been assigned to the after-torpedo room, sleeping on a "hot bunk" schedule. Initially they were desperate for sleep and, when yielding the bunk to another, found a nook on the deck, tossed down a blanket, and slept some more.

While awake, of course, the Corregidor people were amazed at the food available. The crew, for the most part, were tolerant and stepped back to let the half-starved GIs gorge themselves. Döttmer was astonished at how good the fried chicken tasted. But it was very rich, and the first night he threw it up. After that, his system adapted and he couldn't get enough. The crew laughed, as he and the others launched into mountains of the mouth-watering stuff. And mashed potatoes. And butter. And peas. And biscuits and more butter. And gallons of grape juice. Apple pie.

But Ronnie had received a top-secret message about a Japanese task force retiring from a battle off Australia's northeast coast, an area known as the Coral Sea. Ronnie briefed his officers in the wardroom, knowing the two stewards hovering in the pantry would put out the word well before he announced it on the 1MC. Indeed, the essence of Ronnie's message was that Navy flyboys had given the Japs a licking in the Coral Sea. Now, a big fat carrier limped for the Home Islands with bomb damage. She was expected to transit the Sulu Sea sometime tomorrow via the Sibutu Passage off the coast of Borneo. And, by golly, Ronnie slammed a fist on the wardroom table, the *Wolfish* would be there to intercept and sink the sonofabitch.

Ronnie was Lieutenant Commander Roland M. Galloway, the *Wolfish's* captain. When relaxed, he wore an easy, lopsided grin, and the crew loved him. Döttmer never learned his real name and everyone called him Ronnie behind his back and, of course captain to his face. He was freckle-faced, ruddy complected, two hundred pounds and not an inch taller than five nine and had been an All-American fullback at Northwestern. He presided over his officers with broad grins and slaps on the rump; his wardroom talked their crazy version of American football with elbow nudges and roars of mock incredulity. Perpetually sweating, Ronnie wore washed-out khaki shirts with cut-off sleeves. And his shirttail hung out, a major infraction in larger ships of the U.S. Navy. Always clean-shaven, he allowed his officers and crew to wear beards if they were neatly trimmed.

Except for the boot ensign, Mr. Gruber, the officers called each other by first names, which to Döttmer was one of many breaches of military conduct. He was amazed at the lack of discipline in this submarine: It bordered on insubordination. Yet they did their jobs well. In fact, Döttmer had to admit things went very smoothly on the *Wolfish*.

After the third day, Döttmer was given permission to roam the submarine. It was difficult and terribly crowded. With the Corregidor people, men were squished everywhere and the place smelled like a locker-room, especially when they were submerged.

Even so, it didn't take Döttmer long to find what he wanted. It was a room the size of a closet in the after part of the control room. A bakelite label over the door read: *Radio Room. Authorized Personnel Only*. Three times the door had burst open while Döttmer eased by. Lingering, he'd been able to study the cramped little space and its equipment. He was encouraged to see a large radio transmitter. Now, he had to figure out how to get to it.

Escaping Corregidor, he not only had a good chance for survival, but also a good chance to do what he had to do before time ran out. If Epperson's report was correct, time would run out on 4 June, 1942. Midway. Chances were, he figured, the *Wolfish* would still be on patrol when Yamamoto attacked. He had to do something. Now.

Hurry.

On the bridge, Döttmer listened to water sizzle down the port side while occasional wavelets slapped the ballast tanks and shot through the limber holes. Accompanying this was the thunder of the *Wolfish's* four diesels, with the engineers running them at peak output so they could dive at first light in the Sulu Sea's deep waters.

Here, the bottom shoaled to twelve fathoms. It was too shallow to dive, so Ronnie had posted four extra lookouts topside; the two regulars were high in the periscope shears, with the officer of the deck and junior officer of the deck scanning port and starboard. Döttmer stood beside the chief radioman on the bridge's port. Two more sailors were stationed on the starboard side with Ronnie strutting back and forth, binoculars raised constantly sweeping the horizon. This was unlike the Ronnie that Döttmer had met three days ago. This Ronnie was very serious and, for the first time, Döttmer noticed his teeth were rather pointed, almost predatory.

Occasionally, Ronnie yelled to the lookouts to keep a sharp watch. And just not for ships, he boomed with deep resonance. Watch out for logs and driftwood. The Balabac Strait is known for all sorts of crap, he exhorted. Two months ago, the *Pickerel* had lost her pitsword, a speed-measuring device, when she ran over a damned palm tree in broad daylight.

Nobody dared to counter Ronnie about the darkness. If something was there, they'd hit it. If they did spot it, it would be too late.

Lieutenant Sampson was the OOD and Ensign Gruber JOOD. It didn't take long for Döttmer to learn the crew called Gruber Lil' Adolph because of a miscalculated attempt to emulate the moustache of movie actor George Brent.

The *Wolfish*'s crew was lucky. If Döttmer were caught referring to anyone in Germany by the name of "Lil' Adolph," he'd most assuredly be hanging by piano wire in an SS subbasement, wiggling, gurgling, slowly choking to death.

In a way, the joke was on Himmler and his SS thugs. In 1937, his mother was suspected of being Jewish. But Wilhelm Furtwängler, music director of the Berlin Philharmonic, was convinced it was all a bureaucratic mix-up and interceded in behalf of the Döttmer ménage. With extensive records and great bravado, the maestro painted his lead trumpeter and family as pure Aryan to Reichsminister Goebbels, who in turn sold the concept to Himmler. The pressure was off.

But eighteen months ago, while young Helmut was away at naval officer's training, a heated argument broke out between Elsa Döttmer and her talented husband, Kurt. It was a rainy evening and during dinner, the conversation turned to the war. Elsa uncharacteristically screamed that she wanted to return to New York, where young Helmut had been born and lived until age ten learning flawless English with an American accent.

"Why?" bellowed a red-faced Kurt Döttmer, once again sensing a threat to his career with the Berlin Philharmonic. He didn't have to add that little Helmut had been miserable in America. That gang of young thugs, jealous of his dexterity on the violin, had ambushed him on his way home from school one day, beat him senseless, then smashed his left hand in a door.

"Because, Wolfgang is Jewish." Wolfgang was her sister Frieda's husband. The childless couple lived in New York, where Wolfgang Schweitzer worked as a magazine editor.

Elsa beat her little fists against Kurt's chest, "And that's enough to tip everything back the other way. Himmler will find out. He has sources; even in America!" shrieked Elsa.

Neither realized that their son had just quietly walked in unannounced. He wanted to surprise them wearing a fresh navy officer's uniform with shiny gold braid, designating him as a brand new leutnant zur see: ensign. But seeing them like this, he stood in the shadows and said nothing while rain dripped off his new officer's cap and greatcoat.

Kurt Döttmer was astonished. "Wolfgang? Jewish?"

"Yes," cried Elsa.

"That little bastard! Why didn't you tell me?" Kurt raged.

Tears ran down Elsa's face, "I didn't really know until his father introduced himself to me on the tram two days ago. He was on the run and asked me for money."

"Gott." Kurt Döttmer sat heavily on an overstuffed loveseat. He scratched at his moustache for a while, then asked, "Did you give him any?"

"Yes. But all I had were twenty Reichmarks."

Kurt nodded and pat the loveseat. "Sit here, *liebchen*."

Kurt Döttmer took Elsa in his arms and kissed her, saying unconvincingly that Himmler's thugs would lose the scent. At any rate, it was too late. The Fatherland was at war. The border was closed, to leave was impossible.

Then Kurt Döttmer wailed about his son, Helmut. That those damned American hooligans had done him a favor. He always thought Helmut a fairy for playing the violin. The trumpet was a man's instrument he had exhorted his son.

They didn't have money for doctors after the fight. Young Helmut's hand swelled horribly. Papa Kurt figured it was an infection of some sort. Eight months later, they were able to afford attention at New York's Hospital for Special Surgery but it was too late the doctor told the Döttmer's. The boy's ring finger was forever cocked at the joint--a deformity flexion--they called it. And his little finger had no feeling whatsoever.

The violin was out. Secretly Papa Kurt was happy and he launched into a six-hour-day regimen of trumpet lessons for the boy.

Now, he lamented, after all the years of practice and tutoring, Helmut wouldn't be able to perform--wouldn't be able to follow in Papa Kurt's footsteps with this damned war. Kurt had been so proud. Helmut had not only proved himself on the trumpet but on many brass instruments as well. Such promise the lad showed!

"He was wonderful on the violin," Elsa wailed. "You should have let him try again."

"The little bastard was all through," Kurt raged, kicking over a small table and breaking one of the legs. "I gave him his chance. But," Kurt's eyes puffed and he waved a stubby forefinger under Elsa's nose, "he got back at me alright. The little turd had to sign up for the damned *Kriegsmarine*, when he knew damned well I could have got him deferred."

Their shouting rose in timbre, so Helmut let himself out quietly. He had a somber dinner, unsuccessfully tried to find a room elsewhere, and returned home two hours later.

Kurt and Elsa seemed happy to see him. Young Helmut pretended not to notice the broken table and Elsa didn't mention the little water puddles she wiped up in the foyer forty-five minutes earlier.

Later, on active duty, young Helmut had heard rumors about Admiral Wilhelm Canaris harboring anti-Nazi tendencies. So, he answered a call from the Abwehr for intelligent young talent to become reconnaissance and espionage agents. Döttmer signed up and, after intensive training, was posted to a commando unit. On the night before his first taste of battle in the invasion of Greece, Döttmer paced the destroyer's main deck under a moonlit Aegean sky. He was surprised when Admiral Canaris, also out for a walk, joined him. Döttmer didn't even know the admiral was on the ship. Their discussion was stilted at first, and centered on the upcoming invasion. But soon, Canaris learned of Döttmer's background and they talked of music, with Canaris fascinated at Döttmer's stories about his father and the Berlin Philharmonic.

That went on for a long time, and then they discussed the future of Germany with Döttmer detecting a slight edge in Canaris' politics. The rumors were correct, so he seized his chance and told the admiral about his mother's problem. Canaris stopped in mid-stride and stared at Döttmer in silence for a whole minute. With a sigh, he vowed to do his best to keep the matter off Himmler's desk.

Canaris kept his word, and Döttmer grew to love his job. Demolitions, train wrecks, bridges, radios, parachutes, handguns, and knives became utensils of survival that he honed to a sharp edge. Even the killing didn't bother him. Last March, in training for the invasion of Greece, they hired an overweight Cypriot thug to demonstrate hand-to-hand combat. It was from this man that Döttmer learned the garrote, one of the Cypriot's favorites for the silent kill.

Döttmer didn't have a chance to try it out until Canaris ordered him to a new mission assigning him the code name HECKLE. Döttmer was inserted last June into Texas, via cargo ship to Vera Cruz. He crossed the Rio Grande to El Paso where in the train station, he discovered the Cypriot's technique demanded total surprise and overwhelming strength as he executed the real Walter A. Radtke. The garrote worked again with that stupid guard in the Navy radio intercept file room on Corregidor. Then he tried it on Epperson, but the debilitated Navy lieutenant was stronger than he looked and spun away, forcing Döttmer to shoot Epperson with the guard's .45. Luckily an enormous salvo of artillery landed at the same time obliterating the .45's blast. He'd been able to take his pictures and escape cleanly only to have to chuck them over the side when that damned Ingram ambushed him.

Döttmer raised his binoculars and swept the horizon again. To the north, Cape Melville drew rapidly aft. They were making good time and Döttmer moved closer to Chief Hall, a thin, dyspeptic forty-two-year old radioman who continually belched. Döttmer swept again with his binoculars and decided now was the time. He leaned over and said, "Er chief, you guys got something to keep me busy?"

Hall nudged his belly with the heel of his fist and said, "What do you do?"

"Crypto mostly."

"Uh, uh. We're too small. Officers do the crypto stuff here." Hall raised his glasses and scanned his sector. He finished and said, "Sorry."

The chief was being difficult. Try harder, he thought. "I have a good fist."

"Yeah?" Hall's voice rose a little.

"Tops in my class."

"How fast can you receive?"

"Twenty-five words a minute. When I'm on my stride--thirty."

"You there!" shouted Ensign Gruber. He walked up and stuck his nose between the two, saying, "Stop talking and keep those binoculars up."

Döttmer automatically shoved his left hand in the small of his back while Chief Hall propped his elbows on the bulwarks and belched loudly. "Sorry, Sir. Yes Sir. We'll keep lookin', Sir."

"Don't get sarcastic with--"

Just then a guttural voice wafted up the conning tower hatch. "Bridge!"

Gruber gave Hall a look, then stepped over and yelled down. "Bridge, aye."

The voice below said, "Maneuvering Room reports number two main engine on propulsion, Sir. Mr. Sutcliff says we have a full can and are now making turns for twenty knots. Sounding still one-two fathoms."

"Very well," said Gruber. He walked aft, finding Ronnie and Mort Sampson on the cigarette deck, peering at something off their starboard quarter. Döttmer cocked an ear to hear Gruber's nervous report. "Ron--er, Captain, maneuvering room reports battery charge is complete. All four engines on propulsion now. Speed is twenty knots. Sounding, twelve fathoms"

Ronnie muttered something and shifted his vigil to the port quarter. Gruber walked forward. As he passed, he hissed, "Keep a sharp lookout you two."

After he was gone, Hall tossed an exquisitely refined belch into the night. With a nod toward Gruber he said, "Little twit's worked up 'cause we can't dive."

"Yeah?" Döttmer cast a quick glance at Gruber's back. For a moment, he visualized the ensign wiggling under his garrote.

"Just about shit his pants two weeks ago when we were bottomed in two hundred feet off Cebu. Japs throwing ash cans everywhere. Held us down eleven hours."

Döttmer gave the obligatory sigh, then asked. "Why's he take it out on us?"

"Still scared shitless. I don't think he'll do another patrol."

"Does he ever--"

"Better keep them binocs up, sailor," said Hall, with a glance in Gruber's direction.

Döttmer scanned the horizon. After thirty seconds, he found nothing in his sector. "Chief, I gotta tell you. This is my first time on a sub, too. I'm as nervous as Lil' Adolph with nothing to do. Can I help out with something?"

"How fast are you?" Chief Hall asked again.

"Twenty-five words a minute. Thirty when I'm hot. And I send a hell of a lot faster."

"Clearance?"

"Top Secret. You'll find it in my file."

"We're standin' one in three, now. Let me talk to Mr. Chance." Chief Hall hurled another belch, it's ripping vibrato dissipated in the direction of Balabac Island. "Keep them binocs up, before Lil' Adolph blows his stack."

25

7 May 1942
Looc Cove
Luzon, Philippines

The plane roared over. Ingram sat up, looking straight into Bartholomew's craggy face. "What was it, Rocky?"

The chief machinist's mate had relieved him at four thirty. "Float plane, Sir. Zero. Right over the damned trees."

Ingram stood and checked his watch: 9:27. The day was warm and cloudless. The waters of Looc Cove were a deep emerald in the middle, phasing to a brilliant turquoise near shore. But it was hot, with pressing humidity even at this hour.

"Did he see us?" said Ingram.

"Don't know."

The float plane flew over again, lower if that seemed possible. It banked around the cove's edge then headed out to sea. They waited, looking at one another, until the engine's noise disappeared.

"What the hell was that?" Otis DeWitt sat up rubbing his head.

"Zero," said Ingram.

"He see us?" said DeWitt.

"Don't know for sure," said Ingram. "What I do know is that we have to pull this thing deeper in shadows and camouflage with branches. Now."

DeWitt sat up straight, pointed out to sea, and said in a resonant, booming voice, "Lieutenant Ingram. Do you have any idea of how to get through that line of enemy ships?"

In the trees above them, the Cicada flies chirped their shrill buzz as Ingram studied the bilge. At length, he looked up and spread his hands.

"Then maybe we should abandon. Move back into the hills," said DeWitt.

"I don't think so," said Ingram.

DeWitt said, "I would advise you give serious thought to--"

They turned, hearing the howl of a diesel engine. Quickly, the roaring grew to a cacophony of many diesel engines. The men woke and, crouching low, took their weapons in hand as the rumble grew. Even Beardsley whipped out his nickel-plate and waved it toward the cove entrance.

"Jeez, Leon, don't cock that thing." Holloway pulled the B-17 pilot down behind the gunnels.

A blunt-nosed, one-hundred-foot Japanese barge churned by Looc's entrance heading north at perhaps five or six knots. Then another; followed by twenty or so of the narrow-beamed craft. Japanese naval ensigns drooped from each barge's fantail, where a helmsman stood in an enclosed elevated pulpit. Except for one or two crew pacing up and down, the barges were empty.

DeWitt said, "Troop carriers. That's what they used for landing on the Rock."

"Where the hell'd they come from?" said Holloway.

"I'd say Fortune Island," said Ingram.

A destroyer hove into view, and lost headway three hundred yards off the cove's entrance. The Zero zipped overhead again then flew over the destroyer, waggling its wings.

"Why so many?" asked Bartholomew.

"Next week, they invade California," said Sunderland, patting his breast pocket. "God, I need a cigar," he muttered.

"Damn things are empty," whispered DeWitt, staring through binoculars. He exchanged I-don't-know shrugs with Ingram. Finally, the last of the barges howled past and faded toward Manila Bay, leaving the destroyer standing dead in the water off the cove's entrance.

"Mean looking son-of-a-bitch," said Bartholomew, as froth kicked up under the destroyer's fantail. With six-five inch guns bristling from three turrets, she gathered headway then headed back out to sea. She was a *Hubuki* class with a graceful, raked bow and superstructure, moderately low freeboard, and gentle, almost aesthetically situated twin funnels. Three-hundred-seventy-one feet long, the ships in her class were built in 1931 and were the first rivetless destroyers in the Imperial Japanese Navy. With two geared Parsons turbines and four Kanpon boilers, they could sprint at forty knots.

The *Hubuki* reminded Ingram of a lanky cat poking in a dark Chicago alley, sniffing out a barrel of half-eaten fish carcasses. "Brrrr."

Beardsley's hands flailed at space. "What's wrong?"

Ingram hissed, "Somebody dig out the machete. Sunderland. Get up in that tree and drop a couple of branches on us. That damn thing may come back."

A muttering Farwell fumbled under thwarts, found the machete, and tied the scabbard to Sunderland's belt loops. Yardly and Whittaker grabbed Sunderland's torso and handed him up to a branch nine feet overhead. The gunner's mate, with machete dangling from his belt, grabbed the limb and dangled. His feet and legs barely moved.

"Come on, Sonny," growled Farwell.

Sunderland hadn't moved. He still hung from the branch and puffed. "...can't."

"Can't you do better than that?" asked Ingram.

Sunderland swung pathetically. But he could only raise his legs above hip level. Finally, he let go and, even with Whittaker and Yardly trying to catch him, thumped heavily in the bilge, laying on his back drawing great lungfuls of air.

Yardly turned and said, "He's outta gas, skipper. Maybe we should have something to eat."

Forgotten was the *Hubuki* class destroyer as she headed out to sea. The men seemed to surge toward Ingram; their eyes bored into him.

Sunderland, still out of breath, rolled to his chest and pushed himself to all fours looking up at Ingram. His tongue was dry and bloated. Smacking his lips, he managed, "Hell, Skipper. All we want is an hors d'oeuvres or two."

DeWitt said, "This is nonsense. We can be easily captured before the day's out. I recommend we grab everything and move into the hills."

Silence.

Ingram looked over DeWitt's shoulder and out to sea. A light offshore wind ruffled his hair as he raised a hand, saying, "Who's for abandoning ship and moving into the hills?"

DeWitt's hand quickly went up, then just as quickly came down, seeing his was the only one in the air.

"Okay." Ingram nodded to a fallen log; dead foliage had piled against it. "Rocky: You, Farwell, Kevin, and Junior over the side. Pull some of that tumbleweed over here. Can't have the nips spotting us. Soon as you're finished we'll break out the chow." Ingram allowed a demonic grin, "We eat, gentlemen. Corned beef, tomato juice, salmon, rice. Everything, if we feel like it. I say, if Japs come after us, they'll meet us with full stomachs for a change."

Like children on Christmas Eve, the four sailors slipped over the side. Grins quickly became dark oaths as they staggered about, sometimes wading chest high and stepping into slimy mud holes. First, they scooped ooze from the bottom and wiped it over the boat's freeboard. It soon dried to a muddy brown, blending with the background. Then, they slogged the dead foliage back to the boat and covered it as best they could. The aging, grunting Bartholomew was the last to be pulled into the 51 Boat. Still in chief's hat and overalls, he slithered over the gunnel and lay in the bilge, gasping for breath.

Satisfied their position was well camouflaged, Ingram handed Yardly a can opener. "Bones, from here on in you're in charge of rationing. Everything. Food. Water. Medicine. Today, we stuff ourselves. After that, back to rations." He caught Holloway's eye. "And, I want everything in this boat inventoried and stowed properly."

"Yessir," they said. Yardly asked, "Skipper, do I ration for Mindanao or Australia."

Four hundred and fifty miles to the first destination, over nineteen hundred miles to the latter: More than one ear in the boat heard Ingram click his teeth before saying, "Australia."

Sunderland sat before Yardly and rubbed his hands together. "Okay, come on. Let's dig in."

With a nod from Ingram, Yardly ripped open a case of corned beef and handed out the cans. Salmon and tomato juice followed, and for the next ten minutes the men slurped, burped, chomped and grunted. Like voracious Neanderthals looking over their shoulders to the menace outside the cave, they nervously watched the sea and the skies but kept on eating as another Zero zipped overhead.

After finishing most of the tomato juice and half the corned beef, Yardly booted an open case under a thwart. "Enough," he said. "And we don't waste the cans. We keep everything." He held up a gunny sack.

They tossed the cans, with Toliver pitching a juice can from five feet away that made an abnormally loud clank.

"Watch it, jerk," said Farwell.

Toliver, with unshaven, grimy face and holes in his shirt and shorts, raised his eyes to Farwell and held his gaze.

Ingram said evenly, "Say that again, Farwell."

Farwell's lips pressed until they were white. At length he said, "Easy with the clanking--SIR." Farwell gave Ingram a neutral look, then with the rest of the men, found a place to stretch, using a life jacket for a pillow.

Let it go, Ingram thought. Toliver's not too far gone that he can't take care of himself. He hides by acting like a zombie, but Ingram had watched him a moment or two, discovering the man's eyes darted about at times with fiery comprehension. Yet, a rudimentary level of discipline had to be maintained. Toliver was still an officer and Ingram couldn't afford to let his men degrade him.

Ingram made a mental note to take Toliver aside later to see if he could make him animate a little; if not in self-defense, then at least for the good of the voyage. Also, Ingram couldn't risk letting Toliver play the dolt too long. The others subconsciously looked upon him as a drag and a focal point of their troubles. "Toliver? Toliver," he called.

"Damn!" Ingram looked about the boat. It was as if someone had thrown a master switch: everyone, after months of famished deprivation, had surfeited their hunger and fallen back into a deep sleep.

Ingram checked his watch: 1023. Let them sleep all day. Then underway tonight. In fact, that would be standard operation procedure during the voyage. He'd wait until this afternoon before he talked to Bartholomew and DeWitt about how to break through the destroyer picket line.

The sky began to rumble. He looked up seeing formations of Betty bombers flying south at great altitude. The twin engine, mid-wing airplanes marched overhead as if in lockstep, vee after three-plane vee.

Beside him, Toliver stirred then looked up. Ingram had the feeling he hadn't been asleep. Toliver concentrated on the Bettys then said almost conversationally, "Twelve thousand feet, at least. I'd say they're out of Clark Field."

As the bombers' drone crescendoed the crew woke, cursing and grumbling, then rolled over. Farwell smacked his lips then resumed his snoring.

"In a hurry," Yardly yawned, and heaved to his side.

"Nice tight little formations. Damned Japs," hissed Sunderland, thumbing his nose at the sky.

Ingram counted a hundred Bettys then lost track. He closed his eyes but couldn't sleep until the vibrating faded to the south then he drifted off again...but not before he tried to work out a way to get through those damned destroyers...

26

---

7 May 1942
Looc Cove
Luzon, Philippines

A mosquito gnawed in Ingram's ear waking him up. He slapped at it then checked the sun: late afternoon.

Toliver was close by watching. He shifted his gaze out to sea as Ingram again slapped his ears and neck.

Ingram blinked, "Don't know if I'll ever catch up on sleep."

Toliver said nothing. His beard had become wiry, his hair upkept, and his clothing, it seemed, was more filthy than anyone else. But Toliver's eyes: They were red as if he'd been crying for the past two days. Yet they didn't glisten with tears. They were simply red.

Have to start somewhere, Ingram decided. He said softly, "Get any shut-eye?"

Toliver's eyes were fixed on two *Hubuki*s patrolling out to sea. "Ummm."

"Ollie, damnit! Say something."

Toliver looked at Ingram. Then strangely, his left eye stopped tracking and became fixed in its socket.

"Ollie, you're doing this to yourself. Knock it off!"

Toliver's eyes refocused for a moment. "Ummmm." Then the eye quit tracking again.

Ingram leaned close. "Ollie. Forget about the *Pelican*. That could have happened to anybody. I need you, Ollie. We all do."

Toliver's brows knit and his Adam's apple bounced as if he was going to speak. He opened his mouth, but abruptly stopped, looking over Ingram's shoulder.

Ingram sat back heavily and said softly, "Playing the boob won't do it, Ollie. Sooner or later you're going to have to come around."

Toliver said nothing; his eyes remained on the two destroyers.

A few minutes later, the sun's lower limb touched the South China Sea, making the light turn from brilliant reddish-yellow to a pale pink. Strange, Ingram thought, the Cicadas had chosen that moment to stop buzzing. Even the birds were silent. Why was that?

His answer came a moment later when a diesel engine approached from the north. As it grew louder, the men blinked and roused. Watching Sunderland unlimber his BAR and aim toward the entrance, they broke out the other BARs and 03s, braced them on the gunnel, and waited.

It was a barge.

"Good God," said Yardly.

The one-hundred-foot barge was packed with men so tight, they stood almost elbow to elbow. With the sun behind them, it was hard to tell what they looked like, or even what they wore. Dewitt crawled up and asked, "Suppose they're headed back to Fortune Island?"

"Must have set up a staging area there," said Ingram.

Holloway pulled out the binoculars and braced them on the gunnel, twirling the focus knobs.

Ingram asked, "

well?"

Holloway scanned until the barge disappeared behind the point. "They're GIs, all right. Mostly army. Saw a few white hats."

Ingram asked, "How many per barge?"

"Couple hundred, I'd say." answered Holloway.

"And there's--what, ten thousand on Corregidor?" Ingram asked DeWitt.

DeWitt said, "Eleven thousand. Altogether, twenty thousand or so on all four islands."

Ingram said. "That's a lot of barge trips."

"What's on your mind?" asked DeWitt.

"That," Ingram pointed. Another barge, loaded with prisoners, plowed past Looc Cove toward Fortune Island. "That's our ticket," said Ingram.

DeWitt spread his arms and let them drop, slapping his trousers.

"Take a lot of trips to ferry ten thousand men to Fortune Island," said Ingram. "If they run at dark, we go among them and squeeze through the picket line."

Another prisoner-laden barge growled by.

Ingram sat up and said, "Mr. Holloway, let's secure this boat for sea. Yardly. Evening rations. After that, we go."

They broke from under the trees a little after seven and cleared the entrance at full power. Further south, they slid past Point Fuego and the 51 Boat pitched up and down in troughs, with Forester fighting his tiller to keep his heading.

DeWitt leaned close to Ingram and, pointing at the growing darkness, said, "What is all this?"

Ingram said, "I'd say the wind is fifteen knots and building, Major. Could be to our advantage. Make us tougher to spot."

"Is this safe?"

"I imagine. Why do you ask?"

DeWitt gave Ingram a sour look, sat heavily and folded his arms. The men wedged themselves among brackets and thwarts and, even with the boat's rollicking, once again enjoyed the luxury of sleep. But from the way DeWitt was slumped on a thwart, Ingram guessed the major was as green as the 51 Boat's corroded engine bell.

Looking south, Ingram spotted the picket line in place again with the two destroyers stalking across their track. But for the moment, he knew they were safe. Moonrise wasn't until 2 a.m. and, except for starlight, it had become very dark.

Occasionally, Forester stooped over the binnacle to check his course, the red light's glow washed his face, making him look like Bela Lugosi. "Where to, Sir?" he asked.

"Head right for Fortune Island," said Ingram.

"Where is Fortune Island?" asked Forester.

Good Question.

Fortune Island, seven miles off the coast, was narrow, a mile long and only 370 feet high. Tonight, it was not visible at all. In fact, there was no horizon. Except for navigation lights on the picket line, it was now pitch black. Ingram waited while they rose up the backside of a trough and went over the top. "There," said Ingram pointing off to starboard, seeing a barge's white stern light. "Follow that."

Forester got the idea and they swung about five hundred yards aft of a barge, with the 51 Boat still pitching heavily. It was what Ingram wanted to do; follow a barge directly to Fortune then veer off and head around the island's western edge and run south. He just hadn't planned on it being so rough.

"Damnit!" Suddenly, Forester whipped the boat to starboard seeing red and green side lights bear down on them. He threw the rudder the other way to thread the needle between two empty barges. Their exhausts blasted from both sides as they headed back toward Manila Bay.

Choppy seas, combined with barge wakes, made the 51 Boat bounce up and down madly. Forester cursed, trying to hold a descent heading. A minute hadn't passed when Ingram heard a scream amidships, followed by a loud splintering crash. Stepping forward, he found Junior Forester, Farwell, Whittaker, and Bartholomew wrestling a fuel drum that had broken its lashings and rolled aft to crush a wooden thwart like a rotten egg.

"Someone screamed." yelled Ingram.

Farwell puffed, "Damn thing ran over my foot. I think it's okay. It just scared me."

Lucky. Ingram moved back to stand by Forester. In darkness, it took the four wheezing men thirty minutes to capture the barrel and properly tie it down. While they grunted, and cursed, a million things ran through his mind as he tried to organize his thoughts and plan ahead. What if Farwell's foot is broken and he doesn't know it yet? What about medical supplies? Is there enough food? And that damned Buda sounds like King Kong thumping around in a boxcar. It's going to need an overhaul, soon. How do we do that?

But they had the best talent as far as the engine was concerned. More than Bartholomew, Whittaker was the on-board genius when it came to small diesels. If anyone could keep the thing running it was Whittaker.

His mind turned to setting up a watch schedule. At some point, he wanted everybody to take a turn, with five men up at all times. Let's see, a helmsman, engineman, and three lookouts. What if--

A bright light stabbed at them, blinding Ingram, while a diesel engine roared past.

Forester heaved in right rudder and said, "Damnit. Didn't spot him until he was almost on top."

"He see us?" said Ingram, blinking.

"Don't see how he could miss, Sir," said Forester.

As the 51 Boat flopped over another wave, it seemed the rhythm was easier and the troughs not as deep. Ingram supposed things had evened out because they were farther from shore. But he was still blinded and it took a while for his eyes to adjust. Finally, he picked out the stern light of the barge Forester had avoided. It was about a quarter-mile away now, headed toward Luzon.

It hit him. "Damnit!"

"Sir?" said Forester.

Ingram dug under a thwart, finding a chart and unrolled it. He fumbled for a light and was surprised when someone stooped beside him and snapped on a flashlight with fingers over the lens. In the red glow, Ingram recognized Otis DeWitt looking worse than Lugosi in black and white.

"You feel okay?" said Ingram, making a mental note to tape a red rag over the lens.

"I've done better," DeWitt said with a thick tongue. "You trying to find out where we are?"

"That's not the problem," said Ingram. "The problem is behind us."

"Jap destroyer?"

"No. See the stern lights?" said Ingram pointing aft.

"Yes," said DeWitt. "Isn't that what you want?"

"Yes. But, I don't see bow lights. You know, the red and green ones which means the barges aren't coming out anymore tonight. The last bus to Fortune Island is straight ahead."

DeWitt peered ahead. "Where?"

Ingram had to wait until they eased over a swell. "There." When he pointed, he realized the stern light was getting smaller. With all this cargo, the 51 Boat wallowed at a snail's pace. And forward, he heard the men working the bilge pump, meaning they were taking water.

"You think that fellow had a radio?" asked DeWitt, pointing aft.

"If he does, we're up a creek."

"Maybe we better go back."

Ingram didn't want to admit he was thinking the same thing. He peered at the chart and, running a quick D/R, reckoned they were close to Fortune Island. He checked bearings, looking back to where Looc Cove lay and picked off a new course for Forester. But at the same moment, he saw something that made his heart turn cold. "Kill the light, Major."

DeWitt snapped off the flashlight and looked up. "What?"

Atop another crest, DeWitt had his answer. Almost dead aft, bright navigation lights ghosted into the coastline, stopped, then extinguished to a single, dull light. With the realization that a Japanese destroyer had anchored, DeWitt muttered, "Looks like Hotel Looc is all booked up tonight."

Ingram said to Whittaker. "That all the throttle you have?"

"Maybe a little more, Sir," said Whittaker, kneeling beside the engine.

"Do it."

Whittaker puttered, and the engine ran a little faster.

DeWitt clicked his teeth, "We should have gone inland."

Ingram allowed, "Maybe."

Thousands of stars were scattered overhead, allowing Ingram to finally discern the outline of Fortune Island. The barge they followed seemed to have reduced speed because it looked larger. Suddenly, the running lights went out, but he could still see the dark hulk. It seemed to be swinging left.

"I don't like this," muttered Ingram.

"Me neither," said Forester.

Ingram said. "Major. Go forward, please. I want everyone awake and into life jackets. Now."

Without argument, DeWitt stumbled about to rouse the men. Grumbling, they rubbed sleep from their eyes and donned life jackets.

A white light blinked from straight ahead. "Oh, shit," said Forester.

They got us," said Holloway. "Looks like it's on the island."

"What's that mean?" asked DeWitt

"It's a challenge," said Ingram, watching the light blink again: dit-dah, dah-dah-dah.

"He's flashing ABLE OPTION, Sir," said Forester.

"Dead slow, Whittaker," said Ingram. Then he shouted, "Farwell."

"Sir," said Farwell from the bow.

"Got a flashlight?"

"Right here, Sir."

Ingram rubbed his chin. It was such a crapshoot. What to signal? And as his stomach churned, he realized they all looked at him, expecting their skipper to come up with a miracle counter-sign that would somehow let them off the hook. He wanted to curse them for depending on him to make the decision that most likely would kill them all. Why not someone else? Someone smarter who knew all the answers. Someone who could get them out of this. Someone they could all look up to. Someone to whom Ingram could simply say, "Aye, aye, Sir" and do whatever the man wanted. Now, more than ever, he just wanted to follow orders.

He knew when Farwell flashed his response, the Japanese most likely would pounce all over them. Perhaps a seventy-five was sighted on them now. One touch on the trigger and...

He gave a long exhale. May as well beach the boat right here, throw his hands in the air, bow to the Japs, hand over his crew, and take their places beside their fellow Americans. He looked around the boat in desperation. Nobody stepped forward. Nobody seemed to offer a better idea. It was up to him.

The light pierced the darkness again: dit-dah, dah-dah-dah. They were closer, the waves were much smaller, which meant they were in the island's lee. Ingram was sure the light came from a control station on Fortune Island.

Farwell's silhouette was barely visible, yet his jaw stood out like something from Dick Tracy. What sort of muscles did it take to move that thing up and down, let alone eat, he marveled? No wonder they call him Bucket Mouth. He took a deep breath. "Farwell."

"Sir."

"Counter with OPTION ABLE."

"Sir. *OPTION ABLE*. Signal *OPTION ABLE*. Yes, Sir." Farwell's tone carried a tinge saying, "we're-screwed-if-you're-wrong-sir." He punched his flashlight with the response: Dah-dah-dah, dit-dah.

Two more empties roared by as the minutes crawled past.

Soon, Ingram distinguished Fortune Island's low humpback ridge. And the landscape was dotted by campfires, which in a way, seemed pathetic. But there was no challenge. No cannons. No ripping machine gun fire. No banzai charge with sword wielding Japanese crawling over the gunnels and chopping them into glistening, wiggling pieces of meat.

Sunderland muttered, "Real dazzle job, Bucket Mouth."

Just then the boat rose over a ground swell and a shout rose up forward.

"Sonofabitch!" yelled Forester, slamming his tiller over.

"Shift your rudder," shouted Ingram. Forester did it just in time with the 51 Boat's stern barely swinging out from under a barge's bow. It bulled down their starboard side, its bulk radiating heat.

"Pete, full throttle!" shrieked Forester. The 51 Boat surged ahead and, as the empty barge plowed into the gloom, a pair of flashes lit up the night followed by a thunk-thunk somewhere in the boat. "Bastard's shooting at us, Skipper," yelled Forester.

Ingram yelled, "Down everybody! Sunderland! Take that barge under fire."

"Got it." Sunderland propped his BAR on the gunnel and waited until the barges' shooter fired two more rounds. Spotting muzzle flashes right at the bow, Sunderland jammed the BAR's butt in his shoulder, took aim, and cranked out ten rounds on automatic. He waited for a moment and, not seeing return fire, shifted to the helmsman's pulpit and emptied the rest of his magazine into that.

"Enough," said Ingram, watching the barge swing into a lazy circle.

"Three guys on those gut buckets, Skipper," said Sunderland. "Still one to go."

"'Hold on,' I said," called Ingram.

"Skipper!" Forester pointed.

From darkness, a mass lunged toward them. Ingram recognized the graceful lines of the *Hubuki* in a tight turn three hundred yards away lining up to ram them. She was so close she couldn't depress her guns which normally could have chopped them to bits. Barely visible was her superstructure sporting square glass panes in the pilothouse. They glittered in starlight, making her appear like a leering shark.

Ingram swallowed, looking up to the ship as she drew closer.

"Skipper!" shrieked Forester.

Ingram tried to open his mouth to shout, to scream. Anything.

The *Hubuki* combined a backing bell on her port engine, ahead full on starboard, and threw her rudder left full to enhance her rotation. Edging closer, her searchlight clacked on and, almost immediately, fixed them in its powerful glare.

"Mr. Ingraaaam," pleaded Forester.

Ingram's brain shouted at his hand to shield his eyes. But he couldn't even do that.

A powerful hand grabbed Ingram's shoulder and shook it violently. Ingram snapped his head to the side, seeing Toliver's wild beard in hoary brightness. Ingram worked his mouth. But his lips barely moved.

Toliver shook again, stronger this time. Ingram heard a roaring in his ears and didn't know if it was in his head or outside. Miraculously, his hand moved and he raised it to shield the light. "Sunderland!" he finally croaked. "Get that damned light."

Sunderland slapped a new magazine in his BAR and started firing. Junior Forester grabbed another BAR and opened up, with the rest scrambling for weapons.

Sunderland pumped the last of his magazine into the *Hubuki*'s signal platform, and the searchlight fizzled out in a bright puff of smoke. While the gunner's mate cursed and rooted for another magazine, Junior Forester hosed down the thirty-seven-millimeter anti-aircraft gun tubs amidships.

"Shift your fire. Forester, get the pilothouse," yelled Ingram.

Junior pumped in the rounds and they heard glass shattering.

"Skipper!" yelled Kevin Forester.

Ingram turned to see the barge had circled and bore down on them once more. "Number three guy must be on the helm," said Holloway, raising a BAR and firing at the stern pulpit.

Sunderland said, "The guy's laughing at you, Mr. Holloway. He ain't standing up. He's prone or kneeling." He slapped in a new magazine and fired it all at the base of the stern pulpit. Enormous chunks of wood flew off, with the whole structure collapsing like barrel staves without rings.

Ingram gauged the *Hubuki*. Her skipper was good. And she was getting closer. But being near to land, she had to be careful, holding her speed to less than ten knots. Even so, the graceful ship twisted radically using her twin, forty-thousand-horsepower turbines. She was just about lined up to spear them.

Two hundred yards.

One Hundred.

Seventy-five.

"Jesus." said Holloway as the empty barge once again swooped by.

"Whittaker! Lights!" shouted Ingram.

"Huh?" said the engineman.

Ingram dove to the electrical panel, ripped it open, and flipped on the navigation lights.

In the *Hubuki's* pilothouse, men dropped to the deck, shrieking and screaming when Forester's bullets tore through the Plexiglas portholes. No one was seriously hurt, but her skipper, Lieutenant Commander Katsumi Fujimoto, was in a positive rage as he extricated his five-eight, one-hundred-sixty-five-pound frame from underneath a twenty-year-old ensign who wiggled in panic. With his forehead cut by flying glass, blood ran into Fujimoto's left eye as he rose off the deck, shouting. Trying to wipe the warm goo away, he spotted a darkened shape ahead that separated from a lighted boat close to his bow. Fujimoto screeched orders to his frustrated helmsman who, in exasperation, spun his wheel the opposite way and lined up on the dark boat fleeing to port. With great teamwork, skipper and helmsman coordinated engine orders and rudder to cleanly cut the escaping vermin in half.

The lean destroyer was no more than fifty yards away from the shore boat when she lunged through the barge. In fact, the *Hubuki* was so close, Ingram heard her high-pitched ventilation blowers pumping breath throughout the ship. Just then, her horn sounded, and she frantically reversed engines to keep from running aground on Fortune Island.

"Up yours, Tojo," Sunderland's resonant voice echoed against the *Hubuki*'s portside.

Ingram said, "Whittaker! Lights off."

Whittaker hit the light switch as the crackle of rifle fire echoed across to them. Gun flashes winked from the *Hubuki*'s main deck as her men fired into what remained of the barge.

Sunderland said, "Finally found the key to the gun locker. That Jap captain's gonna rip the gun boss alive tomorrow for sure, eh, Skipper?"

An explosion roared five hundred yards astern, illuminating the *Hubuki* lying dead in the water, with the flaming aft section of the barge bobbing alongside. "What the hell?" said Farwell.

"Not diesel fuel," said Bartholomew. "Maybe a barrel of hi-octane gas for an airplane or something."

"Which way, Skipper?" said Forester.

"Outboard side," said Ingram. "Cut it close as you can and head south."

Five minutes later, they cruised within a hundred yards of Fortune Island's western shore where pathetic little campfires glowed dimly. It made Ingram's stomach churn. Americans were within shouting distance, but now, he was leaving them behind: People he knew, people he had laughed with, people he'd fought with. People he had called friend. Several hundred, possibly thousands of friends were there now, trapped, with little hope for a long time to come.

"Poor bastards," said Holloway, running the back of his hand over his cheek.

Forester tended his tiller as the rest watched Fortune Island recede over their port quarter. Fire on the burning barge cast dim yellows and oranges on trees, huts, and tents. But no one was visible. Perhaps, thought Ingram, everyone was curled up asleep or they were too far away to be seen. But Ingram was disgusted with himself, because deep down, he was glad he couldn't see anyone, didn't have to again look into one of those hollow faces.

―――――――――

The other destroyers held their picket line positions leaving the 51 Boat's way clear.

"Skipper?" said Forester.

"One-eight-zero, Forester," said Ingram. Then, "Farwell."

"Sir."

"Relieve Forester. Yardly. Heat some water and fix coffee."

On impulse he looked back again. But whatever it was that bothered him, it wasn't on Fortune Island. It was something besides the specter of hundreds or even thousands of helpless comrades. Ingram turned, seeing Toliver's wiry beard. He, too, stared aft toward Fortune Island, firelight dancing on his pupils.

27

7 May 1942
14E 02.'08 N
121E 31.'40 E

With Fortune Island a mile astern, the 51 Boat plowed, in a mounting squall, toward Mindoro Island. But Fortune's campfires kept glaring at Ingram in silent reproach. The boat rolled and yawed in troughs until, one by one, the miserable beacons drew farther away and mercifully disappeared.

Finally, they were gone.

With Farwell at the tiller and Kevin Forester curled up amidships deep in much needed sleep, the others stood watching the blackness where Fortune Island lay. Aft, near the helmsman's station, Ingram thought about how close they had come to being killed; there would be other times. He hoped they would be as lucky.

And his fellow GIs on Fortune. His shipmates. He wondered about how close he had been to them; within shouting distance he supposed. Seeing his comrades stuffed into barges sapped his strength. In a way, Ingram supposed, he felt guilty that, out of eleven thousand he and eleven others had a chance;

and, as meager as that chance was, Ingram, for the time being, was free. It made him wonder if he really shouldn't be standing among the others on Fortune right now, doing his duty by suffering and dying with them.

It seemed strange that ships on the picket line kept their stations. And he knew the *Hubuki* hadn't rejoined the line, which meant she was carousing nearby without navigation lights. Why the hell hadn't she raised an alarm? Why weren't all of them charging around, pouring gunfire into the night, trying to blow them out of the water, instead of sedately marching back and forth.

Holloway must have been thinking the same thing, for he wiped a hand over his face and said, "What the hell are they doing?"

Ingram said, "Not sure. You can bet she's out there."

"Bastard tried to run us down."

Ingram nodded. "Had us dead to rights and muffed it. Now, time's on our side."

Moments later, a loud WHUMP was followed by a white phosphorescent burst lighting up the night. The star shell, dangled fifteen hundred feet above the ocean's surface about a mile to port. Three more WHUMPs announced another three illuminating shots that swayed in the breeze and descended by parachute. With the wind from the west, the four eerie lights drifted toward the mainland.

"Steer two-seven-zero," said Ingram

Farwell cranked in right rudder and the 51 Boat headed away from the star shell pattern, but she slogged directly out to sea and into wind waves with her sailors clutching for handholds and cursing.

"Bartholomew!" Ingram called.

"Sir!"

"Keep a sharp lookout for that *Hubuki*."

While Bartholomew peered through binoculars, Ingram stooped and rolled out a chart. Otis DeWitt crawled aft and wordlessly snapped on a flashlight. They examined Luzon's Kalatayan Peninsula, where Cape Santiago jutted out, forming the western edge of Balayan Bay. With dividers, Ingram stepped off the distance to the Cape: nineteen miles.

Another pattern of four star shells rolled out further east. Ingram swallowed rapidly, his voice raspy as he said, "Cape Santiago light should be visible dead ahead. Anyone see it?"

No one spoke and Ingram bent to his chart, realizing the fifty-foot-tower's beacon had most likely been extinguished; they would have to wait 'til later for a fix. On the chart, he checked Mindoro Island twenty-six miles to the south: closer, to the southwest, lay Ambil Island, situated a mile off the eastern shore of the much larger Lubang Island. The distance was about twenty miles. Ambil looked safer than Cape Santiago or Mindoro, which was fifteen miles off Luzon's west coast. He said to Holloway, "That's it, then, Ambil Island." He turned to Farwell to give a new course.

"Lubang's full of Japs," DeWitt said, peering at him in weak light. "I imagine Ambil is, too."

In fighting seasickness, DeWitt was doing anything to keep his mind off the boat's wild slamming and the spray whipping past his face. Ingram smiled in spite of their pounding. "You sure?"

DeWitt croaked, "Up until a day ago it was my job to attend daily intelligence briefings with General Moore. Lubang's full of Japs. But," his wiry forefinger jabbed at the Kalatayan Peninsula, "I don't think that is. The best dope we had was they were concentrated as far south as Nasugbu. From there on it's just little garrisons scattered here and there."

Holloway said, "With the Rock falling all that will change."

DeWitt grabbed a gunnel as the boat ran down the backside of a wave and slewed almost a hundred degrees to starboard.

"Shiiiit," said Farwell, pumping his tiller uselessly.

Ingram lifted the chart off the deck, just as a quartering wave tumbled over the starboard rail. Water surged around their ankles and rolled forward to slosh about amidships.

"Got anything better to do than play rubber ducky, Bucket Mouth?" howled Sunderland, yanking the bilge pump handle back and forth.

"Need somebody on the tiller who knows what the hell he's doin'," croaked Kevin Forester, throwing off a water-soaked blanket.

Junior Forester groaned, "Shitty helmsman."

"Junior, you think you're so hot, you get back here," yelled Farwell.

"Sorry, Bucket Mouth. The skipper would just pick me for top watch and dump you back to seaman deuce. I'd hate to see you cry."

"Jerk!"

"Just doin' you a favor."

Farwell was enraged, his voice gargled, "Oh yeah? How bout next time--"

"Bucket Mouth!" yelled Bartholomew.

Off the starboard bow, a dark mountain rushed at them. The boat was in danger of falling off to port and broaching. Farwell heaved in right rudder, then steadied the tiller as the 51 Boat pitched up forty-five degrees. She climbed the peak, the wave rolled under, and the boat dived into a dark chasm, slamming into the trough.

"Jesus, Bucket Mouth," shouted Kevin Forester.

Farwell paid no attention as he concentrated on the next roller. Not caught by surprise this time, he crested the wave then weaved comfortably down the backside. After a while, he was able to make sense out of the pattern and they settled down to a controlled wallowing.

Another series of star shells dotted the sky toward Luzon. DeWitt asked, "Shouldn't we head for the coast?"

Ingram nodded to the star shells.

"Okay, how about Maricaban?" asked Holloway.

Ingram tapped the pencil eraser on his front tooth for a moment, then picked up his dividers, lay down the chart, and stepped off the distance to Maricaban Island. "Here," he said. "Southeast of Balayan Bay. About thirty-six miles. With this sea, it could be a seven hour-haul. We would barely make it by sunrise. And it means we're committed to the Verde Island Passage." He looked up to DeWitt. "The Japs control all of Mindoro?"

DeWitt's campaign hat, barely outlined against the sky, nodded "yes."

"Even the west coast?" pleaded Ingram. He'd been thinking of duplicating Lieutenant John D. Bulkeley's route when the four remaining PT boats of his Motor Torpedo Squadron Three whisked General Macarthur to freedom almost two months before. Apo Island, twenty-three miles off the west central coast of Mindoro, had been Bulkeley's first stop.

DeWitt nodded and added with a thick voice, "You couldn't make Apo, tonight. And the Calavite Passage would be a deathtrap."

Ingram sighed, "We're committed to the Verde Island Passage, then."

"It's shorter," said DeWitt. "Is there moonlight tonight?"

"About two o'clock," said Ingram.

"It'll help us find a place to hide on Maricaban," said Holloway.

"You have a girlfriend on Maricaban or something?" asked DeWitt.

"As a matter of fact, her father owns a brewery there," said Holloway, looking the major in the face. "I'm dying to see her and slop up the old man's booze."

DeWitt said, "Lieutenant. If you're--"

"Come on, you two," said Ingram. Watching the last of a star shell pattern drift into the sea, he said, "Okay. We try for Maricaban. Rocky?"

"Sir!" replied Bartholomew.

"Any trace of that *Hubuki*?"

"Nossir."

"Very well. Major DeWitt, you and Mr. Holloway take the first watch. Mr. Holloway is watch captain. Wake Rocky and me at 0200." Looking up to Farwell, he said, "Come left to one-five-zero."

It took Farwell a minute to ease the boat around and settle on a south-westerly course. With that, she was back in troughs and staggered parallel to waves.

Ingram grabbed a blanket and wedged himself against a thwart. Every-thing was wet, either from the pooping wave or from spray and dew. He settled in as best he could; resolved to being miserable, knowing there would be little sleep tonight. But surprisingly, he relaxed and felt himself drifting...

Someone shook Ingram's shoulder. His Bulova's radium dial said: 2:30. He blinked and sat up to recognize the outline of Bartholomew's chief's hat. Whittaker was at the tiller and the engine seemed to be running well. The water seemed a little calmer, although the boat still yawed and slopped about occasionally. A few miles to the east, a dark Cape Santiago lighthouse was silhouetted by a rising quarter moon.

"Why didn't they wake me at two?" said Ingram.

"We took a vote and decided to let you sleep," said Bartholomew.

"Not again. Understand, Rocky?"

Bartholomew shrugged, "Yessir."

Ingram rose, finding another figure nearby.

"Can we talk for a moment?" It was Otis DeWitt's Texas twang.

Ingram rubbed his eyes, still miffed at not being awakened on time; Bartholomew hadn't done him any favors by not insisting. "What's up?"

"It's that fellow, Radtke," said DeWitt.

With aching joints, Ingram struggled to his knees and shoved his blanket under the seat. "The bastard really did kill Epperson."

"I believe you."

"It wasn't a damned trumpet that changed your mind."

I'll admit, that got me thinking." said DeWitt. "But it really was this." He unbuckled a pouch from his belt and handed it over. "Mordkin went out again the night that PBY crashed and recovered this. It's what that Richardson fellow must have been delivering."

"Dwight said his name was Fowler. Knew him in San Francisco."

"Whatever. Here. Take a look." He covered a flashlight, snapped it on, and handed over a stained leather pouch.

Cocking an eye at DeWitt, Ingram unzipped the pouch. Inside, the papers were moldy and stuck together. He found an ID photo and pulled it out.

"The real Walter Radtke," said DeWitt.

"Nice of everybody to let me and Dwight know," Ingram said caustically. "Who is the fellow that killed Dwight?"

"Have no idea."

"A spy?"

"I imagine."

"Damnit," said Ingram. "Dwight didn't have a chance. The sonofabitch shot him in the stomach. You ever seen a guy shot in the stomach, Major?"

DeWitt's eyes flinched just enough to let Ingram know this man was one who had always finagled staff jobs hiding behind the stars of the men he served. Unlike his fellow officers in the field, Otis DeWitt had escaped the onerous responsibility of ordering men to die, a task all great military leaders ultimately face in their careers. As a "tunnel rat," Otis DeWitt had eluded the horror of Corregidor until the very last days. He had not personally witnessed the consequences of what his superiors had ordered men to do.

Ingram said. "There was a lot of pain. Dwight's last moments were not easy."

DeWitt nodded dumbly toward the pouch. Ingram stared at him for a moment then reached in, finding a folded flimsy paper that crackled when he pulled it out:

.   .   .

TOP SECRET
    04200355Z
    FM: COM OP-20-G HYPO
    TO: COM PHILIPPINES
    INFO: A. CINPACFLT
    B. ONI
    BT
    1. EPPERSON, D. J., LT. USN, 476225; RADTKE, W. A., CT2 USN, 1187526 EXPOSED INFO EXTREMELY SENSITIVE TO U.S. STRATEGIC INTERESTS.
    2. IF TAKEN PRISONER, SUCH INFO COULD FALL TO ENEMY VIA TORTURE RESULTING IN GRAVE CONSEQUENCES TO U.S.
    3. IF CORREGIDOR SURRENDERS, EPPERSON AND RADTKE ARE NOT, REPEAT, NOT TO BE TAKEN PRISONER.
    4. PRIORITIES ARE:
    A) EVACUATION, US FORCES ONLY. PREFER
    SS, AIR, SURFACE OK.
    B) LIQUIDATION
    5. SANCTUARY WITH LOCAL RESISTANCE GROUPS NOT AUTHORIZED.
    6. ADTAKE.
    BT
"To Wainwright?"

"Yes. COMPHILIPPINES."

Ingram read it then said, "Anything else?"

DeWitt dug out the ID photo of a grinning man with hair parted in the middle. The photo was labeled:

RADTKE, W. A., BU2, USN, 1187526.

Ingram looked at the mildewed photo and whistled softly. "The real Walter Radtke. A bugler off the *North Carolina*. I wonder where he is now."

    "Dead, probably."

"Poor bastard. He played with Ziggy Ellman."

"I know. Here. What's this?" DeWitt dug out a section of damp foolscap that had collapsed to a loose wad. He straightened it out finding a pencil had scribbled: "Dwight, is this what you wanted?--Ben."

"Damn," said Ingram. "Dwight must have smelled a rat."

"'Ben' must be Richardson or Fowler or whoever he was," said DeWitt.

"I suppose so," said Ingram. He read the message again. "Look at this." He mouthed the passage, "'Liquidate' if...if they weren't evacuated by sub or airplane. Jesus! 'Liquidate.' As if Dwight was a Trotyskyite or something. Who the hell was supposed to do the 'liquidating?'"

DeWitt shook his head

"Fowler, you think?"

"Maybe. Did you have a chance to talk to Epperson about Fowler?"

"Buddies. They chased women in 'Frisco."

DeWitt nodded. "So, he was doing Epperson a favor."

"But then Fowler carried a .25-caliber pistol with a silencer."

"I see."

"And a stiletto strapped inside his thigh."

"Nasty."

"Some favor. He was probably sent here to liquidate both Radtke and Dwight no matter what." Ingram noticed "ADTAKE" (advise action taken) in item six of the message. "Did you reply to this?"

"No. The pouch came to us soaked. General Moore suggested we lay it aside to dry out. It ended up in a desk drawer and by the next day, well, it was forgotten because of all the crap that was going on. Hell, our crypto section even forgot to log it in."

"'Grave consequences to the United States,'" read Ingram. He handed the flimsy back to DeWitt. "What's OP-20-G HYPO?"

DeWitt looked from side to side and leaned closer.

Ingram laughed. "Don't worry, Major. I won't blab to the Japs."

DeWitt ignored the humor and said, "Those boys in the code-breaking business are a strange bunch. The few I know are dead serious. And the way they act, we're not even supposed to know they exist."

Ingram nodded, remembering how much Epperson had changed since the Academy days.

DeWitt paused, "Ever hear of a guy named Rochefort?"

"Who?"

"Joe Rochefort."

"No...yes. Dwight mentioned him, his boss I think. Who is he?"

DeWitt's voice dropped to a whisper, his tone conspiratorial. "I'm not even supposed to know this. I overheard Wainwright and Moore talking about him once when I was sitting on the crapper. They didn't know I was there. Apparently, Rochefort's a whiz kid. Knows the crypto business backwards and forward. Disseminated very accurate stuff to our G-2 which helped to save lives." He glanced back at Fortune Island. "I wonder which ones?"

The thirty-six-foot shore boat labored up the backside of a wave and staggered along the top. To Forester's surprise, the wave broke and they plunged six feet, crashing in the trough with salt water spewing in all directions.

Like a dog, Ingram stood with the others and shook off water. He took the moment to check their position. The darkened Cape Santiago lighthouse was farther aft and a rising quarter moon washed Luzon in a silvery luminescence leaving the rest of the sky dotted with thousands of glittering stars. He made a note to take a fix soon. Satisfied, he asked DeWitt, "...OP-20-G HYPO. Is that in Hawaii?"

DeWitt leaned against the gunnel and said in a near whisper, "It's a crypto center. Rochefort runs it, and it's connected by long line to the Rock."

Dwight Epperson's face appeared before Ingram in a demented slow motion; as if he were alive and stood alongside Otis DeWitt right now. The apparition's mouth formed an oval saying '...Midwaaaaay.'

"What?" barked DeWitt.

Ingram said. "ONI apparently felt Dwight and Radtke knew something that was...what did that message say-- 'extremely sensitive to U.S. strategic interests.'"

"'Resulting in grave consequences to U.S.,'" added DeWitt, finishing the phrase.

"ONI wanted to rub out Dwight and his sidekick if they weren't evacuated."

"Ummm."

"That's damn hardball."

"Yep."

"Today's May seventh?" muttered Ingram.

"The eighth."

Ingram looked up to DeWitt. "The Japs will hit Midway on June the fourth."

"Huh?"

"With everything they've got. Dwight said their entire carrier attack force will be in on it. The *Kido Butai* or whatever they call it. Three to one advantage."

"In ships?"

"Right."

"My God," said DeWitt.

"If the Japs draw out what remains of our fleet and defeats it, they'll have clear sailing all the way to the West Coast. You can kiss good-bye to San Diego, LA, and San Francisco."

A wave jolted DeWitt off the gunnel, and his hand shot out to brace himself.

"Radtke knows this?"

"Looks like it."

DeWitt glanced at Luzon. "We must get to a radio, quickly."

"I wish I knew how," said Ingram.

Pointing to land, DeWitt clambered to his knees. "There. The Philippine resistance. I'm convinced we'll find one there."

"Not now. The Japs will get us."

"Lieutenant. I order you." DeWitt seemed almost comical as he weaved with the boat's motion, dew dripping from his campaign hat.

"I agree it's a priority, Major. Another is that we survive. Crawling around the Luzon jungle ducking Jap patrols is not going to do it--"

"I said--"

"This is my boat. Remember, Major? I want to get my hands on that sono-fabitch as much as you. Before June fourth. But--" Ingram stroked his chin for a moment. "Wait."

"I'm waiting."

"Alright, I'll meet you halfway."

DeWitt stared at Ingram.

Ingram continued. "Amador. That guy Amador who went out with the first *Wolfish* batch?"

"What about him?"

"You said they were being dropped on Marinduque, right?"

"Yes."

"That means a radio."

"How do you know?"

"The *Wolfish* wouldn't put in there without some form of communication."

"Conjecture. We could lose valuable time."

"Any better ideas?"

"I prefer Luzon. Marinduque is a just a little island, Lieutenant."

"We'll find out soon enough. If not, we move on. I'm not going to needlessly risk my men, Major, on such an obvious target as Luzon. The place is full of Japs."

"You may be risking your country."

"We have time."

"Time. A short commodity." DeWitt sighed and looked toward the horizon. "At this moment, Radtke could be warning whoever he works for." DeWitt shook his head slowly and stuffed the mildewed message back into the pouch. "The 'grave consequences' could well rest at your door, Lieutenant."

28

7 May 1942
Imperial Japanese Army Garrison
Marinduque Island, Philippines

"What a coincidence. We've both spent time in California," Lieutenant Tuga said. With long, delicate fingers, he turned the ring over in his palm, examining it. "U.S. Naval Academy. Nice. Fourteen-carat gold, huh?" He held it close, seeing initials inside the band. "Who's ACI?"

"A friend."

Tuga wound a large handful of Helen Durand's rich, ebony hair around powerful fingers. "You love him?" He squeezed; her hair pulled horribly.

"No!" she screamed.

He yanked twice and threw her head back: It hit the bed's iron frame, hard.

"Yes!" she screamed again.

"Been to bed with him?"

"Yes!"

"That's better. Where is he now?"

"Pensacola."

"Flyboy, huh?

Helen Durand hardly heard him, her pain was so great.

Tuga pocketed Ingram's ring. "So, you grew up in California?"

Helen moaned. Her scalp seemed afire as he prattled on nonchalantly. "For me, it was just four years in California. UCLA. That's in Westwood. Nice place. Near LA. Lots of movie stars. Ever been there?"

Helen heaved another mighty gasp. She'd screamed so much over the past three days...or was it four...she could no longer cry. Like young Doña Valentina at the end, her voice was raspy. After burning her with cigarette butts and slicing her with a razor blade, Tuga's interest in her seemed to be waning. Actually, he'd only been at it for twenty minutes today.

He'd only groped clumsily at her a couple of times. What saved her was that she'd soiled herself the first day: mightily. She had been tied to the bed; they wouldn't let her get up and that was that. The stench was powerful and Tuga didn't like to get too close, except with his cigarettes. And like many cruel men, Helen reckoned, the man needed an audience for his demented acts. But most of Tuga's troops were gone: sent out to deliver invitations to local political leaders and garrison commanders around Southern Luzon and the key offshore islands.

"Printed invitations," Tuga said, as he shoved a lighted cigarette into her right foot instep. "Card stock, the best engraving. Good quality stuff," he said, as he did it again.

Through her screams, Helen heard Tuga's triumphant announcement that Corregidor had fallen. Celebrations were scheduled, the largest being a long-awaited state function scheduled in Manila on May 18. Tuga said reverently, "...Premier Tojo will be there, and so will I."

Her eyes had been squeezed shut. But now, she opened them for a moment and looked around the windowless room. Tuga sat patiently in a chair leaning against the wall, his arms crossed. It was a large hut and occasionally she heard low voices on the other side of a thin wall where a radio squealed. Her arms and legs were tied to the iron hospital-style bed and long ago she lost feeling to her limbs. It was hot, the room was without windows, designed as a large storage area. There was no circulation and a single light burned overhead.

Tuga heaved to his feet and walked over. "Once again, Miss Durand. Where did you grow up?" He waved a lighted cigarette over her left eye.

"R-R-R--Ramona."

"And where's that?"

"South."

"Ah. Near San Diego?"

"Y-Y-Y--"

"How far?"

Helen could see where that was going and pressed her lips.

"Come on, now." Tuga said gently.

"Thirty miles or so, northeast of--ieeeeyagh."

Tuga yanked her elbow straight out and thrust a burning cigarette butt deep in her arm pit. "Come on! Your lover's a flier. He's in San Diego. North Island Naval Air Station. Right?" he yelled.

She tried to scream; tears ran and oh, God it hurt. And he knew it. She was a mass of cuts and bruises. Yesterday, or was it the day before...Tuga had hit her in the face with his fist. Mercifully, it put her out for about six hours.

Alone. The other prisoners had been barged to Fortune Island but Tuga kept his promise. For all the others knew, Helen Durand was dead. She ceased to exist and now was Tuga's to rape as he'd boasted. She found it ironic that her best defense was her own excrement.

Tuga cursed and fumbled at her blouse. "As you Americans say, you can pay me now or you can pay me later."

Trying to avoid his fingers, she lifted herself away.

Tuga grabbed a handful of hair and pulled her face close. "I learned all about dames like you in California. And now I'm going to teach you." He spat and slammed her head down on the bed's tubular headboard and slapped her one way and then the next. Spittle flew as he screamed, "Whore! I stuff you in a bathtub to clean you off. Then I leave you to my men. They would love to jump you, just like that Filipina. How do you like that?"

She squirmed as he reached beneath, yanked up her blouse and fumbled at the catch on her bra. Just then there was a knock at the door. "Come!" Tuga growled, looking up.

Another *Kempetai*, Lieutenant Watanabe, dressed in a loose-fitting, rumpled gray suit walked in. Much shorter than Tuga, he carefully took off and pocketed round, rose-colored glasses. The two spoke in Japanese.

Tuga sucked in his breath and swore. In a moment, both were bent over her. Tuga grabbed her hair. "There is another matter, Miss Durand. I understand you know a man named Pablo Amador."

Helen's mouth was dry, making it hard to talk. She hadn't had anything to drink or eat in at least three days and the cigarette burns hurt. And now, Lieutenant Watanabe, another of Tuga's "associates" stood by. Tuga had his audience and was ready to go for her breasts. Like life-sized rats, four beady eyes stared down; a hand began fumbling with her blouse. Panic welled, her eyes rolled and she breathed hard. Soon, she hyperventilated.

Tuga, in his own little world, wasn't watching. Roughly yanking Helen's hair, he screamed directly in her ear in a loud, resonating voice, "Where is Amador?"

Enough. Mercifully, she lost consciousness.

Kiyoshi Tuga's junior year at UCLA was a bad one. It was 1936 and in February, he'd missed qualifying for the Berlin Olympics by one point. Tuga was crestfallen and embarrassed. His height, he thought, would give an overwhelming advantage. Yet, Takahashi Yokuda beat him out by a point and was selected to represent Nippon in javelin. That was that. No Berlin. No crowds screaming for Kiyoshi Tuga's victory. In resignation, he knew there was a purpose to all this. He would keep up his training. The 1940 Olympics would be in Tokyo. Already, they had broken ground for the stadium. In four years, he could throw the javelin before screaming crowds.

He returned to UCLA a month later. In March, on a rainy, Friday evening, he was trying to make time with a plump waitress in Roger's Westwood Diner on Wilshire Boulevard. The over-painted blonde wouldn't serve him. An incredulous Tuga made a fuss and she called him a "dirty Jap." Men gathered and threw him out.

In April, Tuga thought he had hit the jackpot. Her name was Phoebe Schumacher. She was a sorority queen, a gorgeous blonde, blue-eyed girl who went out with him three times. Then Phoebe accepted his invitation for the spring dance. Joyously, he spent his whole allowance renting a tuxedo complete with white dinner jacket.

Phoebe stood him up. As corsage and boutonniere wilted, Tuga frantically dialed her number over and over.

Busy.

Roger's Westwood Diner notwithstanding, this was the first time something like this had happened. Many times, Tuga had been dumped after the first date. But this time, Phoebe had led him on. It took two days for his rage to subside and figure it out.

The Sunday afternoon before the dance, he'd been invited out to her parent's house in the San Fernando Valley. By the Pacific Electric rail car, it took an hour to reach downtown Los Angeles, transfer to another red car, then another hour to reach the smallish Schumacher ranch in Van Nuys. It was hot in the Valley that day. They sat on a long porch shaded by six pepper trees, sipping lemonades.

What's your major?

Political Science.

What are you going to do after you graduate?

Government service.

Too bad about Berlin. Will you try for the Tokyo Olympics?

Yes.

How nice of your parents to send you here.

Not really, I'm here on a government grant.

Where do you live?

Santa Monica.

No. Back home.

Ah yes, Kuji.

Where's that?

A little town on Honshu's Pacific coast near the northern end.

Amazing. Pardon us for saying this, but your English is so good.

Tuga smiled.

Later, Tuga commented that Mr. Schumacher had a nice place. There was a long silence. Gus Schumacher finally muttered that he raised chickens; he used to be in the real estate business but then came the depression...

The inquisition continued after dinner.

What about your family? What's your father do?

He's an Army officer recently returned from duty in China.

China?

He served with the Kwangtung Army there. The rest of my family, I have two uncles and a brother, are fishermen.

Fish?

Tuga took the red car home that night. Phoebe Schumacher never spoke with him again.

The worst that year was the telegram from Kuji. He was summoned home for his father's funeral.

Colonel Yoshi Tuga had been arrested, quickly tried and executed for his part in a rebellion against the Prime Minister. The Tuga family was disgraced, Colonel Tuga's ashes were sent home three months later. It was a quiet, solemn occasion.

After graduation Tuga went in the army. He hated infantry and lunged at a chance to go into intelligence. Eventually, he was reviewed for secret service, his father's background overlooked for the moment, and accepted into *Kempetai* training the fall of 1939, just when Germany invaded Poland. These were heady times in Japan. In 1940, she consolidated her conquests on Asia's mainland, achieving one of her inner goals of *Hakko Ichiu*--"bringing the eight corners of the world under one roof."

Tuga's unit was very good, rooting out one traitor after another. Working in Tokyo, they became a favorite of General Hideki Tojo who had built the *Kempetai* to its current glory by crushing a Kwangtung Army officer's rebellion in the early thirties.

Tojo worked hard making the army pull together as one; he unified army and country; Tuga, with tens of thousands of others, worshipped Tojo and what he stood for.

As Tojo had wiped out resistance in the Kwangtung Army, Tuga went to work in Tokyo, learning his trade, torturing, maiming, making amends for the embarrassment of his father, always reading General Tojo's works, always mimicking his thoughts, always trying to do exactly what Tojo did.

Shortly after Tojo was appointed Prime Minister in October of 1941 (replacing Prince Konoye), Tuga's unit became an honor guard of sorts and was invited to march a few hundred meters with the general in a ceremony on the grounds of the Imperial Palace. Two and a half weeks they drilled like army soldiers forsaking their gruesome *Kempetai* work.

On the afternoon before the ceremony, Tojo's car swung around and stopped, the general in the back seat watching the practice. Finally, Tojo alighted from the car, a black, 1940 American Packard, and stood with arms akimbo. He shouted, Tuga's squad came to an abrupt and confused halt. Tojo shouted again and pointed directly at Tuga, ejecting him from the squad.

Tuga was not to march with the great Tojo. Hideki Tojo was five foot two. Lieutenant Tuga, was more than a foot taller at six-three. Where Tojo weighed 115 pounds soaking wet, Tuga weighed in at 190.

An embarrassed Tuga was relegated to driving the sound truck. But to Tuga's surprise, Tojo learned of Tuga's embarrassment after the ceremony. He was summoned to Tojo's car and introduced, shaking hands with the general through the open window. Tojo urged Tuga to do his best to support the *bushido* code and the *zaibatsu*, the ruling political party. Then, in a quiet aside, the little man admonished Tuga to report to him if he spotted anything out of order especially among the officers. He gave Tuga a card with a phone number. Tuga fervently nodded and said, "Yes, Sir."

Tojo's car drove off. All Tuga could think of was the next meeting. Tuga knew he would never be allowed to stand next to the miniature Tojo in a ceremony. But he could still report to him and shake his hand whether he was in a car or behind a desk.

Somebody threw a bucket of water in her face. A man was close by, rage etched in every molecule of his skin. Tuga slapped her twice, then hit her in her stomach. "I want to know now, or you die!"

What was he driving at? Helen would have said anything. All she could do was nod.

"Amador. Was he with you?"

A nod.

"Why didn't you tell me?" Tuga shouted.

He slapped her hard. Helen tried to scream, but it came out as a prolonged raspy moan.

"He escaped." Tuga demanded.

"He hid." She passed out.

Another bucket of water drenched her. She woke up coughing.

Tuga was at it again. "Where was he going?"

"...steamboat..."

"I know that, bitch. Where was he going?"

Helen tried to think. What was Tuga getting at? Everybody knew Pablo Amador was going to Nasipit.

"Don't pass out. Answer me." With all his strength, Tuga shook her shoulders.

"...Nasipit..."

Tuga threw her back. "Damn. I didn't realize it. Amador was on that submarine. I almost had him." He said to Watanabe in Japanese, "What was that Filipino's name?"

"Roberto."

"Why didn't he say anything about Amador earlier?"

"He was holding out for more money."

"Well, kill him."

"With respect, Sir. This man gave us Aguilar and Diaz."

"I said kill him."

"Yes Sir."

"Now call headquarters and order a boat. I'm going to Nasipit."

"What about her?"

"No good to me now." Tuga reached down and ran the back of his hand over her face.

They went out. Helen hadn't understood anything except Tuga's last words: "Santo Tomas."

29

8 May 1942
Maricaban Island
Philippines

They crept up to Maricaban, a narrow island two miles off Luzon. It was an hour before sunup as the thirty-six-foot boat worked its way through the reef and anchored in a shallow, uninhabited cove a half-mile south of Sepoe Point, the island's northwestern tip. The day grew humid as they lay thirty yards off a beach carpeted with unspoiled white sand and deep green palms. Otis DeWitt had, by default, been appointed intelligence expert, but he scratched his head and sucked through crooked teeth when Ingram asked about enemy garrisons on the island. Without better information, Ingram was reluctant to allow anyone ashore, so he restricted them to the boat. His sailors passed the day tossing and turning under a thick canvas tarp. With the oppressive heat, they jumped in and swam about for a few minutes. But the water was near the temperature of blood so they scrambled over the gunnel, where water evaporating from their clothes cooled them off. After forty-five minutes the process started over again.

Whittaker and Kevin Forester tried their luck at fishing, but grew tired after an hour or so. Yardly offered rations at four in the afternoon, but they were too hot and too grumpy to eat. And so, seconds stretched to minutes, and minutes mercifully to hours until darkness fell and they weighed anchor, happy to escape "Caldron Cove" as Holloway called it.

With Forester at the helm, they chugged easily through the Maricaban Strait, and by nine-thirty headed into the Verde Island Strait, a major shipping route in peacetime. But it was a tricky passage, known for masses of water surging from the Pacific through the San Bernardino Strait which lay over two hundred miles to the southeast. From there the water ran along Luzon's southern coast and into the Verde Island Strait, accelerating to near eight knots, causing violent rips and eddies. Here, the current would change directions unpredictably, giving sailors great cause for concern whenever they transited.

Tonight, there was a thick overcast and the situation was made worse since buoys and lighthouses had been yanked from service by the Japanese. Ingram was forced to dead reckon in the murk without any navigation references. By ten-fifteen they were almost through the narrows, when dead ahead, he spotted ominous shapes silhouetted against the blackness. He told Forester to come right and was soon astounded to discover they had closed three anchored ships.

"Further right, Forester!" Ingram hissed.

There was no doubt in Forester's mind the ships were Japanese and he needed little urging to swing his tiller further. Ingram was amazed to see two of the ships were the largest submarines he'd ever seen; they were anchored in a nest with exhausts blasting to charge batteries. Nearby, was a sulking destroyer. All three brooded at darken ship like nocturnal predators, eager to spring upon an unsuspecting victim.

Minutes later, when the 51 Boat neared the Passages' southeastern end, Ingram spotted what looked like a campfire near Luzon's Arenas Point. He peered at it for a while, discovering the light didn't draw aft. In fact--my God! The light moved forward, rather than aft, of their beam. Even at full power, they were being set back into the narrows.

Ingram opened his mouth to yell, but he couldn't find words.

"Current!" wheezed Farwell.

"Whittaker!" shouted Ingram, finally discovering his vocal cords.

The engineer bent to the Buda and coaxed out a few more rpm. But it didn't help. The current still shoved them back toward the narrows, where coal-black silhouettes of the anchored Japanese warships again took shape.

"Come on, Pete," Bartholomew urged through clenched teeth. He stood with hands on his knees, peering over the engineer's shoulder. Whittaker ignored him as he beseeched more power from his engine, but it overheated and began sputtering and making clanking noises.

"Overhaul," Whittaker muttered.

Bartholomew nearly yelled, "Screw the overhaul. You get us out of here, Pete, and I swear, I'll give you a new La Salle when we get back to the States.

"Cadillac," corrected Whittaker.

"Hey, what's wrong with a La Salle?" said Bartholomew, nervously looking aft. With the raging current, they had closed to within five hundred yards of the submarines and destroyer.

Whittaker reached in, fine-tuning the fuel flow. "Ain't a Cadillac."

"Yes, it is," said Bartholomew. "My brother-in-law's got one. Ride's smooth as a baby's butt."

The ships were getting bigger. Over the Buda's pathetic laboring, they could once again hear the throaty rumble of the submarine's diesels. And with the menace more imminent, they imagined they could *feel* the resonating thump of those engines.

"Hell with this." Ingram ran forward. "Toss the anchor."

Ingram, Brian Forester, Sunderland, and Yardly all jumped to the bow and cursed and scrambled to shove aside the crates, water tins, clothing and rifles that were scattered over the anchor locker. Working frantically, the four finally exposed the hatch.

Ingram sneaked a quick look over his shoulder, seeing they had drifted even closer to the nested submarines, the Buda's laboring notwithstanding.

A rusty latch squeaked. Sunderland ripped open the hatch and gave a satisfied grunt. "Got the Sonofabitch. Stand back."

Junior Forester said, "Wait. Is--?"

"Outta my way, Junior." growled Sunderland. He heaved and the anchor hit the water with a satisfying splash. Rode and line quickly zinged out of the anchor locker.

"Shit!" said Yardly.

"Huh?" said Sunderland, not realizing he'd forgot to check the anchor's bitter end. It wasn't tied to the boat. In seconds, everything would be gone.

Forester frantically grabbed what was left of a section of coil that hadn't ran. He tried to secure it around a cleat, but the slack paid out, making the line burn through his hands. Ingram, Sunderland, and Yardly jumped in to help. Forester, hissing in pain, had the line almost secure. The other three grabbed a bight and finished manhandling the line securely around the cleat.

The boat lurched. Ingram checked the campfire, finding there was no more sternway. The anchor held. "Shut it off," he yelled in a hoarse whisper.

Whittaker switched off the engine as Forester stumbled aft and sat on a thwart, sucking at his right hand and groaning.

Ingram kneeled beside him. "Stick your hands in the water," he said.

"I'll kill the bastard." Forester said, as he leaned over the gunnel and dipped his hands.

"Even seasoned sailors forget," Ingram mused, patting young Forester's back. "Do me a favor. Wait 'til we get to Australia before you kill him."

Forester said through clenched teeth. "Don't be surprised if he ain't here when you wake up some morning." Yardly made his way aft and dressed the young quartermaster striker's hand. Ingram watched for a while, then double-checked their position as they bobbed with the surge.

It was spooky being this close. Three hundred yards away, the submarine's diesels thundered and the destroyer's exhaust blowers whined as they waited helplessly. To Ingram, the shadows of Verde Island materialized into Imperial Japanese Marines running across the water, waving swords high in the air and shouting "banzai" in a screaming suicidal charge.

Then, strangely, the 51 Boat swung almost violently in the opposite direction. Now they were pointing toward the submarines as the current rushed to the southeast.

Ingram stood quickly and said, "Let's go."

With a whoop, Sunderland, Farwell, and Whittaker hauled in the anchor. Bartholomew started the engine. Kevin Forester grabbed the tiller ready to conn the boat. Soon, they popped through the narrows like a cork in rapids; it was almost as if someone had picked up the 51 Boat and hurled her through the Strait.

It was early twilight when Ingram picked out Mount San Antonio on Marinduque Island. He stood at the helm studying the roughly circular island. The chart had told him it was twenty miles in diameter and lay in an area called Tayabas Bay fifteen miles off Luzon's west coast. By sunrise he eased them around San Andres Point and idled into Calancan Bay looking for an uninhabited cove. He'd conned them only two hundred yards off the coast, but it was still dark inshore, and he had trouble picking out a spot to hide out for the day.

Suddenly, two Zero float planes blasted through Mompog Pass, fifty feet off the deck.

"Down!" cursed Ingram, making sure everyone scrambled for cover.

"What the hell's going on?" muttered DeWitt.

"We're heading for the beach," Ingram yelled, throwing the tiller hard to starboard. "Whittaker. Full power!"

Whittaker cranked in throttle, and the 51 Boat headed directly for Marinduque as everyone cringed on the deck. Bartholomew was curled up in a little ball. Junior Forester lay jammed under a thwart next to Yardly. But Sunderland sat up, propped his BAR and rammed in a magazine.

They held their breath as they drew close to shore and soon, white water boiled about fifty feet ahead. Ingram looked over his shoulder to see the Zeros circling at low altitude, only a mile or so away. He looked ahead to the white water.

Sunderland shouted. "Reef!"

Decision time. He looked desperately at the waves nearby, trying to find a dark spot that would indicate an entrance.

No chance.

Whittaker asked, "Slow down, Skipper?"

"No." Ingram looked over his shoulder. One of the Zeros banked around and headed straight for them. He was sure the pilot had them in his sights. He said. "Everybody ready to jump."

Wait. Here comes a big wave. Ingram wiggled the tiller a little to make sure he was lined up perpendicular to the long comer as it picked them up and carried them toward the reef at dizzying speed. Too late. It was out of his hands.

The Zero continued in its bank just as the ground swell lifted the boat, sending her over the reef and leaving the roaring waters behind.

"Sonofabitch," said Farwell, looking aft.

"What's going on?" sputtered Bartholomew, his teeth gritted.

Farwell said, "See for yourself."

They rose to their feet and gawked. It had all happened so fast, and Ingram was as surprised as anyone else to see the reef's turbulence astern. It almost seemed incongruous to him that he was now motoring serenely in a lagoon, heading for what looked like a dark, sheltered cove. He checked over his shoulder to see the Zeros still circled the same spot. He also noticed the 51 Boat pulled a large, frothy wake over the lagoon's crystal waters.

"Whittaker, dead slow," barked Ingram.

Whittaker throttled back and they coasted toward shore. The Zeros continued to buzz and dip and circle, then suddenly broke and ambled off to the northwest. Two minutes later they were gone.

An indentation in the cove provided a perfect anchorage with thick trees, roots, and vines on three sides while a canopy of leaves stretched overhead. Finding a rock outcropping, Forester tossed out the anchor, making sure the bitter end was properly secured to the boat this time. Whittaker switched off the Buda. Expecting a sweet silence, Ingram heard a distant rumbling.

Suddenly, Bartholomew grinned broadly, whipped off his chief's hat and wiped beads of perspiration from his balding forehead. "I'll be damned," he said.

"What?" muttered Sunderland

"Gotta be a waterfall," said Bartholomew. "What do you say, Junior?"

Junior Forester scrambled over rocks and up to a tree to tie a stern line. "I think so. Mist is rising just beyond those trees." He pointed to a thick grove of coconut palms just yards away.

Ingram said. "Okay, Forester. You and Rocky check on it. Take two canteens each. Major DeWitt. Why don't you grab a pistol and stand guard for them?"

"Glad to," said DeWitt, squaring his campaign hat. With just a little pomp, he strapped on a pistol belt and stepped ashore, where the overgrowth swallowed him along with Bartholomew and Forester.

With the growing light, Ingram decided he was satisfied with their anchorage. In fact, the growth was so thick it was almost like a tunnel. He peered at the dawn's first brilliant rays shining on a small stretch of sand twenty feet away. And, for the first time since Corregidor's siege began, he smelled the ancient Asian odor of dead fish, rotting leaves, and mud. This wouldn't be a bad place to spend a day or two, he thought.

"Whittaker," Ingram said, "Maybe we can beach the boat here and overhaul the engine?"

Whittaker fussed with an oil can and said, "Fine with me, Skipper. She's ready for it, I'll tell you."

"Mr. Holloway," said Ingram.

The tarp had been rigged overhead, and the jaygee was already stretched out ready for sleep. "...uh, Sir?"

"Go ashore and find out--"

"Skipper!"

Ingram looked up, finding Young Forester standing on the rocks. "What?"

"Big waterfall, Sir. Fresh water pool. Like in the movies. Everything except Dorothy Lamour and Jon Hall. Mr. DeWitt says to jump in. The water is fantastic."

"He sent you?"

"Yessir. It's only fifty yards that way."

"Baths?" said Beardsley.

"What the hell's a bath?" growled Sunderland. The nine men looked up to Forester as if he were a messenger from heaven.

Forester grinned. "You ought to see Rocky and Major DeWitt bare-assed. Like a couple of two-year-olds."

"That's it," said Ingram, throwing his hands in the air. "Who volunteers for guard?"

Whittaker stuck up his hand while the others grabbed canteens and five-gallon water cans with guffaws. They poured over the gunnel with catcalls of "...last one in's a rotten egg." Toliver and Yardly caught a grinning Beardsley, as he tumbled over the side. The three stumbled with the B-17 pilot over the rocks, where they clambered up an embankment to follow their shipmates into the palm grove.

Ingram laughed and hooted with the others while they clumped into deep greenery, as if headed toward Coney Island. But laughter soon gave way to thrashing and cursing as they slogged through thick underbrush with clanking canteens and five-gallon water cans snagging on vines.

The sun soared off the eastern horizon just as Ingram broke into a clearing, perhaps a hundred feet in diameter. It was surrounded by coconut palms and jackfruit trees. Hills rose to his left where clean, glistening water spewed through thick undergrowth, tumbled over rocks and fell ten feet roaring into a natural pool. From there it ran through a gravel mini-delta, meandering the last hundred feet to the lagoon.

A ghostly white Bartholomew stood at the waterfall's top, wearing nothing but his chief's hat. With a broad grin, he waved, jumped, and pulled his knees to his chest, smacking the pool with a large splash. Just as Bartholomew hit, Otis DeWitt surfaced, then stretched out to float on his back-spitting water in the air.

The cascading waterfall masked a collective, joyous bellow from the men of the 51 Boat. In seconds, they ripped off their putrid clothes; water containers clanked to the ground and they plunged in, immersing themselves in the healing, smoothness of fresh water for the first time in six months. The last was Beardsley, who yanked off his khakis and staggered about following the splashing sounds. "Any soap?" he asked.

Holloway yelled from the pool's middle. "What's the matter, Leon? Navy guys too dirty for you?"

"Crustiest bastards I ever met," Beardsley shouted, running toward Holloway's voice. He got as far as a foot deep, tripped, and fell on his face, while the others cheered.

Ingram ran past Beardsley, dove in, and swam underwater reveling in the cool layers five to seven feet beneath the surface. He rose, bumping into rocks on the far side of the pool and watched his men frolic back and forth, while the palm leaves turned from a deep red to bright gold to deep green as the sun climbed higher, giving the promise of another hot day. Beneath the rich sunrise, the Forester brothers stood at hip level in the shallow end, backhanding enormous sheets of water at each other. Sunderland pushed Yardley's head under while DeWitt and Holloway crawled up the boulders toward Bartholomew's diving platform. Even Toliver grinned as Beardsley knocked him aside with an elbow then splattered a handful of sand up his back. Ingram looked up into the dawn's brightening sky, thinking it was like he hadn't lived with danger for the last six months, hadn't seen death, nor heard the incredulous screams of the dying, as he and his shipmates jumped and splashed and swam and shouted through the waterfall's unrelenting roar.

Ingram tread toward a sheer drop, not unlike the deep end of a swimming pool where he looked straight up to see a flailing Fred Holloway leap into space and hit the water in an enormous cannonball.

It felt so good. Ingram ducked underwater and pushed off again, pulling deeper with his hands. Luxuriously, he scooped the cold that surrounded him in a fresh, comforting cloak.

Thirty feet away he bumped against another near-vertical rock, kicked off and swam easy laps underwater. At each end, he popped to the surface, took a breath and returned to the cool, enveloping deepness.

After five minutes, he'd swum twelve laps or so and felt lightheaded. Time for a break, he thought. Ingram rose to the surface under Bartholomew's rock and gazed up to see a body fifteen feet overhead perfectly framed against the sky in the form of an impeccable swan dive...

...except the body was...Oriental! Sonofabitch!

He twisted his head seeing three Japanese soldiers wiggling out of their shirts and dropping their pants at the other end! The diver rose to the surface and called to his friends. The water's roar masked his hail but he turned slowly around with a smile on his face and--

Ingram ducked.

He pushed off and went deep, frantically thinking. Damn! Where was everyone? How many Japs were at the other end? Had anyone seen him? He remembered a tuft of tall weeds near the deep end. Aiming for the spot, he rolled to his back and barely broke the surface silently treading with only nose and lips above the surface. Looking behind, he saw the weed tuft and pulled for it, finding the water about three feet deep. It afforded him adequate cover and he squatted in the muddy ooze watching the soldiers lather with soap while the diver leisurely breast stroked toward his buddies.

The diver shouted something as another threw a bar of soap with great strength. Jumping in the air reaching, the man reached, but the soap bar bounced off his hand and flew toward the middle of the pool where waterfall wavelets pushed it on a course directly for the weeds where Ingram was hiding. The foursome laughed and jeered for a minute or so, then the soldier remembered his soap. He looked around the pool just as the errant soap had the temerity to bob through the weeds and nudge against Ingram's right cheek.

He was afraid even to acknowledge it was there lest his eyeball's movements be detected. As if with its own spirit, the bar gently tapped his cheek again. He looked down seeing the label imprinted deeply in the soap: IVORY. Shit. Betrayed by something made in the USA. Slowly, deftly, Ingram reached up and pulled the damn thing under.

The soldier stood at hip level, looking for his soap. After a shout, another bar was tossed, and he caught it this time.

It took the foursome twenty minutes to finish bathing. Then they toweled off, dressed, and vanished into the undergrowth.

Ingram slowly released his breath and waited a full five minutes before he even turned his head. Where the hell is everybody?

Finally, he ventured to shore, finding an inlet he hadn't seen earlier. It was dark, and he tread into it to discover thick vines and grass formed a thick green wall at the far end. His knees grazed the bottom, so he stood in slimy bottom ooze that squeezed between his toes, making him shiver and think of leeches and water snakes and crocodiles.

Stepping on a smooth rock, he rose from the water and gripped the limb of a large, dead tree stump. "What the hell's going on?" he muttered. Grabbing another branch, he pulled himself onto the next rock and jumped on a low, soggy embankment. Looking into darkness, he drew a sharp breath. Two feet from his navel was the muzzle of a Thompson .45 caliber submachine gun. Behind the Thompson was an oriental wearing a planter's hat, a gold tooth, and a large grin. "Welcome to Marinduque Meester Ingram," the man said.

30

The seventeen-mile-wide passage was a major choke-point between the Celebes and Sulu seas. The Philippines lay to the east with its Sulu Archipelago jutting two hundred miles southwest from Mindanao. The Passages' western side was bounded by the Sibutu Island Group, also part of the Philippines, which lay just off Mangrove Point, Borneo's eastern extremity.

Shortly after midday, a thirty-knot southerly blasted through the passage, building tall, well-formed rollers to march north into the Sulu Sea. These white capped wind-waves caromed off the submarine's port quarter, giving her poor rudder control and causing a sickening, almost slewing motion. She chased her target at nineteen knots and could have gone a little faster, but the *Wolfish*'s engineers were nursing the number three main engine again. The nine-cylinder diesel's temperature was up, and it could only run at ninety percent. That, plus a barnacle-encrusted bottom, levied a four-knot

speed penalty on this fleet submarine's hull--in the pre-war days the new
U.S. Navy submarines were called fleet submarines because of their capa-
bility to scout ahead of the main battle fleet.

The war had begun over six months ago, and *Wolfish* was an Asiatic-
based submarine that survived the Japanese attack on the Cavite Naval Base
on December 8, 1941. Since then, she had been pushed to her limits without
the luxury of much needed maintenance, including a haul out and bottom
cleaning.

Kapitänleutnant Helmut Döttmer, now comfortable in a new set of
United States Navy dungarees, was at his general quarters station. It was in
the passageway just forward of the galley, which was part of crew's mess
compartment. Döttmer considered himself fortunate to be stationed here for
GQ. The other evacuees were assigned to the crew's berthing compartment,
the next compartment aft, where they climbed in bunks to sweat out whatever was going on. Indeed, Döttmer had been lucky. Chief Radioman Hall
had given into his plea and tentatively assigned him to radio duties, which
included backup watch stander in the one in three watch section. He was
also backup radioman during GQ, which was why he now stood in this
passage looking through the hatchway into the *Wolfish's* control room. Actually, GQ hadn't yet sounded, but everyone, knowing a pursuit was on, had
drifted to their stations, anticipating the gong.

The radio shack, an area of great interest to Döttmer, was situated against
the portside of the control room's aft bulkhead. The watertight compartment
immediately aft was the galley and crew's mess. Döttmer sat in the hatchway
like a patiently circling vulture, listening and watching and waiting to have
just sixty to ninety seconds alone in the cramped radio shack.

Primary access to the outside was from a ladder in the control room up
through a hatch to the conning tower and up another hatch onto the bridge.
When submerged, the conning tower was crammed with the attack team
where Ronnie commanded from one of the *Wolfish's* two periscopes.

But today, Ronnie was on the bridge with Lieutenant Morton W. Sampson, the *Wolfish's* Operations officer. They stood with feet planted on a
wooden grate scanning to starboard, trying their best to pick out their target
from Bonggaw Island's landmass, one of the westernmost islands in the Sulu
Archipelago. Well above Ronnie and Lieutenant Sampson were two lookouts
strapped into the periscope shears, one responsible for a one hundred eighty

degree sweep to starboard, the other to port. Perched high above everybody on its own mast, was a gadget called a radar antennae that twirled a lonely sentinel. It had been hurriedly installed before they last got underway from Fremantle. No one trusted the damn thing, since it gave false echoes and constantly broke down. Even now, a technician sat with legs splayed, muttering to himself, in the aft part of the conning tower with parts and diagrams scattered all around. Everyone, including officers, called the portly, rather professorial looking man *squatter* since, except for meals and occasional sleep, he'd been there the whole voyage.

Ronnie waved at Bonggaw Island. "Mort, he's in there, damnit. Wipe 'em off and try again."

Sampson took a rag from his pocket, wiped his binocular lenses, braced himself on the bulwark, and carefully examined the verdant green mass of Bonggaw Island. It was warm, almost ninety degrees with as much humidity. But the thirty-knot breeze on their port quarter whipped spray off the tops of the waves, bringing occasional blasts of white water to drench the officer's short sleeve khaki shirts, shorts, shoes and binoculars. Higher in the periscope shears, the two lookouts were free of the spray and remained dry.

"See anything?" said Ronnie.

"Nope," Sampson replied. "She's over the horizon. Must have come further right."

Ronnie cupped a hand to his mouth and shouted up to the starboard lookout, "Babcock, you still have him?"

Babcock lowered his binoculars and called back, "Barely, Captain. Hull down. Just the tops, now."

"Hmmmf." Ronnie stooped over the conning tower hatch and yelled down, "Whoddya think, Gordie?"

Inside the conning tower, Lieutenant Gordon E. Chance, the *Wolfish's* executive officer had been tracking the target through the attack periscope. He stepped forward and, although he could see Ronnie about five feet above him, had to shout over the wind and occasional sheets of water spewing down the hatch. "She's definitely come right, Captain. We have her on three-three-five now, still at fourteen knots. Range has opened to eleven thousand five hundred."

"Hugging the coast." A statement.

"I concur, Captain."

"Anything further on the ID?" asked Ronnie.

Chance was about to say no when, Michaels, a second-class quartermaster, scrambled up the hatch from the control room. Breathlessly, he plopped a copy of ONI-208J, a thick top secret merchant ship recognition manual, in Chance's hands. Partially bald, shirtless and sweating, the thin Michaels pointed with a bony finger. Chance nodded to Michaels and shouted up, "*Yucatan Maru*, class, Captain. One of only one. Eight thousand two hundred tons, three hundred seventy-five feet, fifteen knots."

"What's she draw?"

"Uhhhh." Chance's finger jinked down a dimension table, "Twenty-one feet. The pub thinks she's a refrigeration ship, but they're not sure."

Ronnie rubbed his chin. "Okay. No duds this time. So, let's not leave anything to chance, no pun intended Gordo. I'll want tubes two, three, four, and five forward, and seven and eight aft. Set depth fifteen feet all torpedoes, and tell 'em now, so they have plenty of time to make sure everything works."

"Aye, aye, Captain." Chance drew a deep breath, then said, "Exploders?"

Ronnie said, "We'll give the magnetics another try. But make sure. Pull one torpedo forward and another aft, and check both their exploders and depth engines with a fine-tooth comb."

"Aye, aye, Captain."

"Eight-thousand-ton reefer, huh? Don't you think we should see a destroyer or two? Why don't we see destroyers, or at least airplanes?"

"Dunno, Captain."

"What's the latest on number three?"

"Foggy thinks the exhaust manifold is cracked. He wants to shut it down and take a look." Foggy was the *Wolfish*'s engineering officer, Lieutenant Junior Grade Raleigh T. Sutcliff.

"Jesus."

"What'll I tell him?"

"Negatory. We get the Maru first." Ronnie looked up for a moment, then said, "Okay, come right to three-five-zero and give me a course to intercept by sunset."

"Aye, aye, Captain." Chance ordered the helmsmen who stood in the forward part of the conning tower, "Collins, right fifteen degrees rudder. Steady on three-five-zero."

On the bridge, Ronnie stood and looked aft to check the *Wolfish*'s wake.

Soon, a white knuckle boiled up, a section of extra-frothy turbulence caused by rudder drag. As she turned to her new course, long, marching rollers lifted the submarine's stern, and she took an even more pronounced slewing movement. With no letup in the spray, Ronnie was drenched again, and it took a while to blink away the water. The next time he focused on the gyro repeater, the *Wolfish* had settled on her new course: three-five-zero.

He stepped next to Sampson and pounded a fist on the bulwark. "Damn, Mort. I wanted that carrier. Now, alls we got is a lousy reefer." Something was wrong with the message they had received from COMSUBPAC. Keeping a sharp eye in the Sibutu Passage for the past eighteen hours had produced no tempting targets, no war-ravaged fleet, no fat carriers limping toward Japan's home islands from a battle in the Coral Sea."

Studying the horizon, Sampson said, "So we sink a reefer, and the Nips don't get their ice cream."

"Wonderful." Ronnie raised his binoculars and focused on Bonggaw's lush shoreline. He braced his elbows to counteract the submarine's rolling so he could pick out the tops of the *Yucatan Maru*. "Damn."

"Or maybe fresh tomatoes."

"Wonderful."

"Oranges?"

"Shut up, Mort."

Dominic Federico Lorca, radioman second class, played the fiddle. Döttmer had heard him in the forward torpedo room one night playing something by Bach. He'd squeezed by sweaty bodies, ducked under a stowed torpedo, and slid next to the radioman. "Fugue? G-sharp minor?" he asked.

Lorca's eyes were closed and he barely nodded as he dipped his shoulders and twisted his torso to his music. With a twinge of jealousy Döttmer wondered how could a common thug like this play so well? It was obvious the violinist knew how to take care of himself. He was broad, barrel-chested, having well-muscled biceps. With a nebulous Brooklyn heritage, Lorca had thick, black, curly hair that grew over a heavily pockmarked face and hideously displaced nose. Both of Lorca's arms were tattooed. The left said, "Arrivederci, Tojo" with a black-gloved fist hitting a Japanese caricature over the head; the right bicep sported a bleeding heart that said "Mother".

And yet, for all Döttmer knew. Lorca could have been one of those young thugs that smashed his hand in that tenement house door. And the jerk was able to play the violin while Döttmer was forced into the trumpet.

And now, Lorca stood next to Döttmer in the control room, keeping an eye on the radio room, in case he was needed. For Lorca was the top radio man in the boat. With amazing accuracy, he could send and receive faster than anyone else. It was entirely second nature and to the uninitiated, it looked as though Lorca was goldbricking. He would lay his bleeping earphones--he called them "cans"--one on top of each of his broad shoulders, turn up the volume, and type messages while talking to someone or reading a magazine. It gave one an eerie feeling, as if a squealing phantom sat atop Lorca's shoulders to which he barely paid any attention.

The radio room door burst open. A loud, slashing, belch announced Chief Hall. The slewing submarine made him walk drunkenly, bouncing off bulkheads as he made his way toward the hatch. "Take care of things for a minute, Dominic. I need something to eat."

"Got it, chief." Lorca disappeared into the radio shack.

Hall stepped over the hatch coaming, eased past Döttmer with a nod, and walked into the galley. Döttmer watched the chief grab a sandwich from a pile left out by the cooks and pour coffee that had been brewing since morning.

Hall took three enormous bites and gulped his coffee. With a grin, Hall waved his mug and growled through stuffed cheeks, "Java tastes like shit. Ulcers for sure one of these days." He grabbed another sandwich, walked to a table, and sat facing aft.

Döttmer saw that Lorca had left the radio room door open a few inches and he dared not miss a chance for his first real look. He stepped through the hatch and peered inside the door. Lorca was leaning back in a chair with his "cans" carelessly draped around his neck. Hissing noises occasionally rose from the cans and faded like steam from a Union Pacific engine. He looked up with bored interest then returned to a well-thumbed copy of the *Saturday Evening Post*.

Döttmer stepped boldly all the way in, studying everything, freezing each object in his memory as if he'd be thrown out when Lorca came to his senses.

A giant transmitter was mounted five feet off the deck against the forward bulkhead; six receivers were stacked in twos on the port bulkhead; papers spilled from an open safe to Lorca's left. Behind him were lockers and a bookshelf jammed with technical manuals and code books. At Lorca's knees was a small desk with an Underwood typewriter, a telegraph key, message pads, blank paper, and carbons. A small bulkhead-mounted fan with rubber blades did little more than make flimsies on the message board flutter each time it swept back and forth.

A yellow light indicated the transmitter was on, and a red-and-white striped guard latch was mounted over a switch labeled "transmit." To the right was a tuning knob with several scales, but to Döttmer it looked like he would be able to transmit in the five to ten megacycle range.

Perfect. How about the--

The can's hissing turned to a squeal, then an urgent beeping. Lorca looked up and shouted toward the door, "Priority for Negat-Peter-Peter-Dog from COMSUBPAC. You want me to take it, Chief?" NPPD was the Wolfish's call sign. It was a rather famous one among submariners because the last three phonetics, "--Peter, Peter, Dog," were extrapolated to indicate an overly amorous canine with two peckers.

No answer from aft. Lorca looked up at Döttmer.

"Okay," Döttmer said, and stepped into the passageway. Grabbing on to overhead pipes, he made his way through the hatch. Seeing Chief Hall hunched over what had to be a third sandwich, he said, "Chief, COMSUBPAC has a priority message coming in. You want Lorca to handle it?"

Hall half-turned, his cheeks bulged as he waved. "Uummmph."

Döttmer returned to the radio room to find Lorca already taking the message while glancing casually at his magazine. "Okay?" said Lorca.

"Okay."

Lorca tapped his Underwood and said, "How long you been playing the horn?"

"Ten years."

"Who with?"

"Ziggy Ellman. Backup. They used to call me when someone got sick."

It was a long message. With a practiced hand, Lorca yanked the first sheet from the Underwood's roller and inserted another in one smooth motion, saying, "Me, too. I tried out for the New York Phil. Nuthin'. Six months go by. Then one night a guy got sick and they let me play."

"What was it?"

"Mahler's 'Fifth.'"

Goosebumps ran up Döttmer's arms. Mahler's Fifth. With its emotional trumpet solo, it was his favorite piece. Trying to put it out of his mind, he bent to study the transmitter more closely. It was still in standby. Submarines were on strict radio silence and didn't usually acknowledge messages, especially in a war zone. But it looked like the transmitter would be easy to activate. And once he raised Berlin, he could get Canaris' message off in thirty to forty-five seconds. That was all he needed.

"*Fünf und vierzig sekunden*," Döttmer muttered.

"Huh?" said Lorca, tapping the Underwood.

"Mahler's Fifth. It's my favorite." Döttmer shoved his left hand in the back of his belt, then ran his right over his neck finding it was sticky with sweat. And it wasn't because of humidity in the Sibutu Passage.

Number three main engine took a turn for the worse and began to issue rumblings and clankings uncharacteristic of a Fairbanks Morse, so at four in the afternoon Foggy Sutcliff pleaded his case. Ronnie gave reluctant permission to secure the engine, admonishing Sutcliff to bring the engine back on line as soon as possible. Sutcliff rumbled a vigorous "Aye, Aye, Sir," and with two machinist's mates, rolled up his sleeves and tore into the recalcitrant behemoth.

Thus, with their speed advantage cut by two knots, Ronnie was unable to complete his "end around" and intercept the *Yucatan Maru* at sunset. Instead, he had to settle for an eight-thirty attack. Fine, he muttered to himself, while scanning ahead into the Sulu Sea. Down to seventeen knots. Lousy two-knot differential. Instead we chow down at sunset. Spaghetti tonight; everybody with full bellies, hopefully on the ball. Sound GQ at 2015; surface attack with a four-torpedo spread at 2030; scratch eight-thousand tons and start the movie at 2045. Take a light shower at 2230 and into the sack. It's been a long day.

Ronnie was good at informing the crew on the IMC loudspeaker system, so Döttmer knew the tactical situation by eight-twenty that evening and, although Ronnie hadn't yet sounded GQ, he stood resolutely in the passage way waiting for the general quarters alarm. His vision into the control room was again blocked by Lorca, who stood in the passageway softly talking to Chief Hall in the radio shack.

With the *Wolfish* still reeling in the quartering sea, men hung on to anything convenient. Döttmer was braced against the galley bulkhead and Lorca, he noticed, held his balance by wrapping his fingers around hatch's "knife edges"; the hatch itself was clipped open by a long, screen window-type hooking device. Tonight, they ran the surface attack from the bridge so the control room crew missed out hearing their captain set up the problem, normally heard from inside the conning tower when submerged.

Kimble, an overweight, redheaded storekeeper, stepped beside Döttmer. "Hey Radtke," the man said.

"Yeah?"

"Unclip the hatch?"

"Yeah." Döttmer had done it before, allowing Kimble, who sometimes tidied up after chow, to hang up dish towels and stow a broom and dust pan. Döttmer flipped up the latch-hook and the hatch sprang out a bit, with Kimble swinging it farther away from the bulkhead. Just then, they heard commotion in the control room and looked up to see a man being handed down from the conning tower. The sailor was semiconscious and blood ran down his face.

Ensign Gruber, acting as diving officer, turned to Döttmer and Lorca, saying, "You two. Bear a hand."

Döttmer rushed forward, and with three other men, helped to ease the man down the hatch and onto the deck.

Chief Hall bellowed, "Take him aft and lay him on a table. Call the doc."

"What happened?" groaned Lorca, lifting the man's shoulders.

"Easy with him. He slipped off the periscope platform when they changed lookouts," said Lil' Adolf, dabbing away blood from the sailor's scalp. "May have a busted arm, too. His left."

Döttmer grabbed the man's feet and, with a nod from Lorca, carried the groaning sailor aft through the hatch. They laid him on a table in the mess compartment just as Doc Gaspar, the ship's second class pharmacist's mate, came from back aft and opened his medical bag. He bent over, thumbing away the sailor's hair, examined the scalp wound, and said, "Not too bad. Ten stitches, maybe twelve. Now for the arm."

Lorca drifted back to his place at the radio shack, while Döttmer watched Gaspar gently probe the man's arm. "May have to set this," Gaspar muttered.

Döttmer said, "Is he going to be--"

"Radtke, damnit. I'm talking to you." It was Lil' Adolph, yelling through the hatch.

"Huh?" Döttmer looked up.

"Off and on." Lil' Adolph's moustache bounced up and down as he jabbed a thumb over his shoulder. "You're posted topside as a replacement."

Döttmer looked at Gaspar who said, "Go on. I got it."

"On my way, Mr. Gruber." Döttmer plunged through the hatch. Lorca stepped aside, with Döttmer zipping past and up the control room ladder. As he did, he noticed the rolling sensation increased as he climbed higher in the submarine. But something nagged at his mind as he sprinted through the conning tower. It was forgotten as he dashed up the ladder and stepped onto the bridge into cool, clear night air.

The rich, fertile odor of Asia told him they were close to land. Two lookouts were perched in the shears and Lieutenant Sampson was on the starboard side of the bridge. Döttmer stepped before Ronnie to report. Realizing he'd forgotten a hat, he didn't salute. "Radtke, Sir."

An agitated Ronnie stood at his Target-Bearing Transmitter. Grabbing a handful of Döttmer's shirt, he pulled him close and pointed to a spot aft on the starboard side of the bridge. "Right there, son. I want you to stand right there and keep constant watch on that Jap reefer as she approaches. You can barely see her masts now. Got it?" He handed over a pair of binoculars.

Döttmer accepted them like they were plated with gold. "Yessir!"

Ronnie leaned over the gyro repeater to check their course. The compass card's red illumination combined with pointed teeth, gave his face a demonic cast. "Let me know if you see anything unusual. Anything at all."

"Yessir!" Radtke walked over, braced himself on the bulwarks, and adjusted his binoculars. He found a clear, sharp horizon and almost immediately spotted the ship's masts, even though she ran without lights. What was it that nagged? What--there. "I have him, Captain," said Döttmer.

"Angle on the bow?" barked Ronnie.

Döttmer remembered what that meant from his *Kriegsmarine* basic training. But he first had to juggle the translation.

"Damnit. Target angle--you! What's your name?" yelled Ronnie.

"Port zero--" That's it! Kimble hadn't reclipped the hatch! And Lorca had resumed his position stooping at the radio room door with his fingers wrapped around the hatch "knife edges" to hang on in this seaway. Perfect!

"What the hell was that Sailor?" demanded Ronnie.

"Sorry, Sir. A sneeze, Sir. Angle on the bow; port, zero-one-zero. Opening slightly." And Lorca would deserve it, Döttmer decided. The Italian with the Tojo tattoo was a shitty violin player. And he was from New York. They were about the same age. Maybe he really was one of those who slammed his hand in the door.

Ronnie and Mr. Sampson muttered to one another setting up the attack.

A long, rolling wave pitched the *Wolfish* to port. Döttmer had to hang on. And yes, Lorca, too, had to hang on. He was left-handed; the one he used in the hatchway now, and the one he used for his typing and deadly accurate telegraphic work. When the seventy-five-pound hatch slammed on Lorca's hand he wouldn't be able to do either and, sadly, he wouldn't be able to finger violin strings for a long time. Maybe never again.

Not even Mahler's 'Fifth.'

Döttmer couldn't believe his luck. After sounding GQ, Ronnie had let him stay on the bridge for the surface attack. He tightened the binoculars' focus as the dark, glistening *Yucatan Maru* filled his lenses. She was about a half-mile away, steaming on a course that would take her directly across the *Wolfish*'s bow.

"Range?" snapped Ronnie.

Chance's voice gurgled on the bridge's speaker-microphone, "You won't believe this, Captain. The Squatter has the radar working."

"You're kidding!"

"Range, one-three-two-five." The distance was thirteen hundred and twenty-five yards, a little over a half-mile.

"Sonofabitch," muttered Ronnie as he hunched over his Target Bearing Transmitter. "Wonders never cease. Alright now, stand by for constant observations." He spread his feet a bit for a more comfortable stance and sighted the Maru. "Bearing...Mark!"

"Bearing three-five-zero," said Sampson.

Squeezing his eye tight to the cold rubber eyepiece, Ronnie said, "Range...Mark!"

"Range one-two-five-zero," called Sampson. "One-five seconds to target."

Ronnie's voice was tense as he talked into the speaker-microphone. "Angle on the bow...port nine-zero!"

"Set," said Sampson.

"Fire one!" Ronnie paused two seconds, then shouted, "Fire two!"

Döttmer felt slight thumps, as the Captain fired four torpedoes at two second intervals.

Sampson studied a stopwatch in the pale half-moon, "Perfect setup, Ronnie. Got his ass."

"Damn right." Ronnie checked his own watch in the pale light of a half moon. After thirty seconds, his face turned from gleeful anticipation to abject disappointment.

Sampson reset the timer and pocketed the timepiece. "Shit."

"They couldn't have all missed," gasped Ronnie.

Gott! Döttmer's heart froze. He was surprised when his voice came out in a squeal, "He's turning, Captain. Right toward us!"

They saw a slight flash on the *Yucatan Maru*'s bow and heard a crack. Something whistled overhead and exploded, raising a water column two hundred yards off the port quarter. Another shell zipped from the ship's well deck. Then another from amidships.

Ronnie bellowed, "Reefer my ass. The thing's a damned Q-ship." A Q-ship was a heavily armed ship disguised as a freighter. The Japanese had fitted some with sonar and depth charges. The captain roared, "All ahead flank! Right full rudder! Dive! Dive!"

Ronnie hit the diving klaxon and waited while the bridge crew dove down the hatch, Döttmer first. Air hissed, water gurgled, and more shells screamed overhead, as men plummeted down ladders. Over shouts in the conning tower, Ronnie screamed about his torpedoes--all duds.

The bedlam masked another scream in the control room near the aft bulkhead. The sudden right turn coincided with a pooping wave to cause a twenty-degree port list -- enough to slam the hatch shut and crush four fingers of Radioman Second Class Dominic Federico Lorca's left hand.

31

9 May 1942
Marinduque Island
Philippines

Ingram stumbled almost losing his balance on the embankment. He took deep breaths, fighting for equilibrium and, in the darkness, barely discerned formless shapes. Blinking several times, it came to him the shapes were his men crouched beneath enormous vines and towering hardwoods. Closest was Bartholomew, outlined against a backdrop of near-equatorial jungle, where dappled blacks and grays clashed with brilliant spikes of yellow sunlight and infinite shades of early morning greens and oranges.

The chief held a finger to his lips.

"Pheww. Rocky!" rasped Ingram.

"Shhh. Down, Skipper," whispered Bartholomew.

The chief was naked except for his crumpled, salt encrusted hat, kneeling beside the man with the Thompson. Ingram, feeling stupid with his own nakedness, crouched next to Bartholomew. He squinted. Damn! Here were all of his men; and naked, yet. "What's going on?" he asked.

"Shhh!" With irritation, Bartholomew jerked his head toward his right. Through a small space in the jungle's clutter, he saw four Japanese soldiers ghost by, balancing their rifles over their shoulder in the relaxed, careless way a ten-year-old carries a fishing pole to his favorite summer watering hole. One of the Japanese spoke. Their laughter, thirty feet away, echoed through the jungle, making it seem as if they were within steps.

Soon, they were gone. Ingram's eyes darted for two minutes hoping his eyes would adjust. But he couldn't discern the features of those around him.

Someone whistled. Suddenly, the Thompson jerked upright and the man next to Ingram stood. A planter's hat shaded his face as he held out a hand and bowed, "Augustine Vega, Meester Ingram." Vega was a thin mestizo: half Chinese, half Filipino.

Ingram extended a hand, realizing he still grasped the bar of Ivory soap. Shifting the soap, he gave Vega a slimy right. "Todd Ingram, lieutenant, U.S. Navy. Thanks for pulling us out of hot water."

Vega hissed a gold-toothed smile and bowed again, as the other shapes rose from the mottled background.

Holloway crunched through dead leaves and said, "Before we knew it, these guys had the drop on us. They grabbed our stuff and shoved us in the jungle, I swear, in fifteen seconds. And that was two seconds before the Japs showed up. We thought everybody was present and accounted for, not realizing you were auditioning for a Tarzan movie."

Ingram shook Vega's hand harder. "Thanks very much. There'll be no trouble from us. We'll be quiet and shove off at sunset."

Vega grinned and led them to a small clearing where three other armed Filipinos stood before a pile of soggy clothes, canteens, and water tins. Silently the men separated their garments and wiggled into them. The Filipinos were dressed in threadbare khakis long ago washed white and so riddled with holes, they looked as if they had stood before a firing squad. Shoeless, their feet were wide and nimble as bear's paws.

Ingram one-legged it into wet trousers, saying, "Actually, Augustine, er, Mr. Vega, we'd like to stay overnight, maybe two, so we can overhaul our engine. Uh, fresh water is all we need. Maybe a few coconuts to tide us over."

Vega smiled and hissed and bowed. "Welcome to Marinduque, Meester Ingram."

Ingram cocked his head and said, "Thanks again. Er...can you understand me?"

"Welcome to Marinduque, Meester Ingram." Vega nodded several times, as the gold tooth gleamed under his planter's hat, his eyes invisible.

Ingram hadn't thought to ask anyone before they left Corregidor, "Who knows Tagalog?" Tagalog, a Malay-based tongue interlaced with Spanish, was the language on Marinduque.

He received blank stares. "Ilocano, anybody? Jeez, Bikol?" Ingram asked.

They looked at one another and dully shook their heads.

"What intellect, what international citizens," Ingram said. "You guys impress the hell out of me. Look. Does anybody know--" He stopped in mid-sentence. "Whittaker!" His heart raced and he looked back to Vega. "Augustine. We come in boat. My man guard boat."

The brim of Vega's hat dipped as he smiled and bowed with another ceremonious sweep of his hand.

"Banca!" Ingram waved frantically toward the beach. "Our banca. Is okay? My man okay?"

Vega bowed deeply. "Welcome, Meester Ingram. My mans okay, too. Hate the Hapon just like you. We ready fight, you betcha." He patted his Thompson.

"Whittaker." In frustration, Ingram turned to Holloway and DeWitt, the only one armed. "Grab Sunderland and go down there. Watch out for--"

Another man, a Filipino, stepped forward saying with almost no accent, "Your engineer is fine, Lieutenant." Also, wearing a simple planter's hat, he was taller than the rest, with broad cheeks, thin lips, a pencil-thin moustache, and dark skin. He wore the ordinary clothing of the others but oddly, was not armed. "We gave him a half chicken and some bananas. I think it was too much. He looked ill after four bites."

"Too rich, probably. He hasn't had a decent meal since last December," said Ingram. "What about the Japs?"

"Oh, Alberto and Fernando disguised your boat." He extended a hand. "My name is Emilio Aguilar, lieutenant. As Augustine said, you are welcome here."

They shook. Ingram said, "Is Whittaker still down there?"

Aguilar whipped off his hat, shaking a mane of thick blue-black hair. "He was busy with the motor. If he stays right there, he'll be fine."

Ingram thought there was hesitation in Aguilar's tone. "Is there something we should know?"

Aguilar pointed. "From that hill, we watched your approach. By the sheerest quirk of fate you missed the Hapon's garrison by just one cove. Another small miracle is that the Hapons are gone for a few days except the ones who evicted you just now."

Bartholomew, Holloway, Dewitt, Toliver, and Beardsley stepped up. Ingram nodded to them and said, "You're kidding."

Aguilar said, "Your bathtub is very popular. The garrison swims there every morning. Sometimes, Hapons travel here from the mainland and stay for the day. They lay down mats and picnic."

"Where's the garrison?" asked DeWitt.

Aguilar nodded over his shoulder, "About three hundred meters that way."

"How big?" shot Bartholomew.

"About ninety, plus a few girls."

"Whores?" asked Holloway.

"They bring their comforts."

"*Kempetai*?"

"Yes. We are privileged to have the *Kempetai*. Lieutenant Tuga and Lieutenant Watanabe."

"How many are left over?" asked Ingram.

"An officer and three enlisted, I think. Would you like to see the compound?"

"Please," said Ingram.

With Aguilar leading the way, they walked through the jungle single file. Soon, they trudged up a small hill that rose above the beach. Ingram was out of breath and dizzy by the time they neared the one-hundred-fifty-foot peak. Gasping, he followed Aguilar to a precipice and peered out through thick brush.

Stretched before them were the slate gray waters of Tayabas Bay, with Luzon's mainland fifteen miles to the northeast. Directly east lay Mompog Passage and Santa Cruz Point where Maniuayan and Mompog islands guarded the northern entrance to the Sibuyan Sea.

To Ingram's right was a cove much larger than the one they had ducked into. There was a long pier and motorized patrol-launch. Peaks of thatched

Nipa huts rose over the jungle, and the Japanese ensign fluttered in the breeze. A tall radio antennae protruded from another hut. Ingram shuddered, thinking, if it hadn't been for the Zeros they would have cruised within full sight of the men stationed here. "We were very lucky." Ingram said. "How long have they been here?"

"Four months. It used to be a fishing village: San José. The Hapons threw everyone out and took their belongings, including the food."

A breeze rattled through the jungle and curled through Ingram's hair. In the cove the wind was stronger, making the flag stand straight out and the radio antennae bend slightly. Ingram looked up, seeing haze temper the morning's brilliance. "Monsoons here early?"

"Maybe," shrugged Aguilar.

Below shimmered the pool and waterfall, its cascading waters a distant rumble. In the pond's center--the deepest part--the water was an intense green, giving way to sparkling clarity at the edges where it met white, glistening sands. Beyond was the lagoon and the ocean. Ingram picked out a large stack of palm fronds near tall glistening rocks at the water's edge. "Is that our boat?"

Aguilar nodded. "Your engineer is under there with his chicken dish keeping cool."

Ingram waved DeWitt and Holloway over and pointed out the garrison and the launch. The two grimly nodded.

"The hell with the overhaul. Too many Japs around here," Ingram said.

"Where are you headed?" asked Aguilar.

"We stopped here looking for..." Ingram cut it off in mid-sentence because Aguilar's eyes had narrowed. He was going to say he was looking for a radio. Even mention Amador. Instead, he said, "...looking for fuel and food."

"I see."

"With enough of that, we'll make Australia," said Ingram.

"Why Australia?"

"Is there some place better? China?"

"Mindanao. Your people are there, in the hills with the resistance."

Ingram said, "Mindanao is still free?" The Japanese had invaded and occupied Davao on Mindanao's southern coast months ago. But they had only recently attacked the northern half, concentrating on the Bukidnon Plateau, well known for its sprawling Del Monte pineapple plantation.

"Unfortunately, no. General Wainwright ordered General Sharp to surrender."

"Wainwright. They must have tortured him to make him say that," said DeWitt, shaking his head.

"He was on the radio," Aguilar said.

The others gathered around. DeWitt asked, "When?"

Aguilar said, "Two nights ago, KZRH carried the broadcast. It was General Wainwright speaking. At least that's what the announcer said. He told Sharp he had resumed command of all forces in the Philippines, and ordered him to surrender."

"So, General Chynoweth had to surrender, too?" asked Ingram.

"Mmmmm," said Aguilar. This meant the whole Philippine Archipelago was lost--with General William F. Sharp's twenty-five thousand troops on Mindanao--and another twenty thousand commanded by Brigadier General Bradford G. Chynoweth in the Visayan Islands, the Central Philippines.

DeWitt shook his head. "Sharp was finished anyway. It was more like a capitulation."

Aguilar said, "So now, all of Mindanao is controlled by the Hapons. But many Americans are up in the hills."

Ingram said, "With the Moros?" The Moros, a tribe of fierce Moslem-Malays, lived in Western Mindanao.

Aguilar shrugged. "They're guerrillas, now."

"Better to run with them, than Japs," said Bartholomew.

Suddenly, what looked like fly specks on the horizon materialized into two Zero float planes. Coming from the north, the Zeros circled, as they had earlier when they startled the 51 Boat. One swooped low. Barrel-shaped objects detached from under the float plane's wings and splashed in the ocean.

Holloway shook his head. "Do you think Roosevelt really meant it when he said--"

The sea erupted in twin columns of brownish-black where the Zero made its drop. The second plane curved out of a bank, leveled its wings, and headed for the same spot, zipping over the roiling sea and dropping its load. Soon, two more bursts of charcoal-gray water shot in the air.

"What the hell are they depth charging?" asked Ingram.

"Practice. There is a tethered underwater target."

"That's why they didn't see us this morning," Ingram said. "They were too busy playing with firecrackers."

"Going over that reef was remarkable. I haven't seen anyone do that in years."

"Lucky."

Again, Aguilar looked at him narrowly.

The hell with it, he thought. "Submarines put in here?"

"Yes, one came in here a little over a week ago."

"And they dropped a load of people from Corregidor?"

"Well, yes. We picked them up. How did you know?" asked Aguilar.

"Jackpot, Otis."

Aguilar asked, "You knew them?"

Aguilar had lingered on the word *knew* in an ominous way. Ingram asked, "Is anything wrong?"

Aguilar told them about the massacre at Diaz.

"Jesus." Ingram stepped back, running a hand over his face. "Did anybody live?"

"The ones they didn't butcher, they sent to Fortune Island."

"How many?" asked DeWitt.

"Hard to tell. Ten or so," Aguilar said slowly. "Lieutenant Tuga doesn't like to take prisoners."

"We put thirty people on that submarine," gasped Ingram. "Any idea who survived?"

"No."

"You sure?"

"Why do you ask?" said Aguilar.

"Doesn't matter." Helen. Helen Durand. He put his hand to his cheek, hearing her rich voice, her laughter. Closing his eyes, he saw her wrists and arms as she bent over to sew up his cheek. She was so close he felt her breath on his face. Odd. Why hadn't he thought about her breath on his cheek then? It felt so good. For a second he thought he felt it now, but it was just the southerly stirring over Marinduque.

And that crazy old Filipino telling his stories of Corregidor, the evil magistrate. Ingram was trying to make sense of that while hell itself descended on the fortified islands two miles away. What was that guy's name? "...Amador, Pablo Amador. He--"

"You know Pablo Amador?" asked Aguilar.

Ingram's lips pressed white. He looked down and nudged a rock with his boot.

Aguilar said, "Señor. You said Pablo Amador?"

Ingram rubbed his eyes. He hoped it was the sun. "Who? Yes. We'd just met. You see..."

Bartholomew walked up. "Skipper. What are the chances of starting Whittaker on that overhaul?"

"None, I'm afraid," said Ingram. He pointed to the garrison and told Bartholomew of their plight.

Aguilar said, "Tonight you can move your boat. I have a good spot in mind for you, where you can do the overhaul."

Ingram ran a hand over his face and took a deep breath.

"You okay, Skipper?" said Bartholomew.

"Fine. Mr. Aguilar is right. Let's stretch out in that grove and wait 'til nightfall."

Augustine Vega stepped up. The two spoke in Tagalog for a moment, then Aguilar said, "Oh, no, Mr. Ingram. Not that place. It's swampy. Land crabs, leeches, even pythons. No. You come to my house. Good food. Hot showers while the wood holds out. I have a razor. You can all shave." He thumbed Ingram's cheek tenderly. "...tsk, tsk, I may have something for that, too."

"How far is it?" asked Ingram.

Aguilar jabbed a thumb over his shoulder. "About five miles."

"I see. Tell me. What is it that you do?" Ingram asked.

"Lumber mill. Except the Hapons take our machinery. So now we grow bananas and raise pigs."

"We can't walk five miles," said Ingram.

"We have a truck."

Bartholomew said, "We ought to take Pete. He deserves decent chow like the rest of us."

Ingram looked at Mompog Pass once more. He had hardly known her. She--"

"Skipper?" asked Bartholomew.

Ingram wiped a hand over his face. "Let's go."

The truck, an ancient Ford, bounced through a heavily wooded forest. After forty-five minutes of monotonous switchbacks, they pulled up to the Aguilar home, which was situated at the edge of a stepped meadow. The house stood on the upper plateau, where it enjoyed a commanding view of Tayabas Bay, Mompog Passage, and Luzon, eighteen miles distant. It was a large, four bedroom, single-story structure, done in ranch style with an adobe roof. The furniture was sparse, with only a few pieces--rattan chairs, sofa and table, and reed carpeting covering a cement floor. Except for a crucifix over the fire-place, nothing else decorated the bare white walls. The kitchen was large and homey as was the dining room except, again, there was little furniture.

Without a word, Aguilar's wife, a pensive heavyset woman wearing a shawl, produced bowls loaded with roast chicken and white rice. They gathered outside, at a long, rough mahogany table under a canvas awning. While not totally satiating their hunger the food was good. And they were smart enough not to complain, since the Aguilars were undoubtedly stretching their larder to the limit. But they were surprised when Doña Aguilar laid out jackfruit and bananas for dessert, and poured real coffee.

Later, they took turns firing an ancient wood-burning boiler to heat water for showers and shaving. Ingram took his turn at the razor finding it not quite sharp to begin with. Even so, it produced that wonderful tingling feeling which accompanies a clean face. Then he showered and, with a decent meal under his belt, felt like taking a nap. He stood with Holloway, Bartholomew, and Toliver under a tree as the others threw out mats and began to stretch out.

Ingram scanned the branches overhead. Holloway chuckled, "Afraid of snipers?"

With a last glance in the branches, Ingram unrolled a reed mat and lay down. "I heard of a guy on Cebu. He fell asleep under a tree like this, and the next thing he knew, a python dropped on him and wrapped its coils so fast the guy didn't even have time to gurgle. He was about five feet ten inches in height, but the python squeezed so hard, every bone was broken and the guy was stretched to seven feet."

Holloway gasped.

Ingram said, "And guess what?"

"What?"

"Even at that, the guy was still alive when the snake swallowed him."

Without a smile, Ingram turned on his side and closed his eyes. Holloway carefully examined the branches overhead before he fell asleep.

Something shook. Ingram opened his eyes to find DeWitt kneeling over him. Blinking at the oppressive heat, he checked his watch: almost two o'clock. He'd been asleep over four hours. "Yes?"

DeWitt's voice was soft. "How do you figure this guy, Lieutenant?"

"Aguilar?" Ingram propped on an elbow, running his hand through his hair.

"I'm trying to figure what makes him tick," said DeWitt.

Ingram said, "The Japs took their milling machinery. Ruined their livelihood. So, I guess they don't like Japs."

DeWitt pulled an envelope from his pocket. "This was on the floor of the truck."

"What?" Ingram sat all the way up and took the envelope. It was a high quality, buff stationery the size of a formal wedding invitation. A meticulous script on the envelope invited the attention of: *Don Emilio and Doña Carmella Aguilar.*

DeWitt looked both ways then spat, "What the hell is this guy up to?"

Wide awake now, Ingram pulled out the inner envelope. "The truck, huh?"

"Stickin' out from under the front seat," said DeWitt.

The announcement was printed in black script on high quality, heavy stock; one side was in English, the other Japanese. It said:

The Chairman of the Executive Commission
requests the honor of your company
at a Reception
in celebration of the victory of the
Imperial Japanese Army and Navy

in the Philippines
to be held on
Monday, May the eighteenth
nineteen hundred and forty-two
from five to six o'clock in the afternoon
Malacañan Palace

32

9 May 1942
Aguilar House, Marinduque, Island
Philippines

Gunner's Mate First Class Kermit G. Sunderland snored soundly as Ingram reached under the man's mat and withdrew the .45.--the same Colt MI911AI pistol that the malaria-vexed Sergeant Bruno La Follette had tossed from the Caballo dock in those last, hideous moments. Creeping through the bushes behind DeWitt, Ingram made sure the pistol's clip was full. Then he ran the slide and thumbed off the safety. Insects buzzed in the early afternoon's heat as they crept over veranda and porch and drew up to the front door.

It was wide open.

With a nod to DeWitt, Ingram lead the way through a small entry hall. He peeked around the corner into the living room and saw Aguilar asleep on a couch. Light snoring down the hall could only have been Doña Aguilar.

"Siesta," mouthed Ingram.

They crept up to Aguilar. Ingram took a two-handed grip on the pistol while DeWitt tapped him on the shoulder.

"Uhhhh?" Aguilar blinked at the .45's muzzle. Tearing sleep from his eyes he tried to focus on what was behind the barrel. Ingram touched a forefinger to his lips and said in a low voice, "Just a few questions, Señor."

"Is this the way you treat your hosts?" growled Aguilar.

DeWitt flipped the invitation on Aguilar's stomach and spat, "Is this the way you fight your enemy? By attending their parties--their little victory celebrations?"

Aguilar focused on the rich card stock, comprehension registering on his face. He raised his hands in a gesture of resignation. "May I rise, please?" he said.

Ingram nodded.

Aguilar sat up, lurched forward, and propped his elbows on his knees. Laying his head in his hands, he said in a voice hoarse with sleep, "You are a fool, Major."

"Sure," DeWitt smirked.

"Lieutenant Tuga and his Hapon filth are out delivering these invitations right now. That's why no one is at the garrison to speak of."

"Sure," DeWitt said again.

"You're making a big mistake." said Aguilar.

"Prove us wrong," said DeWitt.

"Alright." Aguilar sighed and rubbed his eyes. "Vargas wants us to form into regions. He calls them DANAs, for District and Neighborhood Associations." When he fled the Philippines with MacArthur, President Manuel Quezon designated his executive secretary, Jorgé Vargas, to take over and work with Japan's occupation forces.

"Sort of like a Nazi cell?" sneered DeWitt.

Ingram flipped on the .45's safety, stuffed the pistol in his belt, and sat.

DeWitt barked, "Lieutenant?"

Ingram said, "Major. Sit down and take a load off."

DeWitt glared at Ingram and sat.

Aguilar said, "Thank you, Señor." Looking at DeWitt he said, "Yes, similar to Nazi cells. And who do you think has been appointed leader of DANA Marinduque Del Norte?"

"You?" DeWitt said.

"Yes, me. Vargas appointed me. No matter who occupies our country: Moslems, Spanish, Americans, Japanese; Filipinos know how to play their games. And Vargas, that son of a bitch, is as good at it as anybody." Aguilar waved the invitation. "Do you think, Major, that Doña Carmella and I will enjoy having to put on our finest clothes and go all the way to Manila for a party..." Aguilar's face turned red and he sputtered, "A stupid party that lasts from five to six in the afternoon?"

"I'm sorry," said Ingram.

Aguilar slammed a fist and yelled, "You two don't know the best part. The best part is we don't have any clothes. How do you like that? Besides taking my furniture and silverware and crystal and milling machinery, the Hapons emptied our closets."

Aguilar's face turned red again. He struggled to control his breathing. "My family has had the mill for over a hundred years. I'm a second-generation college graduate. My father was the first; we went to Texas A&M."

"Now, that was smart," said DeWitt, cranking his twang up a notch.

Aguilar barely flicked his eyes. "We have been the patriarchs of Marinduque del Norte for a long time. But now, I'm just a pig farmer who must borrow clothes for the privilege of traveling all the way to Malacañan Palace for one glorious hour."

Alberto rushed in clacking the bolt on his Springfield. He stood among them, undecided where to aim. Not bothering to look up, Ingram said, "Careful. That thing's loaded."

"Get out of here," bellowed Aguilar.

Alberto had no sooner ducked out the front door than Doña Carmella emerged from the hall. "Emilio?"

Aguilar spoke softly to his wife in Tagalog. Her gaze dropped to the floor; she nodded and went back to her room.

"Did you look in her face?" Aguilar asked.

Ingram coughed. DeWitt, also afraid to say "yes," gazed out the window.

"Until six months ago she was a happy woman. She made me happy. She made everybody happy. She fed us and clothed us and read the bible to us and raised our sons. She fed beggars and sent them into the mill for work. Everybody laughed when she was around. Our children. Our friends. Our workers. Everybody loved Doña Carmella."

Don Aguilar cleared his throat then said, "Lieutenant Tuga and his Hapons came to my mill. It took them two days to take everything apart and haul it away. The day after that they came here. They tied me up and then backed a truck up to the front door and helped themselves to..." he waved a hand, "Our son." Aguilar's eyes turned red. "Ambrosio, thirteen years old, he was brash and outgoing, doing stupid, harmless things. He laughed and was happy like his mother.

"When the Tuga came, one of his men shoved Doña Carmella against the wall while another butted her in the stomach with a rifle. Ambrosio jumped on the soldier's back and..." Aguilar pointed at the window. "Out there. The tree under which you slept. They hung him upside down and used him for bayonet practice."

Ingram's fingers tightened on the chair's arms. DeWitt sucked air through his teeth.

Aguilar took a deep breath and said, "They became tired of that and while Ambrosio dangled overhead, they built a bonfire under him. He lived for another forty-five minutes.

"During all this, they ripped off Doña Carmella's clothes and...did nothing. They laughed at her. While Ambrosio screamed, and roasted they formed a circle and pushed her from man to man. That's all." Aguilar ran a hand over his face. "They laughed at her."

"I'm sorry," said Ingram.

DeWitt said, "I wish we could have done something."

Aguilar said, "And during all this, that bastard Tuga sat in his truck and read a book." Aguilar's eyes blinked. He sat a little straighter and brushed his hair back. His lips twisted into a tight smile. "Don't you think it amusing that we must find our way to Luzon to enjoy the Hapon's 'Victory Party' wearing borrowed clothes?"

DeWitt looked around the room. "Why didn't they take all your furniture?"

"I don't know," said Aguilar. "Tuga knew the expensive pieces. The piano. Our dining table, chairs and hutch. Bedroom furniture. Those pieces came from Spain over a hundred years ago. The crystal was from Ireland. That is what they took."

DeWitt picked up the invitation and turned it over in his hands.

Aguilar said, "That was five months ago. Now, apparently Jorgé Vargas and his masters have decided bygones are bygones and are willing to 'forgive me.' Simply stated, they want me to control things for them in Marinduque del Norte."

DeWitt said, "Tell them to stuff it."

Aguilar said, "Understand this, Major." My response will be closely scrutinized by Vargas and his masters. If I go, the *Kempetai* will think I am their puppet. That's not so bad, except I'll be viewed as such. And in the Philippines, we have our own brand of politics." He looked at DeWitt.

DeWitt said, "What about the HUKs?" The word was from the Tagalog, meaning *HUK*bong Bayan Laban sa Hapon: People's Anti-Japanese Army. Formed earlier in the year by Luis Taruc, the HUK movement was fast gaining enlistments and taking its toll on Japanese occupation forces, particularly in rural areas of Central Luzon.

Aguilar turned red and pounded his fist again. "Taruc is a sonofabitch."

"What? said DeWitt.

Aguilar roared, "He joined the communist party three years ago. We...we...have mutual friends. I got angry with him and told him to quit. He said it was the new thing, the great patriotic idea of the twentieth century. We argued at a dinner party one night. There was loss of face. Over the weeks and months, it became bitter. I finally cut off all communication. I wouldn't be surprised if it was Luis Taruc who sicced the Hapons on us."

"Why the hell would he do that?" asked Ingram.

Waving his hand, Aguilar sighed. "In the Commonwealth, we vote with machine guns and dynamite." He scanned their blank faces. "Did you know of Tee Han Kee?"

"No." they said.

"No? How about Andong Roces or José de Jesus?"

"No."

"Tee Han Kee was vice president of the Chinese Association in Manila. Roces was of the *Manila Tribune*, de Jesus, of the finance ministry. All were murdered. 'Collaborative activities with the Japanese' was the reason, but," Augustine shook his head, "I'm convinced, the killings were personally motivated."

"Now, if Doña Carmella and I don't attend the victory celebration, we'll undoubtedly receive another visit from the *Kempetai*. Perhaps Tuga will be reading Shakespeare while his boys roast me. Or maybe he'll let me off easy and just wire up my balls and spin his little electric generator."

"So, you have no alternatives," DeWitt said gently.

Aguilar nodded and said, "To escape a visit from Japan's thought police,

Doña Carmella and I will probably be forced to go into the forest. That will make the Hapons angry. They will interrogate others. Maybe Augustine Vega will receive benefit of their little electrical experiments. Maybe his wife, Consuela. Who knows? Others will be hung by their feet and..." He raised a hand and dropped it. "What would you do, Major, if this were happening in your home? What would you do if this were Texas?"

DeWitt sat back in his chair and steepled his fingers.

Ingram said, "Things are too tense around here. We'll leave tonight."

"For a number of reasons that is a good idea," said Aguilar. "If your engine needs an overhaul then so be it. Otherwise, I suggest you run. For the next week or so, the Hapons will be in a light-hearted mood. Many parties are scheduled along with our own," he spat the words, "*victory celebration.*"

"Their guard will be down and you can transit choke-points easily. After that, things will become extremely difficult."

"I have an idea, Señor," said Ingram.

"Yes?"

Just then Doña Carmella walked in, carrying a tray with tea service and cups. She placed it before her husband and walked out. Aguilar looked up.

Ingram said, "Come with us. Bring your wife. We'll take you to Mindanao. Australia, if you wish."

Aguilar poured and passed out cups and saucers. "Sorry, we have no chilled lemonade." He paused for a moment, then looked up to Ingram. "I don't think so."

"Sounds like you're out of choices," Ingram said. The tea's scent was wonderful. He sipped and, in spite of the day's heat and humidity, found the aroma fulfilled its promise. His voice was soft, "Please come with us."

Silence. Ingram and DeWitt looked at one another. A minute passed and they sipped tea.

Aguilar opened his mouth to speak, then checked himself. He looked at the door to the kitchen, then back to Ingram. "This...is my home, Lieutenant. Thank you, anyway."

Ingram said, "I'll leave it open. You're welcome to hop aboard, even as we cast off."

Aguilar bowed his head slightly. "Tell me. You're going to Mindanao?"

"Well, we would like to try directly for Australia. But it depends on food and parts for the engine, if it goes bonkers."

"Very well. If you need to go to Mindanao, go to Nasipit. I have friends there."

"Where's that?" asked Ingram.

"It's a small logging town on the northern coast about sixty miles south of the Surigao Straits. Agusan Province. It won't be far out of your way. I'll get word to them."

Something tickled Ingram's memory. Sure, that night on the way to the *Wolfish* rendezvous. "I met someone..."

"Who?" asked Aguilar.

"...Pablo Amador."

"The old guy?" asked DeWitt.

Ingram nodded. "But then, he's probably dead, now."

"You mentioned him earlier," said Aguilar. "The reason I was so cagey is that I wondered if you knew."

"Knew what?" said Ingram and DeWitt.

Amador said, "He escaped and was put on the steamer two days ago. He should have reached Nasipit by now."

"He escaped?" said Ingram. "Why couldn't the--"

Aguilar waved a hand. "I don't know. Something about a secret place in Diaz's that only holds one person. The Hapons set the torch, the place burned to the ground, Amador barely got out, I'm told.

"His family had a big lumbering mill just like me. But the Hapons took everything..."

DeWitt blurted, "We need a radio transmitter. One powerful enough to contact Australia or even the United States."

"It's too bad," said Aguilar. "Fito Diaz ran the resistance. He had a radio. A big Halicrafters."

"Damn!" Ingram stood and walked to the window.

"Why do you need it?" asked Aguilar.

DeWitt said, "Something really important. Do you know of anyone else with a radio?"

"Not on Marinduque. Maybe on Mindanao."

Ingram nodded to a large spotted pig on a long tether strolling among the sleepers outside. "That one of yours?"

"Yes, meet Delores, one of my sows."

They watched Delores sniff at Beardsley's heel and waddle on. Ingram said, "Mindanao. That's over four hundred miles from here."

"Is it so important it can't wait?"

Ingram turned and looked at DeWitt. "Yes," they said.

"You're sure?"

"Yes."

"There may be another way," said Aguilar.

33

9 May 1942
Imperial Japanese Army Garrison
Marinduque Island, Philippines

It was just Ingram, Farwell, and Sunderland. The others stood by the '51 Boat ready to put to sea. Sunderland carried his BAR, Ingram packed the .45, and Farwell carried a Springfield.

Ingram wiped sweat off his forehead and checked his watch: 8:30. He couldn't remember if there was a moon tonight and kicked himself for not checking.

Sunderland sat on haunches, holding the BAR's butt in the ground, and whispered, "Where the hell are they?"

Ingram peered through the bushes as the waterfall gurgled pleasantly to their left. The Japanese garrison stood before them. Once the simple fishing village of San José, it consisted of seven nipa huts, a two-hundred-foot pier, a utility shed, and a freshwater stream that ran conveniently from the waterfall pool through the village's center.

The nipa hut, so called because it was thatched with feathery leaves from the nipa palm, was a single-room structure built on bamboo stilts several feet above the ground. The raised floor had several advantages. It nullified insect and land crab infestation while providing a marvelous natural circulation system through a floor made of split bamboo. This meant a comfortable sleep, even on humid nights. Also, it was a means of corralling livestock. The villagers tossed food scraps and crumbs through the split bamboo flooring feeding their pigs and chickens below. Fires were built in a sandbox in one corner, but there was no chimney, so the smoke escaped out the windows or through floor cracks.

A disadvantage of the nipa system was the ripe aroma. Human and animal feces underneath offended Western propriety, the Japanese sharing this outlook. This was why, according to Don Aguilar, the utility shed had been converted to a latrine.

There were nine nipa huts in San José. Eight were small, perhaps twelve by twelve. The one closest to Ingram was much larger, maybe twenty by thirty. It was a community building with a large porch on three sides; a doorway on the fourth wall gave way to a small room. The Japanese had converted it to their headquarters, and the focal point of Ingram's interest was the fifty-foot radio antenna that protruded through the roof.

"Sssst!" Sunderland waved frantically and they crouched further into shadows.

A Japanese corporal stepped from the headquarters building and sauntered by, smoking a cigarette.

"Taking a leak, I'll bet," whispered Sunderland.

Farwell squeezed his eyes shut and muttered something.

"Bucket Mouth, damnit!" said Sunderland.

"Come on, Farwell," said Ingram.

"Skipper," said Farwell. "I haven't pounded a key for years."

"You're all we got, Farwell. You have to," hissed Ingram. "Now, come on. Say it again."

"Why can't I just write it down?" said Farwell.

Ingram said, "We can't afford to be captured with something that sensitive. It would be our death warrant. And a lot of others, I think, like Aguilar and his people.

"No," Ingram shook his head. "You'll have to go by memory."

Farwell's eyes darted. "I don't read Japanese."

Sunderland spit, "Bucket Mouth! You little bastard. I'll give you two choices. You deal with that damn radio, or you deal with me."

"Easy, Sunderland," whispered Ingram. "Okay, Farwell. One more time."

Farwell ran a finger around his collar. His eyes darted around the camp and his Adam's apple bobbed up and down. Finally, he rubbed his temples and managed, "uh, power on and set to five hundred kilocycles." He swallowed several times.

"Go on."

"Transmit, uh...'To: Any U.S. Intelligence Unit this Net. From: Ingram, Alton C., Lt. USN 638217.' Uh, 'Item one: Escaped Corregidor night of 6 May, 1942. Item two: Now at large.'"

"Right," said Ingram.

Farwell looked up through the trees. "'Item two--'"

Sunderland hissed, "'Item three,' jerk!"

Farwell closed his eyes and bit his lip. "'Item three: Epperson, Dwight G., Lt. USN murdered by Radtke, Walter, CT2, night of 29 April.'" Farwell looked at Ingram. "This is no shit?"

"Bucket Mouth!" hissed Sunderland.

Ingram nodded.

Farwell gulped, looking as if he were in a trance. "'Item four: All info known by Epperson compromised to Radtke, who took Minox photos.'"

"Yes," said Ingram. That was the important part. But he didn't want the message to say exactly what Radtke knew since the transmission most likely would be intercepted by the Japanese.

Farwell seemed a little more confident. "'Item five: Strongly believe Radtke a spy. Item six: Radtke evacuated U.S.S. *Wolfish* 3 May 1942. Item seven: Advise arrest of Radtke before *Wolfish* returns port. Item eight: Advise interrogation by qualified authorities.'" Farwell looked at Ingram. "BT?"

"BT," said Ingram. BT signified the end of a Navy message. "Good job, Farwell. I'm sure you'll do--"

"Shhht," from Sunderland.

The Japanese corporal wandered past on his return trip, zipping up his fly. He mounted the steps and went inside the headquarters building.

"Mr. Ingram," whispered Farwell.

Ingram looked at the quartermaster.

"Your name really Alton C.? I thought they called you Todd?"

"Crimenitley," moaned Sunderland, slapping a hand over his eyes.

Sweat beaded on Farwell's forehead and upper lip, and he fidgeted. Skilled at sending flashing light and semaphore signals, Farwell hadn't been close to a telegraph key since his signalman's course in San Diego, nine years before. His wife and seven-year-old daughter lived in Vallejo, California, and he was scared to death. There was no recourse because Ingram had ordered him to do this: to send this message since he was the best qualified among them. In a phrase, Farwell, Luther A., quartermaster second class, U.S. Navy Bluejacket and ordinary American citizen was scared out of his skin.

Ingram whispered, "My initials. ACI. They called me 'Ace' at the Academy. Now it's just Todd."

Farwell swallowed rapidly. "Uh, huh."

Ingram said, "Alton was my grandfather's name, Farwell. Isaac Alton, on my mother's side. He came west on the Oregon Trail. They--"

"Here we go," whispered Sunderland.

Emilio Aguilar and Augustine Vega walked by. Dutifully trotting behind Aguilar was his sow, Delores, connected by a rope. It was the large, spotted pig Ingram had seen earlier in the day. The two Filipinos walked around the headquarters building into the main compound where the flagpole was situated, an area illuminated by lights mounted on the surrounding huts. Aguilar cupped a hand to his mouth and shouted, "Haaalooo."

Three Japanese soldiers, accompanied by a lieutenant popped into the compound and walked up to Aguilar. They clucked and grinned at Delores who, sensing their intentions, took refuge behind Aguilar's legs.

With great swooping motions, Aguilar and Vega took off their hats and bowed while the Japanese corporal walked out of the hut and leaned on the porch rail to watch and smoke his cigarette.

"That's everybody," rasped Ingram.

"I ain't gonna believe this 'til I see it," whispered Farwell.

It was obvious the Filipinos didn't speak Japanese and the soldiers didn't speak Tagalog. Soon, their discussion became a pigeon Tagalog-Japanese that sounded like forty parrots just set afire. Casually, Aguilar pulled his rope tight, Delores grunted and their harangue rose a notch in intensity with one of the soldiers, a sergeant, occasionally running a hand over the butt of a pistol holstered at his waist.

Sunderland whispered, "Watch the sergeant. He's a hothead. When he's had enough, the sonofabitch is gonna draw that thing. End of discussion."

Farwell said, "This ain't gonna work." He started crawling away on all fours. Ingram and Sunderland caught him by the armpits and pulled him back between them.

As predicted, Aguilar lost control of his sales pitch. They all shouted at one another and the Japanese corporal stepped off the porch and walked over.

Suddenly, the sergeant whipped out his pistol, an eight millimeter Nambu, and pointed it at Aguilar. Aguilar's hands shot into the air and the rope, which was at short stay, jerked Delores's neck. The pig squealed horribly and ran around Aguilar and Vega, winding the rope around their legs. Aguilar shouted something, dropped the rope, and two-stepped out of the bight. Like Aguilar, Vega deftly cleared the rope, and Delores was off. Grunting and squealing, she dashed under a nipa hut, with all five in pursuit.

At the hut, the sergeant shouted, waved his Nambu, and kicked Vega in the rump. Vega dove beneath the hut, while the lieutenant circled around the other side. Delores blasted out from under, dashing between the incredulous lieutenant's legs.

Ingram slapped Farwell's back. "Go!"

With Sunderland standing guard, they burst through the shrubs and up the steps. Inside, the floor and walls were finished with rough lumber. There were two desks, file cabinets and book shelves. A thick drape covered a store-room doorway on the opposite wall. The radio, a five-foot-high freestanding unit, was mounted against the back wall. Farwell ran for it while Ingram peeked out the window to keep an eye on the pig chase.

"Power on?" asked Ingram.

Farwell fiddled with knobs, "Everything is in Japanese but it looks like its warmed up and in standby. Yeah. You say five hundred KC?"

"Right," said Ingram. Five hundred kilocycles was the international distress frequency. He hoped an Allied receiver would be tuned to it.

"Got it," said Farwell. He flipped a guard switch. "This is a good set." He picked up earphones and put them on.

Desperately squealing, Delores ran under the headquarters hut. Ingram and Farwell dove for the floor hearing the Japanese outside shriek at Vega and Aguilar. Peeking through a knot hole, Ingram watched Delores zip right underneath. Next was Vega's back. And, uncannily, the Filipino stopped and looked up at Ingram and smiled, then shot forward again in hot pursuit.

The posse of six formed up on the other side and chased Delores into the latrine.

"Whew." Farwell stood and fiddled with the radio again.

While Farwell worked at the radio, Ingram hunched by the desk. Rising to his knees, he looked at the top. There was an ebony blotter with ornate pen set next to it. A calendar, scrolled with beautiful flowers, lay open on the blotter. Even though it was in Japanese, the month must have been May, because Xs were meticulously drawn through the Arabic numbers up to the ninth.

Tucked in the blotter's lower right corner was a copy of the *Manila Tribune*, dated May 8, 1942. Ingram picked it up, seeing a picture of General Wainwright with one of his aides. Both wore rumpled khakis and were seated in a room furnished in wicker. A microphone labeled KZRH was placed before Wainwright, and behind him stood a Japanese with slicked-back hair, wearing rimless glasses and a well-pressed white suit. The main column quoted Wainwright's radio message:

'By the authority vested in me by the President of the United States, I, as Commanding General of the United States forces in the Philippines, hereby resume direct command of Major General Sharp, commander of Visayan and Mindanao forces, and all troops under his command. I will now give a direct order to General Sharp. I repeat, please notify him. The subject is surrender. To Major General William J. Sharp, Jr. This is the message. To put a stop to further useless sacrifice of life on the fortified islands, yesterday I tendered to Lieutenant General Homma, Commander in the Philippines, the surrender of the four harbor defense posts in Manila Bay. General Homma declined to accept unless the surrender included places under your command. It became apparent that they would be destroyed by the airplanes and tanks which have overwhelmed Corregidor.

After leaving General Homma with no agreement, I decided to accept, in the name of humanity, his proposal and tendered at midnight to the senior Japanese office on Corregidor the formal surrender of all American and Filipino troops on the Philippine Islands. You will, therefore, be guided accordingly and will, I repeat, will surrender all of your forces to the proper Japanese officer.

This position, you realize, was forced on me by circumstances beyond my control...

Farther down the page was an edict in bold block lettering warning all American and Filipino servicemen to surrender at specific points by May 12. After this, the edict stated, the Imperial Japanese Army would not accept their surrender.

Like an awakening ghost, the radio made soft shrieking noises as Farwell tried switches and twiddled dials. Ingram replaced the newspaper and slipped open the desk drawer, finding two neat pads of paper and two pencils. Nothing else. He eased the drawer closed and cocked his head.

Thinking he'd heard a noise in the storeroom, Ingram opened the heavy drape with a finger and peeked inside. It was completely dark, perhaps seven by ten with a small desk at the door; an iron bed was on the far side and a small table stood nearby with instruments of some sort.

Odd, he thought. It's not a storeroom and seems messy. Aren't the Japs always clean? And, peeooow. the smell.

He lifted the curtain, hooked it open, and walked in seeing a gunny sack on the desk. He looked inside, finding wallets, watches, rings, and pocket knives. Reaching in, he pulled out a wallet and flipped it open. There was a U.S. Navy ID card with a photograph of a grinning face. The caption said: Collins. Robert Allen, CDR, USN, 364516. Looking in the sack, a heavy coldness swept over Ingram as he realized what these things were.

"Skipper," said Farwell hoarsely.

"Yeah?" Ingram looked into the main room.

Farwell sat hunched over the telegraph key, his earphones bleeping with static. "Got it cookin.'" He began tapping the key.

"...atta boy." Stepping back in the little room, he returned to the sack spilling its contents on the desktop. Quietly, Ingram swept his hand through the wallets and papers picking up a ring. "Damn," he muttered. It was a United States Naval Academy class ring and his stomach churned as he looked inside the band. The inscription was there, just as his mother had ordered: ACI -- 1937. The ring belonged to Alton C. Ingram, nicknamed Todd ('Ace') Ingram who graduated from the United States Naval Academy in 1937. The last time he'd seen this ring was when he twisted it off his

thumb and gave it to Helen Durand the night she evacuated on the U.S.S
Wolfish.

"Sonofabitch!" Ingram said. That was April 29, Hirohito's birthday, and
the Japanese were plastering Corregidor while he helped her aboard the
submarine. She had kissed him on his cheek; the one she had sewn up--

"Aaaah..."

Ingram jumped. Something...someone was on the bed. In the gloom, he
saw a blanket, a mass hidden beneath; it moved imperceptibly. "Aaaa..." It
was merely a passage of air through a wind pipe.

The blanket shifted, a hand was tied to the frame. It was a small hand. It
was--

"Jesus!" Ingram walked over and yanked off the blanket. Whatever lay
there was human. It moved slightly making him jump. Its clothes were filthy
and unrecognizable and soiled; the stench, a combination of every kind of
human excrement swept around him. Hair was matted in bloody patches on
the forehead and oozing blisters dotted the face, neck, arms, and chest.

The creature moaned slightly. The voice. It was a woman. Ingram bent to
touch her shoulder. "Can you hear me?"

"Noooo." She said.

"Helen!" shouted Ingram

"...Daddy?" she said softly.

"God, I--"

There was a roar; the building seemed to concuss. Something fell over.
Ingram ran into the other room finding Farwell face down on the desk. Part
of his head was blown away and bits of flesh, skull, and blood were splattered on the radio. For some reason, Farwell's eyes were focused on the radio
as if that had caused what had happened to him in his final moment. The
single shot had been so powerful it had ripped open a panel making the
radio spark and hiss. A small fire glowed brightly inside the transmitter for a
moment, then it went dull and lifeless.

Ingram heard a click. Four feet away a Japanese in a rumpled gray suit
stood just outside the window. He wore round, rimless rose-colored glasses
and had just run his Nambu's action--it must have jammed.

The *Kempetai*' s eyes were lifeless, dark pools, as he swung the pistol on
Ingram, aimed at his chest and pulled the trigger.

CLICK!

"*Kuso*," the *Kempetai* muttered, and yanked again at the Nambu's action.

Ingram's hand went to his holster. He tried to pull out the .45--but, *damnit*--the pistol wouldn't move. His hand shook and, as hard as he willed, he couldn't make his hand work.

The man in the rumpled grey suit cleared his jammed Nambu and aimed once more at Ingram.

Three, heavy concussions reverberated throughout the large nipa hut. As if yanked off his feet by a rope, the *Kempetai* flew sideways, his Nambu spinning into the night.

Screams; two more heavy shots. Ingram ran to the window seeing the *Kempetai* face down in mud. He looked back in the room. His hand shook, the butt of the .45 was firmly grasped but it still wouldn't move.

Someone thumped up the steps. "Jesus!" It was Bartholomew. He stood rooted, his mouth agape. "Bucket Mouth! My God!" He grabbed Ingram's arm, "Two Jap barges heading in. About a mile out. Looks like the garrison coming back." Bartholomew gaped at Farwell again and said, "Bucket Mouth?" almost as if he expected Farwell to wake up and return to the boat with them.

The images burned in Ingram's mind. Helen Durand; a hideous mess in the next room, and here, Farwell's head lay on the tiny desk, his hand frozen on the telegrapher's key. His mouth was open slightly and in finality, Farwell looked at peace.

"I tried, Rocky," said Ingram. "I really did."

34

9 May 1942
CinCPac Quarters
Pearl Harbor, Territory of Hawaii

The evening was hot and mildly humid on Makalapa, an ancient volcano that rose over Pearl Harbor. Halfway up the green slopes stood an isolated, but comfortable, four-bedroom two-story house finished in shiplap.

From the home's veranda, one could see the massive expanse of Pearl Harbor. It was a breath taking view of euphoric somnolence common to travel posters. To the east, the day's haze hovered over Honolulu. Beyond Waikiki's golden beaches, Diamond Head jutted into the whitecap-studded Pacific.

Honolulu, territory of Hawaii: It was there to be seen and heard and felt; bold, red anthuriums, crashing mid-day thunderstorms, and spectacular evenings under moonlit skies.

No longer. Six months ago, euphoria came to an abrupt halt, leaving stark reality the only commodity in the islands. Even now, at the dinner hour, Pearl Harbor was abuzz, as a myriad of tugs, oil barges, and ammo lighters frantically zipped here and there tending to the fleet. With barrage balloons overhead, warships of all kinds and sizes stood in Pearl Harbor's lochs and channels. Some entered fresh from the States, eager to pick up the fight, while other ships, blackened relics, staggered on their way back from war.

Directly below CinCPac's house, on the shores of Southeast Loch, was the submarine base, its fuel tank farm intact. To the viewer's left was the U.S. Naval Station with its complex of piers, dry docks, spidery cranes, and ironically, another tank farm untouched in the December attack. Next to that was Hickam Airfield, where four SBDs took off in pairs for bombing practice in the Molokai Channel. To the far right, East Loch was stuffed with tankers, cargo ships, attack transports, refrigeration ships, and repair ships. Mixed among those were two destroyer nests of five each, snugged up to destroyer tenders. Singled out for their own separate anchorage lay a sinister brood of ammunition ships.

A constant reminder of the December attack was the lingering smell. Even to the heights of Makalapa, sea breezes occasionally carried odors of blistered paint, charred wood, and burnt fuel oil. Worse were the days and weeks right after the attack, when the sea breeze carried the fetor of rotting flesh from bloated corpses that bobbed to the surface.

And only a blind man could ignore the carnage before the veranda of the Commander in Chief of the Pacific Fleet: Ford Island's Battleship Row.

With its own sweet stench, fuel oil still bubbled to the surface to curl around hulks that lay on the bottom like freshly killed dinosaurs rotting in their own pools of blood: *Arizona, Tennessee, West Virginia, Maryland, Oklahoma, California.* Less damaged, because it sat on blocks in the Naval base's Drydock Number One was the Pacific Fleet's flagship, the 33,100 ton *Pennsylvania.* Crammed in the same drydock were the destroyers *Cassin* and *Downes,* which erupted in a spectacular conflagration when the depth charges on their main decks blew up. The *Nevada* was the only battlewagon to raise steam and get underway that tragic morning. But with the longest distance to go, she, too, was hit when the second wave of Japanese dive bombers pounced on her, forcing her to beach at Hospital Point lest she clog the narrow channel to the Pacific.

What one breathed and saw was stark evidence of that which obliterated the lives of over three thousand Americans on December 7, 1941. In a single stroke, the Japanese surprise attack killed more servicemen than the combined Naval losses from the wars of 1898 and 1917-1918. Just a quick glance at necrotic hulks in Battleship Row--now swarming with salvage crews--was more than enough to stir one's outrage. The same glance was a grim omen of what the future held.

A regulation forty-six-by-six-foot horseshoe court was laid under a banyan tree beside the Makalapa home of the Commander in Chief of the Pacific Fleet (CinCPac), Admiral Chester W. Nimitz. Four men, dressed in short-sleeve working khaki uniforms were there, two at each end, one pitching, the other three watching. At the risk of losing points, no one spoke as their boss, Admiral Nimitz, hurled the two-pound-ten-ounce shoe. An ounce below regulation weight, the gleaming 73"-by-7e" shoe spun lazily through the air, hit the platform, flipped on its heels, and leaned against the stake.

"Good toss, Admiral," called Nimitz's partner, Rear Admiral Robert H. English, from the court's opposite end. Until a few days ago, he'd been Commander of the submarine base. Now, he was COMSUBPAC, Commander of Submarines Pacific, and was here as Nimitz's dinner guest for an informal "wetting down" party. CinCPac, the gracious host, had picked English as his horseshoe partner. But English didn't know a damn thing about the game. He asked politely, "Does that rate as a ringer, Sir?"

A tight-lipped Nimitz held up two fingers and slowly shook his head. This throw, his second, was a "leaner," and worth two points. Nimitz's first shoe had been well outside the scoring zone.

"Old man is as serious about horseshoes as he is about Japs," whispered the man next to English, Captain Elphege Alfred M. Gendreau, CinCPac's Fleet Surgeon, friend, and housemate.

English tried not to look nervous. He'd known Nimitz a long time. They had served in submarines together in the old days. But tonight, English knew he was being looked over, even if informally, for his newly won job as COMSUBPAC. With a sidelong glance at the *Oklahoma* laying capsized beside Ford Island, he knew he was in the right job. His wife's younger brother had been the engineering officer in that old battlewagon. And now, Hank was gone. No, Rear Admiral Robert H. English didn't want to do anything remotely stupid, such as looking like a dodo on the horseshoe court. As any other American, he simply wanted to do his job: Take the war to the enemy.

But for now, English was required to be the consummate guest under the banyan tree. "Damn! The old man's good," English said as Rear Admiral Milo F. Draemel, at the opposite end with Nimitz, stepped up for his second toss. Draemel, Nimitz's Chief of Staff, was another housemate. "You guys must intimidate the hell out of whoever you have to dinner."

Gendreau, with hands on his hips, watched Draemel close an eye and take practice swings. "Yeah. We do our share of scaring people." He dropped his tone. "It's working, Bob."

English arched an eyebrow.

"The old man is sleeping through the night."

"Finally."

"No pills, either." For the first time in his life, the taciturn Nimitz had suffered insomnia. The sleepless nights began soon after he took command of the decimated Pacific Fleet on December 31, 1941, when a Spartan ceremony was conducted on the deck of the submarine U.S.S. *Grayling*. Gendreau prescribed mild exercise and ordered the horseshoe court installed. Now, Nimitz, Gendreau, and Draemel played often, usually just before dinner.

"How about his hands?" English offered. The last few weeks he had seen Nimitz's hands shaking.

"Pistol range."

English was surprised at Gendreau's quick answer. "What the hell for?" he said.

"A couple of neurologists told me shooting pistols may do the trick. Something to do with hand-eye concentration. So, I'm having a pistol range built in the new CinCPac Headquarters."

Draemel's shoe spun slowly in the air and clanged around the stake: The ringer was worth three points. Worse, it nullified the two points from Nimitz's leaner. Draemel whooped and Nimitz twirled on the ball of one foot and slapped his forehead.

English gave a soft chuckle. "Good idea, Doc. Japs invade the island and we strap him up in a coconut palm with a sniper rifle, bandolier, canteen, and telescopic scope." An invasion of the Hawaiian Islands was a reality. Many visualized hordes of Japanese soldiers, their officers waving samurai swords and yelling "banzai," effortlessly sweeping over Oahu. All dependents had been evacuated to the mainland, and beach defenses were frantically under construction.

Ignoring English's sarcasm, Gendreau took a deep breath and looked at Battleship Row. He said without a smile, "When it comes to that, I'll be up there next to him."

Something in Gendreau's tone made English feel warm. No wonder Nimitz had picked this man for a housemate. Draemel, too. Both were fiercely loyal to the old man. It seemed ironic to English, a commander of over thirty submarines, to hear something like that from one who saves lives. "We'll all be up there with him, Doc," he said.

Nimitz cupped his hands and yelled, "Batter up."

A jeep drove up just as English and Gendreau stooped to recover their horseshoes. A dark-haired young lieutenant commander jumped out and walked up to Nimitz. It was Edwin T. Layton, Nimitz's Fleet Intelligence Officer. Layton handed Nimitz a folder. The two strolled off a few paces and talked.

English checked his watch. Almost seven forty-five. Dinner was supposed to have been served at seven-thirty.

Gendreau caught his glance and said, "Rochefort's late again." Another lieutenant commander was due to join them for dinner. He was Joseph J. Rochefort, who was in charge of the Hawaii--station HYPO's--branch of the communication security section of the office of Naval communications. The main office, formally called Op-20-G, was in Washington, D.C.

English said, "How does the old man put up with his tardiness? I would have fired the sonofabitch a long time ago."

Gendreau gave a long exhale and shook his head. "I think he assumes Rochefort will always be late, so he asks him early and everything works out."

"Huh," growled English.

Gendreau looked across the court at Nimitz. CinCPac quickly nodded, and the Fleet Surgeon took one practice swing. "Don't judge Joe too harshly, Bob," he said.

"Little bastard works his butt off. I'll give him that," said English.

Gendreau flung his shoe with a graceful release. It sailed, bounced off the stake, and skidded to a quick stop, stirring little dust. Draemel held his hands three inches apart: one point.

"The best defense, Bob, is to knock my shoe outside the scoring zone," said Gendreau.

Layton walked back to his jeep and got in. Just then another Jeep pulled up and Rochefort jumped out. The two lieutenant commanders nodded to one another, and Layton drove off.

A steward quickly appeared on the porch. Nimitz said, "Dinner's on. We'll have to pick this up later."

English was happy about that as he walked inside. There would be no later for this game unless they played by moonlight. The islands were under a strict blackout.

Nimitz lead them to the dining room and sat at the table's head. Draemel was next in seniority and sat to CinCPac's right; English was to the left. Gendreau was next to Draemel, Rochefort beside English. They talked of home and movies and children and grandchildren, as a light salad was served. More Smalltalk took them through Mahi Mahi, boiled potatoes, peas, rolls, and coffee.

They lingered over orange sherbet, then sat back as their places were quickly cleared. The stewards refilled the coffee as Draemel and Rochefort lighted cigars. Nimitz cranked the conversation up a notch, "How many?"

"At least ten thousand. Maybe more," said Gendreau.

The other four looked on as Gendreau explained, "Cerebral malaria killed more Japs than we thought in the Philippines."

Rochefort puffed his cigar, blue smoke curled around the ceiling light fixture. "How can you be so certain. You didn't hear it from me."

English smiled inwardly at Rochefort's peevish tone. In spite of the informal setting, a lieutenant commander simply didn't speak to a full captain like that. He sat back and waited for Nimitz to tear his head off.

"How *did* you find out, Al?" asked Nimitz.

English turned red.

Gendreau said, "Garrity. Army G-2. They got some reports from Corregidor a few days before it fell. Apparently, the Japs bombed warehouses full of quinine before they occupied Manila. Tons of the stuff was there just for the taking. Instead, they blew it up, and a lot of their boys died."

English couldn't help it. "So, did ours."

It was quiet for a moment then Nimitz said, "I wish I could have seen Homma's face."

Rochefort sat forward, an impish expression on his face. "How about Yamamoto's?"

This is where Rochefort gets it, thought English.

Nimitz narrowed his eyes and swept the table. Finally, he looked at Gendreau.

The fleet surgeon sighed, nodded, and stood. He quietly said, "'scuse me, Admiral. Reports to go over before tomorrow." He walked around and plopped a hand on English's shoulder. "Hope to see you around for horse-shoes again, Bob. Good night, gentlemen." With a nod, he walked out.

Nimitz reached to the sideboard and recovered the folder Layton had given him. He laid it flat and looked up.

Instead of seeing Rochefort roasted, English realized he'd been sucked into a strategy session.

Nimitz held up a long, two-page flimsy radio message. "Jack broke radio silence. He's on a beeline for home."

Draemel, English and Rochefort sat up. CinCPac referred to Admiral Jack Fletcher, Commander of Task Force 17, just disengaging from a battle with the Japanese in the Coral Sea.

Nimitz allowed himself a small smile, "They sank the *Ryukaku*. The *Shokaku* is damaged and is on her way to Truk. But--"

Rochefort and Draemel threw their fists over their heads and cheered. The *Ryukaku* was a light carrier; the *Shokaku* a heavy carrier, one of the *Kido Butai*.

Nimitz put a hand up. English noticed it shook just a little. "We lost the Lexington."

"But...but, she was okay, they said," gasped Draemel. "She'd just resumed flight ops."

Nimitz flipped a page and pressed his lips. "...mmmmm..."

They fell silent as he ran a finger down the page. "...here it is. Bomb hit ruptured gasoline lines," said Nimitz. "Damn! One-hundred-octane vapors settled deep inside her. Finally exploded. Must have been like a volcano in there. Fires went out of control. They had to abandon and torpedo her."

The three stared. Nimitz continued, "Jack is on his way back." His steel blue eyes flicked to Rochefort. "ETA afternoon of the twenty-seventh. But the *Yorktown* is seriously damaged."

Rochefort stood and braced his fists on the table.

Nimitz looked up and said, "She's trailing an oil slick ten-miles long. The hull is perforated, many compartments damaged. They estimate a ninety-day stateside overhaul."

Draemel stood, turned, and walked to the window. He ran the back of his hand over the blackout drape seam making sure light didn't leak through. "That's it then. Shit outta luck."

Nimitz said, "Sit, Milo."

English started to rise, "Should I leave, Sir?"

"No, Bob. You're part of this. Milo, sit, please."

Draemel threw his hands in the air. "*Lex* gone. *Yorktown* out of action. We're screwed!"

"Sit!" barked Nimitz.

Draemel turned, his eyes red. He pointed toward the west facing windows. "Yamamoto. That sonofabitch has over one hundred fully ready, chickenshit-loaded, combat ships. That includes eight carriers, Chester!"

"Sit!"

Draemel took a deep breath and sat. Rochefort, English noticed, puffed his cigar, watching the others through hooded eyes.

Nimitz rattled his flimsy, "Jack says the *Yorktown*'s engineering plant is fine. Her elevators work, the flight deck and catapults are okay. We can patch her fuel tanks. There's some hull puncturing but we'll get her shored up and arrest the flooding."

"How fast can she be turned around?" said Rochefort, resuming his seat.

Why didn't CinCPac order him to sit? thought English.

Nimitz looked in the distance. "Depends..."

English lost patience. "Admiral, I don't understand."

Rochefort puffed on his cigar and spit a piece of tobacco into shadows. Draemel seemed to remember his own cigar and regarded it as if it were something very important. Then suddenly, he stubbed it out and ran his napkin over his forehead.

"Midway," said Nimitz.

"They're hitting Midway?" said English.

"Their whole damned combined fleet," said Nimitz. "Yamamoto wants to draw us out. Sink us." He faced English. "Would you believe they've named the officer who is to take over the Naval station there on August first?"

"Nossir," said English.

Nimitz said, "How many ships, Milo?"

"Over a hundred twenty, counting submarines," moaned Draemel. "Their whole damned *Kido Butai*."

"Good God!" said English.

"Six carriers actually," said Rochefort, his voice sharp.

The others gave a start. They'd forgotten about the lieutenant commander. He pointed at Nimitz's radio flimsy. "One sunk in the Coral Sea. Another damaged. And two more carriers are going to Aleutians. So, we'll be up against four. Not eight."

"What have we got?" ventured English.

Nimitz said, "Looks like we're down to three carriers."

"*If* we can repair the *Yorktown*," Draemel growled. "And that leaves us with forty-five ships. Total. Sonofabitch."

English looked at Nimitz. "You want submarines." So, this is why I'm here, he thought.

"In spades," said Nimitz. "Everything you've got. I want a double perimeter to the west of Midway. How many can you give us?"

English said, "Admiral, I--"

"How many, Bob?" Nimitz's eyes were like lightning bolts.

"Twenty-five, give or take. I'd have to figure it out. Two en-route for overhaul from Fremantle. Three new ones from Stateside. Five in refresher training. I've got two boats dedicated to the torpedo snafu. They'll be replaced by two 'S' Boats on their way from--"

"Send 'em out," said Nimitz. "All of them. And forget torpedo problems for the time being. We have to go with what we've got."

English hadn't heard. He muttered, thinking aloud. "Let's see. The *Barbfish* is overdue and presumed lost. She--"

"That's Bob Fox's boat," said Nimitz.

It was quiet. At length English said, "Yessir."

"What's her area?" said Nimitz.

"Bashi Channel."

"Oh." Nimitz looked into the distance for a moment then nodded to English.

"--um, what else? The *Wolfish* is in the Sibutu Passage to intercept *Shokaku*. But you say *Shokaku* has diverted to Truk?"

Nimitz nodded.

English said, "Okay. No sense her hanging around Sibutu. Let's toss in the *Wolfish*, too." But then he remembered something, "Uh, Admiral. She has a batch of evacuees from Corregidor. They're supposed to be dropped in Darwin."

"Cancel the Darwin drop," said Nimitz. "Send her right on to Midway. She can offload her passengers there and refuel. Then, station her on the inner picket line."

After a pause English said, "Aye aye, Sir." Inner Picket Line? English had no idea what Nimitz was speaking about, but he knew Nimitz or Draemel would take care of that shortly, and that his "In" basket would be full over the next few weeks.

Rochefort said, "Perhaps we can have the *Wolfish* try and intercept *Shokaku'* s track on her way to Truk. In case she tries to double back?"

Nimitz rubbed his eyes for a moment. "Not a bad idea. Milo?"

Draemel stood, walked over to a side table, and examined a chart. "Not far out of her way, Admiral."

"Okay with you, Bob?" Nimitz smiled.

"Yessir," said English. Nimitz had effectively thrown it into his lap. "I'll divert the *Wolfish* to run past Truk."

"Good," said Nimitz.

English sat back. Who the hell is running this navy? he thought.

Nimitz asked Rochefort, "Have you been able to nail down the time, Joe?"

It was quiet, the bomb dropped. Instinctively, English knew Nimitz was asking Rochefort to commit. A clock ticked somewhere in the darkened house. Outside, a whistle echoed up from Pearl Harbor. English cocked his head at the prolonged blast. It sounded like a destroyer getting underway. Damn tin cans always had a brittle, challenging hoot.

Rochefort's eyes clicked over the three admirals, taking a long pull on his cigar. "Morning of four June. It'll be Nagumo with four carriers of the *Kido Butai*. He'll launch his first strike at 0600 local time."

Draemel gave a long exhale. His shoulders sagged, and he shook his head slowly. Vice Admiral Chuichi Nagumo had led the attack against Pearl Harbor.

Nimitz drummed his fingers. At length he said, "You sure?"

The tip of Rochefort's cigar glowed red. "Best I can do. Layton agrees," he said, exhaling. The smoke didn't quite rise to the ceiling this time. It stayed at eye level and clouded his face.

Silence. The destroyer's whistle hooted again with five short blasts: the danger signal.

Nimitz said, "Okay. We'll go with that. I'll call Ernie King." He turned to English. "That means we need your boats on station by noon of three June, Bob. Can you do it?"

Who the hell is running this Navy? thought English. "Of course, Admiral."

35

9 May 1942
Calancan Bay, Marinduque Island
Philippines

A thin overcast blurred all but the brightest stars. Moonrise wouldn't be until
4 *a.m.*, yet visibility was, for some reason, tolerable. With Don Aguilar and
Augustine Vega leading the way in a small banca, the 51 Boat cleared the reef.
An hour later, Marinduque lay off their starboard quarter and Ingram stood
at the tiller, heading for Mompog Pass.

"Anything Forester?" Forester and Whittaker were keeping lookout astern
in case any one came after them.

"Nossir," said Forester.

"Good." Ingram breathed easier with each deep swell that rolled between
the 51 Boat and Marinduque.

Amidships, Yardly, DeWitt, and Holloway worked over the formless,
groaning shape they had carefully loaded just before pushing off.

Ingram couldn't see what was going on except when one of them occasionally reached for the water jug or yanked something from the medical bag. Growing impatient, he barked, "Yardly."

Yardly rose, walked aft, and stood beside Ingram, wiping his brow.

"Well?"

"Touch and go, Skipper. Those bastards did about everything to her. Beat her up, cigarette burns, razor cuts, cracked ribs, maybe a ruptured spleen. Might be leaking blood internally."

Ingram gripped the tiller in a cold rage.

Yardly waved a hand at the ocean's expanse and his voice cracked, "Out here...we got nuthin'. How can I be certain what the hell's wrong let alone figure out how to treat her?"

There was a long silence before Ingram said, "Did they...well...you know...?"

"Hell, I can't tell. And I'm not going to go looking in there, right now. I don't think there's any discomfort there but we won't know for a while. Right now, she's dehydrated and has a high temperature. Where was she, anyway?"

"Small room, no windows. Maybe a storage area at one time."

"How long?"

Ingram shrugged.

"Well, if those bastards didn't feed her or give her water for two or three days, then that would explain it. She probably roasted in there during the daytime."

The image of that little room swept through Ingram's mind. "Probably did."

"I think she's in heat shock. We're dripping water into her mouth with a rag. But I don't think that's going to be near enough."

"Have you cleaned her up?"

Yardly shrugged. "A little. She still smells like shit. But I wish we had some ice. I have to figure a way to get the temperature down. It's up to a hundred five. Then we have to rehydrate her. And she keeps talking about--"

"Jesus! She conscious?"

"Not really. I--"

"Bones!" Holloway's tone was urgent.

"'Scuse me." Yardly ran back to the huddle and kneeled among them.

"Forester," called Ingram.

"Sir." Kevin Forester stepped up.

"Take the helm. Steer zero-eight-five."

"Yessir."

Ingram moved forward, dropped to his knees, and squeezed next to Yardly. Helen's mouth was open wide and she inhaled in a great wheezing gasp.

Yardly looked sideways for a moment, then put an ear to her chest, lifting her wrist and checking his watch. "Can't tell..."

Helen's chest heaved, her breathing erratic. But then she moaned. "...almost home..."

"What's that?" said Ingram.

"She's said it twice." said Yardly. "Feel this."

Ingram followed Yardley's hand to her forehead, finding it hot.

The corpsman said, "A thready pulse and her heartbeat is erratic, although it's hard to tell with that damn engine pounding in my ears."

Helen's chest heaved again. "Ahhhh..."

"Damn." Ingram bent close to Helen's ear, stroked her forehead and said, "Hold on now, Honey. It's okay now. We'll take good care of you."

"...beautiful..." She gasped.

Ingram said into her ear, "You're safe, Helen. Hurry up and get well. I need you to fix my cheek again."

"...see you." She gave a long sigh, her mouth half open.

Ingram looked at Yardly.

Yardly grew tense. "Damnit!" He ran his stethoscope over her chest. "Can't hear anything. Could we throttle back for a moment?"

Ingram called aft, "Whittaker. Kill the engine."

Whittaker said, "Skipper, it's going really good now. I don't think--"

"Kill it, damnit!" said Ingram.

Whittaker switched off the engine. The 51 Boat slowed, then lay dead in the water, rising and falling on the swells under a gathering overcast. Everyone crowded around, seeing that Helen did not move.

Yardly listened, pushing the stethoscope around her chest. After a while, he shook his head and looked up.

"What?" said Ingram.

"Gone." Yardly choked.

"No!" said Ingram. "Helen you can't," he almost shouted.

Yardly lay a hand on his shoulder. "Sorry, Skipper."

He pressed close, seeing an alabaster-white Helen Durand, hair plastered to her forehead, her mouth halfway open. "What for?" Ingram looked to the sky. "What the hell for?" He almost bit through his lip. Why had this woman's death, more than any of the other grisly deaths he'd seen on Corregidor, affected him so much? Even before the question surfaced, he knew the answer and was angry at himself for being selfish, that he would have to suppress the feelings he had for her. That they never existed. To do it right, he would have to tell himself that she never existed.

Impossible. She does exist. She's right here before me. She did...exist...

"A good kid," Bartholomew muttered. "I guess we ought to get some canvas and sew her up. Let's see. For weights we can--"

Helen's chest heaved; she gave a great gasp.

"Jesus, Bones," said Sunderland. "Do something."

"Maybe she needs artificial respiration," said Bartholomew.

Helen's chest heaved again, drawing in another lungful of air.

Junior Forester said, "I took artificial respiration in lifesaving. All you do is--"

"Quiet!" Yardly slapped his stethoscope over Helen's heart. "Sonofabitch. It's goin'" He grabbed her wrist. "Pulse is back to where it was. She's breathing normally." He looked up. They all crowded around, the farthest man four feet away. "Alright," Yardly said. "Step back. She needs air."

Bartholomew came to his senses and growled, "Back everybody."

Ingram stood and moved away. With the others, he watched Yardly thumb open her right eyelid and shine a penlight. He did the same with the left, then stared at the deck. "That's it," he said.

"What?" said Ingram.

"We got some work to do. And quick," said Yardly. "Mr. Ingram? Mr. Holloway?"

Both said, "Yes?"

"Take her clothes off. Everything. Now, please." Yardly started digging in his bag, pitching packages and instruments on the deck.

"What?" said Ingram, incredulous.

"Now, gentlemen. No foolin'" said Yardly, fumbling with a long tube.

Holloway said, "But--"

"Do it, now. Take my word, it's important." Yardly raised a hand and pointed. "Mr. DeWitt. Mr. Toliver. Get a couple of blankets and soak them in sea water."

"Sunny, grab that bucket, fill it with seawater, and pour it all over her."

"Now?" said Sunderland.

"Yes, now. Hurry up. And keep dumping water on her until I say stop."

Sunderland picked up the bucket, Toliver and DeWitt grabbed blankets and leaned over the side. Ingram's lips were pressed; his Adam's apple jumped up and down as he bent over Helen with Holloway and began tugging off Helen's clothes. Ingram tried not to look but couldn't help noticing her body was covered by thin cuts, some still bled. Prominent were beet-red cigarette burns. A few were festered and oozed pus. And the odor. Ingram gagged as he tore away what was left of her blouse...

"Pants, too?" asked Ingram, barely choking back his rage.

Yardly leaned over. "Yeah. But rinse 'em out and save 'em." He nodded to a tube lying beside his kit and said to Holloway, "Burn ointment. Start dabbing."

"This enough, Bones?" asked Sunderland, gently pouring a bucket of water over Helen's body.

"Keep it going 'til I say stop," said Yardly.

"Okay to start the engine now? We need to get going," said Ingram.

"Okay," Yardly said absently, looking into his medical bag.

"Whittaker," said Ingram. "Start the engine and let's go. Forester, zero-eight-five. I'd like to--what are doing?"

Yardly had Helen's head pulled way back, elevating her chin. Now he stuck his fingers in her mouth then eased a long, rubber tube after it. Without looking up, he said, "...never done this before."

"What?" asked DeWitt, bending close.

"Feeding an NG tube into her stomach. Hope I don't--could one of you hold that flashlight? Thanks; damn thing could go into her lungs. I'm in deep...ah...made it. Sunny, gimme that bottle." He snapped his fingers.

Sunderland fumbled near the medical kit.

"No, you dope, that's rubbing alcohol; there, the bottle on top of...labeled saline...yes..."

Sunderland handed it over with a you-better-know-what-the-hell-you're-doing look.

Yardly held up the bottle of clear liquid. "Here's what's happening, folks.

Team effort. Now. Chop-chop. She's into heat shock and dehydration. That's why she almost died. Temperature needs to come down, so keep pouring water over her."

"And get this damned bilge pump going," barked Bartholomew. He pointed to water sloshing about their feet. "This is your baby, Junior."

"Count on it, Chief." Junior Forester inserted a big lever in the pump and wiggled until it gurgled with great sucking sounds.

Bartholomew leaned over the side watching water squirt out the discharge hole. "Keep it going."

Yardly said, "Worst of all she needs water and a bunch. Right now, pure water would kill her so it has to be saline. I got only one quart, she needs at least a gallon so, Rocky--"

"What? Me?" said Bartholomew.

"Yeah. You're elected. Make up four more quarts," said Yardly.

"How the hell do I do that?" asked Bartholomew.

"You...you. Shit," Yardly stroked his chin, "Wait." He hooked up his bottle to the NG tube, letting the saline run into her stomach. "Try two teaspoons per quart."

"You sure?" said Bartholomew.

"...no."

"Damnit, Bones," said Sunderland.

Yardly whipped around. His eyes glistened as he said, "Not sure. That's the best I can remember."

Sunderland growled, "Bones, if she dies I'm gonna--"

Ingram said. "Get going, Bartholomew. The rest of you shut up. Just do your jobs."

Helen was entirely naked, with Holloway and Ingram cleaning her off as best as they could. Then they had Toliver and DeWitt loosely wrap two soaking blankets around her.

"Sir?" Sunderland stood close with another bucket of sea water.

Ingram sat back, letting the gunner's mate pour another bucket of cold, sea water over her body while Junior Forester worked the bilge pump handle, sending water back into the ocean.

Forty-five minutes later the evening was still warm. Sunderland poured on another bucket of water while the others traded off with the bilge pump. Yardly, with Helen's head cradled in his arm, dumped in his third bottle of saline: Rocky's brew they called it.

Helen coughed.

"Hey!" said Yardly.

She coughed again and gurgled, her hand rose tugging at the NG tube.

Ingram pulled her hand away but she reached again. He grabbed her wrist and held it.

Yardly said, "Helen, can you hear me?"

Helen gave an, "Uhhhgh."

"You're gonna be okay, now. You know you're with friends?"

"Uhhhgh."

"Good. I'll pull the tube, but you have to take more water--at least a quart."

"Uhhhgh."

"Tube goes back in if you don't drink."

Her head nodded slightly. "Uhhhgh."

"Okay." Carefully, Yardly eased out the tube then felt her forehead. "Seems better. Uh...here, Skipper. Do you mind?"

"Got it." Ingram scooted over and lay Helen's head in his lap while Yardly rummaged through his kit. Ingram stroked her hair as the men in 51 Boat grinned and muttered and slapped Yardly on the back. "Gonna be a hell of a doctor, someday," said Whittaker.

"Hey Bones. Can you cure the crabs, too?" said Sunderland.

"In your case Sunny, they're irreversible," said the corpsman. He pulled out a thermometer and stuck it under Helen's tongue while Ingram fussed with the blanket. At length, Yardly pulled it out, flipped on a pen light, and said, "Not bad, ninety-nine. I think we can knock off the wet soaks for the time being. Maybe let her dry off and get her something to wear."

Ingram tipped the saline bottle to Helen's mouth, pulled down her lower lip, and poured a little. He watched her swallow and grinned. "Alright, Yardly. I'm putting you in for the Congressional Medal of Honor."

"Long way to go, Skipper."

"How's that?"

Yardly whispered, "Electrolytic balance is all screwed up. We don't know if that will come back. It's fifty-fifty."

"How long?"

"Couple of days."

"Sure looks better to me," said Ingram.

"Well, for now, yeah. But what can happen with people in heat shock is that their kidneys stop working."

Ingram stared at Yardly.

Yardly said, "No kidney function, nothin' we can do. She'll die."

36

9 May 1942
Mompog Pass
Philippines

Ingram's teeth chattered. He peered in the blackness of Mompog Pass looking for patrol boats. As the 51 Boat rolled and the Buda hummed, Ingram couldn't forget the little soaked heap laying ten feet forward fighting for her life. As a diversion, he forced himself to concentrate on the Aguilars. Quite simply, they had been wonderful. Just before Don Aguilar and Augustine Vega ventured into the garrison with Delores, they had provisioned the 51 Boat with coconuts, cooked pig and chicken, sliced dried beef, boiled fish, jackfruit, and white rice.

Doña Carmella was helping with the last of the load when Ingram, Bartholomew, and Sunderland came on the run half-carrying, half-dragging Farwell's body and carrying Helen. With the Japanese barges headed toward the reef, there was no time to talk. And it didn't take much to convince Don Aguilar the enraged *Kempetai* would select him and his wife for their first reprisal. Reluctantly, he and Doña Carmella agreed to move to the south side of Marinduque with Vega's relatives until things quieted down. They all knew that meant until the war was over whenever that was. But in the end, it was the right move for Aguilar, who admitted his ineptness at playing the political games fast developing in the provisional Philippine government.

The three Filipinos promised Ingram they would bury Farwell in a secret location where his body could be exhumed and returned home at war's end.

Ingram couldn't put Doña Carmella out of his mind. Besides losing her son, she and her husband were now uprooted from their home and livelihood. Everything was gone after giving all they had for a strange, ragtag band of Americans that had crashed into their life.

Ingram realized he hadn't truly known any Filipinos beside those in Manila or Cavite or Subic Bay: Navy towns where his ships docked. He hadn't paid attention to those who told him Filipinos living in the provinces were gracious and friendly and would share everything they had. After meeting the Aguilars he knew it was true. And somehow, he realized Don Aguilar would even give his life, if necessary. After tonight, Ingram wondered if he could do as much.

He ran his hand over his brow, still feeling shaky, and he tried not to look at the land to starboard. To port, he picked out a gray-black shape he knew to be Maniuayan Island. He scanned the blackness for picket ships, seeing none, at least those with running lights. But darkened picket ships were another story as they had learned off Fortune Island.

The Forester brothers were stationed forward as lookouts, as they headed into Mompog Pass. It was only three-and-a-half-mile-wide but, Ingram reckoned it would be too late if they stumbled on a picket now; surprise would be on their side. A look at their wake told him a voracious southeast current had the 51 Boat in its grip, yanking them along at, Ingram judged, ten knots over the ground. This made it possible to quickly squirt through Mompog Pass, but unfortunately, they would be unable to reverse course if something popped up before them, such as a Japanese patrol boat.

Otis DeWitt stepped beside him and said in his twang. "How far tonight, Lieutenant?"

"Umm...good current. I'm trying for Sibuyan Island—about ninety miles..." Ingram said.

DeWitt nodded toward Yardly who sat beside Helen Durand. "The doc says she's sleeping now. She's had enough water."

"Good." After a moment, Ingram told him about the *Manila Tribune*'s article with Wainwright's surrender order and the admonition to surrender by May 12.

"So what if we don't?" asked DeWitt.

"Then the Japs shoot us, I suppose."

"Anything else new?"

"I hope not."

Dewitt moved a little closer. "How did Farwell do?"

Ingram looked over his shoulder toward Marinduque. For a moment, he thought he saw Farwell's face take shape in the misty headland. He wore a twisted grin and his enormous jaw clanked up and down. Then it all changed, and the quartermaster's head lay on the small desk, one eye half-closed, the other all the way open. The transmitter sputtered and arced in the background, causing glistening hair on the back of Farwell's head to catch fire. Farwell's hand was still on the transmit key and—

"Lieutenant?" asked DeWitt.

Farwell's face was gone. Strange. "I don't think he raised anybody. He'd just started tapping the key."

"Damn!" said DeWitt. "We were so close. Did you give it a try?"

"Jap's bullet blew up the radio. Sparks flew and the damn thing arced all over the place. That was when Rocky came in yelling for us to scram."

DeWitt looked into the pitch black off the port side. "Sibuyan Island, you say. How about trying there?"

"No," said Ingram easing the helm as they crested a wave and dove into a trough. He was thankful he had something to do. Steering helped erase tonight's horror from his mind. And the engine ran better. In fact, it purred. Whittaker had worked on the Buda after all.

"No? What do you mean 'no,' Lieutenant? We're sitting on top of something prejudicial to the security of the United States." DeWitt's resonance carried a manufactured tone of incredulous outrage.

Ingram looked back to Marinduque.

Farwell was there again, grinning.

Ingram's voice squeaked, "Anymore flyers like today and we'll all be hanging upside down in some butcher shop."

DeWitt said, "I don't think— "

"Major, damnit," Ingram said. "I want the same thing as you. But we're not taking unnecessary risks. We were lucky to get out of San José. And Farwell was killed doing what I was trying to avoid—involve civilians."

"Farwell was doing his duty."

"What about the Aguilars? And what about their neighbors? You know there will be retribution. Many will be killed indiscriminately."

"That remains to be seen," DeWitt said peevishly.

Ingram felt the bile rising. DeWitt knew better; he was merely trying to win a point. "Do you know how many Chinese have been killed since Doolittle raided Tokyo?"

"What does that— "

"Two hundred fifty thousand, so far, Otis. All in the Chekiang Province where our fliers went down. I repeat. That's two hundred fifty thousand Chinese men, women, and children: Civilians that the Japs slaughtered for helping less than one hundred B-25 guys."

"How can you be so sure?"

Ingram peered over the starboard quarter toward Marinduque. No Farwell. "Epperson. It came over the wire in a fleet intelligence report. Apparently, it's still going on. Chiang Kai-shek is raising hell with the State Department. I'm surprised you didn't get the word."

DeWitt fell silent.

Ingram's voice dropped, "Don Aguilar showed up at that swimming hole. We didn't go looking for him. But I don't want that to happen again. We'll have to be more careful and keep a better watch."

"Finding Helen was a bonus."

Ingram couldn't argue with that. "Yes."

After a pause DeWitt sighed, "Okay. We play it your way." Then he said, "Bartholomew said you did some fine shooting. Sunderland, too."

Ingram ground his teeth. Why the hell couldn't he tell these people that he had frozen? That he couldn't pull that damned .45 from the holster even though, as he ran the terrifying scene over in his mind again, he had had plenty of time. The *Kempetai*' s Nambu jammed. And Sunderland had shot the Jap just before Bartholomew stumbled in. Maybe seeing Helen's mutilated body had made him freeze.

Farwell.

Why the hell couldn't he shoot? Ingram's teeth chattered. "Listen, Otis. There's something you should know. I— "

"Skipper? Can I make a suggestion?" Beardsley wobbled to his feet only to slip. Toliver grabbed an elbow and eased him up.

In spite of himself, Ingram felt like chuckling. Beardsley's accent had become less Des Moines and more Chicago; an almost deliberate copy of either Bogart or Raft; he couldn't decide which one. Quite simply the B-17 pilot was feeling better. Yardly had been changing his bandages each day and it was paying off, in spite of the tropical environment that inhibited healing.

"Shoot, Leon."

"I couldn't help overhearing."

"Lieutenant." DeWitt's tone admonished the B-17 pilot.

"Let him talk, Otis," said Ingram.

Beardsley reached for space. Toliver grabbed the pilot's hand and guided it to the binnacle where he steadied himself. "Just trying to help out, Major." He paused. "I got buddies on Mindanao. B-17 jockeys. Pursuit guys, too. There's a half dozen emergency airstrips near the Del Monte plantation. A few in Agusan Province around Nasipit. We hook up with one of them and we fly out. Be in Australia within a week."

DeWitt folded his arms. "Del Monte? Nonsense. Those people are in prison now."

"Maybe so. Maybe not. Some could be in the hills. But the point is, I flew into at least two of them."

"Flew into what, Leon?" asked Ingram.

"The airstrips!" Beardsley almost shouted. Leon sounded more like Bogart, Ingram decided. And he could tell it was with great restraint that the B-17 pilot had not added "dummy."

Beardsley continued, "It was MacArthur's idea. They carved airstrips out of jungle in case the Japs gained air superiority. All sorts of stuff is hidden in there. Airplanes are in sandbag revetments all covered with camouflage netting. Plans were to use them for night bombing."

"What do you think, Lieutenant?" asked DeWitt.

Ingram said, "Those things gassed, Leon?"

The boat rocked. Beardsley's hand slipped off the binnacle. Toliver grabbed it and placed it back on. "Thanks Ollie," he muttered from the side of his mouth. "Full load. Ammo for all the guns. Bombs on carts ready to go."

It seemed so easy. Turn everything over to the Army with Otis DeWitt stepping in to lead the charge, and one of Leon Beardsley's grinning throttle jockey buddies hauling them to Australia in glory.

Beardsley slurred, "Aussieland, Todd. Think of it. Hot baths, hotter broads, steaks, all the beer you can drink. A deal you cannot turn down."

"Shut up, Leon. Let me think."

Beardsley made a spitting noise.

Ingram rubbed his chin. Weather permitting; they could make the 450 miles to Mindanao in six nights. Up until the fifth day, their track would be the same, until Bohol Island. There they would have to decide whether to run directly east for the Surigao Straits and the Pacific, or to head south another hundred miles for Nasipit, a harbor on the north coast of Mindanao.

Something else came to mind. Amador. He had gone to Nasipit, his hometown according to Aguilar, setting up a resistance cell. "There's a radio in Nasipit," Ingram said.

DeWitt exhaled loudly. "That's it then."

"Okay. We run for Nasipit," Ingram said. "We'll try to hook up with Amador and use his radio. And then dig up one of Leon's B-17s. All we need is someone to fly it."

"I've got friends all over the place, just itchin' to take a crack at something like this," said Beardsley.

"Where, Leon?" asked Ingram.

Beardsley swayed easily with the boat's motion. "Just get me there, Todd. I'll take care of it."

Ingram and DeWitt exchanged glances, knowing there would be great risk looking for a B-17 and one of Beardsley's pilot friends. Most likely, they would reprovision and head for Australia after they made radio contact.

Dewitt said. "Six days. That gives us time."

"Time for what?" Beardsley asked.

"Never mind," said DeWitt.

"Huh?" said Beardsley.

"We're in a hurry," said Ingram.

"How's she doing?" Ingram bent over Helen. She lay on her side; her fist was pushed against her mouth; her knees curled up; definitely fetal.

"Okay so far," said Yardly. "Now. Go get some sleep, Skipper."

"I don't mind." Tonight, he was afraid of sleep.

"Well, I do. We need you whole. Now, go." Yardly pointed to an empty spot.

"Okay." With a sigh, Ingram crawled over and lay on a blanket. Over the past few days he had learned the trick of sleeping on hard surfaces. Even in his debilitated condition he could find enough body fat to wiggle under his ribs, hip, and other areas where bone contacted the deck. With a little finesse, he would brace his feet against the roll of the boat and sleep comfortably, having scrunched fat in the right place.

But tonight, he fell into a shallow, troubled sleep as his mind spewed grotesque images of Farwell's brains splattered on the side of the radio hut. And then cigarette burns popped out all over his body; they hurt like hell, he could feel everyone and Helen grinned at him.

A hand mercifully tapped his shoulder, lifting him from the horror. The Buda's roar ripped into his eardrum and brought back the reality of Mompog Pass and Marinduque Island.

Sunderland crouched over him. "Sorry, Skipper. You said to wake you." He pointed ahead. "Mr. Holloway says Sibuyan is in sight."

"What time is it?"

"About four."

Ingram blinked and ran a hand over his face. The skies were clear and a bright moon had risen, although it seemed more like a thin piece of cheese than the half slice predicted by the *Nautical Almanac*.

Sibuyan's Mount Guitinguitin rose above the horizon like a vampire's tooth. And off the starboard bow were the headlands of Romblon Island. They were well into a flat Sibuyan Sea and making remarkable time. It must have been the current that squirted them out of Mompog Pass farther than he anticipated.

He looked aft, seeing Yardly drinking a mug of tea, sitting cross-legged next to the blanketed lump that was Helen Durand. The corpsman gave an "okay" sign with thumb and forefinger, then drew a blanket around his own shoulders to ward off the morning's dew. Further aft, Holloway stood at the tiller. They exchanged waves. A quick glance around the boat showed the rest were asleep, except for the watch section; Sunderland doubled as aft lookout and engineer. The two bow lookouts were Bartholomew and Junior Forester.

"Okay. Thanks Sunderland," Ingram said. "Wake me by five-thirty. Before, if you spot reefs or Japs." Ingram lay back trying to wiggle fat under his bones. He closed his eyes.

"Uh, Skipper?" Sunderland's voice was barely audible.

Ingram's eyes popped open.

Sunderland leaned close. "Thanks for bagging that Jap."

"What?"

"I didn't see him. I was watching the others chase that damned pig. First thing I know is that Jap's right behind me blowing up Farwell. He could have had me, too. I was wide open."

"His pistol jammed."

"Yours didn't. Thanks, Skipper."

Ingram had to clear this up. "You...you *did shoot* the other two?"

"Right after you zapped Tojo."

"I see."

"I owe you one, Skipper." With a wink, Sunderland scrambled aft and fiddled in the engine compartment.

Ingram rolled to his back, put his hands under his head and watched the boat roll under the stars. What's going on? Who the hell shot that little turd? He eased to his side trying to gather more fat under his ribs.

Four feet away Beardsley snored. Just beyond was Toliver who was becoming known as 'Rover,' i. e. Beardsley's watchdog. Toliver seemed to be with the pilot all the time--helping him walk, helping him feed himself, even helping Beardsley wash clothes. Using a small syringe from Yardley's medical kit, Toliver irrigated Beardsley's eyes and changed the dressing each day. Ingram wondered if he should say something; maybe a word of appreciation would help lift Toliver from his malaise.

But now, in darkness, it seemed as if Toliver watched him. Then his eyes flicked to the stars when Ingram looked over.

Ingram rolled close. "Ollie," he rasped. "Was that you?"

Toliver watched the stars. "Skipper?"

"You followed us and shot that Jap, didn't you?"

"Better sleep, Skipper. Long day tomorrow."

Ingram moved to yank Toliver's shirt lapel, but Beardsley stirred and began muttering; and his foot brushed Whittaker's head.

Toliver glanced again at Ingram, then wiggled to search for his own hat. He settled back and stared at the stars.

37

12 May 1942
U.S.S. *Wolfish* (SS 204)
Bohol Sea

WHAM! WHAM! WHAM! WHAM! WHAM! WHAM!

The depth charges perfectly bracketed the *Wolfish* just abeam of her forward engine room, each exploding within milliseconds of one another. Döttmer and Lorca were catapulted into the overhead and fell on the radio-shack deck amidst a howling tangle of sweaty arms and legs. Lorca screamed with the others from sheer, unbearable physical pain, not terror as the Japanese destroyer hurled its hell down upon them.

Unbelievable. Only moments before they were on the surface, loping at an easy pace with two engines on propulsion and two on battery charge. The boat pleasantly rolled under a dark, overcast night and, down below in the crew's mess, Doc Gaspar played Artie Shaw records on the ship's recalcitrant portable record player. They were steaming on course 055 degrees true at fifteen knots. The Surigao Straits lay twenty miles off the bow, with the narrowest part of the transit due in an hour and a half. After that, Ronnie planned to clear Dinagat and Hibuson islands by sunrise and be well into the Pacific at cruising depth, complying with a mysterious message received two nights ago ordering them to proceed to Midway at best speed to refuel. A Fremantle-based submarine refueling at Midway? Why? "Not that we don't mind being closer to the States, but what the hell for?" everyone asked.

Döttmer, of course, thought he knew.

He and Lorca were jammed together in the radio shack. With three fingers of his left hand broken, Lorca couldn't articulate all the equipment, so Döttmer had been assigned as backup. The Corregidor refugee was at the radio copying a FOX broadcast when someone shouted, "crash dive."

The *Wolfish* nosed under and, within seconds, a Japanese destroyer dropped a six depth charge pattern, a preview of fear and terror Döttmer had never imagined.

And now, his heart raced as people screamed about the boat. His stomach was knotted and he kept swallowing, yet he wanted to vomit all at the same time.

A shout echoed from the control room, "Passing three hundred feet. I can't hold her, Sir."

Ensign Gruber yelled, "I said 'blow negative,' goddamn you!"

Döttmer felt his panic well up. He'd always held a rather clinical outlook that fear was contagious and that all one had to do was simply close his eyes and ears to those so afflicted. But this was all around him in three dimensions. He couldn't stop the smell of ozone and scorched flesh from reaching his nostrils. And incredulously, he couldn't stop the warm flood seeping in his crotch. Disgusted, he knew he'd voided his bladder, and no command existed in his consciousness to make it stop. He couldn't even stop his teeth from chattering. With what rational thought remained, he knew Lil' Adolf's incompetence was what scared him the most. Somebody better do something, quick. Like shoot the little bastard and find a diving officer who knew which side was up.

With depth charges raining overhead, Döttmer thought about the chart taped to the nav table and the soundings he'd seen around their last plotted position: 450 fathoms (2,700 feet). And with all the screaming and yelling, Lil' Adolf had let them slide below test depth. At any moment, the *Wolfish* could implode like a chicken egg run over by a steam roller.

The lights flickered and went out. From the control room pealed shrieks and groans of men calling to God and mother, while others bellowed "shut up!" or, "Gimme that battle lantern."

Get out.

Döttmer reached up and turned the radio room doorknob. It wouldn't budge. He tried to rise. Döttmer was on the bottom of the pileup with Lorca's thigh draped over his chest. It was wet also. Amidst the clamor, Döttmer had a quick flash of Lorca's slicked-back hair and Hollywood he-man image. The oaf used to strut around showing off his perfectly defined chest and arms. And those stupid tattoos: "Arrivederci Tojo" and "Mother." He even oiled his skin.

And now, the debonair, ex-violin playing, Radioman Second Class Dominic Federico Lorca had peed his pants, just like anyone else.

Total darkness. Ozone. The temperature was easily up to 115 degrees. Screaming men were convinced they were going to die.

WHAM! WHAM! WHAM! WHAM! WHAM! WHAM!

The *Wolfish* twisted and worried as if clamped in a shark's jaws. Döttmer heard a loud pop, followed by a high-pitched wail and more screams. But something was different. In darkness, he felt around. He was on top of the screaming Lorca this time.

Incredible.

With the last pattern, the two had been tossed in the air and had changed positions. Döttmer's buttocks now pinned the radioman's bandaged left hand to the deck. With an impulsive heave, Döttmer rose, making sure his weight bore directly against Lorca's stitched hand. The desired effect was achieved. Lorca screamed.

Get out.

In darkness, Döttmer found his feet and pulled the narrow door with all his might.

CRACK! The damn thing opened! He was free. Except there was no place to go. Fore and aft, it was entirely dark. He sensed someone close by on the linoleum deck. Just then, the man croaked. Vomit splattered on the deck. Forward, someone else whimpered.

Suddenly the aft hatch flew open and a flashlight flooded the passageway.

"Make a hole!" a figure growled from behind the jiggling beam.

Döttmer recognized the voice which rumbled through darkness. It belonged to Lieutenant Sutcliff, the chief engineer.

"Inside," the officer rumbled to Döttmer.

Döttmer slammed the door as Sutcliff lurched by.

Soon, the emergency lights flickered and came on, illuminating the stygian cell called the radio room. Döttmer reached over and flipped off power switches, taking everything out of "standby." Not that it mattered, he noted. All the indicator lights were dead anyway.

There was a blast of high-pressure air. From the control room, the chief of the boat yelled over the din, "Number one master vent valve is stuck open."

"Four hundred thirty feet," screeched Lil' Adolf.

"Get out of the way. Secure the blow!" yelled Sutcliff.

Ronnie yelled from the conning tower hatch, "Foggy, maneuvering room still doesn't respond. All ahead flank, damnit!"

Sutcliff grabbed a headset and repeated the order. From aft they heard the motors whine louder. The submarine shook and a loose piece of gear clanked and rattled outside the hull.

Döttmer opened the door a crack, seeing the fourteen men in the control room in various stages of shock. All were bare chested and glistening with sweat. Light bulbs had shattered. Broken glass littered the deck. And it smelled; someone had defecated. One man sat on the deck holding his head as blood ran freely over his fingers and dripped on the deck. The electrical panel arced loudly and threw sparks.

"Another can's on her way in," yelled Collins, the sonarman. He twirled his range knob. "Nine hundred yards."

Döttmer stepped out of the radio shack into the passageway. Lorca held his arm tenderly, struggled to his feet, and followed to watch. It didn't take long for everyone to realize a destroyer was making a run on them again. Her steam turbines howled louder and louder, and her sonar pinging jumped to an eerie high-pitched interval.

"Shifted to short scale," shouted Collins.

"Collins," barked Ronnie from the conning tower hatch. "Give me a mark when she's at four hundred."

"Aye, aye, Captain," said Collins, wiping his brow.

Behind Döttmer, Lorca stood on his tiptoes and asked, "We still sinking?"

Döttmer searched for the depth gauge. His teeth chattering was worse.

He found it hard to form simple words. "Don't know," was all he could manage.

Collins shouted, "Four-hundred yards, Captain!"

"Right full rudder. Starboard back two thirds. Port ahead standard," shouted Ronnie from the conning tower.

"We're sinking through four hundred seventy feet, Captain," Sutcliff called up the ladder.

"Shit!" gasped Ronnie. "Blow safety!"

Three thousand pounds of air pressure blasted into the safety tank, forcing water out and making it almost impossible to hear. Collins whipped off his headphones and had to scream, "She's dropped."

"Hold on everybody," Ronnie yelled as he darted around his conning tower.

"Stern planes jammed," shouted the stern planesman. "No hydraulic power."

"Shift to manual," shouted Sutcliff.

WHAM! WHAM! WHAM! WHAM!

The four-charge pattern was perhaps a hundred yards astern. At that range the explosions were terrific; the stern jumped up and the boat whip-sawed. It would have been terrifying, but after the previous two patterns, the *Wolfish's* crew looked at one another relieved the charges weren't closer.

Sutcliff asked, "Sternplanes?"

The stern planesman puffed at his wheel. "I have control now, Sir."

Sutcliff shouted to his talker, "Very well. Tell the aft torpedo room to rig up a set of falls on the stern-plane linkage just in case."

Lil' Adolf pointed at the depth gauge and sobbed almost maniacally, "Look! We're going up."

"What?" shouted Ronnie.

Sutcliff yelled up the hatch. "We're rising. Four hundred twenty feet, Sir."

Ronnie squatted at the hatch and looked down into the control room. A pencil clenched between his teeth muffled his voice, "Good. Come left to zero-four-five. All ahead standard." Lieutenant Chance, the executive officer, hovered behind the captain, taking damage assessment reports and speaking into sound-powered phones.

"Foggy. Level off at three hundred feet. Don't let me broach," said Ronnie.

Wham. Wham. Wham. Wham. Wham. Wham.

Collins said, "Pattern was dead aft, about a thousand yards. They must have dropped on datum."

"Three hundred seventy-five feet, Captain," said Sutcliff.

"Very well. Can you hold me at three hundred?" asked Ronnie.

"...uh." from Sutcliff.

"Foggy, damnit!"

"Do my best, Sir. Everything's all screwed up in here."

"Foggy, you don't sound too--"

Collins's hands cupped over his earphones and he sat up. "Rain squall!"

"Where?" from Ronnie, Chance, and Sutcliff simultaneously.

Collins spun his dials and bent close to his oscilloscope. "...er, zero-one-zero relative."

"Helm. Make your course zero-five-five," said Ronnie. "All ahead flank!"

"Captain! We can't run at flank for long. Battery's about had it," said Sutcliff.

"Screw the battery," Ronnie shot back. "*We've* about had it. Prepare for battle surface. Collins. Can you tell how far?"

Collins shrugged then held his earphone. "Sounds close and getting louder." It was the best Collins could do.

Helmets were passed up to the conning tower. Ronnie put one on and demanded, "What are the Japs doing?"

Collins said, "Deep starboard quarter, Sir. One-seven-five; fifteen hundred yards."

"Periscope depth, Mr. Sutcliff." called Ronnie.

The chief engineer looked up the hatch. His mouth dropped open. The captain hadn't called him by his last name since he'd first stepped aboard. "Aye, aye, Captain." By working with bowplanes, motors and ballast, Sutcliff coaxed the *Wolfish* to thirty-five feet.

"Collins!" roared the Captain.

Collins jumped but he knew what Ronnie wanted. "Not much louder, Sir. All I can say is it's steady."

"Very well, up periscope," called Ronnie. Soon he cursed softly, then, "...try the attack scope...shit...Mr. Sutcliff?"

"Sir?"

"Periscopes won't rise."

Sutcliff ran to the pump-room hatch, flipped it up, and shined his flashlight inside. "...I'll be a sonofabitch. Captain! Pump room's flooded; damn near waist deep. Must have shorted the periscope hoist motors."

"Well, turn on the damn bilge pump."

"We did. Strainers must be clogged."

"Alright. We go blind, then." Ronnie checked the pitlog repeater (the speed indicator). It was broken, too. A lot of gauges were broken. "We'll wait two more minutes." He clenched his fist. "Go, baby." After a moment he said, "Foggy. How many turns we making?"

Sutcliff got the answer from his talker and said, "Turns for eight knots, Captain. Just about full power. But the batteries have about had it. We'll burn out, soon."

"Can we start engines?" asked Ronnie.

"Main induction is flooded," said Sutcliff. "Gotta drain before restart. Take a few minutes."

"Contacts, Collins?" said Ronnie.

"Just the two cans, aft. Closest one is at about twenty-five-hundred yards," reported Collins.

"Good enough," shouted Ronnie. "Battle surface!"

Air hissed. The *Wolfish* slowly, mercifully, crept to the surface. Her conning tower broke into the night shedding the water that had camouflaged her from her enemy. Ronnie popped the hatch and charged topside as the *Wolfish*, with decks awash, gathered way with a fifteen-degree starboard list.

Döttmer stood back as helmeted sailors carrying ammunition and .50-caliber machine guns, charged past and up the ladder to follow Ronnie out the conning tower hatch. Sutcliff dashed aft to start his diesels. This left Gruber standing in the way of the chief of the boat, who shouted at his Sailors trying to organize his control room from chaos.

Number four main engine thundered into life. Almost immediately, the putrid stench in the boat was exchanged with cool, clean, salt air. Döttmer took a deep breath, feeling the wonderful relief as rich, new oxygen hit his system. He put his hands on a rail, savoring the air when number one main engine barked into action. He looked over at Collins just as the sonarman said, "We're in the squall, now. Japs are three-thousand-yards aft."

The exec scrambled down the hatch and got Gruber moving. Soon, the low-pressure blowers were going, allowing the *Wolfish* to rise farther out of the water and make better speed. "...I said where's Lorca?"

Döttmer looked up to see Mr. Chance standing before him. He straightened up. "Sorry, Sir. I think he went aft, looking for Doc Gaspar. Screwed up his hand."

Chance looked up the conning tower hatch. "Damn. Hall's topside." He ran a hand over his face and said, "Look, Radtke. Can you get this out?" He handed Döttmer a penciled message.

It was addressed to COMSUBPAC in five-digit groups. The exec must have used a one-time pad to set it up so quickly. "Can do, Sir."

"Go! It's important. Let me know when Pearl acknowledges receipt."

"Aye aye, Sir."

Chance slapped on a helmet and dashed up the ladder.

With a look, Döttmer took in the carnage of the control room. Then it hit him. Yes! Here is my opportunity.

He ran in the radio room, closed the door, and flipped on power switches as he sat. Quickly, he hit the "antenna up" switch, set the transmitter to 15.775 megacycles, slapped on earphones, and tuned his receiver. Without waiting, he tapped out Abwehr-Berlin's call sign followed by: HECKLE calling BESSON. HECKLE calling BESSON.

He cupped his hands around the earphones. Nothing. Not even a squeal. Maybe the receiver was damaged. Nothing for it but transmit in the blind. He tried once again. HECKLE calling BESSON. IMPERATIVE YOU WARN—

The door whipped open. Lieutenant Chance's frame filled the entrance. "Any luck?"

"...er no, Sir. But I'm trying."

"Didn't think so. Radio antenna trunk is flooded. All the radio and APR antennae insulators topside are fractured. No way you can get out 'til we rig a wing antenna. Grab a helmet and go help load the deck gun."

"But— "

"Now, damnit!"

Chance wasn't satisfied until he watched Döttmer strap on a helmet and head up the crew's mess escape hatch. Then he turned to deal with Gruber who sat on the stern planesman's bench, his head in his hands.

Döttmer was on deck for only two minutes when a round from the Japanese destroyer's 4.7-inch gun hit the forward engine room nearly blowing the *Wolfish* in half. The submarine sank immediately in 404 fathoms of water, taking with her Lieutenant Commander Roland M. Galloway (Ronnie), her Captain; Lieutenant Gordon E. Chance (who had given Döttmer his life by ordering him topside), her Executive Officer: Lieutenant Junior Grade Raleigh T. Sutcliff (Foggy), her engineering officer; and eighty-six other officers and men, including all those evacuated from Corregidor.

Döttmer flailed in the water for two hours amidst the screams and confusion of men fighting for their lives. After a while, their voices drifted off and he sensed he was alone. But as the new day broke, he saw men around him being tossed among the *Wolfish's* oil slick and wreckage. He would see someone each time he crested a wave. Some signaled, others simply lay back.

The sunrise was a crisp, red-orange and he watched it heave into a cloudless duck-egg blue sky. Soon it climbed over a mountain range on Mindanao, perhaps ten miles to the east. The destroyer was gone, and Döttmer gaped at the sunrise when something thumped him in the back of the neck.

"*Ach! Gott!*" Döttmer was immediately embarrassed that he had cried out in his mother tongue. But he was sure a shark had bumped into him preparing for a feeding frenzy. He spun to face his attacker and screamed again.

It was a fully inflated eight-man life raft.

He didn't realize how tired he was until he tried to climb in. With the greatest of efforts, he pulled himself over the top, then slithered the rest of the way in like a fish and lay on his back for a long time, catching his breath. At length, he rose to his knees to see who else was about.

By noon, he had hauled in Kimble, a storekeeper; a nearly dead Lieutenant Mort Sampson, the operations officer; Ensign Gruber; Chief Hall, a radioman. The last one he pulled in was Radioman Second Class Dominic Federico Lorca, bandaged hand and all. The ex-violin player had been in the crew's mess when the shell hit. And miraculously, he was here to talk about it, except when Döttmer asked him something, Lorca spoke only in jumbled phrases and looked at him with the unfocused stare of the shell-shocked. Perhaps the idiot was still deaf from all the depth charges, Döttmer supposed. What was apparent was that all of his wonderful Hollywood hair was scattered about his eyes and forehead, making him look the fool he really was. But the man's tattoos still glistened on his arms.

There was no water nor food nor medical supplies, and Lieutenant Sampson died at four in the afternoon. He wasn't heavy but it still took three of them to hoist Sampson's body up and over the side where he began his long journey to the deep.

With that, Lil' Adolf drew into himself, leaving Kimble, Hall, and Döttmer the only sane ones left. Lorca, in a way, seemed dangerous as he faded in and out.

By late afternoon it became apparent a breeze was setting them well to the south toward the bight of Butuan Bay, where Mindanao's coastline changes from a north-south axis to east-west.

Döttmer rigged the oars and started rowing. After sunset, two dim sets of lights popped out on the coast to the south, each about fifteen miles distant. With any luck, he could row them to one of the villages, and perhaps find help.

Possibly even a radio.

He looked at Lil' Adolf. The man slept soundlessly, his mouth a wide oval as if he were dead. The hell with it. He roused Gruber asking, "Any idea about those two towns, Sir?"

Gruber, too sleepy to be peevish, blinked at the coast and rasped, "I think that's Gingoog Bay. To the left is Butuan Bay." He fell back, smacking swollen lips. They all needed water. "Pretty sure those lights are Gingoog City, the others are Nasipit."

"Gingoog looks closer," said Döttmer, turning the raft to the right.

Döttmer rowed and Gruber settled back, trying desperately for the sleep that would help him forget his mounting thirst. Soon, everyone was asleep.

Döttmer rowed and rowed. At about midnight he looked up into the night sky and remembered something.

Nasipit.

The old man. ...what was his name?

Amador. Pablo Amador.

During the first ill-fated *Wolfish* rendezvous, Döttmer had overheard Amador tell Ingram he was from Nasipit, and that the resistance movement was strong there. DeWitt confirmed this later with that stupid kangaroo court with Ingram, in the Caballo stockade. DeWitt said the old man was in charge of the resistance in Nasipit.

And that means a radio!

With merely a flick of the port paddle, Döttmer changed course for Nasipit. While the others slept, Nasipit drew nearer. At one o'clock Gingoog City fell behind Diuata Point. At about two o'clock he woke Hall, the belching radioman, who took over pulling the rest of the way. By his best guess, Nasipit was about six miles distant, and they would land about a mile west. There would be time in the morning to find water and scout the place, and make sure they were well hidden from the Japanese. Or perhaps, he could simply turn himself in. That was a thought.

For now, he would concentrate on finding a radio.

Nasipit. The lights grew brighter.

Döttmer lay down, curled an arm under his head, and fell asleep.

38

12 May 1942
Masbate Island
Philippines

They transited the Sibuyan Sea, working past the southeastern side of Masbate Island, where a drizzly daybreak found them two miles south of Cagayan. Kevin Forester stood at the tiller with Ingram and Holloway studying the shoreline, looking for a remote place to land. The engine didn't sound good, the trip was taking its toll on the 51 Boat's little Buda. A hollow-eyed Whittaker constantly knelt before the compartment as if in a perpetual state of worship. Indeed, the engineman's altar was a lump of machined cast iron with the four pistons pumping up to three thousand psi with each revolution. The craggy-faced, third class engineman cursed and groaned as he diligently prayed over his injectors, adjusted linkage, added oil, and strained wax residue out of the diesel fuel. To add to their problems, the binnacle light had flicked on and off over the past two nights and occasionally, the starter motor wouldn't engage, giving everyone a dose of anxiety.

Suddenly, the horizon cleared revealing two destroyers and a cruiser hull-up steaming their way. Forester needed no urging as he swung his tiller and they headed into a swampy little cove, stuffing the 51 Boat on a sand bar about twenty yards from shore. The place was thick with mosquitoes and there was no beach.

Slapping his neck, DeWitt cocked an eyebrow.

Ingram said, "Otis, it's either here or we go back out there and the Japs use us for target practice."

The rain fell in earnest and it became dark. Half the men piled off and slogged ashore looking for coconut and wild fruit. The others rigged a tarp trying to keep Helen and their provisions reasonably dry. The sun broke at midday for a moment, and their cove glistened with almost every shade of green and blue as the rain evaporated and the land sprang into life. A half-hour later, the rain was with them again, drumming as loud as before.

In the boat, Whittaker and Bartholomew cursed and swore at the Buda as water dribbled into everything. During the brief period of sunlight Ingram had called a work party, pushing the boat farther up the sandbar and tipping it on its side exposing the bottom. The rain was warm and it felt good as Ingram stood knee deep in water knocking barnacles off the 51 Boat's bottom and scrubbing the slimy surface smooth with palm leaves. He was dressed only in shorts, and the rain blasted down making little craters on the water as he pounded and whacked. In a way, the rain's throbbing was somnolent; the downpour grew thicker and he felt as if he were by himself.

Suddenly a hand clutched the gunnel. Helen Durand, hiding beneath Whittaker's baseball cap, peeked over and mouthed, "Morning." Her eyes were alive, active, full of life.

Ingram nodded. "Afternoon."

"Really?"

He turned his face up into the downpour. "Hard to tell with this going on."

She looked good. Yardly had reported her temperature was down and she was taking liquids well. She had been sleeping most of the time and this morning she had eaten some crackers.

The rain let up a bit. Ingram managed. "I thought Yardly told you to lie still."

"Lousy patient. Where are we?"

"Near Cagayan. How do you feel?"

"Okay." Her head rested on the gunnel and she looked straight down at him. Whittaker had also given her dungarees and a shirt since he was the smallest among them. Under the ball cap, Ingram could hardly see her sores, but he knew they must hurt. And her ribs must hurt, too, he figured, even though Yardly had taped that as well. There was only one thing left to question and so far, nobody had mentioned it.

Ingram chipped at a large barnacle clump. "Maybe you should lie down?"

"I'm okay. What are you doing?"

"Making the bottom smooth so we can go faster."

She looked toward the shore and started to get up.

Her voice dropped to a whisper, "Look, Todd. Can you put me in the water?"

"Helen, talk about me being a bad patient. You know what Yardly said."

"He's ashore?" Her teeth were clenched.

"Yes. You should wait until--"

She leaned over the side. Her face no more than two feet away carrying a certain grimace like the one covering a child's face before bedtime.

He grinned, "You mean--?"

"Yes, damnit. Get me out of here."

"Alright!" Ingram slogged around to the low side of the boat. He held out his hands, Helen slid down to him and he lifted her gently over the gunnel.

"Oooooh." She shivered in knee-deep water, weak and unsteady. Ingram clamped an arm around her waist. "Okay?"

"Okay." She nodded toward deeper water.

"Right." Ingram walked her slowly forward. She stumbled and Ingram reached to hold her tight. "Stop?"

"No. Just dizzy. Keep going."

"Okay. Hang on."

Soon she was in hip-deep water and they stopped.

Bartholomew noticed first, then Whittaker. Both stood with hands on their hips. Yardly shouted from among mangroves and started running. DeWitt, Toliver, Beardsley, Junior Forester and Sunderland walked around from the boat's high side and gawked.

Ingram and Helen stood facing out to sea. He looked down and gave a tiny squeeze, "Ummm. Water's getting nice and warm."

"Shut up, damn you."

Like a beach lifeguard on his way to the rescue, Yardly ran toward them, the water splashing in great geysers.

"Okay," said Helen.

Ingram turned her around, finding everyone watching. With a deep bow, he announced, "I give you the new, improved Helen Durand, first lieutenant United States Army."

A breathless Yardly drew up. "You mean--?"

"Tinkle, tinkle, little star," said Sunderland in a falsetto. At that the rest burst into applause and cheers.

"How was it?" a grinning Yardly asked.

"My God. You'd think it was my first time ever." She tried a smile and said. "It's okay, Bones. No pain."

"Good." Said Yardly.

"Thanks, Bones." Still wobbly, she rose to her tiptoes and pecked him on the cheek. "I owe you one."

"I'm gonna collect it all!" whooped Yardly, throwing his white hat in the air.

They moved around her with grins and pats on the back.

Helen's eyes glistened as she said, "Never thought taking a pee would be such a big deal." She felt dizzy and slipped. "Uhh. Todd, get me in the boat."

Masbate fell astern and time passed in a regimen of sleeping, standing watch, fishing, or filling water jugs. They skipped along Cebu's coast carefully picking their way through the Visayan and Camotes seas to Leyte. Ingram reflected that, except for the run-in with the Japanese on Marinduque, these past nine days had been kind to everyone, including Helen who was rapidly becoming another member of the crew. Fresh water had not been a problem; each day they found a stream or a waterfall to replenish their water cans and bathe. They caught up on sleep while underway at night. In daytime, when there wasn't much to do except look for water or haul down coconuts, they curled up in the shade and slept, again marveling at the absence of the cannon's roar or shells exploding every fifteen seconds. Their pallor was gone, replaced by deepening suntans and firm muscle tone. Helen was self-conscious about skin sores and kept to herself, but Yardly checked her over each day, satisfied with her progress.

All showed definite signs of weight gain. They had the Filipinos to thank, Ingram's efforts to avoid them notwithstanding. They tried hard to camouflage the boat when beached, but villagers still found them. Like the Aguilars, they shared everything with the Americans.

At sunrise on the fourteenth, the 51 Boat crept into a marsh about two-miles north of Baybay on Leyte. They were totally secluded, Ingram decided. Trees grew to the water's edge, the thick jungle canopy flourished thirty feet overhead, and vines and underbrush obscured one's vision in three directions. Bartholomew pulled guard duty with the rest fast asleep on a tiny beach. Incredulously, four smiling villagers marched up toting copra, boiled fish, and dried chicken packed in camote leaves.

The next evening, they made ready to shove off from a little cove on Bohol Island about five miles south of Cogtong Bay. They were under an overhanging palm grove that grew to the water's edge, and the Buda wouldn't start, so a grumbling Whittaker rolled up his sleeves, taking two hours to clean the fuel strainer and blow out fuel lines. With Bartholomew's help, he had the Buda back together at nine-thirty; and jabbed the start button. The four-banger coughed and sputtered, but refused to catch, sending Whittaker back into the engine compartment, muttering exquisitely composed phrases of blue language.

The men didn't seem to care. Their little beach had been so remote and so pleasant they were, in a manner of speaking, reluctant to leave. But Ingram spurred Whittaker saying, if they pushed off within the next twenty minutes they could still make Mindanao's Butuan Bay before sunrise.

Again, Engineman Third Class Peter Whittaker thumbed the starter. Thick blue-black smoke tumbled out of the diesel's exhaust as he cursed and pleaded. In a rage, he kicked the engine housing and the Buda roared into life. With a cheer, the men piled into the boat, suddenly anxious to be off. As helmsman on the first watch, Bartholomew grabbed the tiller while Ingram arranged himself on the deck. Methodically, he laid out pencil, dividers, parallel rule, and chart, preparing to put finishing touches on a dead reckoning track across the Mindanao Sea to Nasipit.

With Toliver's cupped hands providing a foothold, Beardsley scrambled over the gunnel. Toliver double-checked everyone was aboard and shoved the 51 Boat into deep water. Just then, Beardsley slipped and clunked his head against the corner of the engine housing. He swore softly, raised a hand to his forehead, and wiped blood from a small cut. The boat was well adrift when Toliver crawled in and moved next to Beardsley to check the cut.

With dividers, Ingram stepped the distance to the entrance to Mindanao's Kinabhangan River mouth, when a hand slapped the top of the chart. Startled, he looked up, seeing Beardsley six-inches away. The bandages were gone and Beardsley's face was puffy and crisscrossed with scars. Blood ran from the forehead cut into his left eye.

But the man's eyelids: Although still terribly swollen, they had parted slightly, and his pupils glinted through narrow slits.

Beardsley grabbed a flashlight and shined it directly in Ingram's face, running the palm of his hand down Ingram's cheek. Tears were in his eyes as he blurted, "God, you're an ugly sonofabitch!"

Ingram sat back. "I'll be damned! Can you--I mean..."

Beardsley nodded vigorously. His voice shook and he had trouble forming words. "Ollie yanked the bandage to check...and ...and..."

"Tough break, Mr. Beardsley," said Sunderland, clapping him on the shoulder. "Now you gotta stand watches."

Otis DeWitt reached over and shook his hand. "Welcome back, Mr. Beardsley."

Others crowded around to pump the B-17 pilot's hand and nudge him with elbows.

DeWitt helped Helen to her feet so she could kiss Beardsley on the cheek. "Goils won't fall for you until you start shaving, flyboy," she said in a husky, Mae West voice.

"Weooooww. Lemme at that razor." Beardsley growled, wiping tears with the back of his hands. Then he said, "You dopes. All this snot'll drive me blind..."

"We'll take care of that," roared Sunderland. With a wink at Bartholomew and the Forester brothers they grabbed his armpits and raised him high over their heads. "Hey, hey. My nickel-plate," cackled Beardsley, tossing the pistol to Ingram.

Toliver muscled his way among them. "You dumb bastards! Put him down."

They pretended not to hear and shuffled to the gunnel, making the boat list precariously. Together, they roared, "one, two--"

"Stop!" pleaded Toliver.

"Woof, woof," they yelled.

"He *may* go blind again," shrieked Toliver grabbing a handful of Beardsley's trouser cuff. "You don't know."

Yardly stood and shouted, "He's right. Put him down."

"Shove in your clutch," they yelled.

With Yardley's glare, they stopped jiggling Beardsley, "Just kidding, Bones."

"Spoil sport," laughed Beardsley, writhing over their outstretched hands.

"Stick him over here. I better take a look," said Yardly.

They put him down, Whittaker clunked the boat in forward, and they headed toward the opening in the reef. Vowing he'd never sleep again, Beardsley hooted and screamed and danced as they plowed into the Mindanao Sea.

After Beardsley quieted down, Yardly looked him over and estimated the pilot had close to full recovery in one eye; about half, so far, in the other. He really wouldn't be able to further tell until daylight. He bandaged Beardsley's forehead, irrigated his eyes, and taped a patch over the left eye.

Even so, an ecstatic Leon Beardsley proudly stood bow lookout on the first watch, gaping at sights recently denied him by a Japanese 240-millimeter, four-hundred-pound howitzer shell. Ingram pondered whether or not Army Air Corps First Lieutenant Leon V. Beardsley had been better off not having the use of his eyes during Corregidor's last two weeks of horror.

With the underway routine, they settled down for the night's passage to Mindanao. The others had already fallen asleep, when Ingram lay back seeing Toliver had turned toward him.

Ingram said in a low voice, "Nice job, Ollie."

Toliver's reply was masked by engine noise. Ingram cupped a hand to his ear and moved closer. "What?"

Toliver said, "When I was a kid I found a duck with a broken wing and took him home. My folks said 'no.'"

Ingram watched as Toliver lay back and laced his fingers under his head looking up into the sky. "You see, I took it as a challenge, thinking they didn't believe I could fix that mallard's wing. I told them I wanted to be a doctor."

"And?"

"I read a book. Duck turned out great."

"What'd your folks say?"

"Angry as hell. Duck waddled around and crapped faster than I could clean it up. I had to take him out in the woods and let him go. Otherwise, my Dad said, we would be having duck for dinner."

"Oh, oh."

"My Dad went with me. We tossed that duck in the air and he flew away."

"Were you sad?"

"I thought I would be. But when I let him go, it was beautiful. He circled once, then was gone."

Whittaker stepped aft, opened the engine compartment and fiddled for a moment. The engine noise was loud, but the Buda seemed to be running well. Satisfied, Whittaker closed up and moved forward to where he had been lying down.

Ingram and Toliver lay still for a moment, enjoying the warm, smooth ride under a dark, overcast sky.

Toliver waved a hand toward Beardsley. "That's what my Dad said: 'Nice job, Ollie.'"

Toliver rolled over and faced the bulkhead.

Helen Durand, Leon Beardsley: Both clutched the gilded promise of restored bodies and normal lives. Yardly and Toliver had helped provide that promise. No doubt Yardly would go to medical school after the war, becoming a successful physician in a snazzy neighborhood. Ingram imagined sitting across Yardley's desk twenty-five-years from now. His onetime hospital corpsman would be clinical, devoid of humor, and solemnly pronounce that his patient and onetime skipper was too fat and had to lose fifteen pounds at once, later sending a bill for fifty dollars.

I'd pay every penny, decided Ingram. Yardly is going to make a hell of a doctor.

Maybe Toliver, too. When he thought about it, there were a million things

Ingram wanted to ask Toliver, but now, it seemed, the *Pelican*'s last gunnery officer had divulged enough for the evening. Even so, he decided to try again. "Ollie?"

"Yeah?"

"What about medical school?"

"Screwed around too much my freshman year. Flunked out of premed and took a BS in business. Think I'll go to law school."

39

15 May 1942
Butuan Bay, Mindanao
Philippines

It was a ninety-mile run under a moonless, overcast sky. By 5 *a.m.*, the air was tepid as after a rain, and the rich land-smell of earth and feces and flowers teased Ingram's nostrils, telling him Mindanao's heavily wooded volcanic slopes were near. A dim, yellow light bobbed to starboard where Diuata Point lay. Ingram hoped it was a fishing banca. The coast was perhaps ten miles away with his destination, the Kinabhangan River, a mile east of Nasipit. There, they planned to beach the 51 Boat and figure a way to contact one of Aguilar's people.

He roused everyone for their landfall, and by five-thirty Mindanao's rocky headland loomed close. It was a gray, clinical dawn with the mountains cloaked in a misty five-hundred-foot ceiling. Holloway steered for the Kinabhangan River mouth, now a dark gap a mile ahead in tall bluffs. To their right, the half-mile wide entrance to Nasipit yawned between rocky cliffs. Prominent was the timber mill, conical kiln, and tall, black stack. There were a few unlighted buildings, a long, empty pier, and a church topped by a cross.

A gentle wind scattered the overcast, giving way to a brilliant sunrise, with morning dew casting a glossy green tint to the forests rising up the slopes of Mount Maiyapay, a 2,360 peak that dominated smaller cone-shaped mountains of northern Mindanao. The water was flat and oily with hardly any surge, as they approached the Kinabhangan river mouth which was partially masked by a guano-covered drying reef fifty yards offshore. The 51 Boat entered the river, where sandy beaches ran on either bank for two or three hundred yards. But after two gentle turns, the river entrance was no longer visible and Mindanao's dark vegetation pressed on them with the banks disappearing under dense foliage.

It was hard to see ahead, so Ingram called for idle speed, slowing them to where only the wake's gentle gurgle told them they were in motion. Everything blended and it became so quiet and so tranquil that even the barely chugging engine seemed an encroachment of the still, damp flora growing closer and closer. On either side, their quarter-wake licked at trunkless Nipa palms rising from the banks to blend with the tall forest. Fifty feet overhead, the canopy was separated by mere yards, allowing a brightening dawn to inch through the foliage where creeping tendrils hung to the river's surface carrying blossoms that exploded into unimaginable colors.

DeWitt stood in the bow and pointed to starboard. Ingram spotted the beach, no more than ten yards in length, rising four feet above the river. Good enough. He drew a finger across his throat. Whittaker cut the engine and the boat nosed into soft sand. As the Forester brothers jumped to guide the boat up the beach, Ingram said, "Sunderland, grab a Springfield and stand by."

Sunderland reached under a thwart and picked up a rifle wrapped in rags. "Japs close by, Sir?"

In the jungle's quiet, Ingram's voice was heard by all, "Last word we had is most of the Japs are over in Del Monte, but this place is full of crocodiles."

"Jeez!" A few of the men scampered to high ground while the rest jumped back in the boat. Standing high on a thwart, Sunderland quickly unwrapped the Springfield, then clacked a round into the breach. He crouched, swiveling his head from side to side.

"Com'on, girls." Bartholomew jumped into the knee-deep water and bellowed, "Let's get organized."

Looking nervously over their shoulders, they tied up the boat, grabbed machetes, and hacked out foliage for camouflage, then set out water tins. This time there were only two empties since they had refilled at Bohol the night before.

"You sure about crocodiles, Mr. Ingram?" said Sunderland, peering into dark underbrush.

"So, I'm told," said Ingram. "Major DeWitt. How about you and Sunderland and I going into town?"

DeWitt beamed. After nine days, he was off the damned ocean and once again into his element. "Glad to."

Ingram said, "Mr. Holloway, you're in charge. If we're not back before noon, shove off, head out to sea. Hug the coast and set a course for the Surigao Straits. Got that?"

Holloway said, "Yessir. What then?"

For a moment, Ingram didn't speak. It was so quiet, the silence seemed almost alive as if trying to somehow penetrate their pores and stifle their metabolism.

Kevin Forester slapped a mosquito on his neck, breaking the spell.

Ingram said, "Simply turn right. You'll find Darwin, about fifteen hundred miles due south. Good luck." Ingram allowed a smile. "I suggest you post a couple of guards about a hundred yards out. Okay?"

Holloway gulped. "Yessir."

Beardsley walked up and blurted, "I want to go."

"I don't think so, Leon," said Ingram.

"If there's a B-17 around, Mr. Beardsley, we'll find it," said DeWitt.

"But I landed here. I know where those bases are," said Beardsley. "I know of at least two near here."

Ingram looked at DeWitt and rubbed his chin. "But what about...you know..."

Beardsley said, "I can see great. Look." He picked up a rock and threw it across a small tributary where it thwacked solidly into a stump.

"You sure you were aiming for that?" Ingram asked.

"My eyes are getting better by the minute. I think I'm good enough to fly," said Beardsley.

"Fly, Leon?"

"Well...yes, damnit."

Ingram looked at DeWitt.

He nodded.

"Okay. Leon, you're on. Ollie, you come, too," said Ingram.

Brian Forester went "Arf, arf," earning a cold stare from Toliver.

Sunderland picked up his BAR and hefted a bandolier of ammo. Toliver grabbed another BAR and bandolier, with Ingram and DeWitt each taking Springfield 30-06s. The remaining two BARs were issued to Holloway's lookouts, so Beardsley simply grinned and patted the small of his back.

Ingram reached into the 51 Boat and tossed a machete to Otis DeWitt. "Lead on, Major."

DeWitt caught the machete by its heavy canvas scabbard and stared at it. Ingram spread his hands and said with a grin, "Come on, Army. This is what you've been waiting for. A ground pounder's show, isn't it?"

Helen sat up and waved.

Ingram said, "Call the cops if they give you any trouble."

"Got it," she said.

Ingram grabbed another machete and started hacking his way up an embankment.

It took a half-hour to chop their way to high ground, and another twenty minutes to claw and scramble to the hard-packed, dirt coast road Ingram had seen on the chart. Wary of Japanese patrols, DeWitt lead the men along the road's right side, ready to duck into the shrubbery in an instant. Every fifty yards or so, they stopped and listened, fully expecting a truck loaded with heavily armed Japanese soldiers to career around a bend and pull up before them with machine guns spitting death. But it was so quiet their footfalls sounded like exploding grenades. And stumbling or tripping on a rock earned an evil glance, as if one had poured the last canteen of fresh water into the Sahara Desert.

Suddenly, pigs grunted, a carabao groaned, and they heard chickens cackle.

"Dang!" muttered Sunderland.

They had walked around a gradual bend and, incomprehensibly, found they had stumbled into a small village. The dwellings were set back under trees and were well masked in the growing sunlight. Even in broad daylight the huts would have been impossible to see until they were right on them.

"Sorry," said DeWitt.

"So much for secrecy," muttered Beardsley.

"I said I was sorry," said DeWitt peevishly.

"Couldn't be helped. Come on," said Ingram.

They kept moving, certain that every step was under observation and that every unseen villager's eye was welded to their backs.

DeWitt said softly, "Nasipit should be right down the road."

Ingram nodded. "Whole damned town will know about us in minutes. Let's angle toward the waterfront."

They came to a fork and took the right one. Soon, they saw the lumber mill's black stack and headed for it. After a turn in the road the mill stood before them except--

"Where is everybody?" asked Sunderland.

Benches were overturned, windows broken, the loading dock and pier were empty, trash blew about and, except for birds flying in and out of windows, the mill was barren.

"Maybe too early," said Beardsley.

"Looks like the place hasn't been used for a while," said DeWitt.

They walked up to the mill and stepped inside. A floorboard creaked, making birds flutter squawking out the windows. Empty.

Dust and cobwebs covered lifeless machines, and it was evident a lot of machinery was gone.

Ingram said, "Remind anyone of Aguilar's?"

Sunderland said, "I'm surprised the Japs left anything."

Suddenly the Judas door creaked. A Filipino stepped in, causing the Americans to level and cock their weapons. He thrust his hands in the air, but after a moment said, "Americans." A minute passed, then he lowered his hands and stared with dark, flashing eyes. His skin was a deep olive and his face had an angular, penetrating appearance.

"Do you speak English?" asked Ingram.

The Filipino nodded.

"What's your name?" asked Ingram. It was getting brighter. He and the others eased into the shadows, leaving the Filipino standing in daylight.

"Manuel."

"Is that all," asked DeWitt.

The man swallowed and said, "Manuel Carrillo."

"Where are the Japs?" asked Ingram.

"Plenty Hapon in Malayalam and Cagayan. Some in Masao." The first two cities were over fifty miles to the west. Masao, at the mouth of the Agusan River, was just ten miles to the east.

"Any Japs here?" asked Ingram.

Carrillo shook his head.

"How many in Masao?" asked Toliver.

Carrillo flashed two bunches of ten fingers.

Sunderland hissed, "Down!"

A pickup with a Japanese flag painted on the door pulled up across the street. The driver was a sergeant. A young lieutenant sat next to him and a civilian rode in the back. The three dismounted and walked up to a sturdy, boxlike structure and pounded on the door.

"What the hell?" said DeWitt.

"Lookit the size of that Jap," said Beardsley, referring to a civilian wearing a white suit. Towering over everyone else, he looked to be well over six feet.

"Shhhht!" Sunderland put his forefinger to his lip.

"Get down," rasped Ingram. He waved his Springfield. They dropped to their haunches and peered through a window.

Carrillo muttered something.

"What?" Ingram whispered.

"Damn Hapon here early. I hope they can wait," Carrillo said.

"Is that a butcher shop?" asked Ingram.

Carrillo nodded adding, "And a meat locker, but they ran out of ice."

The Japanese sergeant unholstered a pistol and used the butt to pound on the door. Soon, a large wooden flap was drawn up in front of the building. Two dark figures hovered inside.

Carrillo muttered, "They're late. Damnit the truck."

Two shots were fired, a scream ripped the air, and two Filipinos tumbled out the front door and into the dirt. They were male and female, most likely husband and wife. The woman shrieked as the sergeant and the man in the white suit tied the Filipino's hands behind his back, pushed him to his knees, and wrapped a blindfold around his head. Then the man in the white suit walked into the hut.

"Who is that jerk?" asked Beardsley.

Carrillo's eyes narrowed. "Lieutenant Tuga," he said.

It felt as if someone had grabbed Ingram's throat. He gasped, "Who?"

Carrillo said, "Tuga. That big turd is a *Kempetai*. He's down here from Marinduque looking for--"

Ingram wasn't listening. His body shook and he ran a cartridge into the breach of his Springfield. Then he looked at Sunderland who did the same with his BAR. They nodded to one another and took aim.

Carrillo rasped, "No! Not now. Please. Wait a few moments."

Ingram growled, "That sonofabitch dies. And I'm personally gonna blast his head to watermelon chunks."

"Carrillo stood before him trying to push his rifle down. "Please, Señor. A moment, please. They'll be here. Then you can talk to him."

Ingram barely controlled himself as Tuga stepped from the hut brandishing a large butcher's cleaver, and while his soldiers tied the squirming Filipino's head over an upended log, took a couple of practice swings. "I swear I kill him before he swings that cleaver."

Just then, they heard the rattling and puffing of another truck. Soon, an ancient Ford stake-truck backfired and careened around the corner. It skidded to a halt, pulling with it an enormous cloud of dust. Three Filipinos jumped out and walked to the back where a large pig was secured.

Carrillo exhaled loudly, "Finally."

Ingram lowered his rifle. "Who is that?"

Carrillo touched a finger to his lips and, as they watched, an argument broke out much like the polemics heard on Marinduque the night Farwell was shot. While the debate was in full rage, the sergeant nonchalantly stripped the blindfold off the meatpacker, untied his bindings, and nudged him with his foot. The woman ran into the Meatpacker's arms; they embraced fiercely for a moment then, incredulously, the meatpacker rose to his feet and joined in the argument against the Japanese.

It was four against three, but nobody seemed to be winning. There was another Filipino, Ingram noticed, sitting in the truck's cab. He wore a planter's hat and had long, silvery hair. He looked familiar, but Ingram couldn't place the man. He squinted, trying to see better, when Tuga thrust a pistol in the air and fired a shot. The two groups parted, with the shopkeeper and civilians facing the *Kempetai*. After a few moments, the meatpacker bowed, Tuga handed him some bills, took the pig's leash, and waited patiently.

Carrillo spat in the dust.

"What?" said Ingram.

"Hapon's peso worth shit." He referred to the Japanese Occupation currency which was basically worthless. Filipinos shunned it except in transactions with the Japanese.

The meatpacker bowed again, then walked inside his hut. Soon he returned wearing a full apron and long knife, which dangled from a belt. He held out a hand and Tuga returned the cleaver that had, only moments before, been intended for a different use.

Ingram said, "Bastard doesn't mince words, does he?"

DeWitt said, "I'm surprised he returned the cleaver."

"One butcher to another," said Ingram.

The pig squealed loudly and dragged its feet as the Japanese sergeant pulled it to their truck. Calling to the Filipinos, they half-pulled, half-carried the wiggling pig, while the lieutenant jumped in the cab and started the engine. Suddenly, the three flipped the pig on its back, grabbed its feet, and shoved the head under the left rear wheel. The sergeant nodded to the Lieutenant. The gears ground into reverse, the engine roared, and the lieutenant let out the clutch abruptly, cutting off the pig's last ululating squeal.

DeWitt, Beardsley, Sunderland, and Ingram, although seeing far beyond their measure of grisly deaths on Cavite and Corregidor, still had trouble holding their bile.

They watched from the shadows while the meatpacker deftly butchered the pig then loaded it in the truck. After twenty minutes, it was done. The meatpacker and Lieutenant Tuga bowed to one another. The Japanese jumped in their truck and drove off.

Carrillo rose to his feet and said, "Okay."

Before anyone could say anything, he stepped outside the Judas door and gave a short whistle. Actually, it was more like a chirp. But the three Filipinos saw Carrillo beckon as they boarded their truck. Quickly, they rushed across the road and stepped in the door. In a moment, all stood in the lumber mill's darkness, staring at one another.

Ingram looked at DeWitt and shrugged. Wordlessly, they felt these Filipinos were genuine and trustworthy. Possibly, they could lead them to the resistance.

Turning to Carrillo, Ingram asked, "Do they speak English as well as you?"

The man with the wavy silver-gray hair said, "I hope so. I went to Oxford University."

Ingram's mouth dropped.

"Welcome to Mindanao, Lieutenant Ingram. And Major DeWitt, a pleasure to see you again." He whipped off his planter's hat and extended a hand to Ingram. That fool Tuga looks for me in every nook and cranny, in Nasipit yet he doesn't know who I am face to face."

"Yes," Said Ingram. "Mr.--"

"Pablo Amador. You were kind enough to take me out to rendezvous with the *Wolfish*."

40

15 May 1942
Nasipit, Mindanao
Philippines

Just before noon, a virulent front raged down the Agusan Valley, making Nasipit cringe under jagged bolts of lighting, thunder, and rain. Corregidor's survivors cowered in a corrugated tin hut behind Carrillo's house, a simple-four room affair on the edge of town. The house had a raised foundation where pigs and chickens rooted underneath, but the hut was built over hard packed earth.

Ingram recalled Carrillo had been production manager at the lumber mill as his father had before him. Since the Japanese closed the mill and shipped the machinery back to Japan, Carrillo did odd jobs trying to make ends meet. Two of his foreman stayed on to help. They were both ex-sergeants in the Filipino Scouts, who escaped Bataan the day before it fell.

Amador had sent them to the Kinabhangan River to bring back the 51 Boat's crew, except for Whittaker and Bartholomew who stayed behind to work on the recalcitrant Buda. Now, they were packed inside the fetid hut with Carrillo and his wife, Rosarita, serving generous portions sent over from an all-day wedding feast underway across town.

Using wooden utensils, Amador, Ingram, and DeWitt were clustered at one end of the table devouring succulent pieces of lechon--roast pig, roast chicken, and boiled fish. Helen Durand sat with them. Until today, she had been mostly on liquids, but now, Ingram noted, she attacked a fair-sized pile of rice. Yet, she had a long way to go; Whittaker's ball cap was still pulled over her face hiding the cigarette burns. Some of the sores were crusted, others were infected and ran like open blisters. Poor kid, he thought. At night, she scratched and moaned, and rolled desperately searching for sleep and escape from the constant itching and stinging. Yardley's regimen was to dip her twice a day in salt water, and yes, paint the damn things with Methylate, making her look just like Dwight Epperson.

The rain dwindled for a moment and music drifted through the window; they looked up hearing the strains of "Aloha."

"That's live music?" Ingram asked, his spoon in midair.

Amador replied, "The real thing, fifteen pieces."

The rain eased to a drizzle and they clearly heard the song's last phrase--"...until we meet again."

It was strange hearing this rich music unencumbered by the vagaries of vacuum tubes and capacitors and static and solar flares. Helen's eyes glistened as she said it for them all. "That was beautiful."

Amador reached over, ladled more rice in her bowl, then folded his hands. "The bride and groom are fortunate to be serenaded by the 110th music division of the United States Forces in the Philippines."

"They haven't surrendered?" asked Ingram as he shoveled from a bowl containing the most unsavory looking swill. But it tasted wonderful, and he was afraid to ask what it was.

"The band is Filipinos but a lot of Americans haven't surrendered," explained Amador. "One of your own," he nodded to DeWitt, "is forming a resistance cell near Lake Lanao."

"Who's that?" asked DeWitt, stripping meat off a chicken thigh.

"Colonel Wendell Fertig," said Amador.

"Fertig!" spat DeWitt. "I know him. He's just a light colonel in the engineering corps. What the hell does he know about fighting?"

Amador said, "A lot of people are listening to him: Moros, Negritos,

Magahats, Malays, your own people who refuse to surrender. His organizational skills are worth their weight in gold. Otherwise, we will do the Hapons work by killing each other off. Perhaps if you're here long enough you'll meet him. He passes through Nasipit next week when we discuss how to get things moving here in the Agusan Province."

DeWitt needed confirmation. "So, you are in charge of the resistance here?"

"Ummm."

"When are you going to start resisting?" DeWitt said rather casually. Instantly, he wished he could have tied a string on the sentence and yanked it back, for Amador flashed a terrible look. "Sorry," he said.

"Carrillo, Guzman, and Ramirez are the core of my unit, here. They're brave men. Others will join us," said Amador, waving around the table. "They have much to make up for since the Hapons occupied our land in the name of the Greater East Asia Co-Prosperity Sphere."

DeWitt gave a cheesy smile and said, "I didn't mean anything. I was only worried we had the wrong information about who was running things down here."

Amador looked DeWitt in the eye. "Your information is correct." Then he turned to Helen and took her hands. "I heard what Tuga did to you. It's good to see you on the mend. The man will receive his measure, I assure you."

"When?" asked Ingram.

Amador shook his head slowly. "We must do it in such a way as to minimize retribution. The best way is to fake an accident. But that's hard these days. They investigate everything."

DeWitt said, "You mean..."

Amador nodded. "Randomly, they take ten maybe twenty of our people if one of theirs is killed. Sometimes they just do it for sport." His fists doubled. "Men, women, children. They shoot them, their bodies left to rot. We're not allowed to bury them." Amador's jaw worked. After a silence, he leaned over and took Helen's hand. "Let me know if I can help you in any way."

With a wooden skewer, Helen pushed a piece of chicken across her plate. "Thank you. How about your family?"

Amador said, "Lucky. I got them out before the war broke. They're in New Mexico. My brother has a gas station in Santa Fe." His voice dropped. "Were you at the Diaz's 'til the end?"

Helen's cap bobbed up and down. "You...heard...Doña Valentina?"

Thunder cracked and Amador grew red. "I did."

Ingram snapped his spoon in half. They looked at him. He put the halves down saying, "Why do they do that. What do vermin like--Tuga--hope to accomplish?"

Amador poured water and said, "Tuga? Unfortunately, I know the type very well. There are plenty of Filipinos just like him--ambitious, nothing gets in the way. They steal, murder, rape. Toga's just like them: A cheap politician out to make a mark. He even claims to have Hideki Tojo's ear."

DeWitt fondled a knife. "I'd like to have Tojo's ear."

Helen coughed and pushed away her plate.

"Uh, sorry." DeWitt stood with his plate and nodded toward the Carrillo's kitchen. "More rice anybody?" he muttered.

They shook their heads and DeWitt trudged off. Amador gave a long exhale and asked Helen, "Where do you live?"

"Ramona. That's in California," she said.

Ingram looked up. "A play. Isn't there a play or something?"

She nodded. "A passion play. It's staged nearby in Hemet."

Ingram snapped his fingers, "I remember now. It's about the Indian Girl-- and what's his name?"

"Allesandro," said Helen, with the slightest of smiles.

"Oh," said Ingram. Watching her mouth turn up like that made him feel wonderful.

Amador nodded slowly and said, "I'll plan on coming to Ramona after the war." Then he fell silent and stared at the patterns he'd traced on the tablecloth; the rain drummed outside.

His eyebrows lifted and he said, "We have a passion play, also."

"Here, in Nasipit?" asked Helen.

"Marinduque." Said Amador. "Emilio Aguilar is involved. Everybody is, actually."

DeWitt returned and sat with a full plate of rice. He spooned a big mouthful and said, "You know Aguilar well?"

"An old friend," said Amador. "As one of the Marinduque dons he is responsible for the Moriones Festival."

DeWitt asked, "What's that?"

Amador traced a forefinger across the oilcloth and said, "A Holy Week pageant, actually."

"Yes?" asked Helen.

Rain thundered outside for a moment, obliterating music of the 110th. Amador's quick eyes flicked to the windows and he looked in the distance. Then he said, "It's about a Centurion."

"Roman?" Asked Ingram.

"Yes. A Roman Centurion," said Amador.

Still unfocused, Amador nodded and said, "The centurion's name was Longinus. He was blind in one eye..."

Amador seemed distracted, again. The three Americans waited patiently. At length he said, "All of Marinduque turns out. They rehearse and build sets and make costumes. Each year they change parts so everybody has a chance to play someone. Except Emilio Aguilar." He paused.

"Yes?" said DeWitt in a tone that implied, 'get on with it.'

"Emilio has played Pontius Pilate for five years running," said Amador.

Ingram nodded. Strange. Aguilar hadn't struck him as one who could act or be animated before an audience and hold their attention. He was so serious, so unlike a troubadour. Perhaps that's what war does to civilians, Ingram thought.

Amador continued, "The legend says Longinus is the one who threw the spear at Christ on the cross. Christ's blood spurted and hit Longinus in his blind eye. Instantly it healed, and he could see again. Right there, he professed faith to Jesus Christ. At that the people became angry and chased him. Longinus escaped but they caught him two days later, on Sunday, and dragged him before Pontius Pilate."

Amador took a deep breath and looked at them. "Longinus did not renounce his faith in Jesus Christ. Pilate sentenced him to death and he was beheaded."

"This is in the Bible?" asked Helen.

Amador shook his head. "Just a legend. It originated back in the 1500s. But for centuries, people have come to enjoy the Moriones Festival."

Amador's eyes darted between them. He said quietly, "After the Hapons occupied Marinduque, the people thought about canceling the festival, but decided to continue at the last minute. Tuga and his filth came on the last day--Easter Sunday. It was their first experience with them. They ignored Tuga. He felt snubbed and became angry."

Amador spread his palms. "In the Hapon culture they can't stand to lose face. So, at the beheading scene, Tuga pulled a thirteen-year-old girl from the crowd and carried out a real execution."

Ingram shook his head slowly.

"Aguilar didn't tell you?" asked Amador.

"Not that," said Ingram.

"It was their daughter," Amador said.

Helen covered her mouth, making a choking sound.

Ingram said, "My God. He only spoke of his son."

"It's too much pain for him." Amador's voice rumbled, "What is wrong with simple poor people working together to sing, paint masks, recite a play, laugh a little, and praise God?" Amador's eyes were almost like embers and his upper lip curled over his teeth.

Instinctively, Helen drew close to Ingram.

Amador's narrow frame quivered as his bony finger pointed in the general direction of north. Spittle flew from his mouth as his voice rose to an uncharacteristic roar, "What's wrong with those Hapon bastards? Why must they stick their fat little hands in everything around them?"

He took a deep breath and then said, "Hapons congratulate themselves for their swift metamorphosis from a feudal society to the twentieth century. Yet giving them Western culture is like giving a thirteen-year-old thug a priceless Stradivarius. He smashes it in rage because he won't bother learning to play it. And to save face, he shoots his neighbors because they do know how to play it."

Rain pounded. Ingram twirled one of the spoon halves.

Amador drew a deep breath and exhaled. "Do you know what the Chinese say about this?"

"No."

"It's one of their proverbs. 'He who strikes the first blow, loses the quarrel.'"

"Somebody should tell the Japs it's not so bad to lose face once in a while." It was Toliver, who had been quietly listening.

Surprised, they looked at him.

Toliver said, "I mean, can't they learn to laugh at themselves? Isn't that what all this is about?"

41

15 May 1942
Nasipit, Mindanao
Philippine Islands

The rain let up and ex-Filipino Scouts Guzman and Ramirez dashed out the door carrying a crock of boiled fish to the two engineers working on the 51 Boat on the Kinabhangan River.

Beardsley scooted over while smacking his lips on a juicy chunk of lechon. He nodded toward the door, "They're wasting their time, Todd. Don't need the boat anymore. May as well give it to Amador and his boys." He popped the last chunk of lechon in his mouth. "Damn. That stuff is good."

Carrillo joined them, giving Beardsley a chart of northern Mindanao. Beardsley unrolled it and rapped it with the back of his knuckles. Wiping grease off his lips, he said, "Good chow, Manuel. Thanks."

"Si." Carrillo nodded.

Beardsley continued, "There are three airfields. Two of them are near here, the other close to Esperanza.

"Which side of the river?" asked Amador,

"East side, about four-or five-miles southeast of town. We flew in and out of that one," he pointed, "for two weeks straight. There were camouflaged revetments under tall trees for about ten B-17s."

Ingram asked, "When was that, Leon?"

"Uhh...last August," said Beardsley.

DeWitt snorted, "That's nine months ago. Who's to say the planes are still there?"

Beardsley said somewhat sullenly. "They're there, I say. And I heard they were still there as of two months ago"

Ingram looked away.

DeWitt clicked his teeth as the strains of "Danny Boy" drifted from the wedding feast.

"I'm not shitting you," Beardsley said plaintively.

"Lieutenant," snapped DeWitt.

"Sorry, Sir," said Beardsley.

Ingram raised his eyebrows to Amador and Carrillo.

They looked at one another and shrugged. Amador said, "Maybe so, maybe not. I remember a lot of air activity then, and this damned jungle is so thick you can just about hide New York City."

"There. See?" said Beardsley triumphantly.

"Lieutenant!" barked DeWitt. "Just hold on."

"Yessir," Beardsley said, picking at a piece of bread.

The rain slackened completely and "Moonglow" wafted through. Ingram said to Amador, "That night, as you boarded the *Wolfish*, didn't you say there was a radio here?"

Amador shook his head. "No more. Hapons took it when they stripped the mill. But there's a receiver, I think, in Gingoog."

Ingram tried to hide his disappointment. "How...do you communicate?" he asked.

"Runner. Tom-tom. We're still getting organized." Like Corregidor, Mindanao had fallen nine days before and the Japanese were in the process of consolidating their conquests. "A submarine called last week near Dipalog, I hear. Maybe they dropped off a radio."

Ingram said, "Too far." Dipalog was almost two hundred miles west. It would take too much time and besides, it was Moro country. Even the Japanese were afraid to go in there.

Lighting flashed and thunder rocked the valley, bringing a new torrent of rain to crash on the hut. Amador almost had to shout. "You need a transmitter?"

"Yes," said Ingram.

"I sense urgency in your tone."

"We need a transmitter," Ingram repeated.

Amador leaned forward. "But--"

Beardsley said, "Todd, those B-17s have great radios. I get you up to twenty, hell, thirty thousand feet and you can call anybody you like: MacArthur, Roosevelt, Hitler. Anybody."

"Thanks, Leon. Give me some time to think it over." Ingram exchanged glances with DeWitt, thankful for Beardsley's interruption. They didn't want Amador to know too much.

Sustained conversation was difficult so they fell silent and picked at the remains of their meal. Finally, Ingram said loudly, "Carrillo seemed to know we were coming. Were you expecting us?"

Amador nodded. "Emilio sent a messenger on the inter-island steamer saying you may be coming here. One of my coast watchers saw you head into the Kinabhangan River early this morning.

"Not a bad system." said Ingram.

"Believe it or not, this rudimentary technology works," Amador agreed.

Beardsley said. "Todd, about those planes..."

"You don't give up, do you Leon?" said Ingram.

"Uh, Uh." Beardsley laid the map in Ingram's lap and pointed. "I'll try the Esperanza field first."

"What?" said Ingram almost incredulously.

"Yeah, me. I can see fine. It should be about...here. The closest. How 'bout letting me have Sunderland and a rifle. We'll zip out there and back. Shouldn't take any more than a day, while you guys sit here and stuff your faces. If the planes are still there, it won't take long to check one over. Chances are I can fly us out; maybe tomorrow night. Next day for sure."

Ingram said, "Otis?"

The rain thumped harder and ran into the little hut. For a moment, DeWitt studied a puddle of muddy water growing in the dirt between his feet. At length he said, "Might as well try it. That's one of the reasons we're here."

Ingram said to Amador, "Where are the Japs bivouacked?"

Amador rubbed his chin and replied, "There's a large garrison in Butuan, some in Buenavista. That's where your *Kempetai* friend is staying."

"Roadblocks?" said Ingram.

"Hmm, yes," said Amador. "I know of a route to Esperanza that...wait a moment." He leaned forward and spoke to Carrillo in a rapid burst of Tagalog. At last he sat back and said, "There are roadblocks, at least three on the route to Esperanza."

Beardsley said, "How far?"

"Twenty-five miles or so."

"Hell, we'll hack our way through the forest," said Beardsley.

Amador opened his mouth, but Ingram said, "You wouldn't get two hundred yards."

Beardsley flushed, making his scars become angry red tributaries. He grabbed Ingram's sleeve. "Todd, damnit. This is our ticket out of here. We keep island-hopping and the Japs are going to catch our asses and roast us over a slow fire like--" he waved a forefinger at the window, "--like whatchamacallit's son."

Ingram shook Beardsley's hand loose. "Try going to Esperanza and you'll be the one dangling headfirst over a slow fire."

"Well, at least I'll go out doing something I'm trained to do."

The two stood almost nose to nose. Ingram's voice rose. "You've come this far."

"So what?"

"Who's been taking care of you?"

Beardsley's mouth opened. Then it shut.

"Sit down, Lieutenant," said DeWitt.

Beardsley said, "I only meant--"

"Sit!" ordered DeWitt.

As Beardsley and Ingram arranged themselves on the ground, Amador said. "There's another way."

The rain abruptly stopped as if turned off by a master valve. Amador spoke in soft tones as the band played "I'll be seeing you." The clouds parted and a brilliant early afternoon sun shot through. Ingram looked out the window, seeing a vaporous haze rise off the ground so thick it seemed to hiss.

Sergeants Guzman and Ramirez were back by nine o'clock that evening. The wedding feast was long-since over, with Ingram and the others just finishing a bowl of soup. They crowded around to listen as the ex-Filipino Scouts spoke with Carrillo and Amador in Tagalog.

At last, Amador turned to Beardsley and said, "They found your Esperanza airfield, Lieutenant."

"Hot damn, let's go!" whooped Beardsley.

Amador raised a hand. "The revetments are empty."

"Sonofabitch!"

Amador's hand was still raised as Guzman prattled on. "Were you aware of a secret strip near Amparo?" he asked.

"Amparo? Maybe. I couldn't remember the--"

"There are two of your four-motor bombers there, they say."

"No shit?" said Beardsley.

"One sits on the ground with its wheels collapsed. The propellers are bent," said Amador.

"Oh," said Beardsley.

"The other sits on its wheels," Amador smiled. "Ready to go."

"I'll be damned," said Beardsley.

Ingram swore Beardsley sounded like George Raft.

At three in the morning they rode in the same stake truck used to haul the pig into Nasipit. Carrillo drove with Amador and Guzman jammed in the cab. Ingram and his crew were stacked like logs on the truck's bed with furniture, mattresses, clothing, and pots and pans piled haphazardly over them. Ramirez was splayed on top to balance things out with the whole rig swaying dangerously, limiting their speed to forty-kilometers-per-hour. Two of the roadblocks were unmanned. At the third, the furniture ruse worked, with two Japanese corporals passing them through unchecked.

Whittaker lay near Ingram and lamented about the 51 Boat's engine. "We almost had her running. Why couldn't you give us another thirty minutes or so?"

Ingram burned with his own lamentation. They had left Helen behind. Yardly was against stacking her on the truck bed among everybody, with her cracked ribs and everything else that was wrong.

Ingram was incredulous. "But you said her functions have returned, Yardly. Her kidneys are fixed. She's on the mend."

"I don't care if she's pissing like Niagara Falls," Yardly said." She's not riding on that damned truck with you guys all stacked around and furniture piled overhead. All she needs is a punctured lung and that's it. Besides, she's still too damned weak."

Tears welled in Helen's eyes. Ingram became angry. But Yardly was adamant. Finally, Amador nipped the fuse by arranging for Helen to stay at the Carrillo's. If things went well, it would only take an hour or so for them to send the truck rushing her back to the field. They would build a heavily padded cage around her for the return trip.

Someone's foot continuously jabbed in Ingram's hip as the truck bounced along. And a chair leg had worked its way down his face, bumping his stitched cheek. He said, "Whittaker, you'll get your thirty minutes if the damn airplane doesn't start. Otherwise you'll be in Australia this time tomorrow."

Whittaker muttered, "Never will know if the damn engine runs or not."

The chair leg banged Ingram's cheek. "I'm sure it would have, Whittaker."

"Thank you, Sir."

Ingram's head was pinned, so he said from the side of his mouth, "Leon?"

"Yeah?"

"Can you see out of both eyes?"

"Sure."

"One hundred percent? Both eyes? I thought Yardly said--"

"Todd." The voice was pure Leon Beardsley this time. "What I can't see, you will."

"What?"

"You're flyin' copilot."

"Leon, damnit--"

"Todd. Lemme handle things. Do what I say. We'll be fine."

"You sure?"

"Yeah. Besides," Beardsley lowered his voice to a perfect George Raft conspiratorial, "I'm a veteran of the mile-high club. In B-17s yet. I can handle the thing by myself, if I have to."

"Mile-high club?" Ingram had heard many times the fly-boy legends of sneaking girlfriends aboard an airplane, climbing above 5,280 feet, setting the auto-pilot, and getting laid.

Three times. Even got the clap once to prove it. She was from Bolivia."

Ingram opened his mouth to speak, but suddenly, the truck changed gears, slowed, then lurched horribly for three minutes or so. The chair leg dug deeply into Ingram's cheek again, and a warm stickiness ran down his face. Brush scraped as the truck bounced along, grinding in low gear.

Finally, they stopped. Amador muttered something. The doors opened, and the truck jiggled to the movements of the Filipinos getting out.

"Wheooow," said Sunderland. "Kevin, your feet smell like shit."

Someone twittered.

Amador rasped. "Quiet. The Hapon's camp is not far."

"How far?" whispered Ingram.

Amador said, "A kilometer. Maybe a little more."

In five minutes the furniture was off the truck and they weaved to their feet. Without giving them time to stretch, Guzman lined them up, making each grab the beltloops of the man in front. With Ramirez trailing, he led them single-file into the forest. Ingram stumbled, cursing and moaning several times, as did everyone else. There was no moon and he couldn't see a thing, making him feel vulnerable. The skies had clouded again, threatening rain, and the night was noisy with insects, birds, and the screeching of monkeys.

After a half-hour of stumbling and tripping, the ground became smooth and predictable. Still, Ingram couldn't see anything except amorphous shapes, but he could tell they were out from under the jungle canopy after seeing a tree line framed against a gray-black sky.

Suddenly they stopped. Something was nearby, within a few feet, and it glistened. It was manmade.

"Lookit that," said Sunderland.

"Gimme," Beardsley muttered. Ingram handed him the flashlight and he switched it on.

Before them was a Boeing B-17D laying on its right wing. The right main landing gear had collapsed and the propellers on the two right engines were bent back over the cowls, like a toy broken by a child. They peered up at the nose compartment, seeing a small seat where the bombardier sighted out of the canopy. To the bombardier's left was an electrical control panel, and an oxygen mask dangled over the chair, its hose still gleaming as if someone had just hung it there.

Amador said, "Easy on the flashlight, Señor."

Beardsley muttered, "One minute." With the others rooted in place, he walked along the wing's leading edges, flicking the light here and there, peering in engine cowlings and checking underneath. Then he said, "Where's the other?"

"Across the runway," said Amador

Guzman motioned for them to get in line again. "Not this crap again. I can't see a thing," protested Holloway.

Beardsley said, "Buck up, Fred. Now you know how I felt."

That shut them up. And within five minutes they stopped again. Beardsley flicked on the light; before them stood another B-17D proudly resting on its landing gear. "Australia, fellas," said Beardsley, walking to the hatch underneath the cockpit. He reached up and, with a practiced twist of the handle, opened the hatch and let it flop down. "All aboard for Sydney and points east, you mugs."

While Beardsley chuckled with the others, Ingram circled the bomber with the flashlight. Then he walked up to the B-17 pilot.

Beardsley grinned. "How 'bout it, Todd? You don't mind getting a little airsick, do you?"

Ingram grabbed the flashlight, flicked it on, and shined it to where the left outboard engine should have been. It was gone, propeller, cowling, and all. "I'll be glad to puke in your airplane, Leon. All you have to do is dig up an engine."

42

15 May 1942
Three Kilometers Southeast of Amparo
Mindanao, Philippines

"Huh?" said Beardsley.

Ingram shined the flashlight where the left outboard engine should have been.

"Shit! Number one," shouted Beardsley.

"Señor!" admonished Amador. "Shhh."

Ingram clicked off the light. Beardsley grabbed it, and walked over to the number one engine nacelle and clicked it back on.

"Please!" Amador pleaded as if talking to a child.

"Turn off the light, Leon. Now," said Ingram.

Beardsley did as he was told and ambled back. "Not as bad as it looks," he muttered. "We can still do it."

"We should return to Nasipit before daybreak." Amador's voice almost shook.

"Why?" said Beardsley.

"There is nothing here," said Amador, spreading his arms and flopping them to his side.

DeWitt sighed. "Nice try. Lieutenant. Maybe we'll find another airfield tomorrow. By the way, is there a chance of using the radio?"

Ignoring DeWitt, Beardsley spun on his heel and stood with hands on his hips watching the men line up. They grabbed belt-loops and stood patiently with heads bowed and shoulders slumped. "Hold on," he shouted, "Nobody's going anywhere."

Amador urged, "Lieutenant. Hapons are camped less than two kilometers away."

Beardsley's forefinger waived toward the B-17's cockpit. His voice cranked up as he said, "The hell with the Japs, damnit. Within--"

"Shhhh," said Amador.

"...within twenty-four hours I'm going to fly that sonofabitch out of here. Now who wants to go?" Beardsley said softly.

"How?" said Ingram.

"Grab an engine. Spin some nuts and bolts, start it up, and take off," said Beardsley.

The men dropped the belt-loops and stood straighter.

"Take one from over there?" said Ingram, nodding toward the wrecked B-17.

"Exactly. Let's get to work."

It soon became apparent Leon Beardsley knew what he was talking about. After Guzman led them back to the wrecked B-17, Beardsley clattered inside the fuselage, finding a tool kit. With Bartholomew and Whittaker pitching in, he built a small platform and was soon tearing the cowling off number one engine.

Army engineers had blown up two bridges, making it impossible to bring the stake truck to the airfield. So, Amador sent Carrillo to Amparo to find something to haul the engine and propeller to the other bomber. Then Beardsley, Bartholomew, and Whittaker, they called themselves the "engine boys," spent the rest of the night cursing and racking their knuckles disassembling the myriad of hoses, exhaust pipes, and the fuel and hydraulic lines packed behind the engine, while the others slept.

At first light, their heads turned to a dull, clopping noise. Ingram stood with the others as a grinning Carrillo led a large, cumbersome black carabao around the wing. Using a cat-o-nine-tails, he flailed the animal's back lightly as it pulled a logging sled, a flatbed tobogganlike arrangement used for hauling felled trees. Sunderland walked over and clapped the great beast on its broad shoulders, making dust rise. "Reminds me of a bull we had at home. Won lots of ribbons."

Bartholomew bellowed from under the wing, "What was his name?"

"Socrates."

"What?"

"You know, like the Roman poet," Sunderland said, jumping on the logging sled.

"Greek philosopher," said Yardly, stepping up beside him.

"Let's hear it for Socrates." The Forester brothers jumped beside the other two and Carrillo whipped the big animal, giving them a ride around the B-17, while the others followed with whoops and catcalls.

What an odd picture they made in the predawn, Ingram thought. Boys grown into men who had seen the horror of war up close and, in one way or another, had killed other men. Now, as if nothing had ever happened, they literally pranced on an ancient logging sled drawn by a big dumb animal that was flogged by one who barely spoke their language.

Their voices were husky with sleep and hope and thoughts of home as they shouted obscenities and threw dirt clods. Maybe, Ingram thought, this dawn will indeed bring their first day of release from this hideous war. With the glib-tongued Leon Beardsley and his engine boys, maybe we really will make it.

While they bantered, Ingram inspected the low wing, four-engine bomber at close quarters. It was still in its livery of polished aluminum and lay about a hundred yards off the runway. Furrows of dirt and ripped-steel planking confirmed the right main landing gear had indeed collapsed during rollout. The bomber had ground-looped off the runway and plowed into thick underbrush at the forest's edge. The fuselage and the two inboard engines were riddled with bullet holes. Half the cockpit instrument panel was blown away as was a large section of the top turret Plexiglas. Dried blood was splattered about the cockpit and radio compartments. Someone had hastily covered the flying fortress with foliage, branches, and tarps. But sections of the plane were exposed and Ingram grabbed some dead brush to cover it back up. He asked Beardsley, "Do you know this plane?"

Beardsley finished disconnecting an oil line and looked at the nose where a scantily clad female figure was painted. The name was SHEZ-ABITCH to which Beardsley smirked, "No. But I'd ground-loop too, if they called me that."

The engine boys had disassembled a respectable pile of parts. Ingram picked up a section of cowling and headed for the other B-17. "Come on," he said to the others. Silently, they staggered along the runway with cumbersome components and bulky subassemblies, crossing over to trudge deep in the forest, where one-hundred-foot Narra trees formed a natural canopy over the revetments. In the other bomber's revetment, Ingram carefully leaned the cowl section against the sandbags, noticing the paint jobs didn't match. This B-17 was painted a dull olive-drab, and she, also, had a name on her nose: TILLY THE TERRIBLE. A caricature of an angry terrier with blond, curly hair, wearing a doughboy helmet cocked at a rakish angle, was painted there. Beside TILLY were six bombs which, Ingram supposed, meant she had flown six missions. He returned to the forest's edge pondering which of the two dogs the lesser evil was. Along the way, he came across seven other revetments. Four held burnt-out B-17s that had obviously been torched. Two other revetments contained charred remains of trucks, jeeps, furniture, and GI uniforms. He explored further, finding no supplies around the other revetments. But, returning to TILLY, he found four barrels of fuel, a barrel of engine oil, various boxes of spare parts, and a crated .30-caliber machine gun with ammo.

He walked back to the runway and checked his watch: 0727. He could barely see the other B-17. Figures filed back and forth carrying parts, and he wondered how Beardsley was doing.

As the yellow disk rose higher in the east, Beardsley called them together, announcing everything was off SHEZABITCH, except engine, propeller, and supercharger. "Time soon for muscle, you guys," he said.

The engine boys went back to work while everyone else eventually wandered off. Some lay under trees and fell asleep, others wiggled out of their rags to bathe in a stream that pleasantly gurgled in a nearby forest. But Amador warned about leeches so they settled for throwing rocks.

With hands on his hips, Otis DeWitt strutted about, looking at the men as they lazed. "Lieutenant Beardsley. We're reassured you are fully conversant with this aircraft's mechanical systems."

Leon Beardsley stood under the aft nacelle section with Bartholomew and Whittaker, unbolting the supercharger mounts. All three were sweaty and greasy as they twirled wrenches and screwdrivers. Beardsley said. "You're in good hands Major. Joint Army-Navy cooperation."

DeWitt continued. "And you really know how to fly that thing?"

"Mile-high club, Major."

"What?"

"Yes," Beardsley said, an edge creeping into his voice. "I can fly that thing, as you call it. That should be obvious."

"What's obvious is that we're not going to get anything done until we get organized."

"Oh?" said Beardsley.

"Look at everybody." DeWitt swept his hand around.

Beardsley said. "Be my guest, Major. Right now, I'm just an engine boy." Wiping his hands on a rag, he went back to his supercharger.

A tiny smile crept around DeWitt's lips, as he bellowed orders: Beardsley, Bartholomew, and Whittaker were to continue with the engine detail; Holloway and the Forester Brothers were assigned to check the runway and fill the furrows dug by SHEZABITCH's right engines. After that they were to make sure the rest of the runway was clear for takeoff.

And with instructions from Beardsley, Ingram took responsibility for topping off TILLY's fuel and oil tanks. Sunderland, Amador, Guzman, and Ramirez set up two-man security details at each end of the runway with Yardly acting as corpsman, messenger, and water boy between all four locations. This, of course, left DeWitt free to swagger around getting in everyone's way.

Nevertheless, things went quickly. By nine o'clock the engine boys jury-rigged an A-frame, and with block and tackle, unbolted the three bladed, Hamilton-Standard propeller and lowered it to the logging sled. With

Carrillo swatting and prodding, Socrates dragged the propeller to TILLY's revetment where they unloaded and propped it against the sandbags.

At ten-thirty, Ingram felt a genuine surge of hope as they lowered the one thousand-horsepower, nine-cylinder, Wright R-1820 engine to the logging sled. Soon it was ready. Carrillo whipped, Socrates strained and moaned, but the sled didn't move. Carrillo whipped and whipped again. The carabao bellowed in protest and strained against the harness, but the engine-laden sled didn't budge.

Ingram kneeled for a moment, and sighted the ground, finding a slight incline to the runway. Also, the ground around the sled was muddy from rains. But once they gained the runway, it would be smoother for hauling.

Manpower.

He recalled what they did aboard the *Pelican* after an air attack had unbedded her reduction gear box. "We need everybody. Fred!" he yelled at Holloway who was throwing dead tree limbs off the runway. "Come on."

"What is it, Lieutenant?" asked DeWitt.

"Time to go to work, Otis. Fred! Hurry up," Ingram hollered checking the sky. A front was building and he didn't want to wait lest the ground become intolerably muddy.

Leaving Amador, Ramirez and Guzman on security detail, they lined up in two teams on either side of the carabao and grabbed two heavy manila lines Carrillo had rigged. Ingram took a position at the head of the right-hand column and said, "Come on, Otis."

"Nonsense," said DeWitt.

"No time for that, Otis. Come on."

DeWitt turned and walked toward the runway.

Sunderland, third man in line on the left row called, "Major, if you don't pitch in, I'm throwing your ass out from twenty thousand feet."

"Sunderland, damnit," hissed Ingram.

Sunderland said, "Mr. Ingram, the sonofabitch--"

"Shhht--" DeWitt dropped to his haunches and stretched out his palm. He rasped, "Git down."

They fell to their knees as thunder rumbled over the Agusan Valley. Soon the air was ionized, making hair on the back of Ingram's neck stand on end. Carrillo slapped a palm against his forehead, "My fault. I hear a whistle. Carlos. It is him. But I didn't..."

"Forget it," Ingram whispered savagely.

DeWitt crawled over all fours to him and said. "Jap patrol. Near the other end of the runway." He watched Sunderland take a position behind a tree and prop his BAR on a low branch. DeWitt added, "I'll have that man on charges."

Ingram said through clenched teeth, "Do something like that again, Major, and you won't have to worry about Sunderland. I'll be the one throwing your ass out from twenty thousand feet."

DeWitt's head jerked to him, and his mouth fell open.

"I mean it, damnit. Your petty horseshit is slowing us down."

DeWitt's mouth worked. "All I was trying to do was--"

"Jesus!" whispered Bartholomew, peeking through tall grass.

Two columns of Japanese soldiers walked across the runway's north end. They were about five hundred yards away, making it hard to distinguish faces and uniform markings. Their gait was easy, and a few balanced their rifles on their shoulders. Thunder crackled to the southwest as they walked across the strip and melted into the forest.

Ingram said softly to DeWitt, "You don't follow orders very well, Major, do you? I'm in command here. When those Japs are gone you're picking up that damn line and hauling ass like everyone else. Got it?"

DeWitt exhaled loudly and looked to the ground. "Peacetime mentality. It's hard to break old habits."

It was Ingram's turn to be surprised, more so, when he turned to see DeWitt's attempt at a smile.

The underbrush rattled; Pablo Amador rushed up out of breath. "What happened? We made so much noise trying to get your attention it sounded like the Chicago Zoo."

Carrillo chattered excuses in Tagalog.

"Sorry," said Ingram. "We were distracted. Are they gone?"

"I think so. They missed the revetments, but it's only a matter of time before they stumble on them. Fito is following them while Carlos backtracks--"

Beardsley walked up. "Mr. Amador. How often does it rain here?"

Amador was confused for a moment. He stammered, "...this time of year? Monsoons approach. Two, three times a day. Maybe more."

Beardsley hit his fist in his palm. "That's it. Damnit! That is it. Let's go." He spun and ran to the left-hand rope and picked it up. "Come on you dumb bastards. We're going home."

Ingram ran up behind him and took his place. "What is it?"

Beardsley, this time with a Bogart accent, said over his shoulder, "It rains, Todd. The damned thunder and lightning shoots cosmic farts all over the sky. Then the toilet from the great beyond flushes, making even more noise. Noise, Todd. Noise. Lots of it. We can run up the engines and test without the Japs hearing."

DeWitt walked up, spit on his hands, and grabbed a section of the left rope. Ingram nodded to Carrillo, who cracked his whip over Socrates' rump.

"Ready?" growled Ingram. "One, two, three, mule haul!"

43

---

16 May 1942
Three Kilometers Southeast of Amparo
Mindanao, Philippines

Grunting, sweating, and cursing, the engine boys finished bolting the Wright 1820 in place by one-thirty. The men on the ground cheered as Beardsley strutted along the wing's leading edge, waving and taking deep bows. With a grin he proudly declared. "Takeoff's at sunset, girls. Rain permitting, of course."

The propeller was quickly hoisted and reattached to the engine. An hour later, Ingram, with mud sucking at his boots, stepped to the forest's edge and checked the sky. They had already had two harsh storms and the approaching front promised more, with ominous blue-black thunderheads roiling well over thirty thousand feet. Rain would be on them in less than an hour.

Forty-five minutes later, the rest of the engine was hooked up and the cowling secured. After a quick test of the cowl flaps, Ingram called, "Leon." With a nod to the sky he said, "Storm's almost here. Can you hurry?"

"On my way," Beardsley said as he kneeled atop the wing behind number one engine checking an oil line. He called to Yardly and Toliver just below, "Seems okay. Let's pull the props through."

Standing beneath, Yardly and Toliver grabbed propeller blades and rotated them counterclockwise ensuring oil was evenly distributed throughout each engine.

As they did so, Ingram spoke with Amador. "Good chance we may be on our way. Time to send the truck for Helen."

"Right." Amador turned and gave instructions to Carrillo who soon walked off with thunder rattling in the Agusan Valley.

In the meantime, Guzman took Socrates into Amparo returning forty-five minutes later with food and water for their trip. Beardsley still straddled the number one engine, madly twirling a socket wrench through an open panel. "Todd," he beckoned.

Checking his watch, Ingram walked under the engine. "How much longer?"

"Forgot something," Beardsley said. "Go to the cockpit and take the left seat. Hurry."

Ingram climbed in the B-17's aft hatch, made his way to the flight deck, sat in the pilot's seat and leaned out the window.

Beardsley, still spinning his ratchet, said, "Master electrical panel at your left. See if we have battery power. Try battery one, two, and three, and check the voltmeter." He called to Yardly and Toliver as they pulled number one's propellers. "That's enough. Back away."

Lightning flashed overhead as Ingram groped for the panel. He flipped the switches, testing batteries one, two and three. The needle barely quivered on battery number two. There was no indication of life on one or three. The smell of ozone mixed with a cold rush he felt in his bloodstream. He said. "Nothing."

Beardsley kept twirling. "Try again."

Ingram methodically redid the battery check. The result was the same. "Leon. We have a big problem," he called.

Beardsley leaned over the engine and shouted down to Bartholomew, "Plan B, Rocky."

Bartholomew said. "Got it. Pete, Bones, come on."

Whittaker, Yardly, and Bartholomew ran in the gathering darkness toward the other B-17. While they waited, Ingram scrambled outside and detailed the Forester brothers to clear debris from the revetment, while Toliver and Holloway rolled the empty fuel barrels outside. Then he called Amador over. "Carrillo?" he asked. "It's been well over an hour."

Amador shrugged. "I'll let you know as soon as we hear something."

Ten minutes later, rain had started spattering when Bartholomew, Whittaker, and Yardly trudged up, out of breath. Between them, they carried an eighty-pound, twenty-four-volt battery from the other B-17. Beardsley secured number one's cowling, eased himself to the ground, and ran to the battery access panel where the wing's leading edge joined the fuselage. As he popped open the panel door, wind twirled leaves and dust in small cyclones; lightning flashed and thunder cracked loudly overhead, as the four worked frantically replacing the battery.

The job was done just as the rain fell in earnest. Beardsley slapped the fuselage and said. "Okay. Let's give her a shot." With a practiced swing, Beardsley pulled his feet through the escape hatch just forward of the bomb bay and disappeared inside. Ingram tried the same thing and was surprised his feet made it up and through on the first swing. Once inside, he scrambled up to the flight deck and sat in the copilot's seat.

Beardsley worked the electrical panel muttering, "Only about twenty volts. Maybe so, maybe not." He pointed to a large cellophane-encased card hanging next to Ingram's right knee. "Read that."

Ingram grabbed the card, "Check off sheet?"

"That's right." No Bogart. No George Raft. Strictly Flight Officer Leon V. Beardsley.

Ingram read the first item. "'Doors and hatches.'"

"Okay."

"'Parking Brakes.'"

Beardsley reached to the instrument panel in front of Ingram and yanked a knob. "Set."

"'Controls.'"

He wobbled the control column and pushed the rudder pedals. "Unloaded."

Ingram called the next item. "'Fuel transfer valves.'"

"Checked on my way in. 'Off.'"

Ingram read down the list. Beardsley's hands were a blur as he moved about flipping switches or yanking levers. Finally, they moved into the start sequence. Ingram read. "'Master switches.'"

"On."

"Do you--"

Beardsley said, "hold on." He leaned out the window and yelled, "Back up, Pete!"

Whittaker, standing just below number one engine, nodded and stepped back ten feet. Just then an enormous bolt of lightning flashed through the revetment, with thunder clapping almost immediately. Rain fell in torrents so hard Ingram could barely see Whittaker.

Beardsley pulled in his head. "Go on!"

Amador ran up to the right side of the plane. He looked up to Ingram with a thumbs down. Soon Carrillo joined him.

Ingram leaned out and shouted, "What happened?"

Amador said, "Roadblock. He didn't even get back to Nasipit."

"Damnit!"

"Todd, come on!"

"What?" Ingram pulled back inside.

Beardsley pointed to the card.

Shit. "'Master switches'."

"'On,' I said."

Ingram fumbled at the card and looked out at Amador who had stepped away from the revetment with Carrillo. From a distance, both stood and watched, their hands in their pockets.

"Todd!" shouted Beardsley.

"'Battery switches and invertors!'"

Beardsley crossed his fingers. "On and checked."

"'Parking brakes--hydraulic check'"

"On and checked."

"'Booster pumps--pressure'"

Beardsley pointed to the right side of the panel. "Todd, damnit, do I have to do everything?"

"What?" said Ingram.

"Look at that gauge. What does it say?"

"It says about, I don't know. Is that twelve pounds?"

"Good enough," said Beardsley

Ingram resumed the list. "'Carburetor filter--'" Then it hit him. "Can you see alright?"

"Not a damn thing from my right eye."

"Awww, shiiit."

"Read, damnit."

The rain eased somewhat as they reached the section where Ingram called, "'Prime.'"

"Here we go." Beardsley leaned out the window and yelled. "Clear one!" Next, he wiggled the "prime" toggle, then hit the start button on Ingram's side of the panel.

Ingram expected to see the prop turning. But it wasn't and, he said with more concern than he intended. "You forgot to hook up the starter motor."

"It's inertial. Takes a few seconds to wind up."

"Yeah?"

"'Oh, ye of little faith,'" said Beardsley. He swiveled his head to look out the window while throwing the start switch to 'mesh.'

Number one's propeller slowly rotated. "You didn't forget," said Ingram.

"Count twelve blades."

"...five, six, seven, eight..." Ingram was mesmerized as the blades flashed past. He barely noticed from the corner of his eye that Whittaker had dropped to the ground. "...ten, eleven, twelve--"

"Zippo, baby," urged Beardsley, flipping number one magneto to 'Both'.

Through the rain, Ingram felt a shudder. A black belch of smoke vomited from number one's exhaust pipe.

The propeller became a blur and scythed the air. But then it stopped firing. Beardsley desperately jazzed throttle and mixture levers on the control pedestal. "Come on Tilly, sweet baby. I love you, honey," he coaxed.

With an enormous backfire the engine caught and roared into life. Beardsley settled it back to idle and grinned as Ingram slapped him on the back. He checked oil and fuel pressure. "Battery was the diciest part. It's charging nicely now."

"You okay, now?" asked Ingram.

"We're okay. Ready to roll number two."

"Can you find someone else?"

"What are you talking about?"

"Helen. They couldn't get her. I'm going back."

"Hell, we're just testing engines. Get her later."

"Leon. I think--"

"Come on Todd."

Beardsley reached again and concentrated on priming number two engine. Lightning flashed outside, and Ingram felt two things simultaneously: A rush of air blow over his head and a hand violently shake his shoulder. He turned in his seat seeing Otis DeWitt, his mouth working. His face was white as he pointed to a fresh bullet hole over Ingram's head.

"Japs!" DeWitt shrieked. "Whittaker and young Forester are hit."

"How bad?" demanded Ingram as number two roared into life.

"Not bad. Amador and his boys are holding them off."

"Sunny?"

"He's aboard," said DeWitt, as thunder crashed so loud it felt like it had originated in the revetment. "A couple of Japs got close but Sunny took care of them with his BAR. We figure it's those squads on their return trip."

Twenty men or so, he thought. Ingram turned, seeing Beardsley mesh number three. Then he knew. "Helen!"

DeWitt said, "Shit! Where is she?"

"Still in Nasipit. Truck didn't get through"

Beardsley said, "Why do I have the idea we gotta roll, Todd?"

DeWitt nodded. "It's now or never."

Ingram said, "Wait a minute. We--"

"Bullshit." Beardsley goosed throttle levers and shouted, "Major. Get everyone aboard and pull the wheel chocks."

Rain thundered on the B-17's aluminum skin so loudly that Ingram barely heard number three cough into life.

Otis Dewitt swallowed rapidly; he leaned between them and said. "Aren't you going to test first?"

In spite of their predicament, Beardsley said, "Major, what the hell do you want? A brass-plated toilet seat? Now get out there and pull the damn wheel chocks. Make double sure everyone's aboard. We'll hold until you let us know."

With a gulp, DeWitt nodded and disappeared as number four fired up. Beardsley fumbled under the seat, handed Ingram a set of earphones, and gestured how to hook them up. Finally, they were plugged in; Beardsley's voice was a metallic, "--think of this bird so far?"

Ingram managed to say, "It'll do."

Beardsley pat Ingram's shoulder, "Todd, it can't be helped. She'll be okay."

Ingram looked over and forced a nod.

Then Beardsley's eyes darted over the instrument panel.

"This thing going to work?" asked Ingram.

"Who knows? The list, damnit."

Ingram fumbled with the list; the rain pummeled so hard it almost obliterated engine noise.

"'Brakes.'"

"Locked."

"'Trim tabs.'"

"Set."

"'Tail wheel.'"

"Unlocked."

Two bullets stitched the fuselage just below Ingram's seat. "Shit. 'Vacuum.'"

"Check."

"'Altimeter.'"

"God, I wish I knew."

Otis DeWitt clapped them both on the shoulders and held up two muddy wheel chocks.

Beardsley leaned around and yelled, "Everybody get in the waist and radio compartments. Brace your backs to the forward bulkhead. Got it?"

DeWitt nodded and crawled aft.

Beardsley flipped off the parking brake, and none too delicately, advanced the throttles. TILLY THE TERRIBLE rolled out of the revetment, spraying a large cloud of water behind them.

"Where's the runway?" yelled Ingram.

"We turn at the tree."

"There's millions of trees."

"The one with an oil drum in the crotch."

"We're almost passed it. Come right. It's at our two o'clock."

"Got it. Keep talking, damnit," said Beardsley, revving up the port engines, pulling the bomber into a right turn. Then he let TILLY straighten and thread her way between two enormous Narra trees.

Ingram said,"'Instruments.'"

"Checked. You forgot radio."

"Sorry. 'Radio.'"

"No radio. I think that's about it, anyway." He reached down and turned on the generator switches then said, "Todd," pointing to the deck. "That lever is the tail wheel lock. Flip it on when I tell you."

Something rattled and chattered over Ingram's head. DeWitt popped up between them saying, "Sunderland got the top turret going. Looks like he took out a couple of Japs trying to throw grenades."

The top turret's twin fifty-caliber machine guns rattled again, followed by an echoing war whoop.

Beardsley rolled TILLY on the runway, turned and stopped, with her engines rumbling at a confident one thousand rpm. He looked out the windows. "Where do you think the little bastards are?"

"Don't know."

"Well, look." Beardsley stuck his head out.

Ingram poked his head out the right-side window into an incredible world of sound, as thunder crashed and rain thumped the fuselage. A twenty-knot wind whipped the downpour into sheets almost lacerating his face, while the four Wright 1820s waited patiently in their nacelles for the summons to full power. He pulled back inside, wiping rain off his face, and said, "Not a thing."

Beardsley, whose face was wet as well, grumbled, "Wish we had someone on intercom so I knew what the hell's going on." Then he grabbed Ingram's sleeve. "This is important. When I call 'gear up,' flip this switch."

Ingram followed Beardsley's finger to the top of the control pedestal between the two seats. "Landing gear switch," he said.

"Right."

Beardsley's fingers moved to another switch. "This is the wing flaps. Flip this when I tell you."

Ingram pointed. "Wing flaps."

Beardsley nodded. "Not bad for a snot-nosed Navy--"

TILLY shuddered. A scream ranged from back aft. DeWitt shouted. Someone shouted back. DeWitt stuck his head in between them and said, "Holloway's hit. They've got a heavy machine gun."

Beardsley said, "Shit. I wanted time for a little run-up. Hold on." He stood on the brakes and advanced the throttles all the way. At full rpm, TILLY roared and rattled and surged, spewing great clouds of mist behind her into the jungle. Beardsley quickly flipped through the four magnetos, checking each tachometer. Finally, he shouted, "Tail wheel lock!"

Ingram leaned down and threw the lever as Beardsley released the brakes. TILLY started rolling. "Locked," Ingram said.

TILLY accelerated, and Beardsley quickly pointed to a panel instrument. "Call our speed."

"...ummm. Forty-five...fifty...fifty-five..." TILLY thumped violently as the mains hit a pothole.

"Shit. I can't believe we're still rolling," called Beardsley.

TILLY bounced again, but not as heavily. Overhead the twin .50s chattered, and Sunderland whooped once more.

Ingram bit his lip then said. "...ninety...a hundred...one-oh-five, one-ten...one--"

Beardsley gently pulled back on the control column. TILLY bounced once and left the ground. He grinned and said. "Sweet Jesus. Gear up, Todd."

Ingram looked down to make sure he flipped the correct switch. He'd just done so when the bomber shuddered. The whole right side vibrated and numbers three and four engines misfired and shook violently in their mounts.

"Oh, my God," shouted Ingram. In terror, he looked out, seeing both engines windmill to a stop. They were only about a hundred feet up with the tree line fast advancing.

"Shit!" screamed Beardsley. "Prime! Prime the--" He reached over and frantically jabbed the number three prime button. Then, the two port engines sputtered out.

Ingram heard a horrible scream. He realized it was his own, as they sank back to earth. TILLY smacked the ground with a gut-wrenching crunch at a hundred and five knots. She plowed between two trees, ripping off both wings, and careened into the forest.

PART III

So, I turned about and gave my heart up to despair over all the toil of my labors under the sun, because sometimes a man who has toiled with wisdom and knowledge and skill must leave all to be enjoyed by a man who did not toil for it.

Ecclesiastes 2:20-23

When a man has nothing to do, it means that he has nothing in which to believe; and lacking belief, he has no will, or need for will; and lacking this, he ceases to be a man.

John Keats,
They Fought Alone
Lippencott, 1963

44

17 May 1942
Naval Base Fleet Landing, Kure
Hiroshima Prefecture, Honshu, Japan

Laden with men from the armada, tens of shore boats dipped and wallowed in the bay's choppy waters, eventually converging a few hundred meters off downtown Kure, a dull, shipbuilding city on Japan's Inland Sea. One by one they picked their way into a narrow channel to the Fleet Landing, unmistakable because of the cloud of blue engine exhaust looming above an overhanging shed. The boats lurched against the docks and disgorged Sailors who clumped up ramps and headed into town with exuberant plans for drinking, shouting, and desperate, last minute encounters.

Among them walked a barrel-chested civilian. The weather was overcast, yet it seemed bright to the man, particularly as he looked about seeing the late spring had finally brought greenery to the surrounding mountains and plains. He immediately turned right, separating from pleasure seekers, and strode toward the railroad station three kilometers to the east. With an hour to kill, the five-foot-three, one-hundred-thirty-pound man held his head imperviously as he walked past the sprawling Uraga Shipyards where the yet unpainted upper works of an enormous new cruiser lanced the sky. Pity, she would not be ready in time.

His head was close-shaved, and he wore a tight-fitting light-gray suit, silk burgundy tie, and spectacles. He blended well with passersby, but for insurance, a gauze mask completed the disguise. Though short, he was solidly built, and moved with purpose unlike the sailors and Imperial Marines who darted about impetuously seeking delights of the *pink houses*. Even with the gauze over his face, the fifty-eight-year-old man seemed ordinary, although more than one policeman looked him up and down, wondering why was such a dapper looking man strayed so near the shipyards, as if he were a petty criminal of some sort. But something about his stature, perhaps it was the way he carried his head, made police stop short of demanding his papers.

His name was Isoroku Yamamoto. He was a *Tai-sho*, or admiral, and was Japan's highest-ranking naval officer. This gave him the added honorific of *Rengo Kantai*, or commander of the Imperial Japanese Navy's Combined Fleet. And for this operation, more capital warships were under his command than any other individual in history.

In the harbor, three behemoths of his personal command, Battleship Division 1, tugged at their anchors. Prominent was the giant *Yamato*, his brand-new flagship displacing seventy-two thousand tons. She had nine eighteen-inch guns that could hurl a 1,451-kilogram projectile--an object heavier than a pickup truck-- over twenty-seven miles. The other two battleships, the *Nagato* and the *Mutsu*, displaced thirty-two thousand tons and had nine sixteen-inch guns. Other elements of his main body attack force were scattered around Kure: the light carrier, *Hosho*; a light cruiser, the *Sendai*; nine destroyers, two oilers, and two seaplane carriers. The rest of his fleet, over one hundred warships, was harbored from Kwajalein to Hokkaido, waiting for the order to sortie for the Midway attack.

Months of preparation had gone into this operation. Midway--code named island AF--was roughly 1,200 miles northwest of Honolulu and was the westernmost island in the Hawaiian Island chain. Yamamoto's major objective was to draw out the remnants of the U.S. Navy's battered Pacific Fleet and destroy them. Having done this, Japan could secure her eastern flank and stage forays against Pearl Harbor and America's West Coast with

Yamamoto's vaunted *Kido Butai*. Seattle, San Francisco, Los Angeles, and San Diego would be crushed.

Yamamoto was the sixth son of Takano Sadayoshi, a former samurai. The boy grew up in Nagaoka, in the Niigata Prefecture on the Sea of Japan. It was one of the few oil-producing districts in the country, and Yamamoto grew to learn and appreciate oil production. Later, as an aide to Admiral Ide Kenji, he toured the rich oilfields of Texas and Mexico. And after the successful Midway operation, he looked ahead to seizing them along with California's oil fields too. He'd even asked his staff to draw plans on how to quickly turn them to Japan's use in case of a protracted land battle on the U.S. mainland.

He was about a half a kilometer from the railroad station when he cocked an ear, hearing a train chuff through. Most trains these days were overloaded with material and troops for the war, and the station would be crowded. Instinctively, he tightened the straps on his gauze mask and walked on.

Again, Yamamoto stopped. Before him was a Shinto shrine that stood half block from the rail station. For a moment, he gazed up at two uprights and a double crossbar, a *Torii* gate. He couldn't see the shrine because of shrubbery, but the curving path, laid in a large uniform gray pebble, peacefully beckoned. He rubbed his chin and examined the stone *koma-inu*, or guardian lions that stood on either side of the path's entrance. He was pleased to see the lions were correctly portrayed; the mouth of the one on the right was open, the one on the left was closed, the pair symbolizing the "ah" and "um" of life--universally recognized sounds of birth and death--an extended interpretation from Hindu mythology, contemplating beginning and end.

The sound of Yamamoto clearing his throat was the only outward sign of the deep uneasiness he felt. The distance between the "ah" and "um" figures was a mere two meters, intended to remind the onlooker of life on earth and how quickly it raced by.

"'Beginning and End,'" Yamamoto mused; the *Alpha* and the *Omega*, as he had read in the Book of *Revelation*. For Yamamoto had been exposed to Christian teachings as a boy when he attended church services held by an American missionary in Nagaoka. It stayed with him even at the Naval Academy at Etajima, where he defiantly displayed a Bible, provoking arguments among classmates. And Christianity influenced his thinking as he matured and traveled as a naval attaché in Western cultures.

A train hooted and rumbled through the station. Yamamoto checked his watch, seeing he should hurry.

He made it just as the Tokyo, Shimonoseki, train steamed into the station. Afraid he would be recognized, *Rengo Kantai* tightened the gauze straps over his face, then paced up and down until the train made a complete stop. He waited patiently as the passengers debarked. Most were military, the others aged or bureaucrats looking as if the war's outcome depended solely on what were in their shiny, leather satchels. In any case, no one stood in the same spot very long--they too, were nervous about police, even though they were on authorized travel. And it was hard to tell which civilian in the shadows were either a *Kempetai* or a *Kempetai* informer.

A thin dapper civilian in his mid-forties eased a woman off the train by her elbow. Kawai Chiyoko' s eyes lighted up when she spotted the stocky admiral. With some discomfort, she pulled herself to full height and said softly, "Iso."

"Chiyoko," the admiral of the Combined Imperial Fleet spun on his heel, pulled down the gauze mask, and bowed as passengers brushed past. He had the strongest impulse to kiss Chiyoko right here before the world but that, he knew, would be bad form for *Rengo Kantai*.

Yamamoto retied his mask and said, "Thank you Doctor. How is she?"

"Please," protested Chiyoko. "I'm fine."

"Better than before," Although he was forty-two, Doctor Nomura's voice was almost a prepubescent contralto. "But she wheezes and she's weak. I had to inject her several times."

"What do you think is wrong with her?" Yamamoto muttered in Nomura's ear.

Nomura shook his head slowly. "Infection is all we know. We have ruled out tuberculosis, however."

Chiyoko tugged at Yamamoto's sleeve. "Iso, please."

Admiral Isoroku Yamamoto hoisted Chiyoko on his back and carried her toward the front entrance, with Nomura hurrying to keep up like a dog on a leash. In front, a 1939 black Buick sedan waited. A young lieutenant, impeccably dressed in whites, snapped open the rear door allowing Yamamoto to carefully arrange Chiyoko in the backseat. Making sure she was comfortable, he turned to Nomura on the sidewalk and said, "Find out."

"Sir?"

"Find out what's wrong with her, damnit! Give her tests. Anything. Do you understand? Send me the bills," Yamamoto growled.

Nomura nodded. They'd had this conversation before. Tests had been ordered. Nothing had worked.

"Where will you be staying?" asked Yamamoto.

Nomura stuttered out the answer in a high-pitched squeal. Yamamoto gave a quick nod, stepped in the car, and they drove off.

Kawai Chiyoko had been a geisha in Shimbashi when Isoroku Yamamoto first met her. She worked at the Nojima-ya house under the professional name of *Umeryu* or Plum-Dragon.

Yamamoto, married and a father of two boys and two girls, began seeing Chiyoko seriously eight years ago just before he left for London as naval attaché. And now, Yamamoto was leaving on another mission, and he had to see her again. But she was not well. She'd been suffering from pleurisy since March, and at one time Dr. Nomura and his staff had given up, telling Yamamoto she would die.

To Yamamoto, one day in April was especially bleak. Not only had Nomura phoned with terrible news about Chiyoko, he'd also learned about the American B-25 raid on Japan's sacred Homeland. Rage over the Americans and helplessness over Chiyoko weighed heavily.

As he tucked her into the Buick's backseat, he was glad to have a chance to do something positive. Yamamoto was convinced that he could make Chiyoko well during his four days of liberty, and he was prepared to devote all his efforts to her during that time.

At the inn in the mountains overlooking Kure, they slept on the bed Chiyoko preferred, a large Western-style called a *double*. She was propped up against the headboard to keep the fluid from running into her trachea. Even so, her breath rattled but it would not bother Yamamoto; he was a sound sleeper.

Wearing just towel and sandals, *Rengo Kantai* padded in after forty-five minutes in steam bath, hot tub, and shower.

"Better?" she asked.

"I can't wait to get you in there again," he said.

She stared at the floor in that contemplative way that made her look deliciously innocent and virginal; a countenance Yamamoto loved even though he knew she had been well practiced long before they met.

She smiled at the thought of their lovemaking. "Nomura doesn't think it's a good idea."

"Nomura is full of it," said Yamamoto.

"He thinks it best, Iso."

Yamamoto stood to his full height, sucked in his gut and cheeks. His rib cage actually protruded a bit as he pointed and pulled a face with eyes squeezed almost shut. "I forbid it," he said imitating Nomura's female falsetto.

Chiyoko put a hand over her mouth.

"You are not to bathe." Yamamoto's spine stiffened, his voice was impossibly high, and his elbows were clamped to his sides.

"Don't," pleaded Chiyoko.

The admiral slapped his hands on his hips and wiggled his thick torso. "We need you smelling like a goat to kill the germs."

"Yes?" she twittered. Except for the congestion in her chest she felt fulfilled and wonderful. Yamamoto had placed her in the tub and slowly, carefully, soap-sponged every inch of her body before they made love.

"You are Japan's top secret weapon," the admiral declared. "The *Kempetai* wants you for their very own to kill Americans with your deadly body odor."

"Iso!" she gasped. Chiyoko was not used to jokes about the Thought Police.

Yamamoto shook off his sandals, leaned down on a chair, placed his hands on the opposite corners, and kicked high in the air into a perfect handstand. She'd seen him do it once on the bow of a shore boat. But then he wasn't wearing just a towel which now flipped down, displaying everything.

"Don't point that at me," she declared.

The admiral's orderly, dressed in unmarked whites, quietly stepped in the room picking up clothes and tidying. Chiyoko pulled the sheet up to her neck.

"You may be right, Umeryu." Upside-down, Yamamoto sounded hoarse. "Why needlessly risk your life before such a powerful weapon?" Releasing his grip on the chair, Yamamoto landed lightly on his feet and rolled through a perfect somersault, ceremoniously standing before their dinner table now being cleared by the orderly.

"Come back here. You're getting too old for that," Chiyoko declared.

Yamamoto snatched two saucers off the table, locked his elbows, and began spinning them on outstretched forefingers. Actually, he had to use his left hand's ring finger since the index and middle fingers were gone. He lost them from a turret explosion aboard the battleship *Nisshin* as a new midshipman during the Battle of the Japan Sea against the Czarist Navy in 1905.

With wet towels and soiled laundry draped over his arms, the orderly bowed and silently backed out of the room.

The corners of Yamamoto's mouth turned up slightly.

She knew what he was going to do. "Don't!"

He flicked his wrists making the saucers spin faster.

"Please," she giggled.

Satisfied that her chest didn't rattle, Yamamoto did an about-face that would have made any of his Imperial Marines proud. Then he shrugged off the towel and rolled through a somersault with his arms still outstretched and saucers spinning, ending a half-meter before her. He did another perfect about-face and bowed deeply.

"Stop!" She was laughing. Suddenly Chiyoko fell into a racking, impossibly liquid cough. She sat straight up and coughed harder.

Yamamoto quickly set the saucers aside, sat beside her, and slapped her back.

The orderly stuck his head around the door with his eyebrows raised.

Yamamoto shook his head and the man disappeared. "Chiyoko," he whispered in her ear. Over and over he said it with the spasm passing after several minutes.

Thirty minutes later, Chiyoko was fast asleep. To Yamamoto her face was white, almost the color of the ringed moon that illuminated the rock garden outside. With great tenderness, he brushed her hair and kissed her on the forehead. Making sure her head was elevated and that she rested comfortably, he relaxed against the headboard and stared at the garden. With this position he wouldn't sleep tonight, but it was worth it. Tomorrow, Chiyoko would waken with that look of a sixteen-year-old. They would make love again, then have breakfast and take a walk.

The late night patterns in the rock garden were beautiful. And it was perfectly quiet. No screeching, shipborne exhaust-blowers or bugles or airplane engines, or men screaming orders. It was so quiet he could almost hear the shadows scraping across the perfectly manicured grounds outside.

He sensed his orderly's presence and admitted him with a nod. The man quickly entered, lay a sheaf of papers next to *Rengo Kantai,* and withdrew.

After a lingering glance at the rock garden, he reached to the stack with his free left hand and picked up a twenty-page report. It was a summary stamped MOST SECRET and labeled OPERATION AF. ORDER OF BATTLE.

His right arm was pinned under Chiyoko and, with fingers missing off his left hand, he had trouble flipping pages. Finally, he got to section twelve and studied it, as he had every day for the past two months:

MOST SECRET

Imperial Japanese Combined Fleet, Admiral Isoroku Yamamoto Commander in Chief:

MAIN BODY - ADM Isoroku Yamamoto
   BatDiv 1 *Yamato* - Flagship, *Nagato, Mutsu*
   Carrier Group - *Hosho* (CVL) 8 bombers, 1 DD
   Special Force - *Chiyoda, Nisshin* (seaplane carriers serving as tenders)
   Screen (DesRon 3) - Radm. Shintaro Hashimoto
   Sendai (CL Flagship)
   DesDiv 11 - 4 DDs
   DesDiv 19 - 4 DDs
   1st Supply - 2 oilers

FIRST CARRIER STRIKING FORCE (1st Air Fleet--*Kido Butai*) - VADM Chuchi Nagumo
   Carrier Group - VADM Nagumo
   CarDiv 1
   Akagi (CV, Flag) 21 Zero fighters, 21 dive-bombers, 21 torpedo bombers
   Kaga (CV) 21 Zero fighters, 21 dive-bombers, 30 torpedo bombers
   CarDiv 2 - RADM Tamon Yamaguchi

Hiryu (CV, Flag) 21 Zero fighters, 21 dive-bombers, 21 torpedo bombers

Soryu (CV) (a) 21 Zero fighters, 21 dive-bombers, 30 torpedo bombers

Support Group - RADM Hiroaki Abe

CruDiv 8 - *Tone* (CA Flag), *Chikuma* (CA)

2nd Section, BatDiv 3 - *Haruna, Kirishima*

Screen (DesRon 10) - RADM Susumu Kimura

Nagara (CL) Flag

DesDiv 4 - 4 DDs

DesDiv 10 - 3 DDs

DesDiv 17 - 4 DDs

Supply Group - Oilers, 1 DD

MIDWAY INVASION FORCE (2nd Fleet - VADM Nobutake Kondo)

Invasion Force Main Body

CruDiv 4 (less 2nd section) - Atago (CA Flag), Chokai CA

CruDiv 5 - Myoko (CA), Haguro (CA)

BatDiv 3 (less 2nd section) - *Kongo, Hiei*

Screen (DesRon 4) - RADM Shoji Nishimura)

Yura - (CL Flag)

DesDiv 2 - 4 DDs

DesDiv 9 - 3 DDs

Carrier Group

Zuiho (CVL) - 12 Zero fighters, 12 torpedo bombers; 1 DD.

Supply Group - 4 oilers, 1 repair ship

Close Support Group

CruDiv 7

Kumano (CA Flag); *Suzuya* (CA), *Mikuma* (CA), *Mogami* (CA).

DesDiv 8 - 2 DDs.

1 Oiler

Transport Group - RADM Raizo Tanaka

12 transports carrying troops

3 patrol boats carrying troops

1 Oiler

Escort (DesRon 2) - RADM Tanaka

Jintsu (CL Flag)

DesDiv 15 - 2 DD
DesDiv 16 - 4 DD
DesDiv 18 - 4 DD
Seaplane Tender Group - RADM Riutaro Fujita
Seaplane Tender Div 11
Chitose (CVS) 16 fighter seaplanes, 4 scout seaplanes,
Kamikawa Maru (AV) - 8 fighter seaplanes, 4 scout planes.
1 DD; 1 patrol boat carrying troops
Minesweeper Group
4 Minesweepers
3 Submarine Chasers
1 Supply Ship
2 Cargo Ships

ADVANCE (submarine) FORCE (6th Fleet) - VADM Teruhish Komatsu

Katori (CL flag) at Kwajalein
SubRon 3 - RADM Chimaki Kono
Rio de Janeiro Maru (submarine tender, flag) at Kwajalein
SubDiv 19 - 4 submarines
SubDiv 30 - 3 submarines
SubDiv 13 - 3 submarines

SHORE BASED AIR PATROL (11th Air Fleet) -- VADM Nishizo Tsukahara at Tinian

Midway Expeditionary Force - Capt. Chisato Morita
36 Zero fighters (aboard Nagumo's carriers
10 land-based bombers at Wake; 6 flying boats at Jaluit
24th Air Flotilla - Minoru Maeda at Kwajalein
Chitose Air Group - 36 Zero fighters, 36 torpedo bombers at Kwajalein
1st Air Group - 36 Zero fighters, 36 torpedo bombers on Aur and Wotje
14th Air Group - 18 flying boats at Jaluit and Wotje

NORTHERN (ALEUTIANS) FORCE (5th Fleet) VADM Moshiro Hosogaya

Northern Force Main Body

Nachi (CA Flag)

Screen 2 DDs

Supply Group - 2 Oilers, 3 Cargo Ships

Second Carrier Striking Force RADM Kakuji Kakuta

Carrier Group (CarDiv 4)

Ryujo (CVL) 16 Zero fighters, 21 torpedo bombers

Junyo (CV) 24 Zero fighters, 21 dive bombers

Support Group (2nd section, CruDiv 4) - *Maya*(CA), *Takao* (CA)

Screen (DesDiv 7) 3 dds, 1 oiler

Attu Invasion Force - RADM Sentaro Omori

Abukuma (CL Flag)

DesDiv 21 4 DDs

1 Minelayer, 1 transport carrying troops.

Kiska Invasion Force - Capt. Takeji Ono

CruDiv 21 - *Kiso* (CL), *Tama* (CL), *Asaka Maru* (auxiliary cruiser)

Screen (DesDiv 6) - 3 DDs

2 transports carrying troops

Minesweeper Div. 13 - 3 minesweepers

Submarine Detachment - RADM Shigeshi Yamazaki

SubRon 1 - *I-9*, Flag

SubDiv 2 - 3 submarines

SubDiv 4 - 2 submarines

NORTHERN (ALEUTIANS) FORCE (5th Fleet) VADM Moshiro Hosogaya

Northern Force Main Body

Nachi (CA Flag)

Screen 2 DDs

Supply Group - 2 Oilers, 3 Cargo Ships

Second Carrier Striking Force RADM Kakuji Kakuta

Carrier Group (CarDiv 4)

Ryujo (CVL) 16 Zero fighters, 21 torpedo bombers

Junyo (CV) 24 Zero fighters, 21 dive bombers

Support Group (2nd section, CruDiv 4) - *Maya*(CA), *Takao* (CA)

Screen (DesDiv 7) 3 dds, 1 oiler

Attu Invasion Force - RADM Sentaro Omori
Abukuma (CL Flag)
DesDiv 21 4 DDs
1 Minelayer, 1 transport carrying troops.
Kiska Invasion Force - Capt. Takeji Ono
CruDiv 21 - *Kiso* (CL), *Tama* (CL), *Asaka Maru* (auxiliary cruiser)
Screen (DesDiv 6) - 3 DDs
2 transports carrying troops
Minesweeper Div. 13 - 3 minesweepers
Submarine Detachment - RADM Shigeshi Yamazaki
SubRon 1 - *I-9*, Flag
SubDiv 2 - 3 submarines
SubDiv 4 - 2 submarines

GUARD (Aleutians Screening) FORCE - VADM Shiro Takasu
BatDiv 2 - Hyuga (flagship), Ise, Fuso, Yamashiro
Screen - RADM Fukuji Kishi
CruDiv 9 - *Kitakami* (CL, Flag), *Oi*, (CL)
DesDiv 20, 4 DDs
DesDiv 24, 4 DDs
DesDiv 27, 4 DDs
2nd supply unit - 2 oilers

Moaning softly, Chiyoko rolled over. He jerked awake. He'd fallen asleep for a couple of hours. His right arm was free now and he flexed it, helping the circulation to return. Looking down he made sure she breathed evenly, then ran a hand lightly over her hair. Then he looked at his summary again. As far as he knew, the AF operation was indeed the largest naval attack force afloat in the history of mankind. He really felt the diversionary attack in the Aleutians was unnecessary and preferred to concentrate everything for the Midway attack. But he decided to let his young staff have their head. It would give them the experience needed for planning attacks on the U.S. mainland early next year.

Besides, he knew he had enough forces for this operation--except perhaps for Nagumo's *Kido Butai*. For this engagement, they would be down to four out of the six original heavy carriers. Two heavy carriers, the *Zuikaku* and the *Shokaku*, were casualties of the Coral Sea Battle and definitely would not be available. But that was not of concern to him. Nimitz had only one, possibly two, carriers with which to defend.

He wanted to be with the *Kido Butai*, that's where the action would be. But he knew his position as Commander-in-Chief had to be aboard the *Yamato* with the Main Body Attack Force, six hundred miles behind the four carriers. He gave a sigh. Chuchi Nagumo would have all the challenges. And all the fun. Yamamoto trusted Nagumo; he'd done an outstanding job executing the Pearl Harbor attack. And this operation was well planned. Nothing should go wrong, now.

Besides, surprise was on their side.

Chiyoko stirred once more and fell back to an untroubled sleep. A glance out the window told him the rock garden shadows were much longer. Dawn would come soon. He listened carefully, making sure Chiyoko breathed evenly. Satisfied, *Rengo Kantai* drifted off to his own blissful sleep.

45

18 May 1942
Nasipit, Mindanao
Philippines

Ingram woke with a wracking cough.

"Shhhhhhh." A hand fell lightly over his mouth.

For a moment, he panicked. He wanted to tear away the hand but he was too weak. He shook his head, seeing light patterns like those cast by venetian blinds.

Where am I?

"Stop wiggling, damnit."

It was a woman's voice. His mind was fuzzy and it took a moment to figure it out. *Amazing*! "Helen?"

"Quiet."

"Helen."

"Shhhht." Her response a cat's hiss.

He lay back and groaned.

A hoarse whisper drifted from Sunderland. "Mr. Ingram, damnit. Shut up before I pop you with a crowbar."

Feet stomped overhead. Guttural shouts echoed and shadows flicked through the light shafts.

Those are Japs up there.

Men. Soldiers. Growing fully conscious, Ingram realized Japanese were directly above. His head lay in Helen's lap and her hand still rested on his mouth. He looked up, finding the shadows emphasized her cheekbones. She still wore Whittaker's ball cap which somehow isolated a compelling and basic simplicity. It was much like the cap she wore when they first met. And even in that moment, the enemy just a few feet above, he caught himself admiring the structure of her face, in spite of her sores and in spite of the fact that her eyes darted about, surveying the threat above. Her chin, her white teeth, and the small birthmark on her neck, the way her left eyebrow arched was all a magnificent combination of delicacy and power and self-determination.

She glanced down nervously, smiled for the briefest of moments, then looked up with the light painting dim, parallel streaks over her. Her hand remained on his mouth and perspired exuding, not the odor of sweat, but fear.

He moved. Dirt crunched under his back as he moved. Cutting oil fumes crept in his nostrils. Familiar figures were huddled around and with thick floorboards above he reckoned they were in a basement of some sort. To his right, soft amber sunlight played over mounds of gas masks and helmets. Farther back stood a stack of several long, wooden crates. A box was open, and a cosmoline-smeared rifle barrel glinted inside. Other crates were piled carelessly about labeled "grenades" or ".30 caliber." Another half-dozen stubby crates were labeled "dynamite."

Suddenly two figures, wearing sandals and drab jungle fatigues, stomped not more than four feet above him. There was a rapid burst of Japanese; the figures turned and walked away.

Nearby, someone groaned, but it was quickly muffled.

Another whispered hoarsely, "Okay for water?"

Helen's head jerked in a nod.

Soon, there was splashing, followed by a choked gurgling. Then it was quiet. For a while the world seemed to mark time, as if the clock had stopped altogether. It was hot and stuffy, and flies buzzed around Ingram's face. He put a hand to his cheek wiping off sweat. Half his face was bandaged and his head hurt. "Ohhh."

One of the men cursed not ten feet away.

"Quiet Bones," another said.

"...can't stand 'em," Yardly whimpered.

Something grazed his ankle and bumped his knee. Ingram looked down into two tiny beady eyes. Another glistening pair were poised beside his boot. "Uggggh." Helen clamped her hand hard over his mouth. He spasmed his legs; the rats scurried off. With effort he controlled his breathing. Helen eased her hand away just as they heard coarse shouts outside. Feet thumped, a tailgate slammed, and an engine started. The driver had trouble coordinating transmission and clutch. Someone shouted, the gears clanked horribly, and finally the truck pulled away.

"What time is it?" Ingram rasped.

"Quiet. It may be a trick."

"How long have I been out?"

"Delirious," she said softly.

"Whatever. How long?"

"Almost two days."

"What time is it, now?"

She flicked her wrist and held it to a shaft of deepening amber light. "Five-thirty," she said.

A figure crawled close. "Welcome back, Mr. Ingram."

Ingram recognized Pablo Amador's quiet whisper. "Pablo, what's going on?"

"I think the Hapons are gone for the time being, but Manuel tells me they're planning to convert this into a headquarters of some sort."

"When?"

"Soon. Possibly within the week."

Ingram looked up at the flooring. "How do we get out of here?"

"Ramirez and Carrillo will move the lathe."

"Lathe? Where the hell are we?" said Ingram.

Amador said, "Nasipit. Under the lumber mill."

Ingram's mouth was dry and he tried to swallow. "What happened with the B-17?"

"The motors stopped turning. You crashed."

Ingram broke into a sweat as he remembered TILLY's propellers jerking to a stop; the bomber slamming into the ground. "Anyone figure out why?"

"Lieutenant Beardsley says the gas was spiked with water."

Ingram sank back in Helen's lap. The Japanese had spies throughout the Philippines well before the war. A lot of material had been sabotaged. Suddenly he jerked upright. "Is everyone okay?"

"Relax," Helen said. "You have a concussion."

Ingram felt the bandages again. "Owww. Tell me how to relax with a concussion."

She said. "Your head hit the instrument panel. Multiple lacerations on the right side. You're fortunate they have Novocain here. I had to sew up your cheek again."

"Oh."

"To begin with, it hadn't knitted well. I don't think you took very good care of it." She wrinkled her forehead, imitating a fourth-grade school teacher holding a switch behind her back.

"You sound better," he said.

"I am."

"Much?" He raised his hand to her face.

Helen pulled her head away. "Yes, much better, thank you. "With the back of his hand, he grazed a cigarette burn near her ear. "How are they doing?"

She jerked her head again. "Itch like the dickens."

"Good."

"...ah..."

"What?"

Ingram wanted it off his chest. "Japs surprised us just as we started the engines. They began shooting. We didn't have a choice but to try and go then. I'm sorry. We couldn't get back here to pick you up."

"I know."

"I'm sorry."

"Forget it."

"But--"

"Forget it, I said."

After a moment he said, "You didn't answer my question."

"What?"

"Is everyone okay?"

Silence.

"Come on, damnit," he said.

"Later," she said.

"Rocky," Ingram called quietly.

Bartholomew's crumpled chief's hat took shape beside him. "How you doin', Sir?"

"Fine. Look, Rocky. Give me a casualty report. I want it all. Understand?"

Bartholomew looked at Helen.

"All of it," Ingram said.

"Okay." Bartholomew's voice broke as he whispered, "Mr. Holloway took one in the chest. He was dead before we hit."

Ingram said, "My God." Thunder, lightning and the bellowing of TILLY's engines filled his head. He could almost hear the rain thumping on the B-17's aluminum fuselage as she surged down the runway. He remembered another sound: the chatter of fifty-caliber machine guns in TILLY's top turret. "Sunderland. He got his turret going."

"At the last moment, a squad of Japs tried a banzai charge on the plane with grenades. Sunny nailed 'em." said Bartholomew.

Another image came to focus in Ingram's mind. "Whittaker fell when we were starting up."

Bartholomew nodded grimly. "Pete was hit pretty bad. We got him inside, but I think he was gone by the time we took off."

Another dead. In near darkness Ingram bit his lip then asked, "What about Forester?"

Bartholomew sucked through his teeth for a moment. "Hit in the shoulder. Miss Durand says..." He looked up.

"He lost a lot of blood; we're still not sure," she said.

"You worked on him?"

"That's what I do."

"I mean, you feel that good?"

"Better than standing around and watching people writhe in pain."

"Well, thank you." Ingram whispered, "Everybody else okay?" Bartholomew said, "To a point. We've been on the run. Tired. Hungry. Japs are madder than hell. Between Sunny and Mr. Amador's scouts, we killed more than half that patrol. Next day the little bastards went on the rampage.

They lined up thirty civilians in Amparo and shot 'em outright. Another twenty or so in Cabadbaran. Butuan was the worst. Fifty were machine-gunned. And they left the bodies in the street for the flies and rats. And you know whose doin' it?"

"The jerk in the white suit, I'll bet." Ingram spat.

"Yeah, he struts around and orders people out of their huts to die. You should have seen what he--"

"Shhh," said Amador.

A large shape scraped above them. Amador said, "That's the lathe. Ramirez." He shouted a phrase of Tagalog.

Ramirez shouted back, and with grunts he and Carrillo shoved a large piece of machinery. Soon a section of the floor swung up, flooding the area with late-afternoon light. Ingram saw that most of the men were bandaged, only two appeared untouched. There was something else. Yardly stared vacantly at the ground, Beardsley's head hung down, and Sunderland lay with his back to them.

Toliver's silhouette filled the hatchway. He leaned down and said, "All clear."

"Stinks in here." Sunderland lurched to his feet and hoisted himself out.

Like zombies, the others worked their way through the hatch, then lifted a heavily bandaged Junior Forester. Helen Durand went out right behind them, to make the groaning sailor comfortable.

Ingram was alone so he wobbled to his feet and grasped the edges of the hatchway, finding his chest even with the floor. His head swirled for a moment as he blinked and squeezed his eyes, adjusting to the late-after-noon sun. Dust motes sparkled in the light shafts and Nasipit, at five-thirty in the afternoon, was strangely silent. Looking up, he studied the lumber mill's cavernous ceiling. Its intricate network of rafters and trusses had been created in a more gentler age by architects and engineers and craftsmen not bent on killing each other. Their symmetry mocked him. It was a taste of civilized achievement ridiculously intact in a world gone mad.

He was too damned weak to hoist himself out. The others had forgotten him and stared into space from wherever they collapsed to the floor. The hell with it, he thought. He wiggled, trying to muster the energy, but only managed to raise a leg halfway toward the hatch.

"Come on, Skipper." Bartholomew and Toliver reached down to pull him through, and half carried him to a stack of quilted furniture pads in a corner.

Ingram panted as he sat. "How's Junior now?"

"No change." Helen came over and eased beside him.

Ingram's eyes meandered over a large circular saw, not unlike the type seen in *Perils of Pauline* serials. "You think Tuga is really going to set up shop here."

Her eyes followed his to the saw. With an involuntary shudder she said, "Looks like he has all the right instruments."

She turned to him and said. "I know what's on your mind. Escape. Maybe revenge."

"What's wrong with that?"

"I mean, give your head a few days before you do anything."

"As long as it takes to repair the engine. Any idea where we should hide?"

"Mountains, I suppose. Amador says that's where most Americans are.

"Are they safe up there?"

"I don't know. Amador says the *Kempetai* hunts them down. Almost like tracking big game. And if they come up dry, they go into a village and torture people to make them tell where the Americans are. What they do when they find them is worse than the Bataan Death March."

Bartholomew shuffled over with a large water canteen. He looked at Helen. She nodded, and he pushed it against Ingram's shoulder, "Drink up, Skipper."

"Not thirsty."

"Better try," said Helen.

Ingram took the canteen and surprised himself when he gulped more than half. Gasping, he said, "Thanks Rocky."

Bartholomew moved off saying, "Cold stew in a few minutes."

"Cold?"

"Cold," Bartholomew said over his shoulder. Apparently, they were afraid of making a fire.

The water seemed to course through his system, invigorating every joint. He drank the rest of the canteen, then lay back, wondering if he could afford to stay quiet for the next day or two. He closed his eyes for a moment but something struck him. "What's wrong with those guys?"

"What do you mean?"

"They're avoiding me."

"They've been waiting for you to come to your senses."

Ingram scratched his head. "I don't understand."

"You're the only one who knows enough about navigation to make it to Australia."

Ingram pursed his lips and made a show of saying, "Ahhh, well then. The taxpayers did their best to teach me all about that."

"Otherwise, they would have shoved off without you."

Ingram raised on an elbow. "What do you mean?"

"You don't remember what happened after the plane crashed?"

"No."

She sat upright, straightened her ball cap, then fiddled with the buttons on her sleeves.

Ingram rose beside her, his eyes darting. "I...can't remember. The plane hit. We skidded into some trees. And then I woke up. Here." He paused then said, "In this building is where I next remember anything."

"Talk to Rocky about it." Something in Helen's voice made him uneasy. "Back in a moment," she said. "Have to check on Forester." She stood and walked over to where the young quartermaster striker lay on a stretcher.

Ingram said, "Chief?"

Bartholomew walked over. "Skipper?"

"What happened back there?"

"Back where?"

"The plane wreck, damnit!" Ingram said loudly. His voice echoed in the cavernous lumber mill. From across the room he felt everyone's eyes flick toward him.

Bartholomew took off his hat and brushed it against his coveralls. "Uhhh, Sir..."

"Leon!" Ingram shouted.

Beardsley's head popped up. "Yeah."

"Come here, please. You too, Ollie. We may as well have a damned officer's call. Where is Otis?"

"Out looking for a radio, Sir," said Bartholomew.

Ingram thought that one over. "How long's he been gone?"

"Since this morning," said Bartholomew as the others sat.

Ingram said to Beardsley, "I hear the gas was sabotaged."

Beardsley toyed with his lower lip, then said. "I'd say so. Otherwise, all four engines couldn't have conked out at the same time."

"Damn near made it." Ingram and Beardsley exchanged glances, sharing the feeling of glorious freedom when TILLY's wheels left the runway. "Number one was cranking fine?" he asked, referring to the engine they had cannibalized from the other B-17.

"As good as the day it was built." Beardsley kicked at the blanket pile. "Damn! We'd be sucking up Aussie beer right now. Holloway and Whittaker should be with us."

In the last of the light, he noticed Beardsley's face was still horribly puffed up. Ingram said, "How are your peepers?"

"Twenty-twenty."

"Both?"

"Well, there's still some to go in my right eye."

"Leon, it was worth the try. I'm glad you talked us into it."

Beardsley nodded.

"You get through the crash okay?"

Beardsley said, "More or less. I woke up as Ollie dragged me from the wreck."

"Ollie?"

"I was pinned. Damned control yoke was jammed in my chest." Beardsley nodded to Toliver. "Rover dragged me out. In fact, he dragged almost everyone out. Right, Chief?"

Bartholomew nodded. "Yep."

Beardsley continued, "Methodical as hell. He worked from front to back. Then the plane caught fire. Uhhh...he didn't have time for Pete and Mr. Holloway's bodies. So we thought everyone was out when we heard scream-ing. That's when he and Kevin dove into the fire and pulled out Brian. And that's when..."

Ingram felt himself go cold. "Go on."

"You don't remember?"

"No."

Beardsley swallowed a couple of times.

"Tell me!" shouted Ingram.

Beardsley looked at Bartholomew. "Todd, I--"

Ingram sprang at Beardsley, grabbed at his feet, missed and fell on the floor, while Beardsley jumped back.

Beardsley said, "You took a big hit on your noggin. It made you sort of loony. You were running in circles and damn near foaming at the mouth. It took three guys to hold you down."

Suddenly it came back to Ingram and his breathing came in short gasps, cold sweat stood out on his brow. In his mind, he saw the plane burning. And he heard screams. "I remember. Ohhh shit." He looked over to where Junior Forester lay. "The fire. It was so damned hot. I thought it was too late to pull Forester out..."

"Easy Todd," said Beardsley. "We crashed. People go batty. I've seen it happen."

"How did we get here?" asked Ingram.

"We walked while you and Kevin rode in style."

"How's that?"

"Socrates."

"Speak English."

"The damned caribou. You don't remember riding on that logging skid?"

"Not a thing," said Ingram, reaching out to Toliver. "Ollie?"

Toliver leaned into the shadows.

Ingram said, "You've been looking out for me, just like Leon."

Toliver's face was like granite.

"You shot that Jap on Marinduque."

"It was you," said Toliver.

"All along the way you've been saving our butts, haven't you?"

"You're crazy," said Toliver.

"Come on, Skipper," said Bartholomew.

Ingram said, "I remember now. That night when--"

There was commotion near the backdoor. In twilight, a figure stepped through, supporting another. The second man was shirtless, and his legs almost dragged. Guzman closed the door quietly, while the second figure sank to the floor.

"Bones," someone gasped.

Yardly bustled over, unscrewed his canteen, and eased it to the man's mouth. The first figure spoke with Yardly, then walked toward Ingram with Amador close behind.

The silhouette of a campaign hat materialized overhead. "Welcome back," said DeWitt. "I was worried."

"Thanks, Otis. Find a radio?"

"No. But I found a radioman." DeWitt nodded over his shoulder.

"What?" said Ingram and Beardsley.

"Off a pig-boat. Japs depth-charged her, near the Surigao Straits. The poor bastard was wandering near the edge of town, half-starved; half-dehydrated. Says his shipmates are camped in the jungle, eating monkeys and lizards."

Ingram said to Amador, "Maybe we better round them up?"

Amador shook his head. "Nasipit is becoming the escape capital of Mindanao. Many Americans are concentrated around here. I think that is why Tuga plans to set up headquarters here. He and his thugs can scoop up prisoners and drag them through the streets."

"Isn't he looking for you?" asked Ingram.

"With so many Americans in the hills, that has become a second priority, I hear," said Amador.

DeWitt nodded toward the man who had collapsed near the door. "What about the submariners?"

"We'll find them and look after them. For now, you're the ones we're worried about."

Ingram said, "Time to get out."

"Yes," said Amador.

Helen walked up. "You and Forester have to recuperate, first."

"I think we better head out, now," said Ingram. "Old 51's engine ready to fire, Rocky?"

Bartholomew shook his head slowly, "Still ripped up. And I think we have electrical problems."

"How long to fix her?"

Bartholomew took off his hat and scratched his head. "Couple of days, maybe. It's tough to work out there. Lotsa mosquitoes and creepys."

Amador said, "There are crocodiles in that river."

"Jeez!" said Bartholomew. He threw his hands in the air and spun a circle on the ball of his foot. "I thought you were pulling my leg," he said to Ingram.

Ingram said, "Rocky, we need to fix it, pronto."

"Is there a way to bring it here?" asked DeWitt.

Ingram turned to Amador. "That's an idea. By sea, it would be only a mile or two to the Kinabhangan River mouth?"

Amador nodded.

Ingram continued, "The best deal would be if there were someone to tow us."

Amador spoke to Carrillo in Tagalog. After a moment he said, "Hidden beneath the pier is the only boat in Nasipit. The Hapons took everything else. It's an old workboat, only four meters in length--a gasoline burning one-lunger, Manuel tells me. He used it for night fishing. I'll see if they can try tonight."

"Thanks. Beats lugging tools and parts through the jungle," said Ingram. "Ollie. You and Rocky take--let's see--Sunderland and Kevin Forester. Maybe that'll help get his mind off Junior."

Amador said, "I'll send Ramirez to show the way."

"Shove off after dinner." Ingram turned to Amador and nodded. "Thank them for their help."

"It's our pleasure," said Amador. "That's why we're here. The sooner you escape, the sooner you come back and kill Hapons."

"I hope so," said Ingram.

DeWitt cleared his throat. "About the radio..."

"Looks like we'll have another day or so to look for one, Otis," said Ingram. "While we're on the subject, do you think we should take your refugee along?"

DeWitt and Bartholomew exchanged shrugs.

"Okay," said Ingram. "If he wants, he's in. I'll talk to him after he's had something to eat. What his rate and name?"

"Second class named Lokko or something like that."

"He just might be our ticket, Otis, if we come up with a busted set. Maybe he could fix it. Don't you think?" said Ingram.

The day's-end fatigue uncovered DeWitt's twang. He said, "Don't know. Guy's kind of bonkers. Shell-shock. Maybe."

"What's with the radios, Sir?" asked Bartholomew.

"Just calling for help, Rocky. Our big problem may be fuel. I'd like to scare up another barrel. And we have to figure out how to ease it down from the pier."

"I can rig a set of falls. Maybe use Socrates?" said Bartholomew.

"Alright." It felt good to be getting organized. Ingram felt hunger pangs in spite of pain throbbing in his head and neck. Gingerly, he turned to Bartholomew. "Is that stew really cold?"

"As last week's cat shit," said Bartholomew. "You ready?"

Bartholomew's metaphor was much too vivid. "Just water for now. I think I'll rest."

46

They towed the 51 Boat from the Kinabhangan River and moored her among rotted pilings under the lumber mill's wharf. Bartholomew, Toliver, and the elder Forester puttered with the diesel, but missed Whittaker's touch and grumbled and cursed at one another. After two days, Leon Beardsley rolled up his sleeves, and pitched in using some of the mill's remaining ancient machinery and reconditioned parts. Finally, it was done, and they stood around as Bartholomew thumbed the start button. The Buda caught immediately, giving a confident rumble.

Meanwhile, Ingram ate and caught up on sleep while Otis DeWitt, dodging Japanese patrols, moved furtively around the Agusan Province looking for a radio.

At the end of the third day, Ingram's head and neck aches were almost gone and Helen removed his bandages, except the one over the cheek.

Everyone was relieved to see Junior Forester sit up, drink water, and nibble at solid foods.

On the other hand, DeWitt's stray radioman was still in a daze. He ate and drank, but ran a fever and slept most of the time; so, Ingram decided to hold off speaking to him for the time being.

Late that afternoon, Pablo Amador brought word the Japanese were moving into the mill in a day or two with plans to convert it to a regional headquarters. With that, Ingram gave orders to push off soon after dark.

The late afternoon was finally cooling off and the Carrillos surprised them with a going-away feast. Sitting on the hard-packed dirt floor the whole 51 Boat crew was jammed in the corrugated tin hut behind the Carrillo's home,. First, Mrs. Carrillo served a half-dozen roast chickens--split in half, stuffed with yam slices and skewered together. Then came boiled fish and jackfruit cooked in coconut milk with large roasted seeds as big as nuts. Next were roasted Cassava roots to serve as a bread beside white rice, rough cracked corn, and ripe avocados the size of grapefruit. To drink, Amador produced a bottle of Fundatore brandy and a bottle of Chinese rice wine. Carrillo rustled up ten bottles of native tuba, a coconut-based beer, four unchilled bottles of San Miguel beer, and two bottles of Coca-Cola, equally warm.

It was quiet as they ate and drank their fill by the light of four candles. With panache, Carrillo reached in a pocket and pulled out a Bearing cigar, offering it to Sunderland.

"Wow. Thanks," said Sunderland, with a broad smile. He accepted the cigar and then ran it under his nose. "Ummm, a Bearing alright," he said reverently, stuffing it in his breast pocket.

Carrillo said, "No, no, no," then spat quick phrases of Tagalog to Amador.

"What?" said Sunderland.

Amador chuckled and said, "He says you must light up now, Señor. For good luck."

Sunderland looked up to Carrillo.

Carrillo nodded and beamed.

"Okay." Sunderland pulled the Bearing out and rattled at the cellophane wrapper. Soon, he had it stripped. Then he bit the cigar's end and spit it out with Amador flicking on a gold Ronson lighter.

They all watched as Sunderland took a long, luxurious puff. "Ahhhh." He sat back and nodded and grinned to the beaming Carrillo. "Thanks, Señor Carrillo."

Otis DeWitt watched the last of the sun's golden rays catch rich, blue smoke swirling around the ceiling. "Damn, there are times I wished I smoked cigars. May I?" He reached.

"This one would knock you on your ass, Major," Sunderland said with a smile. People twittered around the table.

DeWitt smiled too. "I suppose." He leaned back, nudged his stomach with a fist, and muffled a small belch. "What do you say, Todd? Time to saddle up."

Ingram said to Carrillo, "What about our hostess?"

Carrillo shrugged.

Amador said, "She was happy to do it. We all are."

Ingram said to Carrillo, "We would like to thank your wife for all her trouble."

"Yes?" Carrillo said, looking at Amador.

"Please. Could you bring her in here?" said Ingram.

Amador explained in Tagalog. With a vigorous nod, Carrillo got up, and moments later returned with his wife, Rosarita, who bore a confused look. Carrillo put his arm around her, and they stood rather nervously before the table.

DeWitt muttered and stood saying, "I outrank everybody so I guess it's up to me." He made a small speech in his best twang and ended with, "Thank you Mr. Amador, Mr. and Mrs. Carrillo, and Mr. Ramirez and Mr. Guzman, and all the wonderful people of Nasipit for your hope, your prayers, your hospitality, and this wonderful banquet. And you can be sure we'll be back soon to help you nail these bast-- er, jerks."

Amador interpreted, and Rosarita, wearing a large smock that concealed her considerable bulk, bowed graciously.

"Ah, come on." Beardsley rose to his feet and stood beside DeWitt. He began singing in a decent baritone, "Good Night Irene." As he bellowed the familiar phrases, veins stood out on his traumatized face like sinuous, red tributaries. Soon, they all joined in. Rosarita, with a gold-toothed smile, grinned and nodded and twirled.

Ingram, feeling he had to do something, unpinned one of his lieutenant devices from his collar and, with a deep bow, walked up and pinned it on Rosarita' s collar. He topped it off with a kiss to her forehead as the others bellowed the last bars.

The song was over. Anything more seemed inappropriate, so they stood for a moment, hearing only the shrill nighttime chirp of cicadas outside.

With a final bow, Rosarita walked out with tears streaking her cheeks. They got up, but she was back in two minutes with mounds of leftovers packed in wax paper and camote leafs. Toliver, Bartholomew, Sunderland, and Kevin Forester accepted them, and with the two Filipino scouts, filed out to finish preparations aboard the 51 Boat.

Except for Sunderland's cigar smoke, the room was nearly empty. DeWitt sat across from his stray sailor. Ingram moved over and sat next to him. He had terrible sun blisters on his lips and cheeks. His long hair was slicked straight back, his eyes drooped, and he had several nick marks where he'd shaved with an old razor. In spite of his condition his stature was lean and powerful.

With a nod to DeWitt, Ingram said, "How you feeling Sailor?"

The man munched a piece of jackfruit and said, "...feels good to eat real chow."

Ingram held out a hand. "My name's Lieutenant Ingram. This is Major DeWitt."

The sailor studied Ingram's hand for a moment. Then, almost as if a light bulb clicked on, he nodded, grinned and shook. He said slowly, "...Lorca...uh...Dominic."

"What happened to you?"

"...dogging a convoy...night...no moon. Destroyer snuck up and surprised us. Held us down. Rain squall. Shit. That was smart. We surfaced in a--

Lorca whipped around and bellowed to the walls, "Chief! Priority message from ComSubPac. Should I send for Mr. Chance, or do you..." He rocked back and forth for a moment, and moaned and held his hand. Then the moaning became a melody with a deliberate cadence. Lorca's head bobbed one way, then the next, as he hummed and slapped his hand on his leg with the rhythm.

"Kid's loony," muttered DeWitt.

Ingram guessed. "Is that Bach, son?"

Lorca hummed louder, then nodded. "Fugue in G Sharp Minor. One of my favorites."

"Do you play an instrument?"

"You bet. Violin."

"Then what happened--" Ingram caught himself. The man's left hand, his fingering hand, was heavily bandaged. The dressing was filthy and blood had seeped through in spots. With a sidelong glance to DeWitt, he knew Lorca wouldn't be fiddling for a while.

Suddenly, Lorca looked Ingram straight in the eye and said almost conversationally, "That Jap was smart. He knew we surfaced in a rain squall. Charged in and hit us with one round. And guess where?"

"Where?" said Ingram.

"For'ard engine room. And I was one compartment ahead of that. Boat was ripped in half."

Dewitt was incredulous. "How'd you get out?"

Lorca shook his head slowly. "I have no idea. First I was talking to Doc Gaspar, then he's splattered all over me and the lights go out. Next thing I know...I'm in a raft..."

Ingram realized the man was looking through him. It was as if a switch had turned off. "Lorca? Lorca?" said Ingram.

"Come on, son," said DeWitt.

Gradually, Lorca's face took on some color. He focused and looked from Ingram to DeWitt. "Feels good to eat real chow."

DeWitt and Ingram exchanged glances. Ingram said, "You a radioman?"

"...radioman?" said Lorca. "That's what I do. Hotshot second class. First class, soon. Passed my test."

Ingram muttered to DeWitt, "Glad the strongest thing we gave him was that Coke." He turned to Lorca. "Where are your buddies?"

Lorca focused for a moment. "Radioman. I pull in broadcasts from stateside all the time. Even got William Winter. You know him?"

"No," said Ingram.

"Ten times better than Walter Winchell. William Winter always tells it straight."

"You betcha," said DeWitt.

"You sure you haven't heard him?" asked Lorca.

"No," said Ingram.

"KGEI. My hometown. San Francisco."

"Nice town," said DeWitt, nodding at Lorca's tattoos. "'Arrivederci Tojo.' I like that. You get those in 'Frisco?"

"SAN FRAN Cisco, if you please, Sir," said Lorca.

"Sorry," said DeWitt.

Lorca's tongue lolled in his mouth. Finally, he managed, "We get Mr. Winter at ten in the morning, which means he's broadcasting at six the night before...or is it...lemme see...that's it. We're submerged most of the time when Winter's on. That's why I can't hear him so much. So that means he's on in the morning. Ten our time. Did I say that?" Lorca grinned.

Ingram called across the room to Yardly. "Did you look him over?"

"Yes, Sir. Seems okay except for fatigue and that hand. Some sort of dementia. Mr. DeWitt may be right. Shell-shock. He responds to food, though. I think time is all he needs."

Lorca picked another piece of Jackfruit and nibbled at it.

"...better not take him," Ingram mouthed to DeWitt.

DeWitt nodded slowly and whispered, "Sorry. Thought he would come in handy."

Ingram decided to try one more time. "What boat you off of, sailor?"

"Boat? I been on lots of boats," said Lorca.

Ingram reached over and patted the young man on the shoulder. "Mr. Amador will take care of you, son."

He rose and said to DeWitt, "I better go out to the boat and see how they're doing."

"Lots of boats," said Lorca. "*Wolfish* this time. Now she's gone. Jap round right in the For'ard engine room. BAM! I was there. You shoulda seen it."

Ingram took two steps and stopped. "What?"

DeWitt too, had half-risen. He stood frozen in place staring at Lorca.

Ingram said, "*Wolfish? Wolfish?*" He stared at DeWitt.

DeWitt nodded vigorously.

Ingram kneeled next to the radioman. "Sailor, did you say the *Wolfish*?"

"Sure. But...she's gone now. Ronnie's gone, too. Neat guy."

With another look at DeWitt, Ingram asked, "You know a sailor named Radtke?"

Lorca swallowed a couple of times. "Radtke. Radtke. Yeah, Radtke. He has a good fist. I liked the way--"

"Did he make it?" roared DeWitt grabbing Lorca's right hand.

The radioman's left hand bounced against the table and fell in his lap. "Owwww." He shrunk back; his eyes darting between Ingram and DeWitt.

"Jesus." DeWitt crawled over the table, his knees knocking aside wooden bowls and cups. Grabbing one of Lorca's lapels he yelled, "Did Radtke make it?"

"Major!" shouted Helen Durand. "Stop this."

"Don't hit me," screamed Lorca.

Helen Durand and Yardly moved close. DeWitt glowered, then let go.

"Where are your buddies?" asked Ingram as evenly as he could.

Lorca put his hands over his face. "They hung the chief upside-down."

"Who?" asked DeWitt.

"Chief Hall," said Lorca. "The Japs nailed him to a tree."

"You mean crucified?" asked DeWitt.

"That's it." Lorca crossed himself. "Like in church, except upside-down. Scared the hell out of us."

"Who else is left?" asked Ingram.

"Not many, two, or is it three? Mr. Gruber could tell you."

"Radtke?" asked Ingram.

"Radtke. Yes, Radtke. He paddled the raft," squeaked Lorca.

"He's in the hills with them?"

"With Lil' Adolf. Yes."

"Damn!" said Ingram, sitting back.

"Please don't hit me," moaned Lorca.

"Don't worry, son," Ingram said. "Here. Lay down." He nodded to Helen Durand and Yardly, and helped the youngster lay back. Soon he was breathing evenly and they draped a blanket over him.

Ingram's head swirled and he knew it wasn't from any concussion. He stood, surprised that he had to lean on the wall for a moment, "I have to go outside and check on things..." He headed for the door. Radtke! That bastard Radtke here in Mindanao. He'd have to stay and track him down, but he didn't want to. Ingram cursed, wondering why it was up to him; why he was the one shackled with this impossible task. He paused at the door and looked back momentarily.

There she was, ball cap and all, looking marvelous. Yet, her head was cocked as she looked at him. For that matter, so were Amador's and DeWitt's.

"Where the hell are you going?" asked DeWitt.

"I need air."

"You what?" asked DeWitt.

"Damnit, Otis, shut up." Ingram walked out.

47

21 May 1942
Agusan Province Foothills
Northern Mindanao, Philippines

"For the last time Radtke, we go when I say we go," said Ensign Gruber.

"Sir, it's been nine days," said Radtke.

Ensign Gruber barely looked like an ensign. His khakis were tattered, he wore no shoes, and he hadn't shaved since the *Wolfish* went down, his George Brent moustache unrecognizable. Radtke didn't look any better.

Gruber said, "We're laying low, damnit. Now fill that jug and let's go."

"He give you anything to eat?"

Old Lumaban, a sun-wrinkled potato farmer, lived in a hut on a broad plain looking over the Butuan Bay, where Döttmer could see Nasipit, a tantalizing six miles to the northeast.

"Another sackful. Ready?" said Gruber, putting away his wallet. "Damnit," he muttered. "Only two bucks left." Lumaban sold them six potatoes every two days. It wasn't enough to sustain them, and none of them knew enough about survival to catch food on a consistent basis. Although, day before yesterday they caught a monkey. Gruber and Kimble held the wiggling thing, which shrieked horribly, until it seemed their eardrums were about to shred. It wasn't until it bit Gruber that Döttmer stepped in and choked it to death. No one knew how to butcher it and the meat was stringy. But they felt better.

The only reason they didn't head for Nasipit was because of what happened to Chief Hall. It was the day after they landed, and Hall had volunteered to go into a little coastal village for food. He bought two sacks of food from a Chinese storekeeper and was belching his way out of the village when a Japanese patrol walked in from the other end. The storekeeper screamed and ranted, pointing to a clump of bushes where Hall was hiding. The Japanese captured Hall with a horrified Döttmer, Gruber, Lorca, and Kimble watching from the distance. They ran into the jungle, hiding in a cave they had found earlier. Hall screamed so loud that night they couldn't sleep. The next day, as they hiked a road into the mountains, they found him crucified: upside-down.

As they trudged past, Gruber and Kimble retched, and Döttmer had trouble holding his bile, too. But Lorca barely blinked at Hall's corpse.

"Don't trust nobody," muttered Kimble as they moved deeper into the foothills.

Döttmer, who had planned to simply turn himself in, was as horrified as the rest and decided to stick with them, waiting for things to sort themselves out.

Three nights later Lorca wandered off. Thankfully, that was one less mouth to feed.

It was late afternoon at their campsite when Döttmer made his decision. He finished his potato and said, "Mr. Gruber, I'm going into town."

"You'll do no such thing," said Gruber.

Döttmer stood, picked up a potato, and started eating.

"Hey, what are you doing?" Gruber shouted. "That's for tomorr--ugggh"

Döttmer grabbed what was left of Gruber's shirt and twisted with both hands, hearing a soft tearing sound. He said through clenched teeth, "Try and stop me, you little bastard, and I'll kill you. Understand?"

Gruber gurgled and nodded desperately. Döttmer threw him into the bushes and walked down the trail. Fifteen minutes later, he looked back, hearing footsteps. It was Kimble, the storekeeper, jogging to catch up. So be it.

Later, they heard feet shuffling behind them and waited in a clump of trees. It was Gruber and they let him pass, figuring Lil' Adolph would make a good point ferreting out any Japs that might be ahead.

As the sun touched the horizon, they gained the narrow coast road, which was no more than a two-wheel dirt track. They were close to Nasipit, Döttmer knew, as Gruber stumbled along about three hundred yards ahead. Suddenly, he disappeared around a bend and they heard shouting and laughter. But the voices were not the guttural commands of Japanese soldiers; the voices belonged to men and women and children. Cautiously, Döttmer and Kimble eased around the bend finding a raised gazebo deco-rated with colorful posters and quilts and streamers. Folding chairs were set up on the gazebo; beside them lay musical instruments. Filipino men and women and children were gathered around a campfire. Gruber sat among them, his face beaming as they handed him a slab of poached fish on a camote leaf.

A thunderstorm rumbled in the distance, and reds and oranges and pinks drenched the skies above Mindanao as Döttmer and Kimble trudged up to the campfire.

The Filipinos closed around them, shaking Döttmer's and Kimble's hands. Ensign Gruber, without a thought for the past said, "About time you got here." With his fingers, Gruber broke off a chunk and ate greedily. He said, "Say hello to Roberto Manolo. He tells me they do this twice a month."

A Filipino with slicked back hair, wearing a peculiar combination of Sam Brown belt, jodhpurs, and knee-high boots, shook hands with Kimble. "All Americans are welcome," he said in obvious delight.

Turning to Döttmer with a broad smile, he extended both hands. Döttmer quickly shoved his left hand behind his back, tucking it into his belt and mumbled, "Thanks for letting us stay."

An uneasy silence was fractured when Gruber said through greasy lips, "Roberto is the leader of the 110th Music Division of the United States Forces in the Philippines. Did I say that right, Roberto?"

Manolo smiled for Döttmer and Kimble. "Submariners, you are safe here, and we have enough food. Please." He ladled a bowl of rice for each of them and handed it over.

An hour later, Döttmer had had his fill of rice and poached fish and burped contentedly. He settled back as the lead violin sounded an "A," the other players taking up the note in organized cacophony. Silence descended as the last of the twilight's glow warmed the western sky.

Manolo stood high on a fallen tree trunk checking lookouts at both ends of the clearing. They waved "okay." He waved back, then stepped down and took his place at the podium. Manolo raised his baton and the 110th Music Division of the United States Forces in the Philippines opened with "The Star-Spangled Banner." The musicians sat stiffly and played while everyone stood with their hands over their hearts. Döttmer watched with fascination as Manolo finished the anthem with a great flourish. Not bad, for only fifteen men; a little tinny maybe, but not bad.

The anthem over, Döttmer sat and leaned against the tree trunk. Gruber kept to his feet and said, "We've pushed our luck far enough. Let's go."

Döttmer, his hands behind his head, looked up briefly and said, "No."

"What? I'm ordering you," said Gruber. "You can be court-martialed for disobeying a superior officer."

"Remember what I told you up in the hills?" said Döttmer evenly.

"Suit yourself." Gruber turned and said, "Kimble?"

Döttmer heard the gears of capitulation grinding in poor Kimble's head. The man had no choice. Finally, he stood with a pleading look at Döttmer.

"Radtke?" Gruber said a last time.

"Get lost," said Döttmer.

Kimble spread his arms, then flopped them to his side and said, "Jesus, Radtke. He'll hang your ass."

"The man's a dolt," said Döttmer, ignoring Gruber.

"We'll see," said Gruber. With Kimble trailing behind, he trudged back into the jungle.

Satisfied he was through with the U.S. Navy, Döttmer muttered "*wiedersehen*" under his breath. He watched Gruber and Kimble move into darkness, and then turned to concentrate on the three trumpeters. One of them played an exquisite King whose beautifully lacquered bell gleamed in the sunset. He tapped his foot, listening to the 110th strike up "Alexander's Ragtime Band."

48

---

21 May 1942
Nasipit, Mindanao
Philippines

The honky-tonk melody of "Alexander's Ragtime Band" wafted through the evening. Darkness closed around Ingram as he headed toward the pier, hardly noticing the music becoming clearer as light zephyrs blew from the west. He walked across the road and onto the pier where he found his crew stowing gear. They were making good progress and he really didn't have anything to add, so he paced for a few minutes, racking his mind over what that radioman had said.

Radtke was here is what the man said! The 51 Boat had to go tonight but he had to stay.

Damnit!

Looking up at the night sky, he took deep breaths, sniffing Mindanao's rich air. A panoply of evening stars popped out, claiming what was left of the day. It was clear, with hardly any wind. The seas would be calm tonight, he decided; a good time to dash up the coast for the Surigao Straits. Except, he wouldn't be aboard.

Toliver looked up from the boat and caught his eye. With a grin, he flipped a piece of canvas off four wooden cases stowed amidships.

Ingram had to squint to make out the labels: Dynamite. Toliver had added two more cases to the ones they found in the *Pima*. Toliver grinned, "Like the Coast Guard says, 'always prepared.'"

"Where did you get it?" asked Ingram.

"Part of Ramirez's stash in the mill."

Ingram drew a breath. "I'll say. Look, Ollie. Could you and Rocky join me in the hut, please?"

"Got a lot to do, Todd," said Toliver.

"Now," said Ingram.

Looking at one another, Toliver and Bartholomew followed him back to the hut, where they sat with DeWitt, Pablo Amador and Helen Durand. Wind blew, the curtains rustled, and strains from the 110th flowed in. This time, they sounded a bit cheesy as they tried the "Waltz of the Flowers." Ingram found it hard to speak and the silence seemed extended despite the music, so Amador offered, "Regrettably the 110th volunteer band hasn't the benefit of Leopold Stokowski," he said with a smirk. "But it's good though, don't you think? A bizarre intrusion of civilization?"

"Where are they?" asked Ingram.

Amador cocked his head and sniffed, "I'd say the little gazebo just beyond the power station," he said.

Helen said, "They sound sad--so melancholy. Not happy, like before."

"Perhaps it's because you have to leave and they're serenading you," said Amador.

Ingram took a deep breath and said, "There's been a change in plans."

"What Skipper?" said Bartholomew.

"Major DeWitt and I are staying. I want you, Lieutenant Toliver, to take command of the 51 Boat. Chief Bartholomew will be exec. You'll shove off tonight, transit the Surigao Straits and pick up Major DeWitt and me in four days."

"Why?" said Toliver.

DeWitt said, "Something very important has come up."

"It has to do with that radioman," blurted Bartholomew.

Ingram said, "Mr. Amador. Is there a place on the east coast where we could rendezvous?"

Amador poured Fundatore and then said, "I don't understand. What is so grave?"

"We can't tell you," said Ingram.

Amador looked up, his expression said "why?"

"If you're captured..." said Ingram.

"Oh," Amador said. He scratched his chin for a moment. "I suppose you could go to Lengungan Island."

"Where is that?" said Toliver.

Amador took another sip and said, "Right off Tandag village at the mouth of the Tandag River." He ran his hand through his white hair and said, "Actually the village itself would be better. I know some people, and it is well protected from the ocean."

"Tandag it is then. How far?" asked Ingram.

"Ummm, forty, fifty miles as the crow flies, across the peninsula. But it's mountain and jungle. It will take two or three days to get there."

"Can you give us a guide?" Ingram asked.

"Yes. The best."

"How so?" asked Ingram.

"Colonel Fertig. As I explained, he'll be calling here next week. Then he goes to the east coast. You can go with him. So the difficult part is for your boat. Now, have you negotiated the Hinatuan Passage before?"

"The what?" said Ingram, drawing closer with the others.

"Hinatuan Passage. You don't have to send them around Dinagat Island, you know," said Amador. "Here." He took a piece of paper, drew a chart and finished with, "Tonight, go no further than Madilao Point. A half-mile beyond that is a small village called Anason. That's where you stay." He turned to Ingram. "Is something wrong?"

Only then did Ingram realize he was absently shaking his head. He quickly said, "You sound as if they'll be expecting them."

"They will."

"How?"

Amador, the scholar from Harvard and Oxford, smiled. "I told you. We have tom-toms."

"I thought you were kidding," said Ingram.

"I'm not," said Amador, his eyes glowing. "Anason," he said, underlining the village name twice. He looked up at Toliver. This time tomorrow you'll be in the Pacific."

The Pacific: Even casual mention of that deep, rolling, blue body of water made Ingram tingle with anticipation. The other side of the Pacific bordered the western shores of the United States. Ollie and the rest of them would be in the Pacific. Helen, Rocky, Yardly, the Forester Brothers, Sunderland, all of them.

Home.

He looked at DeWitt. Both knew their chances were slim to intercept Radtke and keep him from warning the Japanese. Worse, their chances to hike over the mountains and rendezvous with the 51 Boat were, he knew, poor. He shook his head. The Tandag rendezvous, although great in promise, had little to do with what was most likely to happen.

Amador handed the sketch to Toliver who tucked it in his shirt pocket. He said, "You sure about this Todd?"

Ingram nodded, his stomach churning. "Positive. Now you and Rocky better finish loading."

Toliver said, "I think I have a right to know why you're staying."

"Ollie. Don't try," said Ingram. "Now go."

Toliver stared at Ingram for a long time, then said, "Tandag it is, then. Fifty bucks says we get there first." He extended a hand.

"You're on," said Ingram, shaking. "Otis. You better go with them and grab some weapons and ammo."

"Forty-five and a BAR okay?" DeWitt asked.

"And a Springfield," said Ingram.

Right." DeWitt walked out with Toliver and Bartholomew.

Ingram stood and walked to the window. He eased the curtain aside, seeing that it was quiet. Then he realized his fists were balled and he shoved them in his pockets. He felt as if he were drowning. Hold on! he thought.

They were going, he would remain on Mindanao to face almost certain capture. Swallowing several times, he hoped he would be up to it when it came time for the 51 Boat to shove off.

Ingram ran his hand over his mouth. Calm down, damnit! he thought.

A trace of Sunderland's cigar smoke hung in the air, reminding him of a steak and ale restaurant in Pendleton, Oregon. His parents loved to go into town on Saturday nights and eat at the Round-Up Restaurant--so named after the annual Pendleton Round-up, a cattle drive and rodeo. After dinner, his folks danced while he ran outside with his chums, sneaking cigarettes-- and tipping over outhouses.

When he was fifteen, Ingram was chosen by Daisy McDermott--reigning queen of Pendleton High's graduating class--for the Round-Up Restaurant's annual Sadie Hawkins' dance. Daisy was almost eighteen and well developed. Ingram had terminal acne. Why she choose him he didn't--

"You look tired, Señor. Sit, please, " said Amador.

"Want to make sure they think of everything," Ingram muttered, taking a seat beside Helen Durand as she finished the remains of an avocado.

"It sounds like everything has been taken care of," said Amador.

In the distance, the 110th took up Beethoven's "Fifth." Amador hummed the first bars, "'de-de-de dum... Ugh," he said suddenly knitting his brow. "What's wrong with Manolo tonight, anyway?"

Carrillo walked in, moved to the table, and spoke in Tagalog. Amador stood and listened. Then he said, "Manuel reminds me we need a new caché for our weapons in the mill before the Hapons move in. He has a couple of locations he wants to check. How soon before the boat leaves?"

"About an hour," said Ingram.

"I'll be back to see them off," said Amador, walking out with Carrillo.

Outside, the cicadas buzzed their high-pitched incessant, buzz. Inside, Lorca, Yardly, and Junior Forester snored in the shadows.

It seemed so quiet and Ingram was surprised when Helen moved close.

"Easy," she said. "Last chance to look at my handiwork." She lifted the bandage on his cheek.

"Oww, damnit." He jumped away more surprised than hurt.

"Baby," she whispered.

"Am not." He realized she was trying to cheer him up.

She paused as Lorca groaned and rolled to the wall, resuming his snoring. "Their bellies are full."

"Ummmm."

"Nice."

`"Ummmm."

"I'd better change this before..." She rose to her knees to get a better view of the cheek and in that moment shot him the quickest of smiles.

That smile more than nullified the burns on her face. Somehow, he needed to see it again so he reached up to her cheek and stroked it.

"No." She jerked away.

"Sorry."

At length, she leaned in and gently peeled the bandage off his cheek. Her closeness felt good. Then, her breath tickled his neck as it had on Corregidor. And that felt good.

She finished the dressing, caught his eye, and surrendered another brief smile. That felt good, too.

"Finally knitting, Mein Führer," she said in a clipped German accent. "You vill haf der stitches pulled in two days und you vill like it."

"Scar?"

"Jawohl, Herr Leutnant. Von Heidelberg. Seig Heil!" She thrust out an arm in a Nazi salute.

It became quiet and Ingram glanced across the room seeing that Yardly, Forester, and Lorca were in another world, the meal having done its work. Wind carried the music as the candles sputtered out one by one. And now, it seemed as if the New York Philharmonic was playing as each note, each rich phrase of "Night and Day" was executed perfectly.

"Appropriate selection," she said.

"All of a sudden it sounds like a hundred-piece orchestra."

He tugged at her hand gently; she started to move away. But then she stopped and looked down at him. Her eyes. Even with that ball cap he could still see her eyes. With a knuckle of his forefinger he leveled her chin and kissed her; tentatively at first, then fully. His hand went behind her head and he pulled her down to him. In all his life he hadn't felt anything so sweet and close and soft. She was, he knew at that moment, all he would ever need.

They parted and while she looked across the room, Ingram kissed the sores on her neck, her chin, her neck.

"No," she said.

"God, I'm glad you're here," he whispered. Helen filled him with something he knew he could never give back. Nor would he have to, for she could give it over and over again.

"Todd." She reached up and drew him to her kissing him desperately.

Forester groaned and they quickly moved apart. In the shadows, Yardly sat up, unscrewed a canteen, and held it to the bare-chested Sailor's lips.

"...easy Junior." The pharmacist's mate raised Forester's head.

Forester, his body gleaming with sweat, gulped at the canteen. Water trickled down the side of his face and neck. His voice was hoarse as he said, "That the best you can do, Bones?"

"Huh?"

"How 'bout a beer?"

Yardly chuckled. "We don't have any, kid."

Forester's voice was husky. "Saw you guzzling a San Miguel."

"Uhh. That was a going-away party."

"Why didn't you save me any?"

"Uhhh...you're too young."

"Horse crap. You owe me, Bones." Forester settled back, closed his eyes, and drifted off.

Helen whispered, "sounds better."

Ingram nodded as Yardly laid down and lapsed into easy breathing.

Filled with her richness and warmth, he clasped her face in his hands surprised, in a way that he wanted her so much; surprised that he could care so tenderly for someone when he thought he had forever left such feelings in Corregidor's gruesome wreckage. Survival had been utmost in his mind. And yet, as he looked at her, she was, in a way, survival. Unbelievable.

She didn't try to stop him as he raised a hand to her ball cap and flipped it off letting her lush, ebony hair spill about her shoulders. He stroked her hair and asked, "Your middle initial?"

"Z for Zoe."

"What does it mean?"

"Greek. It means life."

Unbelievable. He gathered her in his arms, seeing light dance on her pupils. She knew what he was thinking! She captured him with her eyes, much like when he'd first met her in Corregidor's Hospital Tunnel.

"Here." He reached in his pocket and dropped his academy ring in her hand.

"My God! Where'd you find it?"

He told her as he closed her fingers over it, kissing her on the forehead then fully on the mouth.

After a while he said, "Would you call my Mom when you get to Australia?"

"That's your job. I'll see you in four days."

"In case I'm not there, tell her--"

She put her hand over his mouth. "Four days, damnit. Don't let me down."

"If I don't make it" he said, kissing her ear. "Hell, I don't know. Just tell Mom...ohhh."

"What?"

He choked in the nape of her neck. "God. I don't feel brave."

She held him, stroking the back of his head. "Todd, what's all this about brave? None of us are brave. We just do what we have to do."

"I tell that to my Sailors. Some of us just crap in our pants more than others."

"Well, don't worry about it."

There was a long silence. He took a deep breath saying, "I know." He looked at her. "I feel dumb."

"Feeling chicken is okay. Feeling dumb is a luxury."

He grinned. "Why is that so damned funny?"

"I don't know. Now tell me. Where is your mother?"

"Pendleton." Geez, her eyes. The hell with it. He pulled her tight and kissed her again. They held each other for a moment, then she rested her head on his shoulder.

"What about your Pop?" she asked.

"Gone. Car wreck my junior year."

"I'll call her."

"Thanks. And when I get out of here, I'll--what? Find you in Ramona?"

"Durand Ranch. We're in the book."

Again he kissed her, harder than before, as the music came in stronger than before.

But this time it was a lone trumpet. Its notes were long and mournful and tugged at his mind. In one sense the melody was rude and crass and caustic yet beautiful, rich, and completely fulfilling, and it had nothing to do with Helen and what they were doing--yet demanded his attention.

He pulled away. She looked up at him, her lips still parted.

There it was! He sat straight up and cocked an ear to the window.

"What is it?" She sat up beside him.

"Damnit."

That trumpet. Melancholy notes filtered through the little tin hut. It was a kaleidoscopic recollection he'd hoped he would never hear again. With the notes came the sound of cannon fire, Caballo Island, jail. He pressed his hands to his temples.

"Todd?" Helen searched for his eyes but they were squeezed shut. "Todd!" she demanded.

"I'm okay." He watched her swim back into focus. "For a moment, I thought I heard..."

He put his hand on her shoulders and pulled her toward him-- "Sonofabitch!" DeWitt burst into the room and stepped to the window.

A strong breeze swirled through Nasipit on its way from Butuan Bay and the Bohol Sea. With it came precise, well-turned strains of the lone trumpeter. In the sharpest detail, Ingram imagined the horn's gleaming lacquered brass bell weaving before its master whose notes embroidered the night with his macabre message.

He jumped to his feet and joined DeWitt at the window. He said, "The "Deguello." It's him. He must be sitting in with the 110th. The bastard is still laughing at us."

"Not us. He doesn't even know we're here," said DeWitt, propping a BAR and Springfield rifle against the wall.

"Doesn't matter. The sonofabitch is laughing." Ingram grabbed the Springfield. "Let's take care of this bastard right now. Then we can still--"

Amador and Carrillo ran in and skidded to a halt, wheezing.

"What is it?" said Ingram.

Both stood speechless as their chests heaved.

Helen got up and put her arm around Amador. "Sit," she said. "Both of you."

They sat; Helen poured water and gave it to them. "Drink," she ordered.

Amador gulped and water dribbled down his chin. He passed the cup to Carrillo, then plopped his white-silver mane against the wall. "Lieutenant Tuga," he gasped.

"What?" said Ingram and DeWitt.

Amador spat, "Lieutenant Tuga and his damned Hapons. A whole company. They're moving in tonight. And they just captured the 110th."

"How can they be captured and still keep playing?" demanded DeWitt.

Amador spat again. "I'm sure Tuga makes them play. It's for his amuse-
ment. He likes to see his prey wiggle."

"Now? Tonight?" said Ingram. "But you said--"

"I know. I know. What can I say? They're on their way here, now," said
Amador.

"Let's shove the boat off chop, chop. Get your stuff, Helen." said Ingram.
He started for the door.

Bartholomew caromed into the hut and whipped off his hat.

"What is it?" asked Ingram.

Bartholomew shook his head. "Engine won't start. Battery's dead."

"What?" said Ingram and DeWitt.

"Damn thing's flatter'n a pancake. Won't even turn."

49

Ingram demanded. "But you recharged it."

"Yessir. Worked great two hours ago," said Bartholomew.

"What happened?" asked Ingram.

"Just gave out. Dead cell, I imagine."

"Look, Rocky. We just got word. Japs are moving in tonight."

"No shit?" said Bartholomew.

"So, recharge it again," said DeWitt.

Bartholomew whipped off his hat. "Ask Carlos. The charger belongs to his cousin." The dead battery had been taken to Carlos Ramirez's cousin, a mechanic with a decent inventory of tools.

"And Carlos's cousin lives five miles away," said Amador.

"The hell you say," said Bartholomew.

With mournful strains, the *Deguello* started again. Abruptly, it stopped, a note going sour.

"Rocky," Ingram sputtered, his fists jammed in his pockets.

"Sir?" Bartholomew waited with arched eyebrows.

Ingram's tongue finally connected. "We have to get you out tonight."

"Sir, don't I know it." said Bartholomew.

"You're sure it's the battery?" asked Ingram.

"Nine innings," said Bartholomew.

"Damn!" said Ingram. "Come on." He stepped through the door.

"Todd?" said DeWitt. He almost had to run to catch up.

Ingram stopped and pointed at the hut. "Otis, load Forester. Grab Lorca."

DeWitt said, "You're sending that nut case?"

"Might as well," said Ingram. "Two medics taking care of two wounded sailors aren't bad odds. He looked over his shoulder seeing Helen and Yardly nod "okay."

"But how?" asked DeWitt.

"Don't know. With the tide, if it's on slack. Or rig a sail. Maybe, they can pole or row the damn thing out of the harbor. At least back to the Kinabhangan River. Otherwise, the 51 Boat stays for the rest of the war under that wharf, with Japs goose-stepping overhead." He snapped his fingers. "I know. Let's tow it out with Carrillo's little boat.

Bartholomew muttered, "May as well try." He ran past Ingram toward the dirt road. "I'll wind up the boys."

"Otis. Can you help Bones with the stretcher?" asked Ingram.

"Of course." DeWitt spun and dashed into the hut. Ingram watched him go, amazed the major hadn't complained.

They walked quickly around the lumber mill toward the wharf. Amador said, "I'll speak with Manuel."

"Thanks." In spite of the dead battery, Ingram felt alive. He'd made a decision and something was happening. Part one of his plan would soon swing into action. They would find a battery, he was sure, or at least get the old one recharged somehow. And he and DeWitt would somehow get to Radtke. Maybe even tonight. What worried him was that it sounded as if Radtke had been sitting in with the 110th, making them sound far better than they ever had. And now, it seemed the band was in the hands of the *Kempetai*, Radtke included. Still, one sniper shot could take care of him. And they knew where to look. Maybe. Just maybe they would meet the 51 Boat in Tandag, after all. Maybe he would find his way to Australia and home.

He felt a rush of anticipation. Home.

He walked faster, calling over his shoulder, "Helen, got your gear?"

Helen quickstepped to keep up. "It's all just what Pete gave--"

A truck roared around the corner, it's headlights flashing across the mill.

"Down!" rasped Ingram. The three ducked behind a pile of empty oil drums while Guzman and Helen, not having crossed the road, ran back behind a small ship chandlery.

"My God!" Bartholomew pointed. The truck's headlights perfectly framed DeWitt and Yardly carrying a bare-chested Junior Forester's stretcher across the road.

Ingram was frozen as the truck ground to a stop. Two Japanese soldiers dressed in jungle fatigues jumped out and ran, shouting into the headlight beams. The soldiers quickly fixed bayonets and leveled their rifles at the stretcher party while the truck's doors wrenched open and three more figures stepped into the light. Two were corporals, the other an officer.

"Damn," said Ingram.

There was a rustle behind him. A chief's hat stood out against the blackness. Bartholomew's voice was hoarse as he whispered, "We can take 'em, Skipper."

"We're going to have to. Get Sunny and the others," Ingram said.

"Right here." Ingram turned hearing Sunderland's growl. His BAR was cradled in his arms. Behind, Ingram recognized the tensed silhouettes of Beardsley, Kevin Forester, Toliver, Lorca, and Manuel Carrillo.

"Anybody else have something to shoot with?" whispered Ingram.

Clothing rustled. Beardsley held up his nickel-plated revolver and cocked it. "Best I can do." The accent was Bogart.

"Damn, one pistol, one BAR." Ingram whispered. "Rocky. You and Kevin go back to the boat and grab some--"

A long, horrible scream perforated the night. They looked at the truck, seeing one of the soldiers brace a foot against Junior Forester's chest to pull his bayonet out. Just then, the other soldier plunged his bayonet deep into Forester's stomach, bringing forth another scream.

"B-R-I-A-N," roared Kevin Forester, running toward the truck.

"Do it, Sunny!" Ingram yelled, running after Forester.

Sunderland quickly sidestepped, propped the BAR on an oil drum, and opened fire.

The bullets zipped past Ingram as he and Forester ran toward the lights. There was a guttural scream. One of the soldiers spun and his rifle flew off into the dark. Another doubled up before them, the man's chest a giant red blossom.

Ingram plowed into the Japanese lieutenant, driving a fist into his stomach. The stocky man had drawn a Nambu pistol from a shoulder holster. Ingram grabbed the man's wrist, then drew back and hit him full in the nose, feeling cartilage rupture under his knuckles. But the lieutenant was incredibly strong. Even as blood gushed from his nose, he easily parried Ingram's clumsy grasp at his throat and rose to his knees, tearing his pistol-hand free.

An incredulous Ingram watched the lieutenant level his Nambu. But then there was a roar. The stocky officer seemed to launch into the fetid nighttime air as Sunderland pumped four BAR rounds into him on full automatic. The lieutenant's feet and legs came to rest in the headlight beams, his glistening, ruined upper half masked from sight.

Ingram weaved to his feet. It seemed as though dead, bloody men lay everywhere.

A sobbing Kevin Forester knelt alongside the stretcher, both arms around his brother's blood-soaked body. He pleaded, "Brian, Brian. Damnit. Come on."

Yardly knelt beside Forester and put an arm around his shoulders. He said quietly, "He's gone, Kevin."

Sunderland jogged up and kicked the soldier's bodies, making sure they were dead. "Got 'em all," he said.

"It happened so fast," said a breathless DeWitt. His raised his arms and flopped them to his sides.

"What do we do with these bodies?" said Beardsley, reloading his pistol.

Ingram said, "Let's take them over to--"

Just then another truck, then another roared around the corner followed by a third and a fourth and then three more.

"Shit! Look at 'em all," said Sunderland.

Ingram stood open-mouthed, as the trucks skidded to a halt. Their passengers jumped out among a jumble of shouts and panicked orders. One of the figures running from the third truck was tall and thin and wore a white suit: Lieutenant Tuga.

"Nail that sonofabitch." growled Ingram.

Beardsley said, "The pig-squasher." He carefully aimed his nickel-plate and fired five rounds at Tuga, the bullets digging dirt spouts around the *Kempetai* as he darted behind a water tower with a group of officers.

"Shit."

"Try your other eye, Leon," said Ingram.

"Sonofabitch. Lookit all the gear," said Bartholomew.

"Psst! Check second-to-last truck," said Sunderland.

Ingram strained to see what Sunderland was talking about. Finally, he saw it. The Japanese had jumped from their vehicles and ran swiftly for cover. But three men stood alongside one of the trucks, their hands in the air.

"Americans," said Ingram.

The first in line was tall with an athletic build and crew-cut blond hair. A bashed trumpet hung from his neck by a lanyard. Epperson's killer was about one hundred yards distant.

"Jesus, that's them." Lorca's voice was hollow. "Lil' Adolph. And that's Kimble."

"The one with the trumpet?" urged Ingram.

Lorca swallowed several times. "Yes. Radtke. That's him."

"Sunderland," barked Ingram.

"Sir?"

"See that blond one with the crew-cut?" said Ingram.

"The guy with the busted trumpet?" said Sunderland.

"Yes. Kill him. Now," said Ingram.

"What?" gasped Sunderland.

"Sunderland," screamed DeWitt. "I order you to do it! The man's a dangerous spy."

"...sssir." Sunderland took aim.

The Japanese opened fire. Bullets zipped past. "Down!" yelled Ingram, jumping behind a coconut tree. He peeked around to see Radtke beckoning. Then, Lieutenant Tuga ran toward the Americans with his pistol drawn. Standing before Radtke, Tuga suddenly nodded several times.

"Sunderland!" Ingram yelled.

Sunderland opened up but it was too late. Tuga and Radtke ducked behind the mill. The other two prisoners were quick-stepped toward the meat locker across from the mill.

Bending low, Ingram scampered to the Japanese lieutenant's corpse and snatched the eight-shot Nambu. Stuffing it in his belt, he pointed to the fallen Japanese soldiers. "Grab their rifles. Shoot out those headlights."

Toliver picked up a rifle, then ran to the truck's cab and jabbed the light switch, plunging the road into darkness.

Ingram said, "Sunderland, Toliver. Stay here and cover our retreat. Otis, let's go!" He pumped his fist up and down.

Sunderland's BAR fired on semiautomatic fire and someone screamed from among the trucks.

Forester bent to lift his brother in his arms.

"Kevin. He's gone." Yardly leaned over and tugged at Forester's elbow.

Bullets whizzed over their heads as the Japanese hesitantly returned fire, trying to figure out what they had run into.

Forester whipped his arm away from Yardly. "Leggo, you sonofabitch," he yelled.

Bartholomew yelled from behind a tree. "You're no good to us dead, Forester."

Sunderland squeezed off three shots then said, "Kevin. Damnit. All I got is one more clip. Then we're up shit's creek."

Forester sunk to his haunches and sobbed. "You guys go. I'll hold 'em off."

Ingram dashed up and said, "I'll take this end." He lifted the stretcher.

Forester looked up at him with an unfocused stare.

"Come on," shouted Ingram.

DeWitt urged from the other side of the road, "Forester, damn you. They're bound to open up with a machine gun. Maybe a mortar, anytime."

Dark figures flitted behind the mill and disappeared in the shadows. Ingram yelled, "They're trying to flank us."

DeWitt said, "Sunderland. Lay some rounds in there."

Sunderland cranked off two rounds, then ran out of ammo. Quickly he rammed in a new clip and fired three more rounds. The confident burrrrp of a Type 100, eight-millimeter submachine gun was his answer. "They're going to have us boxed in," said Ingram. He glanced to the left, seeing bandy-legged figures dash among the buildings opposite the mill. "We have to move."

Rifle shots rang out from behind the mill. A woman screamed.

Ingram felt as though his blood had frozen. "Helen!" He looked around in panic. "Where is she?"

"Who?" shouted DeWitt.

"Helen. She was over there." Ingram pointed to where the submachine gun muzzle flashes had originated.

"I don't know, but we better hustle," said DeWitt.

Bullets zinged above their heads and cut through the trees. Now, there were muzzle flashes from the group on the left. Instinctively, Ingram ducked and opened his mouth to yell at Forester, when he spotted the body of the Japanese sergeant who had fallen nearby. A hand grenade was clipped on the man's belt. He stooped and wrenched it off the corpse and held it up. "Otis?"

"Do it!" shouted DeWitt.

Ingram pulled the pin, hurled the grenade and ducked.

An explosion ripped the night, lifting the front end of the third truck off the ground. By the light flash, Ingram saw nobody was in the truck but the detonation set off its fuel tank sending flames curling into the fourth truck where he did hear shouts and screams.

A low, resonant moan filled the night. It wasn't human, and for a moment they looked around trying to see what it was. After another moan, Ingram saw a beast kicking its hind legs. It was the carabao. Bartholomew had used it earlier to lower the fuel drum down to the boat. They had left him tethered to a bollard on the pier.

"Socrates," said Bartholomew,.

Ingram stood and yelled, "Come on." He looked down, "You, too, Forester." Desperately, he scanned the darkness. Helen! Where the hell are you? Last time he'd seen her, she was about fifty yards back, about to cross the road with Guzman.

A wide-eyed Kevin Forester lay over his brother's wrecked corpse, protecting it with outstretched arms, the fire's orange-red light dancing on his face. With a whimper, he looked up dumbly to Ingram.

Ingram couldn't distinguish Forester's low moans from those of the carabao. But he picked up an end of the stretcher and dragged it toward the furiously beckoning DeWitt.

Another explosion tore through the night. Socrates bellowed again as the second truck, a captured American six-wheeler, rose and flipped on its back like a moribund dung beetle.

The blast knocked Ingram over. "Ammo truck," Ingram rasped, picking himself up. The buildings around them were ablaze. One of them, a dry, wooden contraption whose sign announced a ship's chandlery collapsed to the earth. Small caliber bullets aboard the ammo truck cooked off, making the Japanese scamper.

"Now's our chance," said DeWitt hoarsely.

Amador stood to run, but the Japanese fire suddenly resumed, more deadly than before. He dropped behind a tree and shouted, "Wait! Luis Guzman. The Hapons captured him."

A barrage of gunfire stitched the dirt about them. "Move! Now!" ordered DeWitt.

"That means they have Helen," Amador said.

Ingram stood numbly, refusing to let the realization sink in.

"We gotta go," said DeWitt.

Amador needed no urging as rifle fire raked the tree limb just above his head. He whipped off his planter's hat, stooped over, and rushed past DeWitt into darkness.

Ingram froze and looked toward the mill. It was too dark. He couldn't see movement. He'd taken a couple of steps in that direction, when he heard a plaintive voice behind. "Okay, Mr. Ingram."

He looked back. Forester stood at his end of the stretcher, waiting patiently for Ingram to help carry his brother.

"Todd, damnit! Get moving!" shouted DeWitt.

Beardsley, Toliver, and Sunderland ran. A fusillade of bullets followed as they melted into the darkness.

"Now!" DeWitt quickly fired three rounds from his rifle.

"Helen!" Ingram shouted.

"Mr. Ingram?" Forester tugged from his end, tears running down his cheeks.

Socrates gave another long, mournful howl, while Ingram picked up the stretcher's end. With the convoy burning, he and Forester ran into darkness.

50

Trucks rumbled through Nasipit, shaking the ground as they clattered past the Carrillo's hut. One stopped down the road. Shouts tore the night, then the soldiers reboarded, and the truck drove off.

"Sonsabits damn angry," said Carrillo. He lifted the burlap curtain and peered into darkness.

"Little bastards just about outflanked us," said Sunderland, standing next to him.

"Safe here," said Carrillo. "Not so with Luis."

Amador sat on a bench and said, "Pray the Hapons didn't take him alive."

He looked nervously up at Beardsley and Ingram. The two stood in the middle of the dirt floor like eleventh graders staring each other down in the schoolyard. Ingram's hands were on his hips. His cheek bandage had been torn away, and the wound, although well sutured, still suppurated. Beardsley's arms were crossed over his chest, his face puffy and inflamed.

"Who the hell was supposed to watch her?" Ingram demanded.

Beardsley said, "Take it easy, hothead. It was you who ran after Forester like Jack Armstrong with his pants on fire."

Forester jumped up and stepped before Beardsley. "That was my brother the Japs bayoneted you piece of--"

"Shut up, Kevin," hissed Bartholomew. "There's enough crap going on here." He grabbed Forester by the elbows and yanked him to a bench.

Beardsley grunted and sat.

Ingram counted to ten then said, "What was I supposed to do?" He tilted his head toward Forester. "He ran right at them."

Amador's eyes swept from Beardsley to Ingram. "Gentlemen, please. Arguing is not going to bring either one of them back."

"I say let's go after them." said Ingram.

"You mean an assault?" said Amador.

Ingram nodded. "Tonight."

Amador sighed, "Not tonight. There must be two hundred Hapons out there. We don't have a prayer of getting organized. And our guns and ammunition are still under the floor of the mill."

Ingram leaned against the wall and absently massaged his temples.

Amador moved over. "What's wrong?"

"She's right back in Tuga's lap."

With hope in his voice, Amador said, "Perhaps he'll just send her to Santo Tomas."

"I don't think she'll accept this again. I think she'll kill herself."

"You shouldn't think that," Amador said. "Tuga has his hands full. He'll send her away."

"In a pig's eye. She's his late-night entertainment."

"We don't know if she's captured for sure," Amador said.

"Don't we?"

Amador shrugged.

"Well, I'm not going to stand by and--"

"You about finished?" Otis DeWitt's nasal twang was truculent.

"What?" barked Ingram.

"Radtke, damnit. What do we do about the sonofabitch?" growled DeWitt.

"That the guy you wanted me to cut down?" asked Sunderland.

Ingram nodded. He'd forgotten all about Radtke. "Major DeWitt was correct when he said the man is a dangerous spy."

"What'd he do? He don't look like a Jap." said Sunderland.

"We can't tell you," said Ingram.

Toliver's voice cut through the darkness. "Todd. Where would we be if you and Major DeWitt weren't looking for a radio?" Everyone turned to look at him. "Where would we be if you hadn't found it necessary to stop at Nasipit?"

DeWitt said, "Mr. Toliver. We have stated over and over that--"

"Would we be through the Surigao Straits by now?" Toliver softly interrupted. "Maybe halfway down Mindanao's east coast?"

All eyes snapped to Ingram. A minute passed. Ingram said. "Most likely."

"Then why are we still here?" Toliver's voice rang like a courtroom barrister.

Ingram said, "We're here because Leon's B-17 deal seemed like a much better alternate to transiting the Surigao Straits and a fifteen-hundred-mile voyage through enemy waters."

Toliver stood. "And if you hadn't needed a radio nor were chasing this spy, would you have taken up Beardsley's offer?"

Ingram stammered, "Most likely not. But on the other hand, had the B-17 been flyable, we--"

"In other words, we'd be halfway to the Dutch East Indies by now," said Toliver staring at DeWitt.

The major averted his eyes to the floor.

"That's right," said Ingram.

Toliver said, "Skipper. I don't question what you believe your duty is, but I think we have a right to know. After all, some of us have already given their lives."

"Starting with Bucket Mouth," said Sunderland.

Their eyes bored into Ingram.

Ingram said, "Okay--"

"Lieutenant?" said DeWitt, his voice filled with menace. "I forbid you to--"

"Shut up," Ingram shouted. "I'm in charge here and next time you interrupt me I'm going to throw you to the Japs. Understood?"

DeWitt spun on his heel, walked to the far wall, and leaned there glowering.

Ingram took a deep breath. "You might already know about this guy. His name is Walter Radtke. But that's probably an alias. He worked in the Intercept Tunnel in Monkey Point."

"Crypto Whiz?" asked Toliver.

"That's right. He murdered Dwight Epperson, a classmate of mine, who was his boss."

"That the guy with all the scalp sores who came out to the ship one night?" asked Bartholomew.

"That's him," said Ingram.

"I see. And this Radtke is trying to sell something he learned at Monkey Point to the Japs," said Toliver.

"That's what we're up against," said Ingram.

DeWitt said from the corner, "The information is so grave that it will cost us the war, if the enemy finds out."

Sunderland whistled, "So we really have to kill the sonofabitch?"

Ingram said, "The sooner the better. But someone has to warn our people, too."

"Won't have to if we pump him full of lead," said Beardsley.

"Leon, he may have already talked," said Ingram.

Toliver said, "It's too soon for the Japs to have got their radio up and running. Maybe we can still do something."

"That's why you been looking for a radio all this time?" asked Bartholomew.

Ingram nodded.

Forester moaned, sitting with his head in his hands.

"He going to be okay?" Ingram asked.

Yardly replied, "Sprained wrist. I'm going to wrap a splint." He mouthed to Ingram, "He's too upset to notice pain."

Forester moaned again. He jerked from Yardly and stood. His eyes were red and tears ran down his cheeks. "Look, Sunny, Chief. You guys head for the mountains. I'll blow away your spy and catch up later."

Bartholomew said, "Kevin, time's past for heroes."

"But you won't make it." Forester balled his good fist and smacked the wall making it rattle. "I can keep the Japs off you. I'm the key. You should..."

Bartholomew eased Forester back to the bench. "Come on, Kevin," he said. "Time for Bones to splint your arm. It may hurt." He hung a forearm around Forester's neck and nodded to Yardly.

"Okay." Yardly laid two lengths of soft wood on Forester's forearm and started wrapping.

"You're gonna be fine, Kevin," said Sunderland. "We don't need no rear guard."

As Yardly wrapped, Forester sat rigidly against the wall, trying to stuff his knuckles in his mouth. He squeezed his eyes shut and moaned only once.

"Damnit. We have to do something," Ingram said, watching Yardly twirl the tape.

Bartholomew pushed his cap back on his head and rested his hands on his hips. "We have a choice, Skipper? The battery is toasted which means the boat is toasted. With Japs camped in the mill, how the hell do we get out without being shot to pieces?"

DeWitt nodded solemnly. "I believe it's time to consider moving into the mountains."

In exasperation, Ingram asked, "Are you sure they're setting up a full-time garrison?" Ingram asked Amador.

Amador nodded. "That is my understanding. The crates and equipment in their convoy seem to verify that."

Ingram asked, "That means they'll have a radio?"

"Awww, Todd," said Beardsley.

"Most likely," said Amador.

Yardly spun the tape around Forester's splint.

Ingram watched for a moment then shouted, "That's it!" He threw his hands in the air.

"What the hell?" said DeWitt.

"Bones, how many of those splints do you have?" asked Ingram.

Yardly looked up and said, "A couple."

"We're going to need more than that," said Ingram. "Where did you get them?"

Yardly nodded to the corner.

Ingram walked over, stooped on his haunches, and rummaged through a wood pile. Some of the pieces seemed like ordinary shingles. "You cut splints from that?"

Yardly nodded, looking nervously up as a truck rumbled past. The ground shook again and each man seemed to draw into himself for a moment.

"Lot of Japs out there," muttered Ingram.

"I'll say," said DeWitt.

"So, who's minding the store?" said Ingram.

"What are you driving at?" said DeWitt, raising himself to his feet.

Ingram stood and put his hands on his hips. "Get over here, Otis. Everybody, listen up. Here's what we're doing."

The rumble of trucks was now concentrated in the southeastern section of Nasipit, leaving the way clear to the wharf. Keeping in shadows, they crept through a palm grove close to the tide's meander line, their boots crunching in sand. A soft, quarter moon illuminated Ingram's watch: 10:47.

"We'll leave you here," said Amador, drawing to a halt. Amador carried a Thompson submachine gun in the crook of his arm. Carrillo and Ramirez carried Japanese rifles by shoulder straps.

"I wish I could convince you to go with us," said Ingram. "I think your country needs you as a statesman. Not as a freedom fighter."

Amador smiled, "You're being kind by not saying I'm too old."

"I didn't say that. You're educated. Your country will need you when all this is over," said Ingram.

By a tiny margin, Amador's eyes narrowed. He spat, "Education. The Hapons threw education out the window when they started this filthy war."

"But--"

"Let me ask you. Have you ever spoken with your enemy before you killed him. I mean face to face?"

Ingram thought of the *Kempetai* that had shot Farwell on Marinduque. And if his pistol hadn't jammed, he would have shot Ingram, too. Another image swam into his mind. Earlier this evening, a Japanese lieutenant had aimed his Nambu straight at him. "Not yet."

"When you do, you'll find many Hapons educated. They even have college degrees. Some from the United States. But let me ask you. What good is education?"

Ingram could only say, "What?"

Amador ticked off on his fingers: "Tokyo University, Harvard, Oxford, the Sorbonne, and Heidelberg. What have they all taught us to do?" He shifted his Thompson onto his right shoulder.

"Isn't that what everyone should strive for?"

Amador's gaze was hard.

Ingram sputtered. "That we can learn and..." Under the old man's stare he couldn't finish the answer originally in his mind: create a civilized forum for understanding one another and making the best of our lives in a peaceful way. Instead he looked at the horrible scabs on Beardsley's face. "We still have a lot to learn," he said.

"Especially the Hapons," said Amador. "So much for education."

Ingram drew his eyes away and sighed. Presently, he said, "Alright." He looked around, counting heads. Then he said to Amador, "Start your ruckus in about..." Ingram checked his watch, "twenty minutes. Make it ten after eleven. Otis and I'll join you back at the hut."

"Very good." The three Filipinos started to move off.

Toliver stepped up. "Mr. Amador. If I don't see you again I want to say thank you." He offered his hand.

They shook warmly. "Come back to Mindanao, soon, and bring lots of guns," said Amador.

Beardsley grabbed Amador's hand, then gave him a bear hug. "How 'bout some slot machines and a few casinos after the war?" He swept an arm across the night sky. "Beautiful place. Sure beats Havana."

Amador grinned, "Leave the slots to Manila. We'll take the rest."

"Girls?" chuckled Beardsley.

"All you want," said Amador.

The rest of the crew bid their good-byes to Amador, Carrillo, and Ramirez. Amador's last good-bye was at the stretcher. Ingram had wondered about the wisdom of bringing young Forester's shrouded corpse along. But Kevin Forester had refused to budge without it, rejecting an offer of a hurry-up funeral. He wanted a proper burial at sea for his brother, so with splinted wrist, he and Yardly carried the stretcher.

Amador took off his floppy planter's hat, his silver-white mane spilling about his ears. He placed one hand on Forester's shoulder, the other where the sheet covered young Brian's forehead. He said, "My son. An old man's words are not enough to make up for your brother's sacrifice. But what your brother has done, what all of you have done in Mindanao, Corregidor, Bataan, Manila, Cebu, Marinduque, will long be remembered by the Philippine people. God bless your valor, unselfishly given in behalf of my country, and for all countries living under the boot of tyranny."

Forester wiped at his cheek. "Thanks."

Amador turned and said, "God go with you." Soon, Amador, Carrillo, and Ramirez disappeared among the palms.

In the pale light, Bartholomew watched them go and said, "Gonna be embarrassing if this doesn't work."

They moved off toward the mill. Sunderland took up the point with DeWitt as rear guard. Five minutes later they were within one hundred feet of the mill, where it was obvious the electricity was on once again; the wooden structure was lighted up like one of Beardsley's casinos. The enormous double doors stood wide open and inside, nails screeched as men pried open crates with crowbars while others pounded hammers assembling furniture.

Ingram and his men bent low and slogged along the tide line until they trudged into deep shadows. Finally, the wharf loomed directly overhead. It was so dark that when Bartholomew stopped, Ingram nearly bumped into him.

The Chief whispered, "Sunny's peeking over the top."

It seemed like hours before Sunderland materialized out of the gloom and whispered, "Two guards. That's it. They're both in front. We should be okay. Lotsa people inside, making themselves at home. Er..." Sunderland hesitated, "There's another crew on the roof setting up an antenna."

"You sure nobody's on the wharf?" asked Ingram.

"Just Socrates," said Sunderland.

Ingram turned to Forester and Yardly. "Remember, first thing you two do is dig out the oars. I want them ready to go." The oars were stored in the bilge, under food crates and other gear. Bartholomew was certain one was wedged beneath a full drum of fuel oil. The oars would be critical if his plan didn't work.

"Okay, Skipper," said Yardly, glad to have the chance to set the stretcher down for a moment.

They were bunched at the wharf's ladder. Sunderland crawled back up, studied the mill for a moment, then said, "Now!"

Sunderland zipped over the top, followed by Bartholomew. Ingram was third, running at a crouch toward Socrates. The massive beast blinked and switched his tail, as they took temporary refuge behind an ancient steam-driven crane. After a moment, they scampered down a ladder and stood on a log piling that floated alongside the wharf. It was a big wharf, built for ocean-going ships. The top was about twelve feet above the water at high tide and was supported underneath by a forest of creosoted pilings. Tucked among a row of pilings was the 51 Boat, pitching and bucking with occasional wavelets that swept in from the sea.

They wove their way in toward the bobbing boat.

"Damnit!" Yardly cursed, as he and Forester worked the stretcher around a piling.

"Easy with my brother, you dope." growled Forester.

"Doing my best." moaned Yardly.

"Shut up, you two," hissed Ingram. He pointed up. "Sunderland. Stand guard."

"Yes, Sir," said Sunderland, picking his way back to the ladder.

Bartholomew was first to step into the 51 Boat. Ingram followed and started taking off the engine cover. As the others piled in, Bartholomew clicked on his flashlight. "Where?"

Ingram checked the drive shaft, then looked up to the underside of the wharf deck about ten feet above their heads.

He pointed to the drive shaft near the clutch coupling. "There." He looked straight up and pointed. "Ollie. The spring line should be long enough. Tie it off there."

With surgical tape, Bartholomew wrapped four of Yardley's splints around the 12-inch drive shaft and the coupling, building it with tape and wood until it was all roughly four inches in diameter. While Bartholomew worked, Toliver stood on cross members and tied the Boat's spring line directly above them with a bowline hitch, leaving a long tail. He jerked the line twice to test it, then jumped in the boat letting the line dangle directly over the splinted drive shaft.

"Okay, Skipper," said Bartholomew.

"Sunderland?" said Ingram.

The gunners mate's whisper careened throughout the pilings. "All clear."

Bartholomew looked at Ingram. "All yours, Skipper."

"You do it, Rocky," said Ingram.

"Okay." Bartholomew grabbed the line. "How many?"

"Three turns should do it," said Ingram. "Wait 'til we're on top."

"Three it is," muttered Bartholomew, leaning over. He looked outside the boat, gauging its motion in relation to the pilings as it bobbed up and down. He looked out into the harbor, sensing a larger swell. "Hold it...hold...Now!"

Bartholomew quickly wrapped the line three times around the shaft, as the 51 boat rose on the wave. At the wave's crest, he snubbed it firmly, holding the turns around the shaft. The wave fell, causing the line to tighten around the shaft, making the shaft spin. The pistons pumped up and down in their cylinders with a resounding *brrrp*.

The line slacked as the boat rose on the next wave. Bartholomew eased it off. "Damnation," he giggled. "Twenty-two to one compression ratio, and it works."

"Why didn't it start, Chief?" asked DeWitt.

"It would of." He grinned. "I didn't have fuel system on."

"Quiet, damnit," said Ingram, checking his watch. "We wait for Amador." Amador had promised to fire a few rounds and toss some grenades to mask the roar of the 51 Boat's diesel when it started.

Bartholomew whispered, "Let's roll it again. Really get it loose, and heat up the cylinders. Help it to properly fire when it's time."

"Sssst!" from Sunderland. "Apsjay," he whispered.

"I better check," said Ingram. He jumped out of the boat and ran out to the piling.

Sunderland crouched on the ladder and whispered, "Two guy's strolling along the edge of the wharf having a smoke. Almost here."

Ingram pointed to the ladder, indicating he wanted to take a look.

Sunderland lowered himself and stepped aside. Ingram climbed quietly and peeked over the top, seeing two officers walk toward him. Their voices, in conversational tones, reached him and he ducked. Seeing Sunderland, he gave a thumbs up, indicating the pair would soon be past.

The boat thumped against a piling. "Arrrgh!" It was a loud roar of pain.

A lighted cigarette twirled overhead and hissed in the water directly behind Ingram. One of the Japanese grunted. A hand slapped a leather holster. Ingram instantly knew what had happened--as well as what he had to do.

A wave had slammed the 51 Boat into a piling. Someone, it sounded like DeWitt's voice, had wrapped his hand over the gunnel where the boat struck the piling. By now DeWitt's hand could well be broken.

Knowing he would suffer more than a few broken fingers, Ingram dashed up the ladder and started running toward the beach. "Arrrgh!" He mimicked, his hands flailing in air.

The officers shouted. One fired his pistol from twenty feet away. The bullet zipped past Ingram's ear. He felt the wind and instinctively stopped, turned, and raised his hands as the officers ran up.

Just then an enormous bolt of pain surged in the back of his head. Ingram blinked and passed out.

51

Ingram vaguely remembered his feet bumping on rough concrete and being dragged through the lumber mill's double doors. Too weak to struggle, he was dumped at the foot of a large machine, hands and feet tied.

The throbbing in the back of his head was replaced by a gagging nausea, and sweat beaded his forehead and chest. The mill was hot, the humidity intolerable. He lay there feigning unconsciousness, holding down bile while trying to get his bearings.

Finally, he opened an eye, finding he was beside the lathe disguising the trap door to Amador's weapons caché. He moved just a bit to peek into a floor crack. There they were. Cases of rifles and ammunition lay below: .30 and .45 caliber, mortar rounds, grenades, even four cases of dynamite.

"Owwww." Someone kicked him. Slowly, he turned his head seeing a corporal standing over him. The man shouted, gesturing for him to roll over.

Lieutenant Tuga walked up, wearing white suit and white buckskin shoes. Up close, the *Kempetai* looked even taller than what Ingram remembered from the pig squashing incident: well over six feet.

"Nice nap?" Tuga squatted and fingered the insignia on Ingram's collar. "Navy lieutenant, huh? Don't you wear devices on both collars? What did you do with the other? Barter it for food, maybe?"

Ingram was astounded. Not only was Tuga familiar with U.S. Navy uniforms, his English was perfect. It was hard to imagine this was the man who had tortured Helen so horribly. He wondered how many others this creature had maimed or killed.

Tuga brushed his knuckles over Ingram's cheek. "Well?"

"Sold it to help the war effort."

Tuga chuckled. "Funny man. Scrap iron for the poor Japanese, huh? Some effort." He stared directly at Ingram. "Tell me. What do you do, Navy Lieutenant?"

"Toilet-paper man," Ingram muttered. "Hey..."

Tuga removed Ingram's collar device and dropped it in his coat pocket. "I like souvenirs. What's this, Lieutenant?" said Tuga probing Ingram's right cheek. Bracketing the sutured wound between thumb and forefinger, he squeezed.

"Ehhhagh."

"You with the submariners, Lieutenant?" Tuga squeezed a little more. "Or are you the guy who killed my platoon commander this evening?"

Hot liquid rushed down Ingram's cheek. Pain surged over the right side of his face in white-hot sheets. He screamed, knowing he couldn't have uttered an intelligible word had he wanted.

"Lieutenant, huh? Maybe the *Wolfish*'s exec, huh? What's this about toilet paper?" said Tuga, releasing the cheek. His hand rotated slightly as it withdrew, and Ingram saw a blue sapphire set in a gold class ring: University of California at Los Angeles - 1937. Tuga was a man educated at an American University. In his bitter sarcasm, Amador hadn't been far off the mark.

Ingram gasped for air and willed the pain away. Finally, he managed, "I'm a supply officer. I order things like pallet loads of toilet paper."

"Supply officer, baloney. I'll find out when--" Tuga snapped his fingers. "Hey, that nurse. She with you, maybe?"

"What nurse?"

"Helen Durand. What a sweet piece. She's looks good."

Ingram balled his fists, counting to twenty.

Tuga nodded. "That's all I need to know."

"What?"

"How'd you patch her up so well? Last time I saw her she was near dead."

Ingram kept silent; he'd blundered enough.

"No matter. I have her with your boys across the street, saving her for later. Ummm. Hot stuff. Thanks for cleaning the shit off her."

"Bastard!" Ingram couldn't' help it. An enormous wave of frustration swept over him, his worst fears confirmed. Helen was in the meat locker just sixty feet away. And this ghoul was going to do his will upon her.

Tuga leaned close and said, "Tell me Lieutenant, what's the name of your ship?"

"You got it wrong. I'm a supply--yeahhhh--"

Tuga squeezed. The wound pumped and throbbed, with Ingram fighting for consciousness.

A pail of water was dumped on him and he realized he'd passed out. He was on his stomach and blinked his eyes, watching the tall, thin *Kempetai* walk away. Tuga stepped across the room, up a ladder to a mezzanine level, where radio equipment was being set up.

Ingram gagged and choked for a moment, then tried to relax and control his breathing. Images swam into focus. He looked around counting, about twenty Japanese; some were shirtless sweating in the heat and humidity. Many smoked, generating a bluish cloud so thick it was hard to see across the room.

The soldiers were setting up desks, bookshelves, file cabinets, field telephones and map displays. Bunks were being assembled in a far corner with a wooden partition going up around the sleeping area.

Two sets of feet approached. From the corner of his eye, Ingram spotted Tuga's white bucks. The other pair of shoes were black and terribly scuffed. Filthy bellbottom dungarees were draped over them. The man was an American Bluejacket. "He claims to be a supply officer," said Tuga. "But he's a lieutenant. I'd lay money he's your exec."

"No, the exec wasn't on the raft. I'm pretty sure he went down with the sub," the Bluejacket said. Ingram had heard that voice before.

"I don't believe you."

"It's the truth. There were only six of us on that raft. One died before we reached land. Look, I keep telling you. My real name is Helmut Döttmer. Let me use that radio and I'll prove it. It will be worth your while, too. Within hours, you will be promoted to major."

Radtke! Sonofabitch.

"Why is it I don't believe you?" said Tuga.

"I'll prove it. Look. Is he wearing dolphins?"

"What?"

"Dolphins, Lieutenant. A gold insignia submariners wear over their breast pocket."

"Ah, yes. Let's see." A foot caught Ingram under the shoulder and rolled him over.

Flashing his broadest grin at an astonished Döttmer, Ingram said, "Good to see you again, Radtke. How many Japs were you able to kill before they captured you?"

"You!" roared Döttmer. In a flash he was on Ingram, looping a length of loose rope around his neck and jerking violently.

Tuga's voice pleaded. "No! No! We must interrogate. We must..."

Ingram went dim, then dark gray; blackness swam into swirls of blackness into nothing.

He awoke coughing. His neck was raw and he couldn't swallow. Deep, thumping pain ranged in the back of his head, and it took a full five minutes for the floor's wood-grain detail to pull into focus. Moving against his bindings, Ingram discovered his arms and wrists were still tightly secured, but his legs were free, and he was no longer tethered to the lathe. Risking a small head movement, he opened his left eye and looked up. The partition enclosing the sleeping area was almost complete, which meant he'd been out for a long time, maybe a couple of hours. Döttmer and the Japanese corporal who had originally kicked him to consciousness, sat on the floor beside one another about five feet opposite. The corporal loosely cradled a rifle, while Döttmer's eyes bored into Ingram.

Döttmer said, "Five more seconds and your windpipe would have been crushed like..." He cracked his knuckles. "They managed to stop me. You're lucky. You're going across the street with the others as soon as you can walk."

Ingram's voice was hoarse and he needed water. "You're welcome to join us."

"That won't be necessary. The lieutenant believes me, now." He cracked his knuckles again. "Thanks for the practice."

Ingram gagged and brought up phlegm. Finally, he choked out, "Like you practiced on Dwight?"

Ingram was surprised to see Döttmer's face darken. "I liked Mr. Epperson. He did me a lot of favors. Had me set up to go to OCS."

"And then you shoot him."

The man sniffed. "I have a job."

"What's your name?"

The bugler raised his knees to his chin, braced his arms and said. "Radtke, Walter A., cryptography technician second class, 1187526."

"I heard Döttmer."

"Up yours." He smiled.

Ingram said, "What kind of job do you have that makes you betray your country?"

Döttmer's nose flared, "I haven't betrayed *my* country, Lieutenant Ingram. But I've lived in *your* country. I know what it's like." He whipped his left hand out, holding it under Ingram's face. Trying to extend his atrophied forth finger, Döttmer's entire hand shook with the strain. He shouted, "Here is what your country did for me, Lieutenant."

"What?"

Döttmer raged, "My country doesn't let common thugs roam its streets to do things like this. And I can tell you my country doesn't open its gates to racial imbeciles. My country is not one so weak she can't feed and clothe her people. My country is not one of intellectual depravity or religious fanaticism. My country is not one governed by a constitutional system so ridiculous and so cumbersome, it openly invites incompetence and corruption and political cripples. My country is not one so militarily feeble that she cannot keep treaties such as a pledge" he waved an arm around the room, "to defend the Philippines. My country--"

From the mezzanine level across the room, Tuga yelled, "Mr. Döttmer. We're almost ready." Next to him, two enlisted men in white uniforms were hunched over a large radio transmitter. Three others eased through a trap door in the roof and dropped onto the mezzanine catwalk, pulling a long wire. Tuga stepped to the rail, letting the man with the antenna pass. "Rather than wait, I've decided to send your Midway message. Your people first, then mine. What was the frequency?"

Ingram felt as if he'd been kicked in the stomach. Midway! Tuga knew everything!

What really bothered him was the thought of these bastards working together: Radtke and Tuga. Ingram couldn't think of a worse combination than the hideous political systems these two represented. And as soon as those men connected that damned antenna now, the fruits of Radtke's work would be on the airways.

A phrase from the message Otis DeWitt had shown him, rushed with cold precision: *grave consequences to the United States.* The Imperial Japanese Navy would have plenty of time to adjust their battle plan, and spring a counter-trap on the U.S. Navy. Plus, they would have proof that Americans had cracked their code and had been reading their mail, something they had brushed aside as ridiculous two years earlier when so informed by the Germans.

Döttmer yelled from the side of his mouth, "Fifteen point seven-seven-five megacycles."

"Call signs?" asked Tuga.

"I'm HECKLE. He's BESSON." Döttmer stood. "Hold on. You better let me do it. They should recognize my fist." He walked to the ladder.

Ingram called, "Herr Döttmer."

Döttmer stopped and turned.

"Congratulations on figuring out what your country is not. Now, please tell me what your country is?"

Döttmer stroked his left hand for a moment then stuck it behind his back. "My country values creative ability, Mr. Ingram. We don't allow common criminals to run about maiming and smashing its best talent." A wisp of a smile crept over his face. "I could show you some marvelous film of--but then you'll be in a prison camp. Maybe dead." He grinned and walked toward the mezzanine ladder.

"Hey, Fritz!" yelled Ingram. "Show me now. I want to see it, big man. Show me footage on Warsaw or Coventry or Moscow."

Without a backwards glance, Döttmer waved a hand over his head and climbed the ladder to the radio platform. Just then, several trucks pulled up front. The corporal near Ingram grunted, rose to his feet and faced the door, straightening his shirt and trousers. Spreading his feet, he brought his rifle to a loose approximation of parade rest.

A guard snapped open a door, and a captain and lieutenant walked through, followed by many soldiers tossing aside packs and setting their rifles against the wall.

The officers spotted Ingram and headed toward him. They were twenty feet away when something went *Crumff* outside. Gunfire punctuated the night. Screams echoed, as an orange glare lighted the windows. Bullets stitched through the walls ricocheting off machinery.

As he drew his pistol, the captain's torso suddenly turned bright red and he clutched his throat with a horrible gurgle and spun over a desk. The lieutenant ducked and skittered behind a row of file cabinets just as another *CRACK* rattled the mill. The room filled with smoke, and the roar of automatic weapons pounded Ingram's eardrums. Men screamed and grunted, bullets finding their mark.

Struggling against his bindings, Ingram weaved drunkenly to his feet as gunfire rattled closer. He could barely see, but felt the concussions; predominant was a heavy thump, thump, thump.

A BAR. Jeez, Sunderland!

Footsteps pounded close by. A muffled voice shouted, "Todd, damnit?"

"Ollie!"

Toliver's outline appeared through the smoke, a handkerchief tied around his face, and he carried a .45 pistol. He sliced Ingram's bindings with a bayonet. "Grab my belt."

Ingram clutched Toliver's belt and tried to hold his breath. They shuffled along and the smoke spiraled through Ingram's throat and into his lungs. His eyes welled up and tears ran. There was nothing else he could do except cough, hold on tight, and stumble drunkenly behind Toliver. He stumbled and fell at the entrance.

Toliver let him go and wrenched something off his belt. He threw it inside and fell on top of Ingram.

An explosion reverberated inside shoving more smoke out the windows and door.

Döttmer yelled, "I-N-G-R-A-M." It sounded as if it came from the radio platform. Ingram looked to his left just in time. A furious, howling shape slammed past, knocking him over.

Ingram rose to his feet seeing a shape in the smoke. "Ollie?" he shouted at an advancing shape.

"Over here, pansy." Döttmer lunged with a long club. Ingram ducked. The club whooshed over his head, giving him a chance to spring into Döttmer's stomach.

He did it badly. Or perhaps Döttmer was in better shape because he grazed his side and shot across an anteroom crashing under a workbench. He'd barely straightened up when Döttmer was right there above him, a foot poised over his chest.

The kick's pain was unbelievable. Ingram realized a rib or two had broken and he sagged to the floor. But that probably saved him as the club whooshed over his head again. He rolled to see Döttmer above him.

With a flourish, Döttmer pulled out a garrote then reached down grabbing Ingram's collar. Döttmer dragged Ingram out from under the bench. In a flash the garrote was around Ingram's neck.

Ingram's tongue shot between his lips, his head spasming as Döttmer jerked and tugged.

Döttmer's knee went into the small of Ingram's back, gaining overwhelming leverage, bending him backwards. "Uhhh," grunted Döttmer, twisting the garrote with furious strength.

The lights were going out. Yet there was a roaring sensation in Ingram's ears. Bracing his back against Döttmer's knee he launched both feet in the air. His left foot found a purchase on the edge of the workbench, his right in the bench-vice. With the weight, Döttmer stumbled forward, allowing Ingram's legs to bend double.

Everything was darkness, all sensation was gone when Ingram pushed off the workbench. Both flew backward with Ingram landing on Döttmer's chest.

Döttmer grunted, easing his grip on the garrote. Ingram whipped the loop over his head taking great breaths and rolling to his side. Everything seemed white, he couldn't tell if it was still the smoke or his blurred vision. But he struggled to his feet and backed up, soon finding himself against the workbench. Something scraped close by. It was the beet-red face of Helmut

Döttmer. His thick club swung down. Just in time, Ingram stepped to the side, the club crashing on the work bench.

Döttmer swung left to track Ingram, his left wrist landed in the jaws of the open vice.

"*Ach!*" Döttmer yelled.

Ingram stepped in, delivering an enormous kick to Döttmer's solar plexus while grabbing the German's left hand, pinning it in the vice. Döttmer expelled a vast amount of air. Quickly, Ingram twirled the vice shut against Döttmer's left wrist.

Still gasping, Döttmer sunk to his knees. His lips became an enormous oval as he tried to suck air into his lungs. With eyes wide in desperation, Döttmer finally willed his right hand to raise and travel to the vice's handle to rescue his left hand. Slowly he twirled the handle, the jaws beginning to open.

Döttmer didn't see Ingram bring the club down on his head, landing with a hollow *thwack*.

Döttmer fell to his knees and groaned.

Ingram hit him again.

Hanging from the vice by his left hand, the rest of Döttmer's twitching body drooped to the floor.

He raised his club to swing again--

"Todd!"

Ingram turned as Toliver dashed up. An open mouthed Sunderland was right behind.

Ingram held out his hand. "Gimme."

Toliver turned over his .45. butt first.

Ingram secured a grip and fired two rounds into Döttmer. The corpse jinked each time then was still.

Ingram stepped up, making sure the man was dead, then walked into the smoke.

"Where you going?" demanded Toliver.

"Tuga." Ingram's voice was hollow.

Toliver rasped, "Uh, uh. Sunderland!"

Sunderland and Toliver dashed up, grabbing Ingram's elbows. Toliver grabbed his .45 away as Ingram tried to fight them off. There were two more explosions, smoke grenades, but oddly, the smoke cleared for a few seconds.

The three confused Americans gawked at about thirty confused Japanese gawking at them, everyone's weapons pointed in every direction.

Smoke closed around them and they dropped in unison as bullets zipped over their heads.

"We gotta haul ass!" gasped Sunderland, pulling them toward the door.

"That sonofabitch knows," choked Ingram.

"What?" said Toliver.

"Damned Nazi told him everything," said Ingram, rising to go inside.

With a nod to Sunderland, Toliver said, "We'll get him later." They grabbed Ingram by the armpits and yanked him out the front door.

52

21 May 1942
Nasipit, Mindanao
Philippines

Ingram burst from the smoke. Moonlight glistened off the waters of Nasipit Harbor. The air was cool, helping to clear his head as he tripped and stumbled alongside Toliver and Sunderland. "They shove off?" he gasped.

Shouts and sporadic gunfire followed them as Toliver yelled, "Not yet. Rocky's still trying to roll the engine."

That damned Buda. If it started, they could make a clean getaway, the Japanese still unaware of the boat with all the shooting.

Gunfire rang around them, tearing concrete chunks as they spun behind the large steam-propelled crane.

"Down, Skipper," said Toliver, pushing Ingram behind the treads. Bullets clanged above them, ripping jagged holes in the crane's housing. Ingram crawled past Toliver and fell alongside Major Otis DeWitt.

"Had me worried there for a moment, Lieutenant," said Dewitt. He flicked his BAR's change lever to "F" and squeezed off three rounds on semiautomatic. Beardsley and Forester were crouched nearby, also firing BARs. Behind them stood Socrates, his eyeballs jerking in their sockets. Return fire ricocheted about the crane operator's cabin. DeWitt cranked out two rounds and shouted, "More Japs."

Ingram peeked around the treads. Four more trucks pulled up to the mill, a wake of swirling dust behind them. Soldiers jumped to the ground and ran inside.

Ingram coughed to clear smoke from his throat. His voice was raspy as he wheezed, "Helen and the others. Can we reach them?"

DeWitt said, "Amador and Ramirez are trying to bust 'em out right now."

"Let's go help."

"Can't," said DeWitt. "I told him we would shove off right after we got you out. Plus, we're pinned here, anyway."

"I'm not going."

"Yes, you are," said DeWitt.

Ingram pointed at the mill. "Tuga. He--"

A breathless Pablo Amador materialized out of darkness. "There are forty, fifty men in there, now. They can easily wipe us out."

Ingram demanded. "What about Helen? Luis? The others?"

"Still in the meat locker. We were getting ready to charge when that convoy drove up. Too many Hapon, now."

"You mean you can't get them out?" roared Ingram.

Amador shook his head. "Impossible."

DeWitt interrupted, "Why haven't they tried to flank us?"

Amador said, "They aren't exactly your crack, front-line troops. Remember these are bullies and convicts. They'll get to it soon enough."

Suddenly, rifle fire poured from the mill, the noise deafening. Muzzle flashes blossomed and cordite smoke gushed out windows and doors. Over the din, a whistle blasted, with men darting from each side of the mill to disappear into shadows.

"Pretty soon," said Sunderland. "We gotta decide."

Something rumbled beneath their feet. A roar rose from under the wharf accompanied by a cloud of black smoke. Bartholomew jazzed the Buda's throttle, clearing its injectors. "Hot damn," said Beardsley.

Amador shouted, "You must go. Now!"

They ducked again as bullets punched holes in the crane's truss work.

"Otis," Ingram called.

"Yeah?"

"Radtke's dead, but that other bastard knows the whole story."

DeWitt cranked off a round, emptying the magazine. "Who?"

"Tuga."

"You sure Radtke told him everything?"

"Well...I think so."

"You find out who Radtke really was?"

Ingram said, "His name was Dittman or something like that. He was a damned Nazi."

"Figures," said DeWitt.

"What was that, Mr. Ingram?"

Ingram spun, surprised to see the submariner Lorca beside him with a BAR. "You belong in the boat," said Ingram.

Lorca's eyes were clear, his lips pressed with his jaw set in fierce determination. "You said that sonofabitch was a Nazi?"

"Best we can tell," said Ingram. "But he's dead now, son."

"That's why..." Lorca stood, shaking off Ingram's frantic hand. "Radtke, you dirty bastard," he yelled.

"Lorca. Radtke's dead, I said," said Ingram.

Unaccountably, it became quiet.

Lorca rose to his feet and opened fire, emptying his clip. The soldiers in the mill started firing at the same time. Ingram reached up to grab Lorca, but the radioman doubled up and flew back five feet, falling with a grunt.

"Lorca!" yelled Ingram scrambling over to him.

Lorca's face had the opened-mouthed look of one struck hard in the stomach. Ingram thought he was dead, but the man stirred, sat up, and fidgeted at his belly. Finally, Lorca pulled his belt out of the loops and dangled it high in the air. "Can't do anything right you stupid sonsabitches!" He yelled and shook the belt, it's buckle horribly mangled. "Come on, you little--"

"Quiet!" shouted DeWitt.

Lorca looked down at DeWitt, "huh?"

"Get in the boat," hissed Ingram, grabbing Lorca's BAR. He pointed to the wharf's edge.

"Yessir." Lorca crawled to the edge, threw a leg over, and was gone.

The firing suddenly increased in ferocity. Beardsley screamed and rolled over, holding his leg. Ingram barked to Toliver, "Get him below and make ready to shove off."

Thirty or forty rifles must have fired at once, the noise deafening. Then it subsided. DeWitt's voice was shaky. "They're getting ready to rush."

Ingram said "There's gotta be a way to stop that Jap."

DeWitt shrugged. "No grenades. How 'bout dynamite?"

Ingram said, "...like light the sticks and throw them?"

"I guess. Got any better ideas?" asked DeWitt.

Amador said, "Dynamite?"

Ingram said, "Four cases in the boat. Two are yours, remember?"

Amador said, "Quickly. Here is what we must do."

They nodded as Amador spoke. But then DeWitt said, "Jesus!"

Amador said, "It's not original with me. The Moros did it, then Aguinaldo. After that--"

"We don't have a choice." Ingram said. "Come on."

The Japanese started firing and the foursome had to crouch low to the ground with the slugs slamming into the crane and punching holes in the upperworks like invisible jackhammers. Suddenly, the firing tapered off. Ingram took his hands off his ears, leaned over the wharf and said, "Forester, send up two cases of dynamite, primer caps, and paint thinner."

While Sunderland and Dewitt reached for the dynamite crates, Ingram and Amador caught Socrates' tether and drew the moaning beast right up to the treads.

The shooting stopped just as DeWitt hoisted the dynamite crates over the ledge.

A voice called out. "All right, Mr. Ingram. We're impressed." It was Lieutenant Tuga. "Tell you what. Throw down your weapons and we won't harm you. You'll receive fair treatment and will be housed with the prisoners across the street. Otherwise, we have two beautiful seven-point-seven-millimeter type-92 machine guns now being uncrated in your honor. They'll be ready in about three more minutes."

Sunderland said softly, "Doubt if these jerks know how to set up a machine gun."

A loft window just above the main doors squeaked open. "Well?" Tuga yelled as a muzzle mounted on a bipod poked out.

Ingram hoisted a case of dynamite on Socrates' left side and started tying it off. DeWitt did the same with a case on the right side.

"We need more time. Stall them," rasped Amador.

Ingram cinched down his case and stepped back. Sunderland moved up and primed the dynamite sticks.

Ingram yelled toward the mill, "How can I be sure you won't hurt us?"

DeWitt yanked at a hitch on the right side and said softly, "All set."

Tuga's voice seemed offhand, even casual. "To be honest, Mr. Ingram, my boys are very angry for what you've done this evening. But I'll take care of that. You have my word we won't harm you. But if you insist on staying out there we'll chop you to pieces. Now, what is it?"

Sunderland worked quickly with knife and fingers. Amador leaned in helping. He looked at Ingram and hissed, "More time."

"What about my wounded?" yelled Ingram.

"No more crap, Ingram," yelled Tuga. The machine gun in the loft window spewed out five rapid rounds with a great roar. The crane shook and rattled as bullets thumped against it. The heavy gauge glass in the operator's cabin shattered and tinkled about.

There was a loud clack, then a curse from the hayloft.

"Told you so," muttered Sunderland, working his fuses with deft strokes. "Dumb Nip didn't clean off all the cosmoline."

"Hurry, before he does," urged Ingram.

With a grunt, Sunderland twisted the end of a primer cord. "Set."

"Ready?" asked Amador.

"That's it," said DeWitt

Ingram whispered, "Commence fire!"

Sunderland, DeWitt, and Toliver opened up with their BARs. They were rewarded with a grunt inside the hayloft.

They fired again as Ingram lead Socrates into the open, guiding him so he directly faced the mill's double doors, a hundred fifty feet away. Quickly, Ingram stepped behind the beast and lifted its tail while Amador drenched Socrates' genitals with paint thinner. The beast moaned loudly, his eyes twitching back and forth.

"Okay, Sunny!" said Ingram.

Sunderland crawled over, flicked his Zippo cigarette lighter, and held the flame to the dynamite fuses. Satisfied they sputtered correctly, he picked up his BAR and started shooting again.

Amador flicked his engraved gold Ronson and held it close to Socrates' tail.

The beast's rear end caught fire with a *whump*.

Socrates reared up and loosed a mighty bellow, his front feet clawing in space. Then the Carabao came to ground roaring, and galloped for the double doors. Ten feet short of the doors, he stopped and twirled, bucking and kicking his front and hind legs. Then he ran parallel to the lumber mill away from the door, still bellowing.

Suddenly, Socrates stopped, kicked, and charged again toward the doors trailing a veil of blue-black smoke.

"In the boat, quick," said Ingram. They crawled over the wharf as Socrates twirled another kicking revolution in slow motion.

The Carabao, his rear end still afire, broke into a gallop. He didn't quite make the mill's entrance, but hit the doorjamb at full speed, collapsing the frame with a mighty crunch and disappearing inside with a long, mournful bellow. Shouts rang inside. A scream was cut short by a ripping crash--

The mill erupted in an enormous explosion, throwing planks, machinery, and flame in every direction. Even from their refuge under the wharf, Ingram felt intense heat as the concussion whipped overhead, sweeping pallets and loose gear into the bay as if backhanded by a giant arm.

Ingram climbed up the ladder.

"Where you going?" DeWitt shouted.

"Have to make sure," said Ingram. He peeked over the ledge seeing enormous flames roil into the sky. The mill was gone, the palm grove next to it was afire, and trucks were overturned in front as if they were toys tossed aside by a careless child.

Ingram climbed down meeting DeWitt and Amador at the 51 Boat's gunnel. "Well?" said DeWitt.

"Nobody could have lived through that." Ingram said.

DeWitt grunted. "Nothing else we can do. Let's go."

"Shove off," Ingram said, standing back.

"Aren't you coming?" asked DeWitt.

"Negative," said Ingram. "I'm going with Amador to spring out the people in the meat locker," His face darkened for a moment, "If it's still standing."

DeWitt said, "Lieutenant. You are the best qualified to navigate and safely land us in Australia. Therefore, your responsibility is to your crew. Not," he nodded toward the meat locker, "to her, I'm afraid."

Even before the words were out, Ingram knew DeWitt was right. "But..."

Amador squeezed Ingram's shoulder and said, "Go! We'll do our best."

"Come on, Todd," said Toliver.

Ingram looked around the boat. Firelight danced on the eyes of his men much as firelight had danced on the eyes of the poor souls who watched them push off that last, hideous night on Caballo Island. The difference was, the others had given up. They didn't want to go. But these men were survivors; they had earned their chance at freedom. They needed him. And yes, Otis was right, they were his responsibility.

Ingram turned to Amador. "Can you check tonight?"

Amador said, "Don't worry. As you can see, the Hapons have plenty to do besides bothering about what's in a meat locker. We'll get them. The important thing is for you to go. As you told me, *you* know too much, I'm afraid."

"Makes sense, Todd," said DeWitt, quietly. "We do know too much."

Ingram thought about that and decided for once, Otis was right. With a nod, he stepped in the boat. Reaching up he took both of Amador's hands and said, "Take care of yourself, Don Amador. We'll have to have another discussion about the merits of education when this is all over."

Amador grinned. "Over cigars and Brandy?"

"Only if you bring the Fundatore."

"Consider it done," said Amador. "Here." He reached in his pocket and produced a thick envelope. "For my wife, would you mind?"

Ingram stuffed it in his pocket. "Glad to do it. Would you like me to call her too?"

Amador nodded.

"What's her name?"

With a coy smile he said, "Mariveles."

"Mar--I'll be damned," said Ingram, remembering the night he'd delivered Helen Durand and Pablo Amador to the *Wolfish*. The old man had told the legend of Corregidor to them. Mariveles was the nun who had fallen in love with El Fraile.

"Except we got together. We've been married thirty-four years and my daughter and son are with her in New Mexico."

"But now, there's a big marsh between you."

Amador nodded and looked in the distance for a moment. He said, "Tell her I'm fine; that I love her and miss her terribly--that this is going to take much longer than I thought. It's all in the letter." Then he whipped off his planter's hat and jammed it on Ingram's head. "Without this," he said, "the sun will drive you loco. *Via con Dios!*" He scrambled out of the pilings and headed for the trees.

With a little throttle, Forester guided the 51 Boat out from under the wharf, as pistol and rifle ammunition from Amador's weapons caché cooked off.

Soon they were clear and Ingram said, "Step on it, Rocky."

Bartholomew fed in full throttle and the 51 Boat surged into Butuan Bay. They looked back, seeing a waving figure backlighted under the palms by ghostly orange flames. "Thanks for everything, Mr. Amador," they yelled. "We'll be back. We'll be back."

Forester planted his feet and eyed his binnacle, making sure the 51 Boat was on course for Anason. Ingram looked back one last time. Amador's figure still was outlined by flames leaping from what once was his lumber mill. And as they cleared the harbor, Ingram saw to his relief that the meat locker across the street still stood, miraculously unharmed by the blast.

Two hours after clearing Nasipit, they saw just one ship. She was a lean destroyer, steaming southeast at high speed toward a diminishing blaze on Mindanao's north coast, her course taking her within three miles of the 51 Boat.

Three hours later the moon slipped beneath a cloudless horizon and the 51 Boat hove to, rocking in a slow, rolling sea, her engine barely ticking over. The crew rose to their feet and nervously braced against one another, as their captain searched through the *Book of Common Prayer*--the one liberated from the *Pima*. With a nod, Ingram found the passages and started reading. At first, his words were jumbled and uncertain. But he took a deep breath and found a pace. His voice was clear when he read:

...we commend to Almighty God our brother Brian; and we commit his body to the deep; earth to earth, ashes to ashes, dust to dust. The Lord bless him and keep him, the Lord make his face to shine upon him and be gracious to him, the Lord lift up his countenance upon him and give him peace. Amen

There was a moment of uneasy silence; Kevin Forester heaved one long, mournful wail. Then they eased the weighted, canvas-shrouded remains of Quartermaster Striker Brian T. Forester over the side. Ingram found a verse in the Hymnal and read:

> *Now the laborer's task is o'er;*
> *Now the battle day is past;*
> *Now upon the farther shore*
> *Lands the voyager at last.*
> *Father, in they gracious keeping*
> *Leave we now thy servant sleeping.*

They stood for an uneasy moment, then Ingram took the tiller and rang the bell four times. With Bartholomew opening the throttle, the shore boat surged toward a little village called Anason, their next stop before challenging the Surigao Straits.

Behind them, over the 51 Boat's wake, a meteor glazed the sky. But they didn't see it.

EPILOGUE

*The function of command is rightly considered a great honor.
But command without the means or the authority to fulfill it, is a bitter cup.
I think that our political leaders often fail to appreciate this.*

Brigadier General Bradford G. Chynoweth,
Commander, Central Philippine Forces,
Upon receiving General Wainwright's orders to surrender, May 6, 1942

---

*Probably the most valuable thing I learned [from World War II] was that American
lads wanted to know only three things: that the job they were given to do was
worthwhile, that the sacrifices they made were appreciated, and that they had a fair
chance of survival.*

General James H. Doolittle

EPILOGUE

17 June, 1942
Clarence Straits, Northern Territory
Australia

Ingram was excited. They were all excited. They'd hardly slept, and Ingram had little trouble rousing his men and shoving off at sunrise, leaving the Catholic Mission on Bathurst Island astern.

Australia's mainland lay forty miles across the Clarence Strait. With no wind under a steel-gray sky, the crossing promised to be smooth. By comparison, the wind was up two days before, making the trip across the Arafura Sea miserable—twice, they almost capsized.

Five hours later, they saw pall of dark, black smoke over the horizon. Father McGrath, the missionary on Bathurst Island, had warned them that Japanese medium bombers had struck Port Darwin's Stokes Hill oil-tank farm the day before.

By ten-thirty, Australia's low tropical coastline hove into view, with smoke rising from several fires.

One of the reasons for shoving off at first light was to arrive early and not be trapped in a bombing raid. Father McGrath explained about terrible attacks on Darwin underway since February. With great accuracy, the Japanese had sunk the four-stack destroyer USS *Peary*. Worse, the S.S. *Neptune*, a cargo ship stuffed with depth-charges, had exploded in a spectacular conflagration. Oddly, Japanese planes bombed the hospital many times, while leaving the Larrakeyah army barracks untouched. Father McGrath's opinion was that this was a mix-up: that the Japanese bombed the hospital as a preliminary to invasion, thinking they were wiping out the real army barracks.

During the voyage, Ingram worried not as much about his navigation-- that was almost flawless--as he did about whether or not Lieutenant Tuga perished in the lumber mill. He and DeWitt had many times discussed the fate of the U.S. Fleet at Midway if Tuga had somehow escaped the lumber mill and broadcast a warning.

There. My God. Land

Soon, they closed to within three miles of Australia's lush, green coastline. The bluffs were visible now in great detail and Ingram realized Darwin was, most likely, dotted with coastal defenses and flak emplacements. The 51 Boat was close to her destination, but the reality was, after voyaging by night through nineteen hundred miles of Japanese-infested waters, a trigger-happy Australian kid could blow them sky-high.

That low-roofed tin structure on the hill nestled under trees; his mind raced as he imagined Aussie gunners twirling the handles on a three-inch mount, yearning for the slightest provocation to shoot at something-- anything.

Curious, he mused. Maybe the guns were over there on the headland. Houses and church steeples stood out now, but he was sure each structure concealed nervous gunners itching to take it out on someone. Who cared if it was just a little thirty-six-foot boat with seven emaciated Americans?

After clearing the Surigao Straits, the 51 Boat had skipped down Mindanao's east coast, working her way south toward the Dutch East Indies. Bucking the Molucca Sea, she touched on Morotai and Halmahera; then south to New Guinea and Ceram; down Yamdena's east side, into the Arafura Sea, the roughest part of their passage. Ingram navigated them into the Apsley Straits between Bathurst and Melville islands, where they had been greeted by Father McGrath the night before.

Father McGrath shrugged when Ingram asked for news about a Japanese invasion of Midway. But he did warn them to look as unhostile as possible when approaching Darwin the next day. No one on the mainland doubted a Japanese invasion was imminent, fully aware that Australia was the next esteemed candidate nominated for membership in the Greater East Asia Co-Prosperity Sphere.

So, late at night, they fashioned a Stars and Stripes from an old piece of canvas. And now it fluttered from the flagstaff aft. But, Ingram wondered, would the Aussies see it in time? Or would a nineteen-year-old, former sheep-herder now in uniform, yank his trigger, hosing them down with high explosive rounds.

With smoke still roiling from the Stokes Hill tank farm, Ingram opted not to go into Darwin's main harbor because of the boom defense ships. They would also be itching for a fight so, from two miles out, he shifted course to his left and headed for the seaplane launching ramp; an area known as Doctor's Gully. The pristine resort had been converted to an amphib base with two "Black Cat" PBY's squatting on a concrete ramp.

The men had been trying to act nonchalant, but as they closed the coast, pretense was cast aside and they stood and savored the odor of the Australian continent, reveling in the fact that finally, they were free: that they would soon tread on soil without fear of enemy soldiers or dive-bombers or artillery or banzai charges or ghoulish, sexually-depraved thought police.

Ingram's eyes roamed over the black PBYs again. Paint was chipped off the leading edges, making the aluminum gleam underneath, giving them a grizzled appearance. He realized he hadn't seen one setting so peacefully in broad daylight for over seven months: a lifetime. "Those PBYs are American," he said to Toliver.

"How can anything so ratty look so beautiful." Toliver said.

Ingram grinned then said, "Hey, Yardly. Take Old Glory forward and hold her high, where they can see her."

"Yes, Sir." Yardly untied the makeshift flag from the aft flagstaff and took it to the bow where he held it over his head.

Closer to shore, oil slicks littered the surface and Ingram weaved his way through, unable to avoid the heavy stench. Then the 51 Boat plowed through a patch of smoke from the burning tank farm. Bartholomew waved a hand at the carnage and said, "Peeeoww. Worse than Cavite." To them, nothing would ever match the horror of Cavite, but still they solemnly nodded in agreement, as if the chief were right.

Leon Beardsley hobbled to his feet, leaned on his crutch, and pointed, "Getting ready to launch." Even as he spoke, a PBY's port propeller rolled, then spun into life, with a backward blast of oily, black smoke. The starboard engine caught; then the high-wing, dull black, amphibian waddled to the ramp. Almost ducklike, she coasted down the concrete, hitting the water with a splash, where she taxied to a fairway marked with bouncing red buoys.

"Nasty looking," said Lorca, as the Catalina opened her throttles and lunged into her take-off run. Finally, she cleared the water. As the pontoons folded into her wingtips she clawed for altitude and disappeared to the north. They fell silent again, with the wave action more pronounced as they drew close to shore. No one had shot at them yet, and Ingram steered for two flag poles near the launching ramp. With no wind the flags drooped, but still, he could tell one flag was Australian, the other belonged to the United States of America.

"Sweet," said Yardly. "I'm gonna kiss the ground under that pole."

Lorca said, "Man, I'm right behind you."

One hundred yards.

Sunderland made sure his BAR was out of sight, then stood beside Yardly. "Did you know, Bones, that this is the beer capital of the world?"

"Huh?" said Yardly.

"That's right." They drink more beer per capita here than any place else in the world."

Ingram rang the little bell, calling for idle.

Fifty yards.

"No kiddin'" said Yardly.

Twenty-five yards.

Sunderland said, "Pulled liberty here a couple of years ago. Best beer, best women on the planet; bar none."

CRUNCH! Ingram ran the 51 Boat's nose into the sands of the Commonwealth of Australia.

"Tonight's the night," yelled Bartholomew. He threw aside his crutch and flopped in sandy water with a great splash. "The beer's on me, Sunny."

Yardly jumped out with a whoop. Forester was next, followed by Sunderland and Lorca. Like grinning five-year-olds at Christmas, DeWitt and Toliver piled up in the bow to jump off and join their shipmates, throwing sand and splashing in the waters of Doctors Gully.

While the American airmen shuffled up and stood gawking, Ingram jumped after his shipmates falling headlong in chest-deep water with an enormous splash. He whooped and screeched like the others with the final realization he wasn't going to be killed by enemy gunfire, at least in the near future.

A squad of heavily armed Australian soldiers ran up and fanned out, their legs splayed. A sergeant shouted, "Welcome to the Top End, blokes. Where yer from?"

"Corregidor," yelled Sunderland.

The sergeant waved to his squad who cocked their rifles. "You have an officer, maybe?"

Ingram stood with sand and muddy water dripping down his face. "Me."

The sergeant took in Ingram's torn trousers, ripped shirt, boots without soles and planters hat. "That so, Sir?"

Ingram dumbly nodded. "Name's Ingram, lieutenant, USN. We just got in from Corregidor."

The Australian sergeant reached up to Ingram's collar where his lieutenant's device should have been. "Lieutenant, huh?

Where's yer bars?"

Ingram raised his hands then flapped them to his side with a lopsided grin. "Mrs. Carrillo has one. What's left of the other is with what's left of the Jap who took it."

"He's toast, Mr. Ingram," shouted Sunderland hitting Yardly in the back with a sandball.

"Let's hope so," said Ingram.

"Corregidor, you say?" said the Australian sergeant.

"Yep."

Corregidor fell over a month ago."

"Don't I know it?"

"Any ID, Sir?"

Ingram reached in his pockets and came out with a rusty screwdriver.

The sergeant pulled his pistol and fired a round in the air bringing the 51

Boat crew's celebration to an abrupt halt. Their stares matched the incredulous stares of the PBY airmen gathered on the concrete ramp.

The sergeant yelled, "Now then. On yer faces, you AWOL goldbricks."

Sunderland bellowed, "Not me, Jack. I'm going into town for a gallon of ice cold beer."

"On yer belly, mate. Town's evacuated. No beer here." The sergeant kicked the backs of Sunderland's knees. "Down and spread before I blow a hole in yer."

"Aww sonofabitch," moaned Sunderland, sinking in the sand.

Someone kicked Ingram in the back. "That means you, *Lieutenant*."

Beardsley wobbled to his knees then fell on his face beside Ingram. With a grin he mimicked an Aussie accent, "Right-o Bluie. Welcome to the land down undah."

After two weeks, four long plane rides and many long meals, the Army transport *Tasker H. Bliss* gave a deep, prolonged blast followed by three short blasts, backing from her slip in Sydney. At twilight, Ingram fingered shiny lieutenant's bars (they called them "railroad tracks") on his new, starched, khaki collar. He peeked once again through the slightly parted, watertight bulkhead door to the ship's bosun's locker in the forepeak. Great coils of line hung on the bulkheads along with shackles, pendants, and enormous cheek blocks.

But this evening, the normally neat and orderly white painted space, was thick with tobacco smoke. Men, in a variety of uniforms, sat on blankets spread on the shiny linoleum deck. There were four groups, in circles of five to seven. Each group sat around piles of money, as if in pagan worship of some sort. The group nearest Ingram contained four marine enlisted, two Navy aviator lieutenants and Gunner's Mate First Class Kermit Sunderland. He wore a new set of immaculately pressed dress blues complete with campaign ribbons. His sleeves were rolled up and his white hat was perched on the back of his head.

With a broad grin, Sunderland scooped in the pot--there were several twenties--and stuffed it in a bulging, brown paper bag.

A Marine gunnery sergeant, sitting next to Sunderland, tossed cards on the blanket and spat, "Sheyyatt. Deal, Sunny."

Sunderland raised on his knees, gathered the cards and after arranging them, thumbed the deck beside his ear. He nodded as if satisfied the cards really were all there, then took his time lighting an enormous cigar.

"The man said 'deal,' mister," growled one of the flyboys.

Puffing mightily, Sunderland offered a smile and said, "Okay, okay. Now this here's a game of honest poker. None of this stupid wild-card crap. It's a man's game." He took another luxurious puff and blew smoke in the general direction of the overhead exhaust duct.

"Well? What the hell's it gonna be?" snapped the gunny.

"We call it five-card stud; where money talks and bullshit walks. Ante up, girls." Sunderland tossed in a twenty.

Ingram smiled, eased the bulkhead door closed, and walked aft toward the bridge. In gathering darkness, the *Bliss* pulled away from the dock. When Ingram reached the deck below the bridge, the ship had gained sternway, making the wake sizzle down her starboard side. Sydney was blacked out, and there wasn't much to look at, except shadows of the last land he would see for the next two and a half weeks.

And he wouldn't be seeing Beardsley or Lorca in the foreseeable future. Both were recuperating in Sydney's Naval Hospital. DeWitt had stayed ashore, too having been assigned to MacArthur's intelligence staff in Sydney.

The *Bliss* shuddered as her skipper rang up an ahead bell and shifted her rudder. She twisted a bit, gained headway, and plowed toward the submarine boom and the open ocean.

Toliver walked up. "Evening, Skipper."

"Ollie," said Ingram, trying to stretch. His new shoes felt a little tight, the leather soles weren't yet broken in. Like a fool, he'd already slipped twice today. "Was there really something for us?"

"Yep. Came over with the last guardmail." In the gathering darkness, he held up two envelopes. "How are the boys?"

"Bartholomew, Yardly, and Forester are down below watching the movie. Sunderland's in the bosun's locker, playing poker with a mixed bunch-- flyboys and jarheads."

Toliver stiffened. "We better get up there. Jeez, all that back pay."

Ingram chuckled. "Sunderland has it under control." He explained about the paper bag.

Toliver sighed, "You know. I have the feeling he's going to be richer than both of us if he makes it through this war."

"Richer than you?"

"Absolutely."

"How?"

"Real Estate. Can't you see him selling limited partnerships in cliffsides, swamps, and peat bogs to little old ladies?"

"That's what I'm afraid of." Ingram nodded to the envelopes. "Is that what I think it is?"

Toliver handed one to Ingram saying, "This one's for you."

Ingram held it up to the fading light, examining the neatly typed address label. "Yep. Looks like orders."

Toliver shook his own packet close to his ear. "Damn. You may be right. Nothing gurgles."

"You first."

"Okay." Papers rattled as Toliver leafed through his reconstituted service record. "Hot damn!"

"What?"

"Orders."

"Where?"

"Gun boss on new construction. A brand new can. She's the," he held a page up to capture the waning twilight, "U.S.S. *Ammen* DD 527. Bethlehem Steel in 'Frisco. One of the new *Fletcher* class cans."

"You like that?"

"The farther from Long Island the better." Toliver stuffed papers back in the envelope. "Uhhh. Thanks, Skipper for...not...making a big deal out of what happened on the old bird."

"What? Me? You're the one who blew up that Jap on Marinduque. I owe you my life. Hell, you took care of me *and* Leon the whole trip."

"It wasn't me."

"Nonsense."

Fading light barely revealed Toliver's smirk. "Okay. We're even." They shook.

Toliver said, "Now you."

Ingram unsealed his envelope finding several sets of documents. "Uh, here it is. Oh, yes!"

"Oh yes, what?"

"Orders to new construction, like you. She's the U.S.S. *Tingey* DD 539. Exec."

"Where?"

"Bethlehem Steel, San Francisco."

"See you at the *Top of the Mark*," said Toliver, referring to the bar on the top floor of the Mark Hopkins Hotel overlooking San Francisco Bay.

"I'll say. Better save some of your back pay for--what's this?" A brown envelope fell out. It had red strips around the edges, was heavily sealed, and marked:

EYES ONLY LIEUTENANT ALTON C. INGRAM, USN 638217 EYES ONLY SECRET

"What the hell have I done now?"

Toliver said, "They want you to do commercials on the "Jack Armstrong Show." Good for morale. Sell lots of war bonds."

Ingram stepped out to the rail, opened the message, and held it up to the last of the twilight. The return address said: Headquarters, Supreme Allied Commander, South West Pacific Region. "It's from Otis." He took out a hand-written note:

Todd:

Everything here is great. MacArthur thinks I'm a god since I was one of the last out. I have a job for life.

If you haven't seen the newspapers, it turns out we really kicked the Jap's ass at Midway. Everything was...well...as Epperson predicted. June 4th... everything. We jumped them and sunk four Nip carriers. One of our carriers was lost, but that won't be announced to the press for a while. People here are ecstatic. Predict the Japs, now without a heavy attack carrier force, must go on the defensive.

Wendell Fertig was through Nasipit two nights after our little party and sent a situation report. His message was terribly brief, keeping air time to a minimum, avoiding Jap radio direction finders. Most of it was for requisitioning guns and ammo to build his resistance forces. But he squeezed in three small items: First, he advised the Australian coastal authorities in Darwin to keep a sharp eye out for us. How about that? There's always some jerk who doesn't get the word. Next, Amador passed along greetings and confirmed Tuga died in the dynamite blast.

The last item was specifically addressed to you. No one here understands it. It simply says, 'to Navy Lt. Alton C. Ingram, 638217: RAMONA.' Do you know Fertig? What does 'RAMONA' mean? Please let me know if you have a clue. MacArthur and his people are going nuts. They keep pestering me.

Heard you have orders to a new destroyer as executive officer. Good luck. Call when you're back in Sydney.

Best Regards,

Otis

"Hot damn." Ingram muttered. Helen Durand was alive! She had somehow convinced Fertig to get word out and apparently had a good chance of survival. As the *Bliss* met one of the Pacific's rollers, a great feeling of peace swept over him.

"Huh?" said Toliver

"She made it." Helen. Alive. And she had his ring.

"Who?"

DeWitt's message said "EYES ONLY." Ingram didn't know how much he could say.

"Todd," said Toliver, waving his hands in Ingram's face. "Come back to the party."

"Uh, Sorry."

"Who are you talking about?"

Helen's parents should at least know that their daughter was, for the time being, safe. "I've got a job to do," Ingram said.

"We all do.

"The Bethlehem Steel plant is in San Francisco, isn't it?"

"That's what your orders say."

"And that's in California, isn't it?"

"According to my fourth-grade school teacher." Toliver was close to exasperation.

"So is Ramona."

"So what?"

"I've heard it's a nice place to visit."

"Can't beat the *Top of the Mark*," said Toliver.

"I'm not so sure." Ingram tucked the documents back in the manila envelope. He'd tell Ollie later, but for the moment he wanted to savor Helen's
freedom for himself. For the moment, she was safe with Fertig and had a fair
chance of getting out. He'd learned submarines called with regularity in the
Philippines, supplying the resistance with weapons and medicine, and
taking out ill and wounded.

They leaned on the rail just as the *Tasker H. Bliss* slipped through the
submarine boom into the Pacific. She took on the rollers with ease, while on
the bridge a deck above, the engine room telegraph bell clanged as her
captain rang up all ahead standard.

A CODE FOR TOMORROW

Todd Ingram is back in the fight.

After narrowly escaping the Japanese-held Philippines, he is promoted to the destroyer USS Howell.

His new assignment puts him in the middle of two epic naval engagements: the Battle of Cape Esperance and the Battle of the Santa Cruz Islands. But his fight against the Imperial Japanese Navy is just the beginning.

Todd learns that his lost love has joined the Philippine resistance on a nearby island. He sets off to find her...under the watchful eye of an enemy spy in the ranks.

With the war at its apex, Todd must put his life on the line not only for the woman he loves, but for his country, and a world that is perilously close to collapse.

Get your copy today at
severnriverbooks.com/series/todd-ingram

ACKNOWLEDGMENTS

An embarrassment of riches flowed during my research for *The Last Lieutenant*, particularly in the following categories: Historical and submarine nomenclature; the late Alvin P. Cluster, Vice Admiral Patrick J. Hannifin (retired), the late Rear Admiral John H. Morrill, II (retired), Lieutenant John W. Nelson, USN; Medical; Drs. Joseph N. Lambert, M.D., Russell J. Striff, M.D., and Kenneth J. Wegner, M.D; B-17 nomenclature; Robert Armstrong, Richard Bertea and David Tallechet; Radio Procedures; the late Hal Rosenberg and Linde Williams. Music; Drs. Richard Berkmeir and William B. Roberts.

Elsewhere, I benefitted from the help of the Los Angeles Consulate of the Republic of the Philippines, and Orange County Fictionaires. And fortunately, we are served by library systems with incredible capabilities. The Doheny Library at the University of Southern California -- thanks go to Tyson Reyes -- and the Newport Beach Main Library are solid examples and were extremely helpful, more than fulfilling my research expectations.

Every attempt has been made to conform to events of the time and all settings are actual except for the Japanese garrison on Marinduque. Any inaccuracies herein are attributed solely to me

Discovered during this process was the full meaning of "What are friends for?" Thus, unending thanks go to Richard M. Geiler, Larry T. Smith, and Dr. Russell J. Striff, M.D., friends for a long, long time who truly fulfill the essence of that phrase.

Most of all, thanks to my wife, Janine; friend, companion, lover and copy editor extraordinaire; the best ever. They really broke the mold...

John J. Gobbell

Newport Beach, California
February, 2020

ABOUT THE AUTHOR

JOHN J. GOBBELL is a former Navy Lieutenant who saw duty as a destroyer weapons officer. His ship served in the South China Sea, granting him membership in the exclusive *Tonkin Gulf Yacht Club*. As an executive recruiter, his clients included military/commercial aerospace companies giving him insight into character development under a historical thriller format. An award-winning author, John has published eight novels. The books in his popular Todd Ingram series are based on the U.S Navy in the Pacific theater of World War II. John and his wife Janine live in Newport Beach, California.

Sign up for John J. Gobbell's newsletter at
severnriverbooks.com/authors/john-gobbell
johnjgobbell@severnriverbooks.com

Made in the USA
Monee, IL
15 January 2023

6cadc4bd-8db2-4560-8485-ab33fcaeb542R01